About the Author

Maggie Lett was born in Bootle, Merseyside. After attending art college in Newport, South Wales, she worked as a journalist in Tehran and on several titles in London, Berkshire and Yorkshire. In Sheffield she ran Bukowski's Piano Bar with her partner before going on to teach journalism. Virgin Ground is based on stories from her family history.

Virgin Ground

Maggie Lett

Virgin Ground

Olympia Publishers
London

www.olympiapublishers.com
OLYMPIA PAPERBACK EDITION

A CIP catalogue record for this title is
available from the British Library.

ISBN: 978-1-80074-342-7

This is a work of fiction.
Names, characters, places and incidents originate from the writer's imagination.
Any resemblance to actual persons, living or dead, is purely coincidental.

First Published in 2022

Olympia Publishers
Tallis House
2 Tallis Street
London
EC4Y 0AB

Printed in Great Britain

Dedication

To the cast of characters in my family, past and present, on both sides of the Irish Sea.

Acknowledgements

First of all I have to acknowledge a certain sense of guilt on my part, using half-remembered family stories and then embellishing them for more public consumption. It seems to border on betrayal. Yet all this was in a different era, when children didn't really know much about their elders: they belonged to a secret grown-up world. It was only later in life that I started to wonder why someone was the way he or she was, to speculate on what circumstances might have been the driving force behind those half-remembered stories. So this book is based on family facts but they are presented within a fictional framework, in which no doubt many of the explanations I give couldn't be further from the truth.

For all that, Veronica Kelly offered continued support. She was a great help, providing me with many anecdotes which were new to me. She is also the guardian of the original love letters, which I have quoted verbatim in the book out of respect for such a deeply rooted if ultimately doomed relationship.

I would also like to thank Geoff Rowe, Jethro Soutar and Rachael McGill for their patience in reading the manuscript: they also opened my eyes both to the finer points and to the glaringly obvious.

Part 1

All changed, changed utterly;
A terrible beauty is born.

— W B Yeats

1

"Patsy, come on now, you're going to be late for Miss Bourke." The voice lilted over the field and skirted the haystacks and mingled with the sound of the water playing in the river before it finally registered with the intended ears. Patsy O'Kelly looked up at the sound of her mother's call; the girl had been so busy that she'd forgotten all about her music lesson. She pulled her small fishing net out of the stream and saw that it hadn't been a great session, there weren't many tiddlers circulating in her jar, but she emptied her meagre catch back into the river all the same and watched while they swam away, wondering at their simple skill in navigating the flowing river and imagining what sense of freedom was encapsulated in such tiny fish in the relative immensity of so much powerful water.

"Patsy, I don't want to have to call you again," came the summons. "And no doubt you're soaking wet and will need to dry off. Hurry up now."

The old woman who was working in the field as usual smiled and waved as Patsy hurried past. They had seen each other many times and though they had never spoken there was definitely a bond formed between the two of them, like two souls rooted in the same precious landscape. Patsy returned the silent greeting and padded across the meadow. She was normally anxious to get to her piano lesson, music was regarded as very important in the family and Patsy had a promising talent, but today she felt far away. No wonder her fish trawl had been so poor. As she gorged on the visual feast and earthy smells of the countryside and listened to the birdsong as she covered the short distance home, she also heard echoes of her parents talking late into the previous night of bombs and guns in Dublin. That's where her cousins lived. Patsy hadn't really understood exactly what her mammy and daddy were talking about but she had sensed a tightness in their voices. Whatever it was, it didn't fit with either the peaceful life they knew at Larch Hill or with the fun times she remembered having in Dublin and Patsy decided that the grown-ups were probably just entertaining each other with late-night scary stories. Sometimes they would do that altogether as a family of a winter evening, the candlelight adding a delicious shadowy mystery to it all. She herself had yesterday seen two men scrambling through the foliage by the river, for all the world looking as if they were trying to keep out of sight of the men in uniforms running after them like in a game of catch. At least Patsy had assumed it was a game but neither the two men nor the ones chasing them had been laughing so maybe it was scarier than fun. She stored it up in her mind for when it was her next turn to tell a frightening tale: she would come up with some sort of spooky scenario. Maybe that's why her mammy and daddy had started talking about scary things. Maybe they had seen the men too.

Her two little sisters were playing in the yard in front of the gatehouse when Patsy got back. They were covered in daubs of colour and barely looked up when Patsy stopped to admire their work. They were painting pebbles and stones to make a fancy border to delineate the edges of the vegetable-patch and Patsy would have loved to join in but Miss Bourke was expecting her, and the piano teacher regarded punctuality in behaviour as invaluable training for keeping good time in the music. Being late would introduce a sour note to the lesson. The idea made the young pupil smile: she introduced enough sour notes herself when her attention wandered from the keyboard.

A basin of warm water was waiting for Patsy on the kitchen table. She stored her fishing net and jar in the corner cupboard and quickly cleaned herself up, putting on dry socks and shoes ready to leave the house.

"Let me look at you, we don't want you trailing half the field into Miss Bourke's parlour," said her mammy, giving the child a quick twirl and a once-over. "You'll have to do but you're going to have to skedaddle," she said, handing Patsy her music satchel. "If you're lucky you might catch a lift home in the trap with your daddy."

"I'm sorry, Mammy, I've left bits of grass all over the floor."

"They'll still be there for you to sweep up when you get back from your lesson, Patsy. I won't have time to do it, I have a bit of work to do in the big house first."

"Do you enjoy working in the big house, Mammy?" asked Patsy, at the same time checking that she had collected up all the right music sheets for her lesson.

"I wouldn't exactly say that cleaning and cooking for the family who live there is enjoyable," said Lizzie. "But it's work that I have to do so that we can all live here in the cottage and isn't it a lovely cottage with all the beautiful countryside around?"

What Patsy didn't remember was that she herself had for a short time lived in that same big house with her mammy and daddy: she didn't know that for them it was to be the perfect home for the large family they planned. Patsy was the first baby to come along and Patrick had made a beautiful wooden cot on rockers for the new arrival. She'd lie there in it being soothed gently to sleep by the comforting sounds of her parents' voices. Of course she hadn't understood that their talk was generally about having lots of children to fill the house and its ten rooms: many an evening Patrick and Lizzie had sat in front of a roaring fire together, marvelling at baby Patsy lying quietly in the cot while they imagined her future baby brothers and sisters taking their turns in the same cot and then, over the years, filling the house with the sounds of noisy feet, a whole tribe of little ones playing hide-and-seek and slamming as many doors as possible in their wake. A second baby was already on the way and the homely sense of loving security was never doubted. Until, suddenly, the small family had had to move out and swap the main house for the gatehouse. Lizzie's job was part of the deal.

"You always call them 'the family', Mammy, but Da always calls them 'the English family'," said Patsy.

"Yes, well, they are English, of course, but they're kind enough," said Lizzie. "Come on now and shoosh, on your way."

Patsy was propelled out of the door and didn't dare linger this time to look at her sisters busy with the paint-pots but she did sneak a quick glance, which was enough to have her rushing blindly and headlong into two men who suddenly appeared in the yard. All three girls stopped what they were doing.

"Is your daddy at home?" one of the men demanded.

"Mammy, Mammy," called Patsy. "There's someone looking for Da."

Lizzie's face took on an incipient smile as she reached the doorway and saw the Irish Constabulary uniforms seemingly filling the yard with buttoned bulk, belts and batons. "Can I help you with anything?" she asked, at the same time wanting to get the little ones out of the way. "Get along to your piano lesson, Patsy, you're late enough as it is, and you, Molly and Theresa, go on in now and wash that paint off your hands while I speak to the constables. I think we've enough coloured pebbles already to fill a beach." She waited while her daughters scrabbled into action. "So what is it brings you here to Larch Hill, officers? I don't think the English family is at home right now but I could take a message," she said, casually assuming that the policemen could have no call to talk to her. "I'm due in there soon to do the housekeeping."

"There's no need to bother them," said the older of the constables. "We're just looking for any information you might have on two men who escaped from custody yesterday."

"And why would I have any information on men escaping from custody?" said Lizzie. "I'm just here with the children and my husband and my job in the house. I've no information on any thieves or criminals. We're a God-fearing family in this home."

"I'm sure you're as innocent as everyone else we've talked to," said the policeman. "And where is your husband right now, might I ask?"

"You might ask and I'll tell you: he's at work in Rathfarnham, in the bakery, where he is every day. I believe you get a daily delivery at the barracks. He's no doubt baking your tomorrow morning's bread-order at this very moment."

"God, I love their blaa buns," said the younger man, "perfect, I'd say they are, for the perfect bacon butty."

"I couldn't agree with you more," said Lizzie, "not that we get to eat many, silly though it may sound, my husband after baking the things. We have to make do with the occasional over-cooked ones because the rest have to be sold to people such as yourselves but I'm glad you enjoy them, Constable. I'll pass on your good words when my husband gets home," she prattled on. "We all appreciate a bit of thanks for good work done. So I'll let you get on with yours, if you don't mind. If I leave those two girls on their own too long they'll manage to turn the kitchen into a whole bath-house just by washing their hands."

"Who did you say you are? Your name please?" said the senior policeman.

"O'Kelly, Mrs O'Kelly."

"So if I was to ask at the bakery for a Mr O'Kelly, he'd be sure to be there would he?"

"He would," said Lizzie. "Then the minute he gets home I'll have to wash all the flour dust out of his clothes, which is a real nuisance because you know flour and water get pasty when mixed and it sticks to his clothes something awful. Mind you, the wee ones try to help, though they do make more of a mess, God bless them."

"So you didn't see anyone or anything unusual yesterday?" said the policeman, forcing the conversation back to the reason for calling. "You didn't see two young fellers around the place? They fled along the riverbank and that's where we lost them."

"I'm far too busy to be gazing over at the river, Sir, that would be more than my job's worth, but I'll keep my eyes open from now on. I can let you know at the barracks if I see anything. Are they dangerous, these men? Should we be worried? You don't think they're planning to rob the big house, do you? Perhaps you should stay after all and warn the English family yourselves. You're welcome to come in and wait, have a cup of tea."

"I think you're safe enough, Missus," said the young constable. "They were just a couple of Dublin Brigaders we were after and if they interfere with the baker then they'll have me to answer to."

"Be quiet, eejit," said the boss leading the rookie off down the drive. "You're not to be telling everyone what official business we're on."

Lizzie watched as the uniforms lumbered out of sight heading back towards the town. She knew a few members of the local Dublin Brigade and approved of what they did, ambushing deliveries of food and supplies to the RIC barracks and other wealthy houses in the area, then distributing their haul amongst the poor and needy. She was pleased to hear that two of them had escaped being caught.

The cane struck her suddenly and sharply on the thigh and the two coins fell off the back of her hands and rolled across the floor. Patsy bristled. Her attention had indeed wandered, out into the garden beyond the wide window that sat squarely above the piano when the huge lid was closed, framing a lush temptation right in front of her eye-line. A baby grand the piano was, or so she was told, though to her there was little she'd call babyish about it, especially compared to the solemn upright they had at home in the gatehouse. This baby had a strong sweeping curve to it whereas their piano at home was more of a cold street urchin. Her mother was constantly rubbing polish into it, saying it was a precious piece of furniture which brought music into the house and so deserved care and attention, but solemn it looked and rigidly cold, though Patsy had to admit that her mother was right: when it was played, it had a way of enlivening the whole house. Not so the sound of the two dropped pennies whirring on the spot as they settled on Miss Bourke's flagstone floor and brought Patsy back to the present. As ever she didn't know whether to go pick them up or not; she was always tipping the coins off as her hand position weakened and lost their hovering flatness over the keys. Flat hands were good hands, according to her teacher, allowing the fingers to nimble their way deftly to whichever notes they sought with the least effort.

"Do pay attention, young lady," said Miss Bourke. "Forget those coins, they've already gone, leave them, leave them where they are, they'll not harm the floor," pressed the teacher. "Look to your position here and not out on the garden and you might not lose the next ones and you might learn to play well at the same time. Remember that flat hands are good hands," she said, "allowing the fingers to nimble their way deftly to whichever notes they seek with the least effort."

The coins, one on the left hand, one on the right, were Miss Bourke's simple but effective way of training discipline into the hands of all her pupils, not that many of them would ever reach a level where such a thing really mattered: tinkling a few tunes for a jig or a drunken sing-song was what most of them would end up doing and that didn't call for the ability of a maestro, fun though it was. Still, Miss Bourke believed, you might as well try to do it properly from the word go. She gently put two more pennies on the back of Patsy's hands and balanced them to her satisfaction.

"Now, let's hear the scale of B flat major before you go. We'll have two octaves, if you please, Patsy, and let's see if you can get right through without any mistakes, flowing along up and down the piano. And mind those coins, keep them in place. Not too fast now, it's better to do it

18

properly than to hurry and slip and lose the race. Okay, off you go."

That was another of Miss Bourke's favourite admonitions, about hurrying and losing races. Patsy wasn't entirely sure it was a relevant idea, she wasn't competing against anyone but herself, but she didn't mind these regular doses of bizarre wisdom. She liked Miss Bourke and her soft voice, the way she had of half-closing her eyes when she was listening to Patsy play, her head gently bobbing to and fro, the gleam in her shuttered eyes always dancing to whatever tune she was hearing, real or imagined, it was all the same.

"That was very good, Patsy, very good, you've obviously been practising your scales regularly and you must continue to do so. And remember, playing is not the same as practising. Still, I'm very pleased with you. Next week I'm going to give you something new to try. You may find it a bit difficult but don't be put off. I think you'll conquer it with practice and I'm sure your mother would enjoy hearing it in the house. It's by someone called Beethoven, a German composer, and it's called 'Fur Elise', which means 'For Elise'. It's a bit mournful but it's a nice tune."

"Who was Baytone?" asked Patsy.

"Oh Beethoven was one of the greats," enthused Miss Bourke. "He was only ever interested in his music, nothing else mattered to him. Sometimes he'd bash his hands down on the keys when he was playing as if he was fighting the very piano itself, not that I'd want you to do that, Patsy, mind. Then sometimes he would hide under the kitchen table if he didn't want to know what was going on in the street right outside his own window. Would you believe that? And he must have been a bit whiffy too, Patsy; you know he hated to get washed and for whole weeks on end he would refuse to empty his chamber pot and he'd leave half-eaten food lying around all over the place. Can you imagine the stink? It must have been awful, and in the middle of it all that lovely piano being played, and beautiful music being made. But there you go; he was too busy with his music to bother about anything else."

"Do you know any other stories about Baytone?" asked Patsy, completely awed by the idea of this great musician hiding under the kitchen table next to maybe some old dollops of mashed potato or dried up bits of bacon and sausage and smelly old cabbage and next to all that a chamber-pot full of poo in a pool of pongy pee and all the time the man thinking up new tunes in his head.

"Well what else is that he went totally deaf when he was only thirty-three and he still went on to compose operas, symphonies, concertos…"

"Jesus, Mary and Joseph, stone deaf and he still wrote music."

"That's dedication for you and, of course, a wonderful ear, Patsy, and such a great love of music that for him it excluded everything else. He didn't have many close friends and he never took a wife."

"Is that why you never married, Miss Bourke, because you are too dedicated to music?"

"Now, child, that's enough of the questions for today. You get on home and help your mammy with all her chores. And keep up your practice, of course. I'll see you next week."

"I'm looking forward to meeting Baytone," said Patsy. "I like the sound of him. Maybe I'll be very dedicated to music the same as him and never get married."

Patrick was waiting outside Miss Bourke's house when Patsy emerged from her lesson. "Mammy said you might bring me home today in the trap," she called running down the path and hugging him. She was always pleased to see her da: they seemed always to have had a special closeness between them.

"No trap, I'm afraid, Patsy," he said, scooping her up under the armpits and swinging her around above the ground, music satchel flying. "Seamus lost a shoe today so I've had to leave him with the blacksmith. You and I are going to have to walk home. It'll give us a chance to catch up on what we've been doing today. Did you have a good piano lesson?"

"I did and I learned about a famous composer called Baytone who left potties all over the house even when they were full of poo," said Patsy. "But I can tell you something far more important than that, Mr O'Kelly," she confided pompously. "Two policemen called to the cottage today looking for you but I don't know what they wanted as Mammy made me rush off to my lesson."

"Two policemen? Looking for me? Now what on earth could they have wanted?"

"I don't know but I can tell you that I saw two policemen yesterday as well, they were chasing two other men on the far side of the river. I thought maybe you or Mammy might have seen them too."

"Well, I know I didn't, and your mother never mentioned anything," said Patrick. "I tell you what though Patsy, as it's obviously a police matter let's not mention it to your mammy, we don't want her to worry about dangerous men on the loose."

"Sure Mammy never worries," said Patsy.

"You're right there, Patsy. Your mammy is a strong woman in that department."

The walk home from Rathfarnham didn't take the father and daughter long, with her pressing him on how many loaves he had baked that day and how many sacks of flour did it all take, then him telling her all about the horse shedding its shoe and having to be led to the blacksmiths for a new one. Seamus belonged to the English family but the O'Kelly girls treated him like their very own pet. Patsy was relieved to learn that it didn't hurt the horse when the smithy tapped the nails into its hooves.

There were no constables in sight when they got home to the cottage and Patrick in turn was relieved to learn from Lizzie that the policemen hadn't been looking for him in particular and had left after some cursory questioning and a bit of praise for the blaa buns.

"Forget the blaa buns, I've brought a treat home for everyone," said Patrick, steering the subject away from policemen by producing a shiny plump orange out of his bag. "Would you look at this now?"

"Where did you get that, Daddy?" asked Molly.

"What is it?" asked Theresa.

"It's called an orange, Theresa, that's why we name the colour 'orange', after the fruit, and I got it from a customer who came across it, God knows how, I thought it best not to ask," said Patrick, winking at his wife.

"Come along now, girls," she said, clapping her hands, "wherever it came from, such an unexpected treat deserves a proper celebration. Get the prettiest plates out of the cupboard and put a jar of flowers on the table for decoration and we'll have ourselves a little party."

When everyone was seated at the table, Lizzie ceremoniously sliced the fruit up into five portions and placed the small helpings daintily, one on each plate, oohing with enthusiasm and creating such an atmosphere of happiness that each of them enjoyed the meagre offering as if it was manna itself. She smiled at Patrick across the table as she described the fruit in the most exotic terms.

"Plump juicy oranges like these come from very hot countries where the sun is always shining," she told the girls, "Not like here in Ireland, where it's far too cold and wet. Imagine how colourful the countryside must be in those faraway places, covered in lots of trees just dripping with oranges, each of them getting fatter and juicier by the day and turning this beautiful rich orange colour in all that lovely sunshine. A lot of them come from a country called Spain, where they even grow a special kind of orange for making marmalade for you to put on your toast."

"Would you believe that?" said Patrick, relishing his serving, pulling funny faces and licking his lips as if this here was after all the best and juiciest piece of fruit ever enjoyed by anyone anywhere. "Aren't we the lucky ones?" he'd say to the assembled company. "And here's to the Brigaders," he whispered to Lizzie.

2

The gatehouse was a small lodge situated just inside the drive of the large but modest country house at Larch Hill, just outside Rathfarnham, a few miles south of Dublin. The main house had the sort of arrangement a child might draw, with a door in the middle and the windows arranged symmetrically around it: there were two tall casement windows on either side of a pilastered entrance and four smaller paned ones above those on the second floor. The sides of the house were dappled by light delicately dancing through the foliage of tall birch trees; climbing roses straggled their way up the walls and ivy was making good headway up the corners. It was certainly an attractive house, thanks in no small measure to Lizzie's efforts when she and Patrick had moved in as newly-weds. It had a touch of the Regency or Georgian architectural style about it, the sort of house commonly found in the Irish countryside, now usually owned by an English family or landlord. It was grand enough outside and inside but it was welcoming, certainly more of a home than a residence.

Patsy went in there quite regularly: she and her sisters would help their mother with the extra work involved when there were staying guests, or perhaps when the family was hosting a dinner party and there was lots of peeling and chopping and fetching to be done. A couple of other local women were also taken on to help with these formal dinners and there was usually lots of laughter and chatter going on in the kitchen while they got on with their cooking. The guests were always dressed in expensive evening clothes and the ladies' jewellery would glitter in the candlelight, but they generally fussed over the three poorly dressed children helping to wait at table and the visitors always expressed amused delight that the youngsters should be carrying such heavy platters: as if the children had much choice in the matter.

It was an accident of history that the little ones themselves weren't the ones living in the grand house.

It had been loaned rent-free to Lizzie and Patrick by Lizzie's rich

Uncle Christopher, who had apparently had some vested interest in Lett's Brewery based to the south of Dublin. The brewery was called after his family name: even the company's slogan was a play on the name and it was carried on all the drays as they plied the streets of Dublin and the country lanes with deliveries to all the bars; painted in bright letters on the curving board that arched across and over the driver's seat was the legend: 'Let's drink Lett's'. Uncle Christopher had been very fond of his niece, Lizzie, and her brother, Stephen, and made sure they each had a place of their own to live, though while she had preferred the idea of bringing up a family in the country her brother had chosen to live in Dublin itself, along Usher's Quay on the Liffey.

The exact details of Christopher's sudden loss of fortune were never fully established but the effects were only too real. With it went everything, the uncle and all his beneficiaries suffering an abrupt and drastic reduction in circumstances. What was known was that Uncle Christopher was a gambling man and family lore claimed that he had lost his business on the toss of a card during a serious gaming session with a friend who may or may not have had something to do with Guinness. Whatever the truth of the matter, his debts soaked up most of his assets, including the house at Larch Hill.

"It's a bit of a relief, to be honest, it's such a big house to keep clean and I've always been more attracted to the cosiness of the gatehouse," was how Lizzie had reacted when news of her uncle's having to sell their home arrived. "It will be much more fun for us at the moment," she said to Patrick. "We don't have a houseful of children yet and we'll be able to turn the gatehouse into the prettiest cottage in the area. And the girls will still be able to play in the gardens and the fields, we won't have to move into the town."

The fact was they had suddenly needed somewhere to live and the gatehouse came with the housekeeper's position so that was that, Lizzie would have a ready-made job on site, cleaning that self-same big house to supplement Patrick's wages.

What Uncle Christopher did manage to do, however, was to siphon off some money for his niece, who received a small but regular allowance which she had continued to set aside to pay for piano lessons for the daughters.

Once they had moved out, Patsy's father didn't have much to do with the house or its new owners, a well-to-do couple from England, though he wasn't averse to doing odd maintenance work there for some extra money. That was always a problem for Patrick, a shortage of money, a problem shared, of course, by most of their neighbours in the parish. In any spare time he had he would paint pictures — landscapes of the local countryside mainly, perhaps a view or two of the gatehouse, small portraits of the girls or sometimes a personal request for neighbours wanting to mark a special occasion: even the English family had commissioned him to paint a watercolour of the main house in its lush setting. In fact several people had commented on his fine talent. "You should become an artist," they'd say.

But he could only sell his work for little more than coppers and the more generous amount The Family had paid for the painting of the house promised little more than some decent food on the table for the winter months.

"We'll have some good Sunday roasts to look forward to for the next few weeks, Lizzie," he'd said, "and perhaps enough to buy a few presents for the children at Christmas."

But Lizzie had put her foot down. "Not on your life," she'd said. "That money will cover the cost of a piano, perhaps not the best of pianos but a good enough one to bring a regular touch of gaiety into the house and that's the best Christmas present any of us could wish for. Treats on the dinner table are eaten as soon as they're put on the plate and then what have you to show for them other than a full belly, but a piano will remain as a source of pleasure in the home. We'll still manage to eat, there'll still be food on the table," she had said.

The joy of listening to Lizzie play her music and seeing how Patsy had taken to the instrument reassured Patrick that his wife had been right. She had that way about her, a way of turning the poorest of situations into something special.

The Family were nice enough people and they didn't abuse Lizzie by giving her too much work to do for the small wage she received: indeed there was usually a bit of a bonus to be expected when there were staying guests at the house and at times The Family also passed on items of clothing or bed-linen or household utensils, none of them anywhere near being worn out. They had no children of their own so they also lavished affection on the three O'Kelly girls.

No, they were good enough people: it wasn't that Patrick didn't like them but he had a conscience over his easy feelings and relative convenience of living. He was only too aware of the increasing demands for Irish independence and the political unrest already manifest throughout the country. The Dublin Brigade, whose members had fought and died in the Rising, had burst into new life as volunteers flocked to join the organisation following the 1916 defeat. There was a unit based in the Rathfarnham area but Patrick had so far kept out of it. His own opinions were that the English Government had been in charge of his country for too long without contributing much to the populace or to their health and well-being, but his feelings were tempered somewhat by personal experience of The Family and their simple kindness.

Then there was his brother-in-law on the Quays, a Dublin man too, who, like a lot of his compatriots, had joined the British Army to gain some financial security for his family: he needed it after the loss of his uncle's benefaction and he didn't seem to be doing too badly with the so-called enemy, in fact he'd travelled the world with the British.

Nor did Patrick dwell too much on how The Family had been able to buy the big house or on how their subsequent income was generated, they certainly didn't seem to work: the reality was that it was income on which his own family's situation depended.

For Patsy, Molly and Theresa, Larch Hill provided a rich backdrop to a dream of a childhood. There were woods to explore and trees to climb; there were fields of wildflowers to race through and tall grasses in which three small people could have a good game of hide-and-seek; haystacks were the best jumping places ever — a soft landing always guaranteed — and rock-strewn streams of clear mountain water nearby were places to paddle and splash and to dip in cheap little nets for a spot of fishing. Then there was the pony and trap, a favourite with the girls, bought by The Family along with the house but used mainly by Patrick for trips into Rathfarnham to buy in supplies. In their comfortable gatehouse, Patrick recognised that his family had an easier life than many others he knew.

"Mammy, Mammy, there's a leprechaun on the fence," Molly suddenly yelled, her shriek interrupting a family game. They were trotting home from a buying trip in the trap, counting how many different birds they could spy, when little Molly had screamed and hidden under the blanket in the back of the cart.

"A leprechaun, was it?" said Patrick, trying to sound encouraging whilst quickly having to control Seamus with the reins after the horse shied unexpectedly and set off at a bit of a gallop. "And what was the little feller doing?" shouted Patrick, winking at Lizzie on the board beside him.

"Mending his shoes," stuttered Molly.

"Like all good leprechauns," said Lizzie. "Don't mind him now."

Patsy told Molly not to be so silly but her own eyes were on stalks all the same as she tried to catch a glimpse of the miniature cobbler. She herself often saw strange people, so often that by now she took them for granted as just a part of normal life. Her favourite was the old woman she regularly met in the field or down by the river, her silent companion. Patsy first saw her while out playing on the grass in front of the big house: she had told her mother she'd seen a strange woman wearing very old clothes and tending the garden and her mother had just said: "Of course you did. She wouldn't be wearing new clothes for gardening now, would she?"

Then Patsy saw the same old woman in the same old clothes only this time down by the river and she told her mammy again.

"Of course," Lizzie had said, "no one would be wearing new clothes to go down to the river where it can be quite muddy. Who'd want to ruin their good clothes just to catch a bit of fish for supper?"

After several more sightings and the same sort of reaction, Patsy didn't even bother to mention any more either the old woman or the other floaty people she often saw: if her mother was so familiar with them and what they wore, then obviously everyone saw the same things.

But Patsy had never seen a leprechaun, her strange people were wispier and more see-through than a solid person, than a proper little man mending shoes. She was quite jealous of Molly and her leprechaun and she didn't really think her sister was silly at all.

"I'm a bit worried about those two girls," Lizzie said to Patrick that evening. "Patsy talks about seeing some old woman round the place and now Molly says she saw a leprechaun."

"I wouldn't worry about those two," said Patrick. "Molly must have seen something by the road because Seamus certainly did, or else he sensed something not quite right, else why would he have bolted and taken us for an unexpected race down the lane. I thought we were going to spill all the shopping along the road. As for Patsy, that girl has too vivid an imagination. She was telling me that there's a famous composer who plays the piano but never gets washed. She says she plays the piano too so she doesn't see why she should have to get washed either. Fortunately, she wasn't too keen on the idea of getting very smelly and everyone holding their noses whenever she came near, so we can breathe a pleasant, stink-free sigh of relief."

"Actually, I was talking to Miss Bourke and she's very impressed by Patsy's playing," said Lizzie, "especially for such a young child. She said it's of course early days but she thinks Patsy could have the right talent to study the piano properly, at a proper music institute. I like the sound of that; our Patsy becoming a professional pianist. I don't know what that sort of thing costs, though." She cuddled in a bit closer and traced her hand up and down his stomach. "Perhaps you'd better get your brush out, Patrick O'Kelly, get it dipped and put it to work."

"What's this talk about dipping my brush and putting it to work, Mrs O'Kelly. I thought you were a cultured woman."

"So I am," said Lizzie, "but that doesn't mean I can't encourage your strokes."

3

Clothes were being sorted in a most disorganised way as the sisters were told to pack their small drawstring bags, with more frocks and socks ending in heaps on the floor than being carefully folded and packed for travel. A visit to Uncle Stephen and Aunt Mary on the Quays was planned, always a source of great excitement for the youngsters. Patsy insisted on taking a picture she had drawn showing Beethoven hiding under the kitchen table: she had decorated a cardboard frame for it and wanted to give it to her Uncle Stephen as a gift. Molly chose to gather a small posy of wildflowers for Aunt Mary, protecting them in some tissue paper and tying them prettily with a piece of her precious red hair-ribbon; there weren't enough flowers in Dublin, she declared. The littlest one, Theresa, copied her big sisters: she drew a stick family with a blue pencil and picked a small handful of the different grasses which grew along the side of the house drive: she shoved it all into her bag with all the eager disregard an infant could muster. They also chose a couple of games to take to play with their cousins, Kevin and Tessie. All these personal preparations represented an important ritual whenever the family went visiting, giving the youngsters a sense of responsibility for themselves and towards their hosts and at the same time helping to build up the feeling of adventure and anticipation and so infuse every aspect of the occasion with as much pleasure as possible. That way it somehow seemed to last longer.

The girls loved to visit Dublin, to skitter hand-in-hand along the river and see all the ships tied up from all round the world and hear the shouting dockers frantic at their work, bundles and bales of cargo swinging high above them on the end of huge strong rope-nets and being manoeuvred to a safe landing by the muscular men in their shirt-sleeves and canvas aprons: to wander up and down Sackville Street gazing into shop windows where things they didn't even recognise were on display and to gaze at the finely balanced bonanzas of fruits and vegetables and sausages and pies piled in profusion on the carts of the street traders. Best of all, they loved to stand right at the bottom of Nelson's Pillar and get their heads as closely pressed in to the stone plinth as possible to try to focus up the full height and into the sky, especially good fun when it was raining.

But then they looked through the eyes of excited country children, unlike the city's own issue whose lives were too often played out on broken pavements beneath rusting palings bordering broken-windowed hovels flat-fronted straight on to the street. Kids with chubby arms and runny noses had their fun in dirty rain-stained yards and rubble-strewn cobbles. Old battered cans served as both seats and drums while up-turned splintered drawers and boxes served as cots for the babies and pens for the toddlers the older children were set to mind. The newly-arrived Larch Hill contingent were too animated to really notice any of this or the empty gaps in the street, the rubble of former shops and offices settling into seemingly permanent ugly piles years after the 1916 bombardment: for Dublin's own, the ugly reminders of their home city being torn apart had become an all-too-familiar dangerous playground.

Stephen and Mary Lett lived on the south side of the River Liffey in a tall house on Usher's Quay, a tall house in a long row of tall houses in which each doorway had its own steps leading up from the street. Neighbours would gather for a chat and a gossip on the steps and they would greet the Larch Hill visitors with oohs and aahs at how big the little ones were getting, the locals already inured to the rubble of a bombed-out site on Usher's Quay itself. Stephen used to have the use of the whole house before the brewery debacle but now he, his wife and their young son and toddler-of-a-daughter had to share it with various families renting out rooms on each floor. The once-grand house had devolved into a crowded tenement. Stephen had maintained the use of the ground level, which meant that when the visiting girls were in bed they could listen to all the noises from the street, to all the footsteps, some busy, some lingering, to the chatter and singing of people going home from the bars, to the funnels of the ships hooting out arrivals and departures: they would fall asleep to the night sounds of the city. The adults would be in the next room, sitting up late over a glass or two and catching up on everyone's news.

The Dublin visit also allowed Patrick to get together with his brother, Arthur, who had recently returned from Paris where he had been working as a printer on a newspaper but returned home when the unrest was becoming more organised. Patrick left Lizzie and the children at Stephen's house and went to meet him. Arthur was more strident in his political views than Patrick and was already an active Volunteer in the fight to rid Ireland of the British. He welcomed any opportunity to persuade his brother to enlist in the cause and when the two met for a glass of stout in a Dublin bar he didn't waste much time before bringing up the subject.

A new so-called British army had been sent over from England, he said, made up of desperate men recruited from unemployment queues and British prisons. The one lot were tempted by getting some wages at last, the others by the promise of a free pardon if they went over to Ireland to help control the populace. It had been the brainchild of the British Secretary of State for War, Winston Churchill, and so far some 7,000 men had been recruited. As soon as they arrived, they had immediately launched an offensive against small towns and villages across Ireland, beginning with Tuam in County Galway. By November their targets had grown: Tralee was besieged, all businesses there closed and no food was allowed into the town for a week. By December they were laying waste to a large part of the city of Cork. The British Government had evidently approved the idea of so-called 'official reprisals', the attacking and burning of properties of suspected Volunteers and sympathisers, no proof necessary, a policy that was condemned by the King himself.

"They're really rough types, you wouldn't believe even the British would resort to using such men," said Arthur. "They deliberately look for trouble and if they can't find any then they create it and to hell with the consequences because they make everybody else pay and no one in authority seems to have a mind to stop them. They're worse than the soldiers we faced in 1916 because they're not really soldiers, not as we would recognise the term. They're just thugs in uniform. It would be interesting to see exactly what their orders are, assuming they have any."

"There must be someone in proper charge," said Patrick.

"You wouldn't say that if you'd seen them in action, brother. It's all very peaceful out where you live, no doubt, but here the city has been

31

turned into one huge battleground for them to play at cowboys and Indians but for real, with real guns, and we're all the poor red-necks. It's as if they have been given completely free rein to do whatever they like and what they like is aggression, violence and bullying with the butt of their rifles. They don't miss an opportunity, they'll pick on anyone, especially after they've had a gutful of ale, and no one seems to discipline them at all, they get on with their brutalities with impunity and drink as much as they want whenever they want. I don't mind telling you that this enemy is a very dirty one and seems answerable to no one."

"And how many of you are there up against them? Have you any weapons to match theirs?" asked Patrick.

"I'm afraid I can't answer those questions, Patrick, you haven't joined us yet. Notice how I say 'yet' as I'm sure you'll come round. What I can tell you is this: I'm convinced that this time we'll win, it's not going to be 1916 all over again."

"I'm sure the General Post Office will be only too glad to hear it."

"Don't be flippant, brother, the situation is deadly serious. We all have to be careful, whether we're active or not. These Black and Tans, as they're called, respect no one and nothing, neither you nor your own. Do you know they're issued with as many bullets as they want, with no count taken or records kept? That's the simple measure of the situation."

Patrick sat staring into his beer. What he was being told was far worse than any of the whisperings and rumblings he'd heard out at Rathfarnham, unless he'd been missing something; everyone there knew he was no Volunteer so perhaps they too watched what they said in front of him.

"My brother-in-law's in the British Army, he's a Dublin man and he's no thug," he said.

"Where does he serve?" asked Arthur.

"He was a few years in India, I think," said Patrick.

"Then perhaps you should consult the Indians."

The two men supped their drinks letting the implication lie.

"When you get back tonight promise me you won't tell your brother-in-law where we met this evening," said Arthur. "I'm sure he's fine and all that but we don't trust anyone, anyone at all. Now, tell me how things are out at Larch Hill, life in the gatehouse must have been hard to get used to after being in the big house? I believe an English couple bought it from Lizzie's uncle."

The brothers spent the rest of their couple of hours together conversing about this and that. Their lives were quite different but they remained close. At the end of the evening Arthur asked Patrick if he would hide something for him, just for a couple of nights while he was in Dublin.

"Of course, anything to help," said Patrick.

Arthur scanned the barroom casually and when satisfied at what he saw he passed a package to Patrick under the table.

"Why all the secrecy, Arthur, what is it?" asked Patrick.

"Never mind what it is, best not to concern yourself with that."

Patrick felt through the paper wrapping and stared across at his brother who was still casually scanning the room with his drink raised to his lips, all the while smiling as if he was just enjoying a good chat.

"Is this what I think it is?" said Patrick, frozen by the reality of what he was now holding.

"As I said, it's best not to think about it at all," said Arthur. "Just tuck it inside your coat somewhere and forget it's there."

"How can I forget it's there when I know it's a gun that's there?" said Patrick in astonishment.

"Whisht and be quiet, brother. You need to be more cautious." He leaned across the table. "I'm real sorry to land this on you Patrick but I have somewhere I have to go tonight and in the deserted streets I stand a better chance than normal of being stopped by the Tans. I can't be found with that on me."

"But I can, is that it? Is that why you didn't want to wait until tomorrow to meet and me just having arrived at Stephen's with Lizzie and the children?"

"You'll be safe, I promise. I'll have someone follow you back to the Quays just to make sure. You'd better be on your way now, there are plenty of people still out and about, the curfew's not in force until ten so you won't be noticed, just make sure you avoid anything that looks like trouble. I'll give the nod to my friend as you're leaving."

Patrick quickly glanced around the bar but he couldn't spot anyone taking any particular interest in them.

"Best you don't know who," said Arthur. "And I'll see you three nights from now, same place."

"It seems it's best I don't know anything at all about anything at all," Patrick said sarcastically. "I'm surprised you trust me at all as I haven't joined your fight yet."

"It's not my fight, brother, it's all of our fight."

With that Patrick stood up and walked out of the bar. The gun felt huge in his coat and he thought everyone must be able to see him shaking with nerves but to his surprise he did feel a quiet rush of satisfaction to be doing something valuable and positive, no matter how reluctantly. He felt quite proud. He thought Arthur would be proud too.

In the house at Usher's Quay the children had been put to bed but were finding it difficult to get to sleep: usually they drifted off listening to the medley of street noises outside but tonight the normal buzz of voices and the clap-clap of feet passing by on the pavement were joined by loud bangs and booms that were totally unfamiliar. The sisters thought it was fireworks and pestered their mother without success to let them look out of the window.

"Is it like this every night now?" Lizzie asked her sister-in-law when the children had finally been settled.

"More or less it is, occasionally we have a quiet night but more often than not it's like this or worse," said Mary. "People don't feel safe in their beds at night and that's the truth of it. I advised against you coming to visit but Stephen said it'd be safe enough and he was anxious to see you all before he goes back off leave. In a way he doesn't realise how bad the situation is as he's not here all the time."

"It must be terribly frightening for you, especially when he's away."

"Far more frightening for some people," said Mary. "Sometimes we hear shouts and screams when the Tans force their way into someone's home. You hear them hammering on doors or battering them in with their rifles and then the screaming starts. 'God have mercy on those poor people', I always pray."

"What a terrible way to have to live," said Lizzie. "Would you not think of moving or are you determined to stay here? We could make room for you and the little ones in the gatehouse for a while."

"I fear it's going to be more than a while," said Mary. "Anyway, thank you for the offer, Lizzie, but this is our home and we'll stay put. And I must say, I have some sympathy for the men fighting those awful Tans, their behaviour and casual violence toward people here is dreadful."

The women's talk was interrupted by Patrick arriving back at the house. After a few pleasantries he asked Mary if she would be very offended if he called it a night and he apologised that he felt quite tired, no doubt more to do with his few pints, he said, than the easy enough journey from Larch Hill.

Dublin was the same exciting place as ever for the girls. Their Auntie Mary said she was so delighted with their gifts from home that she wanted to treat them to ice-creams from a fancy shop in the city centre: the girls all chose the three-coloured sort like the one sold in their village shop, a delicious biscuit sandwich filled with chocolate, strawberry and banana flavours that totally lived up to its visual promise, Kevin and Tessie wanted just the chocolate. They all sat on a bench in the middle of Sackville Street enjoying their treat, pressing the wafers together and then licking the ice-cream that oozed out round the sides. Two men ran past chased by a posse of brown-clad soldiers who knocked shoppers and bystanders out of the way roughly with their arms and rifles, all the time shouting and cursing. Lizzie and Mary exchanged cold looks.

"Did you see those men playing chase?" said Patsy. "Shall we do that next, Mam, can we, can we?"

"Yes Mam, can we play soldiers chasing too?" said Kevin.

"They're not nice men, those soldiers, they're not playing and you need to keep out of their way," said Mary. "And also it's a bit too crowded for such small people as you to be playing chase," she said lowering the tension. "You can run much faster than we can so we wouldn't be able to keep up. Then you'd get lost and be too late home for dinner and we'd have to eat yours for you and you'd have to go to bed hungry. Imagine that. Nothing to eat until breakfast tomorrow." She turned to Lizzie. "Let's hope the poor men get away without being caught. It's to be several tortured nights in Dublin Castle for them if they don't."

"Is that where they're taken?"

"Yes, the place has become notorious. I think we'd better make our way back before there's any more trouble. It's a sorry state when you can't even sit in peace with the children without men running past with guns. Right, girls and boy," she said, "shall we go back to the house and do a bit of baking? I've some delicious homemade blackberry jam that tastes even more delicious sandwiched in a sponge cake."

"Can we help with the mixing?" asked Molly.

"You certainly can, I'd expect nothing less," said Mary. "Your mother tells me you're great ones for baking. You must take after your Da. Now finish your ice-creams and we'll head home and get started."

The women and children made their way back across the Liffey over the Ha'penny Bridge, the youngsters leaning over the cast-iron railings and squealing at the seagulls floating indifferently on the river. Once off the bridge, Mary pressed the children into silence as an armoured car pulled up slowly and idled a few yards ahead. Accompanying the car was a troop of Tans, tin-hatted and rifle-loaded, escorting a line of prisoners along the riverside wall of the quays. Foul language and racist jokes filled the air while rifle butts were regularly dug into some man or other's legs and if as a result the man's hands strayed from being finger-linked behind his head then he got another rifle jab sharp into his side. Also part of the procession were boys no older than seven or eight, marching along with the prisoners, wielding bits of sticks and aiming their toy guns at the soldiers. Their young Dublin voices sparked hilarity with the British, more oaths, more curses, more hatred.

"I don't understand what's happening in Dublin," said Patsy, gawking and pulling at her mother's sleeve. "Why are they all marching along like that? Where are they going to?"

"Best not to talk about any of that right now," said Lizzie. "Wait until we get home."

"And did you see that sign hanging up while we were eating our ice-cream?" Patsy persisted. "It read 'Select bar upstairs' but there wasn't any upstairs. The downstairs walls just disappeared into the sky. What's happened to all the buildings?"

"Later, we'll talk about it later," said Lizzie.

Relieved to get back to the house unscathed, Mary bustled about trying to make everything seem safe and normal again. She laid a cloth on the table over the good cloth and the baking session began. It was a messy procedure and siftings of flour clouded the room and dusted the floor but soon enough the place was filled with the tempting smell of freshly baked cake.

"Want some now," said little Theresa.

"We have to wait while the cake cools, then we have to cut it in half right through the middle and then spread the jam thickly on the bottom layer," said Mary. "Who wants to be in charge of that?"

They all did.

"Right then. Patsy, you're the eldest so you can cut the sponge, you have to be very careful because the knife is quite sharp and you have to try to get each half as level as you can. Then Molly, you can be in charge of spreading the jam with the butter knife. You, Theresa, will have the responsibility of spooning the jam out of the jar and making sure that Molly has the right amount when she needs it. We don't want a jam sponge with jam only on one side, now, do we. I wouldn't want to be the one to get the slice with no jam. And Kevin, you can set the plates and cups out."

Patrick and Stephen got back from their stroll round Dublin Bay just in time for the tea and cake and the girls glowed with pride when everyone commented on how delicious it was. Patsy was enjoying herself too much to remember to ask her mammy about the line of men they'd seen by the river.

Everyone stayed in that evening, the lamps glowing warmly and the river noises filtering in from the other side of the road. The girls played in their room with their cousins until bedtime and the grown-ups sat quietly round the table. Talk turned to the incident in Sackville Street that day and the parade of prisoners along the quay: it seemed these were commonplace encounters now. There had been another attack on Bandon Military Barracks and the Tans were looking for reprisals. Homes and shops and offices across the city had been raided and searched and looted, people had been interrogated and bundled into lorries and driven away. Soldiers were positioned on street corners, tanks and armoured cars and barricades blocked main and side roads alike, high vantage points and major buildings on the other side of the Liffey had Tans stationed on the roofs, rifles at the ready, as security was tightened.

"I had no idea how bad the situation had become," said Lizzie. "We seem to be living in a completely different country out at Rathfarnham. You must think us awfully ignorant. Has there been no talk in the bakery, Patrick?"

"Ay there's plenty of talk, people are getting very angry, ordinary men you wouldn't think interested in fighting are saying that something has to be done and that we should all be doing it. I didn't realise Dublin had become so difficult and dangerous, a positive war zone, though I suppose it is only a few years since the Rising so the British authorities won't be taking any chances in the capital. What do you think, Stephen, after all you're in the British Army?"

"I am, more's the pity. If I hadn't signed on for so many years, I tell you, I'd be a Volunteer out there in the streets myself with the boys. Selfishly I now have to think of my wife and young family and what we'd have to lose. I'm thinking of moving us all over to Liverpool, Mary has close family there. These Black and Tans aren't like the army men I serve with, they wouldn't get away with their atrocities if they were. It's a few good sergeants they need, that'd sort them out. But then that's not the policy, is it? These men are actually doing just what the British Government has told them to do: terrorise the Irish into submission no matter what it takes. I tell you one thing: when I get home on leave, the first thing I do is to take off my uniform and hang it in the cupboard. I feel too ashamed of any association with these men. Nor, if I'm honest, do I want people here to think I'm not a sympathiser. How could you not sympathise when your country is subjected to so much brutality by armed thugs on a daily basis? No, the executions of the Easter leaders was the tipping point for a great many people, myself included. Those murders in Kilmainham, for that's all you can call what the British did, murder, they did no more than rally ordinary people up out of their armchairs and on to the streets. The executions proved not to be the end of the matter, as was intended, but the beginning of the end. God, would you listen to me?" said Stephen, "I'm sounding like a recruiter myself. What are your thoughts, Patrick? Are you thinking of joining?"

Patrick looked at his wife with concern but he spoke from his heart.

"Let's just say that I've had my eyes opened. I have to examine my own honesty and honour when I see what's happening out there."

Mary decided to try to lighten the mood somewhat.

"There are some less brutal successes amongst all the killings — oh what a poor way to express it. Anyway," she said, "one of the Volunteers' regular targets is the mail coming from England to the various garrisons. The husband of a friend I know works in the sorting office at the Rotunda, so this story is from him, so to speak. The bags are off-loaded from the Liverpool mail-boats and put into vans to be taken to the post office where they're thrown down three deep chutes into the sorting room. The other night the sorters were waiting at the bottom of the chutes as usual and, as usual, looming shadows of the sacks were cast across the tops of the chutes. 'Here it comes,' said the sorters, expecting to catch the bags of mail. But instead of catching sacks they themselves were caught by young Volunteers entering the place down the chutes, who then waited for the mail and helped sort it before making off with all the letters and official correspondence for the Castle and all the other garrisons. The temporary sorters were still making their escape down the road, laden down with the stolen post, when the armoured car drove up from the Castle to collect what was of course already gone. Evidently there were some letters from spies in the haul. Now what do you think of that?"

"I can't believe there would be spies," said Lizzie.

"Sure, there are always spies at work when there's a war on, that's why everyone has to watch what they say and to whom they say it," said Stephen.

"I think you're right there," said Patrick. "I wouldn't like to be in their shoes when they're discovered."

"They'll no doubt get what they deserve," said Lizzie.

"They'll find themselves in a sticky situation all right," said Mary. "Frankly, the stamp of disapproval will be on them." In the ensuing laughter she managed to steer the conversation away from the war going on outside and thoughts of the armoured cars and tanks they had seen and could still hear patrolling outside were forgotten as family chit-chat and memories took over the conversation and whiled away a couple of lazy hours.

As the clock struck midnight the small group decided to call it a day. They had passed a convivial evening but there was another day tomorrow to enjoy, if they weren't too tired to enjoy it. They dispersed off to their various rooms, quietly so as not to wake the children, when abruptly there came loud insistent banging on the door and men's voices shouting to 'open up in there'. It was the nightmare shared by everyone living in Dublin — the night-raid, the bullying, the violence, interrogation at gunpoint, threats, beatings, cold terror. For Patrick it was a bigger nightmare; he suddenly remembered he had Arthur's gun, which was still wrapped in a parcel in his overcoat.

He quickly pulled Lizzie into the bedroom and told her. "Lizzie, I've a gun in my coat. They'll find it and then God knows what will happen. It's not mine I promise you, but they won't be interested in hearing that."

"What do you mean you have a gun in your coat but it's not yours?" said Lizzie in a frozen mix of astonishment and fear.

"Now's not the time to explain," said Patrick, rummaging to retrieve the weapon. "Jesus, what shall I do with the bloody thing?"

The hammering on the door was getting more frantic and aggressive and Lizzie could hear Stephen calling to ask what was the matter.

"We'll show you what the fuckin' matter is, you filthy fuckin' Irish bastard scum," shouted a voice through the door. "Open up or we'll open the fucking door for you."

Lizzie could hear Stephen start to unlock the door.

"Quick, give it to me," she said to Patrick. She took hold of the parcel and tore the paper off to reveal the handgun and the bullets. She rushed into the girls' room and shut the door as Stephen came face to face with the intruders, still remonstrating with them. A hulking squad of drunken Black and Tans had taken over the hallway, looming enormous and frightening in their heavy military topcoats and sinister in their casual regard of their weapons.

"What do you think you're doing? What do you want barging in at this hour of the night?" said Stephen.

"Well now, you Mick bastard, I'd say we're investigating evidence of unwarranted armed rebellion against His Majesty's Government, that's what I'd say we're fuckin' doing here, you fucking Irish cunt," said the squad leader.

"Then you have no cause to force your way in here, let alone use such coarse language," said Stephen. "I'm a serving British soldier and I'll report you for this. What's the name of your commanding officer?"

One of the Tans jabbed him hard in the stomach with the butt of his rifle. "That's the reply from our commanding officer," he said. Stephen keeled over and was booted to the floor.

"What would His Majesty's Government be doing with a Mick like you in his army, you lying fucker? And if you are in the British Army, what are you fuckin' well doing here in this god-awful place?" asked the one in charge. "No, you're not one of us, you're just a stupid fucking Mick."

The squad set to smashing all the crockery off the dresser shelves with great enthusiasm and apparent amusement; overturning and up-ending furniture so roughly that some chairs were reduced to little more than sticks; searching through drawers and cupboards and any containers they spotted, all the time delivering the odd hard kick into Stephen's ribs. Odd trinkets and china ornaments they found were stowed away into their uniform pockets, the remains of the cake were stuffed into their mouths, a few coins lying about vanished, snaffled into their gloves.

"Stop, stop this," screamed Mary. "Look, see, here's his British Army uniform, here it is, it was hanging up in the wardrobe, you can see what regiment he's in, he's due back with them in just two days' time. For pity's sake leave the man alone."

"How do we know it's not a copy of a uniform, or a stolen one?" said the Tan, so close to Mary's face that she could feel all his spit spraying on to her skin and smell the beer on his breath. "He might have acquired it illegally, like, trying to fool us. But we'll not be fooled, will we lads?"

His three cohorts laughed idiotically and copied the boss, spitting gobbies of phlegm and snot down on to Stephen as the three of them pinned him to the floor, so compressing and compacting his chest under their heavy boots that he had to gasp for just the slightest breath. Ridiculously he felt guilty at his sorry situation and embarrassed at being too helpless a man to look after his own wife and home.

In the next room Lizzie quickly smothered the gun in the folds of Theresa's cot blanket: then she threaded the bullets one by one into the tubing of their brass bedstead and hung a cardigan over the end. Then she signalled to Patrick who opened the door loudly and confronted the raiding party.

"Leave that man alone," he bellowed. "He's a proper British soldier,

41

you're the play-acting ones. Look, here's a letter he wrote to my wife, she's his sister. You can see it was sent in the British Army post."

"Hey, lads, look, there's another fuckin' Mick and another room to search. Go and enjoy yourselves," said the boss man.

The three barged into the bedroom cackling and cheering. They laid into the room, pulling everything around as before, ripping and breaking, whatever they could lay their hands on, including the toys and the innocent bits of souvenirs the girls had collected in Dublin, like shells from the shore, tickets from the trams, leaves from the trees in St Stephen's Green. The sisters were well awake by now, scared, sobbing and crying for their mother.

"Look, here are his army leave papers and look at these letters to me," Mary bellowed at the soldier in charge. "Look, why don't you," she shouted as she waved the small bundle in front of his eyes. "I'm his wife and his letters all show the same British Army postmarks, they were all sent through official army channels. You must recognise the stamps. Look, here's his identity card."

The man in charge snatched Mary's letters and examined them roughly, reading out loud for all to hear those private personal messages that a loving husband might write to his wife across the seas.

"Well, lads," he said to his troops, "it seems we have a proper Irish Tommy grovelling at our feet. Sorry, Sir, I'm sure, an understandable mistake, of course," he pursed sarcastically at Stephen. "But you of all people should know we can't take any chances, you being on the same side as us, so to speak, even if you are a bloody Mick, Sir. Help him up lads, gently now, and we'll be on our way, plenty more rich pickings in store tonight, I'll promise you that."

"What about that money you took and all the things you smashed off the shelves?" said Patrick. "You can make good all the loss."

"Really, can we now?" said the man. He walked over to Patrick and stared at him with disdain. "Let's call it your generous contribution to our evening's expenses, shall we, and we'll say no more about it, agreed?

He summoned his men. "Come on lads, you've had your taster, the night's only just begun."

To Stephen he said: "Just a simple misunderstanding, eh? No hard feelings, mate, officer, private."

He loomed over Patrick, sneering and grimacing. "You know," he said, "I think I'll remember your face."

The Tans stormed out of the room with the same aggressive bluster with which they'd arrived but no one in the room relaxed, no one moved or spoke as the hammering on the doors on upstairs floors resounded through the house, followed by the echoes of thumps, shrill voices and screams. Patrick rushed to retrieve the pistol from the cot — he had to do something, couldn't stand by doing nothing while people were being attacked in the rooms right above him by that bunch of cut-throats — but Mary blocked his way.

"What are you thinking of Patrick? There's nothing you can do with one gun except get us all killed and that wouldn't help anyone, not the people upstairs, not us, not your wife, not your children."

The violence went on in the upper storeys until suddenly a thunderous boom was heard from outside the building followed by explosions and the continuing crack of ammunition in a sickening cacophony of sound.

"Mammy, Daddy, come and see. Out the window, look, there's a huge bonfire on the other side of the river."

The adults peered out and watched silently as a tall billowing tower of flames blazed high into the sky over the city and smoke crept thickly over the Liffey waters.

"My God what do any of these people want?" said Mary.

The Black and Tans unit could be heard rushing down the stairs and out into the street shouting obscenities and cursing 'this shithole of a place'. Patrick and Lizzie ran to bolt the door behind them and secure the house as effectively as possible but the squad had already run off along the river to the bridge to enjoy their share of the action. Lizzie turned to her husband.

"I'd better go upstairs and see if anyone needs any help. You tend to Stephen and help sort the place a bit, I'll be back in a few minutes."

"Let me help you, Mammy," said Patsy. Her face was pale with the horror of a night which had intruded into her innocent childhood and drained her of any sense of security.

Lizzie hesitated for a moment then took her daughter's hand and they disappeared up the stairs. Patsy was no stranger to the bloody

43

mishaps that happened on the farms round about Rathfarnham: careless hands got mangled in machinery and fingers were easily severed in the way of the axe coming down to chop the wood for the fire, and often she had peered through barn doors watching cows and sows pushing out their new-borns in a mess of slimy discharge and many's the time she had looked on while her mammy skinned a rabbit for the pot: Patsy found it all fascinating and wasn't in the least bit squeamish, which was just as well: she needed all her stomach control when she went upstairs with her mam. What she had witnessed in the past were everyday things, normal, just part of living in the country. This was different, English soldiers had done all this deliberately, cruelly, to people who were just people getting along as best they could with what little they had. In every set of rooms it was the same: none had been spared: mothers and fathers, boys and girls alike had been beaten and kicked by the drunken men and left groaning and moaning in the debris of their homes. Patsy busied herself helping her mammy, wiping away blood, cleaning wounds and tearing up old garments to fashion makeshift bandages, all the time issuing soothing words of comfort, though no comfort was possible, other than that it might have turned out much worse.

Patrick kept his rendezvous with Arthur a couple of days later and returned the weapon but their conversation this time was very sparing. It was plain to his brother that Patrick had been deeply affected by the Tans' raid. To Arthur, however awful that whole incident, it had been really no more than a routine occurrence of life under the thumb of the Tan mobs but he recognised that for people living in the country in the grounds of an English house it must have been a terrifying shock. Arthur didn't press the point: he didn't have to use any more persuasion for the situation had arrived at Patrick's own door and personal experience was a great lesson in anyone's education, far more effective than any argued propaganda. When they bid their goodbyes, Patrick hugged his brother closely and hard.

"I'll be coming to see you again very soon, Arthur," he said. "Right now, I just want to get my family back home to relative safety but then, well, I can't let this matter lie any longer. You can count me in for whatever you need me to do."

"I'll get our unit in Rathfarnham to contact you," said Arthur. "But you have to realise that once you're in you're in, there'll be no going back."

"There's already no going back. I can't be a bystander with a war going on."

"It'll be dangerous business, Patrick, for you and Lizzie and the children, but we need all the help we can muster. The Rathfarnham men will brief you."

"And no doubt most of them have families too," said Patrick.

"Ay, well you'll probably know most of them already, brother. Let's have one last glass before you set off and maybe raise a toast to your daughter, I believe Patsy was the real little Republican nurse the other night. Here's to you all and we'll speak again soon."

The gun was never mentioned again between Lizzie and Patrick back home at the gatehouse but an unspoken commitment had been established between them. Lizzie had acted quickly and with bravery in Dublin hiding the weapon and her eyes had been opened as horrifically wide as had Patrick's. The sight that greeted her when she had gone up the stairs to help the neighbours on Usher's Quay was an image she could not dismiss from her thoughts: whole families left bloodied and savagely beaten, their homes totally wrecked by the same men who had ruthlessly attacked her brother while all the children were in their beds. It could so easily have been her whole family left bloodied and beaten. For Patrick the violence and the fear and the anger at what might have happened all swirled around in his mind, punctuated by the remonstrations from his own brother about the urgency for armed action against the British. He'd met the local Volunteer's unit as soon as it had been arranged and Lizzie had accepted that her husband would now be out many an evening, leaving the gatehouse as darkness fell and not returning home until the early hours. What he was actually doing was never spoken about, Lizzie would just unquestioningly scrub away any blood and mud clinging to his clothes.

For their two youngest daughters, childish innocence had hidden the worst of the visit to Dublin and they recalled mainly the sound of fireworks and the sight of the bonfire and not the men who had burst into their cousins' home and frightened them all half to death. They were soon re-immersed in the warmth of life at Larch Hill. Lizzie organised dressing-up sessions, when they'd all wear silly clothes or ordinary clothes in silly ways — their mother and father's shoes and hats were always in popular demand — or they would go for rambles to collect leaves and twigs for sticking and making pictures back at the house.

Patsy was less distracted by her new Beethoven piece than she'd expected, she just pictured the composer hiding under his table trembling when soldiers had arrived in his city and leaving it to others to deal with the situation, others like her own mammy and daddy. She had to make herself concentrate on her piano lesson. The composition was something to do with a woman called Elise and Miss Bourke had agreed to tell Patsy another story about Beethoven as a reward for getting on so well with the piece.

"I told you he was a strange man," she told her young protégée. "Do you know what: when his brother died, Beethoven fought with his brother's widow for five years because he wanted to have his brother's son all for himself. For five years! Eventually, maybe because Beethoven was so famous by then, the court agreed to give him what he wanted and the poor mother had to hand over her own boy to someone else. And what happened then, do you think?"

Patsy thought that Baytone would teach the boy how to play the piano so well that he would become famous too.

"You'd think so, wouldn't you, anyone would think so but they'd be wrong, you'd be wrong," said Miss Bourke. "Instead, Beethoven, after such a long battle in the courts to get his hands on the boy, spent his time hitting the lad really hard all the time and slapping him so badly that when the boy grew up he tried to shoot himself in the head rather than put up with Beethoven's cruelty any longer. It's the mercy of God that he didn't succeed. Well now, is that a good enough story for you, Patsy? Can we get on with your lesson now?"

Talk of a gun and shooting made Patsy think back to that frightening night in Dublin.

"Maybe I don't like Baytone as much as I did before," said Patsy. "Is it all right to like his music even though sometimes he was a horrible, smelly, cruel person and a coward who hid under tables?" she asked Miss Bourke.

"His music is his music," said the teacher, "it stands by itself. Sometimes people do bad things or things we don't really understand but we have to try to understand and at the same time appreciate the goodness in them. Beethoven's music was his goodness and that's why we can try to forgive him. Now let's get on."

Patsy wondered what goodness was in the men who beat her uncle Stephen and how she could appreciate anything about them at all after the way they beat up all the other people in the rooms upstairs.

4

The relative calm of the gatehouse was short-lived. The summer days buzzed by with the humming of insects and the singing of birds but the sounds coming from Lizzie were not so sweet. The girls noticed that their mother was constantly trying to clear her throat of something with short wheezy coughs that never seemed to quite do the trick. They noticed it even more when autumn arrived; they usually enjoyed kicking their way through the spread of fallen leaves which crackled over the ground but this year they had to spend more time indoors, their father said it was because the weather had turned colder but they couldn't understand why this year's weather was any different to past years. Their father was certainly busier in the house too, helping with the cooking whenever he was home from the bakery in time and before he went out to his new evening job. Autumn drifted into winter, with its accompaniment of howling winds and driving rain to rattle and splatter on the windows and doors. Even so, normally this was a cosy time of the year, when the youngsters would forget all the fun of being outside and instead enjoy staying indoors: someone would always be ready with a tune on the piano or they might get out a pack of cards for a game or two or piece together a jigsaw puzzle on the floor in front of the fire. But this year the home was very quiet and the children sensed that if they were ever to behave themselves this was the time.

Lizzie developed such a bad cough and sickly pallor that The Family called in their own doctor to examine her. Patrick was vacant with worry but the doctor reassured him that all would be well after a few weeks of complete rest and if the patient was kept nice and warm. As he was leaving, however, he took The Family to one side.

"I don't think she has much longer," he told them. "She is in quite an advanced stage of tuberculosis. I'm not sure the husband is in any fit state right now to receive the news, especially in front of the daughters, but I need to advise you of what to expect. A few weeks at the most, I'd say."

After the doctor had said his goodbyes, The Family at once insisted to Patrick that Lizzie move into an upstairs bedroom at the front of the main house the very next day where she would be much warmer and able to get some good, proper rest away from the busy demands of the gatehouse. They told the girls that they would move the bed towards the window so their mother could look out and keep an eye on them, though of course the children wouldn't be giving their mother any reason to get cross, now, would they? Patrick said he had a friend in Tullamore whose daughter might come to help with the girls while he was at the bakery until Lizzie was better and that perhaps she could also look after some of Lizzie's chores in the big house. The Family told Patrick he wasn't to concern himself on that account: his home was safe and now Lizzie's comfort was the most pressing consideration.

The three girls were delighted to see the beautiful bedroom their mother was to use while she was getting better: there was a cast-iron fireplace with a lovely warm coal fire blazing in it and a deep-cushioned sofa positioned close enough to catch all the heat if you were sitting having a read or a chat. The bed blankets were of the softest and thickest wool they had ever felt and the bed was the sort that you could bounce up and down on and hardly feel the springs. Nor did The Family tell them off when the girls put the mattress to the test. A vase of flowers provided a splash of lovely colour on a small table next to the pillow end of the bed and a jug of water and some glasses on the same table were conveniently close so that anyone in bed having a sudden thirst wouldn't have to stretch far to get a drink. Of course the girls preferred their mother to be at home properly but in the circumstances they happily carried over their well-hugged teddies and rag dolls to keep her company. A few of her clothes were hung in a wardrobe and The Family presented her with a lovely embroidered nightdress to cheer her up and make her feel pretty during her illness and did whatever they thought best to make her comfortable while she was their guest.

The friend from Tullamore sent his daughter over to Larch Hill as soon as Patrick explained the situation. Betty arrived and somehow contrived to lift the gloom in the gatehouse. She was careful not to make any changes that might cause upset, though she obviously had her own ways of doing things, and she managed to fit into the household as easily as a big sister. The visitor was great fun with the children when there was time but nevertheless insisted that Patsy kept up her piano practice. Betty likewise insisted to Patrick that he remember he had three little ones still and not to be moping around too much all the time, he was their daddy and they needed to feel he wasn't too worried about their mammy.

Life at the gatehouse wasn't the same any more but a spark had been ignited with Betty's arrival. She was a happy young woman, very pretty in a country-living way and well used to looking after a home: she lived with her parents and several brothers on a small farm and had as much work to do as any young woman in the same circumstance. She was warm and kind, and she amused the girls with stories of naughty cows which would object to being milked and would nudge her off the stool while she was busy pulling their teats and the milk would squirt out like a white jet all over the place; she described how to turn the milk into butter in the big wooden churn — what hard repetitive work that was, she said, no wonder she had strong arms fit for a man — and she talked about the fun of walking the cows along the lanes when they had to be moved out to pasture every morning, then back again to the barn every evening.

The girls particularly enjoyed Betty's romantic stories of her young man and his timid courting and how he would suddenly get all shy if he saw her unexpectedly while he was working in the potato fields and she passed by with the cows: she always waved the stick at him too and he'd get even more flustered, she said, and the girls would have a fit of the giggles.

For all her rest, Lizzie's health didn't improve. She was certainly more comfortable in the big house and The Family were very attentive but she missed the hectic life of the gatehouse and meanwhile she was getting thinner and the coughing was worse. Patrick would stare up at her bedroom window and his heart would ache with a growing sense of loss, but he tried to heed Betty's advice and be cheerful with his daughters. He still had to work, of course, he still had to get on with everyday living and fetch the supplies from the town, but everything that before had offered at least some sense of fun thanks to Lizzie was now just a routine struggle. Thank God Betty seemed to have an innate understanding of what he was up to when he left the house quietly most nights.

"Come on now Molly and Theresa," he said. "We three'll go to the shops in town and you, Patsy, can spend some time with your mammy."

Patsy felt torn and guilty inside: she wanted to look after her mother but she also didn't want Molly to catch sight of that leprechaun again without her having the chance to see him too. Of late their father had gone out in the trap alone, silently getting Seamus sorted and leaving with what was hardly a cheery farewell so Patsy didn't want to miss out on this trip, the first time in a week or so that their father had invited any company. She was sure the leprechaun would be sighted.

"Are you sure you can manage without me?" she asked, trying not to give herself away. "I can carry much more than Molly and Theresa. I'm older and I'm bigger than them."

"Yes, you are, Patsy," said Patrick, "and that's why I'm giving you the main responsibility of looking after your mother while I'm out and Betty's busy with the chores. Your mammy needed some cheering up when I saw her before and you might make the most of the opportunity of someone actually welcoming all your chatter."

He got Seamus hitched to the trap, Molly and Theresa climbed aboard, poking their tongues out at Patsy, and they set off to town. Patsy watched them go with mixed feelings: she did envy them the trip but their da had said he had chosen her to look after their mammy because she was old enough to be properly responsible, so she liked that idea.

When the trap was out of sight and she could no longer hear the clip-clop of the horse's feet and the wheels turning over the dirt lane, Patsy fetched a book from the gatehouse and took it with her to read to her mother. As she was running up the stairs the missus of The Family was just leaving Lizzie's room and she gently pressed two fingers to her lips to shush Patsy into being a bit quieter.

"Your mother's not having a very good day, Patsy, she seems very tired, so you need to take very special care of her, as I know you always try to do. What's that you've got there? One of your books?"

"Yes Missus, it's one of my mammy's favourites, it's all about a family of little animals living in the woods and she reads it to us in bed at night. I thought I'd have a go at reading it to her instead, though I'm not sure of some of the long words."

"Well, if it's one of your mother's favourites I'm sure she'll be able to fill in anything you struggle with. Go on in now and remember not to make too much noise."

The child stole into the room like a mouse, as she thought, though her attempt at being quiet was perhaps more disturbing than if she'd just walked in normally. Lizzie was stretched out on the settee and greeted her eldest child with a smile.

"Patsy love, you're a welcome sight for these eyes of mine. It's fine and restful here but even too much rest can get tiring after a while, though I know you never sit still long enough for that to be a problem you've ever experienced. Come and sit by me, it's lovely and warm by the fire."

Lizzie spoke slowly and so softly that it was difficult for Patsy to make out everything her mother was saying, especially as it was broken up so much by her coughing. She sat herself down and snuggled into the crook of her mother's arm, which felt less padded than usual, Patsy noticed. Normally, snuggling into her mammy made the youngster feel all cosy and secure and the sisters usually fought to get the best position but this time it just didn't feel the same.

"You feel a bit thin, Mammy, are you going to get better soon?" she asked.

"I am a bit thin now, Patsy, but I'll be up and about very soon and that'll bring back my appetite. Have the others taken Seamus into town yet? I bet you wished you could go with them, I know your daddy has gone on his own lately though I did tell him that you girls must miss the trips to the shops and the ride in the trap. I know you like going into town, don't you?"

"I do, I like to look at everything in the shops and imagine what all the different sweeties would taste like, and I like to see all the people in the street looking different than they do on a Sunday, they're less serious and their clothes are more crumpled, and I like to see my friends from the town and have a laugh with them and talk about things."

"What sort of things do you talk about?"

"We talk about whether we've caught any fish or not and who's had any visitors from Dublin or anywhere and who's had a fight with their brother or sister and if anyone has a new game or a bike or something really special like that and whether we'll ever get to taste all those sweeties in the shop. And we tell each other jokes and any stories we've heard. I sometimes try to tell them about the old woman I see and her old clothes but they never seem interested in her."

"Well perhaps you could keep her as your secret, Patsy. Now. if you're going to read me that book you've brought, you'd better make a start. But would you get me a glass of water first, please, Patsy. My throat feels very dry. I am fed up with this silly cough."

Patsy fetched her mother a drink and helped to hold the glass to her lips.

"Can I just rest my head on your lap while I listen to the story?"

"Of course you can, Mammy," said Patsy, glowing with importance.

Lizzie settled down and put her head on Patsy's lap. The girl looked at her mother's hair splayed out over her knees: she had beautiful black hair which she generally wore pinned up on top in what looked to Patsy like two fat wings of hair pointing out to the sides and held in place by a fancy pin but today it was all just loose. Patsy combed her fingers through it and started to read. Lizzie snuggled into her daughter's knee and imagined she felt Patrick playing his hands through her hair.

She drifted to a time when they were courting, she and her fine handsome young man with his own shock of thick black hair and such strong bushy eyebrows that arched over his big brown eyes; his eyes had a bit of a squint in them but it gave him that look of vulnerability that Lizzie so loved. They would walk out together keeping the respectable distance but, when they were alone, she loved his gentle caresses and his loving murmurings in her ear, the way he would run his fingers through her hair and put his face to it.

Patsy carried on reading quietly but at the same time trying to put some character into her voice the way her mammy always did to make the story come alive off the pages. She worried that her stumbling over some of the words might spoil the effect but when she felt her mother completely relax it made her feel pleased and important and that her da had chosen the right daughter for the job. She was pleased now that she hadn't gone off in the trap. She had finished the book but decided to start again lest the silence suddenly wake her mammy.

The yard resounded with animated voices and happy chaos when the trap arrived home and clocked into the drive laden with the supplies. There was a nip in the air and a cold breeze threaded its way through the group but Molly and Theresa were nevertheless particularly excited: they couldn't help unload and carry the bags and boxes into the kitchen quick enough as their father had allowed them to choose sweets out of the shop for when they got back and everything had been sorted into its place. He said they all deserved a bit of a treat for being confined at Larch Hill for so long, going into town only for Mass on Sundays. It was a rich reward. The two sisters had chosen brightly coloured gobstoppers for Patsy: they knew she gazed at them every time she went anywhere near the shop and had been saving up odd coppers towards treating them all to one each. A surprise bag holding three all for herself awaited her.

"I'll go up and see your mammy and I'll send Patsy down to help you and Betty put all the shopping away," said Patrick. "Don't forget to take the bags into the main house that need going there, only one at a time, mind, I know you're good hard workers but I don't want you straining your backs. Leave the real heavy stuff to me. I'll see to it later. Then when you've done, you can join us upstairs in the main house and show your mammy what you've got. I'll check first and see if she's up to a visit from such a couple of young hooligans."

Molly and Theresa set about the last of the stowing away, supervised by Betty, all the while salivating at the thoughts of what sugary delights were to come.

Patrick climbed the now familiar stairs to call on Lizzie. He did miss having her at home but it couldn't be helped and he knew that The Family had been right and generous with their loan of the bedroom. He tiptoed up to the door and listened outside before going in so as not to unduly disturb anyone but all seemed peaceful. When he crept in, there was Patsy sitting reading aloud with her mother's head cradled on her knees. Patsy beamed a smile at her father. Lizzie didn't move.

"Daddy, look, I've put Mammy into a really good sleep with all my reading. I've already been through the book four times but I didn't want to stop and move and wake her up, she's having such a good rest."

Patrick looked at the still body of his wife. There was no sign of any gentle lifting and falling through her nightdress, no sign of any life, no sign of his Lizzie. He could only stand there in silence, staring, stricken, dreading to admit the inevitable.

"Are you all right Daddy? Did I do anything wrong?" said Patsy. She looked at her father uncertain as to what was the matter, why he wasn't saying anything. "Daddy, have I done something wrong? Should I have kept quiet and just let her sleep?"

Patrick's gaze slowly moved and lingered on his poor ignorant little daughter's face.

"No, you've been a very good girl, Patsy. Come on now, I'll help you to move,"

He very gently raised Lizzie's head to free Patsy.

"See," said the girl, "I told you she was having a good sleep."

"You go on now and find the missus of the house, will you do that for me, and ask her to come up quickly. And tell Betty to come too."

Patsy left the room. Her legs were feeling a bit stiff after being in the same position for so long and with the weight of her mammy's head on them too.

She rushed down the stairs to get involved with the unloading and emptying of bags and boxes, the stocking on the shelves of all the bits of shopping, almost forgetting in her hurry to speak to the missus or Betty, then she managed a wave to the floaty woman in the old clothes, who was just standing watching her by the door.

5

Patrick moved his family to Hanover Street in Dublin. After the funeral, Betty had stayed on at Larch Hill for a few months and tried her best to create some semblance of normality for the little girls but soon the gossip started and it was decided she should best go home. A married man living under the same roof as a single woman was not something the good Catholics of the close-knit Rathfarnham parish could condone, let alone when the wife had so recently passed away. They could see Betty laughing and playing with the children as brazen as you like and they decided that this was a sure sign that all could not be morally upright in the gatehouse.

What the gossips didn't realise was that Betty herself was anxious to go home. She missed her own family and the farm and she hadn't seen her young man for several weeks: their courting was on a serious footing and she wasn't too keen on the idea of her handsome young beau being targeted by any of the other only-too-eligible girls in Tullamore.

What the gossips didn't see was Patrick cocooned in the corner every night all night, ignoring his children in his grief and snapping at them sharply if they interrupted his mourning with the least sound of gaiety. He made no allowance for the fact that the youngsters had lost their mother. He wouldn't allow anyone to play the piano while he was in the house, forgetting the warm thoughts that had heralded its purchase. Far from the debauchery imagined by the village busybodies, Patrick spent his time in a morose silence which became a thunderous weight over daily life in the gatehouse. He received a short letter from Miss Bourke proposing that she might apply for a piano scholarship for Patsy: Miss Bourke was confident that Patsy would reach and surpass the required level and it would save Patrick the cost of further lessons now that Lizzie's allowance had come to an end. But he threw the letter on the fire and allowed no further thoughts about it to intrude on his misery. Sometimes he would suddenly leave the house and just stand in the yard looking up at the bedroom window of the main house, the window of the room that had robbed him of the final weeks of Lizzie's life. He began to hate The Family for that and their pathetic suggestion that Lizzie would be more comfortable in their commodious home. He hated Larch Hill with all its reminders. He hated the gatehouse with all its reminders. He hated his loneliness but welcomed it with open arms and wallowed in its reminders.

Patrick's friend Michael, in Tullamore, had grown very concerned, both over his daughter's good name and over the deepening gloom that had settled over Patrick. And there were the little girls to consider, motherless but with a father too steeped in his own grief to pay them any heed. Something had to be done.

Michael's family had a small house in Dublin which had been empty for some months: the tenant had just disappeared one night, neighbours said into the bowels of Dublin Castle, and Michael had kept it empty just in case the man was able to return but no news had been heard of him since that midnight knock on the door. Michael carefully packed the man's few surviving personal belongings into a box and arranged for a local woman to give the place a good clean. Then he gave Patrick the key so he could move in with his three young ones. Hanover Street was certainly neither as grand nor as green as Larch Hill but it wasn't Larch Hill: Patrick welcomed the change.

Patsy and her sisters, who found innocent comfort in the thought that their mammy was now living in heaven with Baby Jesus and all the stable animals and shepherds from Bethlehem, had grown a bit afraid of their daddy and his black moods. Nothing seemed to please him, they couldn't do anything right, and they couldn't play any of their games without him shouting at them to be quiet. When Betty left the gatehouse, it was if there was no joy left in their lives. She had amused them once again with stories of her young man and said that she had to go home to see him before he forgot all about her and found someone else: they couldn't understand how anyone could forget her, they said, but they accepted that the cows might be upset and refusing to produce enough milk without Betty there to pump their udders in just the right way.

The idea of moving to Dublin promised adventure but also more loss for the youngsters; they had to say goodbye to their friends in

Rathfarnham, to the familiar fields where they used to hide, to the country lanes they travelled with Seamus and to any further chance of seeing that leprechaun, and to the river where they liked to paddle and fish — the Liffey, as it ran through Dublin, was definitely not a river for paddling and fishing. Patsy was also sad to be leaving Miss Bourke but the piano teacher had presented her with a small book about Beethoven to keep; in it she had inserted the name and address of a good teacher in Dublin should Patsy be able to continue with piano lessons there.

Hanover Street brought with it new problems for Patrick: for a start he had to get a job, he had to earn a living for himself and his family, no matter how much he himself was ready to just give up on it all, but that didn't prove too difficult thanks to his contacts in the bakers' union. Then there were his other commitments, far more demanding now that he was close to the hub of the action.

All the same he couldn't leave his three daughters locked up in a house on their own, especially in Dublin, where they might be tempted to get out and explore on their own. They were too young to realise that there were dangers here that weren't much of a problem in the country and that here in Dublin there was also a war going on: that it wasn't normal for a city to be scarred by mountains of debris and bombed ruins and burnt-out buildings, surviving shops all boarded up, armoured cars and tanks and soldiers patrolling the streets day and night looking for any excuse to use their guns. The war had already battered at the door of Stephen's house just round the corner and yet Patrick had brought his daughters to live in this place and the effects were beginning to tell on Patsy. She had started having nightmares and would wake up crying in the night and trembling uncontrollably even when one of her new floaty people tried to calm her: the constant booms of bombs exploding and the sharp cracks of guns being discharged had triggered memories in the child of the raid at Usher's Quay. Patrick would gently lift her out of the cot and cuddle her on his knee.

"I'm frightened of those soldiers coming into our room again," she sobbed, "like they did that night at Uncle Stephen's. Don't you remember, Da, it was that night when we saw that big bonfire on the other side of the river. Will they find us here? Will they know we're here in Dublin again? I don't want them to come into our room shouting again

58

like they did before. I was afraid of them. Why did we have to leave the gatehouse and come here? Was it because you were very sad over Mammy going to heaven to be with Baby Jesus instead of staying with us?"

Patrick looked at his eldest daughter, still such a child, barely nine years old and as innocent of the world as a child straight out of the country would be, and tears filled his eyes as he thought of how he had been neglecting the children in his own selfish grief.

"Yes, I was very sad when your mammy died," he said. "But you helped me, Patsy, you and your sisters. You told me about how happy your mammy must be with Baby Jesus and how she won't be sick any more and coughing all the time so much that it hurt. It's just that it took me a long time to see that you were right. I was missing her too much to realise how great it must be for her now up in heaven. And in a way she hasn't really left us at all. We're all thinking of her every day, and I know I for one talk to her as if she was right next to me in the room. And then when I thought that bit longer, I decided we might all enjoy coming here to live near Uncle Stephen and Auntie Mary for a bit. I know you like playing with little Kevin and Tessie and now they're just around the corner so you can see them as often as you want."

"But what about the soldiers? They might still be round the corner too."

"You're safe here, Patsy," said her father. "I'll make sure nothing bad happens to you, I promise. There are lots of brave people trying to chase away those horrible men and stop them frightening anybody any more."

"Can I help to chase them away too?" asked Patsy. "I could be brave if I had to."

"I know you're very brave. Aren't you already looking after Molly and Theresa for me? Anyone taking on those two little devils has to be brave. But hopefully those soldiers won't have to face you, Patsy, they should be long gone soon," he said.

"Who are they?" she asked. "Where do they come from? Why do they want to frighten everyone?"

"Well now, Patsy, it's very complicated. It's all to do with history. The soldiers are from England and for years and years England has put itself in charge in Ireland, as if it belongs to them. Well of course it doesn't, Ireland belongs to us, to you and me and to all our family and friends, and to all their families and all their friends. And now a lot of us want the English to go home and let us do things here in Ireland the way we want for a change. Of course England wants to keep Ireland, it's such a beautiful country, isn't it Patsy?"

"I want to keep it too," she said, "all the green fields for hiding and the hills for climbing and the rivers for splashing in and the lanes and the leprechauns and the floaty people. But there are lots of other nice things, beautiful things, which I'd like to keep but they're not mine so I can't. And it would be a sin."

"Have you seen any floaty people in Dublin?" asked Patrick.

"I haven't seen my woman in the old clothes, she lives at Larch Hill, of course, but there are some here too and they always wave to me and smile."

"What are the floaty people in Dublin like?"

"Well, there is a man with a long beard who walks up and down along by the river, he looks happy all the time and he's always laughing when I see him. He makes me laugh too. He uses a stick to help him walk and sometimes when he sees me he just suddenly jumps up in the air and clicks his feet together, as if he was dancing, and he waves his stick in the air like a fairy's wand. He's my favourite floaty person here."

"Are there others?"

"Oh there are lots of them, men and women walking about, picking things up off the ground or just sitting looking at the Liffey. There are floaty children too but they all look very sad. I wave to them but they just stare at me."

"Well, that just shows how brave you are, Patsy. Some people would be very afraid if they saw so many floaty people."

"Why would anyone be afraid of floaty people?" she asked in bewilderment. "I'm not afraid of them at all. They're much nicer than the soldiers."

"Well let's not talk about the soldiers any more. You chase them out of your mind and I'll help chase them out of the streets. Agreed?"

"Agreed, Daddy. But I'd still like to help you and you know I've always liked playing chase, I can run faster than anyone."

"Also agreed, Patsy."

Patrick's situation as a widower with three little girls was quickly well known in the street and it didn't take long for a neighbour to knock on the door offering an answer to at least one of his predicaments. Mrs Dowling, who conveniently lived just a few doors away, was a chubby, homely-looking woman, who always wore a floral wrap-around apron, stained with age and bygone cooking dribbles, and who kept her greying wispy hair back with pins. She also smelled slightly of boiled vegetables but she was friendly and chatty. She was, she said, a widow, and smiled her understanding and sympathy for Patrick and the recent tragic death of his wife.

None of us know when we'll be called, she whispered. How sad for himself and the girls, she said. It was always more difficult for men to cope, she believed, but then they had different responsibilities to women, of course, they had to bring home the bacon, though these days so many women had to take jobs as well to make ends meet in the home that it was no wonder so many little ones were running a bit wild in the streets. She herself often needed a bit extra and she'd be happy to look after the girls while Patrick was at work for a few shillings, he wasn't to worry about a thing, she would take good care of them and make sure they had some good home-cooked food inside them, she said. Hadn't she brought up her own brood of eight children and they had turned out all right, right enough, never giving her any trouble, well, not much trouble beyond the usual, children being children, of course, and brothers and sisters will always have their disagreements, they wouldn't be normal if that didn't happen now would they, she said. Patrick merely kept nodding as she talked on non-stop and all the while looked around her and took in every article and item of furniture there was to see in the room, but eventually an arrangement was reached and Mrs Dowling agreed enthusiastically to start work the following day.

At first she tried to ingratiate herself with both Patrick, who above all was relieved to have his child-minding problem solved, and the girls, who weren't quite so easily conned. Mrs Dowling was no Betty and the girls weren't fooled. Mrs Dowling didn't play with them, ever, not one game, but preferred to leave Patsy, Molly and Theresa to their own devices while she stood on the steps talking to the neighbours and that wholesome home-cooked food she had promised turned out to be a bit of bread and butter each in the middle of the day, in the girls' hands, not even on a plate. His daughters were constantly asking Patrick why Betty couldn't come to live with them like before; had she married her young man yet, was that the problem — they wanted to know. But Mrs Dowling was careful with Patrick, ensuring there was always a hot dinner waiting for him when he got home from work and cheerfully staying on late when he had to go to see his brother Arthur: it was no bother for her, she said, weren't the girls great little ones, so lively and busy all the time, and the extra money would come in handy.

Disturbingly the need for extra money got to be a regular feature of Mrs Dowling's dealings with Patrick. She needed to visit the doctor but didn't have the money for any medicine but nor did she want to make the poor children ill by catching her cold, she'd say: could he see his way to giving her a bit more? Then she had such terrible toothache that she might not be able to work for at least a week without the money for the dentist and she wouldn't want him to have to take time off work on her account. And weren't his lovely daughters growing up so fast and with such enormous appetites to match; so she was afraid she'd have to ask for more money to buy in their food, what with the price of even ordinary things like butter and milk being so high, she supposed, because of all the military activity going on all over the place in Ireland, not that she understood any of that side of things, of course, but she did understand the cost of food.

Meanwhile her young charges were telling their daddy how really funny Mrs Dowling was, how she would give them their bread and butter and then disappear for a long time, leaving them to do the cleaning before she'd stumble back to the house singing before falling asleep in the armchair and waking just in time to prepare their daddy's meal.

"You should hear her snore," said Molly. "It sounds like when we were in Uncle Stephen's and there were loud fireworks."

"And she smells funny," said Theresa.

"We call her Mrs Greens," said Patsy, "'cause she smells as if that's all she ever cooks."

"Well, she certainly cooks me plenty of them, I'm getting heartily sick of cabbage," said Patrick, trying to join in with the merriment but thinking that perhaps he'd made a bit of a mistake taking on the neighbour.

The girls thought Mrs Dowling was indeed very funny, though they wished she'd give them a bit more to eat during the day. Patrick didn't find what they had to say in the least bit funny and the lack of food was of particular concern, especially after all the money Mrs Dowling had cajoled out of him. When he took the girls round to see Auntie Mary for Sunday dinner, he asked Mary if she knew the woman.

"What did you say her name was?" asked Mary.

"Mrs Dowling, she lives just a few doors up in Hanover Street."

"Well now, if she's the Mrs Dowling I know, and as far as I know there is only one Mrs Dowling in Hanover Street, you're right enough, the situation isn't funny. It's a shame you didn't mention her to me before, Patrick, as I could have told you then that the woman has a major drink problem: she likes stout and a lot of it. She spends most of her time in the bar round the corner from here, I see her there in the window every time I pass, so while you're paying her to look after the girls, she's actually spending the time and your money in the alehouse. The poor woman was married to a waster who left her with a house full of children to look after but that's no excuse for her now. You need to get rid of her."

"Easier said than done," said Patrick. "I don't know how I'd manage. She was the only one who wanted the job and now I'm not sure if I could trust anyone else after this experience. I should have stayed at Larch Hill. I knew coming here was a gamble and it's cost us the comfort and security of the gatehouse."

"Without Lizzie's job do you think the English people would have let you all stay on living there indefinitely?" asked Mary. "That would have been a gamble too. It was a big house to look after, I often wondered how Lizzie managed it, and I'm sure the owners would soon have needed the gatehouse for a new housekeeper. The bits of maintenance work and fetching that I know you did might not have been enough to swing it in your favour."

"The bloody English family, no doubt you're right, our days there were probably numbered no matter how much they promised otherwise when Lizzie was dying."

"When Lizzie was dying, they were very good to you all, Patrick, and you shouldn't forget that. You can't blame them for your own misfortune. At least here in Dublin you have a roof over your head and family nearby. Your brother Arthur is still around, isn't he? Or did he go back to Paris?"

"No, he's here."

Patrick sat in silence nursing his cup of tea, his head crowded with thoughts, with worry over his daughters' welfare and the knowledge of just how much he had already surrendered to Arthur's persuasion and to his own conscience — he was active with the Volunteers and being on the spot in Dublin meant even more evenings spent away from the house and perhaps more danger arriving at their front door, this time invited by he himself. He doubted he would have Lizzie's calm presence of mind and the courage to hide guns in the babies' cots.

"What are you thinking, Patrick?" asked his sister-in-law.

"I'm thinking that perhaps the only solution is to put the girls in an orphanage. At least they'd be fed and schooled and have clean clothes to wear."

"They would indeed," said Mary, "after scrubbing them all clean themselves after they'd scrubbed the floors and everyone else's laundry."

"That's only hard work but they'd be safe. Isn't there a convent at Harold's Cross where they take in children?"

"There is, run by the Poor Clares," said Mary, "I spent a few years there myself with the nuns." She turned away to hide her face.

"I thought the Poor Clares was a silent order, no speaking."

"Basically, it still is," said Mary, "but the sisters have been running Harold's Cross orphanage for over a hundred years now. They take in children from all over Ireland and they have a school for the children on the site too. Of course the children have to live and breathe the place and work to keep it going."

"Tell me about it," said Patrick. "Did you enjoy your time there?"

"I'm not sure that 'enjoy' would be the word I'd choose. Everything is very strict and there is little to enjoy, unless you enjoy all that hard work. I don't know much other than the basics and it was certainly very basic in my time: lots of children to each dormitory, all very sparse and quite cold; clothes shared out so you never had a thing of your own in case it made you commit the sin of pride, simple food and not much of it, plenty of chores to do and everything punctuated by prayers around the clock. Friendships were frowned upon. The nuns never liked us children to get too close amongst ourselves, told us it left us wide open to the devil and all his temptations."

"Sounds a bit of a harsh way to treat children," said Patrick. "Haven't they been there long enough to learn what children need?"

"Long enough all right," said Mary, "You'd think the Sisters would know better and them having dedicated themselves to God and charitable work. Everything is done in the name of God and the children certainly work for nothing but what they need to keep alive, I'm not sure how charitable an attitude that is. But I suppose when all is said and done the Sisters do provide somewhere for orphans to live other than on the street and the children do get some schooling. Would you like another cup of tea, Patrick? There's plenty in the pot."

"I would," he said. "Go on now."

"Sure the whole order was illegal as far as the British authorities were concerned, never mind the convent," said Mary, filling up their cups and getting into her stride. "The Sisters had to stretch the truth somewhat in order to get the place built at all but of course they always maintained that they didn't actually lie. They declared, for example, that it was destined to house a fine lady and her fine sisters, which was to some degree true, they were all Sisters of course, though just how fine or otherwise a Poor Clare can be I'm not sure, but it was a lie all the same in my book. The whole place was built on dubious foundations. They'd even claimed that the chapel itself was in actual fact to be a ballroom."

"Well, if that's the case they don't sound too bad to me," said Patrick, "telling the odd lie when necessary. It's all politics in the end. That's what I think I'll do then," said Patrick. "I'll call up to Harold's Cross tomorrow after work. Do you think just for a few days I could leave the girls here with you, Mary, it would only be for a few days until I sort all this out; I know you have your own two on your hands all the time with Stephen away but the thoughts of giving anything else to that Mrs Dowling is just too..."

"You know you're welcome to bring them here, Patrick. Just think carefully about whether you really want to hand your daughters over to the full-time care of nuns and their other-worldly habits. There might have been the odd white lie told in its making but there's very little allowed now at the orphanage of anything the Sisters consider in any way sinful, and believe me they know how to make life itself into one long sin. I was an inmate there, don't forget, and I know exactly what it's like. If you're not on your knees praying or in the classroom learning, you're working or washing or sewing or cleaning and always in fear of being found out if you're not doing any of those things to the nuns' total satisfaction. Perhaps Mrs Dowling's not such a bad option after all."

"My mind's set," said Patrick. "I'm sure you're exaggerating at least a little. Tell you what: I'll speak to the priest about it before I go if it'll make you feel better."

"I'd feel better if there was some other way of sorting everything but you're their da and you must do what you think best."

6

Father Murphy was a traditional priest in both his religious faith and in his fondness for whiskey. He adhered devotedly to the teachings of the Catholic Church and blustered his beliefs to the congregation during Sunday Mass in sermons that always lasted a minimum of half an hour, a long minimum. People would roll their eyes heavenwards when he walked out on to the altar and not his co-priest, knowing what lay ahead and how hungry they'd be for their breakfast after their fast since midnight to receive Holy Communion. Father Paddy Murphy relished their discomfort: his philosophy was that as they generally only went to Mass once a week he might as well make it worth their visit. He also enjoyed a glass of Jameson and a generous plate of good food, both enjoyed with equal relish: the result over the years was that he was rather rotund around the middle and his black suit had to stretch itself somewhat round his expanding girth. He had a mop of grey hair crowning a face which regularly lit up with laughter and eyebrows which would arch into each other with mischief. Dyed in the wool Catholic he might be but Father Murphy was a great one for jokes and genial company: dog-collar to the fore, he would tell someone to feck off when he took offence to their behaviour and would chuckle contentedly when he saw the expression on their face that a priest would say such a thing. He was generally a happy man and, being a man of vocation and of prodigious Irish stock, he was devoted to the idea of the good happy Catholic family.

"What are you thinking of, Mr O'Kelly?" he blurted. "Mary is quite right, you don't want to put those three young daughters of yours into an orphanage when they're not even orphans. Haven't they still got their father, you? Sure, in there they probably wouldn't even be allowed to sleep in the same dormitory, even though they are little more than toddlers who have just lost their mother. They need each other and you now, while they're growing, they need a good family environment, not miserable cloisters. The world can be a cold enough place as it is without losing a mother and the warmth of a childhood spent with your own, no matter how poor the circumstances. For all the good work the Sisters do at Harold's Cross, it remains an orphanage, an institution, and an institution is no substitute for a loving home, no matter how difficult things are. There must be some other solution."

"I hear what you're saying, Father," said Patrick, "but I have no other solution to offer."

Father Murphy went to the small cabinet beside his desk and took out a bottle of Jameson's. He poured out two generous measures.

"This might help warm up the brain," he said, handing a glass to Patrick. "Here, we'll put our minds to the problem."

The two men clinked their glasses in health and swallowed a brain-warming gulp.

"Now," said the priest, "tell me more about the situation. As I understand it, basically you need someone to look after your daughters while you're out at work. It seems to me something of a drastic leap to start talking about orphanages. What happened when your wife was ill and you had to work, who looked after the children then?"

"We were living out at Larch Hill then and a friend's daughter came to help out while Lizzie was ill. Betty, her name was, and she stayed on for a bit after the funeral but then had to go home to Tullamore. Then we came here to live in Dublin."

"And how old was this Betty?"

"I've no idea: seventeen, eighteen maybe, just a young girl."

"And what was Betty like? Did she do a good job?"

"Aye, she worked hard enough but of course I was out all day or sitting with Lizzie, so I didn't have much to do with her. She seemed quite pleasant from what I did see of her and the girls certainly liked her. I suppose she held everything together for us, especially after the funeral."

"The girls liked her you say?"

"They did. She always found time to amuse them and it was grand to hear them able to laugh again, as you say, they're only little ones after all. Not that the neighbours saw it that way. I believe the gossip in the town was one of the reasons her father decided to take her home."

"Sure, there's nothing country people like more than an excuse for a good gossip, bless them," said the priest. "They love to give their clear consciences some righteous verbal exercise. I'm assuming, of course, that your own conscience was perfectly clear?"

"I didn't give either the girl or the situation a second thought, to be honest," said Patrick. "All I knew was that the little ones were happy enough. Actually, Patsy asked me the other day why Betty couldn't come to live with us like before."

Father Murphy downed his shot and told Patrick to do the same. The priest stood up, fetched the bottle and poured out a couple more shots for the two of them. Patrick wasn't a drinking man but he had come seeking the priest's help and didn't want to appear judgemental by refusing a second glass. Father Murphy plumped down in his armchair, relished the whiskey sliding down his throat, took all things into consideration and turned to his visitor.

"Well, it seems to me that there's your answer right there," he said to Patrick. "Mr O'Kelly, perhaps it's time you took another wife to look after those three little ones of yours and it would appear to me that you've already found the perfect candidate."

"What? And who would that be?" asked Patrick, somewhat perplexed at the priest's unfolding logic.

"This Betty, of course. You yourself said she seemed pleasant enough and the girls obviously took to her."

"Pleasant enough sure enough," laughed Patrick, "but I hardly know the girl. I've only just buried my wife and I tell you, Father, I truly loved that woman, I know I'd never find anyone to replace her."

"No one's talking about replacing her," said Father Murphy, "we're talking about you being a father of three young ones and facing up to your responsibilities, providing a proper Catholic home for your daughters and a proper home for daughters requires a woman, a mother. Not everybody is lucky enough to have a marriage based on such true love as you describe, Mr O'Kelly," said the priest, "be thankful you experienced it at least once in your life. Who knows, you might find it all over again. I'll bet that Betty actually has a lot in common with your late wife and that's why the girls responded to her the way they did. Was she a warm sort of a person? Did she play with the children, pay attention to them the way children need, the way their mother did?"

"Yes, I suppose I'd have to answer a yes to all of those."

"Then the problem is solved," said the priest. "You're to marry Betty."

"Hang on there a minute, Father, people don't get married just like that, just to solve a problem. And as far as I understood it Betty had a young man she was hoping to marry."

"You leave Betty to me," said Father Murphy, "that's an end to the matter, the little ones need a proper loving home not some orphanage. Now, here's cheers to a successful outcome."

Patrick's objections were waved away in a swirl of alcohol and they clinked glasses again.

"I'll call out to the parish priest in Tullamore this week and get things moving on the Betty front. Her father's called Michael, I think you said. We'll have a little chat, the three of us. I could do with getting out of this place for a while anyway, God knows Dublin's no Garden of Eden right now so I might as well go in search of a wife for you and enjoy a day in the country at the same time. Do you know they've been distilling their Tullamore Dew in the town for a hundred years or so? Now a glass of that would certainly help wash away quite a lot of Dublin's dirt, don't you agree?"

Michael's family lived just outside Tullamore in a single-storey stone farmhouse, set back off the lane and surrounded by all the usual clutter and rusting paraphernalia of a working farm: harnesses and tack for the horses, milking pails and stools for the tending to the cows, churns for butter and cheese, hoes and spades and rakes that had seen better days and a small plough for tilling the fields. There was a motley of buckets and mops and brushes and brooms leaning and lying around the place, precious lengths of old rope that might come in handy, wooden boxes, bits of torn canvas sacking, bottles, scraps of timber and all the other imaginable indications that the people who lived here worked and lived on the land and never threw anything away. The ground in front of the house was of compacted dirt, which turned to mud at the slightest fall of rain, not uncommon in Ireland, of course, so the ground was often muddy. In the house there was a large kitchen at its heart, where the family ate and conversed, kept snug by the fire in the range, above which were hung pots and pans and spoons and ladles. There were always clothes drying in the room: with such a large family living in the house there was always washing on the go. Outside there was a large barn with stalls for the cows and a sheltered run for the hens and chickens that were otherwise constantly squawking and scrabbling and dropping their shit around the yard, small prices to pay for the constant supply of fresh eggs.

Father Murphy arrived at the farm with the local priest in tow and a couple of bottles of whiskey and the two soon subjected Michael to a barrage of pressure, fuelled and eased by the Tullamore Dew: what a fine wife Betty would make for such a good hardworking man as Michael's old friend, Patrick O'Kelly, and what a good mother for the girls, they said; hadn't they all got on so well together already and wasn't it time she got herself a fine husband?

Michael was only too familiar with his friend's character, so no persuasion was needed on that count. His main thought was for his daughter: it was one thing loaning Betty to Patrick to see his friend through the bad times but marriage was a different matter altogether. Betty already had a young man, a popular lad both in the town and with Michael's own family, a hard worker too, and used to their ways. Life with him for Betty would be spent in familiar surroundings, close to home, with all the support of both their families on hand, especially when their own little ones started to arrive.

Michael rolled the Dew around over his tongue. On the other hand, the lad's mother was a known tyrant, a real old battle-axe.

"Jesus, Mary and Joseph what a bitch of a woman," he said out loud and downing another sup. "Sorry about that, Fathers. God forgive me but I was thinking about the future mother-in-law if Betty was to marry her young man here in Tullamore."

"Tell us your thoughts," said Father Murphy raising those eyebrows of his and leaning in closer to Michael as he detected a promising opening, "all your thoughts."

"I'm thinking that the woman would be unlikely to hand over care of her precious son to another woman without a deal of daily interference. Betty might even be expected to move in with them, God forbid, and what sort of a married life would she have then, one of drudgery and nagging and little opportunity for any sort of private married life with a busy-body mother-in-law constantly on watch. The lad himself is painfully shy and awkward, he'd never be able to stand up to his mother even on his own behalf let alone Betty's. He's good-looking enough but hardly a great catch even though I know there would be lots of takers if Betty should leave him now, make her escape, so to speak."

"It could be telling that you used the word 'escape'," said Father Murphy.

"Aye, I did," said Michael.

Then he thought of his good friend Patrick and his three daughters: he knew Betty had loved the girls and they her in return, she obviously missed them when she had returned home from Larch Hill. And living in Dublin might not be such a bad idea for all the troubles there, give Betty a taste of a different sort of life. And Patrick might always decide to move back to the country again after a couple of years, perhaps even near to Tullamore itself. And meanwhile he knew Patrick was a good man, reliable, trustworthy, he'd not overstepped propriety with Betty in any way when she was helping out at Larch Hill. And, well, after all was said and done, it was his good friend they were talking about.

"It's decided," he said. "Betty will marry Patrick."

That Tullamore Dew had certainly gone down well.

The future bride herself wasn't all that convinced. Her memory of the proposed husband was of a sullen man who had forgotten even the simplest joys of life in his depth of grief for his dead wife. Betty had never seen him otherwise. But she supposed that if he had inspired such love in a woman once and a lasting close friendship with her father, then perhaps Patrick O'Kelly wasn't naturally such a hard man. And then there were the girls, Patsy and Molly and Theresa, to whom she had grown very attached during her short time at Larch Hill and the little ones did need a mother. Betty also had two priests and her father to contend with, all with their minds determined on the idea of the union. In the end she had no option but to do what she was told, like a good Catholic daughter, and she prayed God would take care of the rest.

7

Patrick O'Kelly had once felt invincible. He had Lizzie's love, he had his bits of art, and he had the passion to soar to the heavens on both. He had felt invincible, a man able to take on anything life could throw at him, able to ride any storm that blew, safe in the comfort of his two anchorages, his wife and his painting. Now he just felt flat. Everything had crashed down around him at such a speed that it was as if his very being had become buried in the earth along with Lizzie. He could no longer be the man he was, with a natural capacity for enjoying life that came from being happy, but Father Murphy had been right: the cause did not lie with Patsy, Molly and Theresa but with he himself and it wasn't fair to abandon them to some soulless institute, not Lizzie's precious offspring. Patrick had reluctantly agreed that marrying Betty would be good for them, though he fretted at how he himself would take to life with a different woman, a woman for whom he felt no love and she none for him, a woman with whom he had never shared any warmth or intimacies.

Yet here he was, several weeks into the marriage, having to admit to himself that she brought her own feeling of warmth into the household and life was better for it. He couldn't get over the loss of his Lizzie but he was getting used to Betty. He recognised too that he wasn't her choice for a husband and that she had had to leave her young man behind, the whole thing manipulated entirely for his benefit, not hers, and gradually that very realisation of her situation prompted him to view her differently, sometimes, when she wasn't looking, sometimes, through half-closed eyes, sometimes, when a simple gesture of her gentleness caught his eye. He started acting more kindly towards her, had even started having conversations with his new wife that weren't at all as arduous as he had expected. Certainly the children seemed more relaxed with how everything was working out, with how their father had eased off in his temper. He felt it all.

But he needed to feel invincible again, strong, and with the family problem sorted he now sought strength through the compulsions that drove him, which he experienced as flowing naturally off each other. His soul had always sought outward nourishment in colour, in drawing, in trying to give concrete form to the excitement inspired within him by everything he saw, be it the gentle movement of the wind dancing through the trees or the bent backs of the barrow-pushers plying their trade round cobbled streets of poverty or the familiar faces around him, faces hardened by work and life. All were part of the essence of his heritage, its landscape and its people, but, as well as deserving his aesthetic expressions of intellectual love, all deserved his physical devotion also. That after six-hundred years the British were still in control of his Irish heritage only served to sharpen his instinctive stewardship: Patrick O'Kelly was driven to throw off that particular legacy, the British yoke. The raid at Usher's Quay and all he'd witnessed and experienced since had focussed his mind incisively on the foreign will that imposed itself on his own. It was an arrogant, suffocating burden and the violence involved in shedding it from his people and their land posed a moral dilemma that was now answered merely with a dismissive shrug of the shoulders: 'Thou shalt not kill,' right enough, except under extreme circumstances, forgive me Father.

He left his new wife at home with the children. He had a job on with Mick O'Shea, an old friend from childhood: indeed he'd been out with Mick to a social gathering in the parish hall the night he had been introduced to Lizzie. The two men went back a long way.

"You've got the orders then?" asked Mick. "What's it to be tonight, a run or a watch?"

"Neither" said Patrick. "We're going to need transport. Can you get the car?"

"Not tonight, tonight there's a special service with Benediction after and then Father Murphy needs the car to take some important out-of-town visitors or some such home. To be honest I didn't really follow it all when my Ma was telling me. To be honest I don't think she really followed it all herself when Father Murphy was telling her."

"Well then we'll have to see what we can find ourselves."

Patrick had been surprised but not shocked to learn that Father

Murphy was to some extent actively sympathetic towards the Volunteers: the priest would never condone the killings but nor would he condemn the perpetrators and he often loaned his car without asking why it might be needed. "Just don't tell me anything," he'd say as he handed over the keys.

Patrick and Mick had met by the gates of St Francis' church, a pre-arranged casual encounter, unremarkable in its location. It was a spot favoured by Patrick, who made a point always of making his confession in the church before a job. He wanted his eternal soul to be as ready for heaven as his mortal body was ready to send it there should it prove necessary. He had heard all the arguments about what some saw as the contradiction in all this. Top of the list was the one about the gates of heaven being closed to anyone committing the most awful sin of taking another person's life, a right reserved to God alone. This was usually followed by the one about the perpetrator not having sufficient time to repent before he himself caught a bullet. What chance salvation then. There was also the one about shamelessly making peace with God through the confessional box only to have the absolution invalidated because the same grave sin just confessed was already premeditated to be committed again not long after. That went against the very catechism itself. It broke all the rules about receiving the sacrament of penance, it being conditional on both remorse and the promise to not sin again. Then there was the argument about compromising God's representative, the priest, routinely asking him for absolution for activities that by their very nature were more than likely to continue. Yes, Patrick O'Kelly had heard all the arguments. He had also dismissed them all. It wasn't that he refused to take them on board — on the contrary, he saw himself as a good Catholic — rather that he had considered all the points carefully, examined his own conscience in relation to them and reached the conclusion that he was not breaking any of his personal articles of faith with God. He was no murderer but he would kill, he was fighting a just war. It wasn't that he premeditated committing a mortal sin, it was that he was a soldier doing his duty for his country. It followed that he was not compromising God, the priest or anyone else when he went to confession before a job, just preparing for the event of death like any other Catholic.

"I'll see you at nine," said Patrick, then casually shuffling his feet and interjecting a jovial 'get-way-with-you-now' for the benefit of a couple of passers-by. "Wait for me by the canal, usual stretch."

The two men belonged to the same Volunteers company and had worked well together on previous missions. They both owed their lives to each other on more than one count. Now they parted company easily, confident in their dual purpose and experience on the ground.

Patrick went back to Hanover Street and relaxed in front of the fire while Betty got on with some mending at the table. He struggled to reconcile the quiet pleasantness of his home life with his sense of betrayal to the memory of Lizzie. The struggle was waged especially strongly when it came to bedtime: he was reluctant to go up at the same time as Betty and cause any embarrassment, preferring for now to keep everything at arm's length and maintain a modest distance between them; he didn't want her to think he was an animal, desperate for a woman in his bed when the arrangement had really been for the benefit of the three young ones. Still, he had to admit to himself that sometimes when he looked at his new wife putting things away for the night and getting ready for bed, he sometimes felt in the mood for something more than just blankets to get his temperature rising upstairs.

They had a bit of supper in silence and Betty sensed that this would be one of those evenings when Patrick would be going out. She never asked where he was off to or why and he valued the same unspoken acceptance that had evolved with Lizzie. Perhaps the two women weren't so different.

"I'd best be getting myself sorted," he said, "though to be honest with you I'd be more inclined to stay in if I hadn't already given my word. You're making the place very homely, Betty, and I thank you for that."

Patrick studied himself in the mirror in the kitchen. A contented face greeted him after his year of mourning, his large brown eyes smiling warmly despite the coldness in prospect with the night ahead. He looked at his heavy brows, his jutting cheekbones shadowing over the sharply drawn contour of his jaw-line. Perhaps next he would try a self-portrait, he thought. The idea used to strike him as a vain conceit, not helped by. Lizzie calling him her handsome Wuthering Heights hero, but he was no

Heathcliffe, Patrick O'Kelly was not a cruel man.

He had on his old suit and the red sweater, which was well worn for he wore it many times: he liked the vibrancy of the colour even though he knew it wasn't the most sensible garb for disappearing into the darkness in the middle of some skirmish. Then he put on his grey overcoat, buttoned it tightly against the weather, found his gloves, picked up the newspaper and left the house. His gun was in his overcoat pocket. He and Mick had often debated the best place to carry a weapon; Mick favoured the inside pocket of his jacket and that's where he always stashed his revolver: he believed it afforded better immediate concealment should any Tan patrol suddenly take it into their minds to stop and question everyone who passed them. Patrick preferred to have his gun ready to be ditched quickly in the event of a stop-and-search. So far they had both been proved right. After all, they were both still alive and active on the streets.

It was half past eight, a full thirty minutes before he was due to meet Mick, but Patrick liked to take a roundabout route to a rendezvous whenever he was on a job, often stopping casually and apparently innocently absorbed in reading an article in the paper. When finally he arrived at the meeting point he spotted Mick on the other side of the canal. A British patrol was stationed on the bridge nearby so the two men, now both aware of each other's presence, carried on walking in the same direction away from the patrol, still on opposite sides of the canal. Again it was a tried and tested procedure. The next bridge was a minor crossing about a quarter mile further along but that too was under surveillance. Mick would disappear into a corner shop to buy something, Patrick might call into a bar to get some cigarettes, anything to break the pattern of the two men stalking each other in parallel.

It took several bridges before they could finally meet, now a mile or so from where they had originally started and now on relatively open land and Mick didn't like that at all; he didn't like the feeling that was welling up like a warning in his stomach.

"The Tans are a bit too itchy tonight for my liking," he said. "We'd best get away from the canal, we're being far too conspicuous. Come on this way, there's a few dark entry-ways we could get lost in."

As the two men picked their way across the field in the darkness

Mick quietly urged his compatriot to reconsider the urgency of their orders: for the minute Mick still didn't know what those orders were or how urgent they might or might not be, it was considered operationally safer that way on some jobs. Mick was a brave man, a strong conviction in the cause left him unperturbed by danger, but he didn't believe in taking unnecessary chances and tonight he was uneasy. "They're stopping a lot of people," he said. "They must know something's afoot."

Patrick sat down on the ground under the overhang of a sprawling bush to lessen their silhouettes. He cautiously lit them a cigarette each and they cupped them in their fingers to conceal the glow. Nature was enjoying a quiet night; the winter sky was untroubled and unfavourably starry above the biting cold down below but there was an insistent breeze beginning to blow, a harbinger of rain to come. Mick was constantly fidgeting, taking drag after drag on his cigarette without pause.

Then suddenly he leapt to his feet. "Run, Patrick, run, for Christ's sake, the bastards are coming straight at us."

Patrick was momentarily transfixed by the panicked explosion of his friend's voice in the night silence, quickly echoed by the more threatening yet strangely softer sounds of the rushing feet of the enemy stomping across the field.

"For God's sake run, Patrick. Make for the back streets and we'll split up there."

They started to run to safety as the sound of the soldiers' boots lost all semblance of softness and the Tans thudded their way through the grass towards the stumbling men. Patrick saw them at last, seconds before the patrol froze to take aim, rifles held high, primed and ready to fire.

"Stop right there, you Irish cunts," came a shout from just twenty or so yards away. "One more step and you'll be just two more dead Micks to add to our tally."

Patrick and Mick threw themselves flat into the tall grass hoping for some sort of cover, any cover, praying that somehow what the soldiers had just seen could no longer be seen: themselves. It was a vain hope and they knew it. Each fumbled for his weapon, Mick struggling frantically with numbed fingers to extricate his from the inside of his coat while all the time lying awkwardly on it. The two men somehow managed to get out their guns and toss them away low, into the confusion of the grass, and waited.

"Get your fucking hands up," yelled a Tan in a sergeant's uniform, "in the air, now." He had about ten men with him, all impatient for some anti-Paddy action.

"I said get your fuckin' hands up, one at a time, slowly, or you might panic one of my men into tightening his finger on the fuckin' trigger and then none of us would have any bloody fun, would we. Now, stand up so I can see you, you fucking Irish bastards."

Patrick and Mick struggled to their feet, deliberately stumbling away from where they had hurriedly discarded their guns. They knew the weapons wouldn't have landed far away but still had to try to put at least some distance between them.

"Well, well, well," said the sergeant, towering before them. "Who have we got here then, lads? A couple of thick-shit Paddies, eh?" he sneered. Then he smashed his rifle butt into their faces. The two men reeled backwards with the force of the blow and tried to protect their heads as they fell to the ground. Blood was already dribbling down their cheeks. "Let's take a look at the eejits, shall we?" said the sergeant. "Isn't that what they say here in this piss-pot country, 'eejits'?"

"That's what they say, Sarge," said one of his men. "Sometimes they might say 'right eejits'."

"Sometimes they might say 'right eejits', eh? Well, let's see if we've got just a couple of eejits or, better still, a couple of right eejits, lads, cause that's what they are for getting caught so easily. Get that torch down on them."

The beam of light picked out Mick's features first, his lips trembling but his expression maintaining a grimace of defiance. Then Patrick's face came under the small spotlight.

"Well, well, well, look who we have here," said the sergeant. "We meet again," he said to Patrick. "I told you I'd remember your ugly bastard face and then suddenly here it is, and what an unexpectedly welcome sight it is. We'll have ourselves some sport this evening, lads, him and I have got some history," he said to the patrol. "Get them up, both of them," he ordered, "then search the ground. We might not be going back to the Castle empty-handed tonight after all."

Mick was hauled up first, then immediately booted in the back of the knees so they buckled under him and he collapsed to the ground again in pain. Patrick was dragged up next, then immediately the sergeant kicked him hard between the legs and Patrick doubled up in agony.

"Can't you obey a simple order, lads? I said get these two Irish fuckers up."

The men were wrestled struggling to their feet again.

"Right," said the sergeant to the prisoners, "that's more like it, more sociable, like, now we can talk face to face, so to speak. You, Mick the Knees, try not to bend over like that, I'm not talking to the top of your fuckin' head, and you, Mick the Perv, stop playing with your balls like some tosser, we're trying to have a civilised conversation here. Let's start with an easy opener, shall we, one that even you right eejits can understand: where are you off to on a cold night like this? Looking for the republic, are you? Show me where, I'd like to fuckin' find it too, see what all the fuss is about, then I could mow down the fucking lot of you Paddies all in one go, all for King and Country, no questions asked."

"Can't find anything in the grass, Sarge," said one of the patrol, still sifting his feet through the long grass.

"No? Nothing? Now isn't that strange cause I could have sworn I'd seen them holding something and then nothing. I must have been mistaken and I'm not usually mistaken," he said, his mouth spread wide in a comically perplexed grin. He shook his head from side to side very deliberately and tutted. Then the sergeant pulled a pistol from his pocket and casually dropped it in the grass, all the time making a great show of looking the other way. He even managed a playful whistle. Then he looked down at the gun. "Hang on, what's this then?"

Patrick and Mick could only look on helplessly, swaying on their feet, hands behind their heads, now barely upright, shivering with apprehension but trying to hide their fear, struggling to maintain some show of pride while the blood from their mouths and temples ran down their necks and inside their clothes and all the time pain made it difficult for them to control their breathing.

"Well, well, well, what have we here?" said the sergeant, He raised his eyebrows in mock surprise and glanced down at the pistol he had thrown. "Just look at this, men, just fucking look at this. Just look at what these two fucking republicans have gone and dropped."

He picked the gun up and dangled it loosely from his index finger as if taking care not to contaminate a piece of evidence.

"Definitely one of theirs, definitely, wouldn't you say so, lads?" he said. "Get the tin hat," he bellowed.

One of the Tans produced a large metal can and stood awaiting further orders. A feeling of excited expectation quivered through the patrol as their commanding officer looked fixedly from one Irishman to the other, his silent deliberations mottled by the shadow of a loose cloud moving across the path of moonlight.

He finally stopped and looked directly at Patrick, just inches from his face. "I do like your red sweater, by the way," he said, "I like the colour, it's a good colour, a real English colour, red." Then he abruptly lowered his rifle and shot Patrick in the leg. "But you're still a green bastard," he laughed.

Mick took a step forward to try to help his friend. "Put the tin hat on that one," barked the sergeant.

Patrick lay squirming on the ground, his leg on fire where the bullet had seared its way to the bone. Throbbing pain spread throughout his body and for a time he was oblivious to everything that wasn't happening directly to him. Then he registered the cries of Mick: he looked up to see a couple of Tans roughly forcing the tin can tight down on and over Mick's head, forcing it down and over his eyes, catching and pulling his ears down against their natural direction and scraping the skin and flesh off his nose and chin.

Then they stood back, leaving Mick stumbling about in terror in his metal-helmet blindfold. "Look at him, lads, he can't stand up properly, must be drunk," said the sergeant. "I'm told they do like their drink, these Irish cunts, and it would appear the reports are correct. Let's see if we can knock some sense into the drunken eejit."

The sergeant started hammering on the can with the length of the barrel of his rifle, metal on metal clanging and clanking and resonating into one continuous metallic ring of sound. Mick screamed against the reverberating din assaulting his eardrums so directly, over and over and over again, squealing and wrangling around inside the can with no hole of escape. Mick's nerves were shattered. He struggled manically to get the thing off his head to stop the unrelenting barrage of terrible noise.

"Leave the man be, won't you," pleaded Patrick.

"Leave him be? Okay, if you like," said the sergeant. Then he took aim with the pistol and riddled the can with bullets. Mick slumped lifeless to the ground.

"Well, what do you know?" said the sergeant. "The gun they threw away was loaded as well, lads, you saw it for yourselves. After due deliberation it seems to me that this Volunteer here must have been shot as an informer by one of his own, using one of their own guns, wouldn't you say so lads?"

The lads couldn't agree more enthusiastically.

"And I'm thinking," said the sergeant, "that it's a great pity we came upon this little bit of home-grown justice just moments too late to prevent a cold-blooded execution being expedited but not too late, fortunately, to get a round off and catch the murderer with a bullet to the leg as he tried to make his escape. Neat, eh? I told you we'd have sport tonight, lads. Leave that dead fucker on the ground and let's get this other Irish cunt back to the barracks for a bit of good old-fashioned interrogation, Tan style, and then the drinks are on me."

It was several days before Betty found out that her husband was locked up in Kilmainham Jail. She had spent the evening that Patrick hadn't come home in trying not to worry, knowing he was on a job but not knowing where or what so she could do no more than keep looking at the hands on the clock as they crawled around to midnight and then crept into the early hours and then chased each other into a morning which dawned slowly with still no sign of Patrick and still no news. The following days had been filled with growing fear at what might have happened, while all the time Betty tried to persuade the girls that their father had been called away on special bakery work for some big order. When the news of his imprisonment finally arrived, wanted but dreaded, it filled her with apprehension: memories of the Easter Rising leaders being shot in Kilmainham in the recreation yard conjured nightmare images in Betty's mind. Even out in Tullamore she had heard too much about the place, with its harsh cast-iron stairways and thick walls and padded cells that failed to absorb the screams of men being tortured for cruel pleasure before being left to rot. She had heard too much about the enthusiastic brutality of the jailers who had her husband at their mercy. Arthur had called round to see her as soon as he had heard what had happened along by the canal. Betty was only newly married to Patrick but she had seen great good in the man and a re-emerging gentleness with his daughters. His grief for his dead wife hadn't fully abated but there were signs that the two of them could work at their own marriage and make a success of it, and not just for the girls' sake. Now all of that was in doubt. Betty didn't know what to do and Arthur couldn't offer any real encouragement.

"There are talks going on in London and the chances of a peace treaty are very good," he told her. "This war can't last much longer thanks to brave men like Patrick. The British are taking a lot of casualties and world opinion is against them."

"Can I visit him?" asked Betty.

"You can," said Arthur, "but perhaps you'd best leave it for a few days, you don't want them knocking on your door here and searching through all your things. I'll get word in to him for you, tell him you're anxious to see him when he feels it's right."

"I'd appreciate that," said Betty. "I'd like him to know we're here waiting for him to come home. Do you know how he was caught?"

"I'm afraid I don't have all the information, Betty. It's not much comfort I know but I can tell you that his companion that night was shot dead in cold blood by the Tans who caught them. Why they let Patrick live after they shot him in the leg we don't know. One of our friends inside the Castle told us something about a sergeant recognising Patrick from some past incident but I don't know any more than that."

"Was it Mick who was killed?" asked Betty. "I know they were good friends from old and still looked out for each other."

"I can't tell you any more right now," said Arthur. "I'll let you know how Patrick is as soon as I get word."

"Kilmainham sounds like such an awful place, I can't bear to think of Patrick being locked up in there."

"Try to think positively. Like I say, there are talks going on in London right now and there's a good chance of a treaty being agreed. And there is a lot of pressure being put on the British by the Americans so hopefully the jailers won't risk many more bad reports coming out of

Kilmainham. The world is watching, Betty, remember that. Patrick and all the others aren't being ignored by sympathetic people, powerful people, who want to help put an end to all this bloodshed."

Betty looked at the newspaper every day. Arthur had been right, there were what they called top-level talks going on in London. God willing, peace was in sight and her husband would be home.

Then a letter from Patrick arrived: Betty's heart shivered with relief as she recognised immediately his familiar beautiful handwriting on the envelope, the carefully drawn letters sloping forward as if in great optimism and she called the girls to tell them their father was safe and had written to them all.

But she hadn't looked at the postmark: it showed that the letter had been posted not in Dublin but sent from Ballykinlar Internment Camp in County Down. Patrick had been shipped up to Northern Ireland.

By now the girls were only too familiar with the unrelenting routine violence of war in the streets. They automatically dived for cover with everyone else when the Tans let fly with a hail of bullets into a crowd of people in the street for sick amusement; they had seen plenty of stop-and-search incidents accompanied by the ruthless smash across the head with a rifle butt; they couldn't sleep at night for the wailing of sirens, bouncing and echoing through the deserted streets; for the crackle of gunfire, the hollow boom of bombs exploding and then the thud and crash of falling debris. These things went on outside their own door, even as they were rushing to be home and safely inside before the curfew closed everything down to a frightening muffle. No more were they sent to sleep by reassuring sounds from the street. Children are not exempted from the cruel hand of war. There was no point in Betty pretending that all was well; she needed to be honest with the youngsters and they needed to know why their da was still not back.

"You know I told you that your daddy was one of the men trying to chase those awful soldiers out of Dublin?" she said, sitting down in front of the fire as the girls clustered around looking forward to hearing the news contained in their father's letter and perhaps the date when he'd be back. "Well, he hasn't been out of Dublin working like we thought," said Betty. "He was stopped on his way home one night by the soldiers and they took him off to the Castle. Then they sent him up to the North with lots of other men and now they're all locked up in some sort of camp. But you can see that they let him write this letter to us and then they posted it, so I'm thinking everything must be all right and that we're none of us to worry, you're not to worry."

The girls had friends whose fathers or brothers had also suddenly vanished after being taken away by the British and those friends were always boasting about how brave were their fathers or their brothers and how everyone else was relying on them to free Ireland. Now that Patrick had gone too and Betty had told them there was nothing to worry about, his daughters felt swollen with pride that their da was also one of the brave men and not one of the ones relying on someone else to do all the hard work.

"Those soldiers must be really scared if they've had to send all the men so far away," said Molly.

"I did offer to help our daddy," said Patsy. "Perhaps I could have run away quickly in another direction and the soldiers would have followed me and he could have got away. I would have prayed really hard too, to Our Lady: the nuns say she always listens especially closely to young girls."

"We can all pray and then she'd have three of us to listen to," said Molly. "And we'll write lots of letters and send some nice pictures to Daddy, so he knows we miss him."

"Well, Our Lady will listen to me all right," said Patsy. "I've promised her I'll become a Child of Mary when I'm old enough," she said. "And I'm going to ask all my floaty people if they have any friends where our da is who can help look after him for us while he's away up in that camp," she said. "That'll mean lots of help."

"You only want to be one of the Children of Mary so you can wear a long blue veil when you go to Mass," said Theresa, a few years younger but quite competitive where her older sister was concerned. "I've seen you practising. You look in the mirror with a shawl on and your hands joined together as if you were praying but you're not, you're just looking at yourself in the mirror to see how you look."

"That's not so, it's not," said Patsy. "Tell her it's not, Mammy. You know how much I love Our Lady. I want to be like her when I grow up."

"All I'm going to say on the matter is that you've all of you got some very good ideas for your da," said Betty. "We all need to pray very hard. I'll get in a few night lights and we'll keep one burning in front of Our Lady's little statue until Patrick comes home. Would you like that?"

"I want to light it," said Patsy.

"You can all take turns," said Betty. "Now, shall I read you Daddy's letter or do you want to squabble instead?" There was an instant hush. Betty had glanced at the letter quickly when it arrived to make sure it contained no bad news that would worry the children and to see which parts she would need to leave out. "Okay then, are you all paying attention?"

The girls were. "Wait while I just read through the boring bit at the beginning," said Betty and she read silently to herself.

'Dearest Betty,

'We haven't had the greatest start to married life now, have we? I thought we were just beginning to get to know each other properly too and I was feeling sure we were going to make a good go of it after all my early doubts. Now I find myself locked up in a camp in the north, too far from home for any visit to be possible.'

"Here we are now," she said to the children.

"'My thoughts are with the girls and with yourself and it's these thoughts which sustain me here.'"

"What's 'sustain'?" asked Molly.

"It means that thinking of us all keeps him happy and well and stops him feeling too lonely," said Betty.

"Goodness, all that in just one word!" said Patsy.

Betty carried on with the letter.

"'I am, of course, not alone. I am in a wooden hut with 25 other Volunteers in what they call Camp 2. There are lots of us here. Just to give you an idea; imagine 38 huts lined up in rows, each one holding 25 prisoners, and that's just Camp 2, where I am. I believe there are the same number more or less in Camp1. The huts are simple wooden shelters with just planking for floors and that's what we have to sleep on too, usually, just the wooden floor.'"

"Fancy having to sleep on a wooden floor," said Theresa. "Poor Daddy."

"But at least he has lots of company," said Molly.

"I'm going to work it out," said Patsy. "That's two camps, each with 38 huts, that comes to 76, and in each hut, there are 25 men, that makes…" She started mouthing the sums.

"You can tell us the answer later, Patsy. Shall I carry on reading or what?" said Betty.

"Patsy's always got to be the clever one," said Theresa. "I don't care how many men there are, only that Daddy is one of them. Let's hear his letter, Mammy."

"'*The camp was only set up a couple of months ago after that business in Dublin, you may remember, when Michael Collins and some of his men were accused of getting rid of fourteen British spies, permanently. We read about it in the paper. So I suppose we can't complain: hundreds of us taken and locked up for the few, but then God knows how many others suffered earlier as a result of their treason.*'"

"What's 'treason' Betty?"

"It's when someone tells tales on their friends or secrets about them and then these tales are used against them. Let me see now; it's like someone might tell the soldiers here the name of a man who is fighting them so then that man is arrested and put in prison."

"I wonder if that's what happened to our daddy," said Molly.

"If that's the case just let me find the treason man!" said Patsy.

"'*I can't write any more now as there's a great shortage of paper here. Let's hope to God I'll be home before I need to write too many letters anyway, I'd prefer it if we were all together, then I could tell you all about life here. Everyone is trying to make the most of the situation. Someone has even started giving violin lessons. Perhaps I should have a go then I could play along with Patsy and the rest of you. If you have any time, do try to write to me. Of course, all letters are checked before we get them or before ours are sent out so keep your inner thoughts to yourself. I wouldn't want anyone here reading about our private life.*'"

"And that's all from your da for now," said Betty. "It's a relief to know he's all right up there."

"Can we start our letters to him now, Mammy?" asked Theresa. "It may take me some time as I can still only write slowly. I might do a picture first."

"Well, if you all help to clear the table, I'll fetch some pencils and crayons. Patsy, you look for some paper in the sideboard in the parlour, I think it's in that cardboard box with bean tins printed on it."

"How long will it take for our letters to reach Daddy?" said Molly, balancing cups and saucers carefully to carry them into the tiny kitchen while Theresa moved as carefully as a tightrope-walker so as not to spill a drop from the milk jug.

"I don't know, perhaps a couple of weeks, so the sooner we make a start the better." Betty looked up quickly to the small picture of the Sacred Heart on the wall and said a quick prayer, whether of thanks or relief or despair she didn't know.

The months went by slowly, punctuated by the arrival of letters from Patrick, who always managed to find something of interest to relate from the prison camp at Ballykinlar while taking care not to involve any of the more alarming details of the daily brutality. He didn't want the children having nightmares about their daddy's situation and he didn't want to worry Betty: she had enough on her hands looking after three little girls who weren't even her own, though she had written to him that they had started calling her 'Mammy', hoping that it wouldn't upset him too much as she didn't want him to think she was trying to replace their real mother in his absence. Actually, he warmed to the idea, comforted by the knowledge that the children were settling well. He wrote that they would all be amused to see the bulk of him sitting cross-legged on the floor and crocheting along with all the other big men: they were all making small bags out of purple-dyed string for their daughters and he promised his girls one each. The bags had long thin straps attached, so they could be worn round the neck or over the shoulder, he wrote proudly. Meanwhile they had heard news that negotiations were progressing in London on some sort of limited self-government for Ireland so perhaps he'd better get the bags finished quickly.

"Does that mean Daddy will be home soon?" asked Patsy.

"You're only worried about getting your new bag," said Theresa.

"Girls," said Betty, "if your daddy could hear you now, he might decide not to bother coming home to listen to all this arguing. You wouldn't want that, now, would you?"

8

The red-brick terrace house on The Coombe was much smaller than the family had been used to, either out at Larch Hill or in Dublin in Hanover Street, but it had represented a new start for them all before Patrick had been arrested and he hadn't wanted to impose on Michael's generosity as a landlord for longer than necessary, especially as his friend had unexpectedly also become his father-in-law. Small though it was, the house was cosy and homely, thanks in large part to Betty. It seemed inconceivable now that Patrick had ever considered putting his three daughters in an orphanage.

Immediately to the right of the door that opened straight in off the street there was a front parlour where the piano had pride of place. Off the parlour, tucked away in the corner, was a tiny bedroom which Patsy had claimed for herself, saying she needed to be near the piano in case Beethoven — she could pronounce his name properly now — decided to visit as a floaty person to get in a bit of practice. She was sure that he'd be up in heaven and not down in that other place, being such a great composer, as everyone said he was, but somehow she couldn't imagine him being satisfied with playing the harp all the time. There was also a small, tiled fireplace in the parlour: the grate was just about big enough for one meagre shovel of coal but all the same that shovelful offered a warm glow when lit. A heavy wooden sideboard filled the wall opposite the piano, decked with family photos, odd ornaments, bits of simple arty treasures the children had made and always a small vase displaying a few flowers; there was a lumpy but well-loved sofa under the window, perfect for snuggling into and for nosing out of the window at people walking past, and there were two simple wooden-backed chairs on either side of the hearth. Betty had made it all look comfortable and cosy, with some of Patrick's paintings hung on the walls and bits of crochet-work dotted about on various well-polished surfaces, and she had been sure to include a couple of photograph portraits of Lizzie on the piano. She loved the fact that the girls usually called her 'Mammy' now but she didn't want anyone accusing her of trying to take their real mother's rightful place.

A short hallway led through to the back of the house, straight into another small room, dominated by the table, where the family ate, worked, played and read whatever came to hand; a fitted corner-dresser swallowed up the crockery, a few store-cupboard basics as well as all the indispensable clutter invariably gathered by any family. In this room too there was a fireplace, slightly larger than in the parlour but certainly less grand, having no tiles round it at all: an upholstered chair next to it was reserved, kept empty for Patrick to enjoy some peace when he was at home. A few miniature shrines hung on nails in the wall, the Sacred Heart having pride of place: tiny ledges jutted out on each to take a small night-light.

Off the back room, a poky kitchen accommodated the barest essentials — stove, sink, a wooden drainboard with a couple of shelves above and a couple more below, hidden behind a floral curtain, where the pans were stored. The kitchen also served as the family washroom. Towels and flannels were hung on a few hooks along under the bottom shelf above the sink and an enamel basin served both for washing dishes and people. Betty liked always to have a small plant on the window sill.

The toilet was outside in the yard: newspapers torn into squares were impaled on a nail on the wooden latch-door for the necessary wipes and for occasional readings of half-missing stories whenever nature or the need for some quiet presented itself. At the back of the yard there was an open-sided lean-to in which could be found the press, where butter and milk and other foodstuffs were kept cold. Otherwise, the small yard was just a rectangle of bare brick.

Upstairs in the house there were three bedrooms, varying in size from the tiny to the small, two at the back and one at the front, through which one of the back ones was accessed. A window on the landing shed light up and down the stairs. Betty ensured that the bit of lace curtain hanging there presented a clean aspect to passers-by in the street.

The family had moved into the house just weeks before Patrick's capture and even in his enforced absence life on The Coombe had settled into a daily routine divided strictly into school time and home time. There was a world of difference between the two: cold versus warm. The girls were just a few in the regular procession of boisterous, poorly dressed children scuttling along the pavement to St Brigid's Holy Faith Convent School just down the road. Once inside all chattering was forbidden as a sin against God's holy provision of an education to such ill-deserving young hooligans. Weren't they all lucky to be there by the Grace of God? The nuns ran a tightly organised system of indoctrinating their young charges into the unrelenting teachings of Irish Roman Catholicism and woe betide any child who showed any inclination to being wilful.

Nevertheless, most of the Sisters were kindly enough women. (It didn't take more than a few days for the O'Kelly clan to recognise which ones weren't, which ones were to be avoided.) The school day started with an assembly and prayers in a hall dominated by a large crucifix to induce holy thoughts on Jesus' sacrifice on the cross and so get the day off to a good start: assembly included some quiet moments to get the pupils in the right contemplative frame of mind for learning by the Grace of God, and then a couple of mournful hymns were sung before all pupils and teachers made their way to classes in the footsteps of Christ himself. Every lesson was then preceded by a prayer — to the virtuous Saint Brigid and to the holiest virgin of them all, Mary Mother of God herself — and somehow there was time for education to be delivered in between. The midday break was signalled by the sound of the Angelus bell being rung in the convent on the stroke of twelve, another call to prayer, this time in Latin. The afternoon followed a similar pattern until it was time to go home. Freedom. At least that's how Molly and little Theresa regarded it but for Patsy school offered a chance to learn lots of new things, it meant books to read and a piano she could play in peace: the Sisters encouraged her and got her to start practising all the hymns they sang in assembly to the Glory of God.

The music teacher was a stunted sort of a woman, her long habit making her look even shorter, Sister Scolastica by name: rumour had it among the schoolgirls that the nun had joined the order after her fiancé had been killed in some war or other, anyway, something to do with soldiers, ran the gossip, the loss of her great love spurring her to devote the remainder of her life to God. Whatever emotional sadness lay in her past, she was a friendly and gentle woman, with sparkling eyes that nevertheless managed to suggest an air of melancholy. Her young charges thought it all very romantic and tragic. The piano music she taught wasn't as grand as Beethoven's or the other pieces Patsy had been studying with Miss Bourke — her old teacher had regarded music as something spiritual in itself without the need for recourse to the Almighty and his saints for inspiration — but to Patsy it was the playing and the sounds that counted. She came to treasure her sessions with the love-lost nun. Indeed, Patsy became quite besotted with the whole idea of tragic love and the inner calm it seemed to bestow on the soul it left behind.

"You've a lovely touch on the notes," Sister Scolastica told her out of the blue one day. "Perhaps we could start playing some real music, what do you think? Hymns are all well and good and of course they do help focus our devotions and our prayers but they're not really enough for a gifted young pianist like yourself," she said, "but don't you dare tell any of the other Sisters I said such a thing."

"My old teacher in Rathfarnham used to tell me all about Beethoven," said Patsy, "and we had started working on some of his music."

"I'll bet it was 'Fur Elise', was it? Am I right?"

"How did you know that?" gawped Patsy.

"Well, it's a lovely but simple work and an easy enough introduction to the composer. I used to play it myself when I was young. We had a piano in the front parlour and I'd always have to play something for my mother and she did love 'Fur Elise'."

"So did mine," said Patsy.

"Well then we've something more in common," said the Sister. "I think I might have some sheet music for 'Fur Elise' still, I'll see if I can find it for next time."

"I thought nuns weren't allowed to have anything of their own," said Patsy.

"I probably donated it to the library here when I first arrived, with all my other music and books. I don't think God can be against music, do you, Patsy? or he wouldn't have made it so beautiful."

"But I thought that lots of things that are beautiful are sinful," said Patsy in confusion. "They are there to tempt us and test us, not for us to enjoy."

"Well, that's right enough," said the nun, "but I think music is in a different category altogether. Don't you think it's quite heavenly?"

"I do but sometimes I feel I shouldn't like it so much. I'm afraid of committing one of those sins that I don't even know I'm committing."

"Then just think about all those angels playing wonderful music on their harps up in heaven. Maybe your own guardian angel is a fine musician. I don't think you need worry about the temptations of a bit of sheet music in the convent."

"But it's so hard to know what's right or wrong when so much seems to be wrong and when even just thinking about it when you didn't mean to think about it turns out to be a sin."

"Not everything that's good and beautiful and pleasant is sinful," said Sister Scolastica, "otherwise the world wouldn't be such a wonderful place. Just think of all the lovely trees and flowers there are to look at and smell and enjoy in all their variety and delicacy; the bright blue of a sunny day or the drama of a stormy sky when the clouds are bunching up together right above our heads; the sound of water rushing over stones in the river or of the wind howling over the fields, so powerful yet invisible. And what about your family and the warm love of your parents and your sisters, these are all precious gifts to be treasured and valued. Don't we also have a duty to God to appreciate all these things he has given us and to give thanks for them? I've an idea that might help you understand things better, Patsy: why don't you join the Children of Mary? They have prayers and meditations written specially for young girls and to encourage a very close particular devotion to the Blessed Virgin. You're just about old enough and you might find their readings interesting. They also pray to the martyr Saint Philomena, a wonderful example for young women as they grow up. And you get to wear a blue cape. Wouldn't you like that, to wear a blue cape like Our Lady herself?"

"I'd love that," said Patsy, actually slightly embarrassed by her enthusiasm. "I'd already decided I wanted to join. But I'll have to ask my mammy first."

Despite the heavy weight of religion, St Brigid's provided schooling of a reasonable standard for the poor children who lived roundabout in the close-knit streets and back-alleys known as The Liberties, an old district of Dublin in which not many residents had much in the way of money nor the opportunities it could buy. Some years earlier the area had been a popular destination for teams of proselytisers from England, bent on converting the Catholics to Protestantism: in fact it was only thirty years earlier that a ban against the show of any crucifixes in Ireland had been lifted after being imposed by Britain for years, a ban which strangely wasn't enforced on the Catholic congregations of the mainland. St Brigid's school itself had been opened as a counter-measure aimed at protecting the children and their young faith. Religion thus played a major role in the way the school was conducted but the children did also learn how to read and write and do their sums and understand the Gaelic language.

That was the environment in which Patsy was now immersed and it wasn't only Sister Scolastica who realised there was something very individual about Patsy O'Kelly. It didn't take long for the teaching nuns to recognise that Patsy was not only a gifted young pianist but was also way ahead of her classmates in academic subjects: she was inquisitive and intelligent by nature and was blessed with an almost kleptomaniac memory — whatever she learned or was told stayed in her head with little effort or study. The decision was taken that the child should be taken out of the ordinary classes to join the private pupils and so hopefully progress at a quicker rate. And once again it was suggested that Patsy try for a music scholarship.

9

There was much merriment and hustle and bustle going on in the house. It was early December already and Christmas was close on the horizon, though it still seemed too long into the future for the O'Kelly girls. Aunt Mary had arrived with their cousins Kevin and Tessie from Usher's Quay and the youngsters were busy at the table making paperchains and hand-painted greetings cards, the place littered with bits of coloured paper and a pot of paste and brushes, while the two mothers gossiped and giggled in the kitchen stirring a couple of puddings, surrounded by the organised white-dusted chaos of baking.

"Can you pass me the sixpence to mix in, Betty."

"Here you are, Mary, the sixpence you shall have. Do you know sometimes I think this is a bit of a silly tradition because that sixpence could put more food on the table and I always worry that someone might break a tooth if they don't realise the sixpence is buried in white sauce right there on their spoon," said Betty.

"I'm the same," said Mary. "And I also worry that however I try to the contrary I'll get it wrong and not manage to make sure one of the children gets the lucky helping. I suppose in actual fact they're too busy poking about looking for the money to chance putting it in their mouth."

The women exchanged a that's-children-for-you look and got on with their mixing.

"You know, Betty, I think it's grand the way you've taken on the girls and given them so much love and I know it all happened so quickly after their mammy died."

"Well in a way I didn't have a lot of choice in the matter," said Betty. "Of course I could have said no when my da sorted it all out with the priests and Patrick, I was the last to know, that's often the way it is for women as you yourself know, but I'd already gotten to know the girls and the thought of them ending up in the orphanage wasn't something I would have been happy about."

"No more would I," said Mary. "I was in that place myself long enough."

"Then of course there was Patrick, I had gotten to know him too but only a bit, it was only a matter of weeks I was living at Larch Hill and he was so pre-occupied with grief at the time. I knew he and his wife had been very close. I'd met Lizzie a few times and I thought Patrick must be a good husband and father to merit her devotion."

"Well, he's a lucky man that he has you now. I'm lucky too to have you," said Mary. "When Lizzie passed away, I felt I'd lost a good friend, not just a woman who happened to be my husband's sister but a real friend. God, we used to enjoy the craic when they'd come visit us from Larch Hill. Patrick and Stephen would go out for a few jars and Lizzie and I would have a grand time together. Then of course there was that awful night when the Tans raided the place. Did Patrick ever mention it to you? The little ones were scared out of their wits and so were the grown-ups, to be honest. I'm sure that's what made him volunteer. If only they hadn't come that particular weekend."

"I'm sure it was on the cards anyway, Mary, sure there was enough talk and activity going on out round Tullamore. My da was always up to something, all secret and hush-hush and things hidden away in the cowshed or out in the fields, and don't forget him and Patrick were good friends. I'm sure it was no different in Rathfarnham, though perhaps as they lived with the English family Patrick had to keep himself to himself. But he never talked to me much about what had happened that night in Dublin, though of course circumstances were hard when I went to live with them at Larch Hill, what with his wife dying and young Patsy being with her at the time."

"Yes, that must have been awful for the poor little one. Thank God you were able to help."

"And then there's Patrick's brother, Arthur. He was well involved. When he came back from working in Paris, I believe he was active straight away, very dangerous work he did, I'm told, something to do with 'intelligence gathering', they called it. No doubt he wouldn't pass up the chance to recruit his brother."

"Well I know Patrick used to get together with Arthur when they came to Dublin," said Mary. "In fact I think they'd met up that very weekend. I did hear Lizzie say something about Patrick after agreeing to hide a gun for him. I'm not sure where Arthur is now but I don't think he was ever caught."

"Well he was in Dublin when Patrick was arrested because it was Arthur himself who told me what had happened."

"Do the girls know their daddy might be home soon?" whispered Mary. "I read that Ballykinlar had closed after the treaty was signed in London."

"They know that the camp has closed but that's all. I don't like to get their hopes too high. We don't know how long it will take for the men to get back home or even if they'll get home safely. I'm sure the British won't be as quick to set their prisoners free as they were to lock them up, especially just before Christmas. They might see that as too good a meanness to pass up. We'll just have to wait and see."

"Well, what a grand surprise it would be for them if their da was to walk through the door unannounced."

"What about Stephen, is he getting any leave for the holidays?"

"We don't know that either yet," said Mary. "India is a bit far away for a quick visit. It's a wonder we women ever manage to plan anything these days, let alone Christmas. If it wasn't for the little ones, I'm not sure I'd bother with the whole business, though I must admit I do like Christmas myself. I always think there's a special atmosphere everywhere and people seem happier despite whatever's going on. And I always love singing carols at Mass during Advent."

"Not that we need to sing every verse like Father O'Hanlon insists," said Betty. "You can have too much of a good thing, or too much of a good sing, I should say?" The two women laughed. "There, that's my sixpence well mixed in now. Such treasure for the finder. Shall we let it all stand for a while before the steaming, Mary? I could do with a cup of tea."

"Me too and I wouldn't say no to resting my arms and wrists for a bit after all this mixing. It's quite hard work for something basically so simple."

The two women moved to the kitchen table and slumped in their wooden-back chairs as if into the plushest upholstered armchairs imaginable. Never mind the fraying seat-covers and the odd evidence of old food thanks to some careless little mouths: the weight was off their feet and that was all that mattered. Appetite-inducing smells of pudding mixes were permeating the house and, what with the children so enjoying their festive work, all seemed a million miles away from the guns and bombs and smells of fires burning that had permeated the atmosphere of their lives for what had seemed forever. A sharp insistent rap on the door dispersed the mood.

Betty and Mary both froze at the sudden interruption and its portent; both thought all that fear was behind them now that the Treaty had been agreed but you could never be too sure. There were few in Dublin who'd not experienced the terror of the loud door-knock.

"I'd best go and see who it is," said Betty, carefully putting her cup of tea down in the saucer.

She got up slowly, managed a reassuring smile at the youngsters, who had stopped and gawped mid-snips, and she made her way down the hall to the front door. There was no glass in it so she couldn't determine who was outside in the street, she'd no option but to open the damned thing.

"Who's making all that racket?" she shouted, sounding braver than she felt as she turned the lock. She eased the door ajar, all the time expecting it to be shoved into her by some brute in some uniform or other, but there on the step was Patrick. He was back. Betty could only stand open-mouthed, a shy smile creasing across her face, with simple relief that her dear husband was home with his family again in Dublin, safe and looking reasonably well after his imprisonment. He was thinner and quite pale and seemed to have developed a slightly gaunt stoop but he was smiling too, his own simple expression of relief. He held Betty close, a long clutching hug, his eyes closed and his breath warming into Betty's neck as he held her as if no separation would ever be allowed again. "Welcome home," said Betty. "Thank God you're back." Then she put her finger to his lips requesting no sudden announcement.

"Is everything all right out there?" called Mary, standing up and pulling the chair out from under her to go and investigate any goings-on but not wanting to leave the children. She was becoming alarmed at the silence, half convinced that Betty had been taken away as an accomplice and at the same time not wanting to panic the girls. They were still sitting motionless over their decoration's debris, still nervous after hearing that awful hammering on the door, like the past was still present. All eyes were turned in the same direction, all eyes saw Patrick playfully put his head round the door.

Then the laughter started, the cheering, the squeals, the furniture being moved this way and that, the girls elbowing each other out of the way and shoving through to be the first to give their daddy the biggest and best hug ever, all talking at once and bombarding him with their bits of innocent news and chatter, somehow at the same time dragging him to the table demanding that he immediately inspect their Christmas creations.

"Well, would you look at how clever you all are," Patrick beamed. "The house is certainly going to look great this Christmas and I can't tell you how glad I am to be here to enjoy it with you."

10

With her da back home, Patsy felt that all her trust in Mary the Mother of God had been deeply rewarded and her simple but heartfelt prayers answered to a degree she had never really fully believed possible, try though she might. She constantly made silent Acts of Contrition to ease her guilt over such a terrible lack of faith but her soul soared with such confidence and warmth towards Mary now that she decided to double, triple her daily devotions to that holiest of women, chosen by God himself to bear his precious son, Jesus. Patsy now wore her blue Children of Mary cape with a sincere humility. She knew that her sister had been right before and that she had committed the cardinal sin of pride in her posing and pray-posturing in the mantle, but that was before. Even her Brown Scapula and Miraculous Medal, obligatory outward symbols of virtue worn by all Mary's dedicated Children, were tucked inside her blouse to prevent any chance of careless ostentation. Now she was a true daughter of Mary and would strive to follow her Mother's example. She would be modest, kind, caring and, above all, obedient to the will of God.

The weekly sessions of the Children of Mary were held in a sombre meeting room at the back of the parish church, next to the vestry. It was a poorly lit room, the small leaded window allowed in very little light from the outside, and it was always a bit on the cold side, with no fireplace there to facilitate any source of heat regardless of the weather. Wood-panelled walls only suggested some sort of insulation against any prevailing chill but as there was never any heating on in the place the wood had nothing to absorb to warm its surface touch. Holy books and prayer missals and old copies of letters from the bishop lined the shelves in untidy leanings. Church candles were stacked along the top of a dresser, arranged by size, some tall and fat enough for the back of the altar to illuminate the sacred table during a whole week's services, some small red ones used mainly during home visits to the sick or dying.

There were about twenty girls who attended the meetings regularly in this perhaps humility-inspiring environment, all members of the parish. Not that they were all little saints. Patsy knew the ones who lingered on the street corners with the boys and their posturings were certainly not of the praying kind: giggling and pouting, throwing their heads back with eyes wide and wild, tossing their hair about to catch the sunlight and fiddling their fingers through their tresses to look carefree and exciting and enticingly dishevelled, sometimes even playfully pushing one of the boys to incite some frisson of touch. In the meetings, of course, butter wouldn't melt as they listened to the instruction and read the special prayer to the Blessed Virgin, as did all the Children of Mary throughout the world.

"I desire henceforth to belong entirely to you, walking in your glorious footsteps and imitating your virtues: your angelic purity, your profound humility, your perfect obedience and your incomparable charity." That was Patsy's favourite line, the one where she always closed her eyes tightly in concentrated devotion and shut out the world and its promised distractions. She would definitely strive to imitate Mary's 'angelic purity'. What an instantly holy-inducing phrase, though as yet Patsy had only the vaguest idea of what it meant.

At the meetings they also recited the special prayer to St. Philomena, in turn revered for her steadfast purity. Patsy thought Philomena's amazing story could challenge any of the books she had read at school and what's more it was about a real saint, canonised by the Church for her purity. It spoke of a wonderful young girl who defied all attempts to turn her from her personal promise to God himself.

The heroine was a beautiful thirteen-year-old Greek princess who had taken a consecrated vow of eternal chastity. When her father tried to marry her off to the Emperor Diocletian in Rome — of course the emperor had already fallen madly in love with her — Philomena refused to break her oath to God in Heaven and repeatedly spurned the Emperor's marital suit. For her faithful pains she was subjected to those of the physical, brutal, revengeful kind. The beautiful young Philomena was scourged; then an anchor was tied to her and she was thrown into the sea to drown, while at the same time being fired upon with a hail of cruel arrows. She was miraculously saved by God's angels.

What a story indeed, sketchy though it was in parts, being actually based on no more than suppositions when her burial tomb was discovered in catacombs in 1802 by some nuns: the grave contained various images of anchors and arrows, plus a flower which represented purity, and the elements of Philomena's martyrdom were woven together and the praying and attributed miracles began. Declared sainthood followed.

Patsy's imagination fed on it all, as she had once fed on the stories of Beethoven's dedication to his music above all other considerations, including personal hygiene. Just as then she had gone through a period of not washing, now she inwardly fantasised about following in St Philomena's footsteps, relishing the gothic combination of romance and chastity. She would stride towards a pure future with St Philomena guiding her path. Every day she prayed the special prayer, imploring the "glorious martyr" to "obtain for me that purity for which you sacrificed all the passing pleasures of this world so that, by imitating you in this life, I may one day be crowned with you in heaven." Amen to that, said Patsy. Her simple dedication rose to the heavens with the whispering dissipating breath of every devotional candle she lit. Her small bedroom had meanwhile become a shrine in blue and was so full of holy pictures and little statues that it looked like the repository at the back of the church. It enveloped Patsy and her floaty people in closeted spiritual comfort.

It was a comfort she was seeking more and more. Lost as she was in her simple faith that her prayers had been answered with her father's homecoming, at the same time her da had returned from Ballykinlar with a gathering darkness about him that his children found increasingly frightening. He returned to his old job at the bakery but more and more he had no time to play silly games with the girls once back from work. The days of family laughter sitting around the table that they'd all so enjoyed out at Larch Hill and then in Dublin had been muffled into silence by his time in the internment camp. Now, instead of boisterous fun with their da, there was a growing cold distance, impatience. The joy of his arrival home just in time for Christmas had drooped along with the sagging paperchains; the draught of winter had seeped into the house through every nook and cranny of Patrick's humour, the glad-tidings and festive mirth had lifted as no more than a temporary illusion and the coming of spring had failed to blossom in the innards of their small house. As the months went by, Patrick seemed to retreat more and more into a lonely place, a heavy inner world, as if the camaraderie and thrill of fighting with his fellow countrymen had left behind a void, a defeated enthusiasm for life. He had poured out all his pent-up love in his letters home and, if anything at all remained of those gentle feelings after his confinement, what was left had subsequently evaporated with his spirit.

What Patsy, Molly and Theresa were too young to recognise was that their father had changed fundamentally, so fundamentally that his spark for life, his enthusiasm for being with other people and enjoying their company, had all but been extinguished. Patrick had become disillusioned. He was disillusioned with himself, he was disillusioned with those former comrades for whom once upon a time he would have laid down his life without hesitation, he was disillusioned with his country.

A treaty had been signed in London the previous year between the British Government on the one side and Michael Collins and Arthur Griffith representing the Irish on the other. It had led to Patrick's release from Ballykinlar, for sure, and for that he was immediately grateful, glad to get back to The Coombe in time for Christmas with his family. But the treaty declared Ireland not as a republic but as a Free State, as a continuing dominion of the British Empire, and that led to bitter divisions and disappointments among the men and women who had fought together so hard to escape the yoke of Britain. This in turn had led to civil war. Now former comrades were killing each other, they had become entrenched enemies set on defeating the opposing faction. To some the treaty represented total defeat: they had fought and sacrificed life and limb to win an independent Ireland and now their representatives had betrayed the cause by signing the treaty. To others, the treaty represented an interim victory, with Ireland self-governing at least, and their representatives had furthered the chances of establishing a republic in the future. Patrick was no capitulator but nor could he see any justification for Irishmen killing Irishmen.

When Collins himself was ambushed and killed by his own countrymen in June that summer, Patrick retired into himself in shame and sorrow: Collins had been a hero of the Easter Rising. Patrick wanted nothing to do with any civil war, no matter which old soldier-in-arms arrived on the doorstep to seek his support.

His detachment was insidious. He became isolated within himself. He shunned even the comfort of his family and spent most of his free time organising photographs in a leather-bound album which he bought specially, writing the captions in his beautiful, neat hand, the letters leaning forward in contradiction to the backward-looking pictures that absorbed all of his attention back into the past. His concentration was total, as if he was trying to fix the past in place, ensuring it was immune to any further disturbance. Otherwise, he would be outside in the small yard off the kitchen, working with bits of wood, measuring and sawing, nailing and gluing, mumbling to himself as he fashioned what turned out to be a miniature but perfect replica of a coffin.

The finished item, the wood glowing with elbow-grease, the brass plates buffed to a golden shine, was installed on top of the sideboard in the parlour. It was supported on small brackets at either end, each beautifully carved by himself and each bottomed with a fitted piece of felt to prevent any scratching to the sideboard. Betty was under strict instructions to keep the coffin in pristine polished condition. The girls were under strict instructions to behave themselves under pain of either being reported to the Parish Priest or being forced inside the thing by the banshee for any naughtiness and then have the lid closed on them. The threat was scary in the extreme.

The coffin sat there all day and every day, there was no escape, so the youngsters avoided the parlour, once a cosy snug for playing or welcoming visitors. None of them wanted to catch even the slightest glimpse of the box that might swallow them up if their da saw fit, while their noisy chatter in the back room was always tempered when their father was home in case it annoyed him in some way. The threat of the coffin always soured the air. It had an awful, decaying presence. The girls' only respite was when they got back from school and their father was still at work. They couldn't even visit Kevin and Tessie on Usher's Quay any more: not long after Christmas, Uncle Stephen had come home on leave and moved Auntie Mary and the children over to Liverpool after being allocated a small terrace house in Bootle: he felt they'd be safer there away from the violence of Dublin and he not at home as protector but their going was a sad occasion, a loss felt by both families and many tears had been shed. Patsy, Molly and Theresa had no bolt hole now to escape their father's mood.

Betty's heart went out to the children. She told them that they had to be patient and extra loving to their daddy, explaining that he had seen some awful things happen, things it would take a long time to forget — friends shot dead in the street in front of him, friends shot and wounded and perhaps left bleeding where they fell, friends captured and taken away to be locked up, just like he was, then starved and beaten and made to sleep on hard wooden floors with scarcely enough food to feed a mouse. They were grim pictures indeed for youngsters but nothing that was new to them, they had witnessed enough themselves already.

"It's been very hard for your da but you must remember that he still loves you all," said Betty. "We can help him in our own ways and right now, girls, that means being good and quiet while he's at home. But when he's not here, I want you all to be as noisy and busy as you can be. Can we all agree on that?"

The children were delighted that Betty was still as much fun as she always had been. She worked hard to keep some joy going in their lives. She would never contradict anything Patrick said or go behind his back in any way. She had, for example, considered draping a pretty cloth over the coffin while he was out at work then decided on reflection that the situation could turn out worse if on an odd occasion she forgot to hide the cloth away before he got home. But when he was seated by the fire in his big chair, scowling inwardly, trapped within his own-made prison, she would sometimes say something light-hearted and give the girls a surreptitious wink.

It was upstairs at night in bed that Betty felt the full depth of Patrick's depression. He would often talk out loud to himself about how their life had turned sour because of him, all the while just staring blankly, not seeing anything other than his own emptiness. Then one night finally he sought her support.

"It's all my fault, Betty," he told her, his eyes examining the ceiling but lurking somewhere in the shadows of his mind. His breathing was a mix of sighing and wafting, his voice agitating the silence of the night. "I should never have got involved with such a pointless struggle. It was all for what? So that we could win a free Ireland where men would be free to kill each other? And doesn't that suit the British down to the ground? All those years of being called 'stupid Paddies' by ignorant men parading round in their British uniforms and now aren't we just proving they were right all along? I am so sorry, Betty, so sorry I took you away from your home on the farm and all your own dreams only to turn your life into a nightmare, a nightmare I helped to create. I should never have paid heed to Father Murphy and his matchmaking. I should have left you to marry your young man in Tullamore. You'd all have been better off without me and my so-called patriotic duty."

"Stop there now, Patrick," said Betty, turning to face him, looking at his head lying on the pillow beside her and wanting to still the anxiety swirling around inside him. "I won't listen to any more of this. You're a good man, you've always been a good man, and I came here because I wanted to and I've never been sorry, even when you were out at night God knows where and me here frightened to death that you wouldn't come home. But you did, thank God, you're alive, you have three lovely daughters and a wife who loves you, Patrick, yes loves you, loves the man you are. And you don't know yet what's going to happen here in the end. You yourself always used to say that it would be a long struggle and not an easy one, getting a free Ireland. I had my eyes open when I married you, no one forced me into it, and you had your eyes open when you were fighting, you knew it would be hard and bitter, so don't keep going around in circles over what's done. It's of no help to you and meanwhile the girls are becoming frightened of their own daddy. Is that what you want?"

Patrick was quiet, he had no ready answer other than that of course that wasn't what he wanted. He knew Betty was right, he knew he was shutting out young Patsy and Molly and Theresa, knew only too well the heaviness he had brought down on them, and them only children when all was said and done. But... But... What was it all for with civil war raging in the streets? He was drowning in remorse and anger, helpless against the tug, against the tide of violent disagreements. He turned over in the bed and gazed steadily at Betty.

"What can I do?" he asked her. He posed the question simply, with none of the edge of challenge that of late had come to dominate his everyday speech. His voice was soft and pleading.

"I think you must let it all work its way out and it will if you just let it," said Betty, gently pushing a stray curl of hair out of his eyes, ridiculously moved by the mix of deep despair in his soul and that slight cast he had in those serious eyes. "But you have to help it on its way," she said, "and not be tormenting yourself over what was and what is, what you did or didn't do. We still have lives to live and we must live them as best and as happily as we can. Isn't that why you made all the decisions you made?" She could feel his heavy mood starting to ease. "And you haven't done any painting for such a long time. As I understand it you used to be quite the artist when you lived in the country. Why don't you take that up again? It might be a more appropriate way of using your talents than making coffins."

They gazed at each other warmly. It was the first time Betty had suggested even a hint of criticism at the doom-laden replica on the sideboard.

"You're a fount of common sense, Betty," he said. "What normal man would make such a thing and frighten the life out of his family with it? And did I hear you right," he asked, "did you say you love me?"

"You did and I do," she replied, smiling softly at this big fool of a man. "I didn't at first, you know that, but we've won a closeness between us that I wouldn't swap for the country-lane promises of any young man in Tullamore. And I've something else to tell you, Patrick O'Kelly, now that we're getting you into a more positive way of thinking," she said. "We're going to be having our own baby in a few months' time. What do you think of that?"

"I think I haven't been that successful at keeping my distance, then," he said, his eyes lighting up with a happiness he hadn't felt for a long time. "Come here to me now, woman."

In the adjoining room Molly and Theresa were sitting up in bed looking out of the window after lifting a few inches of peephole along the bottom of the curtains and the flimsy nets to watch the men straggling home from The Cosy Bar on the corner along from the house. It was one of their favourite night-time vigils: when either one of them couldn't sleep, they'd wake the other for company in their spying game. The girls were giggling as quietly as they could at the way the drunken men staggered along, stumbling and bumbling to balance themselves as they headed home along The Coombe, heaving at right-angles to their own bodies but placing their feet in a comically deliberate manner, noisy as usual with the odd one adding a bit of singing accompaniment. That was always the funniest and the hardest for the two girls trying not to make a sound, snorting under their breath and doubled up with the struggle of held-in laughter at the a-tonal strains of some Irish rebel song belted out in a slur: this was what some of Dublin's fighting men had become.

The young spies particularly enjoyed seeing the state of the men whose wives would reverently lead them down the centre aisle of St Francis's and right up to the front bench at Sunday Mass. The Cosy Bar was the husbands' escape hole: it was no place for women, and it was no place many women would want to go. Theresa and Molly had of course never been into The Cosy Bar but they had of course snuck in quick glances through the door: they were not impressed by the fuggy dark interior nor by the stale smell of beer and thick cigarette smoke wafting out.

"Don't they look right eejits," said Molly, muffling the sound of her voice behind her hand. "I'm never going to get married. Men are such gobshites."

"You shouldn't say words like that," said Theresa, "but you're right," she tittered, "they are all gobshites. I'm not going to get married either."

"You're not?" whispered her sister. "And what about young Billy O'Mara? I thought you had your eyes set on him?"

"He's not a man, he's a boy," said Theresa.

"Maybe he is now but won't he be growing up into a man when you leave school? Then we'll see how you feel. He'll be in that bar then as often as his da is now."

"Well maybe he won't be like that. Our daddy doesn't go drinking, does he?"

"No, he doesn't, you're right," said Molly.

The two girls lapsed into silence.

"But you know what, Theresa, when I see the men going home from the bar they don't seem to look as fed up as my da usually looks. Is that a terrible thing to say?"

"Yes, that's a really terrible thing to say," said Theresa. "Would you rather we had a daddy who came in drunk every night?"

"No."

"Well then shut up with your nonsense and don't you be such a gobshite."

"I'm not a gobshite and you're just being a meanie. I'm going to lie down."

"Me too," said Theresa tucking down quickly next to her sister and pulling the blankets up over their heads. "I can hear Daddy and Mammy talking. Pretend you're asleep just in case they come in."

But they didn't.

Patrick's daughters picked up on the difference in their da. He was suddenly a lot less grumpy and groany and the atmosphere in the house took on a warmer feel altogether: the girls could do their chores for Betty and chatter at the same time and they could play without being stifled in a creepy silence.

Even the backyard was no longer out of bounds as Patrick spent more of his time in the house; his new project was to put shelving up in the triangular space under the stairs and a door on it to turn it into an extra store cupboard. The girls thought it was more like a whole little room than a cubby hole, a proper den for them to play in.

As the tensions eased, Molly and Theresa became as thick as thieves: their night-time spying crept into daytime too as they played secret agents, which spilled over into inventing stories with their dolls, for which they were constantly sewing clothes and fancy costumes out of bits of rag cut from old clothes at the kitchen table, then acting out their childish dramas in their new under-stairs den.

Even Patsy emerged from her bedroom more, leaving the cloistered comfort of her floaty people to join in with the rest of the household. Everything was becoming a source of joy again and she liked to help in the sewing sessions with her sisters, guiding their fingers to create neat stitching and even hems. She gradually started playing the piano again in the house after months of avoiding the parlour and its coffin: it was still there, still plonked funereally on the sideboard, and for a while she had still felt too intimidated to practise her lessons for Sister Scolastica in the same room but she was no longer afraid of upsetting her daddy and risking the threat of the lidded box being shut down with her inside: hadn't he himself laughed at the whole thing and said it would obviously be impossible to fit a child into such a small thing anyway. She unconsciously learned to ignore the brass-handled wooden casket.

The coffin miraculously became just a part of the furniture, a bizarre ornament: after all, said Betty, not many people could boast their very own mini coffin in the parlour. Talk of the new baby on the way — maybe a little brother this time — made all of them feel as if their family was a proper one again.

Part 2

Did the kiss of Mother Mary
Put that music in her face?
Yet she goes with footsteps wary,
Full of earth's old timid face.

— W B Yeats

1

Patsy swaggered down George Street. She was smiling idiotically, casually striding forward, head held high, her naturally crimpy hair peeping out from under her black beret; she looked like a young woman who was enjoying the most amazing day possible. As indeed she was, it was.

She was just a few months into her job at Jeanette Modes, the most prestigious fashion tailoring establishment of Dublin, and today she had been singled out by the supervisor and promoted for her good workmanship. Her apprenticeship with her younger sisters making their own clothes, starting at doll-size and gradually getting bigger and more elaborate, had given her enough basic experience to get her first job in a sewing room in the city and a permanent position at Jeanette Modes wasn't that long in presenting itself. Tailoring skills came naturally to Patsy. Now she had moved up from invisible hems (important but a bit monotonous) to proper seamstress, which offered the simple but tactile pleasure of feeling her fingers smooth the most delicious fabrics and rich tweeds across the bed of her Singer sewing machine, easing the cloth gently across the needle plate — no puckering, mind — and guiding it out safely the other side into an organised billowing of tamed material.

Sean was going to be so proud of his 'Streaks'. What a funny nickname he had given her, Streaks: she cherished the intimacy the secret name gave to their relationship. Patsy felt her heart quicken as she thought of her young man, hearing it beat out the arresting rhythms and pumping her body full of dramatic musical sounds. It stopped her in her tracks.

Suddenly she caught sight of herself in a shop window and her idiotic grin smiled back, stretching itself from ear to ear as she tilted her beret to a cockier angle over her curls. She thought she looked nicely silly. She was going straight from work to a meeting to hear an address by a women's group about the continuing struggle for women's rights in the patriarchal and strict Catholic society which had taken over control from the British. Women had earned their voice and their right to be heard after the undeniable contribution they had made in the fight for independence, but they had subsequently felt betrayed when De Valera's government had reneged on all the promises of equality for women included in the declaration displayed at the General Post Office during the Easter Rising and had effectively legislated women back to the kitchen.

Now here was Patsy, mesmerised by the strength shown by women over recent years, ordinary women, herself included, winning small but significant gains against the pig-headedness of old-fashioned men and the power of the Church. Patsy was still a devoted member of the Children of Mary and to her way of thinking this superior attitude by men towards women was an affront against Mary the Mother of God herself: it showed a terrible lack of respect. Patsy's growing political awareness had imbued her daily prayer with an edge of determination: "I choose Thee for my patroness, my advocate, my mistress and my mother. At your feet I take the firm resolution of doing all in my power to procure your glory and extend your service." Patsy had no doubt that the service involved was a question of maintaining the dignity and status of women, not subduing them.

Looking at her reflection, she decided that her idiotic grin perhaps contradicted her strength of feeling but was true to the quivering inner turmoil she experienced every time she thought about Sean, her stomach fluttering like a sustained trill on the piano in Fur Elise.

All very well, she thought as her behatted self gazed back at her, but sometimes her reserves of strength seemed very weak indeed: on the hearth if not on the Home Front her voice hardly registered as a whisper.

When her father spoke, all the old male stuff she'd grown up with was upheld: he ordered and she obeyed. Her earnest political voice on behalf of women was like a lie to herself, like so much empty lip-service. She loved her da, of course she did, but over the years he had grown cold and bitter and distant compared to the daddy he had been. She cherished the now-fading memories of her happy childhood days out at Larch Hill, when her father had enjoyed such a great sense of playfulness and would let them all ride round the yard on the horse's back teaching them what he called circus tricks, helping them to lie across Seamus's back with their arms and legs out either side at full stretch, or to trot while facing backwards, them holding on for dear life and nearly falling off with all the giggling and screaming that went on. It was great fun. Then there were some easier times in The Coombe but, with new babies arriving with yearly regularity, life was too cramped and too hand-to-mouth to allow much in the way of gaiety and her da had grown increasingly intolerant of so much intrusion into his own peace and quiet. He had always worked hard, she knew that, but, in the past, when he got home from work and was back at their gatehouse cottage he was as great a da as anyone could want. He was a loving father in those days. The years of war had changed all that: the secrecy, the danger, the urgent searches for different hiding places for guns and grenades somewhere at home: he knew he was putting the whole family at risk but he also knew there was nothing else he could do.

For all that, the Patrick O'Kelly who had been arrested and interned up north in Ballykinlar Prison Camp had been a nicer person than the Patrick O'Kelly who came back.

Not that it could have been easy for the man, his daughter understood only too well, what with losing his wife — Patsy of all people could remember that day vividly — and then having to leave the gatehouse to move to Dublin, but when he had returned from the camp it was to a warm and loving home with Betty, his wonderful new wife and a step-mother in a million to his three daughters. He'd even got his old job back in the bakery. Patsy couldn't understand why he had changed so much, why he had gradually turned so sour. She couldn't accept that he was the way he was just because of the Civil War and his very real sense of betrayal. That was all in the past but his heavy presence was all she knew now.

Patsy shivered and walked away from her window mirror. The bakery. That's where her Sean worked too, Sean Fitzsimmons. In fact, that's how she'd met him, after calling in to give her da his forgotten sandwiches one day.

She had noticed the good-looking young chap in his flour-dusty overalls and he had noticed her and there was something special in the noticing. She wouldn't have admitted it to herself but she then positively engineered further excuses to call to see her da and gradually that something special she had shared with the young baker had become something really special. They had been walking out together for months now and Patsy was giddy with love for her beau. And didn't he write such beautiful loving letters to his Streaks, regular letters, arriving every couple of days between their Friday evening trysts. She had one with her now and couldn't resist pulling it out of her handbag just to hold, to finger the pages he had fingered. She just had to read it again, right there in the street.

My Dear Streaks, It gives me great pleasure to be able to speak to you through the aid of pen and ink. It is only ten minutes to four on Tuesday afternoon and I'll be thinking of you tonight knowing you'll be out to the pictures with Margaret. What a good friend she is to you. Friday night, my time when you dedicate your precious self to me, seems a hell of a long way off. (Please excuse the lingo, Streaks, but that's just the way I feel, that waiting to see you IS hell. I can see that dirty disapproving look in your eye!)

You know, Patsy (I mean Streaks), I envy Miss Margaret Matthews, because she's twenty-one and she hasn't got a father to tell her to steer clear of us poor unfortunate bakers. I'm not so bad, sure I'm not, Streaks, sure I can't be if someone as wonderful as you chooses to spend time with me. And what enjoyable times we have together. Gee, I'm getting all hot and bothered!

Love forever, Sean.

And didn't he have such beautiful handwriting. Of course, her father was against the whole thing. "No daughter of mine is going to end up with a baker's boy, she deserves a better future than that," he'd rule. This was the very same father who had denied her a possible better future when he refused to let her to take up the music scholarship awarded to her several years ago because, he said, it would corrupt her, mixing with no-good bohemian students. Patsy's precocious talent on the piano had fulfilled the promise Miss Bourke had seen back in Larch Hill and she had rewarded all the dedication shown by Sister Scolastica with the recognition the music award brought to her teaching, all to come to nothing because of her father's iron temperament. The sympathetic intervention of Betty had kept the peace but not the scholarship. Now her father was set against her taking up with Sean.

"Shush now, Pat," Betty would say to him. "What's got into you? You've told me yourself often enough that Sean Fitzsimmons is a hard worker and he's a good Catholic too, isn't he always at Mass and Communion every Sunday with his mother? And what's wrong with marrying a man who works in a bakery? Sure I married one myself."

Then Betty would stare dreamily but dramatically out of the window and murmur gently, though loud enough for Patrick's benefit.

"O Mother of God," she'd say, "I always expected that I'd be living out my life in the country working the farm, listening to the birds singing as I brought the cows in from the field, nudging them along the lane with a little push of the stick, them lowing all the way and taking their time, enjoying the saunter home just like myself. Then I'd collect the eggs from the hens for everyone's breakfast before cosying up in front of the range to enjoy the warmth and the craic. But where did I end up instead?" she'd say to her audience. "I'm here, living in Dublin, all of us crowded into this tiny house, seven children and another on the way, and not a cow to be seen. I'm married to a baker, not a farmer, and instead of listening to the birds and all the cows mooing I have to listen to all the man's moaning. And do you know what, Patrick O'Kelly?" she'd say and turn to face him directly. "I made the right choice marrying my baker's man, daft though he sometimes is, so I know that your daughter could do a lot worse than Sean Fitzsimons. So whisht and leave her be."

But he wouldn't leave it be. Away from Betty's remonstrations Patsy knew that her father went out of his way to make life hell for Sean at the bakery, insulting him in front of the other men and always critical of whatever he did, belittling the young man at every opportunity with remarks and suggestions to the other workers that he was not to be trusted, that he was a mammy's boy and, ridiculously, contrarily, that either he was a bit of a gigolo or that he was no sort of a man to be of any interest to any woman. Patrick was forever warning Sean against seeing Patsy, that he'd marry her "only over my dead body".

On the one hand Patsy thrived on what she saw as the fabulous romantic drama of her situation: she was at the centre of some great love story, the innocent young maiden torn between her handsome lover and her unrelenting father, her heart being pulled in all directions, like the heroine of an opera. She glanced at herself again in the shop window. On the other hand she knew too well that she was in Dublin, not in the theatre, and that her Romeo stood little chance against her father. She wasn't smiling any more.

Patsy arrived at the meeting hall and immediately her confident swagger returned. She was surrounded by a crowd of independent-looking women, women of all ages, women of all types, strong but eager women, all bustling and impatient to get into the venue to have a listen and have their say. Some of them were sporting a Tara Brooch, the Celtic clan emblem adopted by the CumannamBan when they were working alongside the Volunteers during the troubles. Their role in supporting the flying columns had always been recognised as vital in keeping the machinery of war going and later they won the full franchise for women, long before all women in England won the vote, but the presence of so many conservative men elected to the Dáil led to women's gains being rolled back, in many cases rolled all the way back into the scullery: married women weren't even officially allowed to have a paid job. Patsy felt herself to be among a gathering of women determined to put paid to that sort of nonsense and to carry on the fight for proper status and equality. She could at least enjoy the thrill of feeling part of it, even though she knew she would crumble weakly when back at home faced with her da. She bought herself a Tara Brooch and pinned it to her lapel. Perhaps it would strengthen her resolve.

She jostled her way into the meeting and waited for a good dose of female enthusiasm, tempered by her appreciation that life was hard for anyone trying to put food on the table, man or woman. A general hush signalled the session was about to start and eyes turned expectantly towards the platform at the front of the hall.

"First of all, I'd like to welcome everyone," said the speaker, a tall, slim, elegant woman oozing self-confidence. She took in the room with a sweeping glance and had a way of making everyone in the room feel that they had been welcomed individually. "I know how difficult it can be for you women to get out of the house when you have men at home waiting for their meal to be put on the table before them and the poor things likely to sit and starve otherwise." She paused as her words were greeted by an appreciative ripple of amusement. Patsy smiled too, though it seemed to her that the well-dressed woman with nicely manicured nails probably didn't spend much of her own time peeling potatoes and chopping carrots to put anyone's meal on the table.

"My name is Eileen Donovan, as you regulars will know," the speaker continued, "though I'm pleased to say I can see several new faces among us tonight, so a very special welcome to our virgins," she said, and another ripple of laughter flowed round the room as heads swivelled this way and that to identify the newcomers in the audience. Patsy smiled too, slightly.

"That's perhaps a fitting bit of levity considering the theme of the meeting, sex, so as we have a lot to get through this evening I'll straightaway introduce our first speaker, Mairead McCreary of the Marie Stopes Clinic in London. For the benefit of our newcomers, I'll just explain that Marie Stopes is at the very forefront of finding solutions for the problem women face during their years of fertility: basically, how can they limit the number of children they have? Her clinic in London was established to help women make their own choices over their rate of reproduction, based on the best medical information available and regardless of any religious dos and don'ts. Again, the emphasis is on the woman's own decision. Mairead will address the new thinking as regards the various methods of birth control available, quite an important subject, I'm sure you'll agree, especially in a society like ours where women are having to pop out babies almost on a yearly basis. There will be time allowed for questions and comments after Mairead has spoken."

A burst of applause welcomed Mairead McCreary to the stand and Patsy too put her hands together but it was out of politeness: she wasn't comfortable. This wasn't what she had been expecting. She thought they would be talking about the situations in which most women found themselves, either unable to work because of their marital status and family commitments or able to work but earning low wages, being treated like schoolchildren and barely allowed to talk even, having to watch the clock when they needed to use the toilet, even during their monthlies. She had a friend who had studied and qualified to be a teacher but she'd been obliged by order of the Dáil to retire the minute she got married. That wasn't right, that was the sort of right Patsy had come to hear discussed. Instead her ears were picking up references to methods of contraception, to spermicides made out of a mixture of soap and oil, to sponges soaked in olive oil to wipe on your private parts before sex, to condoms and cervical caps, and just a passing reference to the method approved by the Catholic Bishops — the so-called rhythm method, using temperature charts to determine when in your cycle you were most likely to conceive.

"You can, of course, just refuse to have penetrative sex, which can be inconvenient if you yourself are in the mood for some serious love-making," said Mairead. "Or there's that old chestnut, withdrawal after penetration but before the man ejaculates into you, sometimes referred to as 'pull-out-and-pray', not a very funny joke for the woman when it doesn't work, and more often than not it doesn't."

Patsy was too embarrassed to stand up and walk out, especially now with her new Tara pin so prominently displayed on her coat: she wondered what the badge must be symbolising these days. She looked up to the large crucifix of the bleeding Christ hanging on the wall above the platform, closed her ears to shut out the talk of penetrations and ejaculations and contraceptions and mentally recited her Children of Mary devotions. She clutched the scapula hanging inside her blouse.

She was disturbed in her prayers by a hand thrusting a leaflet into her hand. "There's no charge," said the girl who was distributing them to every attendee. Patsy read the cover title: *Wise Parenthood: A Book for Married People*. Evidently it was a condensed version of a sex manual Marie Stopes had written in 1918 as a guide to safe and satisfying sex for married people who wanted at the same time to practise birth control. Embarrassed or not, Patsy shoved it quickly into her bag, stood up from her seat and fled from such sinful vocabulary.

2

Some serious construction work was going on in the backyard at The Coombe. Eddie, the eldest of the O'Kelly boys and Betty's first-born, had been working every odd hour he could spare at the Bird Market. It was held in an alleyway behind, aptly enough, the Aviary Pub off Bride Street, conveniently not too far from The Coombe, which was why the job had appealed to Eddie in the first place. He was already working on Denis McCabe's cart going round the cobbled streets of The Liberties shouting, "Coal blocks!", which was one of the only two things he enjoyed about that particular work, the freedom to yell at the top of his voice without getting a belt from his da or anyone else with a mind to it. The other thing he loved about the coal cart was sitting up top and not on the blocks when Denis gave him the nod: Denis had certain regular customers he had looked after since he started his business at the age of fourteen and he liked to deliver to them himself, the 'personal touch', he called it, to reward their loyalty. While Denis was busy adding his 'personal touch', usually accompanied by a cup of tea, Eddie would be in charge of taking the cart round to cater for the non-personal customers. He would sit up on the wooden seat and slap the ropey reins as he drove the ass that pulled the cart along, all the while shouting "Coal blocks! Coal blocks!" to alert potential customers. Eddie liked to make noise, perhaps because he naturally had a quiet, gentle voice, visually out of keeping with the toughness of his general appearance. He worked the streets with Denis a few times a week, sometimes earning a bit extra by going down to the depot with Denis early in the morning to collect the coal and load it on to the old cart. But Eddie's need to earn a few extra pennies to help out at home had sent him scouting for more work and taken him eventually to the Bird Market, which had been there for a number of years though Eddie had never visited the place before.

He was sorry he hadn't. He discovered a different world, small and somewhat frantic but one which was to lead to a lifelong obsession.

Eddie found himself enthralled, fascinated by all the different birds: the variety of their plumage, long tail feathers and short tail feathers, maybe regal crests protruding proudly up from their gobble-gobble heads; the colours of their feathers, some subtle gradations of grey into brown into black, some bright and shocking enough to make you wonder at how amazing the natural world was. Then there were the sounds — innocent chirrupy notes, dancing melodies, strident caws, piercing shrieks — creating a strangely cacophonous harmony from a collection of birds which had come to this grubby backstreet in The Liberties from all over the world. Certainly, the creatures weren't over familiar to Eddie: he had seen pictures of some of them in books at school but up close they were far more fascinating and exotic than he could ever have imagined. He knew seagulls, right enough, and sparrows, crows, pigeons, the usual flyers round Dublin. He could recognise a magpie and of course there were the ducks and swans in the lake at Stephen's Green, but these birds were proper birds, he thought, redolent of far-away places, high sierras, jungles, wetlands, firing his imagination. The market had begun back in the day when the sailors off foreign ships would bring birds ashore to sell and make a few bob and the market had become an established site. Eddie learned that there was a local man who never left his bed but lay in it all day making birdcages to bring home his bit of bacon. Eddie didn't mind the idea of a job which meant you could stay in bed all day long but he preferred being there in the middle of the action with the birds. His plan was to bring some of that action home.

Eddie's birth had deeply affected Patrick, in a good way, and while he felt crowded in and impatient with the brood of children that followed in quick succession he had never lost his deep paternal warmth towards Eddie, a son at last after three daughters. Now he was helping his son to build a pigeon-loft in the yard.

"Be careful with the saw, we don't want you clipping your own wings before the birds even get here," said Patrick.

They had an audience. Sitting enjoying the warm evening and the performance were Patsy, Molly and Theresa while the two younger boys, Ciaran and Mikey, busied themselves handing nails and screws up the ladder to their father. Only the youngest child, another daughter, Annie, was playing indoors.

"How do you know the pigeons will stay?" asked Molly. She wasn't keen on the idea of birds being too close to her. She had seen seagulls apparently attack walkers down by the Liffey and she nursed a secret fear that Eddie's pigeons might swoop down on her while she was going to the toilet in the yard, something she also dreaded when she was out at Tullamore, though there the birds seemed to have enough other places to search for food without bothering people.

"Because they're not ordinary pigeons they're special homing pigeons," said Eddie.

"I'd no idea there was such a species as a 'special pigeon'," said Theresa. "They're just dirty things, vermin, things we normally try to shoo away never mind bringing them home to live right outside the kitchen."

"Which just goes to show that you don't know anything," said Eddie. "Lots of people keep pigeons and they race them too."

"They race them?" said Patsy. "And where do they do that? Is there a special meeting at Dublin racecourse for special pigeons then? You'll have to tell Billy, Theresa. Doesn't he like to put on a bet occasionally."

"It's not that sort of racing, stupid," said Eddie.

"Well what sort is it? I thought racing was racing."

"What they do is all the owners send their birds to a starting point, a different town or city to where they live, carried in cages or baskets, of course," said Eddie, "and then they release the birds when they get to the starting-off point and the winner is whichever bird flies home to its roost first. That's why they're called homing pigeons, 'cause they always fly home, and that's how I know mine will stay here once they get settled in because this will be home."

"How do you get them to settle so they know which home to come back to, that's what I don't understand," said Patsy. "Why would they want to come back to a tiny backyard when there are lots of big parks full of grass and trees in Dublin to choose from."

"A backyard with a toilet that can get very smelly when you lot are after using it," chimed in Molly.

"It takes skill," said Eddie. "I've been learning what to do at the market. There're a few experts there, all right. My boss Jimmy knows all about it."

"It's a very old tradition, training pigeons," said Patrick, carefully easing a corner joint into place to complete the loft framework. "Get me those two-inch screws, Mikey, will you. Now hold them ready to feed me one at a time while I secure this corner." He turned the screwdriver tighter and tighter and the frame held and took shape. "You've heard of messenger pigeons?" he asked. "Because these pigeons always fly home, they are trained to carry important messages back with them. And they're very fast with their deliveries, much faster than the post office. The first ones known from history were used back in ancient Greece to send through the results of the original Olympic Games, did you not know that? Even in those days people wanted to know who had won what as quickly as possible. Well, they're the same things, messenger birds, they're homing birds. You have to make sure you feed them well and provide them with nice clean boxes to roost in," said Patrick, "that's how you make them want to come back."

"I look forward to them delivering their traditional calling cards all over the yard," said Theresa.

"Ugh," grimaced Patsy, "I hadn't thought about their droppings. Why couldn't you have fancied something nicer, like a canary, Eddie, or a budgerigar?"

"Well we certainly wouldn't be in need of a parrot, not with the amount of talking, you silly women manage," said Eddie. "Perhaps we could get a canary, we could hang the cage in the parlour?"

"No more canaries for me," said Patsy, "I couldn't take any more fame."

"Ay but it was a grand article in the paper when you were photographed walking through the dark streets alone but for a bird in a cage," said Patrick. "You weren't going to let the little matter of a curfew keep you from rescuing little Joey from a bombed house on the Quays. The people might have died but their canary lived on."

"And did the bird live on to tell the tale?" asked Ciaran.

"To sing the tale, Ciaran," said Patsy, "canaries sing, that's what they're known for, their beautiful singing. Do they have canaries at the market, Eddie?"

"They do, you should come down and hear them, and it's true that they have beautiful melodic voices. It's like proper music, sure it is. We should get a couple, you could pay the piano for them, Patsy, and they'd sing their little hearts out and the parlour would be filled with lovely sounds, like a bird choir. We'd have ourselves our very own dawn chorus then."

"Isn't it hard enough having to wake up early for work without having to do it with a racket going on in the house," said Theresa.

"How much are they then, the singing canaries?" asked Patsy.

"They're only sixpence each or so," said Eddie, "but I could probably get them a bit cheaper. They put them in paper bags for you to take home. Sometimes it's really funny because you get kids hanging around mithering Jimmy for a canary to take home for free, just one, they say, as a present for their mammy's birthday. 'You wouldn't miss just the one,' they say to Jimmy. To get rid of the kids from the stall Jimmy pretends to put one in a paper bag and warns them to be very careful how they carry the bag home as canaries are delicate little birds and shouldn't be squeezed too tightly, at the same time they need to breathe so the bag has to be open a bit to let some air in. Then when the kids come back and say there was no canary in the bag when they got home, Jimmy just chases them away and tells them off for having let the bird escape. It's funny, right enough, but sad too when you see the kids' faces."

"Are you helping me to build this loft or just wasting your time in idle chatter?" said Patrick. "We'll not be getting any canaries and that's the end of it. Come on now and help me lift the roof struts into place."

"Well I think we've enough mouths to feed without getting pigeons or canaries," said Molly. "I hate the idea even of having all those birds living next to us in the yard."

"Speaking of mouths to feed, I'll go on in and help Mammy with the tea," said Patsy.

Betty was sitting at the table preparing the vegetables for the pot: she looked very tired. Her fifth pregnancy was proving more uncomfortable than previous ones and the extra weight she was carrying — it promised to be a big baby — was draining her energy. For a start she wasn't a slim woman any more: with all the pregnancies happening so regularly she never had time to lose the pounds and look after her own body. As Patsy walked in, Betty was sitting with her eyes closed and letting out deep sighs: her growing belly, wedged up against the table's edge, was straining against the ties of her pinny.

"Here, let me do that, Mammy" said Patsy, taking the knife from her mother and pulling up a chair next to her. "Why don't you go upstairs and have a rest, enjoy a bit of time to yourself even if there's no chance of any peace and quiet with all the hammering in the yard. I can get on and do this."

Betty visibly rearranged her attitude from fatigue to pretended daydreaming. "I'm enjoying myself here already," she said, "just thinking about the pigeon-loft and all the men of the house busy making it together. I think it was a grand idea of Eddie's, they'll all chip in and look after them."

"Well it's to be hoped so," said Patsy. "You've plenty to deal with already without taking on a flock of birds."

"Can you see me climbing up that old rickety ladder and me bursting at the seams? Not on your nelly," said Betty.

"It'd give us all a laugh for sure but maybe a mean one at your expense." Patsy fetched another knife and got stuck into the peeling. "Do you like having so many children?" she asked her mammy. "It can't be easy being pregnant all the time, especially when there are little ones already to look after."

"That's the lot of us women," said Betty, "to keep Ireland populated with good little Catholics and then they can carry on and have more good little Catholics themselves. It's a never-ending process all right. The clergy are all men and they say what's what but it's us women who carry all the responsibility, for nine months at a time. We might complain but then we love the little babbies without a thought of regret. You wait til it's your turn. You'll love the ground they walk on, each of them."

"So I'm told but it scares me too. I like going out to work and enjoying myself with a few shillings to spend and then there's all the different people I come across. You can't do that with a house full of children. Was there nothing you ever wanted to do yourself, Mammy, apart from getting married and having children?"

"Not really, Patsy, the thought would never have occurred to me. Women stay home and have babies and that's the way it is. And I wouldn't part with any of mine. Even this little one I'm carrying now is making himself known. He's so active and determined that's why I'm sure it's a boy."

"But why can't women be just as active and determined and still have the babbies? It doesn't seem very fair that they have to give up so much for the family. A girl at work was telling me the other day that she'd read a leaflet about what they call birth control, ways to stop yourself getting pregnant. Would you never consider that, Mammy, and give yourself some time for yourself?"

"I would not," said Betty. "That sort of a thing is a sin. And I don't think your daddy would approve, never mind the priest. Now let's get the water boiling on the stove. They'll all be in soon and they'll expect their meal on the table. Molly tells me the three of you are off to Tullamore on Friday. It'll be a nice change for her to have some company on the bus. I'll have to get something for you to take to your Uncle Michael."

3

The weekend promised to be a great gas. The three older O'Kelly sisters were in Tullamore staying at Betty's family farm just outside the town and it was a miracle as far as Molly was concerned that Patsy and Theresa had decided to go with her. Usually they weren't interested: Patsy was too busy drooling over her baker-man's letters, in between the times she was too busy drooling over him himself when they went out somewhere together, although she'd deny it, of course, Little Child of Mary that she was, and Theresa had had her prayers answered when Billy from school, now learning on-the-job to be a plasterer, had finally asked her to walk out with him and now she loved nothing better than to play the Little Lady Hostess in the parlour in The Coombe, hair done up in style, just to sit in the front room drinking tea, when all was said and done. No, Tullamore generally was of little interest to either of them.

Molly herself loved it and often went there on Friday or Saturday to stay the night, often with her friend Nora, and they always had a bit of a wild time. They were both full of a sense of fun and adventure. Molly was never alone much, even when Nora wasn't able to accompany her. Apart from all the family and the laughs they had in front of the range fire in the big kitchen — oh how wonderful to have space to move in and Uncle Michael was nowhere near as strict as her da —there were lots of young men living round about and they were all very keen on the young woman from Dublin. Weak at the knees, they went. She brought a touch of glamour to the house-dances held every weekend in some farmhouse or other. Well of course she did, sniped the local girls, who looked on her as unfair and definitely unwelcome competition, with her long dark curly hair and those big brown eyes she had and fluttered at anyone wanting to catch them: after all, didn't the trollop and her sisters work in a ladies' fashion factory so her clothes were bound to show up their measly cotton frocks no matter what ribbons and bows they pinned on for special occasions. Even those skewed front teeth of hers didn't seem to put the queue of suitors off. Why she couldn't stay in the city with all the fancy men there and leave them a clear field with the farm boys they could never understand: they only wished she would. It all proved their prattling point, that the little madam must be a trollop.

To Molly, however, Tullamore was an escape route to adventure and fun. She wasn't looking for romance, far from it, not really anyway. Her eyes might twinkle at the suggestion of her breaking a few lonely hearts but actually she had been writing to her cousin Kevin for quite some time and that's where perhaps her own heart was going to settle, across the sea in Liverpool with its own promise of a new life. It was just that she did enjoy the sense of freedom she always felt in the country, strolling along the lanes and brushing through the tall grasses in the fields, insects buzzing about and the air filled with seeds gently mooching hither and thither in their search for a good landing place, and it wasn't that hard for her to stem the inevitable funny business tried on among the haystacks by the young farmhands. Life in the crowded city prepared her for any of that nonsense. Their attempts at fumbling were somehow imbued with a charming juvenile innocence. (To be honest some of them weren't bad looking at all.) "I might be from The Liberties," she'd say, "but you're not taking any with me."

Theresa's way of dealing with any of that nonsense was to hold her nose in the air even further up than usual, so much further up that it almost disappeared into the high concoction of interwoven curls and strands she managed to construct with her hair, all smooth and well-disciplined and curt, though to be fair to her Theresa had a matching but very funny sense of humour, quips cutting straight to the bone but irresistibly with the emphasis on the funny bone. With Patsy, well, Patsy just didn't seem to notice the affect she had on men and had all the more effect on them as a result. Her eyes were not the deep orb-like pools of Molly's but Patsy had a way of looking up out of half-closed lids that suggested a certain coquettishness, a come-to-bed look some might say. She would have been thrillingly mortified to have it spelt out to her though she wasn't quite as ignorant of admiring glances as everyone seemed to think. Taken as a trio, it was no wonder the lads of Tullamore were smitten by such a bevy of Dublin beauties.

"Where is it to be tonight?" Molly asked her cousin Robert. He was actually one of Betty's younger brothers but they were so close in age to Patrick's eldest daughters that they regarded each other as cousins. Robert always escorted Molly to the local dances when she was staying at the farm. He was a tall, handsome, manly youth, with the strong, tanned arms of a man used to working out in all weathers and eyes that sparkled and laughed at the slightest provocation and he had a way with words that would tremble the heart strings of any sensitive lass. And to a one didn't the neighbours' daughters thereabouts each yearn to be sensitive to Robert and his tongue, even if he did like the sound of his own wit. All of which added fuel to the fire as far as the local lasses were concerned, for when Robert accompanied that Molly one then he wasn't available for any potential shenanigans with them.

"Well, tonight's ball is actually in a proper hall and not among the usual cow-pat riddled stalls in some baleful barn," said Robert. "There was a dance planned in the modest surroundings of the parish hall in Tullamore, where all things modest can be ensured and imposed by the Reverend Father himself, but that had to be cancelled to make way for a wake, so the priest graciously gave his holy blessing for a social event to be held in that small community hall just up the road from here. Very convenient for us and hopefully very convivial for everyone busy tripping the light fandango without the venerable eyes of the priest beading in on everyone. No doubt the stout at the wake will keep him at his proper duties. There should be a good crowd all the same. There are several I know of coming out from the town, unless they're more tempted by the solemn fun of the wake and decide to hang up their bicycles for the veneration of the corpse. Not that I've ever been to a bad wake," he said, "they're always more fun than funereal. In fact, maybe we should take ourselves off there instead. Molly and I could get stuck into the mourning til morning, Theresa you could perch and reign or rain over the proceedings, as the mood might take you, and I'm sure Patsy that you'd encounter lots of ghostly vapours there to keep you busy between this world and the next. What do you think?"

"All very poetic but I think your words are a bit too pat even for a cow man," said Theresa. "A he or a she? We don't even know who the corpse was when alive never mind dead. And didn't we come here to dance? Sure the three of us here are a sufficient treat to attract all the biddies and colleens from miles around for a bitch and a barney let alone your colleagues from the fields. Don't you want to show off your glamorous cousins out from the city?"

"I do indeed," said Robert, "you've got me there, Theresa, and here I was trying to show off our simple country ways in all their manifestations — you can't beat a good wake — but with three such city sophisticates I've my work cut out for me obviously."

"There's nothing particularly country about having a wake," said Theresa.

"What time does the dance start?" asked Patsy. "I want to change out of these clothes after sitting in them on the bus all that time."

"You've plenty of time for all that titivating," said Robert. "The rest of the family will be home soon and then we'll fill our bellies with some good country fare before we head off to fill our souls with some good country fair."

"Can we do anything to help?" asked Molly. "I could at least get the table set. What about the cows? Are they in yet?"

"I'm just about to go and round them up," said Robert. "Grab a couple of sticks, ladies, and we'll get down to some animal welfare. Mind your fine shoes, mind, country lanes aren't paved with gold like in Dublin, more like dung-laden."

"I'm going to stay if that's all right with everyone," said Patsy, "I'd like a word with Uncle Michael when he gets back."

"A private word, is it?" asked Robert.

"In a manner of speaking," replied Patsy. "I'm hoping to sound him out on some things going on with my da and who knows him better than your da."

"True enough, though Uncle Patrick doesn't seem too keen on coming out here much to visit these days. It's just as well Molly here keeps the family flag flying with her visits. Come on now, girls, the cows await."

"I'll do the table while you're gone," said Patsy.

Molly sauntered straight out of the door ready to head off to the field while Theresa carefully tied a colourful scarf over her head to protect her hair and, together with Robert, the two girls set out to drive home the cows. Patsy heard the babble of their voices grow fainter in the murmur of the trees and then just sat to enjoy the peace of the place. There was little chance of peace at The Coombe, too many people charging about all the time in such a tiny house and then the controlling boom of her father's voice to shut them up. Here it was different, though it must have at one time been full of the same noisy shriekings and the same chaos of a family life full of little ones when Robert was growing up. Still, it was a lovely homely place to grow up in.

Patsy looked around the room. She hadn't been to see the family here much herself lately, years perhaps had passed since her last visit. What with work taking up the whole week, nights out at the pictures with her friend, Margaret, and then excursions with Sean taking up the weekends, she never really felt the inclination to come out to Tullamore. Now she was here, she could well appreciate the attraction it had for Molly: the calm, the quiet, the clear air which had a freshness to it despite the pungent farm smells; the sounds of the countryside itself; the absence of their father's dark presence. Her gaze lingered on the photographs hanging on the walls and lined up along the mantel above the range. She mulled over the different faces, recognising family likenesses that were coming through in her own half-brothers, then took a chair out into the yard and sat enjoying the tranquillity of this little corner of Ireland. Then she pulled out Sean's most recent letter from her pocket to take his words into her heart and to hear his voice in her head. Some elements of her life in Dublin she didn't ever want to leave behind.

My Dear Streaks,

Your father and your humble servant were again left behind today after all the other bakes had gone home. You know, Streaks, I think someone's doing this for some reason of their own, there are dark clouds hanging over our youthful heads, my dear Streaks. But we don't mind that, do we? You know, Streaks (I'm serious now!!!) I have never before looked forward to seeing anyone as much as I do look forward to seeing you. That's the word of honour, of the son of a baker and a gentleman.

A certain young lady of my acquaintance sometimes brags about having no heart, well I'm going to prove to her that she has and, unless I'm very much mistaken, a very nice heart at that. I've one consolation anyway and that is that she will be aged twenty on the nineteenth of this month and best of all that she will be twenty one on the nineteenth of

March next year, then I'll be able to stick my tongue out at her father; because it's her I want to look after me as my tide of life ebbs away (Okay, Streaks, I know you want to wallop me on the jaw, and elsewhere, but dear heart, save it till you see your lord and master next Friday night at 7.30 at the usual place, and we shall thence proceed to some mean place of amusement to whittle away the silent passage of a few pleasant hours).

Oh! by the way, I hope you told Margaret what I told you, about getting herself another bridesmaid. You see, Mrs. F (Oh! Excuse me, I thought you were already twenty-one, and that the deed was done) our family is very superstitious, and you have been bridesmaid twice already. So, the next time it must be that you have bridesmaids of your own, that's if your father hasn't bumped me off before then, we're treading on very dangerous ground, But I do love every foot of the way and I love the girl who's on that ground with me.

Adios,

Sean.

P.S. Kiss yourself in the glass for me, will you, I'll bring an envelope on Friday night to wrap it up in. xxx

What a beautiful letter to receive from your young man, thought Patsy, but there was always that same problem lurking, not even in the background but very much to the fore: her father and his attitude towards Sean. It even managed to worm its way into their correspondence.

"And what are you doing out here all alone?"

Patsy shot up out of the chair and ran to give her Uncle Michael a big hug before he had even got through the yard gate.

"Aren't you the one for fancy displays even in your smart city outfit," he said, almost stumbling while trying to balance the hoe and rake and give Patsy a loving hug in return. "I don't know what your Uncle Michael has done to deserve such a huge welcome but welcome it is," he said. "Now get away and come let me look at you."

Patsy laughed as she, a grown woman, twirled and curtsied as she had always done to her uncle, as if he was royalty itself. Indeed to Patsy he practically was; a saviour at the very least. He had been cocooned in her heart since childhood as a warm, caring man, whose arrival always brought with it a lift in tempo, a promise of geniality and a general feeling that, in his presence, all would be right no matter what. Ever since her real mammy had died and Michael had helped the family get through those terrible months, leaving Larch Hill, then moving to live in different houses in Dublin, he had provided a reference point of support. His daughter might be Patsy's stepmother but, to Patsy, Michael was a cuddly, reliable, loving uncle.

"And what's that you're clutching in your hand?" he asked.

Patsy had forgotten she was holding Sean's letter still and the thought of the precious missive and the inquiry about it made her face flush with embarrassment.

"It's a love letter, is it? That would be my guess, judging by your face," said Michael and he gave Patsy such a knowing wink that the blush returned and positively roseated her cheeks. "And who is the lucky man?" he asked. "And does your father approve?" he murmured in a low conspiratorial voice.

"It is, his name's Sean and no, my da doesn't approve," Patsy blurted out and all the curtseying decorum evaporated as her eyes were suddenly wet with a few tears.

"Just let me put these things away and you can tell me all about it," said Michael. "You don't want to be upsetting yourself too much now before the dance tonight. You're here to have a good time, remember, to enjoy yourself and have a break from those Dublin woes."

Patsy followed him into the barn, sat on a hay bale and waited patiently, trying to keep her sobs to herself as Michael hung the tools on their brackets and wiped his hands on a wet cloth left there for the purpose and heaved off his muddy boots in favour of a pair of slip-ons left there for the purpose: it helped make sure not all the muck from the farm went straight into the house. Patsy had already decided to tell her Uncle Michael all about her problems, that was the main reason she had agreed to Molly's suggestion that they all come out to Tullamore for the dance, but Patsy hadn't expected the opportunity to present itself quite so immediately. Nor was it much of a setting for spilling out your heartfelt troubles, what with the crowd of dented churns in the corner, the stinking animal stalls, the dirt floor, the racks of tools and other bits of machinery, not to mention the lacework of cobwebs and the leaky holes in the roof, but it would do and perhaps even delay the intrusion of everyone else even now heading back to the house.

Michael sat down beside the girl and pulled out a small hipflask from his jacket.

"There, have a slug of that and you'll get your tongue going easily," he said. "Just don't tell your father I gave it to you. Now, Patsy, start at the beginning. Who is this fellow?"

"His name's Sean, as I said, and we've been walking out together for well over a year now. He's a baker too and he works with my da, that's how we met, but I know that my da makes Sean's life a misery every day in the bakery. Sean writes me regular letters and in between the beautiful bits he always mentions what's happened that day at work and it's never good if he has had anything to do with my da. Even at home I get sniping about him constantly and I end up feeling guilty about the whole thing. I really like Sean, he's lovely to me and kind and we always have a great time in each other's company, we talk and laugh all the time and he's very respectful and wants us to get married as soon as we can, but I hate upsetting my da, and all his mean comments make me wonder what to do."

"And has your da directly forbidden you to see this young man?"

"No, not yet, but he takes every opportunity to say awful things about him and that he'll never let a daughter of his marry such a waste of a person. What I don't understand, Uncle Michael, is why my da feels so strongly about Sean. He never picks on Molly or Theresa and they're both courting."

"It's the same bakery, you say. What's this Sean's surname?"

"He's a Fitzsimmons."

"And did his father work at the same place?" asked Michael, a hint of a cloud crossing over his features.

"He did but he died many years ago. I never met him. There's just been Sean and his ma for at least ten years or so, as far as I know."

"Well, I'm afraid that's it, Patsy, the problem for Patrick was the boy's father. Your Sean could be the best son-in-law any man could wish for but that would be any man other than your father. Patrick had a history with the older Fitzsimmons and it's no doubt festered like an old sore and it's still eating away at the man. It had nothing to do with the son, your Sean, but the hatred runs deep in your da. I'm afraid there's very little either you or Sean can do about it short of praying for a miracle and it would take a miracle, believe me, for Patrick to change his attitude."

"What was it that happened with Mr Fitzsimmons? Perhaps I could talk to my da about it, show him that Sean and I understand how he feels the way he does but that it's not our fault."

"It would take some talking to achieve that, I'm afraid. You must understand that all the troubles we had in Ireland these years back ate into the very hearts and souls of people. Apart from the loss of the many who died, there was also the loss of unity and loyalty to each other. Terrible splits were caused in families let alone among workmates. People had their opinions and their opinions were fixed, totally closed to any other point of view, and it led to an awful lot of bitterness. You were either on one side or the other and the only middle you'd meet in was when you clashed together in some violent way or other. I know you yourself witnessed many awful things in Dublin when you were a child, what with all the bombings and shootings and your own father being a fighting man, but in a way what was worse were the divisions that came later, with the Treaty being signed and colleagues turning against each other."

"Yes, but what has that to do with Sean?"

"Nothing, but it has everything to do with Sean's father and what he did or didn't do, and your father, and what he thought the man did or didn't do," said Michael. "Your father can be an almighty stubborn man, as you very well know, Patsy, and once he suspected old Fitzsimmons of being less than a true patriot that was it, the man wasn't worth the dirt under his feet."

"What did he suspect him of? It must have been something serious."

"I'm not party to all the details but I think it goes way back. You see, Patsy, the bakery where your father and your young man work now once played a strategic part in the Rebellion. Sure De Valera is said to have had his headquarters there before the Rising itself. That's not important, what is important is that the bakery was a significant centre for the Volunteers and was the scene of a lot of fighting during the Rising. De Valera himself is credited with setting loose the bakery carthorses one night during an attack so he must have been in and out of the place. It was frequently the starting off point for action against the Brits and there was even a priest loosely based there, a Father McMahon, who would hear the confessions of the Volunteers in a bread-van before they went out on a job. Anyway, that's history now, what counts is that it was believed there was one of the bakers working as a spy for the British and, unfortunately for you, your father and some of the other Volunteers always maintained it was none other than Fitzsimmons. Nothing was ever proved but the man subsequently disappeared, believed to have been beaten and left for dead somewhere."

"Are you saying that my da had something to do with Sean's father's death?" asked Patsy, horrified at the immediacy of what her Uncle Michael was telling her.

"I'm not saying that at all. I'm in no position to say that," said Michael. "All I'm saying is that, rightly or wrongly, there was history between your father and Sean's father, a bitter history, which may lie at the heart of your problems now."

The two sat there in silence. This was heavy stuff for Patsy, difficult to take in, hard to accept that the cause she had been brought up to believe in could somehow now suddenly create an impossible wedge between her and her young man.

"So, there's nothing to be done," she said.

"Not right now, perhaps," said Michael, "but give it some time and perhaps your da will come round. I can't advise you on what to do, girl, I can't even say that if your da got to know Sean he might change his mind because obviously he knows the boy already, but wait and see, you never know."

"Ay but we both do know; my father is unshakeable when his mind is made up," said Patsy. "I can't see all the waiting in the world would make any difference."

The sound of mooing and the tread of hooves and hindquarters being slapped could be heard getting closer.

"I tell you what," said Michael, "I'll have a quiet word with your father next time I'm in Dublin and see if we can't smooth things out a bit. Meanwhile you should go on seeing your Sean and enjoying life, never mind your da."

Suddenly the farmyard was full of people. Molly and Theresa were back with Robert and the cows and at the same time the rest of the family arrived back from Tullamore on their bikes. Patsy was feeling greatly reassured by her uncle's offer to intercede on Sean's behalf and it was the easiest thing in the world for her to put a smile on a bright face after her bout of melancholia. Happy chatter took over the place. Michael's wife May was glad of the willing help getting the meal ready for everyone and so indeed were the sons still living at home, Robert and Jim and Joe, who normally had to be commandeered into peeling the potatoes and chopping whatever vegetables were available, usually carrots and cabbage, but this evening could hand over their kitchen duties to their Dublin cousins who were only too delighted to help out. May took charge of getting the big ham ready for boiling on the range and all in all everyone enjoyed the sociability of the occasion.

The girls were staying in a house just up the road from the Kelly farm. It was only a couple of hundred yards away and belonged to another of Michael's daughters, Betty's only sister, Annie, who had married a local boy, Peter, who had been given the plot of land by his father as a wedding gift. It was a new house, still in the process of becoming a real homely home — it was all very tidy compared to Michael's place and The Coombe — and financial constraints had demanded that there was no money left in the pot to provide modern indoor conveniences like a proper bathroom so the sisters had to make do with taking it in turns to wash in a basin on the table, just like at home, where they had to wash in the kitchen sink. Of course they were used to having to use an outside toilet but here it did mean minding the mud and the puddles on the uneven ground around the house.

Patsy put on a simple frock, linen, with a zig-zag design in black and white. (It was one of Sean's favourites so she felt it kept him close.) Theresa was modelling an up-to-the-minute dress, the bright-print fabric cut on the bias to give a swing skirt and allow her to accentuate her small waist, which she set off with a red belt to pick out one of the colours in the floral motif. (Billy didn't approve of her showing off her figure to every man who cared to look but at the same time he was proud to have such a shapely woman on his arm.) Molly threw on a full circular yellow skirt — she liked it to swirl out like sunshine when she was dancing and twirling around — and a white blouse with short puff sleeves gathered in with a trim of lace, which were becoming all the rage. (Her outfit had nothing to do with anyone but herself.) They had, of course, made all the clothes themselves and the look of the three of them was everything that annoyed the local girls.

"What are you going to with your hair, Molly?" asked Theresa, already planted in front of the mirror making minor repairs to her pile-on-top after a few stray strands had been seized by the evening breeze and given a breath of temporary freedom.

"Well I can't hope to compete with your elaboration or Patsy's natural waves so I'm just going to run a comb through and tie it back in a big bow," said Molly.

"You're aiming at the country-girl look, then," said Patsy.

"Well we are after all in the country," said Molly, inwardly feeling that her sisters weren't quite entering into the spirit of a bit of a fun jig in a barn. She was an old hand at this: she knew that all the pins in the world wouldn't keep a hair in place once the men started twirling you around on the dancefloor, usually with little relevance to the beat of the tunes. Whenever and whyever they felt it was time, that was the key for the men and you had to have your wits about you to follow their sudden impulses to fling you round in a spin, arms flailing about up in the air inches above your head (if you were lucky) and always accompanied by a happy but idiotic grin on their faces. It was a hoot, not a grand ball. "You'll be well used to it by the time the night's out," she said.

Robert had agreed to meet them at the gate to Annie's farm but instead he turned up directly at the house. He conjured a bottle of Tullamore Dew from inside his coat and poured them all a wee tot to get, as he said, their juices flowing.

"Are your genial hosts not here?" he asked, bottle poised over two remaining glasses.

"They've gone to the wake in Tullamore," said Patsy, looking at the generous 'wee' tot of drink being measured and wondering if she might not have been marginally more comfortable at the wake herself.

"All the more for us then," said Robert. "Get that down your pretty city throats and your juices will be flowing all the way down to your pretty city feet. Let me see now, what have you on your feet? Towering-tops Theresa! What are they, for heaven's sake? Walking-out-in-Dublin shoes? It's a barn dance we're going to, more Phil the Fluter's Ball than a Viennese waltz. Sure you'll cripple yourself in those things never mind the poor toes of the poor sods you might tread on, regardless of the sods they might still have on their own wee shod of a pair of shoes after a day in the fields. Mind, I admire your optimism all the same."

"Look down on the audience and it's your own standards you lower," said Theresa. "Besides, just because I pile my hair high doesn't mean I'm not prepared to let it down occasionally. I can always melt into the pot and throw my shoes off."

"Now that would be a foolhardy sense of optimism," said Robert. "You'll be needing another slug of Dew here then for that degree of optimism by way of an anaesthetic to numb your own dainties."

Glasses were refilled all round, more toasts were raised to a night of fun and even Patsy's apprehension was getting drowned out. She was already bobbing about in time to the sounds in her head. A bit of musical mayhem was beginning to seem like an attractive idea.

"I see Molly's prepared as usual with her — what was it you called them, Molly — city casuals?" said Robert. "Quite sensible for the tomboy of the party but I can't come to any wise conclusions about your choice of footwear, Patsy. Let's just say they conjure a totally different image of what's sensible."

"I want to enjoy myself," said Patsy, "and to do that I need comfortable feet and you'll please notice that the uppers are sturdy enough to protect even my delicate toes."

"I think the word 'sturdy' sums them up about right," said Robert.

"Isn't it time to drink up and head off," said Molly. "We're already going to be fashionably late."

"And late enough for a grand entrance," said Robert. "Here I am decked out in my Sunday best — rather disappointed, I have to say, not to have received a single compliment from any one of you despite my clear and focussed attention on each of you — and I'll have three glamorous goddesses clinging to me. The minute we proceed royally through the old wooden doors the tongues will be wagging off and the lassies will be slagging off and everyone will be getting stuck into that other vital ingredient of a country dance — the critical assessment of each and every one who has the temerity to attend it. Drink up now and we'll be off. You'd be advised to use the latrine facilities before you go. It's a much better class of outside toilet here than there."

They walked the short distance down the lane to the community hall, a large shed-of-a-place which by now was surrounded by a tangle of bicycles leaning this way and that against the walls, the fencing, the hedges, whatever promised a bit of upright to keep the saddles off the rough ground. They could hear the fiddles going and the bodhran being struck and the singer's voice not so much crooning as crowing, while outside even at this early hour in the proceedings there were already some couples taking the air for a bit of this and that. It was enticing, busy, bustling with life and laughter, luring them into the promise of a great time to be had. As they crossed the yard, all heads turned for a good nose; as they entered the hall, as royally as they could manage with all their feigned pouting, even more heads turned for a good nose, a good shufty, the men down the one side of the hall almost breathless at the sight of the new arrivals, the girls down the other side quietly breathing fire while trying not to betray their disgruntled envy.

Robert directed his party straight over to a group of his friends. He led Molly on to the dancefloor after giving a nod and wink to a couple of mates who were only too delighted to take the hint and sweep Patsy and Theresa out into the press of jigging bodies. This was a country dance with gusto.

Temperatures rose as tempos got hotter and pulses raced as the evening filled to capacity with gaiety and flirting and fun. Even the local lasses forgot their sniffiness: as always there were far more men than women and even Robert spread his charms liberally without the responsibility of having to look after just one cousin, so the country girls were as much in demand as their city sisters. Indeed, they became sisters of a sort as the night went on, certainly girly confidantes, relaxing into easy conversations together during gaps in the music, swapping fashion tips and tales of Dublin for anecdotes concerning some of the dudes prancing around and some of the more lurid tales of life in Tullamore.

Unfortunately, the sociability wasn't to last the night. Two fillies vying for Robert's attention took their competition to a whole new level and set on one another right in the middle of the dancefloor. It was a scrap to behold: hair was pulled and tugged and tangled until it looked as if two crazy birds' nests had turned into helmets of war; slaps and smacks were stung across cherry-dabbed cheeks making their colour rise to unintended heights; skewed punches were thrown without much control to land wherever the fists were lucky enough to make contact; legs and feet kicked and heeled and booted at will, while screaming and screeching and shrieking drowned out the music altogether.

"This was the other vital ingredient of the festivities — a good old barney — which I thought best not to mention in advance to the more inexperienced among us," said Robert to his cousins who couldn't help gawping at the display of fisticuffs. "I wouldn't have wanted to put anyone off with the idea of a bit of a set-to but you seem to be enjoying it all right."

There was no shortage of willingness among the menfolk to get stuck in too, ostensibly to separate the combatants but having more of a laugh than an impact. And the names being called, the insults being hurled, the catcalls hissed through clenched fists... It was just as well the parish priest had stayed in town at the wake. Penance would have demanded more than a few Hail Marys and a set of Our Fathers by way of contrition.

Peace was eventually declared, the feisty opponents somewhat shamefacedly smoothed down their skirts, mortified beyond belief, and the music started up again. The dancing carried on as if there had been no interruption to the proceedings whatsoever. Robert gallantly got both girls up in turn for a jig but he couldn't resist lording it over his friends with a smug look on his face after having been the cause of the mewling.

All too soon it was over until the next time. The yard twinkled with the dim glow of quivering bicycle lamps as the revellers wheeled out on to the lane and mounted up ready for the ride home. The Dublin lot threaded their way back to the farmhouse, sore of foot but merry enough to ignore the protestations of their feet, worn of body but happy enough to linger talking over the evening's fun.

The following day dawned too early. They were tired and hung-over and woke to the discouraging sight of clothes carelessly strewn across the floor and shoes kicked here and there. It was tempting to just turn over and go back to sleep but the smell of bacon frying excited their nostrils and their stomachs rumbled in eager agreement. Also, Tullamore beckoned. The crazy fun of the barn dance behind them, they were now ready to take on the town.

There was a different sense of ease to enjoy in a county town, busy but not overwhelming as Dublin could sometimes be. They strolled around Tullamore looking in the shop windows, where they had to admit (quietly so as not to cause offence) that everything did look a bit simple, basic, compared to what was on offer in the capital, but the grocery shops were truly tempting and they bought some culinary treats to take home. After a couple of hours spent wandering around, they went to sit on a bench by the canal, gorging themselves on fruit cake while Robert explained that Tullamore's town crest showed a phoenix rising from the ashes because in the late 1700s a hot-air balloon had crashed into the place starting a fire which went on to consume more than one hundred houses.

"I'm not sure a town with a whiskey distillery at its heart is a fitting heir to the title of the mythological bird," said Robert, "but there are indubitably plenty of victims with fire in their belly from that very distillery who manage somehow to rise themselves from their beds every morning after the nightly extinguishment of their thirst."

"Their feathers not a little ruffled," said Theresa.

The canal was busy with barges plying up and down and the four of them sat trying to work out how long it would take to walk its banks all the way back to Dublin, maybe even to the Phoenix Park itself, just to consolidate the experience. The weekend had promised to be a great gas and had delivered on all fronts.

All the same the sisters decided not to put their walking hypotheses to the test and, as planned, flagged down the Dublin bus as it passed the farm gates. It was a warm farewell to everyone that drew their visit to a close, with hugs exchanged, gratitude expressed and promises made to return. Equally warm greetings welcomed them home. The delivery of fresh eggs and newly churned butter, potatoes just recently lifted from the soil and home-baked soda bread from the country provided quite a feast back at The Coombe. The house was full of talk as news and gossip from Betty's old home was delivered. Tales of trips into Tullamore on the crossbars of bicycles and hilarious descriptions of the barn dance made the realisation of back-to-work the very next day all the more unpalatable.

There was a letter from Sean waiting for Patsy, his handwriting unmistakeable. Patrick had been at home when it was delivered over the weekend, obviously by hand, there was no stamp on the envelope. The young man had posted it through the door himself, Patrick assumed, obviously shameless enough to feel free to call to the house. Shameless, without scruples however many times he sat in the front pew at Mass as if he was holiness incarnate, hands joined together in prayer, the very soul of goodness rather than the seed of evil. No surprise there, thought Patrick, smouldering with a deep-seated odium. Like father, like son. Putting on one face to hide the true ugly one behind the public mask of decency. Patrick had already realised that not only was Fitzsimmons walking out with his daughter despite the crusade of verbal warfare he launched every day against the young baker, but Patrick was now also outraged that the traitor's son wasn't even going behind his back in writing to Patsy, he was blatant about it, shoving his cursed letters through the door himself. At least the father had had the common sense to try to hide his treachery. Patrick held the letter tightly, as if it was some sort of a spiritualist's medium, channelling some direct link to the traitor himself long since dead and thus entrapping Patrick in memories he preferred not to remember.

"Get rid of this, woman," he said handing the letter to Betty. "I'll not be having all this underhand correspondence coming into my house."

"Give it here," said Betty. "You know you have no right to throw away someone's letter just because you don't approve of the person who wrote it."

"Approval doesn't come into it. You don't know anything about it, woman, so hold your peace. I told you to get rid of the thing," said Patrick. He slumped into his chair by the fire then stood up and strode out into the refuge of the yard.

Betty looked at the letter in her hand and admired the beautiful writing that seemed to reflect the fineness of the lad with whom Patsy was smitten. Betty was completely at a loss as to why her husband was so against his daughter's young man. She understood that sometimes at the bakery a rush of orders would suddenly come in and everyone would have to take on extra work to meet the supply but Betty had never heard any criticism of Sean Fitzsimmons as a worker. Bemused, she stuffed the envelope into the pocket of her pinny. After a few minutes spent creating distracting noises in the kitchen, she went to hide the letter under the pillow on Patsy's bed. It wouldn't do for Patrick to know she was disobeying him; he was in enough of a mood already. Later, after the homecoming meal when everyone decided to call it a day, Betty whispered to Patsy that there was a letter from Sean waiting for her in the bedroom. Patsy's face creased with happiness as she hugged Betty.

"Just don't mention it to your da," said Betty. "He told me to destroy it and we don't want both of us getting into any trouble. I don't know what Patrick's problem is with Sean but best leave it for now, your father's a strange one all right."

Alone in her room, Patsy tenderly put the letter to her lips. She fondled it between her fingers and ran the tips over the writing. She was aware of the subtle disturbance in the air as her floaty people leaned in to share in her pleasure, giving her the reassurance that her vague visions had always given her. When the O'Kelly family had moved to The Coombe, Patsy had immediately sensed the unseen presence of someone in the little room; that was the reason she had chosen it and also how she had managed to persuade her sisters not to choose it for themselves. The floaty people had made themselves properly known to her only gradually, as they gained confidence in the sensitivities and welcoming response of the new inhabitant. They were a brother and sister, killed along with the rest of their family when the weekly wash draped in front of the fire to dry had gone up in flames. Most of the family had died from severe burns when the tattered clothes they were wearing also caught fire but the two youngsters had been trapped in the separate small off-shot room and had suffocated in the smoke. All the same, despite their history of loss and tragedy, they now brought a feeling of calm to the room and Patsy was often aware of their warming presence, quite the opposite, she knew, of what most people associated with beings from the other side. Ireland was a country embroidered with a web of superstitions but not everyone was comfortable with things they believed to be there but invisible. She drew the ghostly children in to her and opened the letter.

My Dear Streaks,

I hate to write this letter for fear of annoying you and you just back from enjoying some time with your family and friends in the country, but I must ask you a serious question, the contemplation of which has caused me a few sleepless nights and a corresponding number of days of anxiety.

You will, I'm sure, understand my reluctance in writing you regarding such a matter of deep importance to me when I tell you that many a happy home and perhaps a whole life have been spoilt by similar trouble — absence — in this instance the absence of your wonderful self.

It seems a life-or-death question to me. I dare not communicate my state of mind to my friends for they are not to be relied on in these matters so I appeal to you, knowing that you like me a little. In fact, I feel I can rely on you and look to you to grant the favour I am about to ask.

Of course, I may be asking a great deal but I ask you to put away all your social joys and work to devote all your time and attention to the proper consideration of my request. (I hardly dare to sign my name for fear of refusal.) I ask you, out of the fullness of my heart and yours and of our friendship, to answer this great question. Do you honestly think you could agree to meet me on Saturday for a full day's excursion which I have planned by way of consolation for not having seen you this whole weekend due to your visit to Tullamore?

Yours with tickets in hand, hoping for the right reply,
Sean F.

Patsy hugged the letter to herself. A whole day to be spent with her precious Sean awaited. She was glad that she had worn his favourite dress to the barn dance, keeping them connected during her '*absence*' and all the while not knowing that he was devoting his energies to organising a special trip just for the two of them. How dramatic his invitation was, poetic even, she thought, as if she could ever refuse such a romantic request. 'Knowing that you like me a little,' he had written. A little? And here she was, her very heart racing at just the thought of him. She didn't know how she would get through the week with all the turmoil swirling around inside her. There weren't so much butterflies fluttering in her stomach as a whole flight of love-doves soaring and diving down into her depths. She opened her handbag, took out a lipstick and smeared a glance of colour over her lips. Then she imprinted a kiss on the seal of the envelope and stowed the letter under her pillow before getting into bed. She got up again almost immediately, retrieved the letter from under the pillow and put it with the others in her drawer: Patsy wasn't sure about the implications of sleeping with a loved one's letter so close to you in bed. Weren't they constantly taught that even having wrong thoughts could be a sin? Patsy didn't want to take any chances, just in case she died in the night with a stain on her soul.

4

Patsy had really settled into her position at Jeanette Modes and loved working in the place. The other girls were hysterical and full of friendly but scandalous gossip and stories of these goings-on and those coming-offs, of course only when the supervisor wasn't in earshot; in fact some of the things they had to say would surely merit a mention in the confessional box. They certainly gave Child-of-Mary Patsy something to counter in her nightly prayers and renewed dedication to purity: she hadn't realised that women could be as coarse as some men in their comments, though she was conscious of the stirrings in her body when Sean was near and her need to fight them off, to be resolute, Mary-like. So, whatever the complaining about returning to work had gone on after the Tullamore weekend, Patsy herself was happy to be back in such a noisy environment and one in which she was regarded with respect, as a highly skilled worker, unlike at home, where she was given respect as the eldest of the tribe but was also treated as a potential fallen woman by her father. All the same, by the time she clocked off from work on Tuesday evening, she was beside herself with impatience.

Tuesday evenings had become a bit of a delicious ritual. She would meet her friend Margaret, her best friend since school, and they would go for a small tea somewhere or, if mood and money were amenable, the treat would be shiny buns and a coffee in the very fashionable Bewley's Oriental Café in Grafton Street. It was the place to go, everyone who could went there and some people who couldn't really afford it, people who had to nurse a cup of tea for a few hours just to be there. The friends preferred a cup of rich, dark coffee, regarded as the height of exoticism and where better to complete the sophistication of it all than a place modelled, according to the papers, with an interior designed to reflect a genuine oriental tea-house and an exterior said to have been inspired by the treasures discovered a few years earlier in the tomb of the Egyptian pharaoh Tutankhamen. That combination would do very nicely for Patsy and Margaret, a couple of Dublin seamstresses with their own designs on having a girly evening of exchanged confidences followed by a night at the pictures.

"This is a grand place, don't you think so?" said Margaret. "There's something about it that makes me walk taller when I come in through the door. It seems to dust me with a coat of exquisite particles that make me shimmer from head to toe."

"My coat has been dusted right enough but not with anything shimmery," said Patsy. "It's probably just odd specks of either talc or scouring powder."

"Let's sit in the middle. We can pretend to be studying the stained-glass windows while we're actually studying everyone else," said Margaret.

They found an unoccupied table, arranged their coats on the backs of the chairs and posed elegantly into their seats. They scanned the menu, just for appearances as they knew in advance what they were having, put the menus back in place and then lit up. Waiting for their order to arrive the two friends drew in the heady pleasures of their first cigarettes of the session. Whenever they smoked in Bewley's, they both automatically assumed particular mannerisms which, they believed, gave them a certain air of elegance. Each held their cigarette aloft in a deliberately cultivated but supposedly nonchalant way — elbows carefully crooked on the table in front of them and fingers asplay on wrists, gesturing circular and oh-so-fascinating patterns in the air — while their mouths were still pouted post-puff in conversation. Their eyes, lowered demurely under lashes, were busy scanning the room at the same time, just like they'd seen Greta Garbo do in the films.

"See that woman over there," said Patsy, not losing her poise while indicating with directional flicks of her eyes the well-dressed, well-manicured woman sitting across the room from them surrounded by a group of young women who seemed to hang on to her every word.

"The one in the fancy red dress?" Margaret peered over in what she believed to be quite a regal, disinterested way. Her gaze travelled back to Patsy. "The one who looks as if she's used to people dancing attendance on her?"

"That's the one," said Patsy. "She introduced that meeting I went to last week."

"The one about women at work?"

"Except that it wasn't about women at work at all, it was about being married and how to make love with your husband without all the pregnancies."

"It was about sex?" Margaret nearly choked on her coffee cigarette. "And you went to it, Patsy O'Kelly?"

"If 'sex' is the word you want to use, yes, and birth control." Patsy couldn't help automatically pursing her lips in disapproval.

They shushed as their coffee and buns arrived. Neat, embroidered hankies were delicately produced out of their handbags ready to apply ladylike little wipes to the corners of their mouths to keep up appearances during the bun feast.

"And did you learn anything?" asked Margaret leaning in when the waitress had gone. "What did they say?"

"I tried not to listen," said Patsy. "It all sounded rather sinful to me."

"Go on tell me the gist, you must at least have caught the gist." By now Margaret was all attention.

"I caught words like 'penetration' and 'contraception' and once or twice they used that word, 'ejaculation'. That was enough of the dirty gist for me."

"You're too holy for your own good, Patsy. I wish I had known what they were going to talk about, I'd have gone there myself. Amn't I getting married soon enough and I certainly don't want a horde of children screaming at my feet. I'm too selfish for all that devoted-mother stuff, dropping a baby nine months to the day after the wedding night and then every year after that. I want himself to myself for a couple of years at least."

"There's always the option of saying 'no' or keeping your knickers up and your legs closed tight, as the nuns would say."

"Who would even want to keep their legs closed to the man they love when they might enjoy a bit of slap and tickle themselves? Sure, I can't wait to get into bed with Duggie, the wedding can't come soon enough."

"Margaret Matthews that's a terrible way to talk and you a good Catholic girl. I can't believe I'm hearing you right." Patsy was trying hard not to look too offended by her close friend's apparent enthusiasm for the whole bedtime business but Patsy's sophisticated Bewley's persona had been overwhelmed by such directness, such open eagerness to do the deed. She didn't think it sounded rude, she thought it sounded positively crude. "And besides," she said, "there's all that sex stuff you have to put up with. There's more to it than slaps and tickles."

"I hope so," said Margaret. "All that 'sex stuff' is what I'm looking forward to. Enough of all that anyway, I can see you blushing from ear to ear. You're too much of a saint for your own good, Patsy. Now, I want to hear all about your trip to the country," she said, "what you did, who you met and whether you've come back longing for a return to the sweet muscular arms of a country man or if you are still head-over-heels for Sean?"

"We had the greatest time." Patsy was relieved to change the subject, "but there was such a beautiful letter from Sean waiting for me when I got home that I'm afraid I soon forgot about Tullamore," she said and she was unable to hide the glow that illuminated her face. "Betty had rescued it for me. My da had ordered her to destroy it before I got home but she hid it in the bedroom for me. Sean has planned an excursion for us on Saturday but it's to be a surprise, I don't know where we're going."

"A trip to paradise, perhaps, but modest and pure, obviously. He's such a considerate young man, your Sean, I can't understand your father's being so against him."

"According to my Uncle Michael in Tullamore it's got something to do with Sean's father and something that happened years back, when my da was a Volunteer," said Patsy. "Uncle Michael wouldn't go into details but he did promise to have a word with my da next time he's in Dublin, see if he can smooth things out. Until he does, I don't know what to do. I'll have to come up with some excuse to be out of the house all day Saturday."

"I can help you there," said Margaret. "I'm busy with wedding plans on Saturday and wouldn't it be the most natural thing in the world for my bridesmaid to be there to help me decide on whatever we decide we're supposed to be deciding. You could come round to our house for an hour or so in the morning, just to add a bit of truth to the tale, or, better still, I can call for you at The Coombe, then we can head off into town together innocently before you go to meet Sean. How about that?"

"Margaret Matthews, what would I do without you?"

"You'd be a complete lost cause. You'd probably already have taken the veil. Now that Saturday's settled, I still want to hear all about your weekend."

The two friends treated themselves to another coffee and Patsy, all elegance and composure recovered, related the story of the dance and the fight over their cousin, Robert: how the local girls had eventually become genuinely friendly; how much the sisters had enjoyed the farm, even getting used to the smell of cow dung, and then their leisurely stroll around the town and small picnic by the canal. Margaret kept interrupting with comments and questions and the time flew so quickly that in the end they had to rush to get to the Camden cinema: there was a solid-fuel stove at the back of the auditorium and Patsy and Margaret wanted to arrive in time to make sure they got seats near the centre away from the blast of heat. That way also they wouldn't be bothered either by the couples canoodling in the back row or by the Ay-Ay man shining his torch along to put a stop to any such furtive shenanigans. Once settled, Patsy and her friend looked forward to a few hours spent in the company of Ronald Colman. Wasn't he just too handsome!

Patsy hadn't had the heart to tell Margaret that Sean had specially asked Patsy not to be a bridesmaid for the bad omen it promised about their own future wedding plans, especially after Margaret had devised the perfect means of escape at the weekend. Round the kitchen table at The Coombe, Patsy was only vaguely tuned in to the family conversation. She had waited to fetch some Hafner's sausages and white pudding for their tea on her way home from Jeanette Modes, waited patiently at the shop despite the long queue because it gave herself time on her own to think. Hafner's was always busy: their sausages and puddings were so intrinsic that quite a proportion of their sales were destined to find their way over to Liverpool and beyond to remind émigré Dubliners of home. This evening, Patsy had welcomed the inevitable Thursday delay as customers stocked up before catching the night boat for their weekend trips, even in the rain. As she sheltered under her umbrella, at the forefront of her mind was the matter of deliberately disobeying her father and whether her conscience could allow it. It was true what she had told Uncle Michael, that her da had not specifically instructed her to end the relationship, yet she couldn't pretend that he hadn't made his opposition perfectly clear. It could be months before Michael came up to Dublin and had his quiet word, meanwhile poor Sean was so intimidated by Patrick O'Kelly at the bakery that he frequently joked about being "bumped off" by Mr O'Kelly.

"That must have hurt, being bumped off like that," Theresa was saying, her words arresting Patsy's attention, as if somehow, they were addressing Patsy's private thoughts. "I can't believe you both just stood there and didn't offer to help," said Theresa. "It sounds like something straight out of a Charlie Chaplin film." Patsy came out of her daydreaming.

"It was a lot funnier than that, believe me," said Ciaran. "We couldn't do anything for laughing. Mikey here near wet his pants he was laughing so much."

"I did not," protested Mikey, his outrage and red face causing much amusement round the table.

"I saw the beginnings of the damp patch myself," said Ciaran. "Don't leave those pants on the floor next to the bed tonight, please, the stink would keep me awake."

"I didn't wet my pants, Mammy, I promise. Ciaran's just being his usual stupid."

"Then again it's pretty stupid wetting your own pants," chimed in Eddie.

"But I didn't," cried Mikey. "Tell them to stop, Mammy"

"Whisht now and let the lad alone," said Betty. "I've washed enough of everybody's wet pants here and not told the world."

"So, what happened next?" asked Molly. "Did anyone get hurt? What about the poor horse?"

"Well, after the horse slipped on the cobbles and the cart overturned, which was funny enough to witness, believe me," said Ciaran, "there was Mr Flanagan and his horse both sprawled on the ground and there were six legs between them waving frantically in the air and cart-wheels spinning so fast you'd think they were about to take off and launch the cart off into space. And the noise! The cries! The horse whinnying!

Everyone tutting and oohing-and-aahing and trying hard not to laugh at the same time. I don't know who made the most din. Meanwhile Mr Flanagan's sacks of potatoes spilt open and there were spuds rolling this way and that, bumping up and down over the cobbles all the way to the bottom of Meath Street," he said. "That's when I decided to help — to help myself to some free spuds."

"Shame on you," said Patsy, at last lost in a drama other than her own. "Poor Mr Flanagan doesn't make much off his cart without you stealing his potatoes."

"Well then shame on everyone else too who stuffed a few into their pockets." Ciaran was not in the mood to be stopped mid-tale. "The next thing that happened was just as funny," he said. "You know Jimmy Owens, himself who carries his bed of nails everywhere in case he decides on an impromptu performance? He put the bed on the ground to collect a few spuds and then that miser O'Rourke, who used to have the corner shop, tripped over on one of the potatoes he was trying to pick up and himself fell flat out on to the bed of nails. Did we laugh! His face went from white to purple and back again."

"O'Rourke? That miser? Serves him right, trying to get something for nothing and him after having had his own business to run. He must know how hard it is for Mr Flanagan to make a living and he didn't have a horse to feed as well," said Molly.

"Only that wife of his; she could be a bit of an old nag herself in the shop," said Theresa.

"She certainly looked a bit like a horse," said Mikey, wanting to reassert his credentials after the wet-pants embarrassment.

"I'll say 'neigh' to that," said Ciaran trying to wheeze like an old nag, his credentials soaring but steering him too close to the mark for his father.

"That's enough now all of you," said Patrick, though even his stern face had cracked into a begrudged smile or two during the telling of the tale. "Next time you see Mr Flanagan, Betty, perhaps you could give him a bit extra to pay for what Ciaran took."

Order was restored round the meal but a sense of bravado kept Ciaran and Mikey nodding and winking at each other conspiratorially and throwing their heads back and baring their teeth as if they were horses. Mikey tried to give his brother a gentle kick under the table but caught his father's leg instead.

"That's enough, I said." Patrick ordered the two boys to leave the room. They could finish their meal later, when they had learned how to behave, he said, even if it meant their food would be cold. "We'll see if cold potatoes go down your gullets as easily as stolen ones went into your pockets."

The two boys left the room obediently, their shoulders going up and down with supressed giggling.

Eddie had enjoyed the story and sympathised with his younger brothers: he thought the whole thing must have been a gas and only wished he'd been there to enjoy the spectacle but he'd gone straight to the bird market after his coal round, otherwise he too would have been hanging round Meath Street. "Do you think we'll be able to finish the loft this weekend, Da? I can bring the pigeons home as soon as it's ready," he said. "Jimmy's earmarked some birds for me and I've bought some seed and scrounged a few water-bowls."

"We can stretch the netting up on the front tonight," said Patrick. "We need to make sure the local cats can't get in, that will leave just the tarpaulin to put on for the roof and the nesting boxes to fix into place. I don't see why we shouldn't be able to get that done by Sunday. The market's open Sunday, is it?"

"It opens all weekend," said Eddie.

"Then I'll pop over Sunday afternoon and help you carry the pigeons home. As long as you promise me again that you yourself are going to look after them. I don't want your mammy having to get involved because you lose interest after a few weeks."

"How could I ever lose interest? They're birds who will live here but also have a life of their own flying wherever they want to in Dublin. They'll be able to explore the parks and the streets and maybe even have a bit of a fly over the docks, fight over some scraps with the gulls, then they'll come home and relax. It's going to be grand having them."

"I wouldn't mind getting a bird's eye view of the city myself," said Patsy.

"I prefer to keep my feet on the ground," said Molly.

"I thought you liked going up Nelson's Pillar and looking at the view?"

"Once was sufficient for the experience," said Molly. "I'm not keen on heights, they make me too dizzy." She whispered to Patsy: "A haystack's as high as I'm prepared to go." Her sister just pulled a face.

"Won't you have to train the pigeons first, so they know where to come home to, Eddie?" asked Theresa. "When does all that start?"

"Right from the off. It's supposed to take about five or six weeks before you can let them out to stretch their wings and have a little explore. That's to give them time to get used to the good food and warmth and smell of their own loft so they'll come back, then you can take them a bit farther afield, gradually getting further away."

"Is that your plan, to take them out to the country and hope they find their own way home?"

"Maybe," said Eddie. "I might get too fond of them just being here to bother with all that. Anyway, I'd need a good basket to carry them in and return bus fare if I wanted to take them out. I'm not sure I want to spend money on that, as it is there'll be the seed and bedding to buy regularly. No, I'm not bothered about the racing side of it, I just want to have my own birds to look after."

"Just make sure you do just that," said Molly.

"Haven't I said I will," said Eddie. "I don't know why you all have to keep telling me what I already know." He sat taller in his chair, glowing with a sense of assumed responsibility.

While the dishes were being cleared off the table, Patrick called his eldest daughter out to the backyard. "Come and sit with me awhile," he said. It was a kindly invitation, with no hint of authority, but Patsy feared another lecture about Sean and grabbed her packet of cigarettes, needing the comfort-prop. She and her father carried a couple of chairs out and he deliberately shut the kitchen door behind them. They seated themselves and Patsy lit up. She inhaled a few drags and wondered at how gently carefree the smoke looked as it curled into the air while she herself felt taut and anything but carefree.

"Now then, Patsy, what's the matter?" said Patrick. "You seemed to be far away in your thoughts when we sat down to eat."

"It's nothing, Daddy, I was just enjoying my dinner."

"Is that right?" said Patrick. "Well, I think there was more to it than that. I notice you keep to your room a lot lately. I thought your trip to Tullamore would clear your head but it doesn't seem to have done the trick. You never used to seek out your own company so much in the house. Is everything going well at work? Haven't you not long had a promotion? Surely that lifted your spirits."

Patsy didn't know how to answer her father and there was silence between them for a few long minutes. There were noises and voices drifting out from the kitchen and over the walls of neighbouring yards, a general buzz of animated talk as people were finishing the day's chores ready for a restful evening, but there were no words passing between Patsy and her da. She let out a deep sigh, stubbed out her cigarette on the ground and immediately lit another one.

"You smoke far too many of those things," said Patrick. "They can't be good for you. Would you not think about quitting? You should quit."

Patsy was shaking. "What I can't quit is seeing Sean Fitzsimmons," she blurted out, suddenly, without thinking, more confrontational than she had intended. How many times had she rehearsed this very conversation and straight away she had fluffed her lines. "You know I love you, Da, and I'd never go against you normally, but Sean means the world to me, and I don't understand why you are so set against him."

Patrick stiffened, failing to hide his instinctive reaction to what his daughter was saying. His back straightened, his face became fixed, he was breathing heavily and looked about to flare up in one of his familiar tempers but Patsy contrarily felt emboldened by what she regarded as his totally unreasonable attitude.

At that moment Eddie came out of the kitchen whistling cheerfully, keen to finish the loft with his da.

"Get back inside, now." Patrick shouted, in no mood for thinking about pigeons. Eddie meekly went back into the house not sure what was going on in the yard between his da and sister but sure that something definitely was. When Betty and Molly looked at him questioning his quick return, he raised his eyebrows and sucked in his lips by way of a warning to the rest of them to stay indoors.

Taking a defiant pull on her cigarette after the interruption, Patsy was determined to go on now that things between her and her father were finally out in the open. "Sean tells me that sometimes you treat him unfairly at work and he feels awkward and embarrassed in front of the other men," she said. "All I can say is that to me he is kind, respectful, and he treats me like a princess, like his very own princess, and I love him for it. He's funny, he knows lots of things because he reads so much and he takes such good care of his mammy that she'd be lost without him, especially lately when she hasn't been well. You know Sean's father died years ago so she's been a widow for a long time but luckily she has a wonderful son she can depend on. I think he's quite wonderful too and I depend on him, in here," she said, pointing to her heart. "Perhaps if you were to explain it to me, I could at least try to understand why you don't like me seeing him. Maybe then I could help put your mind at rest."

Patrick turned his head towards Patsy and stared at her. His face was frozen but it was an expression of despair that stilled his features, not hatred or anger. His eyes moved all over Patsy's face, studying it, every line, every contour, as if being reunited with the person sitting right next to him and needing to absorb everything. "Sometimes you remind me so much of Lizzie, your real mammy, God rest her soul," he said. "Losing her was a terrible loss." At last he lowered his gaze and took Patsy's hands in his own and held them in such a strong grip that she had to fight the urge to free herself. Then he spoke, very quietly, almost as if he didn't even want to hear his own words let alone say them to someone else.

"I killed Sean's father. That's why his mother has been a widow all these years. I shot her husband."

Patsy went white as the truth was spelt out. The colour drained from her face and she looked in horror at her daddy, her own daddy telling her that he really had killed Sean's father, her own Sean. "You killed him?" she stuttered. "Sean's father? Why would you have done that?"

Patsy tried to free her hands quickly and made to get up out of the chair but Patrick held on.

"Leave me be," said Patsy. "You killed Sean's father and now you're attacking Sean himself. Why would you do that? What has Sean ever done to you?" Tears welled in her eyes and she started to sob uncontrollably.

Betty, who had been peering out through the kitchen window to keep a watchful eye on things, rushed out to put an immediate end to whatever was going on but Patrick ordered her too back inside. "Patsy and I have to get this sorted now, the two of us," he said, "this whole Sean situation has gone on long enough and I need to explain myself to Patsy."

"I don't understand the problem with Sean myself," said Betty.

"Perhaps not but right now it's between Patsy and myself," said Patrick.

"Well I hope to God that something gets sorted between the two of you, it's wearing us all down," said Betty and then left them to it.

Patrick looked around, searching for whatever words he could find that might in some way convey his sense of loss, the guilt he had been carrying since his daughter had started walking out with Sean Fitzsimmons. At first Patrick had assumed the relationship wouldn't last, two young people enjoying a first romance and he had hoped it would end naturally, as these things generally did. But it hadn't. And all the letters suggested that Sean was as smitten with Patsy as she obviously was with him. Patrick clung to Patsy's hands. His voice was barely audible.

"It was during all the fighting when I was a Volunteer," he told her. "We used the bakery as a Flying Unit depot. We'd discuss our plans there; we'd guns and ammunition hidden there, grenades, uniforms; men and women helping the cause would come and go, supposedly in secret. We were always very careful. What we were doing was dangerous and we had to take strict precautions, day and night. Then we discovered that we had a spy amongst us, a spy who was reporting to the British in Dublin Castle. They never raided the place as the information they were getting out of it was too valuable to them but the treachery was costing the lives of a lot of men and women. So, we laid a trap. The details don't matter, what matters is that it was John Fitzsimmons who was the traitor and I was ordered with a couple of comrades to make him disappear. We got him into the back of one of the bread vans and drove him out of the city for the execution. I was one of the ones who carried it out. His wife never found out what had happened or why. It's probably best left that way."

"What did she think had happened?" asked Patsy. "Her husband can't have just disappeared and she never asked where he was or why he never came home."

"The Castle reported that he had been killed in a skirmish. It was a routine report, just a list of names and where and when. People were being killed like that all the time and the authorities didn't want to admit that Fitzsimmons was one of theirs, it would have been bad for their reputation, admitting they were relying on spies, and it might have put others off helping them."

Silence descended again. Patrick looked at his poor daughter.

"I know you think this has nothing to do with Sean but every time I see him I'm reminded of the good comrades we lost because of his father," he said, "and of my part in the execution. It was a brutal, cold solution but I make no excuses for that: it had to be done, we were at war, and he was working for our enemy. And now I see the same traitor's son working in the same bakery and laughing and joking with everyone and I think back to when there was no laughing and joking because friends were dying because of Fitzsimmons' treachery. Sometimes the hatred builds up inside me so much, even after all these years, that I want to murder the son of the traitor too. I ask myself why someone with Fitzsimmons' own blood in his veins should be allowed to live."

Patsy could feel through his hands the tension building up in her da.

"Don't you understand, Patsy," he said. "I have to put up with Sean Fitzsimmons at work and cope in my own way, but I couldn't bear the sight of him coming into our home and sitting there courting my daughter, my own daughter, then maybe being a part of the family and me the only one knowing about his father and how he had paid for his treachery. I think this head of mine would explode."

Before Patsy could say anything, Betty came out into the yard again. "Whatever it is you're talking about has gone on long enough," she said. "Now get inside before I take a stick to the two of you."

Patsy took the opportunity to escape and she barged her way through the house to take refuge in her bedroom. Molly and Theresa exchanged looks and went out to ask their da what was upsetting Patsy so much that the tears were streaming down her cheeks but their father signalled for them to leave Patsy alone.

Patrick stayed where he was, swept by the relief that at last he had been able to unburden himself of the knowledge of his role in the Fitzsimmons' incident. It was the first and only execution in which Patrick had been involved and he had been haunted by the face of John Fitzsimmons ever since, the face of a terrified man pleading for his innocent family to be spared even as the firing squad took aim, a family which included a son who was now bringing the horror of the past into the routine of Patrick's everyday life at work and at home. Patrick had never spoken about the execution afterwards, not even with his comrades. Killing in battle was one thing, he thought, but execution was very close to murder no matter how much it seemed justified at the time. He had told his daughter what he done: he hadn't told her that every time he looked at Sean Fitzsimmons he was faced with his own undeniable guilt and that was what he found unbearable.

"Is Patsy okay?" asked Eddie, hovering in the kitchen to keep out of his da's way.

"Did she look all right to you, eejit, banging through the house and slamming doors and all the while crying?" said Theresa. "Is that what being 'okay' looks like to you?"

"Da says Patsy has some thinking to do," said Molly, realising that Eddie was only trying to show a bit of concern for his sister. "I don't know what went off just now between her and our da but, whatever it was, she obviously needs time to herself."

"Time to herself?" chimed in Eddie. "How can she have time to herself when she shares a room with ghosts." Then he went into a hooing and whooing act and raised his arms ghostlike. As he thought, his audience appreciated the touch of levity.

5

Saturday took an eternity to arrive and Patsy was desperate to see Sean. He had written, of course, but she had been giddy with the idea of telling him about the previous weekend's visit to Tullamore while it was still fresh and exciting in her mind. His mother had been ill and Sean hadn't been able to get away for even an hour during the week, what with doing the food shopping and fetching his mother's medications, then the cooking and housework to give his mother a chance to rest.

Patsy had been desperate to see Sean but that was before her talk in the yard with her father. Now she felt as uncertain as she was desperate. The ominous possibility that Uncle Michael had hinted at in Tullamore had encouraged her vivid imagination to seek out and dwell on the worst possible interpretation but Michael had dismissed her fears and she in turn had managed to dismiss it from her mind. That seemed a lifetime ago. Since then, the hint had proved too real a reality. No chat between Michael and her father would ever be able to cancel out the truth of what had happened, neither the fact of it nor the persistent memory.

Margaret called for her as planned. The suggestion was that Patsy was to help her decide what sort of a bouquet to choose for the wedding, which meant going to the flower market in the city centre to look at the different blooms in season. Anything other than those would cost quite a bit more in a proper shop, Margaret commented with conviction, trying to add substance to the subterfuge, then again, she might decide to take a look in the florist's window after all, to compare prices and see what was on offer, then they might go for a cup of tea somewhere, in which case she would be commandeering Patsy for the whole afternoon, so not to worry if Patsy was home late, fulfilling her bridesmaid's duties. Neither of them had reckoned on any complication but one arose from an unexpected source.

"Sure I'd love to tag along too," said Molly. "I love going round the flower stalls and picking some out for a wedding would add a lovely sense of purpose. Can I come with you?"

"Since when have you shown any interest in flower stalls?" stuttered Patsy, grasping for any reason to put off her sister. She wanted her day out with Sean for the sheer fun of it but she also wanted to know how she'd feel in his company after her father's revelations.

"Well of course, Molly, you're not really a bridesmaid so I'm not sure it would fit with the tradition," said Margaret, trying to save the day.

"I didn't know there was any such tradition that said only a bridesmaid could help with picking out flowers," said Betty. "If there is, it seems like a silly one to me. I would have thought that an extra opinion would be welcome, and Molly's always had a bit of an eye for what looks good."

Further discussion was stemmed by the sound of a knock on the door. Ciaran was busy in the understairs cupboard oiling the chain on his bike so he called out offering to get the door. "It's Nora, for you, Molly," he shouted down the hall. "Come in, come in," he said to Nora, "Molly's out in the kitchen trying to wangle her way into a trip to town. You might have just saved her the embarrassment of being refused the pleasure."

Nora, her lips painted like a bright red cupid's bow as usual, bustled into the kitchen as if she had a whirlwind in tow, as usual. "Hello Mr O'Kelly, Mrs O'Kelly, thanks be to God you're looking so well with the bump there, growing nicely, so it is, and hello to the rest of the tribe, and to you Margaret, of course. There's always loads of noise and activity in this house. Are you and Margaret on your way out, Patsy?" she bubbled without waiting for an answer. "I'm here to see if Molly wants to go roller-skating at Blackrock this afternoon, if that's fine with you, Mr O'Kelly and you, Mrs O'Kelly, I know you have your hands full here. We'll behave ourselves, I promise, Mr O'Kelly, I'll see to it personally. It's such a beautiful day it would be a shame to waste it. There's a few of us going, we're to meet up at the rink and if we hurry we can catch the next train and be in time for the afternoon session. It'll be a gas. Then perhaps we can have a walk on the beach and a paddle in the sea. What do you say, Molly?"

"I say 'yes', I love roller-skating. Can I go, Da?"

"I thought you were wanting to go to town to look for flowers," said Patrick. He wasn't comfortable with Molly's friendship with Nora: she was a nice enough girl but when she got together with Molly the two of them were a handful, far too modern in their behaviour to Patrick's way of thinking. And that lipstick! What sort of message did that send out?

"Sure Patsy and Margaret clearly don't want me along," declared Molly. "It was only for something to do on my day off instead of just watching you and Eddie finishing off the pigeon-loft, Da. Can I go, please?"

"Of course, you can," said Betty before Patrick got the chance to refuse. "Go on and enjoy yourself with your friends and the bridesmaid tradition, whatever it is, will have been maintained."

"Thanks, Mammy. I'll just be a few minutes and I'll be with you, Nora." Molly disappeared upstairs.

Nora launched into one of her rambling anecdotes: this one was about two boys who'd managed to get into the Union Morgue to steal the pennies off the corpses' eyes. Her stories were always funny and she had a way of telling a tale but Margaret had an eye on the clock and didn't want to get too drawn into what would no doubt be a long narrative.

"I'm sorry to cut in, Nora, but Patsy and I should be getting off, we've a lot to do. We'd best say cheerio to everyone before we get too involved in the story. Come on, now, Patsy," said Margaret, "we don't want the flowers all wilted before we even arrive."

They left the house amid much chatter, walking down the hall mentioning this type of flower and that type of flower. Mikey, meanwhile, had tuned in to Nora's tale of the morgue and wanted to know more. Patsy and Margaret shut the front door on a gaggle of laughter.

The surprise excursion was a trip to Howth and Howth Island, otherwise known as Ireland's Eye. Patsy met Sean at the railway station, where he was waiting for her impatiently having arrived far too early in his eagerness to see her. Patsy had hesitated at the entrance just to watch him as he paced up and down and kept checking the time. She was trying to gauge her feelings when Sean noticed her standing there and waved excitedly in recognition. He rushed over, grinning from ear to ear. His face was the picture of happiness as he drew Patsy to him and enclosed her in his arms. It had seemed an eternity since they last met and he told her he never wanted such an eternity without her again. He had already bought the train tickets, returns, and he eagerly outlined their schedule for the day, all the time enjoying Patsy's own excited reactions as he detailed his plans. He had indeed been conscientious in his preparation and had a whole list of sights they were to explore together. Patsy couldn't help but relax into his company.

Once in Howth they headed straight for the gardens round the castle, famous for its wild rhododendrons and beech trees and rock-garden and sundial formed out of a multitude of different flowers, hugging the ground in organised segments of varied colour combinations. Sean told her all about the history of the castle and Patsy delighted in his enthusiasm to share his knowledge with her. Then it was time, according to his schedule, to go share a pot of tea and some scones in a small café where Patsy was able at last to tell him about her weekend in Tullamore, omitting the part about how much Dew she had had to drink. He loved the bit about the two women scrapping at the dance but was glad Patsy was far too sensible a girl for such carryings-on. He knew he would never have to worry about her in that respect, he said, holding the door open for her so they could head off to their next assignment.

In Howth village they sought out an 18th century mile-stone, one of ten markers in a series, explained Sean, the first being at Dublin's General Post Office, then he pointed out the imprint of George IV's footsteps on the West Pier. Sean's commentary added so much pleasure to even the simplest things and Patsy revelled in the bits of information he was able to pass on. Then they joined a handful of other out-of-towners on a short boat-trip round Howth Island and everyone marvelled at the number of jellyfish hanging delicately like a layer of living gel just below the surface of the water: it was like a transparent carpet on the sea, said Patsy, though Sean warned that it would be a carpet that could give you a few nasty nips if you walked on it.

Back on dry land, it was time for some fish and chips. They had worked up quite an appetite, with all the walking and the bracing effect of the sea breeze. They chatted easily as they tucked into their dinner and Patsy's nerves over the secret of their shared history evaporated without her even noticing it go. She had a moment of coyness when Sean mentioned them getting married and all the children they would have and she had to take hold of her Children of Mary scapula to keep herself grounded during the suggestions of such intimacies: she didn't want to spoil his mood. He had organised such a grand day and she was loving every minute of their excursion.

They left the café and strode off towards the heathland. Sean pointed out the highest peak in the area, Black Lin. He adopted a croaky voice to explain why the Bog of Frogs was so-called, obviously, he said deep from within his throat, because it's so wet the place gets inundated with the green slimy things hopping around all over the place and Patsy couldn't help but giggle at his hopping antics. He talked about the Bloody Stream that ran through the area and how that got its name from a fierce battle when the Normans beat the Vikings there in the 12th century and he painted a verbal picture of what the scene would have looked like as the stream turned red with blood from bodies split in two by huge heavy swords. They walked along the cliffs from where they could make out the Baily Lighthouse in the distance, which Sean had also researched so was able to tell Patsy that it had originally been built so high up on the headland that when the fog did come down it covered the light so comprehensively that no one at sea could actually see it — how silly was that for a lighthouse! In the end it had to be moved lower down and was then provided with its very own on-site gasworks for fuel.

They turned their gaze to the shore, spotting the different birds swooping round and colonising the rocky shore and Sean identified the guillemots and the razorbills and the fulmars and Patsy was bursting with pride in her young man. Then half a dozen or so grey seals lumbered out of the water; a couple of them stopped to lie and bask on the sand while the others chased away some of the birds to pinch the odd rock for themselves. There was so much to see and, even better, to see together.

From their cliff vantage point, they could look down on the town and its fishing boats and Sean spread out his jacket on the grass for Patsy to sit down and have a rest while they took in the view. Sean didn't smoke but Patsy lit up as, she said, the conditions and situation were perfect to enjoy the perfect cigarette. She savoured the taste, taking the draw deep inside as she drew the joy of her day deep inside.

They sat quietly next to each other. It was so peaceful up on the cliff. They listened to the rhythmic sounds of the sea, to the determination of the birds calling and cawing overhead and, down below, to the drift of voices carried up from the town, to the clanks and creakings of the boats moored in the harbour, to the gentle thunder of a string of horses galloping along the sands as if in a great hurry. Patsy felt she was in heaven and couldn't resist making an inner prayer of thanks.

It was as if Sean had at last managed to catch his breath after all his tour-guide observations when he suddenly broke the silence to pass on yet another item of local interest.

He told Patsy that on July 26, 1914, a cache of nine-hundred rifles and thousands of cartridges had been landed in Howth off a yacht in broad daylight, shipped in for the Volunteers who were already planning the Easter Rising. The yacht belonged to someone who later served in the British Navy, he said, which was tantamount to being a traitor to two countries and loyal to none. Sean speculated on how many people would have been killed as a result of that illicit cargo and questioned what sort of people could shoot other people without giving it a second thought. He was all in favour of Ireland's independence, he said, but not through fighting and killing, through ambushing British soldiers who were really just doing their job and then leaving them to die right there in the street where they fell.

Patsy took out another cigarette, not such a perfect smoke this time. Sean's conversation had changed from one of easy-going information of the many sights and snippets of local history to one of studied criticism of a history much too recent and personal for Patsy's comfort. And still Sean carried on.

He sneered at the fact that the gun-running owner of the yacht, a man called Erskine Childers, a writer, he believed, got maybe what he deserved when he himself was executed by the authorities of the Irish Free State, the very ones for whom he had smuggled the guns in the first place. Some Irish men made him feel ashamed to be Irish, said Sean. He was only glad that he had been too young to get mixed up in any of that awful business: his father had told him all about it when Sean was a child and his father had had the sense to stay out of it too.

A breeze gusted up from the shore. Patsy looked at her watch, a gold watch given as a present from Sean the previous Christmas, and suggested that perhaps it was time to think about heading back to Dublin. She couldn't be home late. She didn't want her father getting suspicious and then maybe Margaret would get into trouble too. Sean had planned a supper treat to round off the day but he agreed that Patsy was probably right and he didn't want to cause any unnecessary trouble with Patrick O'Kelly: the relationship between them was bad enough without further aggravation. On the train home, Patsy pretended to be asleep.

Eddie was in his element taking charge of the pigeons. Patrick had kept his promise and gone to help his son fetch the birds home from the market and now Eddie was behaving for all the world like the resident expert. Sunday morning had been a strange mixture in the house with a clash of atmospheres around the breakfast table after Mass. Molly couldn't be shut up going on about the skating session at Blackrock and how they had waltzed around to the music of Strauss, whoever he was, and how she and Nora had enjoyed the spectacle of sitting up in the gallery and looking down on all the beginners falling over as their skates ran out from under them and them ending with their backsides up in the air like sprawling hippos. Theresa was always circumspect about her activities; she naturally played her cards close to her chest, preferring privacy to letting the world and his wife know what she had been doing: she'd been out to Killiney with Billy, they had walked up through Victoria Park, they had enjoyed the panorama from the Obelisk and that was as much information as she was prepared to divulge. What no one could understand was why Patsy wasn't elaborating on whatever decisions were or weren't reached on Nora's wedding flowers after a whole day specifically dedicated to their pursuit; she was plied with questions but in reply gave only perfunctory answers and eventually people got the message and gave up asking and got on with their own preoccupations. By late afternoon, final adjustments having been made to the loft and the positioning of the nesting boxes completed to Eddie's satisfaction, the household's attention was devoted to the homing of the pigeons and any awkwardness at breakfast was forgotten.

"I suppose I'll have to think of names for them all," said Eddie, carefully putting the cages on the ground ready to be hoisted up the ladder for him to open into the loft. "I can't decide whether to call them after people on The Coombe, I think that would be a gas, I'd be calling to the birds and people would be looking around, wondering who it was calling out their names in the street. Or I could choose grand names for them after people from Irish legends. The pigeons would have a different status then."

"As long as you don't call one after O'Rourke, the miser," said Molly. "It would probably keep all the seed for itself."

"You could have Laurel and Hardy, and maybe a Charlie and a Chaplin," said Mikey. "That'd be good 'cause the pigeons are bound to be funny flapping around up there in a wooden box."

"That's an idea," said Eddie. "And one could be 'Mikey', he'd be bound to get in a flap and give us all a laugh too."

"Let's get them out of these cages and settled in, then," said Patrick. "I'll go up the ladder first Eddie, then you follow. I'll hold the door while you open the cages and that way we can make sure none of the birds escape. Get ready to pass them up to Eddie, Ciaran, carefully now, one at a time. Mikey, you get ready to take the empty cages down from Eddie."

The chain of command got underway and proved a good system. The racket of the birds dominated the proceedings, what with their cooing and the scratching of their feet on the bottom of the cages as they panicked in the kerfuffle, and apart from the odd repeated instructions there was little in the way of extraneous conversation from the humans. Once aloft, the pigeons fluttered about trying to escape their latest confinement and feathers floated hither and thither, catching in the wire netting: eventually they calmed sufficiently to investigate the loft and peace was gradually restored as nesting boxes were claimed. A row of four faces gawped in at them, all peering from a confusion of levels. Clucking noises were attempted and fingers were poked through the mesh with offerings of seed and friendship.

"I think we should all go down now and let them get used to the place," said Patrick. "We don't want any of them to have a heart attack amidst all the commotion."

"I'm going to stay up here for a few minutes, just to talk to them, let them get used to my voice," said Eddie.

"We'll take these cages back to Jimmy in the market when you're done," said Patrick. "The four of us can go and perhaps get an ice-cream on the way back by way of celebrating the birds' arrival. What do you say?"

There were no objections, just happy squabbles over which flavours were best.

It was all too much jollity for Patsy. No one in the family knew she had spent the day out at Howth with Sean so neither her sisters nor her mammy could figure out what was eating her. Patsy saw them exchanging curious glances and decided to take herself off to her room.

The problem was that her mind was running over the same thoughts over and over again, revisiting everything that Sean had been saying and obsessing at how easily he had simply made bold statements without once allowing for her own response, her own opinions, as if he naturally took for granted that they were at one with his.

For a start she hadn't liked his unquestioned assumption that they would get married and that she would then produce lots of babies: she didn't know her own mind on that yet, how it would fit with her dedication as a Child of Mary. In the cafe she had let the matter go and not challenged Sean over it, caught up as she was in the enjoyment of the day and his company.

What she couldn't let go of was his lack of understanding and sympathy for what the Volunteers had done. He sounded very cold, very absolute; his comments revealed a complete lack of empathy for all Patsy had believed in since she was a child, for all that her father had fought for and the sacrifices good people had made for Ireland. Of course she didn't like the idea of killings and ambushes no more than he did, no normal person would, but war was war and, if what her father had told her was correct, Sean's own father was responsible for the deaths of Volunteers. Wasn't that the same as killing? thought Patsy. He had kept his own hands clean while helping the British do the bloody work, killing men who were fighting for Ireland, men like her daddy and his friends, or breaking into people's homes and beating them with guns, ordinary people in poor homes without a stick of decent furniture in them. She had seen it for herself. Her own da had been locked up in a prison camp.

None of which she could ever say to Sean. His father's treason was a secret he had taken to the grave with him and Patsy could never tell Sean that she knew the truth of his apparently peaceful father, the man who supposedly kept well out of the war while at the same time betraying his countrymen and indoctrinating his son that the Rebellion was wrong and the Volunteers just a pack of murderers. Patsy hated that already she couldn't be totally honest with the man who wanted her as his wife and mother of his children.

As the days went by, Patsy couldn't stop the echoes of Sean's words from swirling round in her head, all the time growing in jarring intensity. They refused to leave her in peace. Her father found it impossible not to see the crimes of the father in the son; Patsy was beginning to see through those same eyes. When Sean's next letter arrived, she was faced what was becoming to seem inevitable.

My Darling Sweetheart,

As I write this letter to you, I am thinking of tonight when you and Margaret will be at the pictures and I'll be at my parish Retreat, praying for the only thing I ever really wanted with all my heart, yourself in marriage. That is the thing I want more than anyone in the world could ever imagine. Marriage to you would be the saving of me, and the crowning of me as regards health!

Well, now, darling, last night in bed I had one of the most terrible dreams it has ever been my misfortune to dream. I am going to write it in my own words and let you imagine in what state I awoke this morning. Well, then, as a young husband-to-be to his young wife-to-be, please God, here goes.

The opening part of the dream was in the bakery with me talking to Patrick O'Kelly and Tommy Byrne about horses in a coming race, laughing and arguing about each other's choice of horses, but none of us would agree with the other's selections. The discussion got hotter and hotter and in the course of the argument I dropped out. The other two got really heated over it and I could plainly see Pat O'Kelly's face the whole time they were arguing and if ever the lust-to-kill was in a man's eyes it certainly was in O'Kelly's. The foreman interrupted at this point and sent us over to another table to work. Pat O'Kelly and Tommy Byrne were separated, and Tommy Byrne was put to work next to me.

He started talking to me about you, Streaks, in a jeering kind of a way. I tried not to mind him at first but he insisted on carrying on about you in a coarse sort of a way so I suddenly turned around and hit him as hard as I could, twice in the stomach. He went down, completely winded.

The foreman and the others came running out of the far bakehouse when they heard the commotion, wanting to know what was up, and Pat O'Kelly said out loud, straight, for everyone to hear, that I had attacked Tommy Byrne for no reason at all. The daring of the lie absolutely floored me, and I couldn't say a word in my own defence. Anyway, I knew they wouldn't have believed me over O'Kelly so I remained silent.

After a short time, the foreman ordered Pat O'Kelly, Tommy Byrne and myself to go to the turnover berth and we went without a word. For a full half hour or more we worked there in silence; I couldn't bring myself to talk to either of them, most of the time I had my back to them. Suddenly, without any warning, I heard a scuffle behind me and I turned to see Tommy Byrne lying on the floor in a pool of blood and Patrick O'Kelly standing over him with a blood-stained knife in his hand. Quickly O'Kelly wiped the handle of the knife and then, before I knew what he was up to, he had thrust the knife into my hand. Then he proceeded to shout for help.

Patsy shivered uncontrollably. To think that all this was going on in Sean's subconscious, and so detailed, was to her mind a direct message from the other side as she experienced it. Dreams like this were not to be taken lightly. At their root was so much deep hatred and animosity carried over from the past through the ether of the spirit world that how could a nightmare of such foreboding not be a warning. It couldn't be ignored. She felt the presence of the two floaty children closing in around her.

It didn't take the men long to arrive and they saw me standing there with the knife in my hand and the dead body of Tommy Byrne lying on the floor still spilling out blood. I was held there by them, completely dazed by the whole thing, until the Guards arrived, and I was taken prisoner. Without a word I was led away and charged with murder.

I was thrown into a very dark cell and left there. I was still in a sort of stupor but as the metal door clanged shut something seemed to snap in my brain and I leaped at the door, tearing, biting, scraping and screaming, proclaiming my innocence to the world at large.

The warder who was on duty got fed up listening to me, he couldn't stand it anymore, so he opened the cell door, pulled me out into the corridor and hit me hard in the face with his fist. I fell to the floor and then he kicked me in the side with his heavy foot.

The next thing I remember was being in the courtroom on trial for murder. The evidence was all against me but the only thing that worried me was that you, my Sweetheart, weren't there. I couldn't understand why but it seemed to be only men in the courtroom. Through a haze I heard the judge pronouncing the dread words:

"Sean Fitzsimmons, I sentence you to be hanged by the neck until dead, and may God have mercy on your soul."

I fainted then and had to be carried back to my cell. The next scene of the dream happened in the death chamber, I had to be carried there, my legs wouldn't support me, and I was sweating terribly from fear of having to die such a death.

I was screaming out your name as the hangman placed the rope round my neck, and it started to tighten. The hangman pulled the lever, then my body was pulled up into the air then plunged into the darkness of the drop under the scaffold.

And wouldn't you know it, then the alarm bell rang for me to get up for work.

My Darling Sweetheart, can you imagine the state I was in when I woke up after that dream? But I suddenly remembered one great thing that dispelled the whole ugly thing from my mind — the thought that I still love you, my own darling sweetheart.

Till we meet on Friday I'll be dying to see you again.

Ever in Love with you,

Sean

XXXXX

Patsy carefully folded the letter and put it away in the envelope. She sealed the back with a kiss, tied the letter in red ribbon with Sean's other letters — she had saved every precious one of them — and then knelt down beside the bed, she needed the comfort of prayers. She wrapped herself in her blue cloak, draped the scapula over her hands and dedicated herself to Mary. "I desire henceforth to belong entirely to you, walking in your glorious footsteps and imitating your virtues: your angelic purity, your profound humility, your perfect obedience and your incomparable charity," she prayed. "O Powerful Advocate, obtain for me, from your Divine Son, perseverance in my good resolutions and the grace of being faithful to them all my life. Amen."

A knock on her bedroom door disturbed her holy contemplation and she heard her father shouting to her to come out. His face was red with anger and disgust when she opened the door. "Sean Fitzsimmons told us all about you secret day out in Howth," he said and walked away.

Patsy finished with Sean that Friday. She met him on the corner of Stephen's Green, he full of his usual enthusiasm at meeting her and anxious to outline his plan for their evening together, starting at Kavanagh's Refreshment Bar in Glasnevin, if she didn't think that was too far to go on a Friday evening, and then perhaps a stroll back towards the city or they could hop on a tram and get back into the city quicker and have a night-cap somewhere, whatever she wanted. Her answer was that she wanted to go straight home: she wouldn't be going out with him that night and she wouldn't be seeing him anymore.

He was heart-broken; he pleaded with her; he couldn't understand what had happened, he thought they were of a mind to spend their lives together and now she didn't want to see him anymore. Unless it was because of Mr O'Kelly and his opposition to their being together? Was it because of the bad feeling at work in the bakery? Because if that was the problem Sean could survive that nonsense, he had managed up to now and once they were married surely it would stop. Or was it because of that murderous dream maybe? He should never have written to her of that dream. He should never have told her about it, he knew she was a spiritual person and was deeply affected by what she regarded as omens and portents and things, and he realised it was a pretty ominous dream in that respect, but could they not just forget it?

Patsy surprised even herself as she explained her decision to the young man who had pinned his hopes on a future with Patsy at his side. She was only twenty, she said, but had decided to dedicate her life to God, not as a nun in a convent but out in the world as an ordinary woman living a single life, working at a job she loved and helping her mammy in the house. Marriage and its responsibilities and duties, both the emotional and the intimacy of the physical side, were not what she sought, she said, and it was only fair to tell him now so that he could find someone else. She knew he would make a wonderful husband for some lucky woman but not for her, no matter how much she loved him. She didn't want to be a wife. She didn't want what being a wife meant.

As she turned to leave and hurried away, Patsy knew she was going to cry. She quickened her step and rushed off towards O'Connell Street so that she could get lost in the crowds should Sean follow her: no matter how she disagreed with his opinions about what the Volunteers had done — and that meant her father — she might not be able to resist his pleas again. The bridge over the Liffey was busy with people and traffic so she swerved off to her left and crossed instead on the Ha'penny Bridge, preferring the closed-in feel of the narrow bridge and its almost single line traffic of pedestrians. She turned left off the bridge and walked along the river, sticking to the pavement across from the wharf wall to melt in with the late-shoppers and groups of people strolling along. She kept her head forward. She feared the pull of her loving, caring young man should she see him trying to catch up with her: the pull might prove too much.

Patsy tried to sneak into the house when she got back to The Coombe but a scene confronted her that meant she would have no time to dwell on any heartache or, possibly worse, have to avoid any probing questions as to why she was home so early on a Friday evening. Betty had gone into labour, a couple of weeks early, and the house was in full maternity-ward mode. Two local women, unqualified but very experienced in midwifery, had been called in to assist in the delivery: between them they had seen scores of The Liberties children born, including Betty's own four in the same bed in which she was now puffing and panting and trying to push out her fifth. Eddie and his brothers couldn't believe how much water had to be boiled and how many clean cloths fetched, with Molly and Theresa rushing up and down the stairs constantly from the kitchen to the bedroom with fresh supplies. Patsy was immediately delegated to oversee operations in the kitchen. It was obviously grown-up women's work, mysterious work, and the boys were happy out of it: they had no desire to see whatever it was that was involved. The youngest child, Annie, was crying because her mammy was making what sounded like screaming noises and in all the hubbub Patrick was doing what was expected of expectant fathers: he sat there quietly.

At last, he was summoned up to welcome his new baby, another son, into the world.

"Put the kettle on will you, Eddie?" said Molly, walking into the kitchen with a basket of cloths to be washed which she discreetly carried out to the shed under the pigeon-loft.

"More boiling water?" asked Eddie. He had thought the whole thing was finally over once he heard the sounds of a baby crying upstairs.

"It's for tea, you eejit," said Theresa. "Ciaran and Mikey, you get the cups ready and make sure you don't forget Mrs Flaherty and Mrs Doran, I'm sure they must be parched. Then the three of you can take some tea up to Mammy and Daddy and say hello to your new brother. He might as well get used to your ugly faces from the off. We need a sit down."

"What does the baby look like?" asked Mikey.

"The same as you did when you were born," said Theresa, "though I'm sure he's a lot handsomer than you ever were. Fortunately, he has the right number of fingers and toes and our mammy's fine but tired. She'll need to rest up for a while, especially," she said raising her voice, "after a nice cup of tea, Eddie, do you hear me?"

"I hear you, I hear you," he said.

"Can I go up to see Mammy?" asked Annie, recovered now that the drama was over.

"You can take up a few biscuits in case Mammy fancies something sweet," said Molly. "What about you, Patsy?"

"I'll give this lot a few minutes while I have my tea then I'll go up and shush them out, give Mammy a bit of peace and quiet," Patsy replied. "Does she need anything else?"

"No, she's grand," said Molly.

Mrs Flaherty and Mrs Doran appeared, chattering away about their latest home visit, praising Betty for being so little trouble and lauding the baby for being such a wonderful little bundle of trouble.

"I'll just pop out and get you something stronger to have with your tea," said Molly. She was the least reluctant of the older sisters to step inside The Cosy Bar on the odd special occasion to get a bottle of Paddy's: Theresa was too prim and Patsy too puritan, so they broached no argument. Then it was a toast all round. Evidently the new arrival was to be called John and glasses were raised to wet the baby's head and welcome little John into the world.

"Wait until the next generation starts arriving, by the grace of God," said Mrs Doran. "You girls are old enough to start thinking of being mothers yourselves, I'm sure. Children are such a comfort in a good Catholic home and, you never know, you might be blessed enough to give birth to a future priest. Baby John upstairs might grow up to become a fine priest. Wouldn't that be grand? What an honour that is in a family, a son with a vocation for the priesthood."

"I'd have been happy if just one of mine had had the vocation to be a plumber," said Mrs Flaherty. "Even one with an ounce of common sense would have been a godsend. I'd say 'amen' to that, all right." She raised her glass in the direction of the Sacred Heart picture on the wall. "It's all very well talking about the honour of having a son become a priest, Martha, but what sort of a life would you be wishing on him? A man sworn not to take a wife, as if we women were too unworthy for the holiness of the Church but at the same we're good enough to do all the cooking and cleaning in the priests' house."

"Cooking and cleaning is women's work, you can't deny that," said Mrs Doran. "You couldn't have the priests having to think about cooking and cleaning when they have a parish to look after, it wouldn't be right, Mary."

"It's even more all right for them because they don't have to clean and cook," said Mrs Flaherty, "someone else does it all for them, some woman. Maybe I should have become a priest."

"Now Mary you're just being deliberately controversial. You a priest, that's a sacrilegious statement to make."

"Never mind, Martha, I'll confess it next time."

A faint noise of hushed adult voices and excited children's voices wafted down as the various women sipped their whiskeys round the kitchen table.

"Just listen to that. You don't get any grandchildren from a son who's a priest, Martha, don't forget that," Mrs Flaherty piped up again.

"We're all their children, isn't that why we call them Father?" said Mrs Doran. "Priests need to be free of everyday distractions so they can look after all the families in the parish."

"Come on now, Martha, I can think of quite a few Fathers as easily distracted by a couple of drinks as the next man. Sure the bars are full every day of lost souls looking for redemption in the bottom of a glass," said Mrs Flaherty. "Is there any more in that Paddy's bottle, Molly? I'd like to raise a toast to us women's unworthiness."

"Well I'll join you in that," said Mrs Doran. "Maybe I'll find my own redemption in the bottom there."

"Let us know if you find it," said Mrs Flaherty. "It would give us a good excuse for another refill."

"Perhaps women should go on strike and refuse to do what's always expected of them," said Patsy. "Men don't want to clean and neither do a lot of women, where's the fun in cleaning, and not all women want marriage with lots of babies."

"Sure we do, it's only natural," said Mrs Doran. "Isn't that how we were made? Isn't that our role?"

"Well the good Catholic homes round here certainly keep you and me busy enough in that respect, Martha," said Mrs Flaherty. "There must be lots of bedtime shenanigans going on behind the holy net curtains of The Liberties, judging by how regularly babies are popped out. And believe you me, it's the husbands wanting the shenanigans after the pub and the women who have to then spend months carrying round the result while trying to look after the previous lot. Perhaps Patsy's right, we should all go on strike. The men would be lost, so they would."

"I thought we were all supposed to have been made in the image of God, men and women, equally," said Patsy. "And don't we celebrate the Virgin Birth with Mary, who became the Mother of God and had only one child through the Holy Spirit?"

Mrs Flaherty burst into laughter. "Patsy, love, there's many a conception come about through the intervention of a spirit but usually it's not a holy one," she said. "There's many a woman knows all about that. 'May the spirit be upon you' takes on a whole new meaning when your man comes home from the pub and he's all fired up, so to speak. Then it's your role to roll over and lift up your nightie, sure enough."

"You are getting far too irreverent for such a precious occasion as the birth of a child into the world," said Mrs Doran. "We've wet the baby's head, now I think it's time that we took our leave and left the O'Kelly family here to welcome its new member without having to listen to your nonsense, Mary. You're sounding like a Protestant."

"O heaven's no, I protest and I protest," said Mrs Flaherty, laughing so much she had to wipe the tears from her eyes. "But you're right,

Martha, it's time we left before I get so far down to the bottom of another glass that I drown out my chances of redemption on the way and then where would I be. 'Bless me father for I have sipped'. 'Say three Our Fathers and three Hail Marys, Mrs Flaherty, and I'll call round later to finish the bottle so you'll be free of further temptation'."

The women drained their glasses, gathered up their paraphernalia and made their farewells. "One of us will pop by tomorrow to check on Betty and the baby," said Mrs Doran. "It's to be hoped to God that you all get some sleep after the excitement. Have a good night, now, and God bless."

"Goodnight, now, and thanks for the Paddy's. It went down as smooth as holy water," said Mrs Flaherty.

Molly saw them to the door while Theresa cleared away the glasses. "Those two are better than some comedy acts," she said to Patsy. "Mrs Doran plays the straight one while Mrs Flaherty speaks the funny lines."

"I couldn't say a word, I didn't want to interrupt the flow," said Molly coming back into the room. "And what about your contribution, Patsy? Women going on strike, is that what you suggest? No more babies? We'll see about that when you're set up in your little love nest with Sean."

"I won't be living in any love nest with Sean," said Patsy. "I'm not seeing him any more. I told him so today. So there you have it, my extra contribution to your evening of comedy." She stood up and deliberately avoided the questioning looks of her sisters. "I'll go up and see to Mammy now. You two can sit here and tittle-tattle about me all you like. I'm sure you'll both have plenty to say, even you, Theresa."

6

The house was settling into the chaotic routine inevitable with the arrival of a new member of the family. Patrick made sure the rest of the household helped Betty as much as possible when they were home from work or school, though he either remained a fixture in his chair by the fire or busied himself out in the yard, the squabbling of the pigeons more attractive to his ear than the noise indoors. Annie was the most animated, delighted to find herself no longer the baby and trusted with being in charge of looking after her little brother: true he was lying in his cot most of the time but even when he was asleep she loved nothing better than to keep an eye on him, fussing around, folding and rearranging his miniature clothes, tucking in his blankets, tickling his cheeks and keeping up a constant commentary on what she was doing. She was fascinated by his tiny fingers and toes and liked it when he gripped her finger as if she was the most important person in the world and he wasn't going to let her go. John was the light of her young life.

What hadn't gone unnoticed was that the light had gone out in Patsy's eyes. Betty had tried to talk to her, anxious in case it had been Patrick's interference that had ended the romance with Sean, but Patsy remained non-committal, saying only that she had grown tired of him and had better things to do with her life than devote it to a man.

"You know he is leaving the bakery?" Betty asked.

"I know, he wrote to tell me. He's moving to Sandygrove with his mother," said Patsy. "They're moving into a big house, he says, with an indoor bathroom and electricity. Quite the modern place, he says."

"That could have been your house in the future, Patsy, wouldn't that have been grand, not having to get washed in the kitchen sink and not even able to shut the door properly. And you wouldn't have to go out in all weathers to use the toilet in the yard," said Betty. "They'll probably have real toilet paper too and not bits of old newspapers hanging on a nail behind the door. And I hear his mother isn't too well, a sickly sort of woman, from what I hear."

"Well, she has a fine son to look after her and he can do it without my help," said Patsy, "even with his fancy electricity. I have no intention of marrying a man because he has a big modern house where you can use the toilet indoors with a light on."

"I don't understand why you sound so bitter about him now," said Betty. "I thought you really liked Sean. Did he do something to upset you? Did he get fresh?"

"No, he just got stale, Mammy."

"Was it something your father did? Is that what happened? I could have a word."

"Leave it, Mammy, I'd had enough, that's all that happened. Now I'm going to my room for a lie-down. I'll be out to help with the tea later."

After Patsy had ended their relationship, Sean had still written to her as regularly as in the past but gradually his communications had dried up. His last letter informing her of the move to Sandygrove was a sad but lovely letter, heart-breaking, and Patsy's emotions swarmed in a mixture of concern for the young man she had once cherished and despair at her own resolution to ignore him.

I am coming back out of my prolonged silence to make one more desperate appeal to you to let me return to your favour as soon as possible,' he wrote. *'Last week I made three efforts in one day to write to you but as you hadn't answered my last letters, well, I just couldn't make it. I can't get the horrible feeling out of my system that you have met and are going with someone else. Believe it or not but I just can't get used to being without you.*

He inquired about the friends they had shared and her family: his own mother, he wrote, was really quite poorly but was too stubborn to let him call the doctor.

I don't want to take up too much of your time with details of my family life as I don't suppose it must interest you much now. I've partly got out of the habit of begging favours — you've shown me how useless it is. I've begged and implored you to let me come back but you don't seem to want anything to do with me. Perhaps now and again on a spare night (if you have any) you could drop me a line or two; I'd love it. In

spite of everything and everybody, even in spite of Hell itself, I love you,
   For now, and for all time,
   Sean.

With the letter he had enclosed the guarantee for the gold watch he had given her at Christmas: she had been thrilled to receive such a special present from so special a person and promised to treasure it always. Now she was resigned to treasuring the watch but discarding the man who had given it to her. Patsy was suffering terrible pangs of conscience after Betty had picked her up on being bitter in her attitude to Sean because she knew Betty was right, he didn't merit such scorn in her voice: she would not go back on her decision but he did deserve some sort of response from her. Once back in her room, she rummaged in one of the dressing table drawers and brought out a pad of paper and a pen and she sat down on the bed to write a reply to Sean's so-tender letter: how had she not done so already.

She thought and thought of what she could possibly say but nothing suggested itself: she had treated Sean's feelings of love and care and kindness in an unforgiveable, mean way, she knew that. She hadn't needed to be so abrupt, so curt, finishing with him after so long walking out together and then simply marching off without even a backward glance or a single word since. He had a right to expect more and she would try to make amends. She started her letter but only got as far as *'Dear Sean'* when there was an almighty hammering on the front door. Patsy rushed with the rest of the household to see what was the matter and the door was opened to a uniformed Garda holding Ciaran and Mikey by the scruffs of their necks.

"Is Mr O'Kelly at home?" asked the policeman. Patrick went to the front of the queue. "Are these two yours, Mr O'Kelly?"

"They are indeed and I'm ashamed to see them being escorted home by the Gardaí," said Patrick. "I have no idea what they've done but you have my permission to administer whatever punishment you see fit."

"That won't be necessary as far as we are concerned," said the policeman. "My sergeant recognised the name and address the boys gave at the station and he said he knew you from Ballykinlar and that you would know best how to discipline the two of them."

"Jesus, Mary and Joseph, what on earth did they do to end up with the Gardaí?" asked Betty making the sign of the cross, seeking divine intervention in her worry and embarrassment at the shame brought on the house.

"They were discovered in the Union Morgue trying to steal the pennies from the eyes of the dead, God rest their souls. More a case of terrible disrespect than anything seriously criminal to worry about," said the Garda. "I'll leave them in your capable hands, Mr O'Kelly."

The policeman released his grip on Ciaran and Mikey, who knew from experience that their father's punishment would hurt a lot more than being dragged through the streets by the collar, even if their feet were barely able to touch the ground so tall was their captor.

Patrick marched them through the house and out into the yard, collecting the leather strap from behind the kitchen door on the way, a strap with which the youngsters were only too familiar. One by one they were made to bend over, hands before them leaning on the wall, while their father administered the strap on their buttocks, ten belts each bottom. The boys howled as quietly as they could; they wanted to take their punishment like men but their father had a strong arm and it hurt too much to be able to stay too quiet for too long. The cacophony of the slap-slap beatings and the whimpering cries of the victims and the pointless protestations of Betty rose up easily through the confines of the yard and before long the pigeons in the loft were squawking and flapping about as if the end of their world was nigh and they were desperate to take flight. Eddie raced up the ladder to try to calm them but it was a thankless task and the birds flew about the loft in a loud blind panic and Eddie flew back and forth along the netting in his own 'there-there' panic and in his futile efforts he dislodged the ladder which clattered to the ground and got entangled in the rising strap and the arm holding it. Patrick, red-faced, panting, was apoplectic: a flow of rich Gaelic issued forth as he struggled to free the instrument of punishment from the ladder rungs. Betty was beside herself fussing about the baby trying to get him to sleep, with all the mayhem going on she hadn't realised that baby John was already exercising his lungs at maximum capacity. The noise crescendoed. The odd human head popped up momentarily above the yard wall as neighbours jumped up and down on their spots to catch the entertainment, always a reliable spectacle when Patrick O'Kelly got to work, you never knew what might happen, and the odd small body popped up on to the wall as neighbours' children claimed the best seats to enjoy someone other than themselves getting a good hiding. What a bonus it was to see grumpy Mr O'Kelly trying to extricate both the leather strap, and himself, from the ladder to carry on with the leathering. Their cheering added to the soundtrack.

Then suddenly it was all over. The strapping was finished, the victims' cries subsided into self-pitying moans, the spew of Gaelic was swallowed by the new peace that descended, the loft was gradually becalmed. The only discordant sound still escaping as the O'Kellys and the neighbours filed back into their own indoors was John's crying. Patsy and Molly took on the job of administering to Ciaran and Mikey, who had to be helped limping into the house clutching their buttocks and looking for a soft landing to rest them on, while Theresa saw to the gentler clatter of making tea for everyone. Patrick hung up the strap and resumed his position in the chair by the fireplace.

"You two," he said to the young offenders when they had successfully managed to lower themselves on to a couple of cushioned chairs, "you should be thankful that the sergeant knew my name and that the strap was all you got and not a few nights in the cells and a day in court. I want to know exactly what you've been caught at."

Mikey blurted out first, choosing the time-honoured excuse of shifting the blame on to someone else. "It was Nora's fault, she put the idea into our heads," he said.

Molly couldn't believe what she was hearing. "Nora? You're blaming Nora for the trouble you're in and bringing policemen to our door? Doesn't that beat everything?"

"Well, it was your friend who told us the story of the kids robbing the pennies in the morgue and you all thought that it was very funny when she was telling the tale," said Mikey. "We just went to see what she'd been talking about, that's all, but we didn't take any pennies from the corpses, honest Da, we didn't take any."

"That makes no difference. You were where you shouldn't have been, you had no business being in the morgue," said Patrick. "It's no place for comedy either," he said, "no matter how funny you thought Nora's story was."

Ciaran couldn't help it. Sore bottom or not, wrath of his father or not, he started to giggle to himself. All eyes turned on him.

"I'm sorry but it was funny, very funny," he said. He really couldn't help himself and carried on in the same vein, amusement lighting up his face regardless of the uncomprehending glances directed his way and the discomfort of being seated on a sore arse.

"I've never seen anything like it," he said. "There were sixteen or seventeen stone slabs arranged all in rows and bodies on most of them. They weren't covered up by big shrouds or anything, just bits of cloth pulled loosely across their middles and their heads and feet left there exposed for all to see. And the flies! There were hundreds of bluebottles buzzing around and landing on all the corpses' bits of bare skin and crawling around all over them. Jesus, that must have tickled and these people just lying there dead and not able to shoo them away. It seemed funny to me, all these people virtually naked except for flies covering them and no one paying them a blind bit of notice except for Mikey and me." He giggled again. "Talk about blind, their eyes looked like something drawn in an outer space comic. The pennies looked like robot eyes and as we moved between the slabs the light caught the pennies in different ways and it was as if they were following us and signalling to each other with little flashing winks."

Then Ciaran closed his own eyes and burst into proper laughter at the memory flooding into his mind.

"And then I shouted a warning to Mikey: 'Look out, Mikey,' I called, 'one of the corpses near you just moved'. Well, you should have seen him bolt out of the place, I never knew he could run so fast, and his face was as white as if he himself were a ghost. I couldn't move, I was laughing so much, and that's when we got caught. We were led back through the rows of slabs and that was the worst thing for Mikey, in case one of the bodies 'moved' again. Whoooo!"

Ciaran took in the reaction of his audience, the reluctant but creeping smiles that were starting to crease their grimaces of disapproval.

"I know we shouldn't have been there, Daddy, Mammy," he said, "but we honestly didn't do anything or touch anything, we only looked — in the case of Mikey, of course, you could say that he also ran." Ciaran looked at his brother and made running movements with his legs. "And

I'm sorry to say but it was really very funny."

Patrick wisely presided over a few moments of silence, partly because he himself could see the funny side and needed to wait to allow the right tone of admonishment to enter his voice, then he passed a secondary sentence on his sons. "The two of you can go to early morning Mass every day before school next week to pray for the souls of those poor people lying dead while you were enjoying the spectacle," he said. "And I'll be checking with the parish priest to make sure you don't miss."

The adults in the room were struggling to look serious but Ciaran felt the smile wiped off his face.

Patsy didn't reply to Sean's letter, beautiful though it was, but she had to find ways in which to fill those times in which in the past she would have been enjoying his company. Her weekly Tuesday outings with Margaret had been reduced to just once a month: Margaret was spending more time with her fiancé and they had started fixing up a small house near the canal so most of Margaret's spare hours were taken up with cleaning and painting the place to get it ready for them to move straight in after the wedding. According to Margaret, the walls of the end-terrace were thick enough so that even neighbours as prudish as Patsy wouldn't be disturbed by a single sigh of passion: all the same, as a precaution which Margaret knew would astound Patsy, the couple had decided that their bedroom would be on the outside end of the terrace: not for them any partition wall to facilitate a busy-body to listen up against it, glass to wall to ear. Patsy had been suitably astounded at such intimate planning by her friend but couldn't deny a frisson of envy for such freedom from guilt at purely physical pleasure.

Rather than mope round the house, Patsy volunteered to help out at The Little Flower Penny Dinners café on Meath Street. It wasn't far and they always needed help, especially on a Sunday morning as free breakfasts were given out to the destitute — men, women and children of the parish — who had attended nine o'clock Mass. It was little enough to do to earn a meal. At other times stew and bread were sold for a penny, the philosophy being that even a small charge would nurture an element of Christian self-respect in the needy. The grace of God would surely pass into them along with their food. The café was a bright and cheerful place, if somewhat basic, and provided Patsy with a welcome change of venue from work and home. It also fitted in with her Child of Mary determination to at least try to emulate the 'incomparable charity' of the Virgin Mother so she took to using up unwanted remnants from Jeanette Modes to run up patchwork tablecloths and bits of curtains for the place.

She was surprised and pleased to find that one of her co-volunteers was none other than Mrs Flaherty, the midwife.

"Aren't you the one to keep us guessing?" said Mrs Flaherty when she noticed Patsy. "I thought you were all for women going on strike and here you are, clear as day, doing women's work on top of your job. Are you not married yet? I thought you were near walking down the aisle with a young man, isn't that what your mammy told me? I won't be pencilling you in on my calendar of house-calls just yet then."

"No not yet," said Patsy, "though from what you were saying you have no shortage of house-calls. Is the parish still a hive of activity in the maternity department?"

"Sure The Liberties are productive enough to keep the Pope himself happy and Dublin at least full of good little Catholic souls," said Mrs Flaherty. "There's a non-ending supply born here by the minute. It keeps the priests busy and the shops in business with the steady trade in frilly Christening robes, white First Communion frocks for the little angels and white shirts for the boys, no doubt every one of them a little cherub. At least they wear short pants or there'd be plenty going up to the altar to put their tongues out while their knees were already out of their trousers. All that money wasted on fancy clothes and here we are trying to feed the hungry for a penny."

"I'd be out of a job if it weren't for people buying fancy new clothes," said Patsy, "though I doubt many of ours are sold in The Liberties."

"All the same we've a lot to be thankful for, praise be to God," said Mrs Flaherty. "I know I like to joke about the way the Church carries on, dictating to people non-stop about what they should and shouldn't do in their own homes and if I have to listen to one more gobshite sermon on the sanctity and importance of marriage from a man in a dress who hasn't a clue what marriage is really all about then I think I maybe will become a Protestant. Then Martha could go round telling everyone with an ear to listen that nothing that Mrs Flaherty did would ever surprise her. For all that I am grandly proud of the charity our local people show on a daily basis. This café couldn't exist without their kind donations and prayers."

"I'd say you must be one of the most charitable yourself, Mrs Flaherty," said Patsy. "You've a brood of children at home who need their mammy, a husband and a house to look after, you're always ready to help when a baby's on the way, yet you still find it in yourself to give up your time to helping at The Little Flower. For all your joking, Mrs Flaherty, you're a good and generous woman through and through."

"Through thick and through thin, as they say," said Mrs Flaherty, laughing, "through the thickness and stupidity of some of our reverend clergy and the thinness of most of the wretched bodies they're preaching to, who I'm sure sometimes take the host itself to give their stomachs something to digest while their souls get to work on digesting the lessons from St Paul to the Corinthians, whoever they were, not from The Liberties anyways. Come on now, Patsy, these onions won't slice themselves. Have a good cry over your young man if you want, tears of joy or sadness, no one will notice. Regardless of the excuse of the onions, people here have enough problems of their own to notice yours."

It was a case of constant supply and demand at the small dining room. No sooner had one set of customers finished up their stew than the next were sitting down, pennies collected, spoons in hand, waiting for the next serving. Patsy got to know all the volunteers and all the regulars, the ones who were bedraggled and with feet sticking out of their holey shoes, the ones who tried to keep up meagre appearances despite their poverty but still needed to eat. She learned which family had fallen on hard times through the father losing his job and the consequence of no food on the table, hence their arrival at The Little Flower, and which family had fared better through the sudden windfall of employment and sudden absence from The Little Flower. She heard all the local gossip, tongues loosened by the exercise of having food to moisten, many of the tongues belonging to people who lived on the street and didn't miss a thing. Patsy couldn't believe how much gossip was to be had not five minutes from her own house.

And of course there was the entertainment of listening to Mrs Flaherty. Irreverent she might be but Patsy thought she was far more

Christian than many who sat in the Sunday front pews. The woman took no nonsense from the café's customers but her abruptness was always in the form of a joke. She certainly wasn't there to judge anyone, she would declare, but being poor was no excuse for bad table-manners. "It's no sin to spill your gravy all over the cloth," she'd say, "but you don't have to then lick it up."

"How many children do you have?" Patsy asked her.

"I've two sons and three daughters and a flighty bunch the girls can be at times," said Mrs Flaherty. "I've my work cut out with them and their admirers. But then I suppose they are good-looking lasses, if I say so myself. There's more than a few pairs of eyes watching them fill out. They're good to me, mind, so I mustn't complain."

"Are your girls all going to get married, do you think? Are you expecting lots of grandchildren to come along?"

"Please God they have a bit of a life before all that business. Once you've a family you're trapped for sure and if you pick the wrong man you can't get rid of him. God wouldn't approve, evidently," said Mrs Flaherty. "How he approves so much of what the men make the women put up with is what I'd like to know. And what about you, Patsy? Are you not still seeing your feller?"

"No that's all over, that finished a long time ago. I wanted a bit of life before all that business, as you'd say."

"There's plenty of time, you're still just a girl yourself. You know people generally get married older in Ireland. I'd like to think it was because people had some common sense but it's probably because they spend too much time feeling guilty because they fancy trying a bit of sex and can't admit it. Then suddenly they can't wait for some wedding-night action so they say 'yes' to the first proposal and then it's too late. Mr Right suddenly seems so Mr Wrong, but the deed has been done and the kissing and cuddling that looked so good in the films turns out to be not quite as romantic and passionate as they'd hoped. When did you last go to the pictures and see the leading man grab at his leading lady and him in a drunken haze?"

"My daddy doesn't drink much."

"Your mammy's been lucky with him, then," said Mrs Flaherty, "though he's certainly as up for some bed sport as most men, judging by the number of children he keeps fathering. Doesn't he work down at Boland's bakery?"

"He does."

"Mrs Doran — you remember Mrs Doran? She delivers the babies with me, sure we've been to your house enough times to help bring a new one into the world — well she had a friend whose son worked at Boland's, a nice boy, by all accounts, but she was never a strong woman, always ailing. The boy's devoted to her, says Mrs Doran. He found them a new house to move into, all modern, so I believe, much easier for a sick woman to have an indoors toilet, of course, and he left the bakery, which was a pity because it was a good job and him with both a poorly mother and a big house to look after. Mrs Doran says they even have electricity in the place, that can't be cheap, sure it's not."

"I wouldn't know," said Patsy. "The son must have worked with my da."

"He probably did, right enough. What was the name now? Fitz something, Fitzsimmons, that was it, Mrs Fitzsimmons. Mrs Doran often mentions her, old school friends, evidently. Do you know the name? I believe the young Fitzsimmons is getting married soon but they live quite a way from here so I won't be pencilling them in on my next year's calendar either, unless Mrs Doran feels a sense of obligation when her friend's expecting a grandchild. Did you know the Fitzsimmons boy?"

"I might have seen him at the bakery but I'm not sure who is who there," said Patsy, almost in a whisper. "Is there any more cleaning up to do here, Mrs Flaherty? If not, I think I'll make my way home."

"You take yourself off, I'll be locking up in a few minutes ready to go home and start my next shift. Please God the girls won't have been up to anything scandalous in my absence. See you soon, Patsy, love. The Little Flower will be throwing her roses down on you for sure so let's hope you get the chance to enjoy the bouquet, though it will have its job cut out overcoming the smells of the brewery and God knows what else round here."

Back home in her room, Patsy finally put pen to paper to Sean, congratulating him on his forthcoming marriage and wishing him all the best for a holy and a happy life with his new partner.

His reply arrived a few days later and tore her heart in two.

My Dear Streaks,

I received your note, for which I was very grateful. It was mighty nice of you, although you were always that. It made me realise that at least no matter what I have lost or won I have at least one person whom I needn't be afraid to call friend. Thanks a million, Patsy.

I'm very glad you heard about the engagement because your good wishes go a long way towards making me believe that the world is not such a bad place to live in after all. I still think a whole lot of you, Streaks, I guess I never will change towards you. I told Eileen about you, probably that's why she'll never come into Dublin with me or let me go in either on my own — she's afraid I'll meet you. She's been so decent to me, she's only a kid and I'm very glad that I met her, she helps to soften the lump that you left me with. In fact, she often tells me that I'm still thinking of you and, sometimes, she doesn't be far wrong.

Yours, as long as I read and write,
Sean. XXX

7

Dublin was bedecked with religious ornamentation, the whole of the city like one magnificent fantasy cathedral, a spectacular stage-set, all to the glory of God. Candles were burning everywhere: they were alight in the thousands of grottoes made out of old packing cases or hurriedly mixed sand and cement which had sprung up in gardens and backyards behind the poorest of terraced houses; they were aglow with instant holiness in front of the hundreds of temporary shrines which stood in solemnity in the otherwise humble stairwells of even the most miserable of tenement blocks. Each mini tableau was a makeshift shelter dedicated to Christ himself, or to the Virgin Mary, or to some other saint. The Little Flower had a great presence, the gentle St Theresa of Lisieux being one of the most popular saints in Ireland. Then there was the dedication to the Sacred Heart: statuary and icons populated every building, every window and every windowsill, every shop, bank and business premises, the flames blazing out with love around the heart of Jesus warming the devout inhabitants of the city to their very souls. Dublin had become one huge religious repository. Flowers — some real, some twisted out of tissue or toilet-roll, others made out of ripped up bags which previously might have held a few weighed vegetables — hung across the streets in dancing garlands or waved festooned from lamppost to lamppost along the pavements.

The occasion was the hosting of the 1932 Eucharistic Congress in Phoenix Park, with Roman Catholic dignitaries from all over the world collected in the city for the event. It was one of the most significant gatherings in years on the Church's calendar, the venue chosen to coincide with the 1500th anniversary of the arrival of St Patrick himself in Ireland. Thousands of visitors had descended on Dublin for five days of fervour. Hotels were full, parlours in each home had turned into makeshift bedrooms, unused rooms in widows' houses had been snapped-up and fully booked. Camps were set up on open ground, schools and libraries had turned into hostels and even the town hall had been converted to help accommodate the overwhelming influx of people.

Patsy had attended several of the subsidiary events organised to coincide with the Congress. Her Children of Mary group had held a beautiful devotion in the parish church, the pews filled with Children past and present in a rippling sea of blue cloaks and white veils. She had visited an exhibition in a meeting hall by Stephen's Green highlighting Irish missionary work and confronted a confusion of conscience as to where might or might not lie her duties as a good Catholic. She had told Sean that she wanted to devote her life to God: perhaps, with this exhibition, God was showing her that missionary work would be a rewarding option. At the same time, she knew she didn't want to become a missionary: her devotion was to her faith and she had heard too many rumours about the terrible cruelty perpetrated by some nuns to want to risk joining them either at home or abroad. Patsy had also gone on one of the many retreats held in various local churches, hours supposedly spent in silent reflection and prayer.

Unfortunately, her human side had persistently got in the way of her spiritual contemplation. Matters of her own heart had taken over from the Sacred Heart, which was how she found herself in unfamiliar territory and not heading for Phoenix Park. She was also lurking; there was no other word for what she was doing.

The parish church she was outside now was also abloom with flowers, dotted at intervals along the path from the gateway, spilling up the few steps and framing the stone pillars of the main door that led worshippers straight into the central aisle, where simple but pretty posies had been tied to the carved ends of the front pews. It was a large parish church, vaulted, the vibrant colours of the stained-glass windows shining like a cache of jewels in the sunlight. To the front of the altar on either side, two large arrangements of red and white flowers kept colourful sentry: in the centre of each arose a tall, straight sunflower commanding its petalled farthingale. The sum total made for magnificent theatre.

The cast of players waiting off-stage here, however, were not Church dignitaries but ordinary people wearing their finest raiment as they milled about like small groups of extras chatting happily waiting for their cue: the men sported buff-shined shoes, starched white shirts and freshly-pressed suits, pink carnations secured in the jacket buttonholes and sharp creases down the trousers, blades to a one, cutting a dash; the women flounced in their new print frocks, the least and most expensive they could afford, and stretched their necks bird-like to show off to best advantage their decadent broad-brimmed hats, bought or borrowed. One woman, whom Patsy recognised as Mrs Doran the midwife, fussed around a rather weak-looking figure who needed a stick to walk, though she was obviously a person of significance for the occasion, judging by her fine-tailored cream linen suit and matching lace-trimmed bonnet, to say nothing of her face, which was positively beaming with motherly pride on her son's big day. Then the organ sounded a run of rich, resonant chords and everyone disappeared into the church, witnesses and guests at the wedding between Sean Fitzsimmons and Eileen Brady. Life didn't stop because a dates mix-up had made it clash with a Eucharistic Congress.

The groom lingered outside, checking for the umpteenth but last time with his best man that he had the ring convenient. He had and it was. The two of them exchanged a few words, smiled, shook hands and then hurried into the church still talking, still animated, the best man with a guiding arm around his friend's shoulders. After an eternity of a few minutes, a hire car pulled up at the gate. An explosion of white frills and ruffles puffed its way out of the saloon and Patsy saw for the first time her replacement in Sean's life: a beautiful young bride, standing shyly on the pavement on the arm of her father who held her bouquet as she smoothed down her dress and a bridesmaid lowered a full veil down over the bride's innocent-looking face. An usher rushed round to the side-door of the church and soon the strains of The Wedding March could be heard filling the nave, signalling the arrival of the bride. She processed inside to join her future husband.

Patsy was loitering in a tram shelter which afforded her a clear view of the proceedings across the road. She didn't want to be spotted so she had borrowed one of Theresa's coats, which Sean wouldn't recognise, and her curly hair, 'unmistakeable' he had always said, was well-hidden under one of Molly's pull-on hats. Underneath, Patsy had chosen to wear the black and white patterned dress which had been Sean's all-time favourite and which was a constant reminder of him whenever she wore it. It seemed to her to be sadly appropriate as she watched him go into the church and move officially out of her life. She had read the marriage notice in the newspaper and had crossed the city to see the wedding. The groom was once 'her Sean' and perhaps he was still and forever would be her Sean, 'for as long as he could read and write', he had written. Patsy shivered with pity for his new bride, a prayerful pity but pity nonetheless, whose rebound courtship must have been one of the fastest on record.

When the next tram came along, Patsy decided to jump on it; she had no wish to see the happy couple with their smiling faces leaving the church in a shower of well-wishing confetti and cheerful 'congratulations' but she wasn't allowed the quick, anonymous getaway she wanted. The crowded tram made slow progress; passengers joined in a chorus of complaints to the poor conductor. There was nothing he could do, no more could the driver: the roads were snarled with traffic and there were uniformed police on duty on every corner. The papers had been full of the details of the preparations for the Congress and had warned of inevitable delays for anyone moving about the city. Patsy said a quick prayer for forgiveness at having put a wedding she had no business attending before making sure she was on time for the holy business of the Church.

"You know John McCormack is singing at the Mass in Phoenix Park today," the woman in the seat next to her said. "Is that where you're headed? To the park?" She gave Patsy no opportunity to reply. "I was hoping to get there myself but I'm not sure it's at all possible now with roads so busy. I suppose we should have known. My friend set off real early this morning to make sure she got a good place, though to be honest with you I think she's more intent on seeing John McCormack in the flesh than any of the bishops. He has a lovely voice, wouldn't you agree? My heart just melts when I hear him sing *The Minstrel Boy*."

Patsy knew the song well. McCormack was a renowned opera-singer but he had good Republican credentials and Patsy had heard lots of his nationalist recordings. "I love that tune too, it can bring tears to your eyes right enough," she said, not wanting to ignore the woman's friendliness.

"I've decided it might be better now to head straight for O'Connell Street, there should still be room not too far from the bridge. That's where the Pope's representative is going to give a public blessing," said the woman. "It should be grand. They're all to move in a religious procession all the way from the park right into the city centre, though I'm not sure John McCormack will be with them. Still, you can't have everything when you're late. A blessing from the Pope's man will have to do."

"I'm sure a Papal Benediction wouldn't go amiss for any of us," said Patsy.

"Then there are the big ships," said the woman. "Have you seen them? I have, I went to have a look. That's a sight, all right, especially at night when they're all lit up. There are huge ones, liners, I think they call them, anchored out in the bay and along the quays. The papers described them as 'floating hotels' for all the visitors. I wouldn't mind trying one of those. The nearest thing I've ever got to a hotel is a weekend with the in-laws in a run-down cottage in Wicklow and I doubt you'd get his mother anywhere near a boat so that would suit me fine."

The woman prattled on, about John McCormack, about the ships, about the greatness of the occasion, of Dublin being so honoured to have the Congress hosted in the city and how proud it would make St Patrick himself up there in heaven looking down on all his faithful converts. The journey was slow but the woman's conversation never faltered. Patsy's mind would occasionally return to Sean's wedding or would roam the cliffs above Dublin Bay imagining herself with Sean, staring at the liners and listening to whatever information he had learned about the whole proceedings, but the woman next to her was determined not to shut up.

Patsy decided to get off the tram and walk the rest of the way. She had planned to go as far as O'Connell Bridge but pressing through the crowds already gathered en masse in O'Connell Street was impossible. She sought out a vantage point, such as it was, and prepared to wait.

There was a loudspeaker system relaying the Mass direct from Phoenix Park and even in their thousands the people listened with heads bowed and as one chorused the Latin responses to the liturgy, their murmurings repeated with split-second delays down the length of O'Connell Street. As the Mass drew to a close, general conversations started up while everyone waited for the procession to pass: the Blessed Sacrament was to be carried through the streets from the park to the bridge where an impressive altar had been erected for the Benediction service.

It took a while but eventually the spectators got their rewards. It was a long but inspiring parade, the different coloured vestments shimmering along like a moving rainbow. President De Valera was in the vanguard with the Papal legates: the irony wasn't lost on many in the throng for the same Church had excommunicated that same De Valera for his role in the Civil War.

"All's forgiven now," said a man next to Patsy but addressing no one in particular, "as if it should have happened in the first place, as if you can separate Catholicism from politics in Ireland. You see all these bishops and what-have-you in their fancy embroidered robes and you can't help but wonder if they know anything at all about the place they've come to."

"Whisht, will you keep your gob shut," said a woman nearby. "That's God's representatives on earth you're talking about."

"God's representatives?" said the man. "Leave God out of it, woman. Some of these men don't seem to have an ounce of common sense to call their own never mind pretending to represent God. Which of these Catholic eejits decided to excommunicate the Catholic leader of one of the greatest Catholic countries there is, that's what I'd like to know. If you could tell me that, woman, I'd be all ears, but I doubt you were consulted on the decision. It's a grand show they're putting on all right in all their robes but give me our own parish priest any day. Him you can trust."

The debate was brought to an end with a message over the Tannoy system that Benediction was about to begin. Heads bowed in reverence once again, signs-of-the-cross finger-flitted across torsos, rosary beads were held up to the lips to be kissed as private prayers were whispered to the Almighty and his Blessed Mother. Patsy made a special intervention on behalf of the new Mr and Mrs Fitzsimmons and then a general "Amen" hummed its way from the bridge to be taken up by the congregation.

Part 3

Though lads are making pikes again
For some conspiracy
And crazy rascals rage their fill
At human tyranny,
My contemplations are of Time
That has transformed me.

— W B Yeats

1

Patsy had agreed to stay on later than usual at Jeanette Modes. She had risen in the fashion establishment to become a valued hands-on supervisor, fully knowledgeable in all the techniques needed in both the cutting and the sewing departments and with that unequalled tactile intuition she had where fabrics were concerned: she knew without question which materials would most suit which designs and patterns. "There's no denying your fingers are sensitive feelers," the other girls ribbed her, "but they're wasted on cloth, Patsy, it's time you found some lucky man to start using them on. Feel something worth feeling, why don't you, something substantial to get your hands round and tug into shape. You'd be a different woman altogether."

Patsy went along with the joke: "He'd certainly end up a different man," she said, making scissor motions with her hands and various unsubtle comments on the basic theme of cut-and-run.

She surprised herself sometimes: she was by nature somewhat prudish, she knew that, but somehow the women-only company of the sewing room dispelled her reservations and she enjoyed the often risqué repartee. She thought it was perhaps because she felt safe in that environment, where there was nothing to fear in the way of real sinful temptation, just jokes and jibes. The girls would bait her with unmistakeable innuendoes to prise some priceless aside from her, always accompanied by the scissors mime and shared laughter. It made the working day a happier day.

It was important to Patsy that she had remained popular, still one-of-the-girls. Her rise in the ranks hadn't created any rifts with her co-workers. Unlike her predecessor, Patsy realised instinctively the value of a happy workplace and as supervisor she didn't insist on silence at the machines: the other women repaid her attitude by getting on with their work and not taking advantage of her easy-going nature to skimp behind her back.

Her outgoing personality meant she was also entrusted to deal with clients and customers front of house, both the big buyers and the individual who entered Jeanette Modes with slight trepidation: Patsy inspired everyone with confidence. She reassured the fashion houses that Jeanette Modes would provide them with consistent quality and guaranteed delivery times, while she equally put at ease any woman calling in for a one-off outfit but perhaps feeling intimidated by the reputation of the place.

This evening she was staying on to discuss the designs and fabrics required to win a big order from one of the growing stores in the city. It was a valuable contract for Jeanette Modes: it alone would keep the sewing-room working at near full capacity for months and could well lead to further substantial orders in men's and women's fashions and so greater job security for the women and, with luck, an end-of-year bonus. Patsy was eager to secure it for the company and for her colleagues, please God. She was to meet the buyer for the store, a Mr Jeremy Murphy. She couldn't decide whether or not the name suggested an Englishman or an Irishman, it sounded like a mix of the two and she speculated on what a Mr Jeremy Murphy might look like while she waited for him to arrive. Normally a meeting about such a major contract would involve the owner of Jeanette Modes but he was off to the Abbey Theatre that night, with supper afterwards, an anniversary treat for him and his wife, and he had left his trusted supervisor in charge.

It was as well that Patsy had sent word to The Coombe that she may be quite late home from work because, whoever he was, Mr Jeremy Murphy was already half an hour late. Patsy looked out of the window on to the street to see if she could pick out a likely candidate but it had started to rain and all she could see were brollies moving quickly en masse. She would have missed the rain if she'd left work at the usual time but now she would get wet going home as Annie had borrowed her umbrella and, typical of scatter-brained Annie, had left it at a friend's house.

"Thank you," she said aloud. "Thank you very much, Mr Jeremy Murphy, wherever you are."

"I'm right here, my good lady, and for what are you thanking me exactly?" said a voice. "I haven't extended the least courtesy to you yet,

201

in fact quite the opposite. I'm much later than we had arranged and I'd say that's quite a discourtesy, wouldn't you agree?"

Patsy turned and saw in front of her a rather dapper man, nattily dressed in a suit of broad brown and yellow check tweed and a dark wool Crombie overcoat, which was flapping open as he stood his wet brolly up by the door to drip and relieved his hands of some calf-skin gloves.

"Jeremy Murphy at your service, my good lady," he said, extending his right hand in a most gentlemanly way. "Very pleased to meet you, Mrs? Miss?" he said, shaking Patsy's hand, eyebrows raised questioningly. "I do apologise most sincerely for my tardiness. I hope it won't cause any problems between us. May I?" he indicated a chair.

"Do sit down, Mr Murphy," said Patsy. "And I in turn apologise for my fit of impatience, which you obviously heard so I can't deny it."

"Then we are even, my good lady. I'm afraid I was delayed by the weather. Such a sudden downpour, so unexpected I had to return to my office to fetch my gamp. Then I positively ran from the store to keep our appointment, as much as one can run when there are people sploshing about hither and thither, unseeing under their brollies and poking everyone else in the eye with their spokes and knocking all in their path out of the way in the battle to escape the not-so-heavenly water from the skies. Dear God knows how to rain down his wrath in a very direct manner. And the puddles! There are puddles everywhere to be avoided if you can and the traffic is positively moving at a snail's pace — there was no point whatsoever in me hailing a taxi, a welcome refuge though it would have been — but still making it difficult to cross the road, of course. Then some individual drivers do, of course, delight in locating any of the deep puddles collected along the kerbside so they can speed through them and give us pedestrians quite a deliberate but undeserved drenching as they pass. I got soaked several times, just look at the state of my trousers."

He stuck both legs out straight for a summary inspection of dirty splashes then relaxed back into the chair. "And you are?" he asked, taking a breath and fixing his eyes on the beneficiary of his arrival.

"I'm Miss Patsy O'Kelly and I've been authorised to deal with your requirements and to answer any questions you might have regarding what Jeanette Modes can do for you. 'Your business is our business,' as we like to assure our clients," said Patsy.

"Then let's get down to that very business, yours and ours, and then I'll take you out for a nice dinner at the Gresham by way of compensation for keeping you so late. I think that would be a suitable gesture, don't you?" he speculated. He didn't wait for Patsy to answer but instead brought out a roll of order forms from the pocket of his Crombie and spread them out on the table.

"We know the high standard of work to expect from Jeanette Modes, Miss O'Kelly, that's why I'm here in your fine establishment, so you can forget whatever sales-talk you had prepared and, if you don't mind, we'll get straight down to costings and delivery times," said Mr Murphy.

"Of course, you're the client."

"Indeed, I am, Miss O'Kelly, indeed I am."

It was a big order: it included men's suits and women's costumes, both formal and casual, suitable for indoors and outdoors; winter-weight overcoats for gentlemen, some with a velvet trim on the lapels; a range of ladies' dresses to cater for all occasions, from fashionable smart daywear to more traditional evening ball gowns. Most of them were to be produced in multiples of ten in sizes from small to extra-large "for the discriminating but more casual customers", said Mr Murphy, while some specialist lines were to be made in one-off samples of varying sizes, to be subject to further rush orders if required. Patsy pulled out bales of different fabrics she recommended as appropriate, running her hands over the cloths and remarking on their textures.

"You seem to have very sensitive fingers, Miss O'Kelly," said Mr Murphy. Patsy couldn't help but smile at the reference. "That we have in common. I too love to run my hand over textiles, to feel their softness or to explore the rhythm in the regularity of the woven threads. Such simple tactile pleasures are grossly under-rated, wouldn't you agree, Miss O'Kelly?"

Patsy watched as her client delighted in playing with the materials, gently billowing them into light-catching folds, then smoothing them out again and patting their flatness lovingly with the palms of his hands.

"Then it would appear you must be very happy in your job," said Patsy. She had never before encountered a man with so responsive an attitude to the multitude of properties inherent in even the simplest fabric available: she had always thought it was more of a woman's thing.

"This one, you understand, Miss O'Kelly," he said, holding up a length of vibrant Chinese silk and brushing it against his cheek, "this one conjures the idea of the wearer almost hovering above the floor as she glides easily and without apparent purpose through some exotic but lush surroundings, chandeliers dripping droplets of light to shimmer over her every move and large pot-plants strategically placed to add a verdant setting to her meanderings." He turned his attention to a bale of ebony-dark worsted, with a note of reverie in his narrative: "This would clothe her companion in undoubted sophistication, as if he himself was a reflection of the smoothness of the finely-combed woollen fibres." He paused, eyes closed, lost in the scene of his own imaginings.

"Are we ready to sign the order forms, Mr Murphy?" interjected Patsy, "or are you yourself now hovering without apparent purpose?"

Her companion let out a raucous belly laugh. "I like you, Miss O'Kelly," he said. "Let's get the paperwork done and dusted and we'll head out for some nourishment. You will come, I hope. My treat, at least the store's treat. You can order whatever you fancy and I'll charge it to the firm. After all, you have had to work late on our account, literally as well as figuratively."

Patsy visibly hesitated.

"Come on now, my good lady, isn't it all part of the Jeanette Modes philosophy, putting the client's business first? That's all you'll be doing, no funny business only company business, I promise." said Mr Murphy. "After all, the way these meetings work I'm bound to have forgotten to ask a vital question or two and this way you'll still be on hand to voice the right answer, lubricated, perhaps, by a glass of fine wine. Get your coat, now, Miss O'Kelly, I'll broach no disagreement. You can share my umbrella if we end up having to walk."

"But I'm not dressed for the Gresham, I'm still in the working clothes I've had on since I got up this morning," Patsy objected.

Mr Murphy pursed his lips and nodded his head by way of understanding her predicament. "Wait now and we'll see," he said. He took a step back and studied Patsy's figure, then flipped along a rack of frocks and picked out a smart but simple cocktail-style dress of cerise satin. "I'm sure this one will do splendidly. Slip it on and we'll be on our way."

"I can't just take a dress."

"Of course you can. Bring it back tomorrow if you prefer, plenty of the otherwise impeccable grand ladies of Dublin do exactly that: wear and return unpaid to the store the next day, claiming the dress or whatever wasn't the right fit after all, too tight over the arse, perhaps, or too revealing of their over-plump bosoms, though it was perfectly fine when they tried it on in the store, of course, preening and posing before full-length mirrors reflecting them from every angle and every vantage point. That's how they stay rich, you know: they keep up appearances turning out in a different outfit every night when parading in the city and half the time it's not costing them a penny. If you can't allow yourself to cheat like that — and you don't look like a cheater, Miss O'Kelly, — you can charge it to my company."

Patsy felt in no position to decline Mr Murphy's invitation to continue their meeting elsewhere, albeit in the restaurant of the Gresham. Things were going well over the order and she didn't want to risk losing it now. And what harm could there be? It was only a meal and a drink with a client. If she were to rise even further at Jeanette Modes, these sorts of situations might arise at any time and she'd best get used to it.

She disappeared into the ladies' room, wiped some wet tissue under her armpits for a quick freshen-up and put on the dress. It looked perfect: the colour suited her and the fit couldn't have been better. She combed her hair quickly, put on a bit of lipstick and re-joined the man who was to be her escort for the evening.

"You've an excellent eye, Mr Murphy," she said, feeling quite the impeccable grand lady herself in the satin creation he had selected.

"I can't argue with you there, Miss O'Kelly. Let me take a look at you. Turn around." Patsy did the honours, raising her shoulders and spreading out her 'sensitive fingers' at the end of outstretched arms as she did a twirl. "Perfect," said Mr Murphy. "Won't I be the envy of all the gentlemen in the room and perhaps some of the ladies too, though secretly, of course."

"I'm sure all the women will be just as well-dressed," said Patsy.

"That's not quite what I meant, my good lady, but we'll let it pass. Come on now, let's take on the might of the Almighty together."

Patsy was in a daze for the whole week after her evening's adventure. Her boss was excited and relieved that she had landed such a prestigious contract for the fashion house and her colleagues constantly pored over the designs they were about to start turning into reality: paper patterns had to be devised and cut and replicated in different sizes; threads of cotton, wool and silk in a range of colours had to be ordered: bales of cloth had to be sourced and delivered to meet such a varied bulk order.

For Patsy there was more to it than work, though she was justifiably heady with the professional status her success had bestowed. Her spontaneous night out with Mr Murphy had reminded her that she had almost forgotten how to enjoy herself. Unlike her progress in the workplace, her personal life had plummeted over the last few years. Her voluntary sessions at the Penny Dinners café and her weekly Children of Mary group hardly constituted what even a devout Catholic like Patsy would call a social whirl.

After Sean's marriage, Patsy had indeed fulfilled Mrs Fitzsimmons' fearsome prophecy — three times a bridesmaid, never a bride. Patsy had been up the aisle three times in attendance as a bridesmaid and there were two more outings pencilled in for the future. Her sister Molly was set on eventually moving to Liverpool to wed her cousin Kevin, after she'd spent further wild times in Tullamore on the protective arm of her cousin Robert or having a laugh at the skating rink out at Blackrock with Nora, while Theresa was planning her own walk up the aisle with her childhood sweetheart, Billy. Theresa had never been interested in enjoying 'wild times', she was far too sedate for that, though Billy himself was certainly developing a merry streak. Patsy had been asked to do the honours for both weddings on the distant horizon. Eddie meanwhile was growing into a handsome young man, muscular and capable and with a fine humour about him, none of which had escaped the notice of the local lassies who found myriad excuses to accost him in the street during his coal round or to call at the house on the off chance of seeing him and then drooling when they did. With all this hearts stuff going on, Patsy knew she was already regarded as a potential spinster, still rather young to be called a spinster but unmarried nonetheless and not a courting-man in sight. She had cared little about her somewhat sad reputation, content with her choices in life. Then suddenly one night she had had to work late and everything had changed. Her evening with Mr Murphy had shaken her equilibrium: Patsy had no desire to become a flighty type but nor did she want to be old before her time. She might not be looking for a husband but she did want some fun in her life.

At least her Tuesday nights out with Margaret had recently been resurrected. Once over the first flush of marital bliss and with a baby already a toddler and herself back at work part-time, Margaret was ready to hit the town with Patsy again. She was lucky to have Duggie for a husband — he positively enjoyed spending quality alone-time with his daughter — and a friend like Patsy with whom she could go out and never worry about looking as if they were loose women out on the prowl. That made Duggie feel easier too. The friends slipped so easily back into their seats at Bewley's it was as if they had never been away.

"My God you look grand in that dress, Patsy," said Margaret, noticing that her friend had taken her coat off almost immediately and had stood lingering for all to see as she carefully folded and draped her coat on the back of the chair. "What colour do you call that, cerise?"

"You do," said Patsy.

Margaret had a discreet feel of the cloth.

"And satin, if I'm not mistaken?" Margaret was impressed.

"You're not," said Patsy, suddenly unsure of her choice of wardrobe for the evening. "Do you think it's too much for a coffee at Bewley's?"

"Nothing is ever too much for Bewley's," said Margaret. "And let's face it, where else would Patsy O'Kelly of The Coombe be able to wear such a frock, no offence intended."

"None taken, you've echoed my thoughts exactly," said Patsy. "I have it, I might as well wear it, though not perhaps when I'm doing a shift at the Little Flower."

They elegantly positioned themselves on their chairs and took in the room. They had lost none of their affectations. Packets of cigarettes were elegantly produced from handbags, no rummaging allowed; fingers were wafted in the air, supposedly adding a dramatic dimension to their so-obviously-riveting conversation; menus were studied in a nonchalant way to suggest that treats in Bewley's were not actually treats but merely a matter of routine in their social calendar. They ordered their coffee and cakes while scanning the other customers. Patsy was wearing by far the most enviable frock and she bobbed her curly hair to full effect, inducing a positive halo of bubbles around her head. Oh, such elegant freedom she felt, worrying at the same time if she was committing the sin of pride.

"You'll never believe who's off to Hollywood," said Margaret, consciously raising her head and her voice slightly to share such an irresistible opening sentence with people on the adjoining tables, "or so they say anyway," she whispered conspiratorially. She had dropped the bait: anyone wanting to hear more would have to strain their ears and work for it. "It was the talk of the machine room yesterday but I've not seen anything in the paper about it. Did you hear?"

"Not about anyone going off to Hollywood, no," said Patsy.

Margaret posed, chin up, and drew in a couple of long drags of her cigarette; she exhaled the smoke into the air, tapped a bit of residue into the ashtray, busied herself picking a stray bit of tobacco from her tongue and grinned at Patsy, spinning out the moment. She was a natural at dramatic effect.

"Go on then, Margaret, don't keep it to yourself now that you're after mentioning it," said Patsy. "Who's off to Hollywood?"

"Well, it's none other than Maureen Fitzsimons, you know who I mean? The redhead? Her father owns that big clothing house in Dublin? It was one of the needlewomen there who heard it, then she told her sister who works with us and then of course the sister had to tell us," said Margaret, "so hopefully there's some truth in it as it'll be all over the city by now and the shame for the poor girl if there's nothing to the rumour. You know what it's like, not much gets past the women in a sewing-room, especially when the shush comes and it's 'heads down and stop talking', then beware anyone with anything in any way confidential to whisper as there'll be lots of ears just primed to take it all in."

Patsy was suitably impressed. As gossip went, this was among the more sensational; it wasn't every day you heard of someone you knew going off to Hollywood.

"It's said that she tried her hand at a bit of acting at the Abbey Theatre when she was younger but didn't get far," said Margaret. "And now she's off to Hollywood. Now I'd say that's far enough, wouldn't you? Over the sea and far, far away from Dublin and the Abbey and sod the lot of them."

"You know she went to school in The Liberties," said Patsy, "that fancy girls' school near Thomas Street. That's what a fancy school does for you. Sure we all went to school in The Liberties too but we're not off to Hollywood."

"Well now I don't know about fancy schools but I gather she's a nice enough girl, no airs and graces about her, so I'm told," said Margaret. "Then again how could there be, hasn't she after all been working as a typist in Crumlin Laundry."

"She'll be able to wash her hands of all that now."

The two friends laughed but only quietly, more of a titter really; they had to maintain their poise as the last crumbs of their pastries were dabbed away on their Bewley's napkins and the main business of savouring the coffee began.

"Sure that's grand," said Margaret, sniffing over the cup and taking in the aroma with an expression of expert delight. "It beats the hell out of the smell of nappies and baby puke, I don't mind telling you." The friends sipped their coffees and again scoured the room with their all-seeing eyes. "You never know, Patsy, maybe there's a talent scout in Bewley's tonight and we'll be spotted too and whisked off to cinematic stardom. Would you be up for that?"

"I'm not sure it would be the life for me and God knows what my father would say."

"Just as well it's highly unlikely then," said Margaret, "not that I'd say 'no' to being in a clinch with some handsome film star. 'Take me, I'm yours,' I'd say, then he'd sweep me up in his strong arms and whisk me off to his Beverly Hills mansion where I would lead a life of sheer decadence. I wouldn't have to do any cooking or cleaning, no sewing and mending, I'd just have to tend to myself and my hunking hero."

"Sure, and you'd hate it," said Patsy.

"But I wouldn't mind sampling it in order to make a proper decision on the matter, to love it or loath it based on experience."

Margaret turned to Patsy with a quizzical look on her face. "Maureen Fitzsimons," she said, "wasn't 'Fitzsimons' Sean's name? You don't know if they're related, do you?"

"Sean's name had a different spelling," said Patsy, "two 'm's."

"That's a shame, you could have found some excuse to renew your acquaintance and we could have had a chance to mix with the Hollywood set next time they were in Ireland."

"I don't think renewing my acquaintance with Sean would ever be an option, with or without Hollywood as the attraction," said Patsy. "Even before he was married, she wouldn't let him come into the city centre any more in case he bumped into me."

"'She' wouldn't would 'she'? Isn't 'she' the cat's mother?" But Margaret recognised that a discordant note had been sounded for her friend. "Are you over him, do you think?" Margaret signalled for the waitress to bring a couple of shots of whiskey to the table. "I know you don't approve, Patsy, but it's for fortification," she said, "just in case you need it. And if you don't I do. Wouldn't it be grand if someone invented nappies that you could just throw away in the bin and not have to do all the soaking and bleaching and shit-stain scrubbing. I'd certainly be up for an invention like that."

"Perhaps by the time you're on duty as a grandmother."

They clinked their glasses with a sláinte and savoured their Paddy's.

"Did you know Paddy's is called Paddy's after one of its salesmen?" said Margaret. "Duggie was telling me, and you know how fond Duggie is of his whiskey."

"I assumed it was something to do with St Patrick being the patron saint," said Patsy.

"Well, the salesman was indeed Irish and called after his patron saint, right enough," said Margaret. "Paddy Flaherty was his name, and he was supposed to be the best salesman in the country. I don't know about that but what I do know, according to Duggie anyway, is that Paddy Flaherty would visit all the pubs in Ireland and everywhere he went he'd buy a round of whiskey for the customers. Then whenever all the various landlords ran out of whiskey, they'd write to the distillery in Cork and order deliveries of 'that whiskey Paddy Flaherty sells'. He sold so much like that they decided it was easier to name it after him."

"My mammy's midwife is a Mrs Flaherty," said Patsy.

"Then the business of deliveries obviously goes with the name," said Margaret and the two friends tittered again. "As we are still talking about familiar names," she ventured after another sip, "you didn't answer my question about your Mr Fitzsimmons. Are you completely over him now?"

"Sean was years ago," said Patsy. "I still miss him sometimes, I'd be lying if I didn't admit it, we got on so well together, but I've never regretted finishing with him."

"I never really did understand why you did that," said Margaret. "You seemed at the time to be head over heels about the man."

"I was and then I wasn't, that's all there was to it."

"And what did your da have to say about it, he didn't like the man, I remember. Sure, he must have been pleased?"

"My da has never mentioned it, not once in all this time. He didn't even tell me when Sean left the bakery or why. Now let's change the subject, why don't we," said Patsy. "I haven't told you yet about my night out at the Gresham."

"At the Gresham? In O'Connell Street?"

"The one and only."

"Have you come into money and not told me? You're the sly one." Margaret was all ears, leaning over the table waiting to hear the tale.

"That's how I got this dress," said Patsy. She had been dying to tell someone about her evening out with Jeremy Murphy but there was no suitable confidante at work and she hadn't wanted to get the family, especially Molly and Theresa, buzzing with speculation. With Margaret she could describe the full circumstances of her staying late to meet an important buyer, who he turned out to be, his invitation to dinner and how he had overcome her hesitancy by snaffling the satin dress right off the rail with a cursory but seasoned eye and how, on such the briefest of acquaintance, he had insisted on paying for the said dress himself.

"Praise be to God, and then he whisked you off to the Gresham?" Margaret was open-mouthed.

"We had to walk because there were no taxis, it was a terrible rainy night, but he held his umbrella up over me the whole way, more over me than over himself, in fact."

"Jesus, Mary and Joseph, how gallant, a real gentleman," gushed Margaret. "All the men I know would just leave you to get soaked while they hugged their own miserable brolly to themselves. Okay, and so you got to the Gresham?"

"Sure it was grand, I felt like royalty the way he took my elbow and guided me right across the hotel lobby and into the restaurant. He asked for a table near the window, to afford a view of the whole room — he wanted to be able to see the other diners, he said, so he could pick out which outfits had been bought in his store. The tables were set beautifully, with a small bowl of flowers on each and linen napkins rolled up in silver bands, the cloths were pristine white, not an ironing crease or a fold to be seen, and the glassware was like Waterford crystal. I was immediately nervous at the sight of the different bits of cutlery lined up, three or four different knives and forks at the sides and a motley collection of spoons across the top. 'Jesus,' I thought, 'which one do I use and when?' He ordered the food — I couldn't tell you the fancy names they had for the dishes on the menu — but basically we started with a small plate of fish of some sort. He saw me suffering a bit of confusion and without saying a word he indicated which knife I should use for the fish, a funny flat thing with a point on the end, not like your ordinary knife you'd have in the kitchen drawer."

"I doubt they'd have anything in the Gresham that you'd have in your own kitchen drawer," said Margaret, "certainly not in the kitchen drawers you and I have known. As for the spoons, we've a choice of teaspoon or pudding spoon and that's your lot. Cutlery seems to be a world you have to have been born into, Patsy, and we weren't. Well, go on, tell me the rest."

"He insisted that we have the finest steaks: he asked for his rare but I for some reason of contrary devilment decided to have mine well done, and I was glad I did when I saw how much blood oozed out on to his plate when he cut into the meat, like a pool of weak red gravy. It was accompanied by what they called 'seasonal vegetables' and here was me all the while thinking that you could only have vegetables when they were in season, otherwise they wouldn't be available."

"It makes them sound posher, I suppose," said Margaret, "more special anyway than just 'carrots and cabbage'."

"There was no cabbage, Margaret, now isn't that a strange thing, to be eating in Dublin and not have cabbage?"

"You're obviously low-born, Patsy O'Kelly. You can't judge all menus by what Betty puts on the table in front of your tribe at home.

Let's forget the food order and get down to brass tacks. What was this Jeremy Murphy like? Is he a good-looking man?"

"I'd say so but not in the standard sort of way. He dresses very well, colourfully, you'd say, with a slight theatrical air about him."

"Would you see him as a potential?"

"I don't see any men as potential or otherwise," said Patsy, "you know me well enough not to ask such a question, but it was a grand adventure for sure and honestly I loved every minute of it. He was amusing, quite cynical at times but in an amusing way, and the whole meal passed without a single lull in the conversation. He's very talkative, in fact he hardly ever shuts up, so I didn't have to say too much, though I'd say, we found we had a fair few things in common. I didn't notice how it happened but I suddenly realised that he was calling me 'Patsy' and I was calling him 'Jem', and him an important business client."

"You obviously got on very well together," said Margaret, "and you needed a bit of a lift so here's to Jem Murphy then, to his good taste in dresses and dress, to his above reproach behaviour and to the future — you never know what or who might be around the corner. Don't forget, Patsy, this man knows where you work."

And so he did. There was a bunch of yellow roses delivered to Patsy at work the following week with a hand-written card tucked inside a small envelope: "I'm told that yellow roses represent joy and friendship and I'd like to invite you out again to repeat the joy of our last encounter and to pursue the chance of a promising friendship. I'll pick you up after work on Friday week. Wear your good dress as we may be going somewhere special. With regards, Jeremy Murphy."

Molly was not happy. She had returned from a weekend in Tullamore, joking about how she was 'making hay while the sun shines', only to discover that her particular sun might have already set. The family had received news that Uncle Stephen had not unexpectedly but all the same suddenly died in Liverpool: he had contracted malaria when serving in India with the British Army and the long-term effects had finally taken their toll. The letter also contained news about Kevin, news which Kevin hadn't mentioned in his letters to Molly.

"I don't think they were a lucky family with their health," said Betty after she had read aloud the letter from their Auntie Mary to the girls. "Didn't your mammy die of tuberculosis? And now Stephen of malaria. That's brother and sister both taken young, God have mercy on their souls," she said, "and poor Kevin and Tessie left without their da the same as you were left without your mammy. It's sad enough, all right."

"He was a good man," said Patrick, "a good Irish man even though he served as a British soldier. Necessity drove him to wear their uniform but he was a Republican at heart and he'd never have raised a gun at a fellow countryman."

Memories came flooding back of the beating Uncle Stephen had suffered that night at Usher's Quay when the Tans had invaded their rooms. The children hadn't witnessed the actual physical brutality but the three sisters remembered well how they had cringed in their beds listening to the sounds of the cousins' home being smashed up and the groans from their uncle as he was kicked repeatedly, and Auntie Mary screaming at the men that her husband was a British soldier.

"I remember better that day you came back from Ballykinlar camp, Daddy, and Aunt Mary was here helping to mix Christmas puddings," said Patsy. "That was one of the best Christmases ever. We little ones were sitting at the table — Kevin and Tessie were with us too, all together making decorations for the house — when we heard the awful loud knock on the door and we were all too petrified to move. Then it turned out to be you at the door, Daddy, and we all started laughing at how frightened we'd been."

"I wonder if Mary needs any help," said Betty. "She was very good to me when I moved to Dublin and joined the family and this would be a time to repay her kindness. Perhaps one of you three could go over to Liverpool for a few days."

"It might be better to wait until this thing with Kevin is sorted out," said Patrick. "If he is set on going to sea and Mary is set against it, then perhaps you should leave them to sort it out between themselves. If he does go, then that would perhaps be the time to offer support. And don't forget Mary has several brothers and sisters living nearby in Liverpool so she's not completely on her own. I'm sure the family will rally round."

"I'd been thinking that perhaps Molly could go over," said Betty, realising that the information about Kevin planning on going to sea had come as a bit of a shock to the girl, "but you're right, Patrick, we'd best wait for things to settle."

Kevin had evidently decided to sign on with a ship docked at Liverpool. He had a curiosity about the world, maybe brought on by his father's stories about the different places in which he'd been based, stories about exotic peoples and clothes and their strange customs. Stephen had been particularly intrigued by the different music he'd heard, which to his ear, he admitted, hardly sounded like music at all. Kevin wanted to see and hear and experience his father's tales for himself and had sought out a merchant ship heading out of Liverpool bound for the orient. Stephen's untimely death had forced Kevin to postpone his plans but it seemed he was still determined to pack up and go. There had been no hint of this determination in any of his correspondence with Molly. She knew he had once signed on to a ship in the past, lying about his age to get taken on, but Auntie Mary had found out and had rushed to the docks with his birth certificate, evidently just in time to stop him getting aboard. That wouldn't be a problem for Kevin now and Molly felt her own plans evaporating into thin air.

"Why don't we leave it a week or so and then Molly and I could go over together," said Patsy. She could see Molly's despair and knew exactly why Betty had suggested that Molly went. Betty was a warm, understanding woman who realised quietly what was what. The whole Kevin relationship was never discussed in front of Patrick. It was best to keep him and his strong views out of boy-girl matters. "We could go over on the Friday night mail-boat and stay either a few days or just the weekend, we could come straight back on the Sunday, depending on what we find. And I'd like to see our cousins again, it's been a few years."

"I'd like to see them too but I wouldn't want to go with you," said Theresa. "Their house is even smaller than this one."

"Patsy never suggested you come, Theresa," said Molly, "so whatever you think about the size of their house is irrelevant."

"I'm only saying…"

"Well say no more," said Molly. "I'll ask if I can have a day or two off work, just in case we end up staying. What about you, Patsy, can they spare you at work? I know Jeanette Modes has a big order to meet."

"I don't think it'll be a problem," said Patsy. "There has been a death in the family and that can't be helped."

"Should we buy tickets in advance or will we be all right with walk-ons?" asked Molly.

"I'll call in to the ticket office this week and try to book a couple of berths for you," said Patrick. "I'm sure Mary and the cousins would appreciate you both going over, even if for just a change of company. The trouble with someone dying in the house is the constant stream of people who suddenly feel the need to call in to express their condolences, always lingering with the sadness over a cup of tea. Thoughtful though it is, after a week of these visits you've had enough."

Patsy wrote to Mr Jeremy Murphy to thank him for the beautiful roses and for his kind message and to beg his forgiveness that she wouldn't be able to meet him as suggested because of attending a family matter in Liverpool. She hoped he would 'please regard this as a postponement and not a refusal'.

He replied advising her to 'think no more about it' but how could she not.

2

The crossing to Liverpool was rough and the stench of sea-sick vomit pervaded the whole boat. The air itself seemed solid with it. Even people who normally prided themselves on their steady sea-legs were retching into paper bags. Faces were green, bodies were bent double and the noise of coughing and throwing up and spitting and heaving meant there was no chance of catching even forty winks. A few thirsty stalwarts still managed to stand upright to down pint after pint outside the bar-hatch with whiskey-chasers taken for medicinal purposes: maybe they had the best idea; rolling around drunk, they didn't notice the rolling of the floor beneath them. The dormitory of berths where Patsy and Molly were lodged was particularly unpleasant, with a non-stop chorus of babies crying and older siblings wailing and complaining. There was nothing the poor mothers could do except hold on and get through the night. With two or three children apiece they snuggled tightly together trying to stay on the one bunk without falling off as the ship pitched and tossed in the storm. One by one the children would suddenly throw up, no time for a paper bag to be fetched into place, and clothes and blankets were covered in puke and the berths and the deck floor became awash with the stuff.

"Dear God and we're only a couple of hours out," said Molly. "I'll look like a wreck by the time we get to Liverpool. I think I'm going to be sick myself."

"Why don't we go up on deck for a break, let the wind blow it off," said Patsy. "We can put our bags up on the bunks, they should be safe enough."

"Anyone thinking about robbing tonight will have their work cut out," said Molly. "Everyone's still wide awake."

The sisters hoisted their cases on to the mattresses and stumbled their way along the gangways and up the stairs to the open deck, clinging on tightly to the rope handrails. In the light from the ship's portholes they could make out the distorted shadowy shapes of several people forlornly hanging over the side, no doubt feeling like death as hastily-eaten and undigested last-minute pies and chips made their escape. The sea swell was frightening: one minute the ship's prow would smash down heavily into the waves and the whole boat would dive in after it so that the horizon line towered high above and it looked as if at any moment the wall of water would have nowhere else to go but to inundate the ship; the next minute the ship's prow would miraculously rise from the depths again and all you could see was dark sky through the curtain of rain, as if you were flying through the very deluge itself.

"I'm not sure this was such a great idea," said Molly, walking her hands along the wall in an attempt to stay on her feet. "You were right about the wind blowing away the sea-sickness, Patsy, now I'm just sick with fear."

"It's not a nice crossing, Molly, but we're safe enough. Don't forget these boats are going backwards and forwards between Dublin and Liverpool every night and in all weathers. And see — there are plenty of crew members up here keeping an eye on the passengers. Look, there's a seat over there, under the shelter of the upper deck," said Patsy and she gripped her sister by the wrist to lead her to the bench. "There now, that's better, isn't it?"

They had to hug their coats around them tightly to keep out the biting wind but they were in a relatively dry spot. They shivered watching the people braving the worst of the weather along the side-rail of the ship.

"If one of them fell overboard no one would ever know, you wouldn't even hear a scream over the howling wind. And if they were noticed going over the side, how on earth would the lifeboats be able to find them?" said Molly, shouting to make herself heard. "By the time an alarm was raised and the ship's engines cut, the sea would have carried them miles off course."

"Don't forget you might have to get used to this, Molly. If you get serious with Kevin you'll be back and forth between Liverpool to Dublin."

"That's if Kevin doesn't choose to go on even longer voyages. Maybe he could work for B&I on the Dublin to Liverpool crossing, then even his mammy couldn't object."

"It would hardly fulfil his dream of seeing the world, now would it,

218

more like 'home from home'. Have you not met anyone else you'd be interested in? No one out at Tullamore? You go there so often I wondered if it was more than the country air that attracted you."

"I like Kevin," said Molly. "We got on very well as kids."

"Aye but you're not kids now," said Patsy. "You haven't really seen him properly in years and all that time he's been growing up too. All you have to go by as to what he's like now are his letters and I got the distinct impression that he hadn't written to you about his plans."

"He hadn't and thank you for understanding and offering to come with me without saying anything in front of the whole family. I couldn't stand catching them in their sneaky looks, especially Theresa's. Her sneaky looks are like pouts of disapproval disguised by a forced smile. Butter wouldn't melt unless someone had something to say about her and Billy."

"You have to admit it's not the same, she does at least see Billy regularly. You've ended up set on the idea of Kevin and you don't even know what he looks like these days."

"He sent me a photo of him in his Post Office uniform," said Molly.

"A photo isn't the same," said Patsy. "Are you sure you're not just convincing yourself there's something between you because you want an excuse to leave Dublin?"

"Don't be so silly, I'm not that stupid." Molly turned to Patsy and grinned: "At least I don't think I'm that stupid but you never know."

Before there was a chance for further heart-to-heart there was a terrific flash of lightning and the girls clung to each in horror as a flag mast crashed down on the deck not yards from where they were sitting. Crewmen appeared from all directions to make fast the pole with ropes and blocks while others marshalled the passengers to get them off the deck and back inside.

"You'd best go in now, ladies," they were instructed, "it's dark and there could be some odd men hanging around."

The sisters burst out laughing. "Well, whoever they are they're doing a better job of hanging around than the flagpole right now," said Molly.

They left the seclusion of their bench and followed the seaman escorting them off the deck. The smell hit them as soon as the door was opened and it didn't improve as they descended into the bowels of the ship to find their bunks.

"Would you believe it," said Molly. "What do we do now?"

Their bags were safe, no one had stolen them, but a brood of small children had stolen what were to have been Patsy and Molly's beds for the night leaving their mother at last able to stretch out. The sisters hadn't the heart to reclaim their bunks and curled up as best they could on what little space was still available. Liverpool suddenly seemed to get even further away.

They didn't expect to get any sleep but they must have dozed off eventually because they awoke to find the ferry had stopped moving. It was early, dark still, but they had reached their destination and the boat was already tied up in its Liverpool berth at the Pier Head. The storm had abated and the River Mersey merely slumbered its way around the ship, slopping and slapping against the hull, calm against the hive of activity going on above the water.

There was an exciting buzz about the place, a happy urgency. Patsy and Molly stood on the deck looking down at the hypnotic sights of a busy port at work. From their high vantage point, they watched the preparations get underway to let the passengers disembark. The wooden gangways were lowered deck-to-quayside and a barrage of voices and faces rose up from the landing place to greet the ship and its cargo of visitors and home-comers. The scene was illuminated to the rear and the sides by regimented lines of gas lamps, misty spots of light punctuating the neat geometry of the quiet wharfs around the dock. To the front, everything was alive in the gentle glow of the arrival shed. A thriving populace of dockers, officials, porters, cabbie-hawkers and welcoming-parties moved through the early morning mayhem.

"There's Kevin and Tessie," said Molly, "down there next to the 'way out' notice, behind the woman in the red hat. Can you see them?"

They started waving and shouting until their cousins picked them out along the ship's rail.

"What do I look like, Patsy?" asked Molly. "Do I look awful? Is my hair a complete mess? Don't answer me. I do look awful, and my hair is a complete mess. What will Kevin think, do you think?"

"Jesus, Mary and Joseph, Molly, he'll think you've just come over from Ireland on a very rough crossing, what else would he think," said

Patsy. "We're here, the ship didn't sink, we didn't drown. Now grab your case and let's get off this floating sickroom."

It was an emotional reunion on the quayside: Molly forgot all about her creased clothes and unkempt hair. The four cousins, who had shared significant times during their childhood in Dublin and had helped each other get through the worst of them, felt tears clouding their eyes as they hugged and held and kissed each other and Patsy and Molly passed on their genuinely heartfelt condolences on the death of Uncle Stephen. Kevin said they'd had no time to prepare for their dad's passing. Although their father had been ill, he had been going to see the doctor at the hospital regularly for treatment and it seemed to be keeping the malaria fits at bay. They had all gotten used to the jerky movements he made, "it would break your heart to watch because he couldn't control them and he had been such a strong man", and they could understand most of what their dad said when he spoke "even though sometimes he'd start talking about something totally random", but the end was nevertheless sudden in its coming.

"My mam woke up one morning and Dad was dead, he'd passed in the night without a sound," said Tessie. "We didn't even have the chance to call the priest. We did call him, of course, and he assured my mam that she had nothing to worry about over my dad's soul; he'd been a good man and would surely go straight to heaven. Of course we had a Requiem Mass said at St James', their old parish, and the church was full. But it was hard for my mam, she didn't get a moment's peace with all the hand-shaking and the how-are-yous. Then of course we had to make sure there was always something in, maybe a few packets of biscuits, for all the callers to the house."

"Have we come at a bad time still?" asked Patsy. "Perhaps Aunt Mary has enough to cope with without two visitors from Ireland landing on her for a couple of days."

"I know for a fact that my mam is anxious for a change of company," said Kevin. "She's looking forward to hearing all the news from Dublin and how everyone's getting on, so don't worry about a thing. A change of conversation will do us all the world of good. Has Eddie still got the pigeons?"

"The pigeons are still there," said Molly. "We can amuse you with a tale or two about those, not that my da finds it quite so amusing, especially when his arms are trapped in the rungs of a ladder."

"What?" said Tessie.

"We'll tell you all the details later," said Patsy quickly. She was tired and ready for a proper sit down and a real cup of tea — on the ferry the tea had been strong enough to stand a spoon in — and she didn't want Molly to get stuck into the narrative while they were still standing at the Pier Head with their cases. "Right now, I just want to get to your house and take the weight off my feet. What's the best way to get to Bootle from here?"

"We can take the Overhead Railway, this way, it's not far," said Kevin taking their two cases and leading them out of the passenger yard. "If you look up you can see it. Can you see it, right up there?"

"It is right over our heads, sure enough," said Molly. "Isn't that a grand idea."

"It goes all the way along the dock road and you get a great view of the ships at berth. I love looking at them," Kevin enthused. "I get to go on board some of them delivering telegrams and they have this impatient stillness about them as if the ships themselves are keen to get back into the open sea. I've started collecting pictures of them all and one day I might actually be on one of those very ships. I see you came over on the Innisfallen, quite a new ship for B&I, as far as I know. Was it comfortable?"

Patsy had to answer: Molly was too busy digesting her cousin's comments. "I'm sure it could be but I wouldn't describe our particular experience as a comfortable one, would you Molly? It was far too stormy a crossing and we were hardly travelling first class."

"That's when a ship comes into its own, when it's battling its way through a storm and the captain's trying to keep it on course," said Kevin. "Hurry now, there's a train coming."

The Overhead Railway did afford a panoramic view over both the ships and the frantic activity going on ship-to-quay as cargo was off-loaded or on-loaded by gangs of dockers while, below the train, lorries rumbled along the cobbled road, disappearing or emerging through the huge-pillared gates cut into a stone wall which seemed to run the whole length of the port area.

"See what's going on there, on the Elder Dempster ship?" said Kevin, pointing out of the window to a non-stop conveyor belt feeding up and down from one of the vessels. "It's come all the way from East Africa full of bananas and that's how they get the bananas off. They have men in the hold loading the big branches of bananas on to the belt — it's made of a soft cloth, so the fruit doesn't get damaged — and then when it gets to the quay the bananas are loaded straight on to trains to take them all over the country. It takes three days to off-load one whole cargo"

"Does it really?" Molly's heart sank as she watched Kevin's eyes glazing over. "You seem to know an awful lot about it," she said.

"It's the whole world coming into Liverpool," he said. "There's timber from Canada, tea from China, silks and cottons from India, fruits and spices from the Caribbean and the Far East..."

"And a lot of boring information coming from you," said Tessie, who was only too familiar with her brother's obsession. "Not long now before you can put your feet up in front of a nice warm fire, Patsy. The terminus at Seaforth Sands is just a few minutes' walk from the house."

They could see Aunt Mary waiting for them at the gate as they walked up Bulwer Street. "Girls! Thanks be to God, it's good to see you, I hear it was a very bad crossing last night," she said, throwing her arms around them in turn. "Just look at the two of you, all grown up into beautiful young women." Molly couldn't suppress a blush as Kevin agreed with his mother. "Come on inside now and let's get some breakfast into you. You must be hungry after the journey."

"We brought you some Hafner's sausages and some white-pudding," said Patsy.

"Did you now, what a treat for us, they don't make sausages quite like Hafner's in Liverpool and you can't get white pudding at all," said Aunt Mary. "I'll put the frying pan on and you two can get those shoes off and relax."

"I think we'd better leave our shoes on for now," said Molly, "or the smell might put you off the Hafner's." She saw out of the corner of her eyes that Kevin appreciated the joke. She smiled at him. His mop of red hair — it was more ginger than she had remembered — kinked up over one side and gave him quite an artistic, almost intellectual air, considering he was what they called a telegraph-lad. She liked the impression. Patsy saw her sister's wistful look and gave her a subtle elbow in the ribs.

Auntie Mary's house was on the end of one of a series of short rows of semi-detached cottages down one side of the street, set back behind low walls and tiny front gardens; opposite, were what the girls assumed were red-brick Victorian terrace houses, you didn't see the same style in Dublin where the streets looked squatter somehow. The overall impression to the visitors was that it was rather closed-in on itself compared to The Coombe, except for out the back where, instead of being overlooked by the backs of other houses, a bit of a grassed area ran down to the wooden-fenced embankment of a railway line. It could be noisy but it was private. Theresa had been right; it was a small house. There was a front room with a range, like the one in Tullamore but much smaller and no longer used for cooking; in the same room was the table, where the family ate, positioned right next to the front window so you could see out to the street, a dumpy settee stretched in front of the fire and a couple of squat armchairs also managed to crowd their way in. An upright piano took up most of the length of one wall. The squash of furniture didn't leave much room for moving about and it was a bit of an obstacle course to get from the front door and through to the tiny kitchen but it was as cosy and homely as Patsy and Molly would have expected from their memories of Auntie Mary's rooms in the Ushers Quay tenement. Upstairs there were three bedrooms of varying sizes of small. The welcome surprises were that upstairs there was an indoor toilet while off the kitchen an area had been walled off to fit in a bath. If you left the door open you could almost cook your dinner while having a soak.

"I'm not working today and I thought you might fancy a trip into town as you haven't been to Liverpool before," said Kevin after breakfast the following morning. "We could go to see the Mersey Tunnel. It only opened a couple of years ago but it's supposed to be one of the best in the world. That's behind the George's Hall and St John's Gardens and close by are the museums and whatever, they're all quite impressive, so you can see a lot from just standing in one place."

"Perhaps there's something we could do to help you, Auntie Mary," said Patsy, "that's why we came over. We'd never hear the end of it at home if we didn't make ourselves useful while we're here."

"You go on into town," said Mary, "You can get me a bit of shopping in Paddy's Market if it'll make you feel better, it'll save me having to go to Knowsley Road shops later and listen to more condolences every time I'm in a queue. I know that sounds unfeeling and ungrateful," she said, "and people are only trying to be kind, but Stephen's dying was hardly a shock, and they didn't see how angry and frustrated he got when he couldn't stop his arms from jerking. Like I said last night, that was the hardest thing for him, knowing he'd lost control of his own body and speech and so it was the hardest thing for all of us to see. We were all so helpless. At least he's at rest now." She wiped away a tear with her pinny. "Now go on out all of you and leave me to enjoy some peace and quiet."

"We'd like to visit Uncle Stephen's grave too," said Molly.

"We'll go tomorrow after Mass," said Mary. "He's in Bootle Cemetery and there's a bus stops on the corner that goes in the right direction. It'll be a bit of fresh air before you get back on the boat. It's a pity you could only come for the weekend but I know you're both working women."

The four cousins took the tram into the city centre and headed to the George's Hall gardens to watch the traffic disappearing into the gaping entrance of the Mersey Tunnel.

"It looks like it's only used by cars and lorries," said Patsy. "There's not a horse and cart in sight. I suppose that's progress for you, not that I'd like to be the one having to go in there to collect up buckets of manure," said Molly.

"Never mind horse manure," said Kevin. "Originally they planned to use it as a route to drive animals through from Wales and The Wirral, so you would have had to clean up after sheep and pigs and cattle as well, Molly, all the way from here to Birkenhead. That'd be more than a few buckets' worth," said Kevin.

"Imagine that, having to sweep up miles of rolling pellets of sheep droppings," said Molly, "chasing them all over the ground and trying to catch them before they got trapped in piles of steaming dung and all the time herds of animals coming at you from every direction."

"So speaks the girl who likes to spend her weekends out in the country," said Patsy.

"There are no dark tunnels in Tullamore to get trapped in while shovelling the muck," said Molly.

They turned and made their way up through St John's Gardens to take a look at the George's Hall and then headed towards the market.

"I don't know about anyone else but I'm gasping for a cup of tea and maybe a bite to eat," said Tessie. "We can try the tea-room at Woolworth's, see if there are any seats. We might be lucky."

They had to push their way through hundreds of shoppers thronging with practised eyes round the counters in Woolworths looking for bargains or cheap treats. "The café's on the first floor, follow me," said Tessie.

They were lucky: not only did they arrive just as a family were vacating a table but the table was right by the window so they could stare down at all the activity going on in Lord Street while they relaxed above the melee. The street was crowded: people were jostling their way in and out of the various shops, bags in hand and children in tow: street traders had their stalls pitched right the way along the pavements demonstrating toys dangling on strings or the merits of some cheap gadgetry, perhaps, while hawkers selling straight out of suitcases shouted for attention, waving maybe tins of polish or pairs of boot-laces in the air; some sandwich-board men proclaimed the need to repent as the end was nigh, others recommended the need to visit a particular emporium without delay, presumably while there was still time. Horses and carts, wagons and delivery vans, cars and bicycles contributed to the general commotion, horns tooting and bells brngbrnging constantly while tall and sedate double-decker trams commanded a stately path through the chaos. It wasn't that different a scene to what you'd find in any other city street on a Saturday afternoon but it was a new city for the Dublin visitors and viewing it from an elevated position certainly seemed to lend it a more interesting perspective.

"Do you see that window across the street, the clothes shop next to the jewellers?" said Tessie. "Do you like that style? I think it's quite glamorous. It's all the rage with some girls here after seeing so much of Wallis Simpson in the papers and on Pathé News and wanting to look like her. She's so slim and she's always immaculate and smooth and modern."

"Isn't she the American woman involved with the new king?" asked Patsy. "I thought he had to stop seeing her because she's divorced."

"Divorced once and already going through her second," said Tessie. "It said in the paper that the American Ambassador in London is supposed to have called her a 'tart'. He didn't mince his words but then he is American. Have you seen pictures of her in the Irish papers? I think she's quite smart-looking for a tart, not at all what I imagine a tart is supposed to look like."

"It's a big scandal here and has been for years," said Kevin. "There's a row going on in Parliament over whether the king should stop seeing her or give up the throne. He wouldn't be allowed to marry a divorcee and be the head of the Church of England as king."

"Fancy having a king as the head of your church," said Patsy. "At least the Pope started out as a priest. That makes far more sense to me."

"I thought people were allowed to get divorced here," said Molly.

"But they can't go on to get married again," said Kevin. "The difficulty for the Government is that Edward is very popular with people. He's got the common touch. According to the papers the establishment sees him as a potential threat because he says he wants to be a modern king. That's why the British secret police have been instructed to follow him. I find the whole thing really fascinating."

"Come on, Kevin, there's something much more fascinating than that," said Tessie. "There's what I'd call proper scandal, the juicy stuff." Tessie adopted a real gossip's face. "It's said that Edward's mother, Queen Mary herself, had been told that her son suffered from some sort of 'sexual abnormality' which, she was informed, had been cured by Mrs Simpson thanks to Mrs Simpson having learned some special sexual techniques in a Chinese brothel." Tessie sat back and smirked. "Not the general sort of conversation they'd want to encourage across the meal table at Buckingham Palace, I don't think."

"When on earth was she supposed to have even been in a Chinese brothel?" asked Patsy.

"When she lived in China," said Tessie knowingly. "She lived there for well over a year, lounging around with her rich friends with nothing to do but whatever 'socialites' do — isn't that what they call her, 'an American socialite'? She must have had plenty of time for some hands-on socialite-ising in a brothel. Anyway, I for one don't really care who she is or what she gets up to or who she does or doesn't marry, I just love the way she dresses. She looks very sophisticated, like a cool, slinky glass of expensive wine. The magazines are full of 'the Wallis look' and Liverpool is full of cheap imitations."

Patsy studied the clothes in the window opposite. "They wouldn't be that hard to copy," she said.

"I can see it now," said Molly, "you getting Jeanette Modes to run up a few Wallis frocks for the daring Dublin market. We can go over and take a closer look when we've finished here if you like."

"I'll go in with you," said Tessie, "it's not a shop I'd go into on my own, too posh. Kevin can keep watch outside in case we're followed by the secret police."

Saturday evening was whiled away in front of the fire, sharing yet more precious memories over a bottle of sherry still in the cupboard since the funeral. Aunt Mary had to dab her eyes occasionally because she was either laughing too much or was crying quietly while enjoying anecdotes involving Stephen. Kevin played the piano for a bit of a sing-song and Molly saved her telling of the pigeon dramas until last, not wanting to appear insensitive by introducing a bit of silliness into the remembrances and so managing to end the session on a humorous note before it was time for bed. They were to be up early the next day to go to the cemetery.

Stephen's resting place was still pristine and fresh, a neat rectangle of turf standing out amongst the rows of older plots. The cemetery was generally well-maintained and other visitors were there weeding and tidying their own family sites, replacing withered flowers and quietly murmuring news of the living to the dead. Tucked away in one corner were irregular groupings of leaning gravestones, all weathered and worn, some barely still upright; tangles of weeds smothered forgotten graves, while one or two sculpted angels maintained their heavenly vigil, once elaborate, now chipped and disfigured by time. It was a neglected area but it seemed to serve as a suitably sombre dust-to-dust reminder of what lay ahead.

"It's a shame Stephen's here on his own and not with your mother in Glasnevin," said Mary. "I wanted to have his body taken over to Dublin to be buried next to her but the expense was too much. At least it's a big enough family plot here so he won't always be alone. I'll probably be the first to join him." She was waiting for a headstone to be carved with a fitting message and Patsy promised to have a Mass said, if she knew on which date they were going to fix it at the grave.

"How did you and Stephen meet?" asked Molly.

"How did we meet? That's a story," said Mary. "I was in Harold's Cross, you know, the orphanage in Dublin, with my own sister and three brothers when we were not much more than children. God did I hate that place but at least the five of us were together, we were luckier than some of the children in there, they didn't separate us and put us in different homes. I never knew why we were put in there because my mother certainly was still alive so I don't understand to this day why we were treated like orphans. You didn't ask questions back then. Anyway, Stephen used to work for a man who had a small lorry and they used to come to Harold's Cross every few days to drop off dirty washing and collect the clean laundry. That's how we met. We used to chat in the yard whenever we could, and when there were no nuns around, of course, otherwise we'd all be in trouble and he might have lost his little job. He would bring me a wildflower sometimes, or a couple of sweets, and tell me the odd joke or stories of what was going on outside of our prison, as we thought of it. We got together when I eventually left the orphanage, by which time we were both of courting age, He always used to say that we hit it off over bundles of clothes and that I became his bundle of joy."

They all stood silently for a few minutes, letting Mary enjoy being lost in the past.

"Well, I'm going to bundle you all off home now," said Kevin. "Patsy and Molly have a boat to catch later, don't forget."

Back at Bulwer Street, Patsy and Molly packed their cases ready for the return crossing but they didn't have much and still had an hour to spare. "I'll make you a decent cup of tea before you go," said Mary.

"Molly, shall we go for a walk round the block while the kettle boils, stretch your legs before you have to sit on the boat all night?" said Kevin. "What about you Patsy, will you join us?"

"I'm fine here," said Patsy. "You and Molly go. I want to bend Tessie's ear about the Wallis Simpson look. I have to get it right if I'm to copy the line. We can sit in the garden, that's a big enough treat for me before going home."

"I'll just fetch the magazine I have and I'll see you outside," said

Tessie, conveniently promoted to fashion consultant.

Molly and Kevin let themselves out and strolled up the street towards the docks. Kevin knew where they could gain access at Seaforth and he thought the docks with all the ships tied up would be an appropriate setting for what he wanted to say to Molly: that he wanted to go to sea but that he also wanted her to be part of his future. His idea was that he could sail out of Liverpool or Dublin, whatever suited her best.

Patsy was pleased with the way she had engineered for her sister to spend some private time with Kevin. "Do you think they'll be able to sort themselves out?" she asked Tessie. "I don't know much about their relationship, only that there seems to be one, judging by all the letters that pass back and forth. I know she was disturbed that Kevin hadn't written about his plans for going away to sea when it was obviously something very much on his mind. It came as a shock to her when we got your mammy's letter. I think Molly felt let down."

"Believe me," whispered Tessie, "chances of Kevin signing on a ship are very slim. I'd be surprised if he even got as far as the Mersey ferry. Birkenhead would be too far for my mam. Since my dad died, she never stops with the comments on how she'd be left alone if her only son went gallivanting round the world and she recently widowed. My mam knows how to turn the screw when it suits her, Patsy, and, as regards keeping Kevin at home, that certainly suits her. He doesn't stand a chance. She already stopped him once in the past, did you know that? She followed him all the way to the shipping office and caused a terrible scene just as he was about to sign his form — and she was no widow then. The agent turned Kevin away and advised him to come back another day when his mother wasn't in tow."

"God that must have been embarrassing for him," said Patsy. "I'd no idea Auntie Mary could be so stubborn minded. She's always in such good humour."

"Well she is when she's wrapped in her family but it has to be on her own terms. You've probably only ever seen her with Kevin and me. That's because when we're all together she's a happy woman and she wants to keep it that way."

"Do you think it's because she was on her own with the two of you quite often when your father was stationed overseas? She must have relied on your company."

"You may be right," agreed Tessie. "She'll certainly do her best to make sure she's not left alone again. Shush now and look at these pictures before she comes out."

Kevin and Molly got back in time for a quick cuppa before they had to set off. It had been a busy couple of days but somehow the weekend seemed to be over before it had started and it was suddenly time for saying goodbyes.

"It's been grand having you over. You brought a breath of fresh air into the place and for that I'm grateful," said Auntie Mary. "The house was beginning to feel quite empty and I hate an empty house. You're both welcome to come at any time, any time, perhaps a happier time. Be sure to give my warmest regards to Betty and your da when you get home. I think of Betty every time I bake a cake and if someone knocks on the door in the middle of it I still get a chill."

"At least that's behind us now," said Patsy. "The only loud knocks on the door these days are when any of the boys have gotten into the sort of trouble boys seem to get into."

"I'd love to meet them all," said Mary. "One of these days, you never know."

The Pier Head was full of people when they got off the train, all concentrated in a couple of groups by the wharf railing. In one, a man was orating atop a soap-box, the other platform was occupied by a woman. Swirling around them was a flight of placards held high: "Fight Fascism", "Fight Nazism", one read, "Spain needs your help".

"What's all that about?" asked Molly.

"It's about what's going on in Europe, in Germany in particular and what they're doing to the Jews," said Kevin. "They've taken away all their basic everyday rights and their shops are being attacked. Lots of Jews get beaten up in broad daylight in the street and no one intervenes. Germany says it's now a fascist country, only for pure Germans. Did you not read about Hitler's Nazi rally at Nuremberg? With his huge army? Pathé News said there were eight-hundred-thousand men goose-stepping in uniform. It's frightening. There's talk of him planning to take over the whole of Europe and turn it fascist. Have you not read about it?"

"To be honest I don't pay much attention to the news, I only get the occasional glance at my da's papers," said Patsy. "Things were bad enough in Dublin years ago for me to bother with what's happening now in a country I don't even know. I see the Pathé News in the cinema but often that's when me and Margaret talk."

"Well, it's what everyone's talking about here," said Tessie. "The stories are terrible about what's going on. And the pictures you see of the children: they're all in uniform too and making that salute they make with their arms stuck out in the air, just like mini-soldiers."

"What's that got to do with Spain?" asked Molly. "Has Germany already taken over Spain? Not that I know much about Spain, to be honest, other than the women dancing in long frilly frocks."

"We didn't do much in school about Europe," said Patsy. "Most of the places we learned about were places in Ireland. I think it was to make up for the past, when geography lessons were all about the British Empire."

"The Germans haven't invaded Spain yet," said Kevin, "but civil war broke out there a few months ago. An army general is trying to take over the country and he's getting military support from Hitler. Ordinary people are fighting to hold on to their republic, they're frightened Spain will become fascist too, but they're just ordinary people, they don't have much in the way of weapons and they're up against professional soldiers. Our government has refused to help so there's a recruitment drive going on here asking for people to volunteer to go and fight for Spain and stop the fascists from taking power."

"Are you tempted?" asked Molly, a slight cloud crossing over her face.

"Not right now but you never know. A few of the men I work with have already signed up. They leave for Barcelona in a couple of months' time."

"I can't imagine your mammy being too happy if you decided to join them," said Molly, really expressing her own fears.

Patsy suddenly let out a gasp. "Would you look at who's over there?" she spluttered. "That's the woman who gave a talk in Dublin about married couples and how they could prevent pregnancy."

The speaker on the other soapbox was non-other than Eileen Donovan, looking as poised and well-turned out here in the blustery breeze of the Pier Head as she had in Bewley's.

"What on earth were you doing going to a meeting like that?" asked Molly. "I bet you never told da."

"I went because I thought it was to be about women's rights in the workplace," said Patsy. "It wasn't. I was quite shocked."

Molly and Tessie exchanged knowing looks. "I think we're all a bit shocked and we weren't even there," said Molly.

"I think I'll just pick up a schedule, find out where and when the next meeting is in Liverpool, so I won't miss it," said Tessie. "Don't worry, Molly, I'll let you know what they have to say. It could be relevant in the future," she said, looking at her cousin but tipping her head knowingly towards her brother. "I think we'd better get to the boat now before it sails without you."

According to the noticeboard by the gangway, the forecast was for a smooth crossing with just a slight swell to the south of the Isle of Man.

"Well, it's the Isle of Man so you might expect a slight swell to the south," Tessie whispered to Molly.

The four cousins bid their farewells, swapping hugs and the usual enthusiastic comments and promises appropriate to a departure. Kevin whispered to Molly that he would let her know as soon as he had made up his mind about what he was going to do but she was to know that, whatever they were, his plans would involve her.

3

Christmas was looming and the traditional activities were occupying the different generations in The Coombe. Patsy and Theresa were helping Betty to mix the puddings, with fond references to Auntie Mary following the visit to Liverpool.

"How did things go between you and Kevin?" Betty asked Molly. "You didn't say much when you got back and your father's in the yard now so he can't hear us. Has Kevin signed on a ship yet? Pass me another egg, will you."

"I think he's still trying to make up his mind," said Molly. "We didn't talk about his plans much but he's obviously interested in anything to do with ships. He even knew all about the boat we'd gone over on and there was me thinking it was just a ferry. But Tessie told Patsy that she doubts Auntie Mary would let him go to sea, though whether or not she'd have much say in the matter I don't know, he seems set on it."

"It'd be hard for Mary to lose her husband and then a son," said Betty, "but I personally think she should let him make up his own mind and not interfere. It's not a mother's place to stop a son or a daughter for that matter from choosing what they want to do with their own life."

"Auntie Mary doesn't strike me as the type to lay down the maternal law," said Theresa. "Is this mixture beaten enough, Mammy? My wrist is getting sore."

"That's fine, let it rest now — the mixture, I mean." Betty broke the egg into a bowl and started whisking. "It depends how Mary is now that Stephen's gone," she said.

"She was quite tearful when we were there," said Molly. "She said the house felt empty."

"I'm sure it does," said Betty. "I know Stephen was often away when he was in the army but it's not the same, she knew he was coming back. I don't know why she doesn't take the opportunity to come back to Dublin. She could take over beating the pudding from Theresa and with fewer complaints."

"It was fun when they were all here getting ready for Christmas," said Molly. "We were talking about that in Liverpool and the knock coming on the door."

They grinned at the awful memory. Then suddenly there was a loud knock on the front door and all three of them were stopped in their tracks, not able to say a word.

"I'll go," called Annie from the other room.

Two tall, muscular men were at the door. In the kitchen the women could hear the voices echoing down the hall, along with unfamiliar squawking sounds.

"Do you not recognise your Granddad Michael, girl? And your Uncle Robert? Don't tell me you've forgotten us already, Annie. And here we've come all the way to Dublin from Tullamore with your Christmas dinner."

Betty burst out laughing and hurried out to welcome her father and her brother and the two fine fat chickens they'd brought from the farm, along with a sack of potatoes, butter and soda bread. The hall was crammed with everyone trying to hug their visitors at the same time. Molly was elated: her Tullamore relations were as close and important to her as her immediate family.

"I'll take charge of the chickens," said Ciaran.

"I want to carry one too," said Mikey.

"I notice you're neither of you offering to carry the sack of potatoes," said Michael. "I suppose that's man's work. Where's that father of yours?"

"He's out seeing to the pigeons with Eddie."

"Pigeons, is it? Well now I'll have to take a look at those. Lead on you two chicken heads."

The party headed out to the yard in time to see Patrick and Eddie encouraging several of the birds circling above the loft to come down to roost but a feathered frenzy broke out as the pigeons spotted the alien chickens and skittered over them threateningly, making the chickens take fright and duck into the nearest dark corner.

"I obviously arrived just in time," Michael called up to Patrick. "This is theatre at its best."

"Sure it's you, Michael," said Patrick seeing his friend standing below, "and Robert. What brings you to Dublin? Wait now and I'll come down. Eddie, you can finish off up here."

"We thought we'd try selling some of our chickens at the market for Christmas, make a few bob," said Michael as Patrick climbed down the ladder. "I brought you a couple. They should be nice and moist and there's good meat on them. You've a week or so to fatten them up a bit more."

"Will we have to kill them?" asked Annie.

"Someone will have to do the honours," said Robert, "you can't put them straight into the oven as they are. Do you not fancy having a go yourself, Annie?"

"I do not."

Immediately Ciaran and Mikey offered their services, each out-shouting the other in their willingness to do the deed. "I could chop their heads off," said Ciaran. "I could wring their necks," said Mikey.

"Aren't you the same two the little men who a few minutes ago wouldn't carry a bag of spuds?" said Michael. "How easy do you think it is to kill a chicken, assuming you can catch one, of course. We'll have to get you out on the farm, build up those muscles. What do you say, Betty? Do you want to get rid of these two skinny scruffs for a while? They can come out with Molly next time and she can leave them there."

Ciaran and Mikey all but exploded with excitement, "can-we-Mammy-can-we?"

"I wouldn't wish you two on to the poor cows," said Betty. "Maybe you can go for a week next summer. Let's go in now, I'm sure granddad and your Uncle Robert must be ready for some tea. Where's your wagon, Da?"

"It's outside, will it be all right there?"

"As long as there are no chickens left in it," said Eddie. "They wouldn't be there for long, never mind with Christmas round the corner."

"We managed to sell them all and some vegetables too," said Robert. "Will the horse be okay do you think? He's not used to city streets."

"We can look after him and guard the wagon," said Ciaran, grabbing Mikey by the hand.

"Off you go, then, and be nice to the horse so he'll be nice to you when you come to visit. Horses have long memories if they take a dislike to someone for any reason," Michael shouted to the two disappearing backs. The boys couldn't believe their luck: minding a horse and cart was far more interesting than making stupid paper decorations with their little sister and brother. "So, tell me," said Michael, turning to the assembled company, "what have you all been up to? It's been a month or more since we saw Molly and usually, she keeps us up to date with the news."

"Patsy and I went over to Liverpool, that's why I missed my visit to Tullamore with Nora," said Molly. "Did you know Uncle Stephen passed away a couple of months ago? We went over to see Auntie Mary and our cousins. The crossing was terrible, I thought we'd both be sick or fall over the side, but Liverpool was grand. Have you ever been?"

"Not in a long time," said Michael, "but I remember liking it well enough. Of course the place is full of people from Ireland anyway. It's just like home so I might as well stay at home. And how is your auntie? It's quite a loss losing a husband, or a wife, as we all know."

"She might be losing her son too," said Betty. "He wants to go to sea."

"Why would he want to do that?" asked Eddie. "How could anyone want to spend all their time looking at boring water when there are far more interesting things to do in the street right outside."

"Well I can understand it, I thought of donning a sailor suit and going away to sea once," said Robert. "I fancied the idea of riding the ocean waves, battling through the storms and skimming gently over the calms, Eddie, seeing strange places, strange faces, strange customs, but then I decided that farming in all weathers is challenge enough and that there were plenty of strange places and faces to be encountered around Tullamore. And what stranger a custom could you wish to witness than the weekly dances in the local hall, as the grown daughters of this house well know. Boys and girls lining up like prospective buyers in a cattle market to give each other the studied once-over, the same studied once-over given by the same boys and the same girls every week. Now to me that is very peculiar."

"And what about you, Robert," said Patrick, "isn't it about time you settled down with one of those lasses?"

"After serving my apprentice lining up with the rest of them to study the prospects, I am actually walking out with one of the local girls from those very same dances," said Robert. "You may remember her, Patsy and Theresa, she distinguished herself with some fine fisticuffs last time you came."

"One of the girls fighting over you?" asked Patsy.

Eddie burst out laughing at the thought. "Fighting over Robert, were they?"

"That they were, so I thought I'd better pick one of them."

"Only one of them," said Theresa, "that's very noble of you, though the other girl might not agree."

"Sure they're all friends really," said Michael. "It's a close community and no one can bear a grudge for too long, not even a jealous lass. It's one of those miracles of life, I always think, that in any community eventually there are enough boys and girls to go around. You find the same phenomenon in the newspapers: there's always just the right amount of news every day to fill the pages. And what about you, Patsy? Are you walking out with anyone since it finished with that Sean fellow?"

"No," said Patsy abruptly. "He's married to someone else now."

"That's all in the past," said Betty, neatly changing the subject. "More tea anyone? Tell Michael and Robert what you all did in Liverpool while I get another kettle on the hob."

Molly stepped into the breach and managed to present such an enthusiastic report of their visit that soon Patsy was joining in too. Awkwardness on the Sean front had been averted but the Tullamore relations didn't know the Liverpool relations that well so Patrick in turn subtly redirected the conversation. He hadn't seen his old friend in quite a while and Michael's arrival had sparked a return of the old Patrick; he was feeling positively chatty.

"I'm surprised you came all the way with the horse and cart, it's a long haul," he said.

"We stopped at Maynooth," said Michael. "We've friends live just outside the town and they've a small farm so we could stable the horse for the night and enjoy the craic over a bit of supper. Then it was just a couple of hours on to Dublin first thing this morning to catch the market."

"Maynooth?" The old Patrick was definitely making a comeback.

"It's a sign of how times have changed that the British might still have a King's Representative in Ireland but he chooses to live out in Maynooth instead of in the grand lodge in Phoenix Park," said Patrick.

"Aye, you managed to chase him out of Dublin all right," said Michael, "if only a matter of a few miles away. All the same he has enough to occupy himself with while he's sitting in his country seat; he's been the representative of three different kings so far this year. That must be some sort of a record."

"And there's still a few weeks to go," said Robert.

"The British certainly have plenty on their plates at home right now without worrying about us," said Patrick. "They can't even keep control of their own royal family. Isn't one of them flaunting himself all over Europe with his fancy American woman?"

"Her clothes are grand, though," said Molly. "Her style is all the rage in England, the shops are full of copies. They have a certain risqué air to them too now that she's seduced a king off his throne."

Patrick ignored her frivolity other than to throw a look of impatient disdain in her direction. "Then there's all the trouble brewing again in Germany," he continued as if Molly hadn't spoken. "Perhaps now's the time we should finish what we started in 1916, get the whole of Ireland united into one."

"There's few people in the country who have any appetite for more fighting, I'm sure yourself included," said Michael, "and there's plenty who'd be on the side of the British against the Nazis, whatever that old Blueshirt reprobate Eoin O'Duffy and his die-hard supporters would have us believe."

"What's a Blueshirt?" asked Eddie.

"They were a bunch of fascist eejits who used to march around Ireland in blue shirts giving the straight-arm salute like they were an outpost of Hitler's army," said Patrick. "They think a German victory over the British would lead to a united Ireland. Sure why on earth would Hitler and his Nazis take control of Europe and then turn round and say, 'Okay, Ireland, you're a free country now'? There's no logic in that."

Theresa welcomed the pause in the discussion as the men inwardly weighed up the two sides of the argument; she had no mind for politics. "Isn't Maynooth where the seminary is?" she asked, trying to introduce a chattier note. "If Betty's midwife, Mrs Doran, had her way, that's where at least one of the O'Kelly boys should be headed. She'd no doubt bask in the second-hand glory of having brought a young priest into this world to serve the faithful."

"It doesn't look like the sort of place where anyone would want to spend a few years of their life," said Robert, "not me anyway, not locked away with a bunch of budding holy Joes. It's a huge grey-looking place and the windows would make you think you were in church all the time. Perhaps that's the idea. Inculcate the habit right from the start."

"They have to study somewhere," said Patsy.

"That they do," said Robert, "but I can't see being stuck out in the middle of nowhere would prepare them for life in a busy city parish."

"They need peace and quiet to learn all that Latin and all the scriptures," said Patsy. "They need to be able to concentrate."

"That they do," said Robert, "meanwhile the rest of us have to do proper jobs to pay for them and their cosy situation while all they have to do is concentrate on themselves and their books. And they don't all get sent to work in those busy city parishes, Patsy. It's no accident that well-off families see the Church as an easy career path for their precious sons."

Patsy was feeling undermined and under attack and was desperately trying to remember the various arguments she had been taught by the nuns to counter routine criticisms voiced at the Church: all she could remember was the favourite attack on the riches of the Sistine Chapel in the Vatican in the face of so much poverty, especially in so many strongly Catholic countries — as if the Pope could sell a ceiling because there was a valuable painting on it — and the other one about the priesthood itself and the rule of celibacy — which leaves priests free of their own domestic worries and nurtures self-denial. Neither of which offered much help against Robert's comments, him being a practising Catholic.

"I don't see the priesthood as an easy choice at all," was all she could muster, "it must be an unsettled life, never knowing where you're going to be sent next, never having a family or real friends, and not all priests come from wealthy families."

"But you don't see any of them go hungry like some of their parishioners," said Robert. "And they're happy to take a drink in the pub, sure enough, but seldom put their hands in their own pockets to pay for it. I've yet to see a priest get a round in."

"They're entitled to have a drink the same as the next man," said Patsy, "that's not a sin, if it's in moderation, and you can never tell what good influence the priest might be having while he's taking his drink in the bar, maybe making some drunk think again before going home to beat on his wife."

Patrick couldn't resist jumping in. "We all know that most of the priests working in our churches are devout men doing a fine job, Patsy, but I'm sorry to say that a lot of clergy turn into pompous little upstarts, out of touch with everyday problems but still forever preaching to ordinary people on how they should deal with those problems and threatening them with hell if they disobey. The priests, of course, do what the bishops tell them to do but the result is this: the Church keeps Catholics under control more through a fear of God and the Devil than through the love of a Christ who preached compassion and respect for his fellow man," he said. "I don't see much evidence of compassion or respect for some of the poor souls who live round here. I've seen members of the clergy turn away from a poor beggar in the street because the heavy smell of poverty was an affront to their noses. That place where you volunteer, Patsy, the Penny Dinners café, that's run under the umbrella of the parish but it's paid for by parishioners who often struggle to put food on their own tables. And the higher up the ecclesiastical ladder it goes, the more they look out for themselves and their creature comforts, with their satin robes and their lush living and everyone bowing and scraping before them, 'Your Worship this' and 'Your Worship that'. No wonder they end up feeling so self-important — and it's all done under the guise of religion. Ultimately, it's in their own interests that nothing changes, otherwise people may start to question the whole business and maybe begin to say 'no'. They're no different to the landed gentry, people who think they've a divine right to rule and be obeyed simply because they happen to have been born into money."

"And that's what happening in the world today," said Michael. "It's already happened in Russia. People had had enough of nothing so they decided to help themselves to something and take it from the rich people who'd always had everything."

"But they're communists and can't be trusted," said Patsy. "I don't see that that's got anything to do with the parish priest or our bishops." She was anxious to stem the unexpected antagonism being levelled at a church on which she relied for comfort and guidance.

"Put it this way. How do you, Patsy O'Kelly, know that communists aren't to be trusted?" said Patrick. "Is it from personal experience, based on all the Russians I'm sure you're acquainted with?"

"I don't know any."

"She's right," said Eddie, "there aren't many Russians in Dublin. The only ones I've ever met were off the ships, selling a few birds in the bird market."

"So how do you know they aren't to be trusted, Patsy?" Patrick wouldn't let go.

"Leave it be," said Betty. "We should be enjoying time with our visitors, not ganging up on Patsy."

"Patsy is quite old enough to defend herself," said Patrick. "The trouble is she doesn't always think for herself. Patsy," he said turning fully to his eldest daughter, "you only know communists can't be trusted because the priest tells you so, isn't that right? You're told we have to defeat communism or communism will defeat Christianity and you believe it, because it's the priest who's saying it. I'd like to ask that priest: how come Christianity, which has lasted for centuries, is suddenly so weak that a handful of reds in Russia could destroy it? Didn't Christ himself preach a form of socialism, which is really a form of communism?"

"You're right in what you say Patrick," said Michael. "If communism means a fairer share of the cake for everyone and not just the rich, then I'm all for communism. As it is, it's hard enough sometimes to afford a loaf of bread never mind a slice of cake."

"I prefer cake to bread," said Eddie, "I'm with Uncle Michael."

"So is Germany fighting for socialism, isn't that where the word Nazi comes from, national socialism?" said Theresa.

"Except that their emphasis is on the 'national' and not on the 'socialism'," said Patrick. "Hitler and his Nazis impose their doctrines on people for the national good, in other words for the good of the state, not for the social good. And who controls that state? Why Hitler himself, of course. He dictates what's what and people have to do what they're told or else."

"Or else what, Da?" asked Eddie, who was delighted to be involved in such a grown-up conversation.

"Or else they get locked away in camps, just like the one I was locked up in by the British at Ballykinlar."

"And if your face doesn't fit then watch out," said Michael. "If you're not the Nazis' idea of a pure German national then the secret police will take you away and that'll be the last of you. Gone. And if you're a Jew or a gypsy or any of the others on the not-wanted list then you've no chance at all. There're already thousands being locked up. That's hardly Christian, Patsy, I think you'd agree. They're keeping Europe safe from communism, they claim, but they're actually fascist and racist and proud to be both."

"At least they're not communists," said Patsy, "isn't that worse than fascism?"

"And since when has the only choice available been between either communism or fascism?" said Patrick. "It's not and never has been one or the other. The truth is these people in power want to keep ordinary people under the thumb so that the ruling establishment, whether it be fascist or communist, is left undisturbed."

"I agree with you there," said Michael. "Aren't the papers full of articles from Spain about that army general, Franco, I think is his name, and the Irish papers are calling him the great saviour of Christianity in the fight against communism. And who is he fighting? None other than the very Catholics whose faith he claims to be saving, ordinary Spaniards who go to Mass every Sunday and do their Christian duty. But they had been doing it for too long on empty bellies while all around them were rich landlords and well-fed clergy alike, so they took over and made Spain a republic. Now Franco is fighting to get back to the way it was before, so of course the gentry and the Church are on his side."

"It's the same story over and over. I can't understand how people here don't see the parallels with Ireland," said Patrick. "We fought to become a republic, in Spain they're fighting to save their republic: we fought against the injustice of rich landlords owning the country, in Spain they are fighting that very same situation. It has nothing to do with religion or communism, it's a fight for social justice, a fight to do away with undeserved privilege."

"There was a stand in O'Connell Street the other day run by the Irish Christian Front raising money to support the people in Spain," said Patsy. "I gave them a couple of shillings."

"You what?" gasped Patrick. "They're not collecting to buy food and medicines for the poor," said Patrick, "they're buying weapons for Franco's army to use against the poor."

"All I know is that the priest said at Mass that the Christian Front was doing God's work in helping Spain," said Patsy. "He said that churches there are being destroyed and priests and nuns are being attacked and killed and that what's happening in Spain is a religious war, it's not political. He said that General Franco was only trying to defend the Church. If churches and priests are being killed, you can't possibly agree with that. Hundreds of Irishmen have already gone off to fight with Franco. They can't all be wrong."

"Unfortunately, they can and they are," said Michael. "You with your family and Republican credentials should see that."

"Well, I'm sorry but I don't," said Patsy angrily. "What I do see is that some things about my family and Republican credentials as you call them were at times less than Christian."

Patrick and Michael were silenced by Patsy's bitter comment and it was time for Betty to step in again. "That's been quite enough serious talk from the lot of you," she said. "I didn't even get to hear about the American woman's clothes. Molly will have to describe them to me later. Da, Robert, will you be saying the night?"

"Sorry about all that Betty, you know what it's like when Patrick and I get together, and it's been a while."

"It's been far too long," said Patrick. "Maybe I'll bring Ciaran and Mikey out to Tullamore myself next year."

"I'd love that. I'm glad to see you've not lost any of your interest in politics and the like, meanwhile we'll be on our way," said Michael. "We'll be stopping at Maynooth again on the way back too so we'd best be off, try to get there before it's too dark. The horse would find its way round Tullamore with its eyes closed but I doubt it'll remember the road to Dublin."

"It would have to remember it in reverse," said Theresa.

"It would right enough," said Robert, "unless we travelled backwards for the sake of visual familiarity. Let's see what the horse thinks."

They all laughed as they stood up from the table and made their own reverse journey back up the hall to the front door. A babble of last-minute advice over the feeding and killing of chickens was delivered as the front door was opened but it was opened on to an empty road outside. Ciaran and Mikey were gone, as was the horse and cart.

"Jesus, Mary and Joseph, what have those two got up to now?" said Betty.

"I can see them, look, they're up there past the corner of Meath Street," shouted Eddie and he set off at a run.

"I'd best go help him," said Robert.

"No need to bother," said Patrick. "Eddie works with the coal man so he's well used to handling a horse and cart round these streets."

"Not that he handles a horse, exactly, more of an ass, as I remember," said Theresa.

"Give the lad some credit," said Patrick, "he'll sort it out."

The small audience watched as Eddie leapt up on to the driver's board, grabbed the reins from a very flustered looking Ciaran and took charge of the situation. He expertly steered the cart round across the width of The Coombe and confidently led the run-away contingent back to the house. He even managed to work the horse up into an easy trot for the last thirty yards or so before whoaing to a standstill, right outside the house. He was greeted by a round of applause.

"Well done, young Eddie," said Michael, "there's a job waiting for you on the farm any time you want it."

Eddie was flushed with pride. "Thank you, Uncle Michael, but it wasn't that difficult. I've had worse things happen on the coal deliveries."

"So come on," said Betty to Ciaran and Mikey, "what happened?"

"It wasn't my fault," said Mikey, "honest Mammy. Tell her, Ciaran, it wasn't my fault."

"It wasn't our fault at all, we were just sitting on the board talking silly to the horse when a group of men leaving the Cosy Bar slapped the horse on its rump and clicked at it to move," said Ciaran, "and it did. The men were laughing and calling to it all along the pavement, encouraging it to follow them. I tried to pull him back but I wasn't strong enough. I thought it'd take us all the way into town but it spotted something in the road and stopped to investigate. Fortunately for Mikey and me it turned out to be an old carrot."

"Saved by an old carrot?" said Molly. "Are you sure it wasn't an old sausage? Your story sounds more like a porker to me."

"It's the truth, we swear," said Mikey.

"Well, no harm done," said Michael. "Remind me next time to tie the horse up like the cowboys do outside the saloon. Is there a lamppost outside the Cosy Bar?"

"I'll go and look," said Mikey but before he went and everybody laughed he realised it was a daft idea. "Just joking," he said.

Eddie handed his responsibilities for the horse and cart back to his granddad and uncle and they climbed aboard.

"Hang on a minute now," said Betty as she rushed back into the house. She emerged with a small food parcel and a bottle of water. "Here's something to keep you going on the journey."

"See you for the New Year dance, Molly, make sure you come, I've told everyone to expect you," said Robert. "And I'll introduce you to Kitty properly, no punches will be exchanged, I promise." He slapped the reins and clicked the horse on and the team of visitors started off amidst much cheering and calling and farewelling.

"We had great fun with the cart," whispered Ciaran to Eddie. "Come on in and I'll tell you what really happened. You'd have loved it."

4

The workers at Jeanette Modes had indeed received a welcome end-of-year bonus thanks to the massive order placed by Jeremy Murphy. The contract Patsy had landed had guaranteed well-stocked larders and a few extra presents for the children on Christmas morning but it wasn't to express seasonal thanks that the women were fussing and gossiping at Patsy's machine. It was the bouquet just delivered to her: a beautiful red, green and white arrangement comprising flowers and ferns and stems of berried holly. It was bound in looping bows of ribbon and the women waited excitedly as Patsy took the card out of its dainty envelope.

"Please accept this floral tribute to the passing of the old year and the arrival of the new," she read out. *"I've secured a table at the Gresham for the New Year's Eve Dinner and I hope family commitments will allow you to join me."*

"And who's it from?" came the clamour.

"It's from that Mr Murphy," she said, "the buyer who placed the order we're working on."

"Well now!"

"Aren't they just too gorgeous!"

"Would you just look at them!"

"And the perfume! Just get a nose full of that!"

"They'll have cost a pretty packet!"

"Are you going to go, Patsy?"

"Is she going to go to the Gresham? Of course she is, woman!"

"You'll be getting a personal bonus then, a special delivery, eh Patsy!"

"He wouldn't be a bad feller to catch!"

"You're the quiet one, Miss O'Kelly!"

Patsy hadn't told her colleagues about her first unexpected outing with Jem, thank goodness: then the tongues would really be wagging. Some of the women had been at work when the yellow roses were

247

delivered but no one had paid much attention to them. This bouquet was altogether too extravagant to be ignored.

"We'd better get back to work," said Patsy. "I don't want the invitation to be withdrawn."

She was glad when the women drifted back to their machines and she was left to her own thoughts. She hadn't heard from Jem Murphy since before the Liverpool weekend and had reached the conclusion that his approach had been just a one-off: she admitted to herself that she was glad it hadn't been.

Apart from anything else, the Christmas festivities were over and she had made no plans for seeing the year out. Molly was off to Tullamore for a few days with Nora and Theresa was going out with Billy and his friends. It wasn't that Patsy was fond of partying at New Year but nor did she fancy just sitting at home and going to bed early. Her father had reverted to his usual morose self after Michael's visit so light-hearted or otherwise chat in front of the fire was out, and there was no tradition in The Coombe of counting down the last seconds of the year before raising a cheer, 'cheer' was not something anyone left behind in the house would associate with New Year. Nor had the impact of Patsy's evening with Jem subsided yet, she was still of a mind to go out and have some fun.

Before receiving Jem's invitation, Patsy had agreed to cover the December 31st late afternoon shift at the Little Flower café and she decided to keep to her commitment. The idea was to provide more of a celebratory meal to the customers than the usual daily stew and one of the local bars had donated a few bottles for the occasion to make it more like a small social, the last serving was due on the table at six so Patsy would have time to get home and changed for the Gresham without too much of a rush. She was pleased to see Mrs Flaherty on duty too.

"Why don't you work in the kitchen with me today, Patsy," said Mrs Flaherty. "I think if I have to put on a fixed happy grin one more time this year I'll scream. My season of goodwill has completely evaporated."

"You wouldn't be here if that were true," said Patsy. "All the same I won't bother to wish you all the best, not out loud at least."

The two women got busy preparing the vegetables and putting the meat on to simmer: the meat was always the cheapest available so it took some cooking to get it tender but today they added a couple of bottles of Guinness to the stock to give it a richer taste.

"How was your Christmas, Mrs Flaherty, if I dare ask?" said Patsy. "I saw you had a short break from the Little Flower and I didn't see you at Mass, so I thought perhaps you'd been away visiting family for the Christmas."

"Not at all, if only," said Mrs Flaherty. "In fact it was the other way round, the family decided to land on us for the whole of Christmas so I'd not a moment to spare, what with all the extra mouths to feed — breakfast, dinner and tea, with lots of tea-breaks in between and then a last cuppa and a biscuit before bed. Then they insisted that Christmas morning Mass in the cathedral would be a special treat for them rather than just going to the local parish. Personally, I always like to be in my own church for Christmas but I'd no choice in the matter."

"I do too," said Patsy. "It has a different feel to a Sunday. The candles seem to burn brighter, the altar always looks beautifully decorated and the vestments and surplices have an extra white crispness; then the crib comes to life with the Baby Jesus added and there's that sense of something special in the air. And d'you not think people seem to sing with a lot more joy in their voices when they're singing carols? I know I do. The children are fidgety, of course, but that's only to be expected, they want to get home to their presents and treats."

"This year I for one didn't want the service to end," said Mrs Flaherty. "I wanted to postpone having to do the dinner for as long as possible. Another couple of hymns wouldn't have gone amiss as far as I was concerned, joyous or not. To be honest with you, Patsy, I'm glad I put my name down here for today. It might be more of the same — cooking, dishes, making sure everybody else is happy — but Jesus I needed to get out of the house. Didn't they only turn round and decide to stay over New Year. My brother-in-law had to get back to work but my sister Eileen wanted to stay in Dublin an extra week, God help us. I know what I'll be doing in the New Year, washing sheets."

"So are you not going out tonight?"

"I am not. I'm going to put my feet up and unless someone takes the hint and cooks then there won't be any dinner on the table. What about you, Patsy, are you off out somewhere exciting tonight?"

"As a matter of fact, I am," said Patsy, grinning as much to herself as to Mrs Flaherty. "I'm off to a grand dinner at the Gresham."

"Are you now? And exactly with whom are you going to this grand dinner at the Gresham, young lady?"

"I'm going with a man I met through work," said Patsy.

"Really? I thought it was mainly women you worked with and now it turns out you have males between the bales," said Mrs Flaherty raising a suggestive eye-brow. "Goodness, Patsy, are you blushing? I thought you were set against men and romance."

Patsy's face grew redder as she quickly put Mrs Flaherty in the picture as regards Jem Murphy and filled her in on the details of who he was and how they met.

"Well, you enjoy yourself while you can," said Mrs Flaherty. "Are you keen on this feller?"

"I've only met him once before, actually."

"Only the once? That's great, that means tonight you can be whoever you choose to be and he'll be none the wiser."

"It's too late now," said Patsy, picking up a bundle of leeks to top and tail. "When I met him I was busy being the knowledgeable representative of an important Dublin tailoring institution, determined to uphold the company's reputation and inspire confidence in the client, but that front didn't last long over our meal. We got on too well for any pretence. Not that it had all been pretence, you understand, Mrs Flaherty, I know my job as well as anyone; but I probably had been trying to put on some professional airs and graces because the order was too important to lose and it was my responsibility to make sure that didn't happen. Fortunately in no time we were on first name terms and I could relax, though he did have to help me with which cutlery to use for the different dishes. It was new to me."

"Tell me what he's like, then, this man who knows his way around a table setting."

"Well for a start he's a great one for talking but he has interesting things to say, dreamy things, imaginative things, not know-all things like someone I used to know."

"I like a man who can be dreamy," said Mrs Flaherty. "There aren't enough dreamy men in the world. Most of them think the very idea of showing their soft side means they're not real men, when all we women yearn for is a bit of softness after a hard day's work or, better still, during a hard day's work. It could be worth getting your hooks into him, Patsy, he could be a catch worth netting. Does he strike you as the marrying kind?"

"He strikes me as too independent for all that and that suits me. He seems more inclined to appreciate nice things — you should have seen the way he delighted in the touch of the fabrics in the samples room — and he goes to the theatre and concerts and enjoys a day at the races. I doubt he'd be anxious to swap all that for the routine of a wife bent over the kitchen sink and kids swarming the place. And you know my own thinking on that score already, Mrs Flaherty."

"Well, what more could an independent gentleman want than an independent woman," said Mrs Flaherty. "We'd best get these vegetables on quick; I heard the first customers coming in. We might not get a chance to chat more so I'll wish you a wonderful evening now with your dreamy gentleman and I'll be waiting to hear the details later, next year, in fact. And if you're not interested in him, you can pass him on to one of my girls — he can add a nightmare to his dreams. Of course it would have to be Josie, my second eldest. Her big sister is walking out with a young man now, a plasterer by trade. Did I not tell you?"

"I wonder if my sister knows him," said Patsy. "Her feller's a plasterer too."

"Maybe they'll get plastered together tonight," said Mrs Flaherty.

Patsy was to meet Jem on the south side of the Liffey by the Ha'penny Bridge at half-past eight. It was a clear night and the sky glimmered with stars and the plan was to walk the short way along the river to O'Connell Street, renewing their acquaintance, Jem had suggested, while enjoying the lights and the sounds of people heading out for the evening's entertainments.

Patsy decided she wanted to arrive first, catch her breath, steady her nerves. Not that she was nervous, she told herself, but it had been a few months since they had last met and perhaps her memory had gilded the lily a little over their first encounter. She ambled casually along the river walk, deliberately not looking directly towards the meeting place but rather gazing about her like a Sunday stroller. She felt good. She was pleased that she had taken the time to pin one of the flowers from Jem's bouquet to her lapel; a nice touch, she thought, and wondered if he'd notice.

He spotted it straight away. Before Patsy had time to clear her hair out of her eyes and make those few last twitchy adjustments to her appearance which people the world over seem to need to make when arriving somewhere, Jem had taken her by the hands and held her out so he could get a good look.

"I see you picked out the only yellow rose in the assortment," he said. "I wondered if you'd notice it. Your choice ensures that we will indeed have an evening devoted to joy and friendship. Take my arm, Miss Patsy O'Kelly," he said, crooking his elbow, "and we'll head along the Liffey but perhaps on the other side where there are more interesting if humble sights to behold. Let's cross the Ha'penny Bridge first and toss a few coins into the water as an investment in the continuity between old and new. You can make a wish if you like but keep it a secret, mind."

The river was busy with boats even though it was New Year's Eve and their bobbing lights reflected like dance steps treading in and over the rippling water, the Liffey itself seemed to be alive to the night's time signature.

"It always looks so cosy and intimate inside the boats' cabins at night when you see the lights on," said Jem, "a few hardy souls cocooned in their own little space, protected from the outside but contributing their own simple existence for us spectators to enjoy."

"It wasn't that cosy but it was very intimate on the Liverpool crossing," said Patsy. "The storm and the need to be sick robbed us all of any attempt at personal privacy. I'd have gladly been a spectator looking on from the shore."

"You can delight me with tales of your trip over dinner," said Jem. "For now, I want to know what it is you respond to on this great river of ours. What gets in there to your core, Patsy?"

"The sounds," she said, "definitely the sounds. I love to hear the funnels sounding their horns and the chains clanking and the ropes stretching and creaking when they're casting off. You can still hear the funnels as the ships make their way out of the bay, reaching us mysteriously through the mist or cutting to the ears sharply on a fine morning when there's nothing between sea and sky to stifle the hootings."

"It's the musician in your soul," said Jem. "Unfortunately we might miss the New Year funnel crescendo at midnight this evening, I doubt we'll be able to hear it in the Gresham, but I suppose we could always leave a few minutes before the New Year countdown and come back to the Liffey."

"I'd love that," said Patsy. "I don't get to hear it at The Coombe either."

"Too far away and too many home distractions, I suppose?"

"Too cosy and already tucked up asleep in bed normally."

"Well tonight is to be anything but normal, Patsy, so I propose that we enjoy our dinner and then see how it goes and if we've had enough of fine dining we'll wend our way back to this same spot. Though there is dancing too after the meal. Do you have dancer's feet as well as musician's ears?"

"I think my ears are more in tune than my feet are in step," she said, "but I do love to dance and I do keep good time with my feet even if they're not always in the right place."

"In that case I shall put my name down in your little book for every waltz, quick-step, fox-trot and — what's that one that came over from America years ago? — the Charleston, that's it; we shall flap about together on the dance floor."

The ballroom restaurant at the Gresham was a mix of the sumptuous and the positively frivolous. A huge Christmas tree dominated the entrance as you went in from the foyer then the scene opened out into an expanse of gold and silver, glittering and sparkling in every direction, with tinsel garlands and glass baubles and colourful lanterns illuminating every corner: wherever the eye alighted it seemed to land in a magical Aladdin's grotto. It was elegant and regal and tasteful but the mood was lightened by a net of multi-coloured balloons hung from the ceiling and swaying banners strung across the room proclaiming, in large letters and plump digits, the old year's end and the new year's beginning. An orchestra was playing on a small stage at one end, the brass instruments echoing and reflecting the shiny illuminations. Patsy felt very privileged:

she felt as if she'd walked on to the set of a Hollywood film.

"You're looking quite lovely, Miss O'Kelly," said Jem when they had taken their seats.

"I'm afraid I had to wear the same cerise frock as before," said Patsy. "I don't have a wardrobe suitable for this style of living."

"It's the nicest frock in the place," said Jem. "I couldn't have chosen better myself."

"And I, Mr Murphy, couldn't have chosen a better-fitting hand-stitched, tailored dinner suit for you. You cut quite a dash."

The mutual laughter established a warm ambience between the two of them that wasn't to dissipate as the evening wore on. It was a set menu, just reading it made the mouth water, and Patsy welcomed being able to relax without having to face the challenge of selecting from an endless list of unfamiliar dishes. To Jem the set selection of hors d'oeuvres, starters and mains was all very familiar and Patsy was happy to let him take charge.

"Tell me, then," he said, "what was so important that you stood me up and went to Liverpool?"

"I didn't stand you up," she protested defensively and again the two of them shared a moment of amusement. Patsy explained why she had suddenly had to go to Liverpool, she elaborated on the horrors of the stormy crossing and emphasised the highlights of the weekend, while mentioning the low points without making a drama out of Aunt Mary's tearful moments.

"I was in Liverpool too earlier this year, I went over for the racing at Aintree," said Jem.

"You are a big racing fan, going all that way."

"I am," said Jem. "I like a flutter on the horses like any true Irishman."

"Do you have to go to the course to bet?"

"You used to but off-course betting was made legal here about ten years ago, when the Free State took over," said Jem, "a state of being free to lose your money at a place of your choosing. But I like to go to watch, Patsy, it makes for an exciting day out, seeing the jockeys in their vibrant silks and their tight little arses, stuck up off the saddles as they ride the course like a rushing parade of giant soft u-bends, upturned, and, of course, listening to the horses thunder past over the turf and the crowd cheering them on to the finish. It's one of the most thrilling experiences I know. And it's the only way to get your money's worth out of a bet, especially a losing bet: at least you get to see how your money was lost."

"You must be keen to go all the way to Liverpool to watch a few horses running past," said Patsy.

"And jumping," said Jem, "jumping over some of the most difficult obstacles in the world. The Grand National is one hell of a race and one hell of a spectacle, Patsy."

"And did you win?"

"I won on the National, all right. The winner was an Irish thoroughbred, Reynoldstown, came in at 10-1. It won last year too so there was a lot of disagreement among the tipsters before the off as to whether a previous win was a good thing or a bad: no horse before had ever won the Grand National two years on the run. Anyway, I thought Reynoldstown might be just the horse to do it so I took the chance, even though it was carrying top weight."

"And you came home a richer man than when you left," said Patsy.

"It'd be fairer to say I broke even," said Jem, clearing his throat slightly as the waitress cleared the table for the next course.

"I've never been to see horse-racing, I've never even been to the Dublin Horse Show," said Patsy.

"Then we'll have to remedy that," said Jem. "I'll take you next year, Patsy. You'd enjoy the sounds and, I have to say it, the smells. There's nothing greets the nostrils quite like a dump of horse manure."

"Now that I have experienced," said Patsy at the same time contrarily relishing the smell of the beef bourguignon arriving at the table — mushrooms were a huge treat for Patsy and all swimming in a red wine sauce promised even more of a huge treat. "I can tell you that this smells a lot better."

"Then tuck in, my good lady, as much as your stomach will allow."

They forked their first mouthfuls and Patsy mmmhed at the taste.

"You've not told me yet about your Christmas, it must be rather hectic with so many in such a small house," said Jem. "I've only ever lived with my mother, just the two of us, my father died when I was young and I was an only child, so Christmas has always been a muted affair, not a lot of what you'd call real jollity, Patsy. Of course, my mother has always done her best to make it special, God bless her, she's a wonderful woman, and I like to play my part. We set aside what we call our 'pre-Christmas Day' evening and we have a glass of sherry each to wash down our buttered crackers and some nice cheeses that we wouldn't normally have, then we decorate the parlour, always just the parlour, and put up a small tree in front of the window, 'that way everyone can enjoy it', she always says. And all the time we sing a few carols, the quality of our voices somewhat governed by the amount of sherry we've imbibed."

"That's a beautiful tradition," said Patsy.

"More of a fading beautiful tradition," said Jem. "Time marches on and my mother isn't as able as she was, so I have to do most of it myself now, bar the sherry: she still enjoys her glass of sherry while she fixes the odd cheeky cherub to the tree."

"Do you cook the dinner too on your own?"

"Again, we used to prepare the Christmas dinner and all the trimmings together, we'd each have our own responsibilities as regards the meal, but you're right, Patsy, now I cook it myself. I'm happy to, to be honest, we're very close."

"Christmas dinner is a major production in our house," said Patsy, wanting to lift the conversation: Jem was obviously devoted to his mother and a hint of melancholia had entered his voice. "And this year there was the added ingredient of two live chickens," she said.

"Don't you mean dead chickens?" said Jem, rising to the bait. "Or are you more of an odd bunch than I'd thought."

"Well of course they started off live," said Patsy and she told Jem about Michael's visit from the farm and his offerings for the Christmas table.

"Who slaughtered them in the end? Was it the boys?"

"My da was to do it but only because the boys had worn themselves out chasing the things round the yard," said Patsy. "They certainly didn't want to be caught. No doubt they sensed what was waiting in the kitchen. Da had decided that the best method would be to wring the chickens' necks but holding them still was trickier than he'd expected. He tried holding the first one by the feet but it managed to keep twisting its head back up and pecking my da til he had cuts on his arms and had to let go.

It's a long time since we lived in the country and he'd had to kill a chicken for the pot. I think it must be an acquired skill and one easily forgotten."

"I can imagine that," said Jem. "Fortunately, it's a skill I have never had cause to acquire. I willingly leave them to take care of that sort of business in the butcher's shop."

"Anyway, it was a great gas watching the struggle between man and birds, we were all of us standing there watching and not one of us could stop laughing. My da was getting redder and sweatier by the minute and in the end my mammy had to take over and finish the job. Then, I don't know if you've ever seen a chicken just killed but it can still run around with its head hanging near off, and there we were with two of them running around with their heads hanging off and all of us scrambling to get out of their way, as if they could see where they were going. One of them even rose into the air and took a short flight before crashing to the ground again. It was awful to see but, God forgive me, my cheeks were sore from laughing as much as everyone else."

"I doubt God would hold it against such a good Catholic girl as yourself, Patsy, after all he put animals here on earth for us to eat and to eat them we have to kill them first, though I'm glad I don't have to do the slaughtering. I'm content to collect my meat wrapped up in a bit of paper rather than having to slice it directly off the carcass, even one as small as a chicken. So, what happened then? Was your father in a bad temper after such a public failure? You told me he can be somewhat of a dour man."

"He was fine, he saw the funny side, thank God, otherwise he would have been a terrible heavy cloud looming over the Christmas dinner. And he did redeem himself by hanging the birds to bleed for a while before plunging them into hot water ready for plucking. That's a job I hate so I was glad he took charge. He got the boys involved too so that kept them quiet and out of the way in the yard."

"You're lucky to have such a family," said Jem. "I think I missed out not having even one brother or sister. Is that what you want for yourself, Patsy, a big family?"

She was slightly unsettled by the question although it seemed to have flowed logically within the conversation without pause for hidden motivation. The delivery of individual Christmas puddings, each drizzled in brandy and set alight at the table, gave Patsy some thinking time. All sorts of questions fired through her brain in split-seconds. Should she reply 'yes' or 'no'? She didn't want to put him off with the wrong answer. Was he interested enough in her even to be worried about putting him off? Was she herself interested in him as a potential husband? Could she tell him the truth about her sworn chastity? How sworn was it anyway? Could it be reversed without her betraying what she regarded as almost a holy oath? Was it a fear of anything physical that really lay behind that oath? Was it no more than a contrived spirituality used as an excuse, as a protection against giving in to what her body wanted but what she convinced herself was sinful carnal desire? Was it because of Sean? Was she too young to be expected to keep a secret vow of chastity and her not even a nun?

"I haven't thought about it that much," she finally managed. "This pudding is delicious."

"I wasn't sure about plum pudding complementing the beef bourguignon but it seemed an appropriately festive dessert. A superb end to a superb dinner, I think you'd agree," said Jem. "The dancing is due to start as soon as the tables are cleared and a bit of rhythmic exercise won't go amiss after all this food. I am literally stuffed. But I do realise that you neatly skirted my question," he said, squeezing her hand across the table, "perhaps we're of one mind on the matter."

Patsy wasn't sure what that one mind might be or what the squeezed hand might imply but she was happy to accept both.

When the music was in full swing, they took to the floor for every dance until legs started to give out and Jem suggested some champagne to toast what was, in his words, 'an evening that has out-performed my already ambitious hopes'.

"I'll join you in that toast, Jem. I can't thank you enough for inviting me, I've never been to such a glitzy glamorous party."

"Here's to more in the future," said Jem. They raised and clinked their glasses and bubbled over with enthusiasm. "Now," he said, "we have to decide on more dancing and a New Year countdown here, or on slipping out and going down to the river. What would you like to do, Patsy, your choice?"

"I've no idea, I'm having such a grand time here. What do you fancy?"

"Well, like yourself, I'm torn. On the one hand we're here for a party organised specially to bid a cheery goodbye to 1936 and give a hearty Dublin welcome to 1937, with open arms spread under a cascade of falling balloons and more champagne to add extra fizz to the midnight tolling. On the other hand is the pull of the Liffey, of the crowds of modest but sincere well-wishers in the street and along the quays, people who could never afford to come to a do like this but are determined to celebrate regardless of their lot in life. And let's not forget your ships and their funnels. We could stay here and exchange drunken cheek-to-cheek greetings with perfect strangers and dance into the small hours, or we could cherish the moment in a more personal, contemplative way down by the river."

"I always think New Year is a time for contemplation," said Patsy, "looking back on the year on what you did or didn't do, looking forward to what might change. And I'm honestly not that keen on the idea of kissing perfect strangers even on the cheek. You've painted two attractive pictures but I'd like to opt for the second one, unless that's really not what you prefer."

"As ever, Miss O'Kelly, we are of one mind. Let's go."

O'Connell Street was heaving with people, as if the whole of Dublin had turned out to celebrate with one giant outdoor party. Spontaneous dancing had sprung up here and there along the pavement: couples and groups of friends were jigging and swirling in chaotic reels wherever there were a few buskers singing and fiddling for their supper, more often than not getting paid in a few jars, which was fine with them too. Jem couldn't resist joining in: all the way to the river he was either leaping in the air and kicking his heels together or twirling round any innocuous lamppost they happened to pass. He tried to goad Patsy into partnering him in his gallop but she pleaded sore feet when actually it was her head that was spinning.

"Not much chance of any serious contemplation of the great issues of New Year here," he shouted. "Not to worry, Patsy, we'll be at the river soon enough and you can do all the contemplating you want."

Jem had to call time on his dancing when they got to O'Connell

Bridge, where they had to force their way through a mass of pedestrian traffic moving in both directions all at once before they could edge their way to a less populated space down by the Liffey wall. The Ha'penny Bridge was already full.

"You'll need to catch your breath after that display," said Patsy.

"Aye but my food has gone down a treat," said Jem. "What time is it now?"

Patsy looked at her watch and momentarily flinched at the idea of consulting Sean's present while she was out with another man. "It's already a quarter to twelve," she said.

"Then we've time to consider any resolutions we might want to make. We'll take a moment or two to think then we'll compare notes on what we promise to do but no doubt won't."

They stood once again looking at the water. The flotilla of boats on the river had disappeared into the night and only the ships tied up at the docks were still bedecked with lights from prow to stern. They looked magical and full of inviting promises of adventure in the everything's-possible atmosphere of New Year's Eve.

"You go first, Jem," said Patsy. "What are you going to do differently come midnight?"

"For a start I resolve to see you more often than just once every couple of months," he said. "If you're agreeable then that won't be too hard a resolution to achieve. Of course, if you're not, I've failed before I've started."

"Then you won't fail because I'd like that," said Patsy. "My life had settled into the doldrums until you arrived and shook me out of myself."

"Perhaps I shook you into yourself, Patsy, think of it that way, it's more positive."

"That's my resolution, then, to be more positive in my life," she said. "I know I often automatically see the negative in people just because their behaviour is not what I'd choose for myself, but we can't all be the same, that's not how God made us. And I know I shy away from situations because I see them too in a negative light but I should try to find the positive in whatever life throws at me. God presents us with opportunities, with a life to enjoy, and I should enjoy it, I should recognise opportunities presented as what they are, opportunities to enjoy to the full, to make the most of the life given me."

"There's some heavy stuff there, Patsy. You certainly meant it when you said New Year was a time for contemplation."

"Amn't I the boring one, put it down to the added influence of wine and champagne."

"You're far from boring, Miss O'Kelly," said Jem. "You're a blast of fresh air. Now it's my turn to get a bit heavy. I also hereby resolve to curb my gambling habit — I'd prefer to stop giving my money to the bookies and instead spend it on taking you out."

Suddenly they were aware of a general hush in the noise of the crowd. People were counting down the seconds of the old year until finally a melodious cacophony started up as all the clock towers and church bells across the city chimed and rang in the start of 1937. Then all the ships sounded their funnels. Jem took Patsy in his arms and kissed her on the forehead.

5

'MY FUTURE PLANS ARE AND ALWAYS WILL BE TO MARRY YOU - WILL YOU PLEASE BECOME ENGAGED TO ME NOW MOLLY DARLING - PLEASE SAY YES - THIS MAY ALSO GIVE ME AN OPPORTUNITY OF SPENDING A LEAVE WITH YOU - PLEASE ANSWER SOON - YOUR LOVING SWEETHEART = KEVIN'

The telegram was waiting at The Coombe for Molly when she got home from work. As soon as Britain had declared war on Germany at the beginning of September the previous year, Kevin, along with thousands of other men in Britain, had been required to register for military service and express a preference for which branch of the services he wanted to join. Molly and the rest of the family assumed Kevin would specify the Royal Navy but instead Kevin had surprised everyone by opting for the RAF. He said he could always go to sea but was unlikely ever again to get the chance to work with aircraft. Not that he was called up straight away. After passing his medical examination he had had to wait several weeks before a brown OHMS envelope was pushed through the letterbox at Bulwer Street, ordering him to report for duty for aptitude tests. Enclosed with his papers was a return train voucher and his mam's spirits rose.

"They've given you your ticket home again," she said. "That's got to be a good sign. The papers are calling this a 'phoney war' anyway. It's months since war was declared and not much has happened since then, perhaps you won't have to go away and fight after all. Hitler won't attack us, surely to God."

"The ticket is so I can come home after the tests," said Kevin, "it's a one-off. I'll have to wait and see what they decide I'm to do."

After the tests it was five weeks before the next OHMS communiqué arrived, his official call-up papers, with just a one-way ticket. Kevin was ordered to report for three months of military training and was then to study as an engine fitter. He was disappointed not to train as a pilot as he'd hoped, his eyesight wasn't passed as good enough for that, but Molly and his mother alike were relieved he'd be staying on the ground. At the end of his three months' military training, he was granted a short spring leave before taking up his posting to an airfield in Wales and he wanted to spend it with Molly, as his fiancée.

Kevin's telegram threw Molly into a fit of excitement at the urgency of the romance it suggested. "Can I say 'yes' Daddy?" she asked Patrick. "I've always wanted to marry him, Mammy will tell you. Patsy and Theresa know it too. And I'm plenty old enough."

Patrick looked at his daughter. Of all three girls, Molly was the one who most reminded him of his dead wife, Lizzie, in her eager warmth and sense of fun, and he warmed to the notion of another marriage between the two families, as if it kept that strong thread uniting them still with Lizzie.

"You know it's frowned upon to marry a first cousin?" he said. "Kevin's father was your mother's brother, don't forget, that's very close. I'd have to seek a special dispensation from the bishop before I could give my permission." He saw the flush of happiness pale from Molly's face. "But I have no objection if the bishop allows it and I don't see why he wouldn't, especially in a time of war when no one knows what's going to happen. I'll look into it tomorrow. You can tell Kevin 'yes' but to bear in mind what I've said."

The enthusiasm returned to Molly, now bursting with happiness under a barrage of congratulations. "Thank you, Daddy," she said. "I'll go to the Post Office tomorrow and send my answer. I think it should be a telegram, don't you, so Kevin will know as soon as possible."

Molly was dreading the ferry journey over to Liverpool again, especially as this time she would be on her own. Patsy and Teresa had said they couldn't get the time off but really they had agreed between them that it would better to let Molly and Kevin spend what brief time they had together. To Molly's relief it was a smooth crossing — people said the sea was more like a mill pond than a clash of tidal flows — and she felt reassured listening to the enthusiasm of her countrymen who were travelling over to England to enlist.

But, while Kevin and Molly were celebrating their engagement in Bootle, the RAF dropped the first British bombs on German soil and Kevin was summoned to cut short his weekend leave and immediately report to RAF Pembrey in Carmarthenshire. There was no time for any engagement party. There was barely time for a loving farewell at Lime Street station, especially as Mary had insisted on joining them on the platform to see her son off.

Back in Dublin, Molly was delighted to show off her ring but she couldn't hide the fact that she was sick with worry and, as the months went on and news of the mass evacuation from Dunkirk suggested that Britain was on the defensive, she worried even more. She confided in Nora that she would go back to England as soon as possible to marry Kevin.

"France has formally surrendered," Patrick read out of the newspaper. "It seems the Germans are unstoppable and have England in their sights. I'm glad we're not directly involved."

"How can you say that when you know Kevin is in the RAF?" said Molly, challenging her father with an eruption of passion that took everyone by surprise. "Won't his base be a target for the German bombers? How is that not us being directly involved? And what about Auntie Mary and Tessie in Bootle? They're part of our family, regardless of Kevin and me, and they live near the docks. Won't the docks be a target too? Is that not us being directly involved?"

"That's not what I meant," said Patrick as Molly left the room.

"I'll go and talk to her," said Patsy, "but you might have been a bit more understanding, Daddy. I don't know how you could have said we're not involved."

In August Molly's fears were vindicated and all the O'Kellys shuddered at the news that Liverpool had suffered a devastating three-night bombardment by the Luftwaffe.

"God help Mary and Tessie," said Betty. "And them with no man in the house at such a frightening time."

"Like a lot of families over there now," said Patrick, though it was a somewhat forced attempt at sympathy and he was still relieved that Ireland was out of the mess. Nazis or no Nazis, he couldn't shake his feelings of animosity towards his old enemy.

Patsy made a series of novenas at the parish church; there were lots of local families with relatives in Liverpool and the pews were full. The priest urged people to put aside their old resentment against Britain and to support the many young men from Dublin who had gone to fight the Germans with the British Army, many of them having deserted from the Irish Army to do so. De Valera remained adamant that the Free State would remain neutral but behind the scenes clandestine support and intelligence was provided to the Allies. And when a raft of German spies was caught in Ireland, there were murmurings in Dublin that Germany might renege on its agreement of neutrality and might actually invade Ireland.

Even Patrick was wavering. "I don't know how long we can in all justice stay out of it," he said, "it's a dirty war, hundreds of bombs are being dropped on anyone and anything, people can't sleep in their beds any more. Women and children in France are being killed in their own homes or made to watch their men being shot by Hitler's soldiers. How can we rely on his word to leave us alone when he is responsible for all that cruelty?"

The newspapers in Ireland were heavily censored on the grounds that too true a picture of what was happening in the war would weaken the morale at home to stay neutral but people knew exactly what was going on from friends and family in England. Patrick had received a letter from his brother Arthur and it painted an ominous picture, a picture Patrick couldn't dismiss however anti-British he was. Arthur had been working in a print shop in Paris for several years when the Civil War broke out in Spain. He had gone to fight with the Republicans there but had had to flee back across the border into France when Franco prevailed. Arthur was back working at the print shop when the Germans had goose-stepped their way through the streets of Paris.

'Everything changed immediately, the Germans wasted no time at all,' he wrote. *'I was at the printers and all we could hear outside was the constant stream of military vehicles driving through the city blasting out propaganda and telling people to stay indoors and off the streets. Of course lots of people had to go out, they couldn't stay in work all day and all night, and some of them got fired at in the street as a warning. On the way home I saw there was already a giant swastika hung across the Arc*

de Triomphe and the Nazis not even here a full day. The newspapers and the radio were taken over and a curfew ordered from nine at night until five in the morning. Doesn't that sound only too familiar, brother! As it was, Paris was already practically empty. Trainloads had fled the city a few days earlier and the roads were jammed with people trying to escape south, on foot, in cars, buses, bikes, trucks, carts, you name it — if it moved there were people on it. And as if more proof were needed of who had taken over the place, Jews who had lived all their lives in Paris were being forcibly made to pin on yellow stars. I can't sit back and not do anything with all that's going on, Patrick, I have to help somehow. I'm sure you would too if you were here.'

"What's Uncle Arthur going to do now?" asked Patsy. "Does he say if he's to come back to Dublin?"

"I'm sure he'll stay where he is," said Patrick. "You know your Uncle Arthur, he'll be in the front line of any fight against foreign occupation just as he was here." Patrick picked up Arthur's letter again. "He says he might not be able to get in touch for a while as no one knows whether the post in and out of France will still operate. Meanwhile, he says he'll have to be very careful working at the print shop, that'll be one place the Germans will keep a close eye on, nor does he know if they'll have his name on a list of International Brigaders who escaped over the border from Franco's Spain. I wouldn't put it past them. But he's hoping to go underground with a few of his colleagues and maybe start a resistance newspaper. He says they've already circulated a report of a BBC broadcast by a French General in London urging the French to fight on. So, Patsy, we'll all just have to wait and see. I'm sure Arthur will get word to us when he can."

"We could have a Mass said for him," said Patsy.

"And for everyone else," said Betty.

The family was anxious when Molly returned to Liverpool just weeks later so she and Kevin could be married but no one could see any point in waiting. Only Patsy went with her from Dublin for the wedding because of the danger involved, though Eddie and Ciaran and Mikey had been keen to go and experience the excitement of the bombings for themselves. Patsy had insisted on making a beautiful wedding dress for her sister; as it couldn't be a big occasion with all the family it was more important than ever to make the day as splendid as possible, she said. She created a slender-fitting gown of white shot silk with swirls of seed-pearls hand-sewn down the full length of the skirt. At Molly's request, the design was based on a gown they saw Wallis Simpson wearing in a magazine picture. Patsy made dresses of a similar but simpler cut in pale blue crepe de chine for herself and Tessie to wear as bridesmaids, not too weddingy so they could easily be worn again. Patsy had actually chosen the style with an idea to going out with Jem: she didn't want to have to wear the same cerise one over and over.

The wedding party went to Mary's sister's house in Dryden Street for a small breakfast after the service before Kevin and Molly set off for two nights in Llandudno. It was to be a very short honeymoon before they moved into digs near the airfield. Molly had swapped The Coombe to live in a war zone but she couldn't have been happier.

Traffic screeched and swerved to a halt, people ran this way and that to get out of the way or stood at a safe distance gawking and having a good laugh: a herd of cantankerous pigs had butted down the tailgate and made their escape from the back of a wagon en route to Dublin abattoir and they were now running amok in their panic. The pigs, like everybody else within nose-shot, could smell the bloody slaughterhouse not half-a-mile away and had freaked at the implication. The noise of their squealing and oinking goaded on their own hysteria. Even better, as far as Ciaran and Mikey were concerned, was the sight of the Gardaí stampeding around trying to get the animals under some sort of control. It was not a sight to inspire respect for the uniformed constabulary.

"Let's get stuck in," said Ciaran. "We can pretend we're helping."

The two lads, who were out shopping with Annie and little John, dumped their bags on the ground and charged into the fray. Annie was standing stock still, totally hypnotised by the scene, while John pulled at her hand trying to escape so he could join his big brothers. It was comical but scary at the same time: pigs lived on a farm and here they were behaving like wild animals and Annie could only stand there open-mouthed.

Ciaran and Mikey were having great fun, running and waving their arms about and shouting and hollering at the tops of their voices, shooing pigs this way and that and colliding deliberately with the posse of men who were helping the police to round up the lawless swine. The O'Kelly two soon realised that it was more fun to drive the rogue pigs away from the wagon but they had to be clever about it: they didn't want to be dragged home by a Garda again and get another belting from their da: they were in their early teens but not too old for a hiding.

Eventually all but one of the pigs was back on board. The loose one, which had maintained its freedom by snuffling and snorting around innocently and so had escaped the frenetic round-up, trotted its way casually over to Annie. She froze, unable to move, unable to scare the pig away as it shoved its snout into one of the shopping bags to explore what was inside.

It was now the ensnared pig's turn to panic like its friends and panic it did. The crowd of onlookers cheered and whooped as the poor animal bolted around wildly, blindly, its head caught in the bag, its trotters kicking potatoes and carrots and rashers all over the road and Ciaran and Mikey on the chase again only this time trying to rescue their dinner. They could be in for the belt regardless of the Gardaí. Food was short enough thanks to the stupid war without them adding to it. Eventually the farmer managed to catch his animal, with some friendly whisperings and a tickle behind the ears, and the lone pig followed meekly to join its fellow damned.

Ciaran offered to take charge when they got home: they were late back because of rioting pigs, that was the truth, and he could blame the pigs for the scuffed state of the vegetables, which was also the truth, but he stressed to little John that there was no need to mention the bit about himself and Mikey taking part.

"But it wasn't our fault," said Mikey, "we didn't set the pigs free."

"No, but we helped them stay free as long as possible," said Ciaran. "Best not to mention that bit at all. Agreed, Annie?"

"Agreed," she said, "as long as I don't get into trouble. I didn't do anything."

"Aye we noticed," said Mikey, "but you're only a girl."

No one cared about the pigs or the state of the vegetables when they bustled into the house. Ciaran shoved to the front and was eager to talk about the morning's adventure but the mood in the kitchen was too heavy. Eddie had just announced his decision to move to London. He had been offered work as a long-distance lorry driver after replying to a newspaper advertisement placed by a haulage company which was desperately short of drivers now that so many men in Britain had been called up.

"London isn't the safest place to move to now there's a war on," said Patrick. "You can't even drive. I don't suppose your experience with the cart will get you far."

"Actually it impressed them," said Eddie. "They said I obviously had valuable experience of manoeuvring heavy loads in traffic and should have no problems driving a lorry. They say all training is provided so I'll learn how to drive and then, don't you see, I'll have a recognised skill. While I'm training, I'll be going on delivery and pick-up runs with another driver so I'll be earning straightaway. I'll be able to send money home to help out."

"But London!" said Patsy. "Aren't they getting bombed there every night? Dear God, you could be blown up. We might never see you again."

"The company is based on the outskirts of London, on the east side, so it should be safe enough," said Eddie.

"Isn't that the side where the docks are?" said Patrick. "The Germans bomb them every night, flying in up the Thames and flattening the place. A lorry depot en route would be a prime target."

"But what else am I doing?" pleaded Eddie. "Nothing, I'm nearly nineteen and I'm not doing anything. I don't want to deliver coal and sell birds in a street market for the rest of my life, I need a proper job, Mammy, and this is a good chance, with prospects. I know it means leaving home but all the young ones are growing up and the house is getting smaller even with Molly gone. Besides, who knows how this food shortage is going to turn out, it could get worse if the war goes on and my pay would come in handy."

The room fell into silence and Mikey tried to bring up the matter of the pigs, until Ciaran glowered at him. Eddie tried a different tack.

"I could also help out in the air-raids," he said. "You're proud of Uncle Arthur, Da, and his work in France, well I could play my part too, only in London. They have people volunteering for all sorts of jobs that need doing."

"What sort of jobs?" asked Betty.

"Like making sure people can find their way to the bomb shelters, or helping to clear up after a raid, digging people out of the rubble, or being on the look-out for any German aircraft approaching and then shining searchlights into the sky and firing at them — I'd love that." He couldn't help grinning, relishing the picture in his head, but straight away he realised that talking about people buried under rubble or of him firing guns wasn't perhaps the best way to reassure his mammy.

"My God, would you listen to what you're saying, Eddie," she said. "Talk some sense into him, Patrick. There must be jobs he could find here. What about at the bakery? Is there a chance he could get in with you?"

Patrick studied his son's face quietly for a moment or two. "Are you set on it?" he asked.

"I am, Da. I've given it lots of thought. This way I get to be trained in something and I can also help people, we've all seen the pictures of what it's like in England now. Surely you can understand that. In the past you did what you thought was right and fought the British. I don't want to fight for them, I don't want to join up when I'm there, I promise, I'm not the fighting sort and never have been, but I would like to help. It's ordinary people like ourselves who are losing everything. You always taught us that it was the rich British who kept Ireland for themselves, not the ordinary British people, not the people like us, and it's those people I'd be helping."

"It seems your mind is made up then, Eddie, and I can't argue with your wanting to help," said Patrick. "We won't stand in your way. When do you leave?"

"They want me as soon as possible, I'm to get the Liverpool boat tomorrow night. The boss of the company has arranged for one of his lorries to pick me up at the Pier Head and take me straight down to London."

"Jesus, you're leaving us tomorrow night?" said Betty. "Why didn't you tell us sooner?"

"Because I thought it would be better this way," said Eddie, "less time for us all to get upset."

"Can I take over the pigeons?" asked Ciaran.

"Can we tell you about the pigs now?" asked Mikey.

6

Patsy and Margaret, ensconced in their favourite Bewley's haunt, couldn't decide which film they had enjoyed the most. On the one hand they'd been thrilled having seen Maureen Fitzsimons show off her talents in a really dramatic role as an orphan girl caught up with smugglers in *Jamaica Inn,* a much meatier role for her after the flimsy Irish colleen part she'd previously played. Of course she was known as Maureen O'Hara now but they could forgive the name change as her new one still sounded Irish. As regular cinemagoers they recognised that *Jamaica Inn* was more melodrama than drama but they wanted to remain loyal to the local girl, so it had gone to the top of their favourites list. On the other hand, they had just been swept up, along with everybody else, by the huge Hollywood epic, *Gone with the Wind.* It was the talk of all the sewing rooms and everyone was in love with Clark Gable.

"I think we're in love with Rhett Butler, actually," said Margaret. "I read somewhere that Clark Gable has very bad breath. Not all his leading ladies are enthusiastic for the love scenes and I can't say as I'd blame them, handsome though he is. Are you having another coffee or something stronger, Patsy?"

"You know I fancy a glass of wine tonight. What about you or are you sticking to Paddy's?"

"I don't know if they do wine by the glass here," said Margaret. "If they don't, I'll join you and share a bottle. Unless, of course, you're so well used to wine after all your fancy dinners out with Jem that you can manage a whole bottle on your own."

"Now that would be telling and I'm a one to keep my own secrets," said Patsy.

"Frankly, Patsy, I don't give a damn. Let's go for the bottle."

"I don't know anything about Clark Gable having smelly breath," said Patsy, "but I did read an article in a magazine one of the girls had at work and it said that, for all his stardom, the man is a genuine sort, a

271

really nice man evidently. The article was about *Gone with the Wind* —
isn't everything these days? — and it said that he was so angry when he
saw the signs round the studio for 'whites' and 'coloureds' that he refused
to go back on set until they were all removed and everyone could use the
same facilities."

"I read that too," said Margaret. "Perhaps the rumour about his
breath was started by one of the Confederates who didn't want the signs
taken down. Americans can be very ignorant even these days. Anyway,
Patsy, forget Mr Gable: how are things going in the Jem department?
You've been seeing him a few years now so it must be getting serious.
Are you finally over that other feller who got married or was he really
the love of your life?"

"Well if he was it's too late now, unless I turn into a scarlet woman
and steal him away from the loyal little wife at home. Do you think I'd
suit scarlet?"

"As in Scarlet O'Hara? I don't think so. Red, maybe. Scarlet?
Perhaps that's not the colour for a Child of Mary, though you can be too
wrapped up in your blue cloak for your own good, Patsy, as I've told you
often enough. Which brings me neatly back to Jem. How is it with him?"

"Where to start with Jem… He's great company, always full of a bit
of mischief, and we seem to understand each other without everything
having to be spelled out. I never feel I have to explain myself to Jem, he
seems to know what I'm thinking, and he doesn't judge me for it. I know
I have some odd ideas for this day and age but he never makes me feel
like an old bore. So yes, I like him a lot, he's fun. I told you how he
danced all the way down O'Connell Street that New Year and I thought
it was just because of the occasion? Well, I've since realised it's just
something he likes to do. He'll start to hum *In the Mood* and sweep me
up and call me 'Ginger' and suddenly we'll be swinging our way along
the pavement, he doesn't care where we are or who might be looking. It's
all very silly but we do have a laugh."

"But do you love him, Patsy? Does he make your pulse race?"

"Not really, I'm getting a bit old for all that nonsense." Patsy
couldn't bring herself to tell Margaret that Jem was never one for kissing
and cuddling, that when his lips met her it was through a quick peck on
the cheek and not a lingering kiss. "All I can say is that I'm very fond of

him and we have such good nights out. Sometimes I feel I'm never at home, which is no bad thing right now, what with Molly and Eddie both over in England and Mammy constantly worrying about the two of them."

"Are they both okay? I can't imagine being over there now, it's so dangerous."

"We get odd letters from them both, of course. Molly sounds very happy, she always had her sights set on Kevin, as you know, but she says it is frightening to hear all the planes taking off at night to go on their bombing missions, as she calls them. Eddie is obviously in his element, what with his driving all over the place and his voluntary duties. He's what they call an air-raid warden, which he says is like bossing people around for their own good but in the dark. I'm sure there's more to it but he doesn't write about anything that might scare us."

"So, you have family at both ends," said Margaret. "Molly hears the bombers leave for Germany, while Eddie hears the bombers arrive from Germany."

"Not forgetting my Uncle Arthur, fighting with the underground in France. And did you read in the paper about the Dublin boat being sunk by a mine just after it left Liverpool? It was the same boat Molly and I went over on a couple of years back. The Innisfallen, it was called, I remember particularly because Kevin told us all about it, it was a new ship back then, he said. I thought our crossing was bad enough but at least we didn't get blown up."

"I'm glad to be in Dublin."

"Me too. Perhaps we'll stay in the café this evening and not go to the pictures, Margaret. I don't fancy looking at more awful war scenes on Pathé News."

"That suits me, I don't want be too late home tonight to be honest as I'm dog tired. And we do have the rest of the wine to finish. And this will have to be my last boozy session for a while. I didn't tell you earlier because I didn't want to put a damper on the evening, Patsy, but I'm expecting again."

The news from Auntie Mary was bad. Bootle had suffered its worst blitz from the Luftwaffe so far in the war. For five nights the bombs rained down and mines attached to small parachutes floated down through the sky without a sound until they landed and exploded. Low-flying German planes were even machine-gunning people down in the streets as they ran to find shelter, she wrote in her letter. Mary didn't know how many had been killed or injured or how many homes had been hit but all the houses down the side of the street opposite her house had gone, she said, all gone, reduced to ruins with bits of bodies sticking out from under the piles of bricks, bits of people she used to meet in the street for a chat. She saw the bodies of the paper-boy who used to deliver their Echo and a couple of the lads who used to go round selling bundles of sticks for lighting the fire. Dear God, it was awful to see. The neighbouring street, Akenside, had disappeared, all but for one or two houses at each end and a stretch of cobbled road down the middle. Crowds of people were out the next day trying to clear through mounds of debris, looking to find anyone who might still be alive. God knows how she and Tessie had lived through it, she wrote. They hadn't had time to get to the shelter on the first night so they had tucked themselves in under the stairs and recited the Rosary. They each made a silent confession too in case they were taken without seeing a priest: with all the terrible noise going on above them, they expected to be hit at any minute. And it went on, night after night. Then in the middle of it all a ship in the docks, loaded with tons of bombs and ammunition, had gone up in flames when a barrage balloon crashed on to the deck and set it alight. The fire spread to the cargo hold and the whole lot blew up just as the poor firemen had been ordered to get away. Sadly, they didn't all make it, said Mary.

'Dear God, they were such brave men. They knew what was on that ship and still they tried to put out the blaze and the Germans still dropping bombs on top of them. You should have heard the bang when it blew, I've never heard a sound like it, I didn't know it was possible for there to be such a loud noise. Even the ground shook. Pieces of the ship were found miles away and, wouldn't you know it, people have already been out collecting them as souvenirs. But I can tell you on a lighter note, God forgive me, that Bulwer Street got the best souvenir of all: it now has its very own ship's propeller,' she wrote. 'It was blasted out of the water in the explosion and evidently rotated through the air until it came to land in Bulwer Street. Remarkably it's all in one piece, a huge thing, *with its blades curling up out of the ground just yards from our house. It's great for the kids to climb on. I know it's not funny, but we can't help smiling every time we leave the house. We're thinking of renaming the street HMS Bulwer. Let's hope we're still afloat when you next come to visit.'*

"I don't know how Mary can still joke," said Betty. "We're moaning just because tea has been rationed and we can't have a decent cup."

'On a different note, there's news of Kevin and Molly moving, in case you haven't heard yet. He's being posted to a new air base not a million miles from Coventry so I'm not too happy about that, Coventry is always getting bombed. I gather it's full of munitions factories. Mind you, nowhere is safe any more. You're better off in Dublin. I'd better go now and find my tin hat.'

A few weeks later a squadron of German planes brought home the horror Mary had described when they dropped bombs on Dublin, killing thirty-one people and leaving four-hundred homeless.

"I see De Valera has already protested to Germany," said Patrick. "Churchill said it was perhaps because British equipment had distorted the Luftwaffe's direction signals. The planes had actually been heading to Liverpool again. That makes it all right then, does it?" said Patrick. "So much for our neutrality."

Ciaran and Mikey couldn't believe their luck. Their father had kept his word and taken them to Tullamore: he was to visit just for the weekend but the boys were to stay there indefinitely and work on the farm to earn their keep. Michael needed the help; growing food and rearing meat had become a matter of national urgency — there were even allotments now in Phoenix Park where the polo ground used to be — and Michael was missing two of his grown sons, who had enlisted in the Irish Army. De Valera was strengthening the home forces in case Germany invaded Ireland as a stepping stone for a full attack on Britain. Behind the scenes, the Dáil had authorised talks with the British for joint action between the two countries if it should come to that and Jim and Joe had sought their father's permission to join up. It had left Michael short-handed on the farm but he couldn't discourage his sons' patriotism.

"We may have to turn one of the paddocks over to wheat to help meet the shortage so the loan of your sons would be timely and useful, we don't want the country to run out of bread," Michael had told Betty. She didn't need much persuasion after the bombs had fallen in Dublin and she wanted to help her father. "They'll be doing plenty of digging so their muscles should be well developed. By the time they go home, they'll be carrying sacks of potatoes like experts. Also, we've plenty of butter and meat here for them so you can make your rations at home go a bit further. I hear there's talk of gas being rationed soon so two less mouths to feed should save all round."

Patrick watched as Michael and Robert showed the eager newcomers round the farm and explained their duties. They saw the field they were to turn-over for the wheat and their father was proud that they didn't utter a single word of objection at the hard work ahead. Quite the opposite: they would have picked up a couple of spades then and there had Robert not told them to wait until the following morning when the ground might be softer after the dew. Ciaran was particularly excited to get reacquainted with the horse too and finally felt safe to come clean about what had really happened when they'd been left in charge of the cart on The Coombe.

"We were just sitting there talking to the horse and, to be honest, showing off to some of our friends in the street," he said. "For a bit of a laugh I picked up the reins and made a clicking sound. I wasn't expecting anything to happen, and that's the truth, Da, I was only copying what I'd seen in the cinema. And then Mikey joined in shouting and wooing and so did the other kids and suddenly the horse started to walk and Mikey fell off the driver's board and into the cart, which seemed to startle the horse and make it go faster. The other kids chased us along the road, whooping and screaming and slapping the horse on its backside, it wasn't any drunks from the Cosy Bar, Da, and, Jesus, I didn't know what to do, especially when a couple of cars appeared round the corner from Meath Street. I could only hold on to the reins tighter and pull back as hard as I could but all the time I was shouting 'whoa' the other kids were shouting 'go'. The bit about the horse stopping to eat something on the road was true, though, and that's how we ended up where we did."

"Well, you certainly had the right instincts," said Michael, "and no harm came of it."

"And let's hope it taught you a lesson," said Patrick. "A farm can be a dangerous place if you don't know what you're doing, and I don't want to hear from Michael that the two of you have caused any mischief."

"Can we go to see the cows yet?" asked Mikey.

"We'll go along now and you can help me bring them in from the field," said Robert. "Then in the morning I'll show you how to milk them."

"Will we have to get hold of their udders?" sniggered Ciaran, digging his younger brother in the ribs.

"I don't know how else you can milk a cow," said Robert. "Come on now."

Michael popped into the kitchen to ask his wife if she needed any potatoes brought in from the barn for supper. "May says we're to sit out here and relax and leave her in peace," he told Patrick. "Everything's under control in there. Annie and Peter are calling in later to say hello and they're bringing over a pot of stew so we're off duty for the minute."

The two men sat down with a couple of glasses of home-brew. Patrick, by habit, didn't drink much but he enjoyed a glass now and then with his friend.

"They're all growing up and leaving the nest," said Michael. "My Annie's already married and a third baby on the way and now Jim and Joe have gone."

"What about Robert? Is he still walking out with the girl from the dance he was telling us about?"

"Kitty? He is that," said Michael, "I can't see Robert going anywhere, he loves it here and working on the farm. She's a nice girl, a tough one but respectful, we all get on grand, and there's already talk of them getting married and moving in here. May wouldn't mind. With Annie gone, I think she misses having another woman around the place."

"I've a few of them still," said Patrick, "though of course Molly's long gone — did I tell you she's expecting a little one in a few months' time? — and Theresa will no doubt go as soon as she's married. We've a couple of weddings ahead of us, Michael. I miss Eddie, though, but I understood his decision to move to London. And now Ciaran and Mikey will be here for a bit so that leaves just Betty and Patsy and Theresa and our Annie and little John still at home."

"What about Patsy, how is she these days? I never got the whole story about her finishing with that young baker from your place. I know she was very keen on him at the time."

"I had to tell her the truth, Michael, I couldn't leave her wondering why the situation was so difficult between me and him. Every time I looked at him, I saw his father standing there, waiting to be shot and me with the gun in my hand."

"Did you tell her everything?"

"I did, God forgive me. She still saw the lad a few times after that and then suddenly it seemed to be over, he left the bakery and she didn't tell us anything. What else happened between them I don't know. I do know I felt terribly guilty, I still do, not over what I did in the past, I had no alternative then, but over what it did all these years later to Patsy. You never know how things are going to come back at you."

"Poor girl," said Michael. "What about now? Has she forgiven you?"

"Who knows, we've never talked about it since, and Patsy can be lost in her own world. You know she still sees ghosts, her 'floaty people', as she's always called them. At times I could swear I hear her talking to them in her bedroom. And then she's so Catholic and devoted that I wonder how she gets through life. God knows who she takes after in that department. She has been seeing someone for a long time but we've not met him. I couldn't even tell you his name, now isn't that strange? All I know is that he works in the clothes business but in a store, not in a factory."

"And you've never met him? Is there something odd about him, d'you think?"

"I think anything to do with Patsy can be odd, generally with a religious turn," said Patrick. "Still, she's a grown woman and free to live her life as she wants. She does her voluntary work, of course, and goes to her parish meetings so she's busy but she's quiet in herself. She doesn't even play the piano like she used to. She was always practising when she was young, and she used to tell us little scraps of information about different composers, it was part of Patsy being Patsy. I should never have prevented her from going to the music college, that's when she stopped. I've been too harsh when it comes to Patsy but it's too late to change that."

"Aye but she's still at home, you haven't driven her away, not yet anyway. Perhaps she'll play the piano more with fewer people in the house," said Michael, "she probably didn't want to disturb the young ones when everyone was in the house. Why don't you suggest she teaches Annie? That might get her interested again. Sure you can't beat the sound of real music in the house and Patsy always had a nice touch."

Patrick thought that was a very good idea but when he got home even he had trouble getting used to The Coombe being so quiet: it felt empty with the lads gone, as if someone had opened the door suddenly and the two blustery whirlwinds had made their escape and blown completely away. Annie and little John had always been far quieter around the house; they had taken over looking after the pigeons and loved to sit up at the loft with the birds but even then you never heard a sound above a whisper out of them. Patsy took herself off to the bedroom not long after Patrick walked in and the thought of asking her to teach Annie or John how to play the piano seemed an irrelevance. Betty was busy with housework, as ever, and Patrick was left to sit alone in his chair by the fire, looking back on things he might have done better.

7

Jem was being very strange, not his usual energetic self. He kept looking at Patsy and then averting his eyes, then he'd look at her again. "I think we should have a serious talk, Patsy, there's a matter I'd like to discuss with you," he said. "Let's stroll down to the Liffey and have a chat. It seems to be our special place for honesty."

They stopped at a small shop on the way and Jem bought a bag of sweets and a bar of Patsy's favourite chocolate. "That's to sweeten you up," he told her, but she couldn't imagine what conversation would require her to be sweetened up.

"Upstream or downstream?" he asked when they got to O'Connell Bridge.

"Let's go along the south bank as far as the ships," said Patsy. "Then I'll have something to look across at while you do your serious talking."

There wasn't much river traffic but there were two boats moored at the landing quay across the river, one of which was the Liverpool ferry, the centre of activity. It was too early for passengers to be collecting on the wharf but the sailors and shore-men were at work getting the boat ready to sail and the sounds of their voices drifted over the water. Patsy felt her usual tingle of excitement at the brisk operations going on and her imaginings of the journeys and the destinations ahead. She could quite understand Kevin's obsession with the sea. She tore the foil on the chocolate and put a square in her mouth, lighting up a cigarette at the same time and savouring the sweet-burn combination.

"So, what is it you wanted to say?" she asked Jem.

"It's a delicate subject, Patsy, but we know each other well enough that we can be completely honest. That's how our relationship has matured over the past few years, don't you agree?"

"I do."

"That's the answer I'm hoping to hear from you a few times this evening," he said.

Patsy stiffened involuntarily at the implication and looked at him. "You do?"

"I do, you do… We're getting along grand so far in this serious talk," he said. Almost for dramatic effect, which was typical Jem, he took a toffee out of the paper and formed a small bow out of the wrapper as he started to chew. "There's a little token to be getting on with," he said, presenting the bow to Patsy.

The two of them stood there silently for a few minutes, Patsy dragging on her cigarette, Jem chewing his toffee. They watched as the mailbags were loaded on to the ferry.

"Are you going to get on with it or will I still be waiting when the Liverpool boat leaves and all the chocolate's gone?" she prompted.

"You notice I only bought the one bar," said Jem. "I'm hoping we can get this done and then go for a little celebratory supper."

"You're sounding like a movie script building up to a very particular significant moment," said Patsy but by now she was grinning.

"Don't be too hasty, my good woman, rein yourself in a bit longer and don't' leave the starting gate before the flag is lowered," said Jem. "It's like this," he said, taking out another toffee to scoff. "We've been spending a lot of time together, you and me, I wouldn't exactly say 'courting' though some people would call it that. Here's the thing, and I'm pretty sure we're of a mind: you know from our regular outings, perhaps I should say our regular 'goodnights', that I'm not a one for the physical side of things, for the usual man-woman things, the kissing and all that, and I rather feel that you feel the same. Am I right or have I got it all wrong?"

Patsy wasn't sure how to respond, whether it was some sort of a test or whether Jem was just fishing. "Go on," she said.

"You didn't answer my question but I think I already know the answer. The thing is…" He paused. "I wouldn't mind having a wife — you, that is, I'd like you for my wife — but I wouldn't be up for the bed stuff, for the intimate side of things. What do you say?"

She didn't say anything. She took out another cigarette and lit up, blowing the smoke up into the air with purpose, as if trying to form rings. She didn't know whether to laugh or cry.

"Jem Murphy, is this your way of proposing some sort of marriage?"

she finally asked, turning her gaze full on him.

"I suppose it is," he said, "though I admit it's hardly romantic."

"It's probably the furthest you could get from romantic," said Patsy.

"Believe me, I could probably get further," he said. "Look, I know I'm asking a lot but it's important to me that I am honest with you. I would like to get married but I want to live with you for your close company, which has become a precious and important part of my life. The rest of it doesn't interest me. So the thought of having babies wouldn't be an option. We'd live a life of intimate celibacy, that's how I'd phrase it, intimate celibacy, but I don't know if that's how you'd want to play it."

They stood side by side leaning over the river wall, looking at the water flowing below them, looking for all the world as if they were having a normal everyday conversation.

Patsy puffed on her cigarette.

"Am I allowed to ask why you would want to live like that?" she asked.

"I'm just not the regular sort of a man, I never have been. I dated when I was younger but I'd always known I was a bit different in that respect, I found the whole kissing thing uncomfortable, unnatural for me, as if I was playing a part for which I was totally miscast." Jem momentarily took hold of Patsy's hand and squeezed before letting it drop again. "There aren't many women who would accept me for who I am," he said. "Or what I am." He turned to face her, his expression a mix of embarrassment and expectation. "Do I need to spell it out for you, Patsy?"

Her mind raced at what he seemed to be implying. A rush of thoughts clamoured in her head if she was right: memories of dirty jokes she had heard; 'unholy' comments made about men who liked men in that way; aggressive and mean attitudes; fears that those sorts of men were dangerous and preyed on boys and should all be castrated. Patsy wasn't sure how to react, with disgust or understanding or shock: all she knew was that it was Jem talking, Jem, a good man, whom she loved dearly in her own way, not as thrillingly as she had Sean but then it was the thrilling element with Sean that she had feared deep down and ultimately rejected.

The question had to be asked, though Patsy half knew the answer before she put it. "Is it that you prefer men, physically?"

"I've never put it to the test," said Jem, "and I don't intend to, I like women's company more than men's and your company especially. And I have always had the distinct impression that you yourself are reluctant to get into any physical entanglements so I'd say we could suit each other rather well. I'd have a wife to cherish and you would have a husband to care for you with all his heart."

Patsy waited for his confession to sink in, waited while she thought of all the implications involved, waited while she mulled over her own needs and her own nature, her own hopes for a future that she didn't want to spend alone despite her avowal not to want to take a man as a husband. Finally, she came to the conclusion that the 'intimate celibacy' Jem was proposing was a logical and welcome solution, for both of them.

"You are a strange one, Jem," she said, "but my answer is yes."

"My good woman, let's seal it with a kiss."

For the first time their lips touched: it was a gentle meeting, without passion but full of a genuine warmth.

"Miss Patsy O'Kelly," said Jem. "I love you dearly. Do you want to marry me as much as I want to marry you despite everything?"

"I do."

"There now," he said, "it had its own peculiar element of romance after all. Let's away now to toast our betrothal with a magnum of champagne, my good woman, that's if champagne hasn't been added to the rationed list now that France is under German control."

More than ever it was a time of make-do-and-mend in The Coombe. Food was short, despite the thriving black-market and fewer mouths to feed. Michael managed to get some small sacks of vegetables, extra butter and the odd rabbit to Betty when Ciaran or Mikey had a weekend at home — they showed no desire to move back to Dublin, they were young men now but they still liked catching rabbits — but the standard menu of potatoes and boiled pig's head was beginning to challenge appetites. Nor was there any sign of respite on the horizon. It had been a dangerous and desperate time to be at sea in the Atlantic. Reports said that one-hundred-and-fifty-five Allied ships had been sunk in a matter of just three months, including merchant ships carrying urgent food supplies to Britain. In turn, inevitably rationing in Ireland intensified.

Added to the problems of getting food to cook was the challenge of actually getting it cooked: the use of gas was restricted to a couple of hours a day, one in the morning and one in the evening, with an army of jobsworth inspectors ready to enforce the law. At any moment one of these 'glimmer men', as they were none-too-fondly known, could demand entrance to the house to check for illicit kettles bubbling on the hob or to put a hand on the oven to see if it was warm when it should have been cold. The 'glimmer' was the pilot light on the stove and necessity demanded that even that little flame was enough to cook a stew eventually or, alternatively, to get you into trouble. Young John O'Kelly was one of the boys stationed on street corners to whistle a warning to everyone to turn off the glimmer when an inspector was spotted in the distance. Even the girls skipping in the street had come up with a timely rhyme for their games and Annie was forever singing it when she was skipping in the yard. The ditty had become a normal part of the soundscape but there was no skipping around the desperation in its truth:

"Keep it boiling on the glimmer, if you don't you get no dinner."

All the same they managed a bit of a celebration in The Coombe: Molly and Kevin had had a daughter, the first grandchild for Patrick and Betty, and Patsy, to the family's surprise, had become engaged to a man they had still never met. He was invited to the house for a small gathering to remedy that very thing.

Jem had suggested to Patsy that they could leave after the party to catch a bite to eat in the city, that way Betty wouldn't have to concern herself with putting on a spread in such difficult times, but he didn't come empty-handed. He arrived with a bottle of Bushmills for Patrick and a huge floral bouquet for Betty. There were no proper whiskey glasses, only cheap-and-cheerful tumblers, a few of them cracked, while the flowers looked somewhat incongruous standing gloriously in a make-do vase under streamers of brown fly-paper hanging from the ceiling, their trapped victims still stuck. There was a moment of self-consciousness for Jem when he walked in, dressed in his fine clothes and looking like the fine gentleman that he was, only to find himself in surroundings even humbler than he had imagined for his Patsy. It was apparent to all that

Patsy's fiancé was like a fish out of water in the house, not what he was used to at all, and the small talk of welcome was expended fairly quickly.

"Do you follow the news much, Mr Murphy?" asked Patrick trying to make conversation.

"Please, call me Jem, we'll soon be family. I do follow the news, Mr O'Kelly, and very disturbing it is, with the war going on these past few years. The effects are difficult enough for us in Ireland, even in the clothing trade, but I understand you've a daughter living near Coventry and a son in London, which must put all other concerns to the bottom of your worry list. You must read the newspapers avidly. I can't imagine how people over there can cope with all the attacks, day and night, while we complain about a shortage of tea. On a hopeful note, I did read that the Allies are making progress. They've even invented a bomb which can bounce over water. Can you imagine that? I wouldn't want to see one of them skimming up the Liffey, would you, Mrs O'Kelly."

"Indeed, I wouldn't," said Betty, appreciating Jem's inclusion and making an effort not to vanish into the background, it was after all an occasion for family celebration not for talk of possible disasters. She had even taken off her pinny. "God protect us," she added by way of something extra to say.

"I read that the Allies should be in Paris any day now," said Patrick. "My brother is in France, working with the Resistance."

"He served in the Volunteers with my da," said Patsy. She had never spoken to Jem about the war years in Ireland and for some reason chose today to establish the family credentials.

"Is that right?" said Jem. "Then you're both braver men than I could ever hope to be. My father died in the Rising and I was too young to know what was going on, all I knew was that we didn't have the usual Easter treats and that my mother spent a lot of time crying. You'll think me very ignorant, Mr O'Kelly."

"I didn't know about your father," said Patsy.

"We've a lifetime ahead of us to fill in any blanks," said Jem. "We should never be short of conversation. Isn't that one of the ingredients of a happy marriage, Mr O'Kelly, to always have something to say to each other?"

The expressions on the faces of the two women, after years spent with Patrick's general lack of conversation, dared him to agree but the arrival of Theresa and Billy saved Patrick from having to answer a polite 'yes' and make a liar of himself. The newcomers bustled into the parlour like a warm wind blown up out of the Sahara, laughter and enthusiasm effortlessly taking over where awkwardness had reigned. Billy, who hadn't changed much since Theresa first picked him out for herself during their school days, had the sort of personality that filled a room and brought smiles to everyone's face. His sudden appearance was a godsend.

"So you're Patsy's feller," he said, welcoming Jem with a vigorous handshake. "I'm warning you now, Jem, this is not a family to take on lightly. I was fortunate to grow up in the neighbourhood, so I've never had the ordeal of coming into it all cold, as a stranger, but you'll get used to them. If you can get used to Patsy, and you obviously have, then you can get used to the rest of the gang. Is that Bushmills I can see? You must have brought that, Jem, Mr O'Kelly's not much of a drinking man but I'll certainly join you in a glass if I may, that'll stoke our furnaces."

Jem visibly relaxed, feeling that Billy was a man as fond of enjoying life as he was himself. Initial pleasantries exchanged, it didn't take them long to discover a mutual interest in the horses, accompanied by confidential asides that it would be best not to get too much into the gambling side in the present company. Both admitted that they had promised their relevant fiancées to keep the habit to a minimum but they recognised in each other the likelihood of that never happening.

"Why don't the four of us go to Leopardstown next month for the Champion Stakes," suggested Jem, "Patsy has been with me to a few meetings and she seems to enjoy it. What about Theresa? Would she be up for it?"

"Well now, your Patsy is obviously cut from a different cloth to her sister," said Billy. "Theresa disapproves of the whole thing and she shows it. She adopts a miserable poker face that I swear even puts off the horses. It's many a bet I've lost when my horse had the race sewn up, only to spot Theresa's face at the rails and be put off his stride. A couple of outings with her were lesson enough. I'd rather go on my own or not at all, to be honest with you."

"Not such a good idea then," said Jem. "My mother was the same, God rest her soul. She would even go through my pockets looking for the odd betting slip."

"She's dead, your mother? I'm sorry to hear that," said Billy.

"She died a year or so ago, left me the house and a terrible feeling of guilt that I had spent more time at The Curragh cheering on the gee-gees than I had being a dutiful son at home and enthusing about her knitting patterns."

"Maybe there's a grand racecourse in heaven that will change her views," said Billy. "Now that would be my idea of heaven. Can you imagine it, Jem, an eternity spent with the horses at the track."

"And what would you use as stakes?"

"Sure I don't know, I haven't got that far in the notion but you could perhaps win some time off for good behaviour and enjoy a spell in hell."

"What are you two talking about," asked Patsy, sidling over for some cheerier company than her da and ma, who were still fidgety and unsure of themselves where this dapper man of Patsy's was concerned. Her father had commented curtly on his fancy clothes, as if warning his daughter that a life of profligacy and debt lay ahead; her mother had remarked on his fine manners, as if forecasting a future that would include at least a measure of care and consideration. Patsy didn't want to listen to any more of her father's warnings, she'd had a bellyful of them in the past and right now she wanted to enjoy her little party without his baleful shadow looming over her.

"I was merely suggesting that the four of us might spend some time together, get to know each other better," said Jem. "Perhaps go out for supper."

Patsy was confused. "You mean us with my mammy and daddy?"

"No, my good woman, delightful though I'm sure that would be," replied Jem, always the gentleman. "I was suggesting that Theresa and Billy might like to join us this evening. I'm sure Betty must be ready to put her feet up by now after a houseful of guests."

"I've never thought of myself as a guest," said Billy, "more like a piece of the furniture."

"Not the small coffin, I hope," said Jem, who had been desperate to refer to the bizarre ornament on the sideboard but hadn't until now identified an appropriate opportunity to get it out of his system.

"More like the sideboard itself," said Theresa joining them. "Large, ever-present, full of bits of nonsense that you could throw away and not miss, and yet almost filling the room."

"You see how much she loves me, Jem," said Billy, squeezing Theresa round the waist and nuzzling into her neck. "What more necessary and solid a piece of furniture could you wish to be than a sideboard. Just open my drawers, Theresa, darling, and I'll handle everything you care to put in."

"Billy!" said Theresa. "My father and mother are in the room."

"I'm sure they know we kiss and cuddle," said Billy, removing his arm and sneaking a glance at Patrick to gauge his reaction. "We're only human after all, wouldn't you agree, Jem? And Theresa, your father's hardly ignorant of what's involved, not with his brood."

"That's enough of that," said Patsy. She always got a bit red in the face with Billy's banter. "We should be going if we're going. Are you two coming with us?"

"I'm up for it if Theresa is," said Billy. "We can stop off at a little bar I know for a quick one first. It's not too far for you ladies in your heels and you can be sure everyone'll hear you coming." He turned to Patrick. "Do fancy joining us, Mr O'Kelly? We're off to The Brazen Head in Bridge Street, where one or two of your predecessors put their heads together to plot against the British and them drinking their ale not a stone's throw from the Castle."

"Betty and I will pass on that," said Patrick. "I wouldn't want to get you young ones mixed up in anything revolutionary."

"We promise to keep clear of all that," said Billy, not hesitating to guide his fellow revellers out of the room, "but I'll keep my ears and eyes open in case I hear anything you should know about. Patsy's got a nose for these things too, just like you, Mr O'Kelly. I've seen her in what looks like a CumannamBan outfit."

Billy steered the group off in the direction of the Quays to what was claimed to be the city's oldest pub, an old coach house not far from the Liffey. An arched passage led them under what looked like stone battlements to a cobbled courtyard and the main door opened on to a warren of small rooms: everywhere there were nooks and crannies, perfect, as Billy said, for secret meetings between The Boys.

"Did all that truly go on here?" asked Patsy.

"Shame on you for even having to ask about such a landmark on the road to our hard-won independence," said Billy. "Sure that great Irish hero Emmet himself actually had a room upstairs so he could keep an eye on suspicious comings and goings in the street outside. Appropriately the British hanged him and cut off his head in spitting distance of this, his favourite drinking hole. It's said that his ghost — or is it his head? I can't remember — still haunts the place, though the only one of us four likely to see him is you, Patsy. You've a reputation for that sort of thing, not necessarily an enviable reputation as reputations go but better to have some sort of a reputation than none at all and at least yours is an interesting one. Now is it a Bushmills you fancy, Jem, or are the celebrations over and we're back to Paddy's?"

"I for one am still in a celebratory mood," said Jem, "so Bushmills it is, especially as I can ease off with the small-talk and relax now that duties have been performed, satisfactorily I hope, and the future in-laws are out of earshot. Not that their presence seems to control your tongue, Billy."

"It's too late for me to pretend I'm anything other than I am," said Billy.

"Yes," said Theresa, "a sideboard with lots of drawers."

"And, fortunately, not a coffin, Theresa," said Billy, "or you'd be in for a dead boring life."

They sat at a table near the window, through which they could see rows of barrels lined up and bits of paraphernalia left over from when coaches used to pull in and disgorge their passengers. The Brazen Head had stood in a prime location since it had opened centuries ago at a crossing point over the Liffey and Patsy loved all the history, especially that it was so connected to her beloved river. She was surprised Billy knew so much about the bar but then he was obviously quite a regular as the barman called him by name. Patsy sipped her whiskey, inwardly marvelling at all the different places she had discovered in Dublin since she started walking out with Jem.

"Cheltenham?" she heard Jem ask. "You're thinking of moving to Cheltenham? That's quite a major stake to lay on a racecourse, moving not only house but country."

"It's more of a dream than a plan," said Billy.

"And have I any say in this dream that's not a plan but that you talk about as if you were leaving next week?" said Theresa.

"Would I do anything without a proper consultation," said Billy. "And didn't you love the place when we went over last year, all those grand Georgian houses."

"They have similar in Dun Laoghaire and it's closer to home."

"Ah but home is where the heart is," said Billy "and your heart is with me. And to be perfectly serious, there could be more work there for me than here. England is going to need a lot of new houses when this war ends and construction is my game, plastering is my trade."

"Playing the horses is your game, Billy, and I dread to think what you'd get up to in a racing town."

"Jem, would you ever say something in my defence."

"I have to say I can see both sides of the argument but which side of the track you'd end up on, Billy, is a matter of speculation, perhaps a matter of too much speculation with the bookies," said Jem. "I love the horses too, as you know, but to me the excitement is the whole experience, the magical environment of sights and sounds and smells in which you have the chance to become rich. Or poor, of course, on a bad day, and show me a gambling man who doesn't have bad days or has good days and doesn't know when to stop."

"I'll show you one, right here," said Theresa pointing to Billy.

"Patsy, help me out here with your sister," said Billy.

"I can see I'll be the only one left in Dublin soon," said Patsy.

8

A double-wedding party set off from The Coombe, with lots of friends and neighbours grouped along the pavements, from the house to the parish church, to watch the two brides progress their way to the altar in their beautiful dresses, coyly holding their veils in place as they lifted in the slight breeze. Women passed admiring "you-look-gorgeous" comments and wished them well; even the customers of The Cosy Bar spilled out to raise their own special cheers, pints of stout and ale slopping happily in the air. Warm spring sunshine added its own blessing to the nuptials: Patrick O'Kelly was giving away two of his daughters, though local tittle-tattle had it that no one was as surprised as he was when his spinster daughter Patsy finally found herself a husband. They'd all have to go to watch just to see what the man looked like: they'd heard he was quite stylish.

It hadn't been a straightforward decision to make it a double outing. Theresa had argued for her own special day, she'd dreamt about it for years, she said. Billy, on the other hand, who had found an amiable companion in Jem, persuaded her that it was the best way to get everyone together at once and not expect people to make two journeys, some from a considerable distance away and expensive when times were hard. He said he personally didn't want to see the women turn up twice in the same hats. "It's not as if we'll be going on honeymoon together," he'd said, "you'll not have to share me with your sister."

The O'Kellys had been parishioners for as long as anyone could remember so the church was full for the ceremony and the Mass. A wedding provided hopeful respite from gloomy day-to-day routine. It was an occasion for all to enjoy and the presence of so many crowding into the pews added an extra aura of sunshine. Right at the back of the church clustered a handful of regular customers from the Penny Dinners café, spruced up as well as they could be for Patsy's big day. The familiar somewhat gaunt faces of The Liberties' poor greeted Patsy with nodding heads of approval and ear-to-ear smiles. They weren't there for Theresa but she couldn't help but be swept up in the whole community feel. It wasn't what she had planned, that was for sure, but she glowed as she walked down the aisle, linked to her father, Patsy on his other arm, all three of them the centre of warm and undivided attention, with Annie and John behind them in their smart wedding outfits. It was as joyous as she could have imagined.

The family from Tullamore all made it to Dublin for the occasion, this time crammed into the back of an old, borrowed bus and laden with cakes, jams and hams plus a few bottles of Tullamore Dew and home-brew as a contribution to the table. Robert had his lass, Kitty, on his arm while Jim and Joe, who had turned up in their army uniforms, proved perfect ushers, seating guests in the right places with efficient military precision. May, their mother, sat proudly watching her two sons.

But it was the sight of two muscular young men walking confidently up the aisle to the front pews that had the eligible lasses of the parish gawping and fluttering among themselves as they recognised none other than Ciaran and Mikey: the tearaway O'Kelly lads had grown into undeniably handsome young men any girl would be pleased to catch. The brothers, elegantly done up in their cheap suits, milked their entrance for all it was worth, glancing flirtatiously along the rows and bestowing grins of recognition on their adoring audience as they positively swaggered to their places.

Molly couldn't believe her eyes either when she saw her brothers: she still thought of them as boys. She and Kevin had made the journey up from the airbase near Coventry so at last the grandparents were able to meet their granddaughter, Kathleen. The war was in its closing stages and the Allies were driving the German forces back across Europe, so Kevin had been granted a full week's furlough for such an important family occasion. There was as much cooing over little Kathleen as over the brides. Good-luck farthings and halfpennies were tucked into the pram from people who could little afford it. Certain traditions had to be maintained no matter what.

Tessie made it over from Liverpool but Aunt Mary was still too nervous to make the crossing. *HMS Bulwer is making headway, but I haven't found my sea-legs yet and the tide could still turn*, she wrote to

Betty. According to Tessie, her mother had stayed at home because she couldn't face returning to her home city without Stephen. She felt that to socialise at such a happy event with her old friends would be too emotional when one of the original party was missing.

Unfortunately Eddie wasn't in attendance. In his apologies to Patsy and Theresa, he blamed his "war work", as he liked to call it. They were unaware that Patrick had made it abundantly clear to Eddie that his presence would not be welcomed: he had been away too long without so much as a weekend visit home.

Circumstances dictated that it couldn't be a lavish wedding breakfast but it was a festive celebration nonetheless, staged in the small parish hall and with music provided by a few fiddlers and an accordionist Patsy had managed to commandeer from amongst the Penny Dinners clientele: it kept costs down and provided a few bob for the out-of-work musicians. Mrs Flaherty had offered herself and her daughters to help with the catering, the midwife's presence adding a certain sense of continuity: she had, after all, brought many of the family celebrants into the world — one of them was already eyeing one of her own girls — but she had also developed a strong bond with Patsy over the dishes and vegetables in the café and was only too glad to help out at her friend's wedding.

Patrick chinked his glass and ahemmed a few times for the assembly's attention. He wasn't one to give speeches but he knew the occasion demanded it.

"I'm not a great one for talking," he said, "in fact how Betty and the children have put up with my silence over the years God only knows." A ripple of gentle laughter moved around the room. "As far as I was concerned, the house was full of children who always had too much to say for themselves and so it was easier for me to sit in my chair and say nothing. And that's what I did, for years. The first time I met Jem here, he told me that the secret of a happy marriage was that a couple should always have something to say to each other and, when he said it, I saw Betty and Patsy exchange knowing glances with a nod in my direction. They thought I didn't notice but I did, and it made me stop and think. Jem's right. It's important not to lose that closeness of talking. Even unimportant chit-chat can bring a smile to the face but you have to talk to let that happen; an anecdote related about the day allows your wife or

293

husband to have a share in that day and so feel included in life outside the home. I have been lucky with Betty; she has the patience of a saint where my moods are concerned and hasn't held it against me — not in open conversation, anyway. When I was open to conversation, that is." Another murmur of amusement animated the guests.

"As for Patsy and Theresa, I doubt they'll have many problems in that respect. Jem, whom not many of you know very well, is, I can tell you, a born raconteur, with a way of looking at things that dwells on the whimsical and the interesting facets of life. He enthuses about whatever he comes across in a way that is both contagious and slightly, if I may say this, outlandish. Then there's Billy. Many of you have known Billy since he was a schoolboy so there's no need for me to tell you that he is and never has been short of anything to say. Quite the opposite. But he also has that rare gift that makes him light up a room the moment he walks in and a way of laughing that is also contagious. So I have no concerns about Patsy and Theresa and their future. They have each caught themselves a natural entertainer. As for Jem and Billy, all I can say about your new wives is — God help you if they take after their father. Everybody, a toast, please, to both couples and to a very happy life ahead of them."

Chairs were scraped and scuffed across the floor as everyone stood up, chattering and cheering their best wishes after such an unexpectedly fine speech. Glasses were raised and clinked together almost in unison just as the door of the hall burst open and the priest rushed in. "The war in Europe is over," he cried, "the war is over."

"Well, Jem," said Billy as a great cheer filled the room, "we won't have any excuses for forgetting our wedding anniversary in the future. May the 8th 1945 will go down in history as more than just Patrick O'Kelly getting two daughters off his hands."

Part 4

The sad, the lonely, the insatiable,
To these Old Night shall all her mystery tell;
God's bell has claimed them by the little cry
Of their sad hearts, that may not live or die.

— W B Yeats

1

Patsy was feeling under pressure, everyone was feeling under pressure. The weather was miserable, the country was suffering under one of the coldest spells anyone could remember, and food was still short: the combination of rationing, still in place nearly two years after the war had ended, and a disastrous harvest throughout Ireland the previous year meant that even Michael in Tullamore was unable to supplement the family table in The Coombe. Making matters still harder for life on the farm was that Michael had had to find extra money to sign up for the rural electricity programme that had been rolled out: not only had he to pay for the privilege of just signing up, he also had to pay again to be connected to the very power grid he had approved and was now faced with having to pay for the house itself to be wired up or the whole thing would have been a total waste of time and money. It was a triple expense he couldn't really afford in the middle of everything else. Michael felt guilty over it but he just had nothing to spare for his daughter's family in Dublin. But then nothing was easy anywhere. It was no wonder the newspapers were full of stories about people leaving Ireland in droves.

Patsy had her own worries: emigration wasn't the answer but right now she did want to disappear. It was the abundant family rather than the food shortage that troubled her, that's where she felt real pressure. Molly already had two children, Theresa had one and another due and, as if that wasn't enough, even Eddie was about to become a father. He had stayed on in London and married a Cockney girl and their first baby was on the way. Patsy was bombarded daily by questions and comments about her and Jem and their failure to reproduce. Wasn't it time they got their act together? Were there any problems in that department?

Patsy's response was "there is no act, there is no department" but that was all inside her head. It wasn't a matter easily explained. And for all her vows of chastity and her 'intimate celibacy' arrangement with Jem, which had seemed such a convenient solution at the time, now she herself was fighting off inescapable feelings of regret. When she heard Eddie's baby news, an unsolicited feeling of broodiness washed over her and Patsy had to force herself to adopt an expression of indifference, her face belying the turmoil she felt inside. Constant references to her tardiness in embracing motherhood only served to turn the screw. Even Mrs Flaherty kept asking when she should book herself in for the home delivery.

As she walked home from work, Patsy stopped to look in the shop window she had lingered in front of all those years ago when she was heading off, young and full of confidence, to the women's meeting. She recalled how happy she had been, newly promoted at Jeanette Modes and anxious to share her good fortune with Sean on their next date. The window-stop had become a sentimental ritual on her journey home since then, although it was now to the home she shared with Jem and there was no sweet love letter in her pocket to tickle her heart. There was plenty of conversation with Jem all right, indeed there was never a dull moment, but nor was there ever any romance, no stirrings of anything beyond close companionship, valued though that was. Patsy gazed at her reflection. She looked like a woman who needed a bit of a tickle, she admitted. Instead, she was on her way to a potential probe.

Betty had refused to take 'no' for an answer when she had suggested accompanying Patsy on a visit to the doctor's surgery to find out why no babies had arrived in the Murphy household.

"It could be just a simple problem for the doctor to fix," Betty had insisted. "I'll come with you for a bit of moral support."

Today, after several cancellations and prevarications, Patsy was faced with no alternative but to go to the surgery with her stepmother.

The waiting room was oppressive and crowded. People sat staring blankly at the walls, greedily devouring the few landscape prints tacked up in a feeble attempt to add a bit of cheer to the place. Dog-eared magazines were picked over, flicked through and discarded unceremoniously. Speculative glances greeted every new arrival and diagnosed their likely complaints. Wet handkerchiefs were scrunched and squelched over runny noses while a chorus of coughs, from the phlegmy to the decidedly bronchial, stuttered over the occasional whispered conversations about the prevalence of tuberculosis after the war and whether or not you could catch it even in a doctor's waiting-room. Judging by the worried looks, the assumed answer to that was a decided 'yes'. The patients were miserable, the place was miserable, the waiting was miserable. At least Patsy and Betty had found two seats next to each other, though Patsy would have preferred it if Betty hadn't insisted on holding her hand in front of everyone, and her a grown woman; people would be imagining all sorts of dire diagnoses.

"Mrs Patricia Murphy," came the call eventually. Patsy squirmed as she stood, even your name became public knowledge.

"You wait here, Mammy," she said to Betty, "I'll go in on my own."

"Not at all, I'll come with you. Two sets of ears are better than one."

The doctor was sitting behind a large desk and smiled a tired greeting as the two women shuffled in: he waved for them to take a seat. Patsy noticed the examination bed in the corner and her heart sank. There was no getting out of this now.

"Mrs Murphy, is it? And what seems to be the problem?" he asked, looking from one woman to the other, not knowing which of them was the patient.

"We want to know why my daughter here hasn't had any children yet," said Betty. "She's been married for a couple of years now and her sisters have all produced babies so I don't think there's anything untoward that runs in the family."

"And you, I assume, are the daughter?" asked the doctor looking quizzically at Patsy.

She felt as if she was shrinking. She was perfectly able to speak for herself but Betty had gotten straight to the point without so much as a nod in Patsy's direction. "I am," said Patsy, convinced that the doctor would already have her marked down as a helpless idiot.

"I see you're thirty-six years old," said the doctor, looking at Patsy's records. "It's not particularly old for a first pregnancy but of course it's not unknown for some women to go through the menopause early." He busied himself taking Patsy's blood pressure and temperature. "Good, all quite normal, Mrs Murphy. And are you otherwise healthy? What about your periods, are they regular? Any in-between bleeding?"

"I'd say I'm perfectly healthy," said Patsy, determined to cling to some sort of maturity. "I've no aches and pains, I go out to work every day without getting exhausted and I eat as well as I can considering the food shortages we all have to endure, and my monthlies are normal as far as I'm aware," said Patsy. "I'm afraid I might be wasting your time, doctor."

"Not at all," said the doctor, noting down Patsy's particulars on his pad. "And what about your husband? Is he a well man?"

"He is."

"He's a fine strapping man," said Betty, "with a healthy appetite. I can't imagine the problem being with him but you never know. I've a friend whose husband had a low count or something. Perhaps that's the problem."

"Will you leave it, Mammy?" pleaded Patsy.

"That's always a possibility, of course," said the doctor. "As often as not it is the husband's weak sperm that's to blame. Well, let's get you up on the bed, Mrs Murphy, and take a look at your works, see what's going on down there. I may not be able to give you a categorical explanation today, in which case I can refer you to a specialist. You can take your skirt and drawers off behind the curtain. There's a sheet you can pull over yourself for modesty's sake."

The doctor washed his hands and selected some shiny metal instruments that promised torture to Patsy. She undressed as instructed and pulled herself up on to the bed. She felt unbearably vulnerable. She felt herself blushing from head to toe. She felt embarrassingly unwhole and uncompleted as a woman. She turned her head away as far to the side as she could manage to avoid eye-contact with the first man ever to touch her private parts — and she a married woman! — and she trembled with the shame of absolutely everything about her whole situation. She mentally sought refuge in a prayer to Our Lady, concentrating hard on her spiritual escape but finding no physical relief whatsoever.

"Open your legs and bend your knees up for me now, would you, and then just let them drop down to the sides," said the doctor. "That's right, now just try to relax."

Patsy took a deep breath and dug her nails into her hands in an effort to create a painful distraction from the real pain that shot through her as the doctor inserted a probe up between her legs and into her very soul. She stifled a cry between clenched lips, fisted her hands and pushed her head further to the side and down into the thin pillow. The doctor explored deep inside her with the chosen instrument, moving it this way and that, up and down, left to right, all the time peering in through some magnifying attachment. Patsy's precious sense of self and privacy was shattered. She felt a sudden piercing and was suddenly aware of a trickle of blood escaping on to the bedding and on to the doctor's hands. She heard him catch a breath of surprise. He gave her a knowing but kindly look, retracted the instrument and washed his hands again.

"I'm sorry if that was uncomfortable for you but it's all over now, Mrs Murphy, you can put your clothes back on."

Patsy knew it was all over in more ways than one.

"That was quicker than I expected," said Betty. "I don't know how you doctors can tell anything from such a brief examination. Does Patsy need to see a specialist?"

"No that won't be necessary," said the doctor. "Everything seems fine down there."

"Then what's the problem?" asked Betty.

"I think we should wait until your daughter joins us as these things are quite personal and we shouldn't perhaps discuss it without her presence," he replied.

Patsy fumbled getting into her clothes. Her stockings refused to slip easily over her feet and got caught between her toes, then she caught one of them on the clasp of her watchstrap and it laddered, the ladder running all the way up to the exposed top of her leg. That was the strap on the watch Sean had given her: Sean, who would never have suggested a passionless marriage to the woman he declared was the love of his life, here in his absence. Not for the first time during the proceedings, Patsy didn't know whether to laugh or cry, either at the situation or at herself.

"Come on out now, Mrs Murphy, and we'll get this sorted for you," called the doctor.

Patsy could delay no longer.

"Right," said the doctor, "do you want to tell your mother or shall I?"

"You tell her."

"Okay then," said the doctor turning to Betty. "There is only one way to say this to you, so I'll get straight to the point. The reason why

302

your daughter has not yet had a baby is because she is still a virgin."

Betty started up in her chair, astonished at what she had just heard. "What? But she's a married woman!" she gasped, totally taken aback, hardly able to speak, her mouth hanging open and her head shaking from side to side in disbelief. "Patsy? Is that true? You've never been with Jem in that sense?"

"Yes, it's true and no I haven't."

"But how? I know you've always been lost in your religion and all the stuff they tell you to do and not to do but I have to ask, you do actually know what's supposed to happen between a husband and wife?"

"Of course I know," said Patsy. "This is a private matter between Jem and me. That's why I asked you not to bring me to the doctor's, I knew why I never got pregnant, but you would insist and now we've done nothing but waste everybody's time and you're looking at me as if I'm stupid and to be pitied."

"Don't you worry about wasting my time," said the doctor. "I'm here for your benefit. Tell me, Mrs Murphy, are there any problems between you and your husband that I could help you with?" he asked. "It's not common but it's not altogether unknown either that a couple can experience difficulties when it comes to performing the sex act. I could arrange for you both to see someone if you think it would help, though I admit that the hierarchy in the Church in Ireland wouldn't approve of such a conversation and that disapproval is still important to some Catholics, perhaps one such as yourself."

"We don't have any difficulties, thank you doctor, so there'll be no need to upset the bishops," said Patsy, wanting an end to the whole episode. "We just made an agreement before we married that the physical side was not something we either wanted or needed. It was a private decision reached between the two of us and, Mammy, I beg you to respect that and not to go telling the whole family something personal to me that's none of their business."

"My poor girl," said Betty, standing up and putting her motherly, soft arms around Patsy. "I'm so sorry, so sorry for all of this. You should have told me. What a life you've let yourself in for, Patsy, so much you're going to miss out on, no family of your own, and for what reason?" Patsy started to sob quietly. "Never mind," said Betty, "no doubt you have your reasons. I won't tell anyone. As long as you're happy with Jem, that's what's important."

"Come back to see me if you change your mind," said the doctor, who was already calling for the next patient as Patsy and Betty bundled themselves out through the door. It created a welcome break in the tedium for the people in the waiting room; the mother wasn't holding her daughter's hand any more, instead she was smothering her with hugs as they left the surgery: that must have been some God-awful news from the doctor, they thought, and their own spirits lifted slightly.

Once outside, Patsy pulled herself together. Her eyes were still wet and red but the ordeal was over and at least now everything was out in the open, even if only with Betty. They sat on a park bench despite the biting temperature while Patsy, forlorn and embarrassed, was subjected to well-meaning streams of comfort and advice from Betty. It all fell on deaf ears: there was nothing anyone could say to Patsy that she didn't already know. She offered up a prayer from her Children of Mary devotions: "O Mary, you know my weaknesses and my needs, come to my assistance and obtain for me, from your divine Son, perseverance in my good resolutions and the grace of being faithful to them all my life."

"Did you not hear me, Patsy? I asked if you'd like to come home with me for some dinner?" said Betty.

Patsy squeezed her mother's hand and managed a smile. "No, Mammy, thanks but I'd better get home to fix Jem's supper, I'm already late. The walk home will do me good and I can call in at the shop on the way. Thank you for everything and, please, don't worry about me. I know I got upset but really my life is as I want it, even though I know it wouldn't suit everybody."

"I promise I'll not tell anyone," said Betty. "If you're sure…"

"I am," interrupted Patsy. "Anyway, I've made my bed, as they say."

"As long as it's not too lonely."

"No one could ever be lonely with a man like Jem."

It was sheer coincidence that the house Jem had inherited from his mother was just round the corner from Patsy's best friend, Margaret, but it had come as a bit of a shock to Patsy that it was such a humble, ordinary place, a small terrace house in Warren Street. She had met Mrs Murphy Senior on several occasions before the woman died, always over supper in a nice restaurant so Patsy had never actually been to their home. Judging by Jem's love of fine eating and fine clothes, Patsy had assumed he was quite comfortable financially, so she was more than a little surprised when they moved into his inherited property, a house even smaller than the one on The Coombe. She knocked on Margaret's door on the way past. She needed the company of a friend and had bought a present for Margaret during her lunchbreak as an easy way into some unforced conversation after the doctor's visit.

"I hope I'm not calling at a bad time but I was passing and I wanted to give you something to go with your new gramophone," she said when Margaret answered the door.

"Come in, come in, Patsy, I'll be glad of some adult company while I get the little ones' food ready," said Margaret. "Sometimes I think I'm turning back into a child myself. I spend so much time making baby-talk I forget what proper grown-up talk is like. The sooner we can start our Tuesday nights again the better. Will I make you a cup of tea? Have you time?"

"I have, Jem won't be home for another hour or so. I've a few minutes before I get the dinner started."

"Sure that's great. I'll pop the kettle on and you can show me what you've brought for my musical enjoyment."

"It's that new recording by Josef Locke, *Hear My Song, Violetta*, it's all the rage right now. He's a policeman from the north; the Singing Bobby, they call him, and he has a lovely voice, high, falsetto, I think. Anyway, the song's very catchy. All the women are mad about it at work, they're always singing it, and I thought it would be a welcome addition to your collection."

"Well, the few records I have could hardly be called a collection, not yet anyway," said Margaret. "We've only got half a dozen or so but enough for a bit of music in the house and the children love dancing around. What's this new one called again? I'm completely out of touch since Fergal was born."

"It's called *Hear My Song, Violetta*, a love song set in Venice, all about meeting on a gondola, on the lagoon and under the moon." Patsy raised her eyelids and pouted. "Serenade across the water, it says. Can you imagine that? Being serenaded in Venice by a singing policeman from Northern Ireland?"

"It sounds irresistible: a man in uniform with a brogue! Let's have a listen. I don't mind a bit of romance when I'm mashing the spuds."

Patsy put the needle on the record carefully. "I love the little tin boxes these needles come in," she said. "Are they expensive? Do the needles last long?"

"Not my department," said Margaret, "I just like listening to the records and I leave the rest to himself. Duggie takes care of all the technical stuff."

The two friends sat swaying to the music as they sipped their tea.

"You should get the sheet music for this, Patsy. Didn't Jem get you a piano?"

"He did, it's in the parlour and it's nice to be able to play again, though I'm a bit rusty now. Jem likes to sing along when I play, we're like an aspiring duet in need of a lot more practice, though I doubt his deep voice would suit this song."

"That's grand that the two of you can enjoy such a simple but nice interest together," said Margaret. "Of course that could all change again if you have a family, though if yours turned out to be anything like mine they'd love the music. They'd probably take after you, Patsy, you could teach them the piano."

Patsy's face clouded over and her cup clattered on to the saucer. Margaret stiffened with the realisation that she'd hit a very sensitive nerve. "I'm so sorry," she said, full of concern, "did I say something I shouldn't have? Isn't that just so typical of me, blathering on and putting my foot in something. Tell me, Patsy, what is it?"

They sat in silence for a few months as Josef Locke sang out his tale of love and lovers singing long ago.

Patsy looked up at her friend. "I've just come from the doctor's clinic," she murmured. "Betty insisted I went. I won't be having any children, I can't."

"O Patsy. I don't know what to say." Margaret took her friend's hand. "And how do you feel about that? I ask because for a long time you said you weren't interested in having any babies, so I don't know how to react."

"I'm fine with it," said Patsy, as much to convince herself. "It's a bit final, of course, I won't deny that, knowing that a family isn't on the cards. It was never something I wanted, as you so rightly said, but the fact that it's out of my hands anyway does put everything into a slightly different perspective. Not that I've changed my mind, I haven't, but knowing that I can't makes it different."

"I can understand that. Will you be telling Jem straight away?"

"I will, he's more than happy with just the two of us."

"You've got a good man there," said Margaret. "He adores you and he's so good the way he likes to take you out and show you off at those fancy places in town. Anyway, you can always borrow my two kids if you ever need a reminder of why you never wanted your own in the first place."

At that very moment Fergal farted a mess of poo into his pants and immediately started to bawl.

"Another load of shit," said Patsy, "everything stinks these days."

The two friends burst into laughter.

2

Aintree beckoned. The weather in England had been even colder perhaps than in Ireland: freezing temperatures and heavy snowfalls had forced the cancellation of all race meetings for a couple of months and now horse owners and trainers were to descend on Liverpool for one of the biggest fields ever run over the Grand National course. The prize money was a big draw after such a lean season. There were already more than fifty horses entered in the race and Jem couldn't wait. He had booked a long weekend in Liverpool as a birthday treat for Patsy, with a room reserved in a small but nice hotel not too far from the course, that way it would be a proper treat instead of a few nights making do in someone's spare bedroom. Jem had always promised to take Patsy to Aintree and the decision to run the steeplechase on the Saturday rather than the traditional Friday had meant that neither Jem nor Patsy would have to take too much time off work. Also, it would give Patsy the opportunity to visit her family. Her younger sister Annie was to go with them; she had never been to Liverpool before and, thinking ahead, Jem had thought she would be good company for Patsy while he was queuing to put on their bets and, indeed, hiding the size of his stakes.

Annie was to stay with Molly and Kevin, who were back living in Liverpool in the very next street to Bulwer. That hadn't been their plan but was the result of Auntie Mary's manoeuvrings: she had turned up the emotional lonely-widow blackmail when Kevin talked about staying on in the RAF in the Midlands after the war and he had finally relented and gone back to the Post Office in Bootle. Because of his job and his young family, Kevin had been allocated one of the new prefabricated bungalows put up immediately after the war as a quick solution to the housing shortage: in fact, Akenside Street, their new address, had lost most of its own original housing stock, rows of red-brick terrace houses flattened into piles of rubble during the Bootle blitz. It had been one huge bombsite before the prefabs were assembled there. It seemed a terrible thing to think, in view of what had happened to the previous residents and their homes, but everyone agreed that the new bungalows were very attractive, with their own gardens front and back and all separated from the street by neat waist-high walls: they even had a proper outside coal-shed, big enough for tools and stuff to be stored as well, and the prefabs came with fitted kitchens, including refrigerators and boilers for washing the laundry. To Annie, it was like going to stay in a posh modern house. Even the toilet was indoors and there was a bathroom with a real bath in it and you could lock the door on both. She hoped to have a bath every day.

Jem was pleased to discover that both the Auntie Mary and Kevin followed the horses. They were regular punters with the bookie's runners who collected in a nearby back-entry, with a look-out stationed at each end in case the police appeared and the runners had to scarper. Jem thought that was very funny: off-course betting had been legal in Ireland for a couple of decades.

"It's all much more civilised, none of this subterfuge, skulking around in back alleys and hoping the men in blue don't arrive just as you're about to collect your winnings," he said, "or, even worse, just as you're about to lay your bet on a horse that later romps home at 50-1 without a penny of yours on its back."

"I don't know why they don't change the laws here," said Kevin. "Maybe it's because racing has always been regarded as the 'sport of kings', a rich man's game, and we ordinary working people can't be trusted with our own hard-earned money when it comes to gambling. It all seems like a very Protestant approach to me."

"It's because of ordinary working people enjoying a bit of a flutter and a grand day out that racing is the number one sport in Ireland," said Jem. "You two would love it, you should leave this heathen land behind and move back home. You know the railways even transport the horses to the tracks for free because they make so much money out of passengers going to the meetings. It's a race-goers paradise, right enough. We have so many courses all over the country now because new ones sprang up wherever the trains went, like the pioneer towns which grew up in the Wild West in America with the coming of the 'iron-horse'. Four-legged or running on metal wheels," he joked, "the horse is a powerful force for promoting civilisation."

"Let's hope we manage to pick one with a winning force today," said Mary, "that would be very civilised."

She had bought all the morning newspapers to collect as much information as possible on the form of all the National runners and the three aficionados studied it with knowledge and insight round the table in Mary's small front room. There was plenty to discuss: in all, fifty-seven runners were to line up at the start, indeed it was one of the biggest cards ever for the race, and it sparked the sort of convivial conversation Jem loved. They all favoured the Irish horses: loyalty took precedence even over logic when it came to the National.

Patsy didn't take part in the avid discussions going on, animated and fun though they sounded with everyone getting in their penn'orth of advice and comment, and she was glad Jem was so relaxed with her family. She merely dutifully glanced through the pin-prickers' guides-to-the-runners and nodded occasionally to stay part of the company. Then she discovered a sudden, totally unexpected emotional connection to one of the horses: evidently it regularly trained on the sandy beach at Sutton, near Howth, the very beach she had sat gazing over with Sean on their mystery day out all those years ago. She scribbled the name down and handed it to Jem: it was a difficult name and she didn't want to forget it.

"Caughoo!!" he said. "That's a 100-1 shot. Are you sure?"

"That's the one I've chosen," she said. "I thought you'd approve as it's an Irish horse."

"It's Irish all right but it's only an eight-year-old," said Mary, peering up over her glasses, pencil poised over the papers. "The National isn't usually won by such a young horse so you'll be just giving the bookie your money."

"But it's the one I've chosen," said Patsy, getting a bit tetchy, as if her precious memory was being called to account. "Am I not allowed to pick out a horse for myself?"

Kevin came to her rescue. "It is young but it won the Ulster Grand National last year and it was even younger then. Go with your choice, Patsy, you've as much chance as any of us. There's always that element of luck on the day, otherwise we'd all be putting our money on the same horse and, with weather like this, all the form forecasts could go out the window."

Indeed it had been pouring down all morning, the sort of day when a cosy chair in front of the fire promised a more comfortable afternoon than standing exposed out in the open but time was getting on and the race-goers couldn't postpone going out in the weather any longer. They wrapped up in warm clothes and heavy macs and shivered at the door as they set off to Aintree, Jem's final attempt at persuading Kevin and Mary to join them falling on deaf ears. Annie had already decided earlier not to venture forth and get soaked: she was to stay at home with her big sister, revelling in being in a nice bright house, with huge windows looking out on to all the gardens, and she loved playing with Molly's two little girls — Annie had been a little mother even as a child — and their dog, Bonzo, which beat pigeons any day of the week.

The bus heading to Aintree was packed upstairs and down, it was already standing room only when Patsy and Jem boarded. The pervasive smell was a suffocating mix of cheap perfume and wet clothes as people pressed and jostled together without enough space for so much as a draught between them; the pervasive sound was an intoxicating mix of excitement and enthusiasm for one of the most eagerly awaited days on the Liverpool calendar. Bad weather or not, people were determined to enjoy the first running of the National on a Saturday, the schedule having been changed at the request of Prime Minister Atlee. He was a popular figure on the bus to the course and, just as everyone piled off at the appropriate stop, the rain stopped too and a great cheer went up in Atlee's honour.

The high spirits weren't to last. The rain had stopped falling all right but it was immediately followed by a heavy fog, which descended over the Aintree course like a clammy cloak muffling the proceedings. It pierced right through to the bone and made the cold seem even colder. Visibility was so poor that people who had paid for entrance into the spectator stands were rewarded by a hanging blanket of mist through which they could make out only two of the famous National fences. It was very disappointing and promised less of a spectacle and more of a damp squib. Jem had bought advance tickets to the stands as part of Patsy's introduction to Aintree.

"What do you think, Patsy?" he said after the first couple of races. "Shall we stay here where it's a bit warmer and we can get refreshments, or would you like to walk along the course to get more of a view of today's magnificent steeplechase?"

"What's it like along the course? Is it worth putting up with the cold?"

"I'd say it is, especially for your first ever Grand National, which should by decree be as grand as possible. We can go stand along the rails either next to one of the big jumps or between a couple of them, so you'll see the runners taking off as one and landing more as a desperately disorganised rabble. And if one of them decides to walk along the face of the fence instead of jumping it, it will cause several others to come a cropper at the same time, so reducing the field in quite a dramatic way, hopefully not by any of the horses we've backed, though it is an exciting possibility in the spectacle."

"So you can actually see the horses racing past, close up?"

"You can indeed, my good woman," said Jem. "Not only that but you also get to hear them: the thundering rhythm of their hooves galloping en masse over the ground, squelching deeply into the mud and the jockeys urging them on, and then the sudden lull when they all lift off into the air to jump a fence, and just seconds later that wonderful clomping thud as they land on the other side and the thunderous rhythm starts up again, and all the while you hear them snorting and snotting through their nostrils and you see their startled eyes bulging with the effort of the race."

"Let's go, then," said Patsy. "You can't experience any of that from here, neither sight nor sound, and I don't want to miss out. I'd rather shiver."

"Take my arm then, my good woman, and I'll steer you round the course. We'll buy a souvenir umbrella first, just in case the heavens open again. We'd be a bit wet but rain might disperse this fog."

They made their way out of the stands and skirted the enclosure to cross to the other side of the track. Officials and racing gentry stood about in sodden groups, their status shrouded in anonymity by the mist, which seemed to hang heavier beyond the glow of the stands. The murkiness of the day washed everything in a miserable grey: only the jockeys' riding silks added moving splashes of colour to the palette.

Jem steered Patsy past the early fences until they got to Becher's

Brook. "This is one of the most famous jumps," said Jem, "named for a man after my own heart. He was, of course, called Becher, a Lord or something, and he was unsaddled when his horse landed at this very fence and the man had to take shelter in the brook behind the jump or risk being kicked to death in the stampede of the oncoming field. Afterwards he testified that it wasn't too bad being submerged, except that he normally preferred his water with whiskey in it. Like I said, a man after my own heart." Jem produced a hipflask and passed it to Patsy. "Let's toast the man with a drop of his own poison and warm ourselves at the same time."

They walked on further over the soggy ground, the wetness beginning to penetrate up through their shoes, the mud cloying around the bottoms of their legs. Jem found a space for the two of them by the rails where the course headed out into the country. They could follow the indistinct shapes of crowds of people shifting about incoherently in the fog and could make out the looming foliated bulk of the fence immediately on their left and the vague dark barrier of the next jump off in the distance.

"We'll stand here, by the Canal Turn," said Jem. "It's not a bad spot and it's a challenge of a fence. We'll be able to see the horses approach and witness them soar way above us and up high into the mist before they sail balletically over the brush, stretch their legs clear and steady to land on the water-logged turf, only to have to change direction abruptly without losing their footing or their balance, ready to plough on to the next fence, Valentine's."

"Valentine's! O how romantic," said Patsy, "a fence dedicated to love. Only courting couples should be allowed to approach it, arm in arm and gazing into each other's eyes by a monstrous monument to Valentine's Day."

"You are such a romantic soul, Patsy, and wouldn't that be a fabulous idea. They could have race marshals patrolling and demanding that all couples within kissing distance of the fence provide loving proof of the state of their hearts and whether or not they were in it to the finish. Unfortunately, the naming of the fence has nothing to do with Cupid's bow but is yet another example of the bizarre magic of the National," said Jem. "It's said that back in the middle of the last century a horse called Valentine jumped that very fence but went over it hind legs first. Now, Patsy, try to even conjure a picture of that in your mind and your mind will boggle, I guarantee it. I've seen my share of horses jumping and I just can't imagine the equine acrobatics that must have gone into that one."

"You seem to know a story about every fence," said Patsy.

"I'm a racing man, my good woman, knowledge of the obstacles is par for the course. And I can tell you that you can enjoy all of this twice, because they have to do two circuits before the finishing straight."

"Jesus, Mary and Joseph, the horses must be exhausted by the end."

"It's not regarded as the greatest steeplechase in the world for nothing," said Jem. "Now you can understand our comments on your decision to put your shirt on an eight-year-old and his chances of not only completing four miles or so of fences but completing them ahead of far more experienced horses."

Patsy smiled to herself as she thought of her experience of watching the horses on the beach at Howth.

The fog was filtering everything into a hushed quietude but they caught the announcement over the Tannoy system that the horses were lining up at the start. Along the rails spectators could only listen and wait, a buzz of anticipation electrifying the atmosphere as every head was turned to the left, necks strained, waiting to catch the first glimpse of the runners.

And suddenly the noise of the hooves could be heard thumping over the ground and the charge of horses emerged frantically and suddenly out of the all-enveloping mist, solidifying as they raced past, determined in their powerful forward thrust, up and over, sprawling and sliding over the muddy turf as the jockeys, tight bums bobbing in the air and feet clenched and kicking in the stirrups, fought to angle their mounts on landing to smooth out the sharpness of the bend and encourage the horses to recover their stride. It was every man on every horse for himself. Some jockeys were unseated, flung without dignity out of their saddles and down to earth as their horses tumbled in the mud and then headed off, riderless and reins-free, to re-join the charge and hamper their stable-mates with their erratic weavings. The runners could be seen rising over Valentine's before dissolving at full height once again into the fog and the mire.

Jem produced his hipflask again. "Did you enjoy that, Patsy?" he asked, grinning with his own adrenaline rush of the chase.

"I've never seen anything so thrilling and yet so fleeting," she said. "I couldn't make out where Caughoo was, I was too busy watching the whole thing. What about your horses? Could you make out any of them?"

"I got lost in the moment too and paid little heed," said Jem. "And anyway, it's too early to call. They'll be coming round for the second circuit in a few minutes so you'll have that fleeting thrill all over again."

The murmur of the crowd had increased with the excitement and soon the horses were galloping towards them again, rising as before, sinews straining and muscles bulging as they raced on past, the cheering rising in unison with the runners to a deafening pitch as punters urged on their hopes of reward. There were fewer contenders this time round but the level of urgency was if anything greater than before, each jockey pleased to have survived this far and perhaps sensing they could be in with a chance.

From where they were standing, it was impossible for any of the spectators along the rails to see right across the course to the winning line, they just had to wait for the announcement of the result. When it came, the winner of the 1947 Grand National was declared to be none other than the 100-1 outsider, Caughoo. Patsy had won.

The whole family was gathered in the prefab having their tea and all talk was of the National. Only Patsy had secured a win with her gutsy pick, for all the experienced studying of form that had gone on that morning, but she had bought chocolates and a bottle of whiskey out of her winnings for everyone to share in her luck. Caughoo's victory hadn't been secured without controversy so there was plenty to discuss. The jockey beaten into second place had accused Caughoo's rider, Eddie Dempsey, of cheating: Dempsey had, according to his accuser, hidden on his mount behind a fence, concealed by the fog, and hadn't actually run the first circuit, instead joining the race when the field was already depleted on the second time around and the other horses were beginning to tire. According to the race officials, photographic evidence showed that Caughoo's rider had done no such thing and had indeed completed the full course and come home a worthy winner. It had been a good day for the bookies but there were many punters who still claimed Caughoo's victory was a farce.

"It's just sour grapes because their horses didn't win," said Patsy. "We were there, and the fog wasn't so bad that the crowds along the rails wouldn't have noticed a horse just standing there at a fence waiting on its own and jigging about the way horses do on the spot, then suddenly galloping off again when the others arrived. Surely the other jockeys would have seen it too yet only one of them made the accusation."

"Well, we'll never know for sure," said Jem. "I for one am prepared to give Patsy credit for her astute selection. It was foggy and misty out on the course all right but she has a point about the unlikelihood that no one else but the jockey beaten into second place would have noticed."

"And where was this jockey that he could see what he said he saw and none of the others did?" said Patsy.

"Well obviously we weren't there, we had only the radio commentary to go by and it certainly sounded like a plausible complaint," said Auntie Mary. "Sure, the horse was too young, and his jockey knew it. He had to do something to improve his chances."

The discussion was interrupted by a howling noise right outside the window, a cross between the mournful cry of a lone wolf on the prairie and the chest-thumping jungle call of Tarzan.

"I know who's responsible for that racket," said Kevin laughing eagerly as he immediately got up from the table and hurried to open the front door.

"I knew it was you," the others could hear him say, "who else would be daft enough to howl into the night like an animal in distress. Get in quick before the neighbours fetch the police or the cruelty-to-animals people."

The culprit was a friend of Kevin's arrived unexpectedly to stay. He was a Dublin man, Mike O'Dowd, who was working his way up to gain his captain's ticket in the Merchant Navy. His ship had docked in Liverpool and he had decided to take Kevin up on his invitation to stay any time he was in port. Sleeping on solid ground was a welcome change from the rolling of the ship, even with seasoned sea-legs. There would be no problem over sleeping arrangements. Annie was in with the girls and Mike had a camp-bed permanently stored in the house for his impromptu visits: it wasn't the first time he had stayed.

"Come in, Mike, a new addition is welcome. We've been arguing about the Grand National result but I think the debate has also run its course. Patsy here won but her success was spoilt by talk of cheating during the race, cheating by the winning jockey. Poor Patsy's under fire and further argument might spoil her sense of satisfaction altogether."

"Nothing could spoil my victory," said Patsy, "and I've the winnings in my pocket to prove it."

"And nor should it," said Mike, shaking her hand and congratulating her on her astute selection. "Now who have we here?" he asked, wrapping the company in an infectious smile, open-mouthed and full of neat white teeth. "There are several faces I don't recognise but friendly expressions on all of them and none of them as cut-throat looking as my usual companions."

"We've got family over from Dublin for the weekend," said Molly, "so you'll feel right at home." She went round the table introducing everyone and Mike's enthusiastic greeting of the young O'Kelly girl brought a bright blush to Annie's face: she wasn't used to receiving the flirtatious attention of such a manly man. A chair was found for the new arrival and he shoved in right next to her.

"I've the best seat in the house," he said as he winked at Annie. Her cheeks went even redder.

"If anyone's noticed the tall canvas bag standing up in the corner in the bathroom, here is the man responsible," said Kevin. "That's Mike's bow and arrows. He leaves them here so he can get in some practice along the shore when he's in port for a few days."

"I have to keep my eye in and my arms strong," said Mike. "Do you like a man with a good eye and strong arms, Annie?"

"Sure what use is a good eye," said Annie, finding her composure and matching Mike's humour in her own flirtatious way. "I'd prefer a man with two normal ones. And good arms, is it? You should see the arms of my brothers and that's from carrying sacks of potatoes and digging the land. There's not a bow and arrow in sight on the farm in Tullamore."

"Ah but you'd be glad of my good eye if we were out in the jungle and a lion charged through the bushes bent on attacking us," said Mike.

"I'd save you from being mauled in a horrible death and we'd have something you could cook for my supper."

"Get away with you, Mike, shooting lions in the jungle? Is that what you do?" asked Jem.

"So he tells us," said Molly. "Where do you think he learned how to do that howl outside the window?"

"From Tarzan himself," said Mike, "just before he dove into a jungle pool and played with the crocodiles. Now, young Annie, wouldn't you like to go swimming in a jungle pool with me there ready with my bow and arrow to keep you safe from the crocodiles? Would you like to be Jane to my Tarzan and live with me in a leafy cabin up in the tree-tops? We could drink coconut milk and you could swaddle yourself in furs."

"I'm not sure I'd like the feel of fur right next to my skin, far too itchy," said Annie. "Unless you're actually trying to make a monkey out of me, of course, in which case perhaps Cheetah would be my role, a faithful friend rather than a kitchen skivvy having to cook the beautiful wild animals that fell to your good eye."

"I doubt you'll ever let yourself be a skivvy," said Mike laughing. "Now, tell me all your news, everyone."

The whiskey was going down a treat, especially as Mike had turned up with another bottle and a carton of cigarettes. A pack of cards was produced and Mike enthralled them all with tricks. Then he asked Annie if she had any money, preferably a note.

"Why should I be giving you any money when your tongue is already well silvered," she said, "or do you expect me to pay for the privilege of listening to all your blarney?"

"Go on now and don't be such a mean young lady," said Mike. "Where's that generous spirit I thought I'd identified?"

Annie pulled a ten-shilling note from her purse. "I hope you realise how many hours I have to work to earn that," she said.

Mike put the note in an envelope. "I'm going to rekindle that generous spirit I saw in you," he said, and he went over to the fire and threw the envelope into the flames. "What does money matter?"

Annie couldn't believe what he had just done and rushed over to try to grab her precious note but the envelope was already burning. She was almost in tears. Mike had taken the joke far too far. She sat in front of the fire watching her pay go up in smoke.

Mike went over to cheer her up. "Let's see if we can rescue the situation," he said, poking about in the fire and managing to retrieve the charred remains of the envelope. "There you are, no harm done," he said, producing Annie's ten-shilling note, totally intact, out of the burnt paper. "And what's this?" he said, poking around a bit more. "There's something else there. Well, would you believe that!" and he handed a small red rose to Annie. Her blushes knew no bounds.

All the rain and fog had dispersed when they woke the next morning. Patsy and Jem had arranged to meet Annie at their hotel but she was some quarter of an hour late when she arrived.

"That man threw me over his shoulder, climbed up the drainpipe with me on his back, then put me on the roof of the house," she blurted out breathlessly when she finally met them. "Then he left me there. Thank God it has a flat roof. All the neighbours came out to watch and have a laugh at my expense. I was mortified but I couldn't get down. And there he is stood on the ground looking up at me and playing a jig on a penny whistle. Was I supposed to dance, do you think? Finally Molly ordered him to help me get down because she knew I was coming to meet the two of you, so he climbed back up the drainpipe, stood on the roof, beat his chest and entertained the whole street with one of his Tarzan calls. Then I was back over his shoulder and he carried me down. Everyone applauded and cheered and I had to take a bow before running in to the house to hide with the embarrassment of it all. That man is crazy."

"But he's great fun, so he is," said Jem. "And I think you loved it all. Just think how much you'll have to tell everyone when you get home. You never thought you'd be meeting a real live Tarzan. He has certainly had lots of adventures and he gave you a bit of an adventure of your own. Come on admit it, Annie, it made your weekend, never mind him setting fire to your hard-earned ten-shilling note."

"Kevin told me Mike is a member of the Magic Circle in London," said Patsy. "He must keep them all entertained on the ship."

"He's entertaining, all right," said Annie. "He suggested we all meet this afternoon on the shore so he can do some shooting. I asked him why we would want to stand there watching him pull his big bow and he said we'd be able to look for his arrows for him in the sand. According to Kevin, what you have to do is walk up and down in straight lines, a couple of feet apart, and keep your eyes peeled."

"And did you agree to go?" asked Patsy.

"I think I sort of did, but you don't have to if you don't want to," said Annie. "I fancy taking the dog for a walk. Molly says Bonzo loves going to the shore."

"We could all go," said Jem. "We could get some fresh air and I can maybe take my shoes and socks off, roll up my trouser-legs and have a paddle in the brown waters of the River Mersey. How could we resist such an invitation? I like this Mike O'Dowd fellow and who knows what else the afternoon could have in store. What do you say, Patsy, it's your weekend treat? You could spend the whole day with your sisters and cousins, out by the sea, watching the gulls dodge Mike's arrows."

"I hope he's not planning on shooting any birds for Annie's pot," said Patsy.

The whole family bar Auntie Mary went on the expedition. The shore was just a ten-minute walk from Bulwer Street and the dog was let off the leash as soon as sand took over from tarmac. Concrete anti-landing-craft pyramids still lined up along the water's edge and a series of gunners' pill-box turrets hidden among the sand-hills were ugly monuments left over from the war, reminders of the very real possibility of a German invasion along the Mersey. Now they provided Bonzo with good sniffing territory and he cocked his leg on as many as he could: the pervading smell of the pillboxes was of stale urine, irresistible to the mongrel, and he explored inside every single one and added his own contribution.

The tide had recently gone out, leaving a long stretch of flat beach for Mike's shooting. His bow was easily five or six feet tall and it took a lot of strength and expertise just to pull the string taut, let alone tight enough to arch the bow to take an arrow. He checked to make sure no one was lingering on the beach in his sightline and fired off a few missiles. They soared into the sky in a sweeping arc before dipping down and landing in the sand, but he had only shot a few arrows when disaster struck, there was an almighty crack; his bow had fractured in the middle, leaving a dangle of limp string and two lengths of splintered wood. Mike exploded with rage. It was a relatively new bow. It was supposed to be top quality. If he had been hunting when the bow failed, he would be dead.

"So, you really do hunt with it?" asked Annie innocently, only to be greeted by a face of Mike that none of them had seen before.

"What else would I use a bow and arrow for?" he said. "Just to amuse you on the shore?"

"Okay Mike, let's find your spent arrows and we'll call it a day," said Kevin. He was sympathetic to his friend and could understand his anger but it was nobody's fault and he didn't want the weekend soured: the visitors would be going back to Dublin the following night. He organised the group across an imaginary grid over the sand and the search for the arrows got underway. It wasn't as difficult to find them as everyone had imagined because the sand was flat and damp still after the tide and soon all had been recovered.

"Thank you all. I'm sorry for losing my temper," said Mike. He gathered up the broken bow and shoved it back in the sheath. "I bought the blasted thing last time I was in Liverpool so tomorrow I'll go and play hell with the poor salesman in the shop. It'll be a different sort of target practice." Then his broad grin broke out again and he turned to Annie: "Now you see what sort of a man you're really dealing with."

Their last night in Bootle was a musical affair. Kevin had a natural ear for picking out a tune on the piano and he played all the popular songs of the day. Those not affected by stage fright sang their party pieces to an appreciative audience, who joined in with the choruses, and Patsy unearthed some sheet music to play her part. Mike and Bonzo added a few howls of their own and it wasn't long before neighbours were knocking on the door to join in and the evening turned into an impromptu party. A rousing rendition of 'Happy Birthday to You' had Patsy in a bit of a dither as the centre of attention while a squeeze round the waist from Mike had Annie in a different sort of dither.

"We'll both be sailing away tomorrow night but I'll hear your siren's voice calling to me over the waves and I'll see your beauty in the stars," he said to her. "Though come to think of it, the waves will be lashing the ship and there won't be any stars. The weather forecast doesn't auger

321

well for any of us ploughing through the seas tomorrow night. I'll just think of you instead, vomiting up over the side."

Annie was heartbroken to be parted so quickly from Mike, a man who seemed to offer everything she could wish for — romance, attention, fun, adventure, strength, bravery, and no doubt passion too.

Molly noticed her sister becoming very subdued when it was time to leave to catch their boat the following day. Annie had asked Mike if there was an address she could use to perhaps write the odd letter to him and he had replied with a flirtatious joke but no address. Molly took Annie to one side and told her that Mike had been engaged to a childhood sweetheart in Dublin for several years and they were planning to marry as soon as his next promotion came through.

"What's that to me?" said Annie with a shrug. "The man's too much of a selfish idiot and what woman would ever want to trust such a flirt. I pity the girl he's engaged too. Hasn't he been giving me the nod all weekend? Don't worry, Molly," she said grinning and owning up, "he didn't fool me one bit with his great sense of humour and his sparkling eyes and his gorgeous smile and, you know, all his tricks."

3

The Irish tricolour was flying high from every vantage point in Dublin and street traders had done brisk business selling smaller versions of the green, white and gold flag to decorate window ledges, doorsteps, cars and carts. Every home displayed its Irish credentials. Billowing cascades of matching balloons bobbed in shops and banks and offices. Printed portraits of Irish leaders throughout history took pride of place on hoardings and lampposts and shamrock symbols blossomed everywhere. There wasn't a surface left without some sort of decoration for the occasion: it was 1949 and thirty-three years to the day of the Easter Rising and at last the new Republic of Ireland was proclaiming its hard-won independence from the British crown with a military parade in O'Connell Street. A twenty-one-gun salute had been sounded just after midnight on the bridge, delayed by a few minutes, according to the papers, because of the number of people who had broken through the safety barricades to be closer to the action and now, later in the day, the same crowds were swollen by yet more spectators for the parade itself. The biggest flag of all was hoisted in pride of place across the full width of the pillared portico of the General Post Office, where all those years ago Patrick Pearse had read aloud the Proclamation of the Irish Republic. Now the President of the Republic, Sean O'Kelly, was to officiate at the march-past of the Irish Army and take the salute. There were two Tullamore representatives in the parade, Jim and Joe, who were marching with their comrades.

Michael and May were among the thousands lining the street for the celebration. Their sons had written to say where to look out for their battalion and May was swollen with pride that both her boys were taking part. It more than made up for losing their sons' help on the farm. The cheering was thunderous as the soldiers marched past: independence at last after hundreds of years of being subject to the British.

Patsy and Patrick, however, were not there. As an active member of the Volunteers, Patrick had been invited to join his former comrades in the victory parade but he had declined. Instead, he asked his eldest daughter to accompany him on a visit out to Larch Hill, their first visit since the family had left for Dublin not long after Lizzie had died in the young Patsy's arms. Patrick never ever spoke about their life out in the country, he shunted such memories to the back of his mind, always determined not to risk making Betty uncomfortable with talk of his dead wife. But thoughts of Lizzie and their days living in the gatehouse with their three young girls stole into his mind every day. They were happy times, infused with a sense of freedom and relaxation, full of music and humour. Lizzie had the knack of finding an opportunity for humour and joy in everything, even, he remembered with a smile, in sharing that one precious orange between the five of them.

"Has it changed much, Daddy?" Patsy asked, the two of them standing in the lane and staring up at the house. There didn't seem to be anyone around, the place looked as if it had been empty, for a while. "I thought it was all much bigger but I was only a child at the time."

"It was life that changed," said Patrick. "Maybe we were all children then, certainly we were more innocent." He stood there silently for a few minutes. "The gatehouse looks as if it's more of a storage barn now than a home and I'm surprised to see the big house looking so neglected and overgrown," he said. "The English family who lived here were quite particular, they liked to keep the front of the house well maintained, always a fresh coat of paint round the windows and doors and the front walls whitewashed regularly. And the garden was always kept in good order, nice and tidy but with a wild feel to the planting, it was a lovely burst of controlled nature to greet you first thing in the morning. All that was part of my job, of course, they didn't do much hard work themselves, the husband and wife, only gave instructions to your mammy or me as to what needed to be done and when, inside or out, but they were fair employers, I suppose. They showed a lot of kindness when your mammy was ill, God bless her."

"I have only vague memories of the day she died, though I don't know what's a real memory and what seems like a memory but is actually just something I've been told and it's become lodged in my head," said Patsy. "What I do remember particularly vividly is being really uncomfortable when Mammy was lying across my knee and I felt a bit cross because I desperately needed to move, God forgive me, but I was afraid of waking her knowing she was ill."

"I don't think I've ever forgiven myself for leaving you with her that day, and you so little to have your mammy die on your knee."

"You had no way of knowing what was going to happen," said Patsy. "Mammy had been in bed for weeks, so that was nothing new, and we needed stuff from the village and we children couldn't have gone there alone, either walking or in the trap. Don't feel guilty on my account, Daddy. I think I was actually the lucky one, I was with Mammy when she passed, when she was relaxed and warm and just drifted away while I was reading her a story. And what was the alternative for her? More weeks, maybe months, of that awful cough. I remember how much it seemed to convulse right through her." Patsy opened the gate. "Shall we go in? I can't see there'd be anyone who'd object."

They walked up the short driveway and stopped to peer in through the windows of the gatehouse. They were both overtaken by a sudden rush of emotion, as if nothing had changed and they were actually looking in on their old life. Through the accumulated rubbish they could see a pale shadow where the colour of the wall had faded behind the piano. Patsy started humming a bit of what she could remember of a Beethoven piece her old teacher had introduced her to.

"What's that you're humming?" asked Patrick.

"It's some Beethoven."

That simple reference lightened the mood. Patrick started to laugh and recounted the tale of when Patsy gave up washing herself because she said Beethoven never used to wash so why should she.

"You always had a mind of your own but it was always set on some outside influence," said Patrick. He walked round the cottage and found an old horseshoe. "Poor old Seamus," he said, "what he had to put up with."

"Thanks to you insisting we children could use him as a plaything."

They picked over small piles of debris lying on the ground. Small potato tubers were growing wild among the weeds and small rocks which the children had painted poked hints of faded colour through the overgrowth. Odd scraps of water-stained fabric reminded them of the pretty curtains that Lizzie always insisted upon and a couple of rusting spoons and a fork brought back images of the three girls doing a bit of random digging in the earth.

"You and your sisters were always keen to help with the vegetables but I'm not sure your gardening contribution would have kept the family fed," said Patrick.

"We had a great childhood, Daddy, we were spoilt with all the freedom we had and the countryside right on our doorstep. And you and Mammy seemed so happy. Like all children I thought it would never end but of course everything does."

"I'd say it ended too soon," said Patrick.

"You never mention my mammy."

"There's a lot of stuff I never mention but it's not because my mind and heart aren't full of longings and regrets. Sometimes I ache inside so much that I can't even just be pleasant to anyone, to anyone at all. When your mammy passed, I know I changed. Perhaps I should have talked about it more but who could I talk to? You were too young and I could hardly talk to my close friend Michael about how much I was missing my dead wife when I was about to marry his daughter so my children would have a mother. Betty has been a godsend and God knows she has tried over the years to get me to share my feelings. I just can't, Patsy, they're too painful. I think of your mammy and I ache, I think of all the terrible cruel things I did as a so-called patriot and I ache. I think of what I did to you and Sean Fitzsimmons and I ache, both of yourselves completely blameless but made to suffer because of me and my own guilt. And the only way I can cope is in being silent."

Patsy put her arms around her father. "Well, I'm not a child now," she said. "I'm old enough to know you can't lock everything away in silence because then you're silent with the people who love you and you make their lives hard and none of it is their fault. I'm here and you're my daddy and precious to me. You're more important to me than a young man I knew in the past. You said yourself I've always had a mind of my own and, if I'd had a mind to, I would have kept on seeing him regardless of your feelings."

Just then Patsy saw her old floaty friend, ever dressed for a day in the fields, and the old woman raised her spectral head and gave Patsy a friendly wave and a smile of recognition. Patsy waved back. There was something very reassuring in the old woman still being there.

Patrick turned towards the main house. The front door was secured with a padlock and the window shutters were closed so there was no chance of taking a look inside. He pointed to one of the upstairs windows and his eyes filled with tears. "Once she got in that room she never came home, not alive anyway," he said. "That was such a disappointment to your mammy. She knew the English family were being kind and quite sensible suggesting that she would be more comfortable in the big house but I'm sure she knew she was going to die in there. Perhaps she didn't want to die in the cottage and her absence be even more tangible to us all when she'd gone. And like a fool that day I went off in the cart and never got to speak to her again. You're right, Patsy, you were the lucky one and it's taken me all these years to realise that."

Patrick stood quietly looking up at the window. "You know once upon a time that was actually our bedroom, your mammy's and mine," he said. "Little did I realise at the time that she'd die in it so young. We had great plans for that house."

"I never did get to hear the story of why you had to move out," said Patsy, anxious to turn thoughts away from her mammy's death.

"Lizzie's uncle owned it and he had let us live there rent-free, but then he lost all his money and had to sell everything, including the house," said Patrick. "We were always given to understand that it was because of his gambling but I don't know the details. I don't remember much about my in-laws, the Lett family, God forgive me, but I do know that your mother had been used to a much better standard of living before she married me and had to settle for a simpler life with a baker. She always maintained an elegance about her. I sometimes worried that working in the big house amongst all the fine things would make her dissatisfied and would turn her against me. I remember getting paid for a small painting and your mammy choosing to spend the money on buying a piano rather than on stocking the larder and for a moment or two I saw it as an indication of her desire for a different life to the one I could provide but I was wrong, thank God. She was too good a woman to be influenced by fancy living."

They were suddenly aware of someone crunching up the drive from the lane, it was a man but no one they recognised.

"Can I help you with anything?" he said. "Are you interested in buying the old place? It's been empty now for some years and you can see it's quite run down but structurally I think it's sound. To be honest I don't know who has responsibility for selling it now. The English vicar in the village has a key and he asked me to keep an eye on the place, that's how I came to notice you looking around."

"We used to live here, in the small cottage," said Patsy. "There was an English couple living in the main house when we left."

"Aye there was right enough, that's going back a bit. They've long gone," said the man.

"Did they go back to England?" asked Patrick.

"They did. Things became very uncomfortable for them during all the fighting, and it wasn't because of the local Volunteers. From what I understand they were reasonable people, popular enough in the village despite being British, but then you'd know that better than me if you lived here with them. It was when a unit of Black and Tans descended on the place and demanded the use of the house as a free barracks that their life changed. They were real ugly men, violent and coarse, thugs, if you ask me, drunk more often than not and shoving their weight round as if they owned the place and pulling their guns on innocent people in the village just for the laugh of it, from what I'm told. And they wouldn't leave the poor woman of the house alone, English though she was, pestering her with all sorts of innuendos and grabbing a hold of her as she walked past, so I'm told. The local police were powerless to help and in the end the couple decided to leave. The Tans were delighted, of course, they had a free run of the house then and no one able or willing to challenge them at the risk of getting a bullet in the back. Since then the house has been neglected. Would you like to take a look inside? I can fetch the key."

"No thank you," said Patrick. "The house itself doesn't hold particularly happy memories for us, grand though it used to be. As my daughter said, we lived in the cottage and worked for the couple. We were just curious as to what it was like here now after all these years."

"Well, feel free to wander," said the man. "If you change your mind about the key just ask for me in the village, Keenan's the name."

"Thank you very much, Mr Keenan," said Patsy.

They watched him check that the door of the cottage was still secure and then he was gone.

"No one escaped the cruelty of those years," said Patrick. "Was it worth it, do you think, Patsy, all the killings, the sacrifices, the destruction, all to win independence which probably would have come anyway in the end? The British have given India independence and we might have been next. Instead, we've had war and civil war and the lasting bitterness of the divisions that caused between friends and families. Sometimes I think it was all a stupid complete waste of life, for the living as well as the dead."

"You can't honestly believe that Daddy. There was an uprising of sorts in India too. The British didn't just give up all their wealth and good living there because they lost interest. They were losing power and status and they knew it."

Father and daughter strolled around the gardens, each lost in their thoughts, and crossed the field to the river where they tossed a few pebbles into the water. The place had lost none of its soothing magic despite the unhappy memories.

"Let's go home now, shall we," said Patrick. His eyes were wet with tears.

By the time Patsy and Patrick got off the bus back in Dublin, the crowds were beginning to disperse after the parade. The atmosphere was full of good humour and a buzz of animated conversation bounced along the pavements with the people making their way home. It had been a great day and the air of celebration was still tangible. People were happy but hoarse after the non-stop cheering for the country's past heroes, for the desperate acts of bravery committed in the name of Ireland, for the hard-won victory against an occupying force and for their great hopes for a better future now they had control of their own affairs. Paper tricolours were still clutched with pride and families skipped along the ground with merry purpose. In the onward rush, Patsy didn't notice the family stop suddenly directly in her path. The woman was pushing a pram and singing and cooing in the general direction of the gurgling occupant, the man was holding a toddler up across his shoulders and was obviously in the middle of making some funny remark to the small boy running alongside him when he stopped abruptly in front of Patsy and Patrick, the colour draining from his face. He let go one hand off the toddler's leg to raise his hat politely.

"Mr O'Kelly," was all he said. Then he replaced his hat and glanced quickly at Patsy before gathering his family to hurry along. It was Sean Fitzsimmons.

Patsy abandoned her father, left him standing in the street with just a hurried excuse of having to get the dinner started. She didn't want him to see how upset she was, not only because of their talk out at Larch Hill but also because it would be like a betrayal of Jem. Back in the house she had no dinner to prepare. Jem was out at one of his business dinners and she had only herself to look after but with no appetite to satisfy. She went upstairs to the bedroom and took out a lidded box from the bottom of the wardrobe. She lit up a cigarette and stared at the box on her knee. It was where she kept her treasures — the small bag her father had crocheted in Ballykinlar, the book about Beethoven that Miss Bourke had given her. Then she opened the box and took out a small bundle, still tied carefully in bright red ribbon, and one by one she read all of Sean's letters.

4

Annie had begged Patsy to go with her down to the great banana bonanza along by the North Wall of the docks, just to see what mayhem was going on and at the same time they could stroll along the Liffey together. She wanted to talk to her big sister about "a personal matter" and the banana business at Alexandra Basin would be a perfect excuse to get out of the house 'to discuss things'.

"What banana mayhem?" asked Patsy. It wasn't a story Jem had read out from the paper though she did recall some of the women at work making lots of jokes about looking for bananas and who would find the biggest one to stuff in their gob. One of the girls had made suggestive sucking motions with her fingers in her mouth and Patsy hadn't joined in the chatter, though she had done her best to look both suitably amused and shocked. She was conscious that she was getting somewhat withdrawn with her colleagues in the workroom: she tried to relax into the banter like she used to but more and more her mind drifted into a state of emptiness.

"Don't tell me you have no idea what I'm talking about," said Annie. "You must be the only person in Dublin who hasn't heard about the bananas. You just wait until we get to the Basin. I bet half the city's population is there. Shall we cross on the Ha'penny Bridge or further along?"

"Let's go further along," said Patsy. The Ha'penny Bridge had tarnished for her, the magic rubbed off completely via a significant departure and a happier but perhaps ill-fated arrival.

As they walked on the quays, there was certainly a steady increase in the number of people heading in the same direction. There was also a steady increase in the number of Gardaí going the same way. The attraction was a tide of bananas floating in the water and available for free to anyone who could fish them out. Patsy couldn't believe her eyes. The water was positively a sea of brown and yellow as far as the eye could see.

"Where have they all come from?" she asked, quite astounded at the bizarre scene.

"Evidently a ship arrived loaded with tonnes of bananas to deliver to the Tropical Fruit warehouse," said Annie, "but, when the time came to unload them, the fruit company refused to accept the delivery because they said the bananas were already too ripe to sell. Instead of taking the bananas away, the ship's crew just dumped the whole lot of them over the side and into the dock and then sailed into the sunset. It didn't take long for the news to get around."

Annie was right. Hundreds of people were lined up several deep along the basin trying to nab some of the catch. An assortment of implements was in play — buckets and brooms and mops, fishing nets and garden rakes and, bizarrely, the odd pick-axe — anything that could hook on to a bent banana or drag a hand of fruit to the side; there was even a flotilla of rowing boats being oared frantically from the direction of Ringsend ready to land the unexpected booty. Scores of children were running around screaming and squealing with all the excitement and the promise of getting to enjoy a rare treat. Bananas had been a scarce commodity during the war years and after and, though they were now available, they still came at a price: only those whose belt-tightening during the lean years would hardly measure one notch could afford such a tropical luxury. The sight of so many bananas floating about right in front of them, free and there for the taking, had induced a frenzy of greedy fun in the crowd, even if the bananas were past their best; it was like a mad holiday outing, as if the citizens of Dublin had decided to initiate a new festival. The Gardaí had their work cut out: they had to try to control the crowd and at the same time keep an eye on any banana-hunter who might topple into the water in their quest.

"It's a great gas," said Patsy. "All we need is a brass band and a few balloons and the party could go on all day, not that I personally have any intentions of leaning into the water. Do you know anyone who might be banana-fishing? We could offer to buy some."

"As a matter of fact, I do," said Annie.

Patsy turned to ask her sister who it was but held her tongue when she saw that Annie was blushing and curling in her bottom lip under her

332

top teeth.

"As a matter of fact that's what I wanted to talk to you about," said Annie. She blushed even more.

"About someone who'll risk life and limb for a few free bananas?" joked Patsy and the joke hit home.

Annie laughed and flashed a huge smile at Patsy. "I've already put in my order, both for the fruit and for the life and limbs that go with it," she said with a wink. "I'm just waiting for the delivery."

"Annie O'Kelly!" said Patsy. "You sound like the women at work. It obviously is an extremely personal matter you want to talk to me about. Well, I'm all ears but I'm not sure this is the right place to speak about anything confidential. Shall we go back into the city and get a drink somewhere or is your banana-fisher waiting for you here with his catch."

"I'm his catch," said Annie girlishly, "and anyway, he's more of a banana-boatman than an angler, though I must say he's very good at reeling me in."

"Irresistible bait, judging by your expression. So can we go or do you want to stay?"

"We can go somewhere else," said Annie. "I'm to meet him later. He's in one of the rowing boats so he'll not be free until this evening, sink or swim, bananas or no bananas."

They left the melee behind and made their way back along the river to the city centre. It was a warm April day and they came across a small café with views out over the river.

"Come on in here, there are free tables by the window," said Annie, though actually most of the tables were free. "It's not very busy today, I suppose most people are down at the Basin. We won't have to worry about any prying ears. I'm not ready for my da to know about Matt."

"So that's his name, he of the irresistible life and limbs," said Patsy, settling into her chair and pulling out her packet of cigarettes.

"Can I have one of those?" asked Annie. "It's a treat to be able to smoke without hiding. My mammy gets cross with me at home if she even sees me with a cigarette, that's why I don't carry any in my bag. She goes on about how bad they are for me and what a terrible waste of money too. If I did light up in front of her, there'd be no pleasure in it at all."

"There are times when a cigarette is exactly what you need and this is one of them. I'll go and order. Perhaps we'll have some toast with our tea. I'll ask for extra butter though they might not have enough to spare. These days there's never enough of anything, though in truth there hasn't been for years. We were always lucky to have Uncle Michael there to give us food off the farm."

"We can offer to pay for extra butter," said Annie. "There are only ourselves and a couple of other customers in so there's hardly a rush on. Pity we don't have any bananas to barter with."

"Not yet anyway," said Patsy. She went to the small counter, exchanged a few pleasantries with the waitress and returned to the table able to report that the butter negotiation had been successful. "Now, start talking. What does this Matt fellow do? Does he have a job?"

"He does and he doesn't," said Annie, her face showing a mix of embarrassment and amused pride. "He's involved in trade, you might say, that's why he had the rowing boat, he's involved in what you might call 'off-shore' trade, 'on-the-side' trade."

"Might you also say he's involved in what you might also call the 'smuggling' trade?" asked Patsy.

"You might," said Annie, "but you might not mention it to my da, whatever you might call it." The tea and toast arrived and Annie kept her eyes focussed on buttering the bread and stirring the milk and sugar into her tea. "The problem is," she finally said, "there are no jobs Matt can get, there are no jobs anyone can get. I only got mine in the sewing factory because Molly and Theresa had worked there and their reputation helped me get a position. Lots of girls were trying to get in. And then there's our brother, John; he got into the bakery because of Da. There are just no jobs."

"So, Matt and his friends — I assume he doesn't do his off-shore trade alone — decided to create jobs of their own."

"That's right, and who can blame them. You can understand why I wanted to talk to you about this in private, Patsy, I'm not happy about the situation but that's the way it is."

"How long have you been seeing Matt?"

"I met him not long after we came back from Liverpool. I obviously can't resist a man connected to the sea. Don't you remember Mike?"

"I do and I remember how you were quite taken with him, until you found out about his fiancée," said Patsy. "That means you've known Matt for what? Three years, is it?"

"Almost, it'll be three years in August, the fourteenth, to be exact. He used to get odd labouring work at the docks but it was all very hit-and-miss, it usually depended on how well your face fitted and how many drinks you bought the labour boss in the pub. Matt always thought it was a very unfair way to go about things so he got together with some friends in the same boat, so to speak, and they had a word with some of the sailors off the ships about how and what could be brought into the country on the sly, like, and they decided that's what they'd do, go into an unfair business of their own."

"He must mean a lot to you, Matt, I notice you still know the date you met."

"Do you remember the date when you met Jem?"

"I recall the occasion because it was at work. We had a meeting in the factory to discuss an order for his store and then he took me to dinner to cement the deal."

"And cemented you into his heart in the process," said Annie. "That's far more romantic than how I met Matt: we literally bumped into each other in the street and I fell over."

"So he picked you up?" grinned Patsy.

"He did and that was that. Now I don't know what to do because he wants us to get married and I want to too but there's the matter of his work. I haven't figured out how to explain it to Mammy and Daddy without making Matt sound like a criminal."

"Well, I suppose he is," said Patsy. "Whatever the jobs situation is, he is breaking the law."

Annie didn't appreciate the comment. "I thought you of all people would understand," she sulked.

"The only thing I understand," said Patsy, "is that, if you love Matt, then you should marry him, whatever anyone else says. It's your life and you might as well live it with the man you love. You'll always be sorry if you don't, always sorry, the regret will never go away, take it from me."

Patsy sounded as if she was making some sort of a confession and

Annie didn't know whether or not to pursue the matter. Her sister's face looked downcast, perhaps shadowed by some regret of her own that had never gone away, but before Annie could ask Patsy carried on talking.

"After three years, or almost three years, you must know your feelings, so we'll just have to come up with some explanation that sounds convincing but isn't actually a lie," said Patsy. "Otherwise, you'll have to elope."

"I suppose I am old enough to marry without permission," said Annie giggling. "Wouldn't that be romantic? Running off with a smuggler and becoming his bride?"

"Matt could row you out to sea, catch a waiting boat and then smuggle you off to an unknown destination where he would make an honest woman of you."

"But how would I make an honest man out of him?" said Annie. The two of them laughed at the idea.

"No marriage is without its challenges," said Patsy.

"So speaks the older sister with all her years of experience. I thank you for that," said Annie, "I knew you were the very person I needed to talk to."

"Here's to love and romance," said Patsy and the sisters clinked their teacups.

"What's he like, Matt? Tell me about him."

"I suppose you'd say he's the rough and ready type, very manly and capable, like Mike O'Dowd was — those qualities always appeal to me — but in a less officer-class way, less of the gentleman and more of the street corner," said Annie. "He weighs things up and then goes with what he wanted to do in the first place, no matter how scatty. He's fun, totally unpredictable, I never know what to expect next, like his 'off-shore' work, though that did come as a bit of a shock. And he has the most piercing eyes, I feel positively naked when he looks at me in a particular way."

"That sounds like a dangerous combination for a daughter of Patrick O'Kelly," said Patsy. "What does he deal in? Is it the usual cigarettes and alcohol?"

"He doesn't tell me. He reckons what I don't know won't hurt me or him. But I'll ask him tonight if he can get you some cheap ciggies."

"Where are the two of you off to this evening?"

"We're going to a bar, more of a club, really: you have to know it's there. It's hidden behind a heavy door and when you give a special knock a slot opens in the door and they look at you to decide whether or not to let you in. Of course, they know Matt and me now," said Annie. "I like the place, it's quite dark and it has a slight hint of danger, which I find exciting, there's all sorts of types hang out there, some who seem to have cultivated the knack of never showing their faces, but you can dance and they play a lot of American swing. Do you like to swing?"

"I do," said Patsy. "In fact, I'm getting Jem to fix one up in the yard, one of those with a frilly top, and padded cushions."

5

The Gorgeous Gael Jack Doyle was fighting the US beer baron Two-Ton Tony Galento at Tolka Park football ground in a wrestling exhibition challenge some sports correspondents couldn't take seriously. The Dublin event was regarded more as entertainment than sport. Doyle had never fulfilled his promise as one of the strongest heavyweight boxers ever to come out of Ireland: as an amateur he won twenty-eight fights in a row, twenty-seven of them by a knock-out, and earned himself respectable kudos as the British Army champ but, after turning professional and getting a shot at the British Heavyweight title, he blew it, choosing to spend hours in the pub drinking before the fight. He could barely stand up in the ring let alone box. That became a familiar trademark with the man from Cobh, drunk to the point of incapacity, and it wasn't long before his boxing career careered out of existence. Be that as it may, the gate at Tolka Park was a sell-out. Doyle was a larger-than-life figure: now overweight and out-of-shape, he remained a celebrity in his home country, the man who had put his Cork city on the Hollywood map, landing himself a film contract thanks to his good looks, good physique and beautiful tenor voice — he sang at the Royal in Dublin and on stage at the London Palladium. The fact that his few screen appearances were less than noteworthy didn't trouble his Irish fans. They still held him in some esteem, unaffected by newspaper stories about how violent he was out of the ring or by the fact that he had swapped boxing for wrestling as an easier way to make money to fund a life he described as being devoted to alcohol, women and slow horses. His enduring popularity attracted a capacity crowd to the Dublin stadium. Jem had had no difficulty persuading Patsy to join him in ringside seats. Doyle's rendition of *South of the Border* was a particular favourite of hers. It was another record she had bought for Margaret's collection.

The ring was assembled in the middle of the football pitch and a scratchy gramophone played a selection of Doyle's recordings over the loudspeaker system to get everyone in a partisan mood. There were a couple of bouts on the card but little attention was paid until the Gorgeous Gael himself made his way through the adoring crowds, wearing what could only be described as a somewhat dingy off-white robe that had seen better days but all the same waving his arms in the air like the champ he never quite became.

"His lifestyle has certainly taken its toll," said Jem. "Look at the size of the man, he must be well over thirty stone."

"He certainly doesn't look anything like the picture they used on the poster," said Patsy. "I didn't realise he'd be twice the man he was. I remember seeing him strolling down O'Connell Street a few years back with his glamorous wife on his arm and hundreds of people following in their wake. He threw smiles and kisses in all directions and we all loved him, our very own film star just walking down the street like a normal person."

"I think Hollywood had had enough of him," said Jem. "You know he's supposed to have thrown a punch at Clark Gable and knocked the man out cold."

"No, I didn't know that. I'm a big fan of Clark Gable but then show me a woman who isn't. Look at your man now in the ring. There's no comparison. And he could have gotten himself a decent robe, he can't be that broke."

"I wouldn't be so sure," said Jem. "He's a big spender all right, though they say part of his trouble is his generosity. He doesn't like to drink alone, and his habit is to make sure he's not drinking alone by buying a round for everyone in whatever pub he goes into."

"Still, he's Jack Doyle. We forgive you, Jack," shouted Patsy up to the ring. She laughed at herself entering into the occasion. Her reward was a personal wave from the hero, or so she liked to think, as he took off his gown and virtually wobbled round the canvas.

The first four rounds were more pantomime than wrestling prowess as the Gorgeous Gael and Two-Ton Tony danced and wove around each other, making half-hearted grabs in turn. Patsy and Jem were seated right next to the newspapermen's bench and Patsy heard one of the reporters comment that all the American had to do was get a grip on one of Jack's double chins and the fight would be over.

But he didn't and it wasn't. In Round Five the opponents simultaneously lunged, met in the middle of the ring, four arms and four legs somehow knotted in attempted wrestling holds, and the two fighters crashed through the ropes and on towards the press stand. Two-Ton Tony himself was no small man and the sports commentators tipped their benches and tables up in a blind panic to escape the combined weight of some seventy stone thumping down on top of them. Jem made himself into a barrier between Patsy and the fracas as Two-Ton ended up flat on his back on the floor underneath the hulking bulk of Jack Doyle. Chaos broke out. Jack's Irish supporters heaved him to his feet and tried to hoist him back into the ring, all the time the referee shouting at them not to touch the man or the fight would be forfeit. Meanwhile poor Two-Ton was unable to move; lying badly injured, prostrate and helpless and unprotected on the football turf, he was suddenly surrounded by a mad pack of children pinching and poking him and jeering in his face. As some sort of a strong stretcher made its way through the melee to take Tony's heavy mass of flesh to an ambulance, the home fans finally managed to get Doyle back into the ring. The referee had become redundant. The fans declared the Gorgeous Gael to be the Gorgeous Winner, taking turns to hold his arm up in a victory salute, whereupon the whole ring was invaded by spectators, all celebrating and cheering the success of a man who seemed totally oblivious to whatever was going on. No one was bothered about an official result: the Dublin crowd had turned out for a grand night and they had got one. It would be the talk of the city for months.

"When I bought ringside seats, I didn't realise we'd be so close to the action that we'd be a part of it," said Jem. "Are you okay Patsy? You didn't get hurt?"

"I got sprayed with Jack's sweat, that's about all," she said. "I won't wash for a week, though I suppose it could be Two-Ton's sweat so maybe I'll wash it off after all. Is that it now, is it over?"

"It is, my good woman, that's the card finished, which is just as well as I can't see order being restored here any time soon. Shall we make our way out?"

They shoved a path through the horde of fans, some of them still trying to get into the ring, and made their way across the pitch towards an exit. It was like swimming against a tide of human flotsam, fortunately all good-humoured.

"I never knew wrestling could be so entertaining," said Patsy. "Having said that, I hope the American isn't badly hurt."

"There is a school of thought that says wrestling is all theatre and not much pain," said Jem. "Sure they practice their moves together sometimes and can agree in advance which holds they're going to go for and when, so they can each have their moments of glory. It could be that it's only the last few rounds that count."

"I can't see that being the case this time. I can't see they would have planned to fall out of the ring together in such a heavy spill right next to the newspapermen."

"I'm looking forward to reading their first-hand accounts tomorrow," said Jem. "It's not often the reporters get to play their own role right inside the story. This time they were literally on the receiving end of the news. Now, let's go for some food, my good woman. I fancy going out to Kavanagh's Refreshment Bar at Glasnevin. They do a fine coddle which will warm us up a treat after all these hours out in the fresh air. Let's treat ourselves and not bother with the tram, look at how many people are already queuing at the stop."

Jem was looking to hail a cab when a young well-dressed man approached him and made to shake his hand, his face illuminated by a smile stretching from ear to ear. "Jeremy," he said, "what a wonderful surprise. I didn't expect to bump into you here. Have you been to the wrestling? Not exactly fine specimens on show, you'd agree?"

Jem shook the man's hand though he seemed somewhat taken aback by the encounter. "Hello, Peter," he said. "Yes, I've been with my wife, Patsy here, but we're in a bit of a hurry right now so I'll catch you another time, what do you say. Sorry to rush off so abruptly. I'll be seeing you, Peter." He took Patsy by the arm and led her off. "There's a cab there now," he said. "Let's make sure we beat everyone else to it. We don't want Kavanagh's to run out of coddle before we even get there and I've quite an appetite."

The bar was a bit of a Dublin institution though Patsy herself had never been there. The name on the façade spelt out "Kavanagh" but it was more widely known as The Gravediggers: it was right next door to one of the main gates into Glasnevin cemetery and the gravediggers themselves habitually used the back door of the pub, a direct link to their place of work, and had evidently evolved a special system of knocks to indicate their orders so the publican could have the drinks laid out on the bar ready.

"So the drinks are as well laid out as the late arrivals," said Patsy.

"Aye, a case of down the hatch for some and down and out for others," said Jem, pushing through the swing doors with Patsy following in behind: she didn't want to go into a strange place first. Kavanagh's wasn't what she had expected — she hadn't really known what to expect — but her immediate impression was that she was glad she was with Jem: it was rather dark and basic, all wood and glass-panelling, dimly lit and low-ceilinged, more of a man's bar, she thought, than somewhere she would enjoy with Margaret. Bewley's was definitely more their sort of establishment. The pub was busy with a mix of locals and visitors to the cemetery but Jem found an empty table and put in their order for coddle. The smells coming from the kitchen suggested the stew would live up to his recommendation.

"Was this one of your regular haunts before you got married?" asked Patsy.

"Not a regular haunt but I've been a few times," said Jem. "There's often good craic in here. Singing and dancing are prohibited but poets and storytellers are welcomed and you can hear interesting tales well told. What would you like to drink, Patsy?"

"Something warming but refreshing," she said. "I'll have a port and lemon."

While Jem went to the bar, Patsy was able to have a proper look at the clientele. Perhaps her initial impression had been a bit hasty, she thought, and decided to suggest an outing here with Margaret after all. It was dimly lit and rather basic, with its wooden benches and tables, but the mix of customers was comfortable. Probably because of the stream of mourners, thought Patsy: anyone taking the trouble to visit a family grave could hardly count as reproachable in their behaviour. By the time Jem returned with their drinks she was feeling pleasantly relaxed.

"Who was that Peter fellow who came up to you in the street outside the Park?" she asked.

"No one important, just someone I know through the store or I would have made the proper introductions," said Jem. "You know how I like to show off my good woman." He squeezed her hand and brushed a curl back behind her ear and she revelled in both the compliment and the simple, loving attention.

"Well, you'll get the chance now," said Patsy. "He's just walked in with another man."

Jem involuntarily made to turn his back slightly but Patsy had already waved over to the two young men and signalled that there were a couple of chairs at their table.

"Are you sure we won't be intruding?" asked Peter.

"Not at all," said Patsy. "We both enjoy company and where better than in a cosy bar."

The proper introductions were indeed made, though it seemed that Jem already knew Peter's friend, James.

"Did you enjoy the wrestling, Mrs Murphy?" he asked.

"I'm just Patsy," she replied, "and yes, I enjoyed the whole spectacle very much. We were seated right next to where the two giants crashed out of the ring but fortunately they didn't land on us. We'd have been flattened."

"What'll it be?" Jem asked the newcomers, resigned to the fact that they were settled at the table.

"I'll come with you to the bar while I make up my mind," said Peter. "The gleaming bottles on display might inspire me as to what to imbibe today."

The two men went off to the bar leaving Patsy alone with James.

"How did you and Jem meet?" he asked.

"We met through work. I'm at Jeanette Modes and Jem came in one day to place a big order for his store. We hit it off straight away, but we didn't start walking out immediately, that was some months later. It seems a long time ago now. What about you? How did you and Jem meet?" she said.

"Oh, we've known each other for a year or so now, after we met in a club in the city."

"I thought Jem said he knew you from the store."

"Well in a way yes, I suppose that's right," said James. "The club is

343

for businessmen and that's where we do our, well, our business."

"All very informal, then?" said Patsy. "That's the modern way, no doubt, not like when he first came to Jeanette Modes and we went through the designs and fabrics for the order, though come to think of it Jem did have an almost casual way of placing the order and then he took me to the Gresham for — I'll never forget his way of putting it — for some 'nourishment' he said."

"That certainly sounds like Jem," said James.

Jem and Peter got back to the table with an extra round to save having to queue again. "I ordered you a coddle, James," said Peter, "we could all do with a warming infusion after our afternoon's excitement."

"I'm always ready for a good coddle," said James raising his eyebrows and pouting his lips and they all laughed, though Patsy felt that her amusement was of a slightly different nature.

The coddle was served and enjoyed and the rounds kept coming. An easy familiarity had descended on the table when suddenly Peter stood up and clinked his glass to gain the attention of the bar. With his attentive audience all ears, he began to recite an impromptu ode to the day's big sporting event.

"We'd all gone along to Tolka Park, many of us just there for the lark
And to see Jack Doyle, the man of the hour, and if he could still wield his terrible power.

He entered the ring bathed in perspiration, sweaty but carrying the hopes of the nation.

His robe, well, it had seen better days, probably because of the man's betting ways."

The pub erupted in applause and calls of encouragement to continue.

"Two-Ton Tony was to be his foe, a beer-man by trade, and boy did it show"

Peter stuck his stomach out and wobbled his belly by way of accompaniment.

"But which of the he-men would come out a winner, would Jack pay the price for being such a sinner.

They grabbed by the arms, all flabby and fat, and they clung by the legs, but it all fell flat

For neither the Yank nor the Gorgeous Gael could do much more than get chased by the tail."

"Get that man a drink," shouted one of the customers.

"Where was I now?" said Peter.

"Come on, Peter, this is better entertainment than the real thing," said James.

"Just give me a moment," said Peter, wetting his whistle most dramatically. "Right now, here we go:

Then the bout erupted like a scene from Hell, though exactly what happened no one could tell

As, tied up as one, they flew from the canvas, with Two-Ton down first, I have to say, *on his big ass.*

The newsmen scattered, their drinks all splattered, their chairs they clattered but none of it mattered

For the crowd in the ring had the Irishman's back and they declared it a victory to our man, Jack."

Glasses were raised in a general toast to "Our Man Jack" and it was as if Kavanagh's was full of old friends, with people talking and laughing together as if they had known each other years and didn't just happen to be in the same place at the same time for the same recital. The drinks piled up on the table in front of Peter and his friends, who were by association equally rewarded with free drinks. They were all getting happily tipsy, jokes and funny anecdotes being swapped back and forth. Patsy was in such good humour after such a grand day out, she couldn't remember her hesitation in first walking into the bar several hours ago, nor did she notice the familiarity going on between her three companions.

She interrupted the flow around the table with a toast of her own. "Jem, James, Peter, here's to you all, you're great company."

"Indeed, we are," said Peter, "indeed we are."

By the time they got home, Patsy was in a singing mood, treating Jem to a rendition of *Hear My Song* but substituting 'Violetta' with 'Jeremy Murphy'. "Doesn't it make you feel romantic," she lulled into his ear, leaning into his shoulder as he jiggled to get the key in the door.

"Well, it's a warm night and we've a moon all right but I hardly think a street of red-brick terrace houses in any way resembles an old lagoon," said Jem, "but do carry on, I like listening to you sing, though I have to point out to one as musical as yourself that you are beginning to slur your

345

words slightly, only ever so slightly, of course, you being so musical and all. We'll no doubt be able to tell from the neighbours' faces tomorrow if they too appreciated your late-night performance."

Patsy almost stumbled down the hallway: she wasn't as used to drinking as Jem and he insisted on escorting her out to the yard so she could use the toilet first and then leave him to lock up the house. Upstairs in the bedroom, she was feeling very giggly as she struggled to get undressed: she couldn't easily get the zip open on her dress and found herself twisting and contorting like a rubber doll in the effort, which she found hilarious — didn't she sew the blasted zip in herself: she tripped over her feet kicking off her shoes and snorted as she overbalanced and bumped into the dressing-table, making all her little bottles and jars jingle with the shock, then she fell backwards on to the bed clutching the toe of her silly stocking, which stubbornly refused to part company with her left foot and somehow had her leg stretched so that it waved about in the air, held straight and rigid by the bow-string stocking she still gripped in her hand. Now that was the funniest yet, she thought. Her cheeks were sore with the hilarity of it all. She extricated her left foot, pulled herself upright, pushed her shoes safely out of harm's way and tossed the offending stocking on to the floor in the corner without a care in the world. She resumed her tribute to Josef Locke as she took off her brassiere and stepped out of her panties, then she caught sight of herself in the mirror and stopped laughing. She studied the naked image in front of her, momentarily wondered if it was a sin to look at yourself like that, and then she touched her nipples. She drew her hand away quickly feeling tremendous guilt but then she cupped her breasts and she felt her nipples again, marvelling at how they had suddenly become hard. A thrill passed through her body. She heard Jem's footsteps on the stairs and quickly got into bed, peering over the covers as he came into the room and got himself ready for bed. She was acutely aware of his presence.

Jem took his clothes off slowly in that precise, meticulous way that he had, taking care of his clothes was a matter of pride with Jem, the cornerstone of his fastidious approach to his appearance; he wanted to look the best that he possibly could as a matter of habit. He carefully draped his trousers and arranged his jacket on a hanger, smoothing out any creases before stowing the suit in the wardrobe: he took off his shirt,

346

assessed the armpits with a brief sniff, pulled a face, and then consigned the shirt to the laundry basket. Still without making a sound so as not to disturb his wife, he folded each item of clothing as it came off and put it away in the correct drawer or straight in the basket for a wash. Patsy watched his every move through half-closed eyes: his every muscle flex, his strong arms, his head bent as he concentrated on his nightly routine which, as usual, closed with a quick run of the comb though his hair. He got in between the sheets, gave his nose a good blow and tucked down.

Patsy waited for him to settle then whispered: "I had a great day, Jem, every bit of it. I loved the wrestling and all the cheering of the crowd, and the drama, of course, and wasn't it great fun in the bar with Peter and James? I did like them, such good company. You should invite them to the house one night, I could make something special." She nuzzled in and felt Jem's body stiffen. She stole her arm across his chest, caressing his skin with her fingers as she pushed them gently through the front opening of his pyjamas, then guiding them down to his waist, marvelling at the feel of his flesh over his downy stomach, and on down when Jem abruptly grabbed hold of her hand and just as abruptly shoved it away. Then he turned on to his side and lay with his back to her. Patsy went very, very still; she was afraid to move even to get her hankie to wipe the tears.

6

The telegram that arrived at The Coombe wasn't for Molly this time; it was from Molly. Annie had gone over to Liverpool to visit her sister but she obviously hadn't stayed long. Instead of the postcard they had perhaps expected from their youngest daughter, Patrick and Betty had opened the door to receive news which they could never have imagined.

ANNIE GONE TO GRETNA GREEN TO MARRY MATT — COULDN'T STOP HER — MOLLY

Patsy had been summoned immediately and asked if she had known of the planned elopement for planned it obviously was, said Patrick: even in Scotland there were rules, you couldn't just turn up and get married whatever the reputation of the place as a destination for runaway couples wanting to get wed.

"Did you know anything about this?" he demanded, waving the telegram in her face the minute Patsy walked through the door

"Anything about what?" she said.

"Let her read it," said Betty. "I'm sure Patsy doesn't know any more about it than we do and shouting at her won't help."

But Patsy's face dropped when she read the message and it was only too apparent that the news hit her more with stunned recognition than with outright shock.

"You seem to have had some prior knowledge judging from your expression," said Patrick. "I hope you weren't a party to this scheme."

"No, I had no idea what Annie was planning but it was something we joked about a while ago. That's all it was at the time, a joke, but perhaps it settled in her mind. You know what Annie's like: whatever's not what everybody else does, that's what appeals to her."

"I'd say that was a very odd thing to joke about," said Patrick. "Where would the idea even have come from unless there was something already in the air," said Patrick. "There must have been more to the conversation than you're telling us. You, of all people. Patsy, I thought could be trusted with a matter such as this."

"And where do I come into it, being trusted with a matter such as this?" said Patsy. "What Annie decides to do is nothing to do with me. You're very quick to point the finger just because you didn't know what your own daughter was up to. Perhaps you should pay more attention to what's going on around you instead of sitting brooding in the chair all the time making everyone's life a misery. You told me you were finished with all that. Annie simply said that Matt wanted them to get married and that she did too, that's all, and then we joked about them running away to do it and she thought the idea sounded very romantic. It was a silly, innocent joke and that was the end of the conversation. I think you're being very unfair to say I had anything to do with it. Annie's a young woman, you can't expect her to live in the shadow of the past like you, in the shadow of you looming large over everyone from the authority of your sacred chair in the corner. She's not as easily controlled as I was. I'll not bear the consequences of any more of your warped influence."

"That's enough," said Patrick.

"Dear God, Annie has eloped and all you two can do is argue," said Betty. "None of us is to blame, she did what she did herself, I'd just like to know why. Maybe she thought we wouldn't approve of her marrying Matt." Betty's face suddenly drained of all colour. "Oh my God, Patsy, you don't think she's pregnant, do you?"

"No, I'm sure she's not, I just think she wanted some excitement in her life and she's in love."

"She always avoided the subject when we tried to find out exactly what the man does for a job," said Patrick calming somewhat after Patsy's attack. He knew she was right. It wasn't her fault that Annie had chosen to run off. "I had my suspicions that all wasn't as it should be in that respect. He never seems to work regular hours and seems to be away a lot at night. Can you at least tell us what he does for a living, Patsy?"

"I can't tell you that, no." Patsy chose her answer carefully, she didn't want to lie outright to her parents but nor did she want to get Annie into any worse trouble, though it did seem that the situation couldn't be any worse as far as Patrick and Betty were concerned. Patsy herself couldn't help but admire her sister; Annie certainly wasn't going to give up the man she had set her heart on.

"Well, I'm sure she'll come home sooner or later, and we must make sure she's welcome when she does," said Betty. "Patrick, I'll not have you attacking her and Matt and chasing them away with your black temper. I'll not let you banish our daughter because of the way she chose to get married. From what Patsy said, it was Matt who suggested getting married, he wanted to do things properly, and maybe he was the one who suggested they got married quickly to keep it all proper. What's important is that they are getting married. They could just as easily have started living in sin."

Patrick held his peace and went to sit in his chair.

"Will you be all right, Mammy? Is there anything I can get you?" asked Patsy.

"You go on home now. Your da and I will no doubt have more talking to do, not that he ever does any of the listening."

It was three weeks before Annie returned to The Coombe, with a new gold band flashing on her finger and a shiny new husband linked through her arm. She looked elated with happiness and was thrilled to have such a great adventure to recount. She and Matt had spent just a couple of nights in Liverpool — "separate rooms, there were no shenanigans" — and had actually tried to persuade Molly to accompany them to Gretna but her sister couldn't get time off work at such short notice. Then they took an early train up to Scotland, a magical journey through 'such wild and beautiful countryside', before arriving in the tiny village of Gretna Green and booking into a small local hotel: "Separate rooms, there were no shenanigans," Annie was determined to stress. Patrick had been right, no one could just turn up in Gretna Green and get married, they had to prove residency in Scotland for at least three weeks prior. Fortunately, in Matt's line of business — still not specified — he had contacts in Scotland and was able to arrange for proof of residence to circumvent that particular rule.

"I suppose it costs a few pounds to get someone to help you break the law?" asked Patrick rhetorically.

Matt didn't rise to the bait. "Actually, I didn't pay anything, Mr O'Kelly," he said, "but I would gladly have paid a fortune to have young Annie for my bride. As regards breaking the law, it seems to me there's not a whole lot of difference between three days and three weeks anyway: if you can marry after three weeks, why not after three days? A bit of an illogical law, I'd say, just time and numbers that really don't mean very much at all when your heart's set on getting married."

"And was it in a church?" asked Betty.

"You'll never believe it, Mammy, it was in a blacksmith's forge, of all strange places for a wedding, so we stood before a small furnace that was all ablaze and were surrounded by horseshoes hanging everywhere on nails, now wasn't that a lucky omen?" said Annie, her eyebrows raised at the astonishment of the venue. "The blacksmith performs the ceremony, in front of witnesses, of course, and to seal the marriage he bangs his hammer on the anvil and that's that, you're legally married."

"Legally perhaps but not in the eyes of the Church, not in our eyes," said Patsy. "Are you going to make your vows before God and the priest too?"

"We've already done that, so you don't need to worry about my eternal soul," said Annie. "Matt sorted all that with a priest in Liverpool through another contact."

"And being a priest, of course, he certainly didn't provide his services for free," said Matt. "No doubt our not-inconsiderable contribution to the parish funds went straight to the off-licence."

"There's no need to be so clever," said Patrick. "That's how the priests might conduct themselves in Liverpool but they don't behave like that here."

"Come off it, Mr O'Kelly. You must know different priests to the ones I know."

"I'm sure of that," said Patrick.

"Molly and Tessie were able to come to the church too and be the witnesses," said Annie, ignoring her father's sniping, "so the family was represented. God, we had a grand time. Of course, we didn't have a traditional wedding breakfast, we went to the Woolworths restaurant after the church, would you believe, and then we went to a pub for a proper toast, but to me it was perfect, really special. Mammy, I wish you had been there, it was the most exciting wedding I could ever have dreamt of."

"Your mammy would have been only too pleased to attend your

wedding had she known there was going to be one," said Patrick.

"Are you not even going to congratulate us, Mr O'Kelly? I think at least a hint of best wishes to your daughter wouldn't go amiss," said Matt. "I'm madly in love with the crazy girl and we've done things properly even if a bit unexpectedly."

"Come here and let me give the two of you a hug," said Betty opening her arms wide, determined to make Annie's homecoming a happy one. "You have my very best wishes. It was only that I was so worried and surprised when I got Molly's telegram telling us what you'd done."

"Clearly Molly's telegram wasn't as honest as we'd supposed, telling us she couldn't stop you when obviously that wasn't an issue," said Patrick. "She put out the welcome mat and knew for two whole days what you were up to, Annie, but she waited before letting us know and then deliberately sounded as if she was taken by surprise and helpless in the matter. She was complicit in the whole thing. There'll be no welcome mat here for her next time she wants to come to Dublin."

"Daddy, would you stop with all that nonsense," said Patsy. "First it was my fault, now it's Molly's fault. Why don't you just take a look at Annie's face and see how happy she is. She married the man she wanted to marry, that's all that's happened."

"Can we shake hands for Annie's sake, Mr O'Kelly?" said Matt.

"Please, Daddy," said Annie. "I'm home, amn't I, safe and still your daughter. Matt took good care of me all the time we were away, and he never once behaved in an improper manner. But Matt is my husband now and that's the way things are, so you can either turn your back on me or you can join in with the rest of the family and celebrate my good fortune in marrying such a wonderful man."

Patrick did turn his back but only for a few seconds. He pulled something out of his pocket and turned to hand some money to Matt. "Perhaps my new son-in-law would nip next door to The Cosy Bar and buy a bottle of something suitable for a toast."

7

It was a shocking end to Marian Year. The whole of 1954 had been declared a twelve-month celebration dedicated to the Virgin Mary by order of Pope Pius XII himself. Not only were the special devotions to the holiest of mothers winding down but it was also the run-up to Christmas, the special feast of families, yet a baby had been snatched from his pram in Henry Street while his mother had turned her back momentarily to buy something for the Christmas festivities. It was almost four years to the day that a baby had been taken from its pram in the very same street.

"I can't understand how anyone could do such a cruel thing," said Patsy when Jem read out the article from the newspaper. "Is it a kidnapping for ransom does it say?"

"It doesn't go into many details, the Gardaí have only just started their investigations, but I'd say it's unlikely to be a kidnap," said Jem. "The mother seems just an ordinary young woman, out shopping on her own and pushing a pram round and her loaded up with bags of provisions she's had to carry herself. I doubt she'd be doing that if she had the sort of money that would attract a ransom demand. Rich women don't trawl their progeny along Henry Street in some battered old pram. It looks battered in the newspaper photo. Surely a kidnapper would target a family who could afford to pay."

"Why else would someone steal a baby?" said Patsy.

"Someone who didn't have one but wanted one, I suppose," said Jem. "The incident four years ago apparently didn't involve any ransom demand and the child was never found."

"Do the police think the cases are connected?"

"They say they are investigating the possibility but I wonder how they could tell after all this time. Presumably they investigated four years ago and where did that get them."

"Or the poor mother who had her baby taken," said Patsy. She wondered how she would feel in that poor mother's place, forever imagining what her child must look like growing up, imaging her child by now calling another woman Mammy, if he or she was still alive. In her heart of hearts Patsy herself sometimes imagined how any children of her own might look like by now had she not agreed to her pact with Jem.

"I see Tayto have brought out a new flavour of crisps," said Jem. scanning the page. It was his habit sometimes to sit and pick out interesting items in the paper to read to Patsy. It was a routine they both enjoyed. "It says here that their new line of cheese and onion flavoured crisps are selling like hot potatoes. The reporter must have thought long and hard to come up with that line. Have you tried them yet, Patsy?"

"Tried what?"

"These new Tayto crisps. Are you not listening to me or what?"

"I was still thinking about the baby being stolen," said Patsy, sitting staring into the fire. "Imagine losing your child like that."

"Well God forgive me for saying so but at least that's something we'll never have to worry about."

"Do you ever think about it?" said Patsy. "Ever regret that we don't have any little ones?"

"Not in the least," said Jem. "I'm very happy and content to have you all to myself, my good woman, why would I want to share your attention. Besides, I'm far too selfish a man to want my lifestyle interrupted by noisy brats running round the house. We wouldn't be free to enjoy ourselves as much as we do, Patsy, think about it."

"I do," she said.

Jem turned the page of his newspaper. "We'd better order in a stock of American flags for the store before there's a run on them. There's an American senator coming to Dublin for a visit next year with his wife. Someone called John Kennedy, no doubt playing the Irish card with the American voters. What is it with these people that they always try to establish some Irish ancestry? What time did you say Billy and Theresa are coming round?"

"This evening, after they've put the children to bed. Annie is baby-sitting for them."

"Now Annie is a real little mother in the making. It's a pity that Mike fellow we met in Liverpool was already taken, they got on very well and he was quite a character."

"I think Annie thought it was a pity too at the time though she's found her match now. Shall I pour you a drink yet or do you want to wait?"

"Will you join me?"

"I'll have a small drop with you."

Patsy poured them each a drink and sat down again in the small armchair by the fire: Jem was in the big chair, as his spreading waistline demanded. Married life was suiting him in more ways than one. He had a comfortable home and he had a good woman with whom to share it. He was used to that sort of domestic arrangement after spending years at home with his mother but Patsy was much better company, more stimulating, with opinions of her own, even if they sounded naïve at times, what with all her religious beliefs but an amusing outlook which often contradicted her instinctive prudishness: he often caught her out of the corner of his eye either mouthing a silent prayer or crossing herself after she'd made some slightly risqué remark.

"Are Billy and Theresa coming round for a reason or is it just a social call? Not that it's important, it will be a pleasant evening regardless and we won't even have to leave the warmth of the fire. There's certainly a December chill in the air."

Jem returned to his newspaper. "Well would you look at that? The world is going crazy and none crazier than America. It must be all the Irish immigrants making their mark: only those with no sense would have chosen to leave our emerald isle for such a country. You keep up with the music world, don't you Patsy? Have you ever heard of this singer? Elvis Presley, he calls himself while everyone else seems to call him Elvis the Pelvis."

"All I know is that the young girls at work drool over him and his quiff."

"A quiff, is it? Well, I don't think it's his quiff is the problem unless that's a euphemism for something totally different that sticks out. It seems there is a movement started in America to get him banned from public performance on the grounds of indecency. They say he gyrates his hips and thrusts himself forward on stage so much in front of audiences of screaming young women that it's like watching him simulate sex with them. Would you believe it? It doesn't make clear whether it's the simulation or the stimulation that the holy Joes object to. Now tell me they can't be Irish Catholics behind that fuss and nonsense, Patsy. You can't beat a good Roman Catholic when it comes to seeing the perils of sex everywhere."

"I wouldn't mind casting my expert eye over the potential perils of his gyrations, is there a photograph?" asked Patsy, stifling an ironic comment about what kind of a good Catholic expert she could possibly be with her total lack of any sex of any kind anywhere. Jem held up the paper for her to see. "Well, he certainly has smouldering eyes," she said. She scanned the article. "He used to sing in his local church," she commented, "like the Everly Brothers, they're very popular too."

"Say no more," said Jem. "You never know what goes on under those chasubles or behind the sanctity of the closed vestry. We're none of us deaf to the rumours."

"Stop that now, Jem. You're being too smart and too disrespectful." Patsy made the sign of the cross over herself and went into the kitchen to prepare supper for the visitors.

"I'm sorry, Patsy. I'll say no more."

By the time Theresa and Billy knocked on the door, Jem was fast asleep in the chair, his empty glass lolling in his hands resting on his stomach. He woke up with a snort and a start to see the dimpled grin of Billy mocking him from not two feet away.

"Well, your man certainly knows how to enjoy his day of rest," said Billy.

"There speaks the man who never dozes in the chair," said Theresa. "Instead he falls into a virtual coma, unconscious of life going on around him, his belly heaving and his mouth hanging open and dribbling out God knows what strange substances."

"Let me take your coats and you get yourselves warm," said Patsy. "I'd no idea how cold it was until I saw your breath illuminated at the door."

Jem stood up from the chair and offered it to Theresa. "It's grand to see you both, especially on a Wenceslas night like this. And I needed waking up from my own particular coma, Theresa. I might have slept here until morning and Patsy would have been too considerate to disturb my slumbers," he said. "Let me get the glasses filled and you can satisfy my eager curiosity. I'm sure you said there was something momentous you wanted to tell us, or maybe not, I'm still barely awake and might have made the whole thing up in my sleep."

"We do have some news for you," said Billy, "all to do with an old dream of mine."

Slaintes exchanged and tumblers toasted, the four of them sat in front of the fire, warmed by the flames and the conviviality of familial friendship. The small dimensions of the parlour added to the air of intimacy, just right for the imparting of the big news.

"We're leaving Dublin," said Billy. "We're going to live in Cheltenham." He waited for the announcement to sink in, Patsy's face a picture of shocked disappointment, Jem wearing a look of amused incredulity. "I was right about the job opportunities and I've been offered a permanent contract with a construction firm that's just been taken on to build a huge new housing estate, a major development, hundreds of houses and a small local shopping centre on a site on the edge of the town."

"But can't you find work here?" Patsy said, thinking only of the plan to leave Dublin.

"You've a short memory, Pat," said Billy. "Have you forgotten the march in Dublin a few months back? Hundreds of unemployed men marching through the city to demand jobs? Then they all sat down on O'Connell Bridge and traffic was brought to a stand-still for hours, nothing could move, buses couldn't get through to take home people such as yourself who have jobs, it was chaos. You must remember that. And who could blame the men for trying to do something about their situation? You say look for a job here, Patsy, but there are sixty-thousand people out of work as it is and there's nothing so special about me that I'd be at the front of the queue if a job was being handed out."

"But you have a job," said Patsy.

"But for how long?" said Theresa. "I don't particularly want to move but we have three children now and there's no security with Billy's firm any more. They've laid people off already. I can't live like that, worrying if he'll come home from work one day with his last pay packet. The

Cheltenham job is a godsend in the circumstances. And when it's all finished, a number of the new houses will be offered to company employees like Billy to buy or rent. It's a great opportunity."

"If it's so great, why are they taking men from Ireland and not local men?" Patsy argued.

"Well terribly sad though it is, the fact remains that a lot of British working men were lost in the war," said Billy, "England needs to recruit from elsewhere or the country could grind to a halt waiting for the next generation to grow up."

"There is of course a tradition of Irishmen going over to do the heavy work for the British," said Jem. "Wasn't it Irish navvies who built their railways?"

"And now those railways are being staffed by people from Jamaica," said Billy. "England has had so many jobs to fill that hundreds of people have had to be shipped in from their Commonwealth to work on the railways and particularly to work in the hospitals too. Now they need men with building skills."

"Are you sure it's not just the racecourse beckoning?" said Jem. "Following the horses is one thing, following them with lock, stock and furniture is a different thing altogether."

"The proximity of the racecourse is just the icing on the cake," said Billy, his chubby face creasing into a rosy expression of sheer joy at contemplating the cake.

"In all fairness, what you say makes absolute sense," said Jem. "It's a very pretty, very smart place, Cheltenham, and to be offered a new modern house there would be a fine thing for the family. And I might even persuade Patsy to go over for the racing. You enjoyed Aintree didn't you Patsy? In Cheltenham you could visit Theresa same as you visited Molly in Liverpool."

"That sums it up nicely, doesn't it? Everyone's leaving and I'm left here but I can visit them so you can have an easy conscience going to the races," said Patsy. "And the only children I've got, all my little nieces and nephews? All living miles away in England. Eddie's over there too, I've never even seen his daughter and the poor child born with facial abnormalities. Ciaran and Mikey are talking about moving to England too. Why don't you take them with you to Cheltenham, Theresa, it's obviously such a great place — plenty of jobs and, what was it you said Jem, very pretty and very smart."

The room fell silent under her outburst and Patsy realised she was getting ridiculously upset and left the parlour before she burst into tears. She hurried into the kitchen and started bustling about, setting the table for supper and stoking up the fire in the back room.

"I'd better go and help," said Theresa. "You two stay here until I call you."

She found Patsy distorting her face in all the ways people do when they're trying not to cry, her bottom lip was gripped firmly under her top one by the teeth to stop the quivering and her mouth tugged itself left to right.

"Patsy, I had no idea you would get so upset," said Theresa. "This move isn't my idea, it's all driven by Billy, but I must admit I've had enough of living with no proper bathroom and having to go outside into the yard to use the toilet. I want a better home for my children. You must see that."

What Theresa saw was that her sister was struggling to hide something far more personal than the news of a family member leaving Dublin.

"Oh, Patsy, what's the matter really?" she asked and then the penny dropped. "Is it that you and Jem have no children of your own? Surely that's nobody's fault. God mustn't have meant you to have any."

"God has nothing to do with it, Theresa," Patsy snapped. "You know nothing about it so you can keep your religious homily to yourself. It's my own fault, not God's."

"I don't understand."

"And why would you? You've had it easy, haven't you, marrying your childhood sweetheart and popping out the babies. There's been nothing complicated about your life, you got what you always wanted and who you always wanted but I wasn't allowed to marry the man I wanted, my father made sure of that. But you don't know anything about what went on so, like I say, you can keep your religious there-there to yourself."

"Are you not happy with Jem?" asked Theresa. "I thought the two of you had a grand life together."

"Your idea of 'together' and mine are totally at odds," said Patsy. "Now please leave me to get on with things. Go back into the other room and talk to the men about all your exciting plans and I'll call you when it's time to eat."

Patsy turned her back and made to look busy.

"I'm sorry for whatever it is, Patsy." There was no reply, no getting through the barrier that had grown up between them. "Do you think maybe Billy and I had better go?"

Patsy sank at the table, her head resting on her hands. "Yes, just go," she said. "I'll be all right. I'm probably just over tired, we're very busy at work. I think I need an early night. I'm sorry for all this and I really do wish you well with your move."

Theresa tried to hold her sister but was gently shrugged away. "I'm sorry to have to tell you while you're upset, Patsy, but Ciaran and Mikey have already asked to come with us. Billy's got them labouring jobs on the same site." With that she collected the coats from under the stairs and disappeared into the parlour and after a few minutes could be heard leaving the house with Billy. In the front room, Jem poured himself another drink and stayed where he was. He would have to think of some way of lifting Patsy's spirits while fighting down his own feelings of guilt. Perhaps he could take her to the annual showing of Maureen O'Hara's Christmas film, *Miracle on* some street or other, he knew Patsy was a big fan of the Irish actress, then he remembered it was about a mother and her young daughter and he decided that perhaps wouldn't be such a good idea. He'd have a look to see what else was showing.

"It's great to be able to get out again, even for just an hour or so," said Margaret, settling down to enjoy a healthy slice of barm brack fruit bread with her cup of tea. "It's ages since we last had the chance and God knows when I was last at the cinema."

"I went with Jem just before Christmas," said Patsy, "but he sees things with different eyes to you and me so our post-film conversation tends to be of a more critical nature — how good was the dialogue, was it delivered well, how fine an eye had the director."

"Jem definitely is a man with an artistic frame of mind," said Margaret. "How's your cream cake? It looks appropriately gooey but then you're all right with your figure, you never seem to put on weight no matter what you eat."

"I'm long past caring about that," said Patsy. "Self-indulgence is gradually replacing holy indulgence on the menu."

The two friends had broken with tradition and gone to Clery's department store restaurant for their girls' treat, though it was only on the rare occasion nowadays that they could get together for a proper social session, the sort you wore your favourite lipstick for and maybe a hint of rouge. Life had changed, though more for Margaret than for Patsy. Margaret was juggling work and an increasingly busy home life. Patsy had fewer pieces in play to juggle and found herself having to fit in with her friend's schedule if she wanted to go out instead of sitting in someone else's kitchen just round the corner from her own. Today she had had to work right through her midday break so she could leave early to keep their date at Clery's but she didn't want to have to explain that to Margaret. She didn't want to spoil the day.

"Thank God for a bit of good news too," said Margaret.

"What news is that?"

"They found that little boy who was snatched before Christmas while his mother had gone into a shop. She'd only gone in to buy him a teddy for Christmas morning, would you believe, and the poor child ended up in Belfast of all places. A woman had come down all the way to Dublin to steal a baby, the same woman who took a baby from its pram in the same street four years ago. That one was a little girl. She must have wanted one of each. At least we can all shop in Henry Street with an easy mind again. I must say the whole thing put me off taking any of my kids along there."

"Was it because of the £100 reward?"

"Not at all," said Margaret. "It was because the poor baby wouldn't stop crying during the whole of the train journey and the woman apparently didn't know how to cope with it all. Another woman got suspicious and reported it to the Gardaí. When the police eventually traced the kidnapper to her home in Belfast, as well as the missing baby there was a little girl there who had exactly the same birthmarks as the child who had been stolen in Dublin all those years ago and indeed that's who it was. Now that's what I call good news."

"I have some news too but it depends which way you look at it whether it's good or not," said Patsy. "Theresa and Billy are moving to England; they're going to live in Cheltenham. Billy's been offered a permanent job there and the possibility of a brand-new house."

"And how could that not be good news?" said Margaret. "I wouldn't mind that myself. My brother-in-law's taking his family off to London in the summer. Somewhere beginning with a P. Pimlico? No, sure isn't that an up-market red light district, according to the papers? Anyway, wherever, he says there's more work there for him and the schools are better for the kids."

Patsy decided to change the subject. "Do you ever shop here at Clery's?" she asked.

"Not really, though I did bring the children to the Christmas grotto. They particularly liked tearing up and down the grand staircase and I was so embarrassed that I rushed them out of the store without looking at any of the displays. What about you? Do you and Jem come dancing here?"

"No, Jem always says that working in a store is enough for him, why would he want to spend his time off in one."

"I can see his point."

The restaurant was getting busier by the minute, with people standing by the entrance waiting for somewhere to sit. As soon as Patsy and Margaret had finished their tea and cakes, people began to approach them to ask if they were leaving soon and they began to feel uncomfortable taking up a table.

"We should go," said Margaret. "I much prefer Bewley's, do you? We've still got an hour to ourselves, let's head over there and have a chaser. Have you time?"

"I've probably got more time than you. Jem's working late at the store, stock-taking, I think, so he'll be late home. It'll be a supper from the chip shop for us."

"I suppose they have lots of stock-taking to do after Christmas and the January sales," said Margaret. "Shops need a never-ending supply of stuff to sell because people seem to have a never-ending need to buy. Just as well, Patsy, or we'd all be out of work. Come on and let's get out of here."

As soon as they stood to put their coats on, two couples appeared and Patsy and Margaret hurried away leaving them to fight over the empty table.

"We chose the right time to come," said Margaret.

"And the right time to leave," said Patsy.

They walked down O'Connell Street and were just on the bridge when the photographer who worked the pitch every day stopped to take their picture and handed them a ticket. "That will be a nice one," he said, "you both have such lovely smiles on your faces walking along, happy looking. The print will be ready to collect at the studio tomorrow, a nice reminder for you ladies of your afternoon out."

Patsy took the ticket and said it would be her treat. "The number of times he has taken my picture and I've never yet bought one," she said. "If I get this one, I won't have to feel guilty any more, the man's only trying to earn a living like the rest of us, God bless him."

"His name's Arthur," said Margaret. "He's Ukrainian. He came here from Kiev to escape the anti-Jewish crackdowns so you should feel very guilty at not having supported the poor man before today."

"How do you know all that?"

"Because there's a woman at work who buys a photo from him every fortnight without fail so she knows all about him because they inevitably have a chat every time now, they've become like regular old friends," said Margaret. "She has been doing it for a few years. She puts all the pictures in an album and writes a little note underneath each one, including the day and the date it was taken, and if anything special happened that day that might explain either the expression on her face or why she was wearing whatever she was wearing, bits of information like that. She says it's also a good way of keeping tabs on how she looks and whether or not she has put weight on or needs a hair-cut."

"What a grand idea," said Patsy, "like keeping a visual diary without having to go to the trouble of describing anything in words, though I don't think I'd be wanting to see so many photographs of myself: having a mirror is bad enough for showing how the wrinkles wrinkle their way into your skin gradually and how the chin slowly but surely starts to sag. Does your friend have a particular day? Is she bothered by the weather?"

"She gets her picture taken every other Friday regardless of rain, wind or shine. It's even turned into a bit of a game between the two of them. If Arthur spots her coming, he sometimes tries to snap her before she's had time to put on a pose or he'll suddenly surprise her by jumping out from a crowd and snapping away. That way, he says, she gets to see her face in all its guises.

"There can't be many guises left after all these years," said Patsy. "And what about your colleague, does she play any games?"

"She does. If she sees Arthur getting his camera into position, she puts on a really silly face, walking along looking like an eejit or like something from a horror film, and she holds it like that until he's done. It all sounds like a hoot. I'm quite jealous. What a grand idea to come up with in the first place."

"Snap," said Patsy. "I was about to say exactly the same thing."

"We can snap out of it now and have a shot of a different kind," said Margaret.

They had arrived at Bewley's but loitering outside and looking very agitated and not a little grumpy was Margaret's son, Fergal.

"Mammy thank God you're here, I've been waiting ages," he said. "Where have you been? I thought you always came to Bewley's with Mrs Murphy so I ran all the way here. You have to come home, Daddy has to go out, Granda's not well and next door couldn't come in and sit with us, not knowing what time to expect you back."

"What's the matter with Granda?" Margaret turned to Patsy and sounded quite concerned. "The man's getting on a bit now and his health hasn't been too good lately."

"He had a bit of a fall," said Fergal. "Granny says it's not too serious but she asked for Da to go over and help him up to bed."

"I'll come along with you now and perhaps we can all stroll round to see Granda, cheer him up, shall we? I'm sorry Patsy, we'll have to have that shot another time. I'd best rush on. They're showing *The Quiet Man* again at the Tivoli next week, I'd love to watch it a second time, do you fancy it?"

"I do. I think Maureen O'Hara and John Wayne make the perfect wild Irish couple and who wouldn't want to live in a little cottage like that in Mayo?"

"Anyone who wants to be warm and dry," said Margaret. "I'll have to go now."

"Go on," said Patsy. "I'll call round in the week with the photograph. Here," she said to Fergal, "here's a shilling for all your hard running."

There was still no sign of Jem when Patsy got home so she lit the fire and put a couple of plates in the oven to warm for their chip supper. After an hour or so she turned the oven off and made herself a cup of tea and buttered a slice of bread. She was on her way up to bed when Jem finally rolled in, his breath blasting out almost solid whiskey.

"Was it stock-taking at the bar?" she quipped and carried on up to bed.

Jem was too merry to call up his apologies but not too merry to pour himself another drink and slump in front of the fire. He hummed to himself, cackled with mirth, downed his Paddy's and then soberly stared into the dying embers. "It's all dying, we're all dying," he said and gradually fell asleep.

It was a couple of days before Patsy was able to call into the photography studio, determined to be pleasant to the man who, she now knew, had had a difficult life.

"Ah," said Arthur as she produced her ticket, "one of the women with the beautiful smiles. You and your friend certainly brightened my day. I remember particularly because everyone else seemed somewhat down after the Christmas festivities and then you two walked along with your beautiful smiles. I hope you like the photograph and that it will bring back happy memories whenever you look at it."

"I've no doubt it will," said Patsy. "I don't suppose you did two copies as there were the two of us?"

"I printed up two copies just in case," said Arthur. "I'll put them in separate holders, one for you and one for the other lady."

Once outside the shop — she had been too embarrassed to do it in front of Arthur in case she didn't like the picture and it came across as anti-Jewish — Patsy had a look at the snapshot. It was a lovely warm portrait of two friends out together enjoying themselves and Patsy felt a simple glow of satisfaction flush over her. Margaret had been her good friend for most of her life and the easy closeness between them had been caught perfectly by Arthur and his camera. How lost she would be if Margaret decided to move to England too: the idea obviously appealed to her and she already had family members heading that way. Patsy lingered over the photo and her eyes moved across it to take in the whole scene. Suddenly she had to pull the print closer to get a better look: there in the background, unmistakeable, was Jem, walking along by the Liffey with Peter, heads together, bodies leaning in, the easy closeness between them caught perfectly by Arthur and his camera.

8

It was a fascinating letter but it failed to put anyone's mind at ease. How could it? Sitting round the table at The Coombe and listening to the letter being read out, all the family could really think about were the newspaper reports of the ambush of an Irish Army unit serving with the UN peace-keeping force in the Congo. The Press was vivid with horrific speculations about the mutilations and cannibalism supposed to have taken place. And Jim was out there, in the Congo, Michael's son, that's where he'd written home from. Jim was part of the first overseas posting for the Irish Army since it had been founded thirty-eight years ago and the country had given the soldiers a bumper send-off with a parade in Dublin. But within months of their arrival in West Africa, one of the platoons had been massacred while trying to repair a bridge at a river crossing. They had been shot with poisoned arrowheads and then reportedly hacked to death where they lay. Jim had written his letter before the killings had been reported in the papers and now his parents were sick with worry. Africa sounded like a beautiful place but also a savage, dangerous place. In a desperate attempt to create some sort of a spiritual link to his son, Michael had driven to Dublin from Tullamore with Robert to attend the funeral cortege of eight of the soldiers killed in the ambush. As the trucks carrying the coffins drove slowly through the city and on out to the cemetery for the burials, a heavy silence weighed down on the city muffling the shuffling presence of the hundreds of thousands of people lining the street.

"Any one of them might have had a son in one of those boxes. We might have," said Michael, back at The Coombe describing the scene to the family. "It was supposed to be a peace-keeping operation, for God's sake. They were only trying to mend a bloody bridge."

"At least we know Jim's safe," said Betty.

"He was when he wrote the letter," said Michael. "But, if it's true the platoon was ambushed because they were mistaken for mercenaries fighting in the civil war, then who's to say the same thing won't happen again. Jim's letter hardly describes a stable situation for all his apparent wide-eyed enjoyment of the whole adventure."

'*It took us four days to reach our base from the coast,*' he had written, '*and that's struggling through brush and bush in temperatures so hot I thought someone had opened a baker's oven and shoved me in. And don't forget we're wearing our regular uniforms not the fancy safari suits that you see in films. Oh no: we might be in Africa, but we're still decked out in woollen tunics and hob-nailed boots. Can you imagine it? In this climate? All the same the countryside is quite beautiful, I never thought in a month of Sundays that I'd ever be looking out over fields planted with cotton, you should see them with their heads bobbing in the air bursting open to show their stuff. It's very pretty but unfortunately not suitable for our farm at Tullamore, though you could always give it a try, Da. You could have the first plantation in Ireland.*'

"I wonder if any of the cottons we use come from there," said Patsy. "I'm going to check. It would feel different in my hands if I knew it came from where Jim is stationed."

"I don't know how you can even think of such a thing," said Annie.

"I wish I was there," said John. "Give me the letter here to read."

"'*We have no real base, we're living in tents that can get very stuffy but sometimes we're lucky and find a few deserted huts to sleep in but that's only if we're lucky. Most of the villages have been burnt to the ground and the natives long gone. We do see the odd woman and child watching us from behind a tree in the distance but the only men we see are warriors and when we see them it's certainly not from a safe distance*'," read John. "Here now, here's my favourite part," he said. "'*One day we were out on patrol — our main job is just being there to keep the different fighting sides apart — when we were suddenly charged by about a hundred tribesmen, some wearing leopard skins or some other animal skin and their faces painted with different patterns and colours. Jesus, they were frightening, and they were all armed with spears and bows and arrows, a few of them had guns, and you should have heard the terrific noise they made as they charged. Thank God our interpreter was able to explain that we came in peace. The stories they told us were terrible, about pygmies attacking their villages. Pygmies, would you believe? I've yet to see one.'* I should have been a soldier instead of a baker," said John. "I'd rather see painted tribesmen and pygmies when I'm at work than bread and buns."

"It's a bit late for that now, thank God," said Betty. "And what about the awful things Jim's seen, never mind your painted tribesmen. Are you also anxious to see the bodies he's seen, people ripped open and their legs cut off and their heads cut off? Is that what you'd like to see? Thank God it's only Jim there and not Joe as well! I didn't think they'd stay in the army all this time."

"Soldiering seems to suit your brothers, Betty," said Michael. "I can't see them ever coming back and being able to settle on the farm."

"What do you make of it all, Daddy?" asked Patsy.

Patrick had been very quiet while the letter was being read out. "Don't get me started," he said. "What's not in Jim's letter is what's going on in the place and that's the usual one of greed. The Congo is rich, there are diamonds and minerals there for the taking and lots of people prepared to kill for that taking and for the wealth and the power that brings. It's the same story in a lot of these countries: they win their independence from the European colonialists but instead of the ordinary people benefitting it's the few who seize the opportunity to grab control and keep all the benefits for themselves. And there's always a few of them so then they have to fight it out between themselves, and God help the villages in their path. In a way it's understandable, the Congo has been looted for years by Belgium and the local people have had nothing and now they want it all. Unfortunately, most of them won't get anything."

"You're right there, Patrick," said Robert. "I read a report about one local leader who travels round with a convoy of fifty motorbikes, all of them ridden by armed men. You can't tell me he's driving around in search of peace. And meanwhile those poor cotton farmers have to survive as best they can."

"Well, I hope to God Jim survives. I don't know why they had to send the Irish Army there," said Patsy. "I thought we were supposed to be a neutral country."

"We're still part of the United Nations," said Robert. "Like my da says, we're supposed to be there keeping the peace, not fighting on one side or the other."

"Some peace!" said Patsy. "How often does Jim get to write home?"

"He's tries to write every few days but of course it depends on the army's postal system in the field," said Michael. "Sometimes we don't get anything and then we get three or four letters at once."

"Well, I'm glad you brought his letter to share," said Betty, "even though it's unsettling. We'll all be anxious until he comes home safe."

"We can only hope that this terrible massacre will serve as a lesson if it was, as they claim, a case of mistaken identity, though with the UN being accused of taking sides in the conflict I don't feel too optimistic," said Michael.

"We should all make a novena for peace in the Congo," said Patsy.

"Yes, well, you go ahead," said Robert. "There are such terrible things going on I sometimes find it hard to give any credence to any of that praying stuff. Why does God stand by and let it happen — all that comes into my head, especially when I think of those soldiers just buried today who were there on a peace mission, just ordinary sons and husbands and fathers trying to do a good job for people hundreds of miles away. And what was God doing when our fathers were fighting to get rid of the British? Didn't God allow the occupiers here in the first place? I'm afraid I don't have your simple faith, Patsy, though I'm happy to hedge my bets knowing you're praying for us all."

"I think we should change the subject before we get bogged down in who believes in what," said Michael. "It doesn't do to dwell too much on trying to figure out what either God or man is up to. Even the Pope can't tell us that. So, Annie, how's married life treating you? Are the little ones keeping you busy?"

"They are but it's a big help living here, my mammy's able to look after them while I go out to work, Matt is away with his job a lot of the time," said Annie, sneaking a sly glance in Patsy's direction. "He's doing lots of overtime so we can afford to get our own place, so it's a godsend me still living here at home. I couldn't manage otherwise: young Marie is a little madam already, she can't wait to go to school, and baby Michael has been a real early walker so now he's into all sorts of mischief around the house. I can't wait for them to visit the farm. Look at what it did for Ciaran and Mikey."

"It sent them over to England," said Patsy so curtly that all heads turned to face her.

"Patsy, what's that all about?" asked Patrick. "That sounds very rude towards your Uncle Michael and his hospitality, giving Ciaran and Mikey a home and work, a chance to grow up."

Patsy reddened. She was acutely aware of how she had ended in tears in front of Theresa when she learned that all of them were off to Cheltenham and she didn't want to start sobbing again. "I'm sorry," she said. "Uncle Michael, you know that's not what I meant at all. It's just that I miss the family and so many of them are in England now. Our country couldn't wait to get rid of the British and these days, it seems, people can't wait to move over and live with them again."

"I don't think I'd ever want to leave Dublin," said John, "except if I was a soldier and could go to Africa. I'm sure they must need someone to bake the bread."

"Well, your father was a baker-soldier in his own way, John, so you'd be following in his footsteps," said Michael.

"I'm sure your girlfriend would have something to say about that," said Betty. "She loves going round on that scooter thing you ride. You know," she said to Michael and Robert, "John and Eileen go all over the place on it."

"What sort is it?" asked Robert. "I thought about buying one for nipping into Tullamore. They seem to be all the rage."

"They are. Sure we belong to a big club, it's a national club just for scooters and we go on rallies and outings, it's grand," said John. "Then every year the priests hold an annual blessing in O'Connell Street and thousands of us congregate for the occasion."

"Trust the Church to get involved, they like to control their congregations, all right," said Robert. "They can't leave anything alone. Remember years ago, Patsy, when they'd even organise dances to keep us all under their watchful eye."

"I agree with you there," said John, "but actually most of us just regard the blessing as a great excuse to parade around the city and show off. Eileen always says she feels like Audrey Hepburn in *Roman Holiday*. Did you see that film? We loved it, we went to see it several times. Anyway, the blessing is really a big social get-together and, if it keeps everyone happy to throw holy water everywhere, well that's no big hassle. My scooter's a Vespa. I could put you in touch with someone if you were serious about getting one."

"I'll think on it," said Robert. "Of course, if you went off to Africa to bake bread for the army you could leave the scooter behind and I'd look after it for you."

"I'm probably far too old now to join up," said John.

"What's it like for you now working in the same place as your father did?" asked Michael.

"It's okay except for when they go on about the old days and the comings and goings of the Volunteers," said John, "but they still talk about Mr O'Kelly with hushed respect, or it could be hushed something else on the quiet as they know he's my father. There's one man there, been there for years, so he has, Tommy Byrne, and he talks about some young feller who used to work there years ago and how my da made this poor man's life such a misery every day that in the end he quit his job."

"I think I'll look in on Marie," said Patsy, not wanting to listen to any conversation about the bakery and her father: memories had already flooded instantly into her mind. "I'll see if she's awake for me to read her a story." As she was leaving the room, she heard murmured comments about the pity in it that "Patsy would have made a great mother". She shut the door with a bang.

It was always strange for Patsy entering her old room. Marie had taken it over — talk of ghosts inhabiting it had stopped when Patsy moved out so there was no superstitious fear involved for the child — and pictures of ducks and animals covered the walls and stuffed toys were tucked in on all sides of the bed. Marie was sitting up in bed with a book.

"Hello Auntie Patsy," said the child, a beam of welcome lighting up her face.

"Would you like me to read you a story?"

"That'd be grand," said Marie. "Mammy usually reads to me but she couldn't with all the visitors."

"They're still talking so I thought I'd come to see you," said Patsy. "You know this used to be my room?"

"I know. It's a strange room, don't you think? It's not like the others in the house. When I first slept in here, I was a bit scared because I thought someone was in here with me but hiding. Did that ever happen to you? Then Mammy read me a story about a little girl who had imaginary friends she used to talk to, so I stopped being scared."

"And do you have imaginary friends to talk to?"

"Don't tell anyone, Auntie Patsy, I'll only tell you because this used to be your room, but there's a boy and girl I talk to in here sometimes. They're not scary at all. They've become my imaginary friends. Were they here when it was your bedroom? Did you talk to them?"

"Well don't you tell anyone either, Marie, and I'll only tell you this because it's your room now, but yes, they were here then too, and I used to whisper to them so no one else in the house would hear me. And you know what? They're not scary at all. I always thought they actually looked after me and I miss them now that I live with Uncle Jem. So next time you're talking to them, give them my regards, won't you, and we'll just keep it between ourselves. Now, what would you like me to read?"

"Can't you tell me a story instead? I know all my books almost off by heart."

"Okay, let's see now. Did I ever tell you the tale about when we used to live in the country and your Auntie Molly saw a leprechaun one day when we were all out in the pony and trap?" said Patsy. "I didn't? Well now's as good a time as any to remedy that."

9

Mrs Flaherty was mopping the floor at The Little Flower Penny Dinners when Patsy called in to say hello. It was a couple of years since Patsy had been to the café though she had felt guilty all that time about not helping out there like she used to. She timed her visit to coincide with the end of the shift: she couldn't face the litany of repeated how-are-yous to and from customers, preferring instead to catch Mrs Flaherty alone.

"I wasn't sure you'd still be working here," said Patsy, taking her coat off and grabbing a dry cloth to run over the wet floor in the wake of the mop.

"I'm still here, all right, where else would I be," said Mrs Flaherty. "Somebody has to keep the place going." She noticed Patsy redden. "My God, Patsy, I didn't mean that as a dig at you," she said. "You put more than your share of time into this place. A couple of my daughters come now too so the hungry are still being fed and the moaners still being told to stop complaining and mind their manners. Anyway, tell me all your news, girl, how's life treating you? I've given up waiting for the call in the middle of the night."

"I'm grand," said Patsy. "I never made the call either so there are no little Murphy's at home. I've no excuses for not working here other than that I just got out of the routine. And what about you? I thought you might have handed over the reins here by now."

"The truth is, Patsy, the only thing I know about is cooking and looking after people so that's what I do. And it gets me out of the house, especially now that my little ones aren't little any more and they live in their own homes with their own children. I'm a grandmother several times over now but the house is too quiet for me, I just can't get used to not having the place alive with hustle and bustle and that's one thing about the café, it's never quiet when it's feeding time, you know what it's like yourself, it's the proverbial zoo. You're in a different situation, you're set up with your sewing skills and you must have great gas at work with the other women, but I've only ever been able to do housework, so I still do it outside the house as well as in. It's like a social life too in here, this is my gas, never a dull moment, and I get great pleasure out of seeing the appreciation on people's faces when they get a hot meal put in front of them for a few coppers. That's the floor finished so let's have a cup of tea. Just wait now and I'll switch the front lights off. It's been a busy day and I don't want any waifs knocking on the door hoping for a late bite."

Patsy stowed away the mop and bucket and Mrs Flaherty busied herself with the tea. "There are a couple of slices of cake left over," she said, "no point in leaving them to get hard. Isn't it funny how old biscuits go soft and old cakes go hard? No doubt there's a scientific explanation for that."

The place hadn't changed since Patsy's days as a regular volunteer. It had been given a fresh coat of paint and an extra sink had been installed and some additional shelving but otherwise things were much as they had been.

"I've missed coming, I don't know why I stopped," said Patsy. "There are so many different people in and out, not to mention all the characters who've been managing to exist somehow in The Liberties for years."

"Well of course some of the regulars you knew have died off, some of them have moved away altogether, a few have been saved by their children finally getting proper jobs and being able to give their parents a decent place to live," said Mrs Flaherty, pouring the tea, "but there are still a lot of the same old faces you'd recognise, older, of course, but probably no wiser. But enough of that, tell me how you're getting on. You're obviously still in Dublin. I see Betty occasionally in the street and she keeps me up to date with anything major. I understand Annie is expecting her third and even John is about to set the date. He hasn't rushed into anything, God love him. Then there's what happened to your cousin from Tullamore a couple of years back. Wasn't that dreadful getting captured in the jungle? Jesus, his mother must have been frantic. I've added a little something to the tea, Patsy, just to warm up the conversation."

"Yes, they were held hostage for a month after a long siege, so we were told," said Patsy. "Jim wrote home to say they were attacked by thousands of tribesmen but the Irish commander managed to get an important message through to their headquarters that they were running out of whiskey."

"Would you believe that? That's Irishmen for you."

"Well they needed something to drink. The water they were sent during the siege was in old petrol containers so they couldn't drink a drop of it."

"Well, we'll enjoy our drop now, Irish fuel, so they say. I feel a need of it, to be honest with you, especially with all this business going on in Cuba. It's hard to sleep easy at night for fear of us all being blown up before morning by a nuclear bomb. It's to be hoped the Americans and the Russians sort it out between them."

"Thank God there's a Catholic in the White House," said Patsy. "We have special prayer vigils organised at Saint Kevin's but I'm sure President Kennedy will know what to do."

They sat down at the small kitchen table. Patsy wasn't sure why she had come. Mrs Flaherty was not a close friend but she was someone Patsy was able talk to outside of the family and Patsy didn't know whether or not she had come to talk and, if so, about what. "I'm living in Portobello now," she said, "still working in the same place. I'll no doubt be there until I'm ready to retire."

"And why shouldn't you be? You've always loved being a modern woman with a career of your own and your own money to spend, such as it might be, I know nothing pays well these days. But did I detect a hint of regret? I never know when people use words like 'still' and 'same' in the same sentence."

"I don't know," said Patsy. "Being here in the café is a reminder of how hard life is for some people and I have no right to complain, it's just that two of my sisters and three brothers have all moved to England, they're making new lives for themselves and I'm still doing the same old thing. When I was growing up, I thought everything would be more interesting than it actually is. You know my father refused to let me take up a music scholarship to study the piano when I was young? Even the nuns at school tried to make him change his mind, they said I had real God-given talent and it would be a sin to waste it, but he still said no, he said it would be too dangerous for a young girl, too immoral. What a chance that could have been! I might have become a concert pianist, Mrs Flaherty, can you imagine that? Instead, I'm still sewing seams and stitching plackets and living in a house that's even smaller than the small one I grew up in. I don't even have the pleasure of watching children of my own change as they grow up. Even my godchildren are living in another country."

"Do you still play the piano?"

"I do but not very often. Jem likes to hear me play but my fingers don't move the way they used to and that puts me off. It's too much proof of how time has passed."

"And how is Jem? I was only in his company that once when you got married but he seemed to be a very entertaining type of man, quite cultured."

"He is that," said Patsy. "He's not very well right now, that's partly why I called in today, I'm not used to him being poorly and I needed some fresh air. My feet just led me here."

"I'm glad they did," said Mrs Flaherty. "I always enjoyed listening to your ideas and opinions. You've always had things going on in your head, Patsy, not the normal things most of the young girls have in their heads around here. They take their path in life for granted, God bless them, but not you. I still remember the shock on Martha Doran's face that night your brother John was born, and you suggested that we women should go on strike until men started doing their share of the housework and looking after all the children they kept fathering. I could see Martha booking herself into a Novena specially to offer it up for your wayward soul."

"I remember," said Patsy. "I don't think all the glasses of Paddy's helped; I couldn't keep my mouth shut even though I could sense Mrs Doran beginning to get fidgety."

"Beginning to get self-righteous and holier-than-thou, you mean. She sees things only in black and white, always has done: the black is whatever goes on outside the holy umbrella of her Church, the white is the good Catholic doing whatever the priests tell him or her to do, even when to any normal human being what they say is often patent nonsense. Still, she's a good woman and her prayers have been answered: her son joined the priesthood after studying out at Maynooth."

"She'll definitely be happy then. How is she herself? Are you still delivering babies together?"

"Not any longer, she has terrible problems with her knees and all that bending over beds and between legs isn't easy for her. I think the last baby she delivered was for her friend's son, the one I told you about who was getting married. I think it was the weekend of the Mass in Phoenix Park. He has three little ones now."

"Fitzsimmons?"

"That's right, Fitzsimmons. So, I don't see Martha as much as I used to, God bless her. Do you fancy another wee drop of something, without the tea this time? I've half an hour before I have to head off home."

"Then I'll have one with you," said Patsy. "Maybe by the time I get back Jem will have fallen asleep."

"He's poorly, you said. What's the matter, a cold, is it?"

"I don't know and of course he won't go to see the doctor. He had a mouth ulcer for a couple of weeks and then it seemed to develop into a rash and he got a couple of lumps. And he's not comfortable down there, round his privates," said Patsy pointing discreetly in the appropriate direction.

"What about when he passes water?" asked Mrs Flaherty. Her face was no longer relaxed despite the Paddy's. She was weighing up all the symptoms Patsy described.

"He said it burns a bit when he goes to the toilet. I got him some cream at the chemists in case it was piles but it didn't seem to help," said Patsy. "The poor man's not himself, he's all aches and pains and he's been off work for a couple of weeks. That's another reason I needed to get some fresh air, I'm not used to him being around the house so much, he's normally out and about."

"Is he?" asked Mrs Flaherty but it was a rhetorical question. "What about you, Patsy? Have you picked up anything from him do you think?"

"No, I'm right as rain. I shouldn't really tell you this, it's rather personal, but to be honest with you, Mrs Flaherty, we don't sleep in the same bed any more. Jem's in the parlour on a small put-you-up. He gets quite feverish and said he doesn't want to spoil my night's sleep."

"That's good to hear, Patsy. You know I've heard of men getting sick

378

like this and you should get your husband to consult the doctor before it gets too serious. And you must look after yourself, Patsy, keep your distance as much as you can. I know that's not what a wife wants to hear but you must take care. And make sure you wash your hands well after touching him, even better would be to wear some rubber gloves when you're helping him. I've got some I can give you."

"But, Mrs Flaherty, this is Jem we're talking about, in the name of God, my husband, I can't be washing my hands every time I touch my husband. He's only a bit rundown, he probably caught some sort of a bug. I'm sure he'll get over it soon, please God."

"Meanwhile why don't you do something to please me, Patsy: take care of yourself and don't take Jem to the surgery, get the doctor to come to the house. I'm sorry but what you describe is no joke and could be very contagious. I hate to ask but we've known each other a long time: is it possible Jem has been cheating on you with someone, someone who might have passed something on to him during, you know, sex?"

Patsy quickly picked up her coat. "That's a ridiculous, horrible thing to suggest," she said. "Jem's not interested in other women. Anyway, I'm sorry but I to have to rush off now, Mrs Flaherty. I'll call in again some time."

Patsy did rush off but the rushing stopped the minute she left the diner, she was in no particular hurry to get home. The place wasn't the haven of innocent conviviality it used to be. No reference had ever been made to her spurned approach to Jem the night of the wrestling match and Patsy felt she was living within a managed silence, a vacuum that was slowly but surely sucking the last vestiges of womanly love out of her. She thought of the times her husband came home late and the worse for wear but always in a great mood and she tried to forget the directness of Mrs Flaherty's question. The implications were too awful to bear.

The commode was in the corner of the backroom near the fire and, no matter how much Patsy tried to disguise the thing with fancy drapery, it remained a commode and looked like a commode. It had become such a painful struggle for Jem to get out to use the toilet in the yard that they had had to install the chamber-pot contraption in the house. It wasn't a small, discreet thing, more like a grand throne designed for comfort which Patsy had found in a second-hand shop — she didn't want to think about its previous occupants — and there was no space for such a large extra piece of furniture in the front parlour, which had become Jem's permanent bedroom. The only option was to lodge it in the backroom, where, of course, they ate all their meals and where, with the parlour out of commission, they now spent all their evenings. It wasn't the pleasantest of living arrangements. It was also rather smelly, especially as Jem was having problems with his bodily functions, having to pee and shit frequently, which had never been a problem he had in the past, and he still suffered that awful burning sensation. Patsy had just as frequently to then empty the bowl down the outside toilet, occasionally seeing spots of blood in Jem's urine. She had long since taken Mrs Flaherty's advice and got in a supply of rubber gloves. Jem had consistently refused to see a doctor but, whether he liked it or not, Patsy had called in to the surgery to ask the doctor to call round.

Jem was diagnosed as having third-stage syphilis: he had left it too late for any effective cure, his liver and kidney were already diseased and failing, but the doctor put him on a course of penicillin to alleviate the symptoms. The awful prognosis was that Jem should expect a gradual loss of sight and the onset of deafness and he could go on living like that for years. The doctor also insisted on testing Patsy for syphilis: she was clear.

The house was run like an isolation unit, Patsy would allow no one, not even Margaret, to visit to witness her shame — shame at the conditions in the house, shame that her husband had caught a venereal disease and all that implied, plus a warped, self-conscious sort of shame that she hadn't caught it too because of the simple fact that she was in a marriage where no physical love was ever part of the deal: she couldn't face the thought of being on the receiving end of anyone's pity were they to find out. Even Betty had assumed that by now Patsy and Jem had sorted out whatever was the original problem in that department. Without either visitors or the Jem of old for companionship, loneliness at home had taken on a heavy new dimension for Patsy. It was no longer just the rejection of the marital norms, which Patsy had after all accepted from the outset, it was that the daily life she had enjoyed with Jem, his animated conversation, his humour, his enthusiasm, was being eroded along with the man himself. Jem was thin, emaciated looking compared to his past stature, his pallor a mix of grey and yellow. He would slump vacantly in the armchair, drooped and drooling, his eyes not focussed on anything, a terrible look of guilt and resignation on his face, and Patsy sitting opposite him by the glow of the coal fire, drifting in and out of unformed memories and thoughts which she didn't want to capture.

"I can't tell you enough how sorry I am for ruining your life, Patsy, for taking your life," he told her during one of his lucid moments. "What a catastrophic misfortune for you to have agreed to my proposal. It must have been the magic of the Liffey that did it. You kept your side of the bargain, a bargain with the Devil, and what did I do? I turned my back on your needs while for my part I was fulfilling myself with a man, something I fervently promised you I would never do. May God forgive me, may you forgive me. Well, I'm being punished for it now all right, though I can't even take my punishment like a man. I rely on you for everything, even for wiping my arse. I've become the baby you never had."

"You're rather large for a baby," said Patsy.

"I am that," he said, "and I don't have the innocence of a baby, just the guilt of a dirty old queen. I meant to keep my promise to you, I hope you can still believe that, Patsy, you were the one woman I hoped would keep me on the straight and narrow, but these depraved urges would never leave me alone and in the end I had to satisfy them."

Patsy looked at the man who had once been so dapper, so meticulous and fastidious in his garb, so charming and entertaining and interesting in his approach to whomever and whatever was going on around him: a man who had looked after her, cherished her as an equal, made her laugh and made her cry. She felt herself melt with sympathy at the dishevelled image before her.

"You're not in the least depraved, Jem, I won't listen to you talk like that about yourself," she said. "You're the way God made you, that's all, and you know well my feelings about God and his divine mystery, though I might agree to the use of the word 'dirty' now that you have to use a commode which I have to empty and scrub and disinfect."

"My good woman," said Jem, "you maintain your humour in all of this hellish situation. You truly are as magnificent as I've always

381

believed. If only I'd been the proper man you deserved."

"Who's to say what we do or don't deserve," said Patsy. "You were and you are my man, as you are, Jem Murphy, one of God's creatures who grasped the life God gave him with both hands."

"Unfortunately, these hands grasped more than I had intended."

"Let's not dwell on that image," said Patsy. "Having to flush away your stools is about as much image as I can handle these days."

"Would you say you've had some good times with me, Pat? We enjoyed ourselves, didn't we? It wasn't all spoilt by our agreement?"

"I'd say you treated me to some grand times, Jem. We've had a lot of laughs together and fun and we've done all sorts of different things, I've been to places and occasions that I would never have gone to without you in my life. I am grateful for so much that you made possible, Jem, you swept me along with your infectious determination to make the most out of life and I was glad to join you."

"Most people, of course, think that to make the most out of life you have to have a family of your own, so I failed in that respect. You asked me once if I regretted not having any children, well the answer now would have to be 'yes', I do regret it, little ones around the place could have been an enriching experience for the two of us and might have kept me out of temptation," he said.

"Except that you couldn't bring yourself to go through the basic requirement needed to have children, not with me anyway."

"I tried once or twice, I honestly did, mentally anyway," said Jem. "I'd look at you lying next to me in the bed and I'd feel full of love for my Patsy. But then I would start to make a move towards you, to run my hand over the curve of your shoulder and investigate the sensitivities of your neck, and from seeming the right thing to do it suddenly would all seem so wrong, not me, so I would stop. It would have been dishonest. Then perhaps you would have been led to believe that I was a changed man, come to my senses, all would be normal from then on when I knew it wouldn't be, I couldn't change who I am. And I was frightened too that I'd start to kiss you and be repulsed by it all, not by you, Patsy, but by the very idea of being with a woman. I didn't want to find myself turning away in disgust. I did that to you once and the remorse was unbearable. I couldn't even bring myself to mention it later. I really am so sorry."

"To be honest with you, Jem, I am sorry too," said Patsy. "Sometimes I'd look at you asleep in bed and I'd look at your beautiful strong arms and your chest lifting and sinking with your breathing and I'd want so much to be in those arms and to have that chest pressed into mine. I wanted to know what it would be like at least once in my life to be wrapped in a man's body. But there are plenty of women who have all that and have to put up with drunken husbands climbing on top of them whether they're in the mood or not and maybe getting a black eye into the bargain. I never had to worry about that with you, Jem, thank God, and just think, I saved a fortune on not having to buy sexy nighties."

"You should buy them anyway, for yourself," said Jem, "enjoy the silkiness next your skin and appreciate the silly prettiness of dainty lace trimmings. It would have to be French lace, of course, then you would feel très coquettish."

"Not much point in that on my own," said Patsy.

"Have you thought about that, Patsy, about being on your own when I'm gone?"

"I don't want to hear you talking like that, Jem Murphy. The doctor said you can live for years."

"He also said I'll be going blind and deaf. Who would want to carry on for years like that? I couldn't read the papers to you any more and I wouldn't be able to hear if you read them to me instead. That's not life, Patsy, that's just not being dead, especially after all the great things we've done together. I'll just end up more and more helpless. You'll have a real big baby to look after."

"If you insist on me treating you like a baby then I will. For a start you can do what you're told and be quiet."

He did but the quiet was interrupted by tell-tale gurglings from his innards and Patsy flew to whip the drape off the commode in time. A hiss of piss and the straining of Jem trying to pass what counted for solids broke the silence. Patsy put on her rubber gloves, wiped him down and carried the potty out to the toilet. Leaning over the bowl to clean it, her eyes welled up and she had to linger until her emotions had subsided.

"There you are," said Jem when she returned to the house, "life as we now know it. Perhaps I should wear nappies."

"So I can stand over the pan boiling them clean?" said Patsy. She

383

took off her gloves and put them back on the hook in the kitchen.

"The fact is that we do need to discuss the future, whether you like it or not," said Jem. "It doesn't have to be a morbid conversation but there are things you need to be aware of for when the time comes. For example, there are papers in a box at the bottom of my wardrobe which are the titles to a plot in Mount Jerome cemetery, out at Harold's Cross. My father bought it years ago and he's buried there alongside my mother. There's room for me and then for you when you join me."

"When I join you? I thought you said this wouldn't be a morbid conversation. I'm not ready to die yet. Haven't I a big baby to look after, a baby getting old before his time."

"Now Patsy, leave me be. I've always taken care of you and I will in the future. In the same box you'll find a letter to my bank, a will, if you like, the bank has a copy too, giving you the right to my savings and my pension. Neither are very large sums, I've never been a rich man and, as you know, what I've had I've liked to spend, but there should be enough to see you through."

"See me through to my end, is that what you're saying?"

"My good woman, you were always too stubborn for your own good. Just remember what I've told you. Now, on a lighter note, shall we have a drop of Paddy's to cheer us after all this morbidity?"

"The doctor has forbidden you to drink any more whiskey because of your medication and, besides, we don't have any."

"I'm sure one drop won't hurt after a lifetime of abuse," said Jem. "Perhaps you could bring some in with you from work tomorrow. By then my cup will be flowing over, my chamber-pot by any other name, and you'll need a tot to anaesthetise your nose and visuals. Right now, I'm sorry but I need to use the blasted thing again, then perhaps I'll take myself off to bed."

Patsy and Jem both went through their motions.

10

It was a blessing for Patsy to go out to work, though she worried about leaving Jem alone for too long. She had finally fully confided in Mrs Flaherty and the erstwhile midwife had kindly offered to call in a couple of times a day to see to Jem's needs but still Patsy felt disloyal in keeping her job on. A lot of women didn't work at all once they had a husband, let alone a sick one, but, being confined to her isolation unit so much, Patsy felt that life was passing her by and she relied on her sewing colleagues to keep her both sane and at least vaguely up to date with what was going on in the world beyond Warren Street. Liverpool was in the news, evidently, having become the centre of a music revolution with a band called The Beatles and Patsy neatly assumed that Molly's daughters were fans so that she could join in the conversation and impress her colleagues with her tenuous family link. And Russia and America were involved in some sort of a Space Race, sending rockets up into the skies, would you believe, first with monkeys and dogs and finally with men on board. The sewing room had a great gas talking about what it would be like in space with all that floating around with your skirts blowing up over your arse to show your knickers and whether or not they might soon be called on to ditch the traditional suit and run up space-suits instead, made to order or ready to wear for a night of star-gazing on the Wicklow Mountains, your very own rocket-man by your side primed for take-off above the waters of Glendalough, St Kevin turning in his grave. Down on Earth, Patsy was feeling just that: down, earthbound.

"You should have been there, Patsy," said Bernadette in the sewing room, talking to Patsy across her Singer, "it was just like you'd imagine being in New York would be, it was amazing, I never thought I'd ever get to see a real one for myself. And the noise? Sure, I haven't heard the like since… well, I've actually never heard the like. You should have come with us. We all went for a Guinness and a Jack Daniels after, to keep both flags flying, so to speak, but by the time we fell out of the bar it was more stars I was seeing than stripes, I have to admit. Are you listening to me Patsy? Have you heard a word I'm after saying?"

"I'm sorry but my mind's at home, Bernie. You know Jem's not well at all, the house is like an intensive-care unit in a hospital," said Patsy. "What was it you said?"

"I was talking about the big parade last evening, a motorcade, I think they called it, and President Kennedy standing up there in his open top car waving to us all and with the brightest smile you can imagine. My God, he's a handsome man. I didn't realise he had such a mop of blond hair. He's come to visit his ancestral home, the commentators said, some place I've not heard of in Wexford. I can't believe we actually have an Irish Catholic as President of America. And there was a ticker-tape welcome for him, papers streaming down thrown by all the people crowded in every possible window and some even on the ledges and the rooftops. It was a positive snowstorm of ticker-tape, just like in New York."

"I doubt they use rolls of Dublin bus tickets for their ticker-tape in New York," shouted Siobhan from the other side of the table.

"Well, they had to use something," said Bernadette.

"And where was all this?" asked Patsy. "I've no idea any more what's happening outside my own house. I knew President Kennedy was coming for a visit but the dates and details got filed away among Jem's temperature charts."

"They drove down O'Connell Street and then over the bridge," said Bernadette. "We stood there waiting for what seemed ages and then suddenly we knew they were on the way because the wave of cheering got louder and louder and then suddenly, there he was, right in front of us. According to the papers this morning the crowd broke through the police cordon in Duke Street and surrounded Mr Kennedy's car. God I'd have loved that, I may have got to shake his hand or at least touch his sleeve or his car, but of course we were still over in O'Connell Street."

"That was a pretty stupid thing to do, mobbing his car, I'm surprised no one got shot," said Siobhan. "There were security men everywhere and they were all armed. I bet they had their guns drawn when the car was mobbed."

"That's because there had been three death threats, it said in the papers," said Bernadette. "There were two direct to the police and one to the newspaper. They're not going to take any chances after that are they, not with the President, not with him being a Catholic and all, you know what some of those Orangemen are like."

"Trust me to miss out on all the excitement," said Patsy. "And was Jackie there? They always look such a lovely couple."

"She's at home in the White House," said Bernadette. "She's about to have another baby so she couldn't make the trip. It's a pity, I would have loved to see her in the flesh, she's so glamorous and elegant."

"That'll be from the French side of her family, French women are always very chic," said Siobhan. "Doesn't she look grand in those little box-suits she wears? I think she does, I'll have to make myself one of those."

"Maybe we should suggest a new line to the boss," said Patsy. "We could launch a Jackie range."

"Would that be instead of the space-suits or alongside?" asked Siobhan.

"I don't see why we couldn't combine the two," said Patsy. "We could trim the jackets in silver and sew on bits of tasselled piping and maybe a zig-zaggy electric motif on the front and market them as being out of this world."

"Guaranteed lift off at any social occasion," said Bernadette. "You'd have to get one yourself, Patsy. Isn't your husband always taking you out to proper social occasions?"

"In the past we used to go out all the time but he's not up to it at the moment. But Jem's a big fan of Jack Kennedy so I'm sure otherwise we'd have been out in the city last night joining in the celebrations."

"I doubt that would have included a Guinness with the girls," said Siobhan.

"No," said Bernadette, "it would have been some fancy dinner somewhere with all the big-wigs of Dublin."

"Maybe so," said Patsy, "but these days a Guinness with you girls would have been good for me, though to be honest with you I've never really acquired a taste for the stuff. But I like the smell of the brewery, it gives the city an individual atmosphere."

That set the women off on talk of the pervasive Guinness fumes that always hovered in the Dublin air, which in turn set them off on talk of pervasive smells that were anything but pleasant, just stinks. All too familiar with those of late, Patsy sank in on herself at the thought of having missed out on a night of laughter and joking with her colleagues while she was stuck in nursing Jem and tending to his chamber-pot: it would have been a real tonic to go out and enjoy herself, she might even have enjoyed a glass of Guinness. Then she asked God to forgive her for having such selfish thoughts. "Dear God, I'm sorry," she prayed. "I accept this Cross you have given me to bear, far less of the Cross you bore for me, a sinner, and I pray for your help so that I can carry my Cross cheerfully and without resentment, so that I can offer it for your greater glory, Amen." Then she felt for the Children of Mary scapula which she still wore round her neck: "O Mary, conceived without sin, I wish this day to place myself and Jem under thy protection."

But at home Jem was deteriorating, slowly but undeniably. Patsy had to shout to make herself heard but Jem often asked her to play the piano: he said that the reverberation of the notes helped him to hear the music. It comforted him to be able to still hear his good woman playing some of the old songs, which in turn conjured pleasant memories, which in turn worsened his depression at his increasing invalidity.

"I could murder a drink," he was constantly complaining, "anything to help numb the numbness of the overwhelming anaesthetic of hopeless illness."

Patsy finally relented and bought a bottle of Paddy's on her way home from work. They could enjoy at least a glass together and both gain some respite, she from the routine drudgery of nursing and he from the humiliating need to be nursed. She had consulted Mrs Flaherty first, not knowing the potential risks of mixing whiskey and penicillin.

"The poor man hasn't much to keep his spirits up," said Mrs Flaherty. "It seems to me that, if it's something you always enjoyed together, then where's the harm in an occasional short measure if it brings a bit of joy back into his life. You know, Patsy, when you're out at work he has nothing at all to sustain him. It must be a terrible long day for him, terrible, the hours taking their time to drag on and all the time him wondering if you'll be back soon. I always feel guilty when I have to leave him alone. If it was me, I'd go ahead and have a drink with the man. It's all very well the doctor advising against it but we both know Jem's not going to suddenly get well, God bless him, better to make his life as bearable as possible while he still has it. I can't see the real harm in him enjoying just a wee drop."

When Patsy handed the glass to Jem that evening, his eyes lit up. "My good woman you bought some," he said, "now that really does call for cheers."

"You know why Paddy's is called Paddy's?" she asked.

"I've been drinking the stuff for many years but you've got me stumped there, Patsy. Don't tell me an upstanding Child of Mary such as yourself knows something about Paddy's whiskey that I don't."

"It's called after a travelling salesman called Paddy who used to work for the distillery in Cork. He'd go all over the country selling the whiskey," said Patsy. "Everywhere he went, he would treat whoever was in the pub to a whiskey, like a free sample, I suppose, and it proved very popular, and sales of the whiskey increased no end. The customers were so used to Paddy and they liked his brand so much that they started asking for a 'Paddy's' in the bars and the publicans started ordering supplies of 'Paddy's' from the distillery. So, they decided to make it official and call it after their most successful ever salesman, Paddy."

"My God, Patsy, that's a good yarn," said Jem. "Who told you that?"

"Margaret told me once when we were having a night out."

"I like Margaret, you should have more nights out with her, never mind me, I'd manage, sure it wouldn't be every night. You need to get out, Patsy. You have a full-time job and your patient here is very demanding: it's important that you still get time to enjoy yourself. I'm afraid I've become a real burden."

Jem looked at Patsy as he waited for a response but she was miles away.

"What did you normally do on your nights out?" he intruded.

Patsy retained a faraway look. "We'd normally go to Bewley's every Tuesday, that was our night: we'd drink posh coffee and eat delicious buns and we'd chat about things, swap stories about what we'd been up to, gossip about film stars. Then maybe we'd finish off with a Paddy's before going to the pictures. I used to love going to the cinema with Margaret. We're both on the same wavelength when it comes to films."

"Why did you stop your Tuesdays?"

Patsy's lower lip curled down momentarily. "Margaret got married and had children," was all she said.

"But now, what about now? Surely her children are old enough that she can go out on the odd evening."

"Everybody's life changes, Jem. We can't just turn back the clock or try to repeat the same things, you can't recapture that spirit you had when you were young."

"No," said Jem, "you can't, but it doesn't mean you have no spirit left and that spirit needs to fly, you need to fly, Patsy, you need to escape this trap I've sprung on you."

"There's no trap," she said, "it is what it is."

Jem suddenly bent double and Patsy uncovered the commode and helped him over to it. The familiar sounds of splatterings and splashings, the familiar stink of wee and shit, the intimate fumblings of carer and cared-for imprisoned together in a tiny backroom put an end to the conversation. Patsy fetched her rubber gloves, wiped Jem down, lifted the potty and took it to empty in the outside toilet. Jem watched her move quietly about, resigned, uncomplaining, the same routine repeated many times night after night with what he could only describe as a kind of loving devotion, though he was owed no such thing from her. He was heartbroken.

"When Mrs Flaherty calls in tomorrow tell her I'll stop by her house after work," called Patsy from the kitchen as she was putting the whiskey in the cupboard and rinsing the glasses. "It's pay-day and I want to give her something for all her trouble. I know she always says 'no' but I'm going to insist."

"She's very kind and she might be insulted if you try to pay her," said Jem. "Perhaps instead of giving her money you could buy her a treat which she wouldn't be able to refuse, some good lean pork and a few bottles of Guinness to enjoy with her husband, maybe. No need to rush home on my account, Patsy. Mrs Flaherty always leaves me in fine fettle and you may need to queue in the shops, people will have a bit of money in their pockets for the weekend."

"That's a grand idea. You're a genius in the thought department, Jem. I shouldn't be too late back, if you're sure you'll be okay for an extra half-an-hour or so."

"Take all the time you want, Patsy, a bit of hustle and bustle is what you need, and I'll keep myself entertained. But for now, I think it's time I called it a night."

Jem had been right about the queues. It had been so long since Patsy had called in at the butcher's in town that she had forgotten how popular it was on a Friday but the wait was worth it: Mrs Flaherty was thrilled with the generous piece of pork and the stout.

"My God it's a while since I saw a joint like that," she said. "I'd put it straight in the oven but for the fact that it's fish day and I still observe some of the Church's rules, though why an all-merciful God would condemn you to hell for eating a bit of meat on a particular day of the week I don't know."

"I don't think it's supposed to be a sin to eat meat on a Friday, more of an exercise in self-denial," said Patsy.

"You'd know the finer points of the teachings on sin than I would, Patsy. Whatever it is it's denying us a tempting roast and I'll not deny that," said Mrs Flaherty. "Still, I can rub salt and pepper in the skin and leave it overnight and we'll have a fine feast tomorrow with lots of crackling. I do love a good bite of crackle," she said, nudging Patsy in the ribs with her elbow and guffawing with laughter. "Thank you, Patsy, though you know you don't have to pay me anything to help with Jem. You've a lot to cope with and I'm only too willing to help."

"I don't know how I'd manage without you and your friendship, Mrs Flaherty. Anyway, I'd best be going, I don't like to be too late, and Jem does need to use the chamber pot rather often, as you'll know. How was he when you left this afternoon?"

"It was hard to tell. One minute he'd seem totally lost inside his head, thinking hard, so to speak, the next he'd be the usual chatty Jem. It's such a crying shame, Patsy, what's happened to the man."

"It's more than a crying shame," said Patsy, "it's just shame, really, his and mine."

"Whisht, now, that's all between just the three of us so go home and have as nice an evening as you can, between your latrine duties, of course." She walked Patsy to the door. "Did you decide on the whiskey?"

"I did, I bought a bottle of Paddy's and we had a drink together last night."

"And was it nice?"

"It was, except that Jem got a bit morose and starting telling me all over again what to do when he's gone."

"No harm in being practical, I suppose, he has plenty of time for these things to weigh on his mind and he'll be anxious on your behalf."

Patsy made her farewells and stepped smartly along the pavement. She felt rude brushing past people and almost ignoring their easy greetings, but time was getting on and she was eager to cheer Jem and tell him how successful had been his suggestion over the meat. She was pleased she had bought a joint for the two of them as well and a couple of apples to make the sauce: Jem insisted on having apple sauce with pork, it was the only way to eat it properly, he'd say, apple with pork, mint with lamb.

The house was always quiet when Patsy got home and first opened the door but this time there was no cheery call from Jem to welcome her home. She glanced into the parlour; sometimes he had a lie-down after Mrs Flaherty's visit, but he wasn't in bed. Patsy shut the parlour door softly and went down the hall. She didn't know whether or not she was imagining it but the smell seemed worse than usual and her nose shrank as it hit her nostrils. "We'll have to open the window for a bit, Jem, it's a bit stuffy in here," she chattered as she walked into the backroom. There she found Jem slumped quietly in his chair, but he wasn't asleep. Jem was dead, the empty bottle of Paddy's on the floor beside his chair. His trousers were soiled and stained with dark patches and the acrid smell was almost overpowering in its sadness.

11

There weren't many people at the funeral, deliberately so: Betty and Patrick were there with Annie and John; Margaret was there with Fergal; Mrs Flaherty was on hand to offer her private knowing sympathy to Patsy and the church benches were otherwise dotted with the handful of parishioners who always turned out for a Requiem Mass. Patsy had decided against holding a wake or having an open-coffin vigil in the parlour for people wanting to pay their last respects: she wanted to protect Jem's dignity and not let anyone see his deterioration, she knew he'd hate that. The burial was at Mount Jerome cemetery, according to Jem's instructions, and, after the ceremonial sods of turf had been thrown down on to the coffin, Patsy urged the few mourners to go on home and leave her for a while on her own at the graveside.

She stood there unable to cry. Her mind sought its usual comfort in prayer and she mentally summoned every spiritual verse to do with dying and the departed that came into her head but the words were garbled, more of a ritual protection against proper thought than anything sincerely recited. Her own life flashed before her, as if it was her own death she was mourning.

"Are you all right, Mrs Murphy? I don't want to disturb you."

Patsy felt a hand gently rest on her shoulder and she looked up to see James, the friend of Jem's whom she had met at The Gravediggers pub after the wrestling match.

"I didn't know you were here," she said.

"I only came to the burial, I'm not a church-going man, especially not for funerals, especially not for the funeral of a good friend, it's too upsetting," said James.

"And how good a friend was he?" Patsy spat out, not meaning to sound so accusatory.

"Not the sort of close friend you're obviously imagining in the circumstances. That would be Peter, him and Jem were the intimate ones,

393

a genuine couple, if you'll forgive me for saying so. Me? I am strictly a woman's man but I grew up with Peter and he was my closest friend since childhood."

"So that's who it was, Peter, I thought perhaps it might be; I saw them together once in town, and yet he didn't come today," said Patsy.

"Peter passed away last year, Mrs Murphy. I'm afraid in the end they killed each other and not in the nicest possible way."

"No, not the nicest possible way to go," she said, staring down at the coffin and picking out for the umpteenth time the engraving on the bronze plate, the somehow anonymous starkness of the name and span of Jem's years written out in curving letters, his birth to death linked by no more than a fancy hyphen. "I'm sorry if I sounded as if I was blaming you, James, and I'm sorry you lost your friend."

"We've both lost people important to us, we just happen to have the same ones in common, Mrs Murphy, even though we're not personally connected. Do you plan on staying here much longer or would you like to join me for a drink, we can toast Jem, on his way."

"You know, I was going to go straight home but, yes, I would appreciate that, the emptiness of the house isn't something I look forward to," said Patsy. "It will be the only bit of a wake in Jem's honour, God forgive me. I didn't want people to see how he was at the end, looking at his sick body and keeping their true comments to themselves."

"Then we'll just wait for the coffin to be covered and then let's go and honour the man. I suggest we take a taxi over to The Gravediggers and do the honours there. It was always one of Jem's favourites and you and I did after all meet there, Mrs Murphy."

"We did and I'm sure that by the end of the evening you were calling me 'Patsy' so let's get back to where we left off and call it a good beginning."

"Agreed, Patsy. The Gravediggers might be next to a different cemetery but we'll make sure all the spirits are well represented."

"I'll feel right at home, then," she said. "Did you know people have always laughed at me because of my habit of communicating with spirits other than the ones you find in a bottle. Did Jem ever tell you that?"

"Indeed he did, and it was one of the peculiarities he loved about you," said James. "He always said you were a most unusual woman.

We'll see if he manages to come through the ether after a few tipples. Come along now, we don't need to see the last spade of earth being shovelled. Perhaps we'll enjoy a plate of coddle too at the pub but whether to keep the various spirits up or down we'll have to wait and see."

The Gravediggers was of course alive and buzzing with conversation, a good-humoured crowd already settled in for the late afternoon craic. Patsy and James decided on a Paddy's each as being the most appropriate send-off for Jem and Patsy was pleased that the table they'd sat at all that time ago was free. She was reminiscing in her head when James arrived with their drinks.

"Here's to Jem," he said raising his glass.

"And to Peter," said Patsy raising hers, "may the two of them rest in peace."

"Though what sort of peace will be reigning in heaven with their arrival can only be guessed at."

They clinked their glasses and drank the toast but Patsy's face had taken on an inward expression. The waitress arrived with the coddle and they started on their meal.

"Can I ask you something, James?" said Patsy. "It might sound a bit odd but it's something that has been on my mind constantly since Jem took bad and you've just made me think of it again."

"Go ahead," said James, braced for perhaps an intimate question regarding the departed friends.

"Do you think the fact that they were homosexual would stop Jem and Peter being allowed into heaven?" said Patsy. "I've prayed and prayed for Jem's soul, all the time knowing that the life he led was regarded as terribly sinful by the Church and worrying that he may be condemned to an eternity in hell."

James took her hand. "Patsy, you crazy Catholic, isn't that sort of ignorant teaching one of the reasons why I'm a believer but not a church-going man? Just think about it now: Jem was a good man, Peter was a good man. Why on earth would God punish them for what was, after all, love? It might not have been what most people regard as the usual or accepted sort of love but that's what it was: they were two people who loved each other, they just happened to be two men. Isn't God supposed be the very element of love?"

"Thank you, you're right and you've set my mind at ease. I thought the same myself, or at least that was what I'd been hoping, but we're never supposed to question what the priests tell us and it's a hard conditioning to shake off. Sometimes I think I've spent my whole life doing what I was told was right but wondering sometimes about where, what you might call, the humanity of it all had gone. It's as if everything there is to enjoy about being alive has been deemed some sort of sin. I'm sure that wasn't God's intention but it's made me quick to judge people and what they do on that basis. That's hardly what I'd call a Christian approach, it certainly wasn't Jesus's approach."

"I think the important thing is to be an honest person and to wish no one harm," said James.

"On that measure Jem failed," said Patsy abruptly. "He wasn't honest with me. We got married on the understanding that he would never give in to his temptations as regards men but he did, and it killed him and robbed me of…"

"Robbed you of what, Patsy? I understand that you married Jem with your eyes open to the situation. On what measure do we judge you on your motives for agreeing to marry a man with whom you knew you'd never live as a proper wife? Was that being honest, either with yourself or to Jem?"

"I wonder if I've ever really been honest with myself," said Patsy, "never really known how much I let my life be governed by genuine beliefs or by simple fear. You know I loved a young man very much when I was young. I'd say he was the love of my life but I wouldn't want to sound like a character in a romance novel. He wanted us to get married but I backed away. I remember even now the night I just left him standing in the street after breaking with him and the heartache I went through for months, years, after. His father had had some serious history with my father — it's not my place to go into details — and my father was completely against the whole relationship and I used that as an excuse to myself but perhaps it was because I was afraid of how the young man made me feel when I was with him, me having taken a personal vow of chastity."

"And how was that?" asked James.

Patsy's face was suddenly transformed by what could only be

described as the same sort of comical dirty look she would adopt in the sewing room. "Physically excited," she said, a slight blush reddening her face.

"And you thought that was wrong?"

"As a devout blue-caped member of the Children of Mary I saw it as a sinful betrayal of the standards of the Virgin Mary," said Patsy and she turned to look at James and laughed at how ludicrous the confession sounded. "Amn't I the one?" she said. "But that is partly why I married Jem, so that I'd never have to cope with anything physical. I'm probably the only widow to have remained a virgin through all her years of sleeping in a marital bed but, now listen, James, only one other living person knows that and I'd like to keep it that way, both for Jem's memory and for myself. It is a bit embarrassing really. What happened was that my mammy insisted on accompanying me to the doctor's surgery to find out why no babies had come along after me being married for a few years. You can imagine her face when the truth was revealed."

"And yours," said James. "Pity the poor doctor having to spell it out in front of your mother."

"I'm sure there's no training for that particular situation at medical school," said Patsy. "I set the precedence that day, right enough," she said, emptying her glass with a dramatic gesture. "Can you stay for another drink, James? I'd like to get the next round in, unless there's somewhere you need to be."

"I'm in no hurry but perhaps you'd prefer me to go up to the bar, you being a Child of Mary with a status to uphold. Shall I get the same again?"

"Yes please, but hold the coddle this time."

"Now can I ask you something, Patsy?" said James, back with the drinks. "Can I ask you to forgive me for being basically complicit in the matter of Jem and Peter? I felt very guilty that first time Jem introduced you as his wife, knowing what I knew and yet sitting at the table, all of us having a good time and you being the only one in the company who didn't know what was really going on. Peter was my friend but I still felt guilty then and I've felt guilty ever since, especially knowing how much you had to put up with when Jem was sick. I saw it first-hand with Peter, though he spent his last few months in a hospice. Can you forgive me?"

Patsy raised her glass. "Here's to friendship and loyalty and no more guilt," she said. "Peter and Jem were together, that wasn't your fault, it's the way it was. Maybe the guilt belongs to the rest of us for trying to dictate what's right and what's wrong."

"Well, I'll add to that toast, if I may," said James. "I'll add our friendship and the honesty between us."

"That's a grand idea. Sláinte!"

"Sláinte is táinte!" said James.

"I'll take the health but you can keep the wealth," said Patsy drinking the toast. The two of them were as relaxed as any pair of familiar friends.

"Are you married yourself, James?"

"I am and we've three wonderful children, two sons and a daughter, not so young now, of course, they're trying to make their own way in the world and it's hard to let go. Childhood passes quickly; one minute you're changing nappies and singing lullabies, the next you're complaining about the type of clothes they wear and the type of music they listen to. Babies become adults, become their own people and, if you're lucky, they remain a real part of the family through their own choice. Is that something you regret, not having children?"

"I never used to but gradually a sense of absence has been growing. I've lots of nephews and nieces, not that I see much of them, they all live in England."

"You have? Well now, that's something to be thankful for even if they don't live round the corner. You'll never be short of someone to land on for free accommodation," said James and the easy understanding between the two of them erupted in laughter again. "I think that calls for another Paddy's."

A group of people chattered through the door of the pub, all dressed in black from another funeral and obviously pleased to be freed from the grimness of the graveside. A few tables had been set aside for them and a small buffet laid out.

"Did I tell you that Peter insisted on being buried wearing the tie that Jem had bought him?" said James. "He and Jem bought each other matching red ties one Christmas, bright red, very seasonal, oh it was a long time ago, and they always tried to wear the same ones whenever they went out together because, they said, the ties added a touch of festive flamboyance to any outfit, whatever the weather, whatever the occasion. Peter said before he died that he wanted to wear that tie for his funeral so that he and Jem would always be tied together. I thought that was a very touching, very loving idea and we respected his wishes."

"God forgive me," said Patsy. "Jem made exactly the same request but in the end I put a blue one on him so he'd look more sober in his coffin. The man's not long buried and I'm afraid he'll already be turning in his grave."

"Well, he was never a one to keep still for long," said James.

The Gravediggers was getting noisier and Patsy was getting proportionately merrier. "I think it might be time for me to leave," she said. "It wouldn't do for me to be legless leaving my husband's funeral and I don't want to presume on your kindness too much. Besides, I think I've said enough; I don't want to get overly confessional and spoil what's been a lovely couple of hours."

"I need to get back too but I've time to see *The Merry Widow* home," said James, humming a short melody from the operetta.

"Isn't that the final waltz?" said Patsy. "Very appropriate for a merry widow tripping home from her husband's funeral. You must be a musical man?"

"Not particularly but I do have a love of opera and classical music. I could take you along the next time there's a concert on in Dublin, not that there are many operas staged here. Kathleen, my wife, she hates opera and classical music in general, she reckons it's all too way above her and posh. She's been to one or two concerts with me but I'm afraid I failed to convert her. Even the Spanish drama of *Carmen* hit the wrong note when we went to see it in Cork. It was Peter who used to accompany me, he was a real classical music and opera fanatic, so I've lost my regular companion, you'd be doing me a favour if you came. Jem said you were a one for all sorts of music. Perhaps you'd like to come to one of the Friday evening concerts in St Francis Xavier Hall, they're free, which is always an advantage, but they're quite good. The conductor's from Budapest, I think."

"I'd love that," said Patsy, "I didn't even know about them but I suppose that was perhaps because Jem went with Peter sometimes too."

They took a taxi back to Patsy's house but James didn't linger "Let me know if Jem gets in touch," he said. "I've always wondered what's on the other side."

Patsy was glad to plonk herself down in a chair and put her feet up.

The house had an almost tangible permanent stillness to it now that Jem was buried, there was a finality to it, a sense that this was it, this was how it was going to be. She thanked God that Jem was no longer suffering and asked that he be allowed into heaven without too much delay in purgatory, despite his earthly inclinations, and she prayed for the strength to manage on her own: she had never before lived alone and the thought of starting that so suddenly was scary.

All the same it had been a sad but not miserable day and she was already looking forward to a musical outing with a new but unexpected friend. She started thinking of what to do now that she was a widow, of what changes to the house she could make to give it a fresh look and cheer herself up after Jem's confinement — God forgive her, the man was only just put in his grave — but first of all she needed desperately to go to the toilet, all that drink had filled her bladder to bursting point.

She hurried out to the lavatory; it was hard trying to run with her legs virtually crossed and even harder pulling down her drawers quickly enough to avoid spillage and she sat down on the seat more than a little relieved. It was a shit-hole, she thought looking at the bare brick walls and the chipped concrete floor, there was no other word for it. Then she suddenly hit on the perfect idea of what to do with her new freedom: she would decorate the outside lavatory and flush away all the unpleasant memories of emptying and scrubbing shitty chamber-pots. "I'm going to reclaim the toilet," she said out loud and giggled, "I'm going to decorate the outside toilet and make it the most luxurious outside toilet that anyone could imagine." Pleased and amused at the audacity of her decision, she went back into the house and poured herself a drink. When the alcohol finally took its toll and she fell fast asleep, Patsy had a strange dream of Jem up in heaven conducting an orchestra of angels and her sitting in the front row with Peter.

Part 5

Things said or done long years ago,
Or things I did not do or say
But thought that I might say or do,
Weigh me down, and not a day
But something is recalled,
My conscience or my vanity appalled

— W B Yeats

1

There was a distinct sickly yellow-grey feel about the house. The commode had gone back to the second-hand shop and the lingering smell of the thing, and its previous contents, had nearly dissipated but even a couple of months after Jem's passing there was still a sense of the intensive care unit about the place. Patsy had decided to go out and buy the biggest bouquet of flowers she could afford, big enough to have a small arrangement in the parlour, which had been reclaimed after its spell as a bedroom, and a larger bunch in the backroom, where she spent most of her time. In the florist's, she had chosen a mixture of flowers in warm colours, rich reds and sunshine yellows and royal purples, to add at least a hint of vibrancy to the house. She stopped in front of her shop-window and unconsciously moved both her head and the bouquet this way and that as if trying out different poses. Then suddenly she was stopped in her tracks as she looked at herself and froze at the recognition of a lonely woman with little to look forward to. It was a wonder the flowers didn't wilt in her arms there and then. It was expecting too much that a bunch of cheerful blooms would change anything, she was thinking, when a cheerful voice interrupted her dreadful silence.

"A special day, is it, Missus?" she heard, at the same time seeing the reflection of a scruffy lad sidling up to her on the pavement. "I thought maybe it was, what with the flowers you're carrying. You don't often see such a beautiful bunch walking down the street unless it's a special occasion."

"It is indeed a special day," said Patsy, who had always felt an innate respect for the young, particularly the poor young. She hated the way most people dismissed them with a cuff or a derisory word as if the children were already up to no good and not worth the time of day. "I decided to treat myself and the flowers are my treat." She greeted the boy with a warm smile.

"You're much too pretty to have to treat yourself to flowers,

Missus," he said, affecting a flirtatious note in his comment.

"And you're much too young to be approaching a strange woman in the street and trying to sweet-talk her," said Patsy. "What is it you're up to? Begging, is it?"

"No, Missus, I just liked the flowers, I swear that's all it was, but a penny wouldn't go amiss. Perhaps I could buy my mammy a flower too."

"Does your mammy like flowers?"

"She does, she loves flowers, but we never have any proper ones in the house, only a few wild ones I pick for her in the park, sometimes, or from along the side of the canal."

"And does she like those?"

"Well, she always hugs me when I give them to her and says how precious they are, as if they were a bouquet as beautiful as yours, but I know she's only pretending. What are a few dandelions other than a few dandelions?"

"It's the thought of you picking them for her that makes those dandelions so precious. Did you not think of that?"

"I suppose."

"Next time you pick some, you should look at the dandelions in your hand and you'll see what beautiful flowers they are too, with their proud little heads of fine yellow petals, splaying out like a burst of sunshine in the dirt that gradually turns into a delicate fluffy little ball that you can hold up to the light and see through and then blow away into the wind to tell the time. I'd like to know who decided dandelions were just weeds. If you lived in the desert, a few clumps of dandelions would be a wonder in their own right, don't you think?"

"I've never been to the desert but now that you mention it, Missus, I can imagine how pretty dandelions would look growing up out of all that sand."

"If you promise me, you'll always try to remember that image, then I'll give you a few flowers out of my bunch for your mammy, would you like that?"

"I would and I promise to remember," said the lad. "I like you, Missus, you can forget I asked for a penny."

Patsy carefully pulled a few blooms out of her arrangement and took off the small ribbon that held them neatly in place. "You hold my flowers while I tie these up nicely for your mammy," she said.

"Aren't you frightened I'll run off with them all? Most people would be."

"Well, if you do," said Patsy, "then we've both of us lost a new friend and you shouldn't lose new friends so carelessly, you should look after them and hope they become old friends." She finished the ribbon with a nice bow and handed them to the boy. "There," she said. "Now your mammy might get a bit suspicious when you give them to her so you must tell her that a kind woman in the street gave them to you because she wanted to share her happy day. Tell her it was a Mrs Murphy who was celebrating just being alive. Will you do that?"

"I will, she's going to love them, Mrs Murphy, and we'll all be able to enjoy looking at them in the jar."

"I'm sure they'll bring a lovely splash of colour into the room," said Patsy. "And who have I been talking to? What's your name, young man?"

"I'm Sean," he said.

"Is that so? Well, young Sean, you've a good strong Irish name there so here's a penny for you too as you've been such excellent company."

"You don't have to give me a penny. We're friends now."

"The penny is from one friend to another, to buy a little treat, a present from one friend to another. Off with you now so your mammy can get the flowers into water before they start to droop. She's lucky to have such a good son, I would have liked one just like you."

Patsy watched as the boy ran off, holding the stems of the flowers carefully in one hand and protecting the heads with the other. She was ridiculously pleased when he stopped and turned to give her a wave before heading off round the corner. His sudden appearance in front of the shop-window had managed to dispel the fear of loneliness that had crept over her at the thought of taking her flowers home to an empty house: the sudden shiver had been replaced by an inner glow which stayed with her all the way home. Even putting the key in the door no longer seemed to echo and for the first time in months she walked down the short hallway without dreading taking that first step into the back room: the commode was long gone and so was Jem but today his absence seemed less heavy. She fetched a couple of vases and arranged the flowers.

405

"All right then, yes, I am in a good mood, I made a new friend today," she said in the general direction of what had been Jem's chair while she was putting a match to the fire. "You would have liked him, a young boy named Sean. Of course, the name wouldn't mean as much to you as to me, all that was before your time, but that's not really the point. The point is that he was a nice young boy, good to his mammy. I gave him a few flowers to give her. Mammies are important. I don't remember my real mammy too well, I just have particular memories of her. I still hear her playing the piano, she'd a gentle touch on the keys. And I remember how she used to share out a piece of fruit between us all and we'd feel it was a great treat. Lizzie was her name. And I remember the day she died in my arms. Of course I didn't know she was dead, I was only a child, I thought she was asleep lying there with her head on my knee and not moving. But I've probably told you all this before."

Patsy tended to the fire, holding a sheet of newspaper in front of the grate to suck the flames into life. It was something you always did, people always did, but she was always wary after a couple of occasions in which the newspaper itself had caught fire and thrown her into a bit of panic. It had happened once when she was a girl out at Larch Hill and her favourite doll had been blackened beyond repair and Patsy had had a healthy fear of fire ever since. She was extra careful since Jem had died, knowing she'd have to cope with any sudden blaze herself if the newspaper caught and had to be bundled into the grate quickly.

"Did I mention I've plans to turn the outside lavatory into a small palace?" she said. "I think I deserve it after all the shit I had to put up with. God forgive me, I'm getting very careless with my language. It won't really be a palace, of course, it's only a small toilet after all, there's not much space in there for creativity, but it's going to be very special. I haven't decided yet on exactly what I'm going to do but I'll definitely buy a new bowl and cistern. They're sending men into outer space and I'm still flushing the toilet with a worn wooden knob on the end of a bit of old rope. And after all the flushing away of Jem's contributions even the bit of rope has become little more than a frayed length of string, you can all but count the fibres. I'm surprised you put up with it all these years and didn't think about having a proper bathroom put in upstairs, especially knowing how you always loved a bit of class. Of course you

406

might have thought about it in the past, how would I know. I suppose lack of space is always the problem in these old houses. Maybe that's why you had so many fancy evenings out at restaurants, so you could use their facilities, I know I always did when we went out; I'd have had a proper bath there, given the chance, which of course I wasn't. But I made sure to make the most of what was on offer; I loved the handle-flushers and the lovely clean sinks with hot running water and fancy pink soaps and bottles of nice smellies to perfume the place and the boxes of pretty tissues always on the side for the customers to use when they wanted to delicately dab the corners of their freshly-painted lips. I'd put on a fresh coat just for the excuse of using one of the tissues. Isn't that just too silly? Anyway, I won't be doing much of that any more, no, I won't be doing that at all any more, so I won't. God rest your soul, Jem, but you'd no business leaving me a widow so soon, you and your fancy man."

There were so many magazines about home interiors to choose from in the newsagents that Patsy ended up spending much longer in the shop than she had intended. The proprietor was beginning to give her funny glances as she flicked through the pages of various publications, no doubt convinced she was reading his stock for free with no intention of parting with any money.

Her problem was not with forking out any money but on which magazine to fork it out on. She wanted ideas for wall colour combinations and fittings for a modern bathroom, hoping to get inspiration for her new project. Of course all she really needed to investigate were the latest fittings available for a toilet, she didn't have a bathroom, so she might as well have gone straight to a plumber's shop but that wouldn't have been any fun. Patsy finally made her magazine choice and surprised the shop-owner by buying not one but two magazines when she added a movie glossy to her home interiors purchase. His cold glance was replaced by a customer-special smile.

"Enjoy your decorating and do come again," he said as he gave Patsy her change. "I myself hate the whole business of painting and all the mess it involves but my wife loves to linger over the magazines, just as yourself, and then it's me who has to get busy putting her latest fad into practice."

"Did I linger too long, do you think?" said Patsy directly. "You seemed to look at me a bit suspicious."

"Not at all," he said. "A fine lady such as yourself is entitled to take her time making her choice. Mind you, it's true that we do get people coming in to read what's on the shelves and then they march out, bold as brass, without having bought a thing. How they think that will help us stay in business I can't imagine. But my wife tells me that I have developed that very suspicious look that you mentioned, and she says it's almost become my natural expression and not a very attractive one, God forgive me. The need to watch the coppers is a hard thing indeed, especially under the critical gaze of my good wife."

Patsy left the shop and decided to treat herself to a Bewley's coffee and do a bit more lingering over her magazines, after all she had no reason to rush home any more, no one's dinner to get on the table, no one to tell her about his day or to ask about her day, no day to share with anyone, just an empty chair.

It was a slightly different crowd in the coffee house than she was used to, there was little glamour and scant posing going on; instead the Saturday afternoon clientele was much like herself these days, women past their prime but still eager to be out in the city, smartly-dressed from the most conservative shops — there were several tweedy suits in evidence — and Patsy noticed one woman in particular, decked out in a fur coat, her lips brightly but carelessly painted in a cupid's-bow flamboyance. Then she realised it was none other than Nora, Molly's old friend, sitting comfortable and relaxed and perfectly at home in what were obviously familiar surroundings. Nora was smoking tipped cigarettes, the filter well-stained from the thickness of her lipstick, and she sat happily bobbing about in her seat to the background music as her eyes wandered around the room. Patsy was about to signal to Nora when a woman approached her own table and blocked her sightline.

"Is it Patsy O'Kelly of The Coombe?" she asked, and Patsy recognised Mrs Doran, the midwife, now needing a stick to help her walk, her back and shoulders so hunched over they upset the balance on the poor woman's legs.

"Mrs Doran, hello," said Patsy standing up. "I've not seen you in a long time. I thought you must have moved away for good. Would you

408

like to join me? I'll order you a coffee or is it tea you prefer?" she held out a chair for the woman.

"I'll just sit down for a minute or two, Patsy, I'm actually meeting my daughter here but I'm a little bit early. I'm so slow at getting round these days that sometimes I over-compensate and leave the house much too soon and then the bus comes on time and speeds along and I arrive ahead of time, like today. It's become a weekly fixture for us both, meeting here, an opportunity to catch up, mother and daughter. I get to see Déaglán during the week: he's busy in his parish of course but I try to get over to St Kevin's for morning Mass if he's on duty and if my knees aren't playing me up too much. Thanks be to God we're all still close."

"Are you telling me your son's a priest at St Kevin's? In Portobello?" asked Patsy. "Sure that's my parish, it must be Father Dec then?"

"That's what the parishioners call him," said Mrs Doran. "I do too in front of them, I think that's only right, to maintain that respectful distance between priest and laiety, otherwise he's still just Déaglán to me."

"Well, I'm glad your prayers were answered and you got a son into the priesthood," said Patsy. "And isn't it grand that you have such a regular arrangement with your daughter."

"We try never to cancel the arrangement, it's only once a week after all and life is so busy these days that you have to be firm with yourself and set aside time for family and reflection, don't you think?"

"I do," said Patsy. "Years ago, I used to come here every Tuesday evening with a friend of mine, that was a fixture too for a long time, our girls' night out, we'd call it. We'd feel very independent, very modern. We'd have something to eat and drink here and then we'd go to the pictures. I'm sorry to say that most of our reflections were concentrated more on the Hollywood gossip scale of importance than anything worthwhile but they were precious times."

"God is at his most kind when he puts such good friendship our way," said Mrs Doran." I know you used to help out at the Little Flower Penny Dinners café with Mary, Mrs Flaherty, do you remember her?" asked Mrs Doran. "I used to deliver babies with her, including some of your mother's, if I'm not mistaken? Mary and I were great friends, God

409

bless her, even though we didn't always see eye to eye on what you might call Church matters, though it was actually in church that we met. I remember she had a real jaunty knitted hat on that I couldn't take my eyes off — of course we were very poor in those days and a jaunty hat was something to behold — and she noticed me looking at her and admiring her hat as we filed out of the pews after the last blessing. Do you know, the very next Sunday she gave me one that she had knitted herself out of bits of wool she managed to get her hands on? 'Now this is a good woman,' I thought to myself. We were friends ever since."

"That sounds like the Mrs Flaherty I know. We became very close working together at the café and I couldn't have managed without her constant help when my husband was sick," said Patsy. "I'm sorry to admit that I haven't seen her since his funeral a few months ago. Time seems to have taken on a muffled feel since he passed, what with having to burn all the bedding and his clothes and scrub the house from top to bottom — he had been quite ill, poor man. I hardly had the time to properly mourn his going and then there was all the matters to sort out with his bank. Since then I seem to have just been drifting along in a daze. I never even gave the café a thought, God forgive me, but I'll make it my business to call in and help Mrs Flaherty again this week, I'll get myself back on to her kitchen rota, I'm sure she would still appreciate the help."

"I'm sure she would if she were there, Patsy. You obviously haven't heard," said Mrs Doran, her eyes moistening. "Mary herself passed away these two weeks back, it was very sudden, God rest her soul. All that hard work she did all her life for her family and others finally took its toll. She died peacefully in her sleep, so that's a blessing to thank God for, she never suffered or got ill, God just took her soul one night up into heaven. I'm sure she'd go straight there and Saint Peter would open the gates wide for her, none of that purgatory nonsense for Mary Flaherty, she was too good a woman and thought only of other people, never of herself, all the time I knew her. I miss her terribly and, you know, I even miss the bit of irreverence she always had. I'm sure half the time it was just to keep me on my toes for she was as Christian a woman as you could ever wish to meet."

Patsy felt incredibly sad, both for Mrs Flaherty's passing and for her own guilt at having lost touch, and also for the terrible loss evident in Mrs Doran's grief. Patsy stretched out her hand and gently squeezed her companion's arm. "I am so sorry, I wish I had known, I've been so out of touch, unforgivably so," she said. "Where is she buried? I can at least go and visit her grave."

"She's out in Glasnevin but I'm afraid I can't tell you which is the grave site, you'd have to ask in the little office there. I hate to have been the bearer of bad news, Patsy. I didn't know the two of you had become so close. However much she liked to talk, Mary was never the one to gossip."

"We've both lost a true friend," said Patsy. "I wish to God I'd gone to see her before it was too late. She put herself out so much to help me and Jem and then what did I do to say 'thanks'? I just stopped calling in to see her, may God forgive me."

"I'm sure Mary would have understood your circumstances. Your husband died, you said?"

"He did, after being sick for a long time. Towards the end he couldn't leave the house or look after himself and, of course, I had to keep my job going but Mrs Flaherty used to call to the house every day to see to his needs."

"That sounds just like Mary. Thank God there are people like her in the world or where would we be. I had another friend died too recently," said Mrs Doran. "I suppose we're all heading the same way."

"Was it another good friend who passed?"

"Yes, she was, we'd been friends since schooldays and we stayed close all our lives, thanks be to God. She had been a widow for years, her husband died back in 1920, I think it was, God rest his soul, and she never had good health herself, but she wasn't on her own; God had blessed her with a devoted son and he really looked after his mammy, even when his own three children came along. Well of course they all lived together in quite a big modern house, so that was some help, what with all the convenient fittings they have these days and the daughter-in-law being on hand to help out. A nice girl he married. They'd a big wedding, I remember, the same weekend as the Ecumenical Congress and that must have been a good sign, I always thought, getting married during such a holy time in the city, though to be honest with you at the time I was slightly cross that I had a wedding to go to and had to miss the big service in Phoenix Park. That must have been quite a grand occasion. Did you manage to get to it yourself? Oh," said Mrs Doran glancing over towards the door, "there's my daughter just come in now, just in time to stop the conversation getting too bogged down in the past. That's what I have to be careful of at my age, looking back too much, we've all got to carry on as best we can with the life God gave us, isn't that right, Patsy? So, I'll be wishing you good day and thanking you for your company while I was waiting. I really must try to get my timing right."

"I'm glad it wasn't right today," replied Patsy with a smile, "otherwise we might have missed each other. I'll remember you to Mrs Flaherty when I go out to the cemetery. Look after yourself, now."

Mrs Doran went to join her daughter at another table and Patsy was alone again. Her coffee had gone cold and her cream bun seemed to have soured on the table. She pretended to flick through her magazines but they too seemed to have lost their gloss after all Mrs Doran's news.

Patsy quickly gathered together her things and left the café, in too much of a hurry to hear Nora calling to her and then rapping on the window to catch her attention as she rushed by. Patsy wanted to be home, preferably without the bother of the journey to get there.

2

Ireland was reeling. Just five months after his triumphant visit and motorcade parade through Dublin, where he had been welcomed and cheered by tens of thousands of ecstatic people, President Kennedy had been fatally shot in another motorcade, this time in a US city, his poor wife clutching his bullet-ridden body as his heart pumped out the life-blood from him in the back of their car. No one could believe it, the Catholic President assassinated without mercy or regard for the goodness of the man, for the feeling of hope his religious faith had brought to the world. Hadn't he saved that world from a nuclear war? The whole nation was stunned. It was experienced as a very personal loss, as if one of Ireland's own true sons had been gunned down. A National Day of Mourning was declared and special services and Masses were held in churches throughout the country, rosaries were offered up in practically every home and night lights were kept burning before statues of the Sacred Heart and Our Lady. President Kennedy's death had brought Ireland to its knees. Patsy had queued for hours with other mourners at the US Embassy in Merrion Square, each anxious to register their acute sense of sorrow in a book of condolences. There was little talking as they waited, only hushed whispers, memories exchanged of his beautiful smile, of how he waved back to the crowds so enthusiastically as he drove through the city, of how much safer they all felt with him in the White House especially after seeing what a fine man he was in the flesh, of how at-home he looked during his visit. The general feeling was that he should have stayed 'at home'. Once inside the embassy, emotions took over and the condolence book filled with shakily penned messages, as if everyone had forgotten how to write. The ink was splotched with the wet of tears, including those of Patsy, whose faith had been momentarily tested that God would have allowed such a terrible thing to happen. Too many people were dying before their time.

"Oh, dear God, what is it you've decided on this time?" was the question that beset her mind the following day, though she immediately recoiled at what sounded like a bad-tempered challenge to the Almighty. All the same she wondered if there was to be no end to the misery as she frantically slipped her key in the lock at The Coombe. Betty had sent her an urgent message to say that Patrick had been taken ill and was in hospital. Patsy had rushed round to the house immediately, her mind filling with questions about what might have happened to her father.

"What's the matter, Mammy? Is it serious?" she asked as she flung open the door into the back room.

"Patsy, thank God you're here," said Betty, who was trapped at the kitchen table with Annie's son Tommy on her knee. He was playing with some toy soldiers on the table, concentrating on his imaginary war game and oblivious to the panic in the room, and he managed but a garbled greeting to his Auntie Patsy as she walked in. "Annie's already at the hospital and I thought perhaps you could go in and relieve her so she can get home to the children. Your daddy kept asking for you when I was there earlier but I couldn't get a message to you sooner. Patsy, the doctors don't seem to know how long he might have."

"Jesus, Mary and Joseph, but what is it?"

"It's something to do with a bit of shrapnel that has been in his body all these years," said Betty. "To be honest I don't understand it all. They said something about a splinter of metal that had been lodged in some soft tissue in his body and after all this time it has now caused a tumour to grow in his chest. Here, I wrote down the name they called it somewhere. Can you get off my knee now, Tommy, I need to look for something for Patsy." The child grumbled and slid on to the floor making dramatic moaning sounds as if he had just been shot as part of his game. "Will you stop that now, Tommy," said Betty, the tone of her voice telling him that this wasn't an order to be disobeyed, even if in his game he was the general. She rummaged around on the mantelpiece and retrieved a slip of paper for Patsy.

"Malignant fibrous histiocytoma," Patsy enunciated slowly. "I've never heard of that."

"Nor me but I do know what a tumour is and that's what it is in ordinary language," said Betty, "and this one is evidently bad enough to have its own name."

"Can't the doctors just remove the shrapnel and the tumour?"

"They can but they say that sort of major surgery into his chest could be quite dangerous for a man of your daddy's age and fitness. We all know he's been sitting in his chair too much these past few years. We should never have got rid of the pigeons, at least they kept him going up and down the ladder regularly. The blasted bit of metal has been in him all this time and now he's perhaps too old to have it taken out. I don't know what to do, Patsy, the doctors need permission to go ahead and operate or not and they need to know soon."

"And what does Da say?"

"You know your daddy, he doesn't say anything, he just lies there suffering in silence and we all know how sullen he can be when he sets his mind to it. Maybe that's why he's anxious to see you, Patsy, perhaps he'd prefer to talk to you about it than to me. It was hard enough for me to get him to see the doctor but in the end he couldn't deny the pain he was in and he couldn't pretend there was no big swelling when we could all see it with our own eyes. It was strange, Patsy, the lump was very warm when you touched it. Sometimes I thought I could see it growing bigger right in front of me."

"I'll go to the hospital now," said Patsy. "Does John know? Has he been in to see Da yet?"

"He's working a double-shift at the bakery today to make up for yesterday's short hours for the day of mourning but I've told Eileen to let him know."

"Is she going to go to the bakery to tell him?"

"She is but she has to wait until the children get home from school."

"I tell you what, Mammy," said Patsy, "I'll take a taxi to the hospital and go via the bakery to collect John. You and Tommy can call round to let Eileen know she needn't rush out with the little ones, it's a long walk for them anyway. When John and I have had a word with the doctors, we can decide whether we need to get in touch with the family or not. We could do with a telephone. How much easier it would all be if everyone still lived in Dublin."

Patsy walked up to Hanover Street hoping to catch a taxi and was in luck: one pulled in after only a few minutes of waiting and she was soon walking into the once-familiar entrance to the bakery. Primarily she was worried about her father but still a wave of memories and Sean washed over her — how could they not? — and she struggled to push it all to the back of her mind. She was recognised by one or two of the by now old hands and was bombarded with best wishes for Mr O'Kelly as someone went to fetch John. The anonymous image of him appearing in a whitened silhouette in the doorway, covered in flour dust, made Patsy's heart jump instinctively but any fleeting memories of happier days and another flour-dusted silhouette were buried as she hastily told her brother about their father being in hospital.

"I've got my scooter out the back," said John. His Vespa was a bit battered now but John still lavished attention on what he referred to as his 'collector's item'. "I'll just tell the foreman I'm going to have to leave it here overnight, it should be safe enough. Unless you fancy hopping on the back, Patsy? We'd get to the hospital quicker."

"We might but I might not get there in one piece and then there'd be your father and me to worry about. There's a taxi waiting and the meter's running, so you need to hurry," called Patsy.

"Here now," said the office manager as John went to see to his scooter. The manager took some money out of the petty-cash tin and handed it over as a contribution other than flowers to Mr O'Kelly's hospital stay. Patsy couldn't help thinking of what John had said about Tommy Byrne and his gossip, they obviously still talked about the same Mr O'Kelly making a young baker's life so unbearable back in the day that the young man had quit his job.

"Thank you, if you're sure now, that's very kind," she said accepting the money from the manager. "I'll be sure to tell my daddy and pass on everyone's good wishes. It's a great help, so it is, taxis aren't the cheapest way of getting about but sometimes we have no alternative. I suppose I could have climbed on to the back of John's scooter but it wouldn't have been either easy or a pretty sight — I'm wearing a very straight skirt."

It took best part of half an hour for the taxi to weave its way through the city traffic but finally they arrived at the hospital. Patsy and John were directed down a long green corridor to a small but bright side room where they found their father, decked out in a crisp hospital nightgown with a small all-over dot pattern, lying almost to attention in a well-tucked bed: various machines were plugged in and connected to Patrick who hadn't yet worked out how to move without disconnecting them. Annie was looking out of the large window which gave a panoramic view over Dublin and she was attempting to make small talk with her father, describing all the places of interest she could see and relating anecdotes of things she remembered doing in the different places as a child, but Patrick just lay there, staring up at the ceiling and giving poor Annie no encouragement whatsoever in her efforts. She raised her eyebrows with relief when Patsy and John walked in. Patrick merely stared at them and put up with their hugs and gushes of sympathy.

"I'm not sure if he's really with us or not," said Annie in a whisper to Patsy: it wasn't unknown for their father to hear everything even when he pretended a total lack of interest or was supposedly otherwise occupied, in this case with John's undivided solicitations. "He hasn't said much. He even ignored the doctors when they came in to examine him again for the umpteenth time. He just lay there and let them get on with their probings and listenings. I don't know whether or not he knows where he is or, if he does, he just doesn't care. Patsy, I think he wants to go, I think that's what it is."

"He's a stubborn enough man to have made up his own mind even on when to die," said Patsy. "You go on home now and see to the children, Annie, it's hard for Mammy right now having to look after little Tommy while she's so worried. Tell her I'll call in on the way back from the hospital. I assume Matt's away on some sort of business, is he?"

"You know Matt," said Annie. "I'd be the last person to know. He's not at The Coombe, that's for sure. He'll just turn up unannounced, as he does, with a wallet full of money, though I have to admit it does come in handy. I just don't ask where he gets it." She put on her coat and gave her father a farewell squeeze of the hand. She was surprised when he actually looked her in the eye and squeezed back. She was sure she detected a sneaky smile. "You're an old fraud so you are, Daddy," she said. "I'll be in tomorrow to see you. Perhaps I'll bring Marie and Michael and Tommy to entertain their granddad. They might have more success than me." She couldn't tell if his expression suggested that that would be a good idea or whether it was wry resignation to the inevitable.

Not long after Annie had left, Patrick put a hand on John's arm. "You go home to your wife and children too," he said. "I'm happy that you came all this way to see me, I've been blessed with good sons and daughters, but I want to talk to Patsy. Give my love to Eileen."

"I will. And all the men at work send their best wishes, Da," said John affectionately. "They even paid for our taxi here so you've not to expect any flowers, they said. I'll try to pop in tomorrow. We're on double shifts at the moment but you're well respected at the bakery still, revered almost, which always amuses me knowing what an old tyrant you can be. Anyway, I can't imagine them refusing to let Mr O'Kelly's son off for a few hours to visit the man in hospital. Shall I bring you a few cakes in?"

"That would be nice, as long as the nurses let me eat them. I think maybe they've put me on a special diet," said Patrick, "they don't want to feed the lump. You'd best go now. It'll take time getting home on the bus."

"I'll see you and your lump tomorrow," said John. "Have a good night's sleep if you can in this place. Hospitals are always far too lit up even at night. You'd think they'd see enough of the sick during the day without having the spotlights on them all night too. I'll have a word with them on the way out."

John hugged Patsy, gave a sympathetic smile and left the room, shutting the door gently behind him as he gave a last wave through the little window. Patrick beckoned Patsy to bring the chair over to sit next to him. "My voice isn't as strong as it used to be," he said, gripping her with that powerful strength that the elderly sick always seem to muster, however serious their condition. His fingers were like pincers clamped on to Patsy's arm.

"Now Daddy, what are we going to do about you?" she said.

"That's what I want to talk to you about. You of all the O'Kellys have a way of looking at things in black and white, Patsy, and that's what's needed now, an appreciation of the situation in black and white. Betty gets far too upset for a proper discussion but we all have to be realistic," said Patrick. His voice trailed off. "I have to be realistic."

He sucked in on his lips and a look of resignation and despair shadowed his face, the face of a man who was used to being strong and in control but now found himself helpless and totally reliant on others, on strangers in white coats who bustled about with instruments and folders and a knowledge that was beyond his simple grasp. He looked lost and drained, as if he had deserted himself. Patsy suddenly, for the first time, recognised that her father had become an old man, shrunken before her. How had she not noticed it before? She almost cried.

"The way the doctor has explained it to me is this," he said looking at her, speaking slowly but forcing his voice to sound matter of fact. "The biopsy showed that the tumour is cancerous, and they can operate to remove the lump and the metal but that wouldn't be any guarantee that the cancer wouldn't return. It's highly possible it has already spread beyond what they can see, so I'd have to have more tests to find out and then perhaps more treatment, whatever that might entail, maybe more hours of surgery and then more tests again. The fact is that they can't cure cancer, we all know that, you know it and, more to the point, I know it; there is no cure, that's the black and white of it. And all this testing and treating and recuperating could go on for months and months and still with no guarantee at the end. I'd never be a well man again, just a patient trying to get by on diminishing hope. What sort of a life would that be? I'm not a young man, Patsy. My body can't fight back like it used to. It's old and tired. I'm tired too. I've not always been a good man, as you yourself know, and the past catches up in the end, so they say. I might be at my end now. I've been responsible for other men's deaths and perhaps the time has come for me to be responsible for my own, or at least to let the cancer take its natural course."

Patsy started to interrupt with what she hoped would be encouragement but Patrick shushed her.

"Let me just finish," he said, "I need to talk about it, it helps me to clarify in my own head what I'm faced with." He paused and signalled to his daughter that his mouth was dry for want of a drink of water.

"The immediate thing would be the initial operation," he continued, "which the doctors say would take a few hours, and then there would be what they call a post-operative period, during which time I'd be living what sounds to me like a no-life sort of existence." A hint of the absolute determination for which Patrick was well known returned momentarily: "I've never been a dependant man and I'll not start being one now," he said. "So, after this post-operative period, the next set of tests would start and the whole cycle would begin again, the whats, the ifs, the discomfort, the helpless humiliation of being little more than a human specimen on which tests are performed and assessed and reperformed and then assessed again and all the while the family trying to cheer me at my bedside instead of getting on with their own lives."

He sipped more water.

"And there you have it, Patsy, that's the way things are, and I don't know whether I'm up for all that. I don't know whether I want to go through all that... palaver." He smiled at the use of the word. "That's the situation I find myself in, that's the situation which I can decide to accept or reject," he said. He looked directly at Patsy and then turned his face away, never easing his grip on her arm as his eyes swept over every insignificant detail in the room.

"But you can't give up, Daddy," said Patsy. "If the doctors think the operation might work, then surely it's worth a try."

"Sure the doctors never actually say what they think as such, they only tell you what the options are and the possible outcomes and potential complications. They give advice on the whys and the wherefores, all right, but they're very careful not to commit to an actual opinion on what you should do, they want you to make up your own mind."

"And have you made up your mind?"

"I have," said Patrick, his eyes rheumy. "I've had a good life, Patsy, a long-enough life. I don't want to end it as an invalid, traipsing backwards and forwards to the hospital and dragging poor Betty and the rest of you along in the wake, if you'll forgive the unintended reference. I don't want people having to wait on me hand and foot. You had enough of that with Jem and he was a much younger man than I am."

"And does it not matter to you what your family thinks? Doesn't it matter that we would all urge you to have the surgery and at least take the chance that it would be successful? Put your trust in God, Daddy."

"God owes me nothing," he said, "but I love you all and I owe each and every one of you for the life we've shared together. You've all been on the receiving end of my stubbornness, you in particular, Patsy, God forgive me, but I'm going to exert my will this one last time and I'm relying on you to explain my wishes to Betty and to your sisters and brothers. Will you do that for me? That one last thing?"

"I've never liked the word 'last'," said Patsy, "it's too final."

"Surely you can understand my feelings?"

"I can but I don't want to," said Patsy. "I can't imagine not having you here."

"Not having me here to ruin your life a bit more?" he said.

"We've been over that before, Daddy, and I don't blame you any more now than I did the last time we talked about it. You said you hadn't been a good man but I don't believe that for a minute. What you did fighting for Ireland and what you believed in was good, was it not? You gave us a grand life when we were children in the country: that was what a good man, a good father, would do. Your heart was broken when Mammy died but you married a wonderful woman so your daughters would have a mother, you refused to put us in that orphanage; again, that's what a good man would do and that's what you did."

"We did have an idyllic life out at Larch Hill, didn't we, though we all worked hard for it. Even you youngsters waited on table when the people in the big house were having one of their so-called dinner-parties, and Lizzie, God rest her soul, probably worked harder than any of us and then didn't have the physical strength left to get over the consumption," said Patrick. "As regards fighting for Ireland, that's what set me on the downward path I could never climb up from. Sure, we fought for our independence and at the time that was something to be proud of but it came at a cost to us all, we became murderers, killers, as if someone's life meant nothing just because he was on the opposite side of the fence — or was suspected of being. I'm so sorry about Sean Fitzimmons's father, Patsy. Not that it's only us Irish. Look what's just gone on in America: what sort of stupid people shoot their President?" he said. "Where was the sense in that? Where is the sense in any of the violence we perpetuate against each other? There's no sense: no humane sense; no religious sense; no political sense and yet we still do it and I've been as guilty as anyone, God forgive me. You must pray hard for my eternal soul when I've gone, Patsy, I know I can rely on you for that despite what I've done."

The door opened and a nurse arrived to check on her patient, putting an end to the conversation. "And how are you this evening, Mr O'Kelly, still playing hard-to-please?" she said. "And you'll maybe be Patsy, the daughter he's been waiting all day to see?" she said turning to Patsy.

421

"Well, he might be in a better mood now that he's seen you. I've to make your father comfortable for the night now so I'm afraid visiting is over for today. You can come back tomorrow after the doctors have done their rounds."

The nurse busied herself with the paraphernalia to take Patrick's blood pressure and temperature and he immediately sank back into his human specimen mode.

"We'll talk more tomorrow, Daddy," said Patsy. "Please don't do anything silly before then."

"I can't imagine Mr O'Kelly ever doing anything silly," said the nurse, "he's one of our quieter patients."

"You'd be surprised just how silly this man can be," said Patsy, leaving the room quickly so that her father wouldn't see how upset she was. She hurried down the hospital corridor, anxious to get out into the street as quickly as possible and was relieved to see a queue at the bus-stop: a bus was obviously due. People were chatting as they waited, some in lowered tones about loved ones sick in the hospital across the road, others happily oblivious to the worries consuming their fellow passengers. Patsy herself was replaying her father's reasoning over his decision not to have the operation and his heart-breaking plea for her to explain his wishes to the family.

She called in to The Coombe as promised after the hospital visit but she stayed only long enough to tell Betty that Patrick had agreed to have the operation. They had now to wait for the doctors to set the date but it would be sooner rather than later, babbled Patsy: they wanted to get the tumour out to prevent further complications. Betty was overjoyed, Patsy was full of guilt at betraying her father's possibly dying wish. She prayed hard, begging God to intercede to change Patrick's mind so that her deception, which was meant well, would be at least only temporary.

Once home, she set the fire and put a match to it, hoping that this evening it wouldn't be reluctant in its catching. The week's catalogue of bad news had left her cold and chilled and she wanted nothing more than to sit in front of the hot coals. She made a pot of tea and sat down, staring into the grate: the wood was succumbing to the first flames and the tell-tale spits and crackles of successful ignition were music to her ears.

"I suppose I should tell you all about the day but I haven't the heart just yet," she said, addressing Jem's chair. She supped on the tea and had a biscuit. "I know you want to know but you'll have to wait. Just be patient." She laughed. "Be patient? That's a funny thing for me to say in the circumstances, as if I haven't spent enough time today surrounded by people who can't be anything but patient right now. Patients have to be patient, they've no choice in the matter, they're patients, unless of course they want to scream and rant against the holy quiet of the wards. My father's not the one for that sort of behaviour, of course, but dear God I wish he'd be a bit more patient right now. He's decided to just give up and die."

Patsy poured herself another cup of tea. "Everyone's gone or going," she said aloud. "If they're not dead or dying they're away living in a different country, so the effect is the same, they've gone." She looked around the room and shook her head. "And I'm left with you for company," she said towards the chair, "not even Jem but his mother, my mother-in-law. God must have had fun with that old joke. It's certainly on me, all right, I didn't see that one coming, but I suppose it was always your house, yours and Jem's, and now you have to share it with me." She lit a cigarette.

"Tell me, I've always wondered: did you know about your son and his preference for men? You didn't, you say? Well at least you were spared that. A woman such as yourself, a lady, I should say, though from humble stock, as I believe, a lady nonetheless, would have found all that rather hard to accept. And here's me accepting it from the start and putting up with our so-called intimate celibacy deal, though his behaviour in his latter years did come as a shock, I have to admit. I was robbed by that, robbed of the little dignity I had tried to preserve in the whole sexless marriage." She had another biscuit.

"Sorry, Mrs Murphy Senior," she said, "I shouldn't insult your ears with a reference to sex. You probably found the whole thing as distasteful as I once thought I did. And it's not as if the deal between Jem and me was your fault." Patsy felt her attention caught by some sudden disturbance in the air around the chair. "Or was it?" she said, staring at the vacant seat. "Come on now, you must have known, he was your own son after all. Maybe you did know what was what and you saw me coming, maybe you saw me coming as a gift of an opportunity to protect your own and his dignity, mine wasn't important, was that what happened? You met me and gave him the green light? 'Marry the woman, Jeremy dear, hide your secret shame, no one will guess if you're married.' Is that how it went between you? And me the... what is it they call it in the American films... the fall-guy? Is that all I was? Your fall-guy? Well, it doesn't matter now anyway, Mrs Murphy Senior; you've gone, your son's gone, everyone's gone and I'm still here, with only myself and ghosts for company."

She drank the last of her tea and went upstairs and got ready for bed. It was cold upstairs and she was glad to snuggle into her long flannelette nightie and tuck herself well in under the eiderdown. The bedside light was still on and she looked around the room: at the dressing-table mirror in front of which she had looked at herself naked and guiltily ventured a touch of her breasts; at the empty wardrobe where Jem's clothes were always hung neatly, the drawers in which his clothes were always folded neatly, the laundry basket where even his dirty clothes were always stored neatly. She remembered the awful humiliation and self-disgust she felt when he rejected her physical approach that night.

She climbed out of bed and fetched her special box out from the bottom of her own wardrobe and took out the small string bag her father had made, putting it to her lips as she prayed hard for him to get better. Then she took out the bundle of Sean's letters, handling them with love and care and fondly fingering the ribbon that still held them tied neatly in a precious little parcel. She climbed back into bed and read each one, more ghosts, vanished messages from the past.

When the Liverpool boat docked in Dublin a few mornings later, three O'Kellys disembarked, having travelled over to Ireland together after a frantic round of consultations to coordinate their visit to see their da in hospital. It had been easy for Eddie and Theresa, who both had telephones at home and had arranged to travel up to Bootle together in Eddie's car. Molly had had to call on the good nature of the only neighbour in the street to have a telephone, a Conservative councillor (his politics were considered odd for someone who not only lived in a Corpie house but a prefab at that) who had had the phone installed to facilitate his official duties. Ciaran and Mikey were to follow from

Cheltenham in a few days for a long weekend in Dublin with the family. It was a few years since many of them had been home and, though it wasn't the best of circumstances that brought them back, they were glad of the unexpected opportunity for a family reunion.

Eddie suggested that Molly and Theresa go straight to The Coombe to let Betty know they had arrived safely; he wanted to go direct to the hospital to spend some time with the father he hadn't seen for a couple of decades. Not that it was entirely Eddie's fault: Patrick O'Kelly had long been in the peculiar habit of suddenly banning individual members of the family from visiting The Coombe and it wasn't always clear why or why the ban was just as suddenly lifted. Molly had been on the receiving end of such a ban for her supposed involvement in Annie's elopement to Gretna Green but at least everyone knew that was the reason and it was only imposed for a (somewhat arbitrary) year or so. Annie herself had experienced her father's dismissal after she arrived home as a married woman, the banishment delayed because of Betty's pleadings not to risk losing their daughter but then imposed anyway, seemingly for no new reason. That ban lasted a mere few months, cancelled with the news that Annie was pregnant. Theresa had once arrived at the very door of The Coombe only to have it shut in her face by her father, who told her that Betty had enough to do without looking after visitors who felt they could just arrive at any time on the doorstep and expect to be fed and watered: that one was put down to a bad mood of the moment and didn't last even a day. With Eddie, the original exile, no one really understood what had gotten into his father's head other than perhaps a deep disappointment that his first son had left home so young and had never returned. Eddie had been the first of Patrick's children to move to England and maybe there lay the problem, his son going to live with the enemy: by the time the rest of them went, the toing and froing of people between the two countries was the norm. Eddie, on the other hand, was apparently never forgiven and it was understood in the house that no one was to refer to Eddie in Patrick's presence. That ban had never been lifted.

So, as he knocked on his father's door at the hospital, Eddie took a deep breath; he didn't know what to expect, a welcome or a rebuttal. As luck would have it, he walked into Patrick's room just as the doctors were finishing their rounds and were informing Patrick that his operation had been scheduled for two days hence. When the doctors had gone, Eddie broke the awkward silence by being Eddie: he made silly pigeon coo-rooing noises and jerked his head backwards and forwards over and over, all the time his face creased into an ear-to-ear cheeky grin. His father couldn't help but smile at the familiarity, both of the pigeon references and of his son's easy knack of diffusing a situation with that perennially happy face of his.

"I've missed you," said Patrick.

"And whose fault is that?" came the reply, spoken as a kindly teacher might address a naughty child. "Not to worry, Da, I'm here now whether you want me here or not. Does the ban still hold?"

"Don't," said Patrick, "I'm feeling pathetic enough lying in bed all day without wanting to be made to recognise how stupid I am too. Sit yourself down."

"Not until I've had a look over these charts," said Eddie, unclipping the doctors' notes from the bottom of the bed and making a pretence of studying them. "Yes. Yes. Mmh, I see. Quite right. Yes." He clipped the board back on the bed rail. "Well that all seems to be in order, Mr O'Kelly, you're coming along nicely, they seem to be on top of the problem." Then he cupped his father's face in his hands and the bond was re-established between the two men.

"So you've given us all a scare and we've all come running," said Eddie sitting down. "Theresa and Molly arrived with me this morning, they'll be calling in to see you later today, and Ciaran and Mikey will be here for the weekend. Hopefully you'll have come round from the anaesthetic by then. I heard the doctors say you'll be under the knife the day after tomorrow."

"I will," said Patrick, "and I don't mind telling you I'm not looking forward to it one bit. It seems the Black and Tans left me with a souvenir, a delayed shrapnel explosion in my soft tissue, so I'm told."

"Well, you'll get rid of that the same way you got rid of them," said Eddie. "How are you coping with it all, Da? I'd be liar if I said you looked in the best of health but that's only to be expected; you are in hospital."

"I'm coping, I suppose, but it's very boring in here. I've too much time to spend with my thoughts and nothing else to occupy my mind. I'd actually persuaded myself not to have the surgery but to let everything take its course but Patsy managed to talk me out of it, though she doesn't know that yet."

"I'm glad she did or perhaps it would have been many more years again before you and I spoke, and it wouldn't have been in this world."

"We would never have spoken again, Eddie, that's the truth of the matter, but never mind about all that," said Patrick, "as I say, I'm tired of thinking about my health, or lack of it, and no doubt your sisters will be demanding every last detail when they come in and I'll have to go through the whole business again. So tell me, how's your family? You've a daughter, I know, is she an O'Kelly or is she a Londoner?"

"Well, we can't deny that she has missed out on the greening influence of her O'Kelly grandparents and she hasn't spent much time with the O'Kelly contingent living in England, just the odd visit, so a Londoner she is with an accent to prove it."

"You've only the one child, so I believe?"

"Only the one. Poor Julie was born with a few problems round her mouth and jaw that we had to get sorted and it turned out the problems might be hereditary, so we decided to stop at the one."

"And you got no support from me at such a difficult time, I'm ashamed to admit. Is the child all right now?"

"Julie's fine, Da, though she's not a child any more, and you'll be pleased to know that she loves helping me with my birds. I never lost that interest I had in our pigeons at The Coombe, that all stayed with me. I've lots of feathered friends now, a couple of dozen, I'd say, in a big aviary I built tucked away in the corner of the back garden. I've no pigeons though, which is maybe a good thing, there are enough of those things already in London, aiming their little white parcels on innocent pedestrians, but I remain thankful to our humble Dublin pigeons for what they taught me, them and the bird-market. God, I used to love working up on the loft with you, Da, though perhaps we won't mention the day you got runged by the ladder. That was a great laugh at your expense."

Eddie looked at Patrick for a nod of amused remembrance but his dad's eyes were beginning to close and Eddie lowered his voice to lullaby pitch.

"Is the bird market still there, Da? I loved that bird market and the characters who'd hang around and the busy noise there was always about the place. I collect canaries now. During the mating season it's like listening to a choir of nature herself when one starts to sing and then the others all join in. Of course, it's only the cocks that sing, trying to attract a mate. The hens make a sort of cheeping sound, maybe it's one cheep for a 'no', and two for a 'yes'. That'd be a hoot, if we were talking about owls. Then when the chicks are born, hatched and fledging, there's a comical way in which to tell which little canary is male and which is female because you can't tell just by looking at them, that would be too easy."

Patrick was now fast asleep.

Eddie stood up quietly and carried on talking as he left the room. "To tell which is male and which is female, you have to gently tap the nest and the females generally look straight at you while the young males just bow their heads and stick their arses up in the air. Twas ever the way, eh Da, with females and males, and with that eternal image in mind, I'll leave you to rest."

3

Ciaran and Mikey never got to see their father. Patrick died in his sleep the night before the operation. Betty had been in earlier to visit, bearing a holy card for the special Mass that was to be offered in the parish church the following morning while he was on the operating table. Patsy and her three sisters had called in later but weren't allowed to stay long as Patrick had to be prepped for early surgery the next day. Patsy herself had spent most of the previous night on her knees at the side of her bed, thanking God for his intervention in making her daddy change his mind over the operation: now it seemed that God had listened to both her and her father and had answered both their prayers: she hadn't proved to be a total traitor to his wishes with her deliberate lie to Betty, while Patrick himself was spared the 'palaver' that he had so dreaded.

The family was gathered in The Coombe waiting for the funeral cortege to arrive. Patrick was laid out in his coffin in the front parlour where a small wake had been held the previous night, when friends and neighbours had called to pay their respects and empty several bottles in toasting Patrick's soul on its way. It was as sociable and funny a wake as any, the miniature coffin on the sideboard particularly providing the inspiration for several macabre comments, some of them quite irreverent to the occasion but they sparked some welcome laughter, nonetheless. Patsy and Molly had also come up with an appropriate prop after sorting through an old cardboard suitcase of their father's possessions. It was a hand-grenade, fortunately the empty casing of what had been a dud hand grenade, and that led to some of the funniest remarks along the lines of: "He bit off more than he could chew when he pulled the pin on that one: he forgot to spit the damn thing out." It was also decided during the banter of the wake that the casing should be buried in the coffin along with the corpse, then it would be reunited eventually with some of its missing parts. The lid was now on the coffin, the grenade safely stowed inside along with a few family photographs, small locks of everyone's hair and a couple of Patrick's wood-working tools — in case, it was said, a terrible mistake had been made and he needed to hack his way out. The funeral service was to be held in the parish church and the burial out at Glasnevin.

"God knows what people will say when they see the state of us," said Theresa. "Not many of us look dressed for a funeral, there's hardly a black outfit amongst us and we're the main mourners."

"I'm in black," said John, "though I admit I had to borrow this outfit from someone at the bakery. Is it too baggy, do you think? He's a lot bigger than me. We had to spend our spare cash on getting something suitable for the kids to wear."

"At least it meets Theresa's criteria, she can nod in your direction and hold her head high in front of the neighbours," said Ciaran. "Anyway, we didn't come over to be mourners, we came to cheer Da into getting better," he said. "None of us knew we were coming over for a funeral. Mikey and I had to leave straight from work and we didn't even pack ordinary suits, let alone black ones. Mind you, I don't think we have a black suit between us."

"I have a black sweater, and trousers, that's about all," said Mikey. "Oh, and a pair of black socks."

"I'm glad it's a pair of black socks you've got and not just the one," said Eddie.

"I did wonder about bringing something dark to wear just in case, knowing how serious the situation with Daddy was," said Molly. "Then I thought of how awful it would be to turn up at the hospital to wish him well and me sitting there all dressed in black. That would have been terrible. We were all hoping we'd have Daddy for at least a few more years after the operation."

"Actually he would have hated that," said Patsy. "The doctors explained it all to him and he explained it all to me. The operation was never going to fix him and he faced years of tests and treatments, 'palaver' he called it. He actually told me the other day that he definitely wasn't going to have the operation. I don't know what changed his mind but I can't help feeling his going was the best way it could have happened for him personally."

"Is that what he wanted to talk to you on your own about?" asked

John.

"It was," said Patsy, "he didn't want to talk to Mammy about it and upset her more than she was already. To be honest he was very depressed about the future as he saw it. He was so determined not to have the surgery that I really was surprised to hear he'd changed his mind."

"It was probably for the best then," said Eddie.

"That's all right for you to say, you saw him," said Ciaran, "Mikey and I were too late."

"And we came all this way," said Mikey.

"O for God's sake," said Theresa, "was it a lot of trouble for you then, Mikey, coming 'all this way' with your black socks?"

"I didn't mean that…"

"Leave him alone, why don't you," said John. "The important thing is that he came, isn't it?"

Any further argument was interrupted by the sound of horns and car doors opening and closing outside the house. The funeral cars had arrived. Annie looked out from behind the curtain and saw they weren't the only vehicles pulled up at the kerb. "Jesus, Mary and Joseph, Matt," she whispered to herself, "what the feck are you up to now?"

Parked in behind the cortege was Matt's blue van and he was hauling something out of the back with a rather dodgy-looking character. As the door of the house was opened to let the funeral ushers in to fetch the coffin from the parlour, Matt barged past them unceremoniously, carrying a crate of stout under one arm and some bottles of Paddy's clutched by the necks in his other hand, "for when everyone is back at the house" he told Annie. He set them roughly on the table and rushed back down the hall and out into the street.

Then, as the coffin was finally being carried solemnly out of the house by the ushers, watched sympathetically by the silent mourners and the few inevitable gawpers assembled on the pavement, Matt and his friend shoved back through, hustling the lot of them out of the way, and quickly pushed a path in through the crowded doorway, knocking both ushers and coffin aside and rushing on down the hallway without so much as a word. They were carrying two brand new television sets, still in their boxes, which were barely concealed under raggy lengths of oily cloth snatched up at the last moment for the purpose. Matt also had a bag hanging from his arm.

"Matt, what on earth are you doing?" cried Annie. "It's my da's funeral or had you forgotten? I'd have thought the fact of the funeral cars being outside would have given it away."

"I know all that," said Matt, rushing out to the yard and then back in again. "I just thought that a new television would help cheer Betty up. I got one for Patsy too now she's on her own but on the quiet, like. I won't mention it to your mammy until she gets back from Glasnevin, it'll be a nice little surprise."

Annie could only stare at him in disbelief. "A nice little surprise for when she gets home after burying her husband?"

"Did I do wrong?" asked Matt, somewhat bewildered. "I meant it for the best."

"I know you did, and it was a grand gesture," said Annie relenting, "but your timing could have been better."

"Diversions," said Matt relaxing. "It's all about diversions when there's a delivery to make."

"And are you coming to the Requiem Mass with us or is that another diversion for you to be rushing off again to deliver something else on the quiet?"

"Of course I'm coming to the Mass to see your father off," said Matt. "What a notion. My friend's going to drive the van back to the garage. Best if I don't tell you his name."

"And what's in that bag? You thought I didn't see you sneak out into the toilet?" asked Annie.

"I bought some toilet rolls. Now that your father's gone, I thought we could join the modern age and stop wiping our arses on squares of old newspapers. You'll thank me for it when you've got a touch of the runs."

Televisions and alcohol left dumped and no further deliveries arriving to delay the proceedings further, the coffin was installed with all due if belated respect in the hearse, the family members climbed into the cars and the funeral procession set off at a suitably slow pace.

When the cortege arrived at the church, a military guard of soldiers in vintage Volunteers uniforms had taken up position on the church steps, half a dozen or so former comrades of Patrick's, standing square, rifles

432

to shoulders. On the topmost step were Jim and Joe, in their army dress uniforms. An officer pulled apart from the small guard of honour and solemnly draped the Irish tricolour over the length of the coffin while the rest of the men stood to attention. The acting commanding officer of the makeshift unit was none other than Arthur O'Kelly, returned to Dublin from Paris to attend his brother's funeral, his surprise appearance eliciting excited disbelief and wide smiles out of the grim faces of the mourners, at least out of the faces of those in the family who knew him: Arthur had never left France after the war ended so there were several O'Kelly's who didn't recognise the foreign-looking stranger as their uncle. Betty held out her arms to him and they stood quietly but stiffly hugging for a few moments.

"I'm glad to see you, Arthur. How did you know to come?" she asked.

"I'm still in touch with the organisation and they keep tabs on all the former members," said Arthur. "Unfortunately they didn't let me know that Patrick was ill, they keep only records of the deaths. We were instructed by the defence ministry to drape the flag on his coffin as a tribute to all he did for the country."

Betty merely shrugged at the gesture: "It seems about right that they would only keep records on the deaths. It would have been better if Patrick had heard from his brother occasionally while he was still alive," she said and made her way into the church at the head of the family.

The pews were full. As well as family and friends, parishioners and neighbours, there were several men from the bakery turned up in wrinkled suits with a large arrangement of flowers shaped, kindly but bizarrely, like a cottage-loaf. There was a wreath of wheat ears and grasses and wildflowers from Tullamore: Michael was too frail himself to make the journey into the city after a bout of pneumonia and Robert's daughter was expecting his first grandchild any day so everyone was busy attending to her as well as looking after the other children and the farm. Among the flowers there was also a shamrock formed out of orange and white flowers and green foliage sent by the customers of The Cosy Bar by way of apologies for any noisy inconvenience caused to Mr O'Kelly over the years. In fact one of the pub's more senior customers delivered the floral tribute to the church personally. He was already the worse for wear when he got there and, overcome by the sight of the old soldiers standing to attention in their IRA uniforms, he broke out into song with an unsteady but emotional rendition of *The Soldiers' Song*, his voice carrying into the requiem quiet of the church. He was just a drunk singing and everybody knew it but his lilting voice and choice of song, filtered and floating through the motes suspended like little dots in the still air above the nave, sounded a very moving, very raw last post for the one-time freedom fighter now gone to meet his maker. The disapproving tuts that had greeted the drunk's arrival gradually turned into appreciative nods of approval. A small round of applause followed the end of the song; the irony wasn't lost on the congregation: Patrick O'Kelly was well-known for his sobriety.

During the service, Arthur gave an impromptu eulogy, honouring his brother as a man of great bravery and integrity and loyalty to the cause of Irish independence. He said he had felt a touch of guilt originally over the fact that he had drawn Patrick into the conflict but his brother's subsequent fierce dedication and qualities as a soldier had served to illustrate the deep-rooted patriotism already growing inside. That patriotism continued to drive him in his fight to rid Ireland of the British. Many in the congregation puckered their lips at this reference to the past, glorious though it might have been, it was perhaps going a bit far, they thought, to spit out the word 'British'. They all had family members living over in England and making perhaps a better living for themselves there than they would have had they stayed at home. Arthur had been away from Ireland for a long time in Spain and France, dedicating himself to trying to overthrow oppression, so he hadn't been in his own country when the fighting had stopped and people had had to get on with a new normal life. The years of transition had passed him by. It was just now beginning to dawn on him how much things had moved on. His psyche was stuck in an old Ireland which no longer existed. His eulogy did not rouse the congregation as he had expected.

It was Eddie's short speech that diffused the situation. He made no bones about what a difficult man his father had been, as everyone in the church knew only too well, he said.

"I'm sure there's many of you sitting more comfortably in the pews without Patrick O'Kelly glowering at your every overheard whisper. I used to hate it when I was a boy and I'd get a fit of the giggles during Mass and I'd bite my knuckles and clench my teeth in an effort to stop the sound escaping until the fit had subsided. But Da always knew, he could tell from my body tensing and shaking from the effort of smothering the laughter, and then I'd be in for it later. I won't spell it out, you'll be able to imagine it well enough for yourselves. He was a hard man, he was always in charge in his own home, he ruled not so much with an iron glove as with a face set in steel, some might call it a poker face, especially considering the hours he'd sit in front of the fire, but you would also catch that face creasing into a beautiful smile when he thought no one was looking and he'd heard some witty remark, when to go by appearances he wasn't even listening."

Nods of recognition bobbed along the front benches.

"He was truly devoted to Betty here, my mammy, she never had to worry about him coming in drunk from the pub or taking a hand to her and for that we were all of us grateful, for a grumpy man he did like his peace and quiet at home," said Eddie. "He was also devoted to the rest of us. He didn't always know how to show it, in fact quite the opposite, but the very fact that those of us who escaped him by going to live in England all rushed back the minute we heard he was ill shows how deeply we all cared for the man. He loved us all and we all loved him. Patrick O'Kelly, husband and father, you're already missed."

Only the immediate family went out to the cemetery to pay their final respects and witness the coffin being lowered into the ground and, as if on cue, the heavens opened just as the priest finished his closing prayers. A biting sleety rain fell from the late November skies. "And Amen to that," said Eddie, "Da's obviously just arrived in Heaven." The downpour was far too heavy for any dawdling, reverent or otherwise, or for any careful arrangement of wreaths on the mound. The gravediggers had to get to work straight away to fill in the hole before it filled with water and mud and it was left to them to put the already rain sodden flowers atop the grave. The stone would be installed at a later date.

The O'Kelly party splashed their way through the lines of graves at Glasnevin and hurried into the bar next door, wet and shivery but animated by the sudden rush to get in out of the rain. James was waiting for them inside; he had helped Patsy organise a buffet for the family to

435

save Betty the trouble of preparing something at home and he led them to a few reserved tables while Patsy introduced him as the old friend of Jem's who now escorted her to concerts put on in the city.

She related the story of the grand evening they'd enjoyed in The Gravediggers after the Gorgeous Gael fight and what craic there'd been. Everyone was particularly impressed by the tale of Peter's impromptu ode, which James had remembered and entertained them with at their tables while they tucked into their soup and bread and fat pork sausages. The anecdote lightened the mood and soon old family stories were unearthed and recalled and, in the telling, Patrick O'Kelly was transformed posthumously into one of the softest and gentlest and funniest men you could wish to meet.

"I've got one now," said Eddie. "It might not be up to the Gorgeous Gael standard but I'll do my best." He stood up at the table, ahemmed and took a mouthful of beer.

"We've just buried the patriot, Patrick O'Kelly, a fighting man not known for his levity.

Patrick hadn't been there for the Easter Rising but, a baker by trade, he'd seen the yeast arising."

Appreciative groans greeted Eddie's terrible pun.

"So, he'd donned the uniform and fought the Tans, with guns and grenades and with his bare hands.

Until he was caught and he paid the price, locked up in the North, a place ridden with lice.

Or so I'm told.

And then he became a family man, siring lots of young Catholics, like a good Irishman."

"Now don't be embarrassing Mammy," said Annie but Betty was already shaking with laughter, at Eddie's accompanying suggestive gestures as much as the verse.

"And to keep them in check he made a miniature coffin, no really, he did, I'm not joshing.

"He was a strange man was Patrick O'Kelly.

"It lay in wait on the front-parlour dresser, there to swallow us up if we'd done too much messing

And we avoided that box, we avoided that room, we avoided him too when himself was at home."

"Sorry, Da.

"But he loved us all and we'd great times too, keeping pigeons, killing chickens, he was the glue.

So, we're gathered here to remember Patrick O'Kelly, who was generally known as a difficult fella,

But he's a hard act to follow, a real one-off, and I've no doubt in heaven, he'll show them who's boss.

"And we'll blow the lid off that bloody miniature coffin. To Patrick O'Kelly."

Everyone stood to drink the toast and in doing so noticed that all the other customers had stood up too. "To Patrick O'Kelly," they said in unison and so The Gravediggers' inebriated customers sent the sober patriot, baker, husband and father on his way to join all the other souls buried next door.

There was a wintry draught blowing right through the Warren Street house: Molly and Theresa were shivering with the cold. They had been staying with Patsy while they were back in Dublin and it was their last evening, bags packed and ready to go, but it promised to be a chilly few hours before it was time to leave to catch the Liverpool boat. The problem was that the outer doors and windows were all wide open. With his usual sense of timing, Matt was busy installing the television for Patsy and he had to shout instructions up from the front parlour to his anonymous friend on the roof who was directing the aerial this way and that to find the best picture. His ladder was stretched up from the pavement and a constant mumble could be heard from passers-by having to step into the road to avoid their seven years' bad luck, making signs of the cross for extra protection.

"It's warm in here even with the doors open," said Patsy, who was standing right in front of the fire, the cheeks of her arse toasting nicely in the glow of the coals and she oblivious to the fact that she was blocking any heat from getting into the room.

"It would be if you moved out of the way," said Theresa. "The rest of us are freezing sitting here. It's like being in a polar region. Look, my breath is turning to ice as I speak."

"Will you not shift over a bit?" said Molly. "Don't you have an electric heater we could plug in while the house is open to the elements?"

"You've lived in England too long," said Patsy, "you've become soft."

"Who's become soft?" asked Annie barging in: she had called round to see how Matt was getting on and to say cheerio to her sisters.

"We're the soft ones because we're sitting in the cold while Patsy warms her behind," said Molly.

"It is cold in here," said Annie. "Move out of the way, Patsy, let's all have some of the fire. Anyway, I've something to show you all and it would be easier on the table." She pulled their father's photo album out of her bag and set it on the table. It was a large leather-bound volume, crammed with portraits and scenes, each one identified by a caption written in Patrick's beautiful script and positioned within hand-painted watercolours of decorative foliage and flowers. "I didn't know Daddy was such a good artist," said Annie. "This is like a book of treasures and to think I've never seen it before."

"He was always painting when we lived out in the country, when our real mother was still alive, long before your time, Annie," said Molly. "Local people even used to ask him to paint something particular and then they'd pay him. The last picture he ever did, as far as I know, was a painting of the outside of the house on The Coombe, detailed to every last brick, sort of realistic but not real at the same time, I'm sure there must be a fancy term for it. He even stuck tiny scraps of lace in the windows, like curtains, and peering out from behind three of them he glued on photos of me and Patsy and Theresa."

"'The terrible trio' was how he described us when he did it, I remember that," said Patsy. "I remember that we all looked quite glamorous looking out of the windows, posing with sultry looks for anyone who cared to glance at us. I wonder what ever happened to that painting."

"I can tell you exactly where it is, God forgive me," said Molly. "It's in our coal-shed in Bootle, fortunately on a shelf and not in with the slack."

"You should fish it out," said Theresa. "I only vaguely remember it but I'd like to see it again, remind myself of when we were all quite

438

glamorous, before we lost it all in having kids. Of course, you've kept your figure, Patsy." Theresa shut up quickly, remembering how upset her sister had gotten once before when the subject touched on the children she didn't have. "Let's have a proper look then," she said, positioning the photo album so they could all see.

Loose inside the front cover were two photos of Patrick himself, one looking very serious in his Volunteers uniform, no surprise there, and one of him looking just as serious but it made his daughters laugh: he was wearing voluminous silk boxing shorts which went way below his knees and a pair of boxing gloves and he was posed as if he was ready to knock the stuffing out of all-comers. The slight cast in his eye robbed him of any sense of real threat.

"I didn't know he used to box," said Theresa.

"Nor did I," said Patsy.

"Maybe it was one of those studio portraits where they used to have clothes for you to choose from," said Molly.

"Imagine the Patrick O'Kelly we knew going through the racks of clothes, discarding the top-hats and the fancy dress outfits and instead picturing himself as a master of the pugilist's arts," said Annie.

She started turning the pages slowly and the sisters pointed at people they knew and were amused by the clothes and the hairstyles, adding substance to the pictures with tales of who did what and when and where and what a gas it had been. They didn't recognise some of the faces, even with the help of the labels, but then they didn't know everyone out at Tullamore, they said, or some of their mother's family, other than Uncle Stephen and Auntie Mary.

They started to speculate on who their distant relatives might be — they remembered some talk of a brewery being lost at cards — but Patsy chimed in that her own nieces and nephews were just as distant, in fact, she had never even seen Ciaran and Mikey's growing brood so she wouldn't be able to recognise them in photos either. None of them ever came to visit their poor Auntie Patsy, she complained, but there was no time for her sisters to offer words of reassurance because suddenly the sound of the television came through loud and clear from the parlour and they all went to investigate.

"Let's hope Matt's fixed a better picture on your set than he managed

439

on ours," said Annie. He had, they were greeted by a good picture and only intermittent snowy interference.

"That's all sorted now," said Matt. "You'll be able to watch Gay Byrne's *Late Late Show* now, find out what everyone else is talking about."

"He used to be on one of our channels but I hear he's very popular over here but quite controversial," said Molly.

"Aye, well anyone who broadcasts talk of the Catholic Church having an unhealthy influence in Ireland is bound to be controversial," said Matt. "No subject is taboo for Uncle Gaybo. He's even had people on his show talking about divorce and contraception. You'd never think the man was brought up in The Liberties, where we've little sign of divorce and little evidence of contraception, judging by the number of kids running round." Matt started packing away his tools. "And would you believe one night his guests were talking about homosexuality? On an Irish television show? Not that a church-going woman such as yourself would know anything about that, Patsy. Still, there's always room for more education."

"Is it all done? Can we shut the doors and windows now?" asked Annie. "We'll be frozen solid soon."

"I'll just take the packaging out and my tools and you're all set to do whatever you want," said Matt.

"Thank you, Matt, it'll be good company for me in the house when everyone's gone," said Patsy. "Tell me, do I owe you anything for the television and your trouble?"

"No charge and no trouble at all," he said, "you're more than welcome, just don't get square eyes by watching too much. The telly's grand in its way but you can't beat real live humans for genuine company. We'll just stow the ladder now and be off. Have a safe journey back to England, you voyagers, and hopefully we'll meet in better circumstances next time. Do you want a lift back, Annie, or are you staying for a bit?"

"I'll stay and see Molly and Theresa off. I'll see you later. And thank your nameless friend."

"That's his name all right," said Matt and he headed for the door.

"Matt, wait," called Patsy. "I didn't pay you for the television and your time."

"Keep your money woman, haven't I already told you. I've not changed my mind in the last minute or so," said Matt, shutting the front door behind him.

There was just over an hour or so to go before Molly and Theresa would have to leave to catch the boat and Annie produced yet another contribution to help the wait along.

"This was still in the house since the funeral and I thought we girls might as well share it," she said, taking the top off a bottle of Paddy's and fetching four glasses from the cupboard. "We could all do with warming up after having such a chilly time of it, thanks to Patsy soaking up all the heat. It might be a while before we're all together again so we should make the most of the occasion."

They clinked their glasses and settled round the table. Patsy took out her cigarettes and passed one to Molly — Theresa had never smoked but Molly enjoyed the odd one — and Annie stood up to fetch a light from the fire to save on a match.

"Will you just look at him there?" she said, taking down a photo of Jem from the mantelpiece. "He was a very handsome man, your husband, Patsy, and such a dapper man too, always smart and well turned-out, but then your Billy is a fine dresser too, Theresa. I don't know about Kevin, Molly, I only really remember him in his postman's uniform."

"That doesn't surprise me, sometimes I think he lives in it," said Molly. "When he's on earlies he puts it on first thing because he's straight out to work, then when he's on lates he puts it on first thing too so he won't have the bother of changing later. I hate that uniform, it looks grubby and greasy no matter what I do, and I hate the way it just hangs there, baggy and droopy, shapeless. You lose all sense of there's a body inside. The trousers always have a smelly look too, even though they're not."

"I think that about old men's trousers," said Annie. "They've lost all contact with the poor man's crotch yet they still manage to look as if they've been in the vicinity for far too long. They make me imagine a pair of dirty underpants flapping loosely inside with God knows what stains on them."

"Mother of God, it never ceases to amaze me what must go through your head," said Patsy.

441

"What's it like for you here on your own now? Do you miss Jem?" asked Molly.

"The house is much quieter, of course, but I'm still working so I've not had to get used to being on my own all day as well as night," said Patsy. "I'll have to let you know when it happens."

"Billy was very fond of Jem," said Theresa. "He used to love it when you both came over and he'd have someone he regarded as a knowledgeable companion to go to the races with," said Theresa.

"Of course I never went with him every time," said Patsy. "It never interested me that much to have to ask for time off work."

"No, you're right, sometimes he brought a friend with him, Peter, I think his name was, a nice enough chap, very sociable."

"And did they stay with you?"

"Of course they did, though they had to share a room, it's not a big house, but it was no big deal for them, long-time friends and all that," said Theresa.

"That was very convenient for you all then," said Patsy.

"Does Billy still follow the horses?" asked Molly.

"He doesn't just follow them he chases them, chases them with a pocketful of money I could do with for the housekeeping, to be honest," said Theresa, her face wrinkling in a frown. "He's on a losing streak that's gone on for so long he convinces himself his luck is bound to change soon, 'the law of averages', he likes to say and his face chubbys out with that cheeky smile of his, so he keeps on betting more and more but it's good money after bad, if you ask me. His luck will have to change soon or we're in trouble. This is just between the four of us, mind, don't worry Mammy with it, but you know we might have to sell the house to pay off his debts. The man works hard and he does every minute of overtime he can get but it's all going to the bookies."

"You might have to sell your new semi?" asked Molly. "That's a lovely little house, I'd love a house like that. I love the lay-out of the prefab and it's grand having a garden front and back but the walls are very thin and it's hard to warm the place up. And I'd prefer to sleep upstairs. We've had lots of problems with peeping Toms, especially at the girls' bedroom window, well, they're young women now, of course, so I suppose there's something more to peep at. We've even had underwear stolen off the washing line. Mind you, whoever did it left my knickers behind, he only stole the girls' bras and pants. That tells you what my underwear is like."

"Well I can see us having to move back into an old terrace house," said Theresa, "no insult intended to you, Patsy, but we have got used to a better standard and I dread having to go backwards," she said. "You're lucky your Kevin's not addicted to the horses, Molly. I know him and Aunt Mary have always liked a flutter but a flutter is a flutter, not a rain of notes just going down the drain. You know, at least when Jem was with Billy at whatever course it would be, I always felt that Jem could keep Billy in check. You should have come to live near us, Patsy. We'd all of us have been quite comfortable by now and you'd have had a proper bathroom with an inside toilet."

"Jem used to set himself a limit when he went to the races and he wouldn't go over that limit," said Patsy. "He said he'd prefer to give his money to the theatre box-office or spend it on a meal for the two of us in a nice restaurant rather than give it to the bookies."

"You were lucky with Jem, Patsy, he did like to take you out to nice places, you'd have plenty of occasions to get yourself dressed up," said Molly. "I miss all that, going out and enjoying the city, being with people enjoying themselves. God, I used to love my weekends in Tullamore, what a laugh we had at those dances in the local hall. It was usually me and Nora, of course. I used to love dancing and swirling around to the music and the two of us the centre of attention with the country boys. But Kevin's more of a stay-at-home sort of man, which has surprised me after all those years of him talking about going to sea to see the world."

"But isn't that down to his mother?" said Patsy.

"It was in the past but you can't keep blaming someone else for you not doing what you wanted to do," said Molly. "Kevin and Tessie have known for years that Auntie Mary was always manipulating them but it's made no difference, she's a strong woman and her influence isn't easily shaken off. When she threw that letter of Tessie's into the fire, the one offering a £10 passage to Australia, I thought then that Tessie would at least leave home in disgust but she didn't and she's still there. I gather she's walking out with a divorced man now, from North Wales, I believe. The girls love to get him to pronounce that really long name of some

Welsh town."

"I didn't know she wanted to go to Australia," said Patsy.

"It was a plan hatched with a group of girls she worked with in the factory. They all applied for the cheap passage and they were all accepted but Aunt Mary wasn't going to allow that, so she threw Tessie's letter on the fire. The other women all went and Tessie was left behind."

"A lot of us get left behind," said Patsy but her comment was drowned out.

"Maybe you live too close to Aunt Mary," said Theresa. "The next street is hardly far enough away to create any real distance."

"But it has been very convenient," said Molly. "Mary called in every day to see the girls in from school when they were little and she'd look after them until I got home from work. I can't fault the woman in that respect. And she is very funny, she has a great sense of humour and the kids loved her being there. She used to tell them jokes her father used to tell her, all to do with farts, would you believe."

"Farts? Can you tell us any?" said Annie. "I'm sure my lot would laugh themselves silly, the very word 'fart' seems to them to be the funniest joke ever."

"There is one I remember, a silly one. Here we go now: how do you puzzle a fart?"

"I don't know," said Annie, "how do you puzzle a fart?"

"Sit on a cane-bottomed chair and it won't know which hole to go out of," said Molly. Everyone laughed at the joke, simple though it was. "I told you it was silly."

"My kids would love it," said Annie. "Trouble is, I'm not usually very good at remembering jokes."

"I was never really a party to all that joke-telling," said Molly. "Even now I sometimes feel like an intruder into Mary's little family set-up."

"Speaking of intruders," said Annie, at last seeing an opportunity to ask a question that had been simmering inside her since Molly had stepped off the boat, "does that Mike O'Dowd character still stay with you when he's in Liverpool, Molly?"

"He does, that's partly why Kevin couldn't come over for Da's funeral at the last minute. He'd already arranged for Mike to come and stay. Also it was hard for him to get off work at such short notice. Don't tell me you still think of Mike?"

"I thought he was great fun," said Annie. "I think he was the first man who made my heart leap. I loved his stories and all the magic tricks he did."

"Isn't Matt up to plenty of tricks of his own?" said Patsy. "How else could he suddenly make two television sets appear?"

"Well, none of us will be seeing much more of Mike," said Molly. "He married his childhood sweetheart here in Dublin a few years back and they're moving to Canada later this year. He earned his captain's ticket and was on good money but now, he says, he wants to keep his feet on solid ground and raise his family. I understand he's been offered a good job in Toronto, still to do with shipping but not at sea, so you'll have to go over to Canada if you want to meet up with the man of your dreams again."

"I was just asking," said Annie, "I'm quite happy with the man I've got, even if his tricks are more to do with sleight-of-hand than magic. He is a bit of a rogue."

"Rogue or not, it's thanks to him that Mammy and Patsy have new televisions."

"I forgot to pay him," said Patsy. "Tell him I'll fix up with him next time, Annie."

"We went through all that and he told you to forget it," said Annie. She was about to refill their glasses when they heard the local church clock chime. "My God look at the time, we need to be on our way if you're to catch that boat. Are you meeting up with the others on board?"

"Eddie, Ciaran and Mikey should be down near the quay already, they wanted a last drink in the city before going on board and John's gone with them," said Theresa. "What is it with men that they have to be so predictable all the time. Everything has to start and finish with a drink." She put her glass down. "Are you coming to see us off, Patsy?"

"No, I've said enough goodbyes lately, I've had my fill of them. Annie's going with you so I'll call round to The Coombe and keep Mammy company. It's been a grand couple of hours, so it has."

"It was once you moved your fat arse from in front of the fire," said Annie. "I'll leave the Paddy's, we've started it and you can finish it, you can get drunk later."

445

Coats were put on with an urgency, suitcases and bags were claimed and picked up, last hugs were exchanged and within minutes the leisurely camaraderie had been replaced by frantic hurryings out of the door to get to the bus stop. Patsy stood on the step watching as the trio clip-clopped their way down Warren Street in their high heels and disappeared round the corner after a last fond wave, then she exhaled a deep sigh and went back into the house. She put on her coat to leave but as she was shutting the front door she rushed back in to fetch the photo album so she could go through it with Betty, who might enjoy putting some names to more of the faces. It would be a connection with Patrick but light.

4

In the days after everyone had gone, the house in Warren Street was oppressively emptier than ever. The liveliness which had temporarily filled the place even against the funeral background dissipated as quickly as it had erupted, replaced by a loneliness and a solitude that peopled every corner of every room with the shadows of absence. Even James, who had proved a valued friend and called to visit Patsy regularly in between their concerts and musical outings, was moving down south with his wife to be near their children: they'd all had enough of Dublin, he told her at Patrick's funeral, and he had found a comfortably large residence in the countryside for them all to share, not far from Cork, where they would all be able to breathe in some fresh air. The place needed a lot of work doing, evidently it was a bit tumbledown, so it would be best part of a year before they left Dublin.

"It will be like one big commune," was how James had described it, "but it's sprawling enough that we'll all have our own front doors so we won't be falling over each other all the time. Then if any of them get married and have families of their own, it will be a good start for them not having to worry about finding somewhere to live."

It sounded perfect and, in the midst of The Gravediggers chatty conversations, Patsy had wished James and his family well but really she was bereft at the news and envious of his future surrounded by a growing family. Hers was shrinking. Her own family since childhood had split apart, her parents both now dead — despite her age she felt like an orphan — and her lifetime sisters living miles away across the Irish Sea; her husband was dead too and the friend she had inherited was leaving Dublin. "Some of us do get left behind." The comment haunted Patsy like an inevitable Lesson for the Day. She prayed as fervently as ever but got no solace.

The acute immediacy of it all sent her reeling backwards to those months following Jem's passing. They had been months of silence and

447

their muted echoes now quietly stole through the house like an intangible will-o'-the-wisp. Patsy tried to break into the darkness by immersing herself in music. She had retrieved a book of her father's, a compendium of lyrics, diligently transcribed in his flowing handwriting, its contents and beautiful presentation belying the man's insistence that he had no interest in popular songs. Some of the ones in the book hinted at a clinging nostalgia for the days at Larch Hill, when Lizzie would play the piano and sing while Patrick himself sat drawing; happy days as yet untouched by war and death. Nostalgia for Larch Hill grew out of all proportion in Patsy's head. She bought a collection of song music and practised and sang them constantly, her father's lyrics book propped up in place next to the scores. Eventually a pounding on the party wall of the house would be heard while she was playing and Patsy was delighted that her neighbours wanted to join in with a bit of drumming, until they finally knocked on the door and asked her to keep the noise down because they couldn't hear the television. She ended up switching on her own telly.

Patsy decided to resurrect her plan for the outside toilet. James had looked over her paint charts but had suggested that instead of matching this and that pastel she should let herself go completely over the top and just do whatever she had a mind to. By way of inspiration, he had borrowed a book from the library to show her: it was full of bizarre paintings and sculptures by a Spanish artist, Salvador Dali, and Patsy had been completely won over by the colourful craziness of it all. She had decided to ditch the egg-shell-blues and powder-puff-pinks and instead opt for bold patterns and rich textures — Jem would have approved of that — and to create a wonderful space rather than just a tastefully decorated lavatory. Her father's sudden illness and death had made the whole project seem ridiculously unimportant but right now Patsy needed a touch of the ridiculously unimportant. She decided on a jungle theme: the more ridiculous the better.

"Do you have anything with pictures of Africa or wild animals?" She had gone back to the newsagent's where she knew there was a good selection of magazines. The shop owner, who prided himself on remembering his customers' faces, recognised Patsy as the woman who had spent quite a few pounds on home-decorating publications. He adopted no suspicious look this time but he was intrigued by her change of reading matter.

"Did you give up on the decorating ideas?" he asked, "or are you going on holiday, a safari, perhaps? My wife would love to go on one of them. She's forever nagging me to take her on what she calls an exotic holiday instead of a long weekend in Bray. Although sometimes we go to Killarney, it's beautiful there by the lake but probably not what you'd call exotic. The only things I have in about Africa or wild animals are really children's magazines, aimed at the youngster in school, otherwise there's the National Geographic, that's for adults, a bit specialist, I suppose, we don't sell that many, to be honest with you, but it does have some good stuff about different places in the world. You'll have to have a flick through to see if any of the articles are what you're interested in."

"It's just photographs I want," said Patsy. She didn't want to tell the newsagent what she was planning, she knew how crazy the mention of a jungle look in the outside toilet would sound. "Unfortunately I'm not planning a safari trip, though that sounds like a grand idea. You should surprise your wife and just go ahead and book one."

"I'm afraid I'm in the wrong business for expensive holidays," said the newsagent. "The only safari trip my wife is likely to have is a trip on the city bus out to Dublin Zoo. You go ahead now and browse and see if there's anything suitable."

Patsy started in the children's section but the illustrations were generally drawn or cartoon-like, nothing sufficiently realistic to fire her imagination. In the National Geographic there was a feature on a desert in West Africa and another on the tundra region of Northern Canada, not the sort of extreme hot or cold settings she would want for an outside lavatory, but towards the back of the magazine she found the perfect answer to her search: it was what they called a photoshoot documenting the wild animals and vegetation in India. Just the patterns on the tigers and the different greens and shapes of the plants had her reeling with ideas.

"I'll take this one," she said, handing over her money to the shop owner.

"That's a grand choice," he said, glancing over the contents on the cover. "I'm glad you found what you needed, and you can escape from the dripping wet of the jungle to the sandy wastes of the desert or the snow-covered forests of Canada when you want a change of scenery. See, it's catching, I'm already getting on your wavelength. That's one of the things I love about this shop: people come in with all sorts of interests to read about and it makes me wonder too about all the different things going on. That's what I tell my wife: I tell her there's no need to go anywhere when you have it all at your fingertips in your very own paper shop."

"And does that convince her?" asked Patsy.

"Not in the least. There's no convincing her of anything, not by me, anyway."

Patsy thanked the harried husband for his help and left the shop and headed to Bewley's to study her magazine over a nice coffee and a cake. She walked along enjoying the fresh air, the company of the crowds on the pavement and the general sense of busy life going on around her, people with places to go and things to do. "And all with their own problems, their own ups and downs, hidden from the rest of us with our own problems, our own ups and downs," she was thinking as she hesitated in front of her familiar window to study the various reflections of passers-by, when she suddenly heard her name.

"Is that you, Mrs Murphy?" an insistent voice called to her. "You've no flowers today, I see."

"And isn't that my young friend Sean?" she said turning to see the familiar face of the young lad. "Are you out begging again?"

"I have to do what I can after school finishes but there's no future in it. I do odd jobs when I can get them but I haven't got one today. Is that a magazine you've bought there?"

"It is, it has articles on places all over the world."

"It must be grand to be able to travel and see those places for yourself," said Sean. "But you have to be rich to be able to do that and you have to have a good job to get rich. I can't see myself ever being in that position."

"If you work hard at school, you can do anything you set your mind to," said Patsy, "then you'd be able to buy your mammy lots of beautiful bouquets and maybe take her on a fantastic holiday wherever in the world you both fancied. Meanwhile it's possible I might have a little job for you but it wouldn't make you rich, I could only pay friends' rates and you'd have to get permission from your mammy. I want to do a bit of decorating but I'm too old to climb ladders so I can't reach the top of the walls. Would you be interested in helping me do that?"

"I would and my mammy is sure to say yes. She loves it when I get a bit of a job to do. She says it teaches a person responsibility."

"And she's right. In the end we all have to take responsibility for ourselves in this life, that's why you need to work at your lessons, young Sean, and give yourself some options on what you want to do. Well, let me write a small note to your mammy so she'll know I'm not a kidnapper. You know there were lots of babies kidnapped a few years back in Dublin, over in Henry Street."

"I'm no baby, I could fight off any kidnappers, just let them try," said Sean, "and I promise you, as a friend, that I'd do a good job."

"I've no doubt of that," said Patsy. "Come with me now, I'm going to Bewley's and I can buy you a cup of tea and a cake while I write the letter, it won't take long."

"Bewley's? They might not let me in, Mrs Murphy. I hang around outside there sometimes hoping people might give me their change on the way out but the waitresses always chase me."

"They won't chase you this time, you'll be my guest and they know me, I've been going there since I was a young woman," said Patsy. "I started going there with a friend, well before we were married, and we'd have maybe a coffee, then a glass of wine or a whiskey and then we'd go off to the cinema. Our 'girls' night out', we'd call it."

"I wouldn't mind a whiskey with my cake," said Sean.

"I'm sure you wouldn't but then your mammy would smell it and she definitely wouldn't let you come and decorate for me. Which would you prefer? A whiskey now or some money later for a job well done?"

"Tea it is," laughed Sean. "Do they do cream cakes?"

"They do all sorts and you can take your pick because it'll be my treat. You can call it your first business meeting: we shall be discussing what you have to do and how much I'm to pay."

Sean did elicit a few disapproving stares when the two of them walked into the café but Patsy held him by the hand and let him choose where he'd like to sit. When the waitress approached their table, glaring at Sean as if he was about run off with the cutlery or cause some sort of mayhem, Patsy merely smiled and asked the waitress to tell Master Sean what sort of cakes were on the menu today. He was allowed to order two.

"This is a grand place," said Sean, "but it's mostly old women in here."

"That's because they feel comfortable here, even if they're on their own. It's not always easy for women of my age to enter a place alone. We grew up in an age when that was regarded as the sort of behaviour nice girls wouldn't do."

"Isn't that just too silly," said Sean.

"Of course it is but we grew up surrounded by lots of silly ideas about what women should or shouldn't do," said Patsy. "Fortunately, that's changing. Have you any sisters?"

"Two, they're both younger than me."

"Well, when they grow up, I'm sure there'll be lots of things women will be able to do that we weren't allowed. Now, let's get down to the business of our meeting."

While Sean was stuffing his face with the cakes, Patsy explained what she was planning. Through his young eyes, her idea didn't seem in the least bizarre and he said he'd love to feel he was in the jungle when he went to the toilet: theirs wasn't out in the yard but it was on a cold landing with only a small window you couldn't see out of and when he was stuck in there waiting for a poo to come it would be grand to imagine himself having an adventure. They looked through the photo-shoot together, awe-inspired by the pictures. Sean babbled a stream of suggestions for painting the walls; he said they could include a tiger with multi-coloured stripes on one side, maybe peering through some tall leaves, and maybe there could be a small monkey or two, hanging upside down in a tree, keeping an eye on the big cat from the opposite wall, and maybe a snake could be coiling itself round the handle of the door and maybe they could put in some strange insects crawling across the floor.

"You're full of much better ideas than me," said Patsy. "The sooner we get started the better. I want to buy some green material and thread short bits through it, like a rag-rug, so it will look as if the toilet-lid is made of grass, and I want a full-length curtain for the door to keep it a bit warmer in the winter. Maybe I could find some leopard-print fabric

452

or a print with big leaves and flowers on it, that would be better camouflage for a snake, wouldn't it. I could make sure the snake wasn't hidden, though I don't know how easy it would be to do my business with a snake waiting to spring on me."

"Especially you with your knickers down," said Sean and they both giggled at the thought.

"That could end up as what they would call a real sting in the tail," said Patsy.

She wrote the letter to Sean's mother, detailing where she lived, the name of her parish church and what she wanted Sean to do. He knew Warren Street; it wasn't that far from where he lived just along the canal. Patsy said he could call around at any time and put a note through the door with his mammy's decision and perhaps he could jot down some of his ideas so she could start getting in the paint and brushes.

"Go on home now and get busy on those designs," said Patsy. "I'm expecting great things from you."

"Thank you, Mrs Murphy, for the cakes and everything. I'll be calling round soon, I hope." Sean ran a wet finger over his plate to pick up the last of the cake crumbs and then left, smiling cheekily and puffing out his chest at the waitress on his way out.

Patsy was about to order a whiskey when she heard her name called yet again.

"It's Patsy, isn't it?" After all the recent loneliness of the house, Patsy was suddenly being spoilt for company. There before her was a familiar lip-sticked face from the past, a face that promised humour and sociability and proved that not everybody had gone. It was Molly's friend, Nora. "I saw you in here a few weeks back but you were busy in conversation with someone and then you rushed off. I knocked on the window but you were obviously in a hurry, you looked a bit shaken, to be honest with you, so I decided it was best not to follow you down the street."

"Nora, what a lovely surprise," said Patsy standing up and hugging the woman, discreetly, or so she hoped, avoiding coming into too close a contact with the red-greased mouth. "I was upset that day, right enough, I'd just heard about a dear friend who had died and I hadn't even known to go to the funeral."

"Is that right? You're having a poor time of it then: I hear your daddy passed away recently too. Shall I join you? I don't want to intrude, you always seem to be talking to someone or other whereas I'm usually in here on my own. Are you expecting anyone else?"

"I am not, you've just seen me in unusual moments," said Patsy. "Do sit down. Will you join me in a Paddy's?"

"Sure that'd be grand."

Patsy called the waitress over and ordered the drinks, a bit cross that she had to ask for the table to be cleared and wiped, as if the waitress was still reproachful that Patsy had brought a street boy into the establishment. "Some of these new girls don't practise the same standards as in the past," she commented, deliberately in earshot of the waitress. She pulled out her packet of cigarettes and offered one to Nora.

"You do smoke, I seem to remember," she said to Nora, who nodded in assent.

"I do but it's a dirty habit," said Nora. "The trouble is I enjoy it, not the smell it leaves in the house, especially in the winter when it's too cold to open the windows for some fresh air, but I put up with that for the simple pleasure it gives me sitting down to enjoy a cigarette and a cup of tea and we have to grab all the simple pleasures we can, that's what life has taught me. What good is a cup of tea without a ciggie?"

Patsy lit the two of them and took a long drag on her cigarette: she hadn't wanted to light up in front of Sean, didn't want to set a bad example to the boy, and was gasping for a smoke. "What life has taught me is that I've had enough of death," she said. "My husband died too these few months past. I suppose that comes with getting older, you start losing people, but I didn't think I was in that age bracket just quite yet."

"Age has nothing to do with it," said Nora. "You know my husband died years ago too, years ago, and he was still a relatively young man. It wasn't age or sickness that killed him, it was a car. I can almost laugh about it now, it was so long ago, but he was knocked down and killed one evening crossing the road right outside the house on his way back from the chip shop with our supper. How unfair is that! I haven't been to Mass since. How could God let such a terrible thing happen to a good ordinary family man carrying home a feckin' bag of fish and chips? A man with three young children at home? It beats me. The priest came visiting after a few times, of course, telling me the usual stuff about God's great plan, that we can none of us understand his workings and how God wanted my Donal up in Heaven with all the angels, but I'd have preferred my husband to be down here on earth with me for a bit longer. That was my great plan. Now I can't even eat fish and chips without death being on the plate. But I love fish and chips so I do, I just add more salt and vinegar to take away the bad taste. What about your husband, Patsy, how did he die, if it's not too upsetting to talk about?"

"He was very ill for a couple of years, confined to the house," said Patsy. "Like you I can laugh about some of it now, like he couldn't go to the toilet outside, it was too far for him to walk, so we had to have a commode in the back room. It was always smelly in there, it really stank, and I'm not talking stale cigarette smoke, unfortunately, and then I'd have to clean him up after he'd finished and lug the chamber-pot outside to the lavatory to get rid of the mess. I spent a fortune on rubber gloves."

"I can imagine. My God the things we end up doing for love. We none of us imagined any of this when we were off dancing and having a good time," said Nora shaking her head. "And my God I used to love going roller-skating with Molly, racing round the rink without a care to the future. To be honest I was surprised she married her cousin in Liverpool and not one of the lads from Tullamore. My God some of them were handsome enough to be in the pictures, real good-looking lads, they were, fine and muscular with all that outdoor work they did, and we had them buzzing around us city girls like bees to a honey-pot, as they say, and Molly did so love being in the country with the trees and the fields all around her. But she gave up all that."

"I suppose there's an element of surprise in a lot of marriages, we all give up something," said Patsy. "We grow up and make decisions that would have seemed unthinkable to our younger selves."

"Still, we make our choices and have to get on with it and Molly sounds happy enough. Are you still working?"

"I am. I'd miss the company of the girls in the workroom and I like the routine of it all, it gives a point to the day before I go home to the empty house, I haven't settled into that whole situation yet. But I've decided to do some decorating now that Jem's gone, brighten the place up after all the sickness that went on there. That boy I was talking to is going to help."

"Sure that's grand," said Nora. "I have plenty of company, too much sometimes: I turned the house into a bed-and-breakfast not long after Donal passed and I have my regulars as well as the odd weekend booking when there's something special going on in the city. August is really busy with the Dublin Horse Show. It's a lot of work but we can have grand craic of an evening. The men usually bring a bottle or two back to the house after the pub at night and then the singing and the recitations start. It's a gas, so it is, I'm certainly never lonely. But home is like a business now, my place of work, so to speak, so I make sure I get out of the house every day. I come here to Bewley's regularly, it makes me feel as if I'm still a part of Dublin."

"I feel like that when I go out to the concerts in St Francis Xavier Hall. There's something about crossing the bridge over the Liffey and seeing the lights and the boats moving on the water before heading up O'Connell Street and looking at the people walking up and down in the shop lights, it makes me feel alive. It puts a spring in my step. I go with an old friend of Jem's; his wife doesn't like classical music so he has no one else to go with: it's a chance for me to wear something nice and it's company for him. It's always better to go to these things with another person, then you can talk about it afterwards instead of just keeping all your thoughts and opinions to yourself, it adds to the pleasure. I used to love all that going to the cinema with Margaret. You remember my friend Margaret?"

"I do, she was a nice girl altogether, you and she were very thick from when you were at school. Do you not see her any more?"

"Sure, she only lives a matter of yards away so we try to get together regularly, though it was difficult when Jem was ill. I didn't really want people coming to the house, what with the smell and the commode and the whole business, and I had to be in of an evening to look after himself. God rest his soul, but hopefully with Jem gone now I'll get back into the swing of things. Anyway, you should try the concerts, Nora, they're free and they're on most Friday evenings."

"Sure I'm like your man's wife," said Nora, her cupid's bow suddenly aiming south. "That sort of music's not for me, I like a good melody and maybe a nice manly voice singing something romantic.

Anyway, Friday nights are busy and I'm usually in the kitchen cooking dinner for the..." She stopped mid-sentence. "God forgive me, Patsy, here I am chattering on and not a proper word of sympathy for your da passing. I was so sorry when I heard. I did sneak into the back of the church for the funeral but I didn't want to intrude on the family's grief so I didn't follow you all out, though I would have liked to say a quick hello to Molly."

"I know she planned on calling to see you before going back to Liverpool but as it turned out she never got the chance. We were back and forth to the hospital and none of us expected Daddy to die so suddenly, especially the night before he was due the operation. Then we had a funeral to arrange instead of just hospital visits and then everyone had to rush back to England. They'd only planned on staying for a long weekend."

"It was a good turn-out at the church," said Nora. "I could have done without his brother's IRA stuff during the service, each to his own but I think we all could have done without that, Patsy, though the old soldiers in their uniforms did add a grand touch. I suppose it was all part of who Mr O'Kelly was in the past. I did enjoy Eddie's short address. He summed up your father right enough. He loved you all and he was certainly a grand husband to Betty but he was a hard man all right, Eddie had him nailed. You know he once banned me from the house for a few months because I happened to mention a few boys stealing pennies off the eyes of the bodies in the morgue? I got the blame when Ciaran and Mikey did the exact same thing and got caught. Your father instructed Molly to inform me that I was no longer welcome in the house: I'd encouraged his sons to get up to mischief and so got them into trouble with the Gardaí, he said. God, we had a laugh over that one. Let's drink to the old tyrant," said Nora.

They toasted Patrick's memory and lit up a couple more cigarettes.

"At least his passing quickly was for the best, God love him," said Nora. "There aren't many people who recover from cancer. I'm sure it was hard on Betty but seeing him linger and suffer would have been worse," she said. "Weeks after the accident, I actually started praying that my Donal would die in his sleep. I couldn't bear looking at him in the hospital, a fine figure of a man but his body all broken and him sedated into unconsciousness because of the pain and the doctors not able to offer any hope of recovery. I wanted him to die for his sake and he did, God rest his soul."

"God forgive me but I think it was a blessing when Jem died too," said Patsy, "and I think he must have been blind drunk when he did because he'd emptied nearly a full bottle of Paddy's when I was at work so he must have just drifted off."

"Was he supposed to drink? I assume he was on medication. I don't actually know what it was he died of."

"Some sort of blood poisoning," muttered Patsy, "I could never pronounce the name. He wasn't really supposed to drink but we'd enjoy a glass together of an evening."

"He was told not to drink but he emptied a bottle of Paddy's when he was alone in the house?" said Nora, her eyebrows arching and her red-red lips puckering into a question. "Now wasn't that a strange thing to do. Was he a careless man or was it deliberate? Do you not think that was a strange thing to do, Patsy?"

"I don't think about it." Patsy called the waitress over. "I'll get this," she said to Nora, the tone of her voice considerably cooler than it had been, "it's time I went. I've to study up on what paint I need to buy. Maybe we'll bump into each other again." Before Nora could say another word, Patsy had upped and left.

The house seemed to have an ominous feel to it when she got home. She tried to put Nora's comment to the back of her mind but it kept returning to haunt her.

5

The boss at the sewing factory had insisted that Patsy take a couple of weeks off work after Patrick's funeral, and he was only being sympathetic but Patsy hated being off and she couldn't wait to get back to the sewing room. She had always liked going to work, liked the very fact of going to work and liked the work itself. The days at home were dragging and dragging her down with them. She was half-heartedly glancing at her National Geographic, chain-smoking while she fought to keep Jem's chair out of her sightline lest the image of him slumped dead by the empty whiskey bottle filled her mind's eye. Her enthusiasm for the jungle project had somewhat evaporated in the recognised substance of Nora's words and she was working hard to reignite any interest at all when, as if it was predestined, there was a knock on the door and Patsy opened it to see young Sean standing on the step with a woman.

"Hello, are you Mrs Murphy?" asked the woman.

"I am and you perhaps are Sean's mother?" said Patsy.

"I am, Connie Mulhoney," said the woman. "Sean gave me your letter and told me some bizarre story about meeting a woman in the street and going to Bewley's with her for tea and cakes to discuss him helping her to paint an outside lavatory like a scene from the Indian jungle. Now that's a story you don't hear every day so I thought I'd better find out for myself what he was talking about, who was this woman, and make sure he wasn't giving me a bit of the blarney as an excuse to get out of the house. He always did have a vivid imagination."

"When you put it like that it does sound more than a little bizarre but it wasn't his imagination," said Patsy nodding her head and grinning uncontrollably, "it's all true, Mrs Mulhoney, it was no blarney. But I'm glad you called. It was very wrong of me to invite your son to drink tea without asking his mammy's permission and it's been on my conscience ever since. I wouldn't want you thinking I was some sort of a pervert or a mad woman. That's why I wrote the note and included my address.

Would you like to come in? I'd rather you had your mind set at ease."

"Well just for a minute or two," said Mrs Mulhoney, ushering Sean in ahead of her. "So, it was true too that you gave him the flowers?"

"It was me all right," said Patsy closing the door behind them. "I had a whole bunch of them so it was no big thing." She took them into the parlour and offered to make them some tea so they could get to know each other properly. Sean was very excited to see the piano. "Can you play?" Mrs Murphy. "I'd love to be able to do that." Patsy told him to play around on the notes while she put the kettle on and his mother warned him to be careful and not press too hard in case he broke anything.

"I doubt he'd break anything, pianos are very strong," said Patsy. "You should see the way professional pianists have to bang away on the notes at times and, when you hear some of the best music composed for the piano, you'd wonder how the instrument could survive such a beating. But your mammy's right, Sean, you need to be gentle at first while you find your own touch. You have a go now and I'll do the tea."

Patsy prepared a nice tray, with a pretty embroidered cloth, a patterned china plate covered in a selection of biscuits and a small matching milk jug and sugar bowl: it was something Jem had insisted upon when they were having tea in the parlour; he always said that the simplest of servings became special with a bit of special attention and Patsy had quickly learned to appreciate his point. So she enjoyed the excuse to do more than just pour out cups of tea today: having visitors to entertain was a welcome treat and she liked hearing the hesitant piano sounds drifting down from the parlour. Of course they were somewhat disorganised but gradually you could hear that Sean promised a natural feel for the instrument.

"Here we are now," she said carrying the tray into the parlour and she was pleased to see the favourable reaction to how pretty it looked on the faces of her guests. "Help yourself to milk and sugar and tuck into the biscuits, as many as your mammy will allow, Sean."

"You've gone to a lot of trouble, Mrs Murphy, but I thank you for it, I don't feel so guilty now for calling to your house," said Mrs Mulhoney. "It's so nice see a bit of effort put into something so simple. I try to tell the children that they should always do the best they can whatever it is they're doing. We're poor people but we don't have to be poor in attitude."

"Of course I've only met Sean out of your children but straight away I took to the spirit he shows so I'd say your advice is well heeded," said Patsy. "I do hope you give him permission to help me with the painting, it would only be after school or at weekends and I would pay him for his trouble. But it's only an outside toilet, when all's said and done, and not worth interfering with his schoolwork."

"But it's already helped me learn more about India," said Sean. "I told the teacher about the photos in the National Geographic magazine and first he lent me some books about India and the different animals and plants there and then he lent me one about how India was once ruled by the British, just like we were, but it said that, thanks to the British, India has railways going all over the country, even right up into the mountains and they're very high mountains. I'd like to be an engine driver on some of those trains. And did you know they have what they call a monsoon season, when it rains fair to flood the Liffey?"

"You'd have to have a good umbrella there then," said Patsy "and a good pair of wellington boots."

"Can you explain to me why you want to paint an Indian tiger in the toilet, Mrs Murphy, if it's not too rude a question," asked Mrs Mulhoney. "I can't pretend I'm not a little intrigued now that I know what Sean said is true."

Patsy explained about Jem and how the house was for so long like a hospital ward that she needed to do something silly. "It's just a bit of nonsense really," she said, "but I told Sean about it and his enthusiasm made me think, well, why not? And I could give him a bit to eat too while he's here, I wouldn't expect him to work on an empty stomach coming in from school."

Mrs Mulhoney turned to Sean. "Do you want to do the job then?"

"I really want to, Mammy," he said. "I've got all sorts of designs in my head already and I've been drawing out some of the patterns I saw in the India books."

"Well, you can do it whenever Mrs Murphy says it's convenient," said his mother.

"That's grand," said Patsy. "The sooner we start the better. And when we've finished the project, if we're not sick of each other by then, I could give you a few lessons on the piano, if your mammy agreed."

"I'd love that too," said Sean. "Could you show me how to play something now?"

"I think for now we've taken up enough of Mrs Murphy's time and eaten enough of her biscuits, young man," said Mrs Mulhoney.

"And it would be better to start with a proper lesson," said Patsy. "When I was a little girl, I had lessons and the teacher made me play with pennies balanced on the backs of my hands to make sure I maintained the right position. I thought at the time that she was mad but she was right, it was very good discipline. We can try that and see how you get on."

Sean's face dropped. "Would I have to bring my own pennies?"

"No, I'd make sure I kept some on the piano ready. But your mammy hasn't agreed yet. There would be no charge, of course, Mrs Mulhoney, you wouldn't have to pay me, my reward would be the pleasure of introducing Sean to being able to play and maybe develop an interest in music."

"It would be something special for him if you could do that, Mrs Murphy. Life hasn't been kind to us, Sean's father died several years ago in an accident on the docks and I don't have money to spare for anything other than the basics. I never expected an opportunity for piano lessons to come Sean's way."

"It would be important for him to practise between his lessons. Do you know anyone with a piano? If not, he could come here a couple of times a week on his way home from school, twenty minutes or so would be best, it wouldn't be any bother as long as I knew when to expect him."

"I think we need to get the painting done so I can start," said Sean. "What a friend you've turned out to be, Mrs Murphy."

"Sean that's a bit forward," said his mother.

"Don't be cross with him, it was me who told him we were new friends," said Patsy.

It was arranged that Sean would call in the following Saturday ready to get to work on the lavatory and the Mulhoneys took their leave. Patsy watched as they walked down Warren Street towards the canal and again Sean turned to wave before disappearing round the corner. There were a few neighbours standing chatting on the pavement and Patsy, who had been known for keeping herself to herself over the last few years, surprised them with a friendly nod and a smile in their direction.

"It's a beautiful day, isn't it?" she called over, which confused them even more as the sky was weighed down with clouds and a breeze was getting up. The neighbours exchanged puzzled looks — the woman had obviously lost it with the death of her husband — but they returned Patsy's greeting and kept smiling to her as she shut her door. Then they made the most of the minor encounter to fuel a bit of gossip.

Back in the house, Patsy cleared up the cups and saucers and carried the tray back to the kitchen. She washed up the few dishes in the sink, singing to herself 'like a young slip of a girl', she thought, and then stored everything away in the cupboard.

"It's none of your business. Can't a woman sing in her own house when she wants to?" she said to the chair. She rummaged in her sewing box for the tape-measure, rummaged in a drawer for a pad of paper and retrieved a pencil from behind the clock on the mantelpiece. "I'll be outside if I'm needed."

She went out to measure the floor area and the walls of the toilet and then sat on the seat awaiting inspiration, until the cold and the rain drove her back inside. She saw that a scribbled note had been shoved through the letterbox.

"*Mrs O'Kelly, I did knock but you must have been out. My mother told me to make sure to call so I'll try again later in the week. I hope Wednesday morning after Mass will be convenient.*"

It was written on St Kevin's Parish Church paper and signed by Father Dec.

Patsy made sure the parlour was spick and span and the fire glowing in the grate for the priest's visit. She had dithered about whether or not she should attend the Wednesday morning Mass but had decided against it on the grounds that it might look as if she was trying to make a good impression — she didn't normally go to morning Mass as she had to go to work — and also that she might feel obliged to wait for Father Dec after and then it could be awkward making conversation on the way back to Warren Street. She would feel far more comfortable at home, after all she didn't know the man. She felt guilty that she didn't even know how long he had been based at St Kevin's but it wasn't long and he had arrived at a time when she had enough to deal with without fussing around the new priest like some of the women parishioners. They didn't so much fuss as flutter, that was Patsy's opinion, with their eager invitations to dinner and their light way of talking as if the man was automatically an old friend just because he was a priest. In fact, in Patsy's opinion, all that familiarity had an air of irreverence about it. She preferred to keep some sort of distance, especially bearing in mind what personal weaknesses were revealed in the confessional box and it would be easy enough to recognise the speaker's voice. She was busy filling the kettle when, as if unexpected, the knock on the door made Patsy jump. She had a last check round the place, quickly kicking her slippers out of sight under the chair, and went to open the door.

"Mrs O'Kelly, at last we meet," said the priest at the door.

"Hello Father Dec, do come in, I'm sorry I missed you last time, I was in the yard and I obviously didn't hear your knock," said Patsy.

"Aye well it's not too far to come," said Father Dec. "As I said in my note, it was my mother's prompting that brought me here but I'd have got round to visiting you sooner or later. It takes a while to get to know all our parishioners individually."

Patsy led the priest straight into the parlour and indicated a chair by the fire. "Ah, you're a musician, I see," he said. "I play a bit myself but finding the time's the problem. We've a piano in the priests' house and I can guarantee that, as soon as I sit down to play, someone will need a home call with Holy Communion or a hospital visit or Last Orders, though fortunately that one isn't every day or we'd be running out of parishioners. I brought these for us to have with a cup of tea, assuming I'm offered one of course. I shouldn't presume so much. Occasionally I've called to a house and been virtually shooed away off the doorstep quicker than if I'd been the Devil himself."

He handed a paper bag to Patsy and could see immediately that she wasn't familiar with the contents.

"They're bagels," he said. "Have you not tried them? They're like doughnuts, round with a hole in the middle, but they're not sweet, they're made out of bread."

"No, I've never eaten one of those."

"I often buy them. I get them in the Jewish bakers on Lennox Street, do you know the one? The Bretzel Bakery, it's called, a small family business."

"I know the shop but I've never been in," said Patsy. "To be honest, I assumed it was just for Jewish people."

"Not at all, sure they'd never sell enough to keep going if the shop wasn't for customers of all faiths."

"Well, I'm happy to try one on your recommendation, Father. What do I do with them? Just put butter on or what?"

"I love them split in half and toasted," said Father Dec, "then the butter can melt in. But just buttered is fine, save you going to any trouble."

"Sure how is toasting a bit of bread what you'd call trouble. I've to brew the tea yet anyway. I won't be long."

Patsy disappeared down the hallway and was surprised when the priest followed her, insisting that he help with the bagels. She was relieved that she'd cleaned the back room as well as the parlour, just in case, and wasn't shamed by any untidiness.

"By the way my name is Murphy now," she said. "Your mammy knew my family on The Coombe and we had a close mutual friend in Mrs Flaherty, you probably knew her, but my married name is Murphy. My husband passed away last year, God rest his soul, but really it was a blessing as he was very ill."

"Mammy told me. And then your father died," said Father Dec. "A bad few months you had, losing so many loved ones."

"It was bad, but I've been to enough funerals recently and heard enough of the routine words of comfort so please, Father, don't talk to me about God's plan and how we can't understand it," said Patsy. She realised she had sounded rather short. "God forgive me, I'm sorry, that sounded incredibly irreligious and rude."

"No it didn't and I wouldn't dream of adding to the litany of comforting words, Mrs Murphy, I'm not even sure God has all these plans they talk about. I think God just let's things happen and lets us get on with it, but perhaps he keeps an eye on how we do that," said the priest, buttering the bagels and arranging them on the plate. "Maybe that's the only type of intervention there is, a watchful eye to see how we get on with our lives and how we cope with all the challenges. Some people face the everyday difficulties that come with being very poor but they remain as honest as the day is long. Some people are rich but are so greedy for more that honesty goes out of the window. You can understand why non-Catholics question the immense wealth of the Church when so many of its members live in poverty."

"I agree with you there, Father," said Patsy. "It's hard not to see their point. Sit down now and I'll bring in the tea. Would you like it in here or in the parlour?"

"Another tricky question, Mrs Murphy," he said. "You see, I'm normally a kitchen-man myself but I can appreciate the special effort people put in to enjoying a good excuse to use the parlour. So, which is it to be?"

"If you're a kitchen-man, then the kitchen it is," said Patsy setting down the tray on the table. She had warmed instantly to this man, Mrs Doran's son, the answer to Mrs Doran's prayers but obviously not cast in the same traditional Catholic mould as his mother. Patsy said a quick prayer of thanks that she had thought to light the fire in the backroom too, just in case.

"Personally, I have never liked the idea of having lots of money," she said. "Of course we all hope we'd be generous with it but I can see how easy it could be to slip into the pattern of getting used to having nice things around you and then wanting more and more. I'd just be glad of an indoor lavatory, that would be my idea of rich. I had a friend once and she used to say that her idea of being rich wouldn't involve having a big car and a big house but just being able to go into a good restaurant without having to check the prices on the menu before even opening the door."

"Well bagels are cheap enough. Are you enjoying them, Mrs Murphy?"

"I am, I'll have to try the Jewish bakery myself. My father was a baker all his life but of course they never made anything like these."

"They're unleavened, they don't use yeast at all, as far as I know."

"Unleavened! That sounds straight out of the Bible," said Patsy.

"Well there you have it," said Father Dec.

"I wonder why they opened a shop here in Portobello, it seems a strange choice of location."

"Not really. You know Portobello has quite a Jewish heritage. A lot of Jews had to flee the pogroms in Eastern Europe at the end of the last century and a lot of them, especially from Lithuania, apparently, ended up in Dublin and they settled in this area. In some quarters it's still referred to as Little Jerusalem. I suppose it was more reassuring for them to stick together after their flight from persecution and then arriving in a completely foreign country where people spoke a completely foreign language."

"It's hard to think of Ireland as a foreign country," said Patsy. "I've only ever been over to England and that's hardly what you'd call foreign."

"It must have been difficult for them, refugees we'd call them now. Of course, they brought useful skills with them. Haven't they always had a great reputation in the tailoring trade? You're in that business yourself, as I understand from my mammy, so you might be interested to know that the very first treasurer of the tailors' trade union in Dublin was a Jewish man who lived in Portobello, in fact he lived right across the street from you, at number 14. There you are, history on your doorstep."

"Right across the street? Well would you believe that! I never knew any of this and I've been living here for nearly twenty years," said Patsy.

"I made it my business to learn something of the locality when I was posted to the parish here," said Father Dec, "otherwise I would have been just as unaware of it all as yourself."

"When I was growing up it was all about Irish history and fighting for our independence from Britain and my family experienced enough of that history, not only right on the doorstep but even inside the house."

"And many Jews living around here were active supporters of that same fight," said the priest. "There was one Portobello woman in particular, an artist, so I believe, who hid ammunition under the vegetable patch in her yard and she and other Jewish women, all members of CumannnamBan, believe it or not, smuggled all the ammo over to the General Post Office during the Rising. God forgive me but I can't remember the woman's name and she a true heroine of Ireland. Her father apparently was the optician mentioned in Joyce's *Ulysses*. In fact, the fictional hero of the book, Leopold Bloom, was also supposed to live in Portobello, so the area has literary as well as historical connections. Have you ever read *Ulysses*?"

"No, I thought it was supposed to be dirty."

"I think you're probably old enough to read it and decide that for yourself," said Father Dec. "After all it's considered a modern classic and not just in Irish literary circles. To be honest with you, Mrs Murphy, I never could see the point in the Church treating people like children with a list of what they could and couldn't read, in this case partly because of a scene in which a woman talks very candidly. It seems to me just further proof that men are actually frightened of women."

"Frightened? Isn't that a strange thing to say?"

"Not really," said the priest. "If you think about all the different religions in the world, they're all governed by men, and it seems to me that their rules are often designed to keep women in their place. What are the men afraid of, do you think? I think they're afraid of the power of women. We priests can't get married because a wife would be a distraction from our duties. But then we can't have women priests either, so women are always kept on the side-lines, even though a lot of them I'm sure would make perfectly good ministers and representatives of God. In some religions, the women can't even pray in the same part of the temple or the mosque as the men in case again they prove to be a distraction. In other words, it's the men who are weak and easily distracted. Religions often require their women members to cover their heads, so that their hair doesn't prove a distraction. How sad is that as a comment on men? Even here it's uncommon for a woman not to wear a hat or a scarf in church. It seems that men are so easily distracted that rules have to be enforced to keep even women's hair out of sight. So it's the men's problem really, would you not agree?"

"I didn't think it was my place to agree or disagree," said Patsy. "I was brought up knowing my place and there's a comfort, a security in that. I'm surprised to hear a Catholic priest talk like you. You seem to doubt an awful lot and yet for all that you decided to become a priest."

"I became a priest to love and serve God and his followers," said Father Dec. "I admit that I often got into heated arguments at the seminary with what they referred to as my 'modern ideas' but my answer to that is that we live in modern times. Old rules aren't necessarily relevant. Perhaps an analogy would be motor cars and road traffic. Years ago, you could just walk along the street and maybe just have to dodge a horse and cart or a bicycle, everything was slow-moving. Now it's all much faster and we need speed limits and traffic lights and parking signs and all that. New rules had to be introduced for the modern world to function safely and I think the Church needs to examine some of its old rules and adapt."

"But you could argue that we need the old rules and regulations more than ever simply because everything is more complicated and dangerous, because today the road to salvation is full of diversions and side streets and fast lanes and maybe they're all just dead-ends," said Patsy. "We need reliable signposts to guide us away from taking the wrong path. I think all these modern approaches are getting out of hand. It's as if anything goes now and I'm not sure too much freedom of behaviour is a good thing."

"Too much of anything is not a good thing, Mrs Murphy, and I agree that we need reliable strictures by which to live but to me those strictures come through God Himself, we need God more than ever but we're in danger of actually putting people off and deserting God through the Church's apparent lack of what I'd call basic compassion. It's all 'don't do this' and 'don't do that', which is all very negative, without any understanding or allowance made for people to be people. There's a lot of traditional teaching preached from the pulpit that seems to me to deny who we are, as men and women, if you like, and it's an approach that I just can't go along with. For example, I find it very puzzling that we can lock a young girl up in a convent because she's pregnant but not married: while she's there she's little more than free labour and when she comes out she's regarded as a fallen woman, meanwhile her baby is whisked off to America whether she agrees to it or not. But the man, the other half of the coupling, he gets off scot-free in this patriarchal religion of ours, he's not so readily identified and he doesn't get shoved away in a priory. Even when she marries a woman is expected to bear the responsibility for the birth rate in the family. She is told that contraception is a terrible sin, instead she must say 'no' to her husband, even when he comes in drunk and maybe violent from the pub demanding his marital rights. Would such a man listen to a simple 'no', do you think? The result is that she has to spend most of her life being pregnant and in between using her body to feed the babies while your man is probably back in the pub. I know that's not all men, Mrs Murphy, and thank God it's not, but it's enough of them in this country of ours. Meanwhile the modern world is overpopulated as it is. To me all this detracts from the simple but true worship of a merciful God. Human beings are complex creatures, with genuine concerns and needs and drives, that's how God made us, and people can have a lot to put up with, whether in their own lives or in the troubled world at large, and God forgive me, but I can't see how fobbing them off with what are sometimes just old platitudes repeated over and over is of much value."

The priest paused and smiled at Patsy. He noticed she had taken on a rather faraway, pensive look. "Forgive me for all that," he said, "but once I get started... I hope I haven't offended you, Mrs Murphy. My intention in coming here wasn't to lecture you on my opinions but merely to say hello and enjoy a bagel with a cup of tea."

"I wonder if the world isn't just too modern," said Patsy. "Nothing is straightforward any more; everything seems open to question. There are things we were always taught were sinful that I'm no longer sure about. Things happen and you end up finding it hard to see where is the sin that was supposed to be there, where is the badness when it's a good person you're dealing with. You go through your life being taught — and believing — that something is good or evil and then experience teaches you that not many things are so cut and dried, there are shades of good and evil and, if there are these shades, where is the line to be drawn that condemns someone for what you would call being a human being."

"Was there anything in particular you had in mind?" asked Father Dec, easing seamlessly into a priest's role.

"Only my whole life and whether or not I wasted it because of the things I was brought up to believe," said Patsy. "Perhaps it's that — and God forgive me for saying this — perhaps it's that I gradually started to think about how so many of the Church's rules seem obsessed with the physical side of life, sex, I suppose we must call it. How many female saints have been canonised because of their purity, their chastity? Even Our Lady was a virgin mother. If that doesn't add up to a pitiful dismissal

470

of the vast majority of ordinary women, then I don't know what is."

"Would you care to elaborate?"

"I've been a Child of Mary all my life, Father, and I've said my daily prayers, sincerely asking for help to remain pure. I even made a vow of chastity when I was young. And where has it left me? Pure but alone. It's all very confusing. For example, no one would argue that murder and theft would ever be right, we don't have to be told that, we know that murder and theft are morally wrong, but we have to be instructed in a whole list of rights and wrongs to do with love when surely expressing love must be morally right yet we're made to feel it's dirty. For men it can be a pleasure but for women it's somehow associated with sin and laden with guilt. We're told that a baby is a gift from God, so the young girl locked up in the convent to have her baby is really being punished because she had sex, even though it would appear it was with God's blessing because it resulted in the gift of a baby. Divorce is not allowed but annulment is and I'm not sure what the difference is — both mean the official end of a marriage made with the same vows. I'm sure it's because divorce allows for people to get married again and that means going on to have sex with a new partner, otherwise what's the difference between divorce and annulment. And why is contraception wrong? Because it allows for women to enjoy the physical side of their marriage without the possibility of babies. And why is homosexuality wrong? Because again it means sex without babies, even though it can be based on real love, real genuine love between two people who have found each other and love each other despite all the difficulties."

"It sounds like a subject close to your heart, Mrs Murphy," said Father Dec. "You made a vow of chastity when you were too young to really know what it meant but you're a widow so you were obviously married. Did you and your husband not…?"

"No," Patsy broke in. "We didn't. I had taken a vow of chastity and he, God rest his soul, was a homosexual so our marriage was more of a convenient agreement."

"And now you feel regret?"

"It's not so much regret as thinking of what a more normal life would have been like with children of my own. And, God forgive me, at times I hated Jem, resented him for an arrangement I had fully agreed to," said

471

Patsy. "My husband was a good man, Father, a kind and honest man, very caring and considerate, and I used to worry that his soul would have gone to hell because he was homosexual. That was an awful thought, but I don't believe that any more. What I do worry about, Father, is that in the end he might have deliberately hastened his own death, maybe to spare both me and himself from the prospect of him ending up deaf and blind and even more helpless than he was already."

"How did he die, Patsy, what exactly did he do?"

Patsy chewed on her lips and hesitated before answering. "He drank a whole bottle of whiskey while he was taking very strong medication, something the doctor had strictly warned him against. Was that suicide, Father? Will Jem have been condemned straight to hell?"

"I hope I can put your mind at rest on at least that count," said the priest. "I don't believe for one minute that God in his infinite justice would see fit to punish such a man. I've no doubt other priests might tell you differently but, like I said before, sometimes I wonder if they believe in the same God that Jesus Christ told us about, the one who is all merciful and understanding and forgiving. In all likelihood Jem drank the whiskey simply to alleviate his pain, his situation, which would be perfectly understandable. Doctors can sometimes seem over cautious, that's their job, and I think we can all be guilty of not appreciating the seriousness of their advice. Jem probably thought he was doing no harm. I think you should rest easy on the matter, Mrs Murphy."

Patsy suddenly looked relieved but embarrassed. "I offered you tea, Father, and here I am treating your visit like a confessional."

"And I offered you bagels and treated you to a dose of my 'heathen' modern ideas. So, we're even, Mrs Murphy. I have to be going now, do my rounds of the sick of the parish, but I hope I'd be welcome to call again. More often than not I'm with parishioners who see me coming, so to speak, and they turn on their religious fervour thinking that's what I'd called for when actually a good discussion and exchange of opinions is always more interesting. We belong to a living Church, after all, and talk keeps it and us alive."

"I'd like you to call again, Father, but I'll get the bagels next time," said Patsy.

Part 6

Out-worn heart, in a time out-worn,
Come clear of the nets of wrong and right;
Laugh, heart, again in the grey of twilight;
Sigh, heart, again in the dew of the morn.

— W B Yeats

1

Patsy decided to try on the cerise cocktail-dress that Jem had picked out for her that first time they went to dine at the Gresham after sorting an order for his company at Jeanette Modes. She remembered how he had immediately known her dress size and what colour would suit her, not one she would have normally chosen for herself but he had an eye and he had been right. She hadn't worn the frock for years: the only time it registered in her consciousness was when she flicked through her wardrobe but tonight she wanted to wear something special. That it had such a strong link to Jem was an added touch. She was going to the Feis Ceoil national music competition in the city with James and it was to be their last musical soirée together before he moved to Cork with his family. Of course she would never have met James had it not been for Jem, so it seemed appropriate to wear what she always thought of as Jem's dress. It amused her as she took the frock off the hanger to think of how something so essentially female as a dress could be so closely associated with a man in Patsy O'Kelly's cloistered mind: from even further back over the years, she still had a black-and-white geometric patterned one that was forever a connection with Sean Fitzsimmons.

She was looking forward to her evening out. The morning had been spent painting with her young helper, putting a basic undercoat on the freshly-plastered walls of the lavatory — Matt had sent one of his men around to do it — and then in the late afternoon sketching in the outline of their design with tailor's chalk. She'd had a good all-over strip wash at the kitchen sink but it had taken a while to get the paint off her hands and then she needed a good application of hand-cream before she trusted herself to take hold of the satin dress: she didn't want any rough bits of skin pulling any threads out of the smooth material. Now the question was whether or not the thing would fit her. According to Theresa, Patsy had kept her figure, thanks to not being stretched out of shape with pregnancy, Patsy remembered with a touch of resentment, but now she would be glad if her sister's comment proved to be true. Only fitting in on would tell.

First of all, she put on a change of underwear, her best to sit without rucks under the dress, then the big moment arrived, and she slid the frock over her head. All was well, it fitted as if Jem had just picked it out for her off the rail. She didn't even have to struggle with the zip. She titivated her hair and put on some make-up, thinking, as she did her lipstick, of Nora and what drove the woman to slap a cupid's bow across her face. It was a mean thought and she immediately regretted it, thinking instead of how the cupid's bow was a colourful symbol of Nora's natural effervescence. Patsy gave herself the once-over in front of the mirror, turning this way and that to gauge the overall effect when she caught herself looking directly at herself, eye-to-eye: life wasn't so bad, she told her direct gaze, she had indeed been through a bad patch but she was coming out at the other end. It would be her last outing with James but she wasn't going to spoil it by being miserable at his going.

Once downstairs she had a look at the clock and decided she had time for a sit and a cigarette. "Not that it's really any of your business," she addressed Jem's chair, "but I'll tell you anyway as you asked, give you something to think on, Mrs Murphy Senior, while you wait for me to come home. That is if you put in an appearance then, it'll be late when I get back. I'm going out with one of your son's old friends to a music competition and I wanted to look nice for the occasion. He's sending a taxi to collect me. You recognise the dress? It looks nice? Well thank you for your approval. Yes, Jem chose it, so he'll be with me in spirit, which will make a bit of a change from your spirit, I suppose. You know, I've yet to figure out if there's any pattern to your being here, whether it's just on a whim from the other side or whether it's because you're stuck here on this side but have different places to go to as the fancy takes you. Oh, there's the taxi now so I'll love you and leave you. As I said, I'll be late back so don't wait up."

Patsy didn't spot James outside the hall at the prearranged door: groups of concert-goers swarmed outside the venue, some togged out for the evening in their finest finery, adding a touch of cognoscente glamour to the occasion, others more bohemian in their arranged-scruffiness appearance, the sort her father had been so apprehensive about all those years ago when he refused to allow her to take up the scholarship. Both approaches looked harmless enough but interesting and invigorating to Patsy. She was excited to be a part of the throng. The Feis Ceoil was a grand gala that had become a major event on the Dublin music calendar but Patsy had herself never been before so she hadn't really known what to expect or, indeed, what to wear. Jem had been several times, no doubt with Peter, and all Patsy had gleaned was that the competition was started at the end of the last century to encourage interest in Irish music after years of neglect but that was about as far as her knowledge went, other than that the festival had developed into much more and that Jem always dressed up for it.

"Hello there, Patsy." She heard James's voice before she felt his hand on her arm and turned to greet him. He stood back and gave her the once over, obviously admiring what he saw. He was wearing a dinner suit and Patsy was glad she had opted for the cocktail dress. "I hope you haven't been waiting on your own too long," he said. "I didn't know what time to tell the taxi: sometimes they arrive on time, sometimes if they're not busy they arrive early to get the booking out of the way. Then I was a bit delayed. We're in the middle of packing up the house, as you know, and Kathleen needed my brute force to move a couple of boxes."

"I've not been here long," said Patsy, "just long enough to enjoy looking at all the people. It certainly attracts a mixed crowd."

"It's always very popular, I was quite lucky to get a couple of tickets in the stalls," said James. "Do you know much about the Feis Ceoil?"

"Not really," said Patsy, "only from odd comments Jem made. It's not really the sort of thing you're conscious of growing up in The Liberties, at least I wasn't aware of it, I wouldn't like to cast aspersions on any of my neighbours who might have been far more in the cultural know than the O'Kellys ever were."

"I'm sure there are people from all parts of the city who'd be interested but of course you do have to have a few pounds in your pocket to enjoy some of these things and I'm lucky enough never to have been poor," said James. "You'll have heard of John McCormack, no doubt. He sang in Phoenix Park during the Eucharistic Congress Mass?"

"I certainly have heard of John McCormack, who in Ireland hasn't, and him with such a beautiful voice. Unfortunately I missed him that time

478

in the park." Patsy refused to let her mind dwell on how she had spent that day spying on Sean's wedding. "What's he got to do with Feis Ceoil?"

"He won it one year," said James. "He beat James Joyce, the writer, would you believe. Joyce had a good tenor voice too and he entered the competition but the story has it that he marched off the stage in a temper because he was asked to do some sight reading. He wanted to know what that had to do with being able to sing and he criticised the committee for making it one of the rules that all entrants had to sing a piece from sight. All the same he managed to win a bronze medal."

"That's the second time recently someone has mentioned James Joyce to me," said Patsy. "I've not read any of his books but evidently Portobello, where I live, of course, is well represented in *Ulysses*, is that the title?"

"It is and you should read it, if you can get a copy, it can be hard to get hold of in Ireland because of the language and the sex," said James. "That's Ireland for you, always looking for something to be scandalised about, always preoccupied by the temptations of the flesh."

"Jem used to say that Ireland loved getting her knickers in a twist when it came to sex."

"He had a point," said James. "It can be a fine line between titivation and the sheer relish of being scandalised. You know even Feis Ceoil isn't immune. One year there was actually a walk-out. One of the set-songs had the word 'kiss' in it more than once and some of the singers withdrew from the competition rather than repeat such an objectionable word in a song. Of course, a few years later the country was at war with the British and then with themselves but that didn't seem half so objectionable. You have to wonder at our priorities."

An invisible signal seemed to spur sudden movement on the pavement and everyone started making their way into the concert. Patsy and James were shown to a row halfway down the auditorium and fortunately the people in the seats in front didn't have either big heads or big hats to spoil the view. After everyone had sat down, a hush fell over the theatre, broken only by an unrehearsed but familiar chorus of coughs and throat-clearing, and the proceedings began. Patsy settled into a delicious, musical heaven, appreciative of all the performers and especially of those who obviously had to overcome a last-minute fit of nerves, for these were all accomplished in their fields but the combination of a sense of occasion and the competitive edge was bound to release a flutter of butterflies on stage. She wondered how she would have coped had Miss Bourke's predictions of her young Larch Hill pupil becoming a concert pianist ever come to fruition. Right now, she had only to forget the past and its promises and enjoy the evening.

The programme swept the audience along and it was clear from the applause, which ranged from the generous through the enthusiastic to the ecstatic, exactly who on stage had won as far as the people in the seats were concerned. A young tenor by the name of Frank Patterson had everyone enthralled and, indeed, when the results were announced, he had won first prize in several sections. Ireland had a new golden boy.

"That was wonderful," said Patsy as she filed out with James at the end of the competition, her sentiment echoed over and over by many other voices in the general buzz of approval jostling its way out after the concert. "It's hard to believe there is so much music going on in the country, so much undoubted talent. I felt quite envious. It's made me want to sit down at the piano and start practising again, though I'm not too sure my neighbours would appreciate it. They've already made their feelings known on the matter."

"How was that?"

"How was that, was through various bangings on the wall, and finally a knock on the door asking me to stop. Evidently, I was interfering with their television viewing."

"What imbeciles!" said James. "You should practise round the clock and with the loud pedal down. Come on, let's find somewhere for a welcome nightcap. Is there anywhere you fancy? We can take a taxi, if we can find one, though I see a few chauffeur-driven cars pulling up so we could be lucky."

"I'm in your hands, though perhaps somewhere in the general direction of home might be easiest. I like that place that looks for all the world like a small castle from the outside, near the Quays."

"The Brazen Head?"

"That's the one. Jem and I went there after a small party my mammy had organised at home to celebrate our engagement. We were with my sister and her husband, the ones who moved to live in Cheltenham. Jem and Billy got on very well, two horseracing fans."

"And another James Joyce connection," said James "He was quite a regular there at the same bar. The Brazen Head it is, then."

The pavement in front of the concert venue was as crowded as it had been before the show, as if everyone was reluctant to call an end to what had been a fabulous evening of entertainment, full of eager speculation as to who might or might not turn out to be a winning entrant. There was a lot to talk about: did the judges make the right choices in the end? People had to make up for all their own opinions and comments that had had to be left unsaid during the performances, agreeing and disagreeing but all welcoming the arrival on the scene of the young tenor, Frank Patterson, surely to become a household name. Chatter and laughter filled the air with a lively enthusiasm that was palpable. It was Dublin at its best, thought Patsy: she wondered why anyone would want to leave but again shoved the question to the back of her mind so as not to put a damper on the evening. She was only vaguely aware of being guided along by James' arm about her to a less busy spot on the road where it didn't take too long for a taxi to pull up. Soon they were sitting in the pub, drinks in hand.

"I shall miss our little outings," said Patsy.

"Me too," said James, "very much. But you know sometimes Feis Ceoil is held in Cork instead of Dublin and there's no reason why you couldn't travel down. Kathleen would love it and it would give you a chance to see the new house."

"How is the packing going?" asked Patsy.

"Slowly, that's all I can say. We have another few days before the removal van comes so we need to get a move on."

"And is all the work finished on the new house?"

"The major work is but it's a strange thing when you're moving house: one minute you seem to have all the time in the world and suddenly you're off and whatever's not done is just not done. We'll be living in a bit of a building site for a few months at least, I'd say, but Kathleen is keen to go, no doubt quite glad of having the chance to get things sorted exactly as she wants. The children are already squabbling about which part of the rambling residence will be theirs. What about you? Can you see yourself moving from Warren Street now you have no ties there?"

"Well, James, I do have a silly tie there though it's not of my choosing," said Patsy. "You asked me once to let you know if Jem ever got in touch — you knowing my reputation for seeing spirits and such like. Let me say right now that Jem hasn't been in touch so I've no message for you there. But you'll be amused to hear that I'm stuck with his mother."

"Jem's mother?" James almost spat out his drink, he started laughing so much.

"The one and only. She puts in regular appearances, poor woman. I'm not sure if she wants to make sure I'm looking after the house or whether she's still there because she's in a sort of limbo."

"And does she talk to you?"

"Not in so many words," said Patsy. "Let's just say that she sits there in Jem's old chair by the fire and manages to communicate what she wants to say. She's a nosey one all right, with her questions, and she does like to comment on whatever I happen to be doing."

"Is she nasty?"

"Not always, she did say she thought I looked nice tonight, but I think that's because she knows Jem chose this dress for me."

"Well, she was right, you do look very nice, quite the beautiful woman, I'd say, and Jem always had instinctive good taste when it came to clothes," said James. "I just can't imagine what it must be like to live with a ghost."

"I think we all do, it's just that not everyone sees them. I believe that everywhere — not just old houses, as a lot of people think, or places where something awful has happened — but every single place on this earth retains traces of the past, of the people and the events that took place on that one same spot through the ages, and occasionally those traces can be picked up across the surface of time."

"By someone like you who has the gift?"

"I don't know that that means, 'someone like me'," said Patsy. "I don't feel like a someone, I don't feel I have a gift, it's just an awareness I've had since I was a child. It's never frightened me, though I did learn to keep it to myself because I know it can frighten other people or make them think I'm some sort of a crazy woman."

"I don't think you're crazy at all, but I suppose people are always afraid of what they don't understand or can't see for themselves," said James. "I hope there's nothing of that sort in our new house, it is quite old."

"If there is, I'm sure you won't even notice it," said Patsy. "You must be looking forward to the move."

"I suppose we are, especially now," said James. "If you ask me there's going to be trouble flaring up soon with the North and Dublin's bound to get brought into the conflict. I'm too old to want to live through any of that again. It was bad enough when I was a child and I wouldn't want my own having to go through that violence."

"Is it getting that bad?" asked Patsy. "I know they started a lot of internment a few years back and my father was convinced the whole thing would blow up again too and not just along the border. I can't understand why there's still so much hatred on both sides. I suppose there's still a lot of people wanting a united Ireland and a lot of people in the North still totally against it. I haven't been following the news lately as much as I used to, I've had enough bad news to deal with at home."

"I agree with your father. There seems to have been a pattern developing up in the North. There'll be some relatively minor incident of paramilitary activity, which is inevitably followed by tighter restrictions being introduced, and then a more serious incident in retaliation to that, which all repeats itself and repeats itself again, each time the situation worsening. I admit I used to laugh at the stories you'd read in the newspaper of the odd telephone box being blown up along the border, I thought that was the work of some crazies trying to hold on to the glories of the past, but it's not so funny now. Then there are all the civil rights protests going on, Catholics demanding a fair election system, one man/one vote, and who can blame them. For a start they'll never get on the housing list any other way, there's an awful lot of discrimination goes on, but I can't see the Protestants agreeing to give up their control without a fight."

"I wonder if it would have been peaceful by now if there'd never been partition," said Patsy.

"There's always a chance it might have but there's also a chance it would have been a lot worse," said James. "Who's to know how bad it's going to get now. In that regard at least I'll be glad to get away to Cork."

"Well, I'll be sorry to lose a friend," said Patsy.

"Me too, very much so," he said, taking her hand briefly before letting it go. "You seem to be getting on all right anyway. Is life settling down?"

"It is. I'm still working, which I love, and I happen to have bumped into a few familiar faces recently, which was very welcome after being cooped up in the house so much while Jem was ill. I had a visit too from the new priest at St Kevin's Church. He's the son of a woman I know quite well, a midwife, in fact, who helped my mammy deliver several of her babies, and I think she'd asked him to call and check up on me after Jem and then my da passed away. Father Dec, he's called. He's good company, not at all like your everyday priest. He brought some bagels with him to have with a cup of tea. Have you ever tried them? They're Jewish. We had them toasted and buttered and they were delicious."

"No, I've not had one, but it sounds as if they'd be a nice change from the usual slice of toast and marmalade for breakfast. How's the jungle-in-the-toilet project progressing, by the way?"

"It's going very well. I had a modern low-flush toilet and cistern installed and young Sean and I sketched in the design on the walls today. He has some grand ideas. They do get more outlandish by the minute but to be honest I'm glad to go along with whatever he suggests. I might have given up on the madness of it all by now without him and gone back to safe but boring pastels, as you called them. It's good to have him helping me. I like having young company in the house."

"Well, I can understand that if the alternative is your dead mother-in-law. You never know, the tiger in the toilet might prove enough to send her on her way," said James. "Otherwise you could ask Father Dec to perform an exorcism."

"Time" was called from the bar and they had to finish their drinks. James helped Patsy on with her coat and they made their way back through the pub courtyard to the road. They both tried but the easy animation of their normal conversation was already sounding forced in the finality of the short walk: neither would admit it even to themselves, but the taxi seemed to take a quiet eternity to arrive. Then the taxi pulled up and sad goodbyes couldn't be postponed any longer and, though they were accompanied by firm invitations and acceptances to visit, both Patsy and James knew this would probably be their last meeting.

"I will definitely keep in touch," promised James as he hugged Patsy closely before pulling away quickly and helping her into the taxi. "I'll send you the address just as soon as we've settled in."

"You do that," said Patsy. She kept looking and smiling out of the window as the car drove away and he stood waving from the pavement. She kept looking until he was out of sight, disappeared altogether, invisible, vanished into the past.

2

It was a bit of a squash in the lavatory when Patsy and Sean, the two nascent artists, were at work on their jungle murals. They agreed early on not to keep apologising for elbowing and bumping into each other as there was no room to stand on polite ceremony. It wasn't too bad when Sean was up the ladder and Patsy was working on the bottom of a wall, otherwise a certain amount of contortion was necessary. Sean, a budding Rousseau if ever there was one, proved to be a talented hard worker and his eye for design and colour reminded Patsy of Jem when it came to clothes. She had taken Sean on a buying trip into the city so that he could supervise which paints to buy, though he was always mindful not to choose the most expensive. The small test pots of different colours available in the decorator's shop would be perfectly adequate, he had told Patsy, and would save on waste. At last, after several weekends devoted to the project, the whole thing was really taking shape. The background greens and browns had been blocked in and it was time for Sean to be allowed to work on his own on what he called 'the fine art' of the scheme, the detailed foliated landscape and the animals themselves.

"This is your last chance to suggest any changes," he said to Patsy. "You don't have to accept everything I say, you know, and are you sure the snake will be to your liking up the door?"

"It will and perhaps it will frighten off any mice or insects," said Patsy. "As for the rest, I can already see how good you are at all this. My efforts would have been pitiful by comparison. You carry on and I'll get to work on the sewing."

Annie's husband Matt had sourced the new toilet for Patsy and had it installed by another of his nameless contacts. He had also managed to find a large piece of what he called butchers' grass, the sort of artificial greenery you saw in the window displays of butcher's shops, and Patsy wanted to add fabric flowers to it as a warm covering for the floor. There was enough to allow her to make her toilet-seat cover too. For a curtain she had decided on a very deep brown on to which she could also applique similar flowers to keep the theme going. Sean approved, saying the floor and seat cover would pull together by echoing each other at different levels, the whole lot set off by the top-to-bottom length of the floral curtain.

"You sound very knowledgeable," said Patsy, impressed by the boy's concentration and dedication.

"I've always loved to draw and paint," he said. "Of course we only have what you might call scraps of paper in the house and some old paint boxes from Christmas presents we were given years ago when my da was alive, but the little rectangles of colour are worn down into bare dimples in the middle. There's not much paint left. I went into one of those posh artists' shops once and I couldn't believe how expensive everything was, but I enjoyed looking at all the different kinds of paints they had and brushes for all different types of work. I'd love to know what you do with them. I wanted to ask but I didn't like the way they looked at me from the moment I walked in so I didn't ask."

"Like the waitresses at Bewley's?"

"Just the same," said Sean. "It always makes me feel cross when I get those looks. This time I was cross and disappointed too because I only wanted to know things, I wasn't going to steal anything."

"Well, they are just ignorant people, and you mustn't mind them," said Patsy. "Now I'm definitely going in to start sewing and maybe in half an hour we can have a tea break."

They worked for the whole of the afternoon with just the one break for tea. When they decided to call it a day, Patsy went to inspect the progress outside and was pleased to be greeted by the life-sized tiger, which had gained its first lot of purple stripes. The same colour traced in segments what was to be the snake coiling up the door and Sean had painted a small cluster of flowers in the same colour in the bottom corner behind the toilet.

"I think I have some purple remnants that would be a grand match for the paint," said Patsy. "Now let's get back into the house. Your mammy will be here soon and we don't want to miss her knock."

Mrs Mulhoney had arranged to meet Sean at Patsy's house so he could help with the weekend shopping and she had his two sisters in tow:

the middle child, Maureen, an interesting-looking girl who had a bit of a tom-boy appeal about her, and the youngest, Veronica, who had an auburn mass of curly bubbles above quite an angelic-looking face. They were all anxious to see the jungle-toilet out in the back-yard after Sean talking about it so much and it was a noisy procession that traipsed down the hallway and straight out of the back door. They were all amazed at how amazingly amazing it was. Patsy left Sean to be the tour guide while she poured out some lemonade for the youngsters to enjoy in the yard. She sat down with Mrs Mulhoney for a chat over a pot of tea.

"You must be very proud of your children," said Patsy.

"I am but it's a bit of a struggle, as I told you last time," said the mother. "I'd love nothing better than to be able to give them the best, I don't want them getting into trouble just because we're poor, but you yourself know how it is, money doesn't grow on trees and people can be very cruel with their assumptions just because your clothes have seen better days."

"I'd love to be able to help," said Patsy, "but I don't have that much myself."

"Oh, forgive me, Mrs Murphy, I wasn't hinting. God, I'd hate you to think that. I feel quite ashamed if that's the impression I've given you."

"I know you weren't doing anything of the sort, Mrs Mulhoney. You were just stating the facts. I was brought up in a house full of children myself and my father was only a baker, so I know what it's like trying to make ends meet and there's a family to feed and clothe. As regards the children getting into trouble, I don't think you need to worry about Sean. He's a very honest boy, he seems to have a healthy understanding of how the world is but he doesn't let it get him down, and I believe he has real artistic talent. He's very creative. I hope they encourage him in school. I can't really do much for you on a day-to-day basis but, with your permission, I'd like at least to buy Sean a book of drawing paper and maybe some watercolour paints. He was telling me he'd been to an art shop in town but he left when he saw how the assistants were looking at him as if he was a thief."

"He would be delighted with that and so would I," said Mrs Mulhoney, "but only if it's part of his payment for the work he's doing here."

"That's what we'll call it then. I'm sure he wouldn't like to think of himself as a charity case. I don't know your daughters, are they a help to you?"

"They are, they have to be really. Maureen especially likes to look after her mammy, she's full of energy and mischief but she's quite the little mother herself. She likes nothing better than taking care of her brother and sister and she's the one they go to if they have a scratch or a cut. Out come the bandages and the ointments and the plasters and then she carries out the examination, all very serious, mind."

"She sounds like a good doctor in the making, or a nurse. And what about Veronica?"

"Her big preoccupation right now is that she is to make her first Holy Communion in a couple of months' time so she sits at home practising her catechism and walking round the house with her hands joined and pointing up to heaven. She manages to keep a straight face but at the same time she deliberately jitters her head to shake her curls, so she looks a bit demented, to be honest. She's a great laugh. Then she says she has to practise sticking her tongue out to receive the Host and of course she chooses her moments."

"Has she planned her white dress?" asked Patsy. "The little girls all seem to like dressing up for the big day. I suppose in a way it's their first big day on the public stage."

"We'll have to think about that," said Mrs Mulhoney. "There's a second-hand shop where they sometimes have used Communion frocks, so I'll have a look in there. Hopefully I'll find something. Veronica knows we won't be making any special trip to Clery's like some of the girls at school."

Patsy poured more tea. "Now that's something I could help with," she said. "Would you not let me make her a dress? I can get some white cloth at work — there's often a bale-end that's far too short to be of much use so it wouldn't cost you anything — and Veronica could come here to be measured and I could run up a dress at home for her on the machine, it wouldn't take me any time at all. I'm afraid you'd have to sort the veil and the headdress yourself but at least you wouldn't have to worry about the frock. And it would be much nicer for Veronica to have her own new one."

Mrs Mulhoney's eyes almost welled up. "You've already been very kind to us. I can't expect that of you," she said.

"I don't see why not," said Patsy. "All I'd be doing is a bit of sewing and I'm well used to that." Before Mrs Mulhoney could raise any further objections, she was stopped in her tracks by the children bustling back into the house, emptied glasses clinking as they were deposited on the table and all the talk being of tigers and snakes and jungles. The lavatory had proved a great success.

"We'd better be off now, children, or all the shops will have closed," said Mrs Mulhoney getting up. "Thank you for your hospitality, Mrs Murphy, and for your generous thoughts."

Patsy led the way down the hall to the front door. "I'll see you next time, Sean." Then she turned to the sisters. "Veronica, I understand you're making your first Holy Communion soon? Would you like me to make you a special dress for the occasion?"

"My God, I'd love that," she screeched with excitement, before sticking her tongue out and giving Patsy a demonstration of her holy way of walking. It was too late for Mrs Mulhoney to intervene over the dress now that Veronica knew and she could only sneak in a look of pleased disapproval at Patsy.

"You'll have to come round again to be measured," said Patsy. "Perhaps, Maureen, you could bring your sister, give your mammy a bit of a break."

The family set off to the shops and Sean again paused to wave before turning the corner. Patsy went back into the house feeling she had had a good day. She lit up a cigarette and finished the drop of tea still in the pot, it was cold but wet, and decided she had earned a lazy evening after all the painting and sewing. She would get fish and chips for her dinner and sit and eat them on her knee in front of the television. Then she would put her feet up and settle down with Gaybo for his late show. Bugger Mrs Murphy Senior, she could sit and haunt herself for a change.

3

It wasn't in the back of a Black and Tans wagon but Patsy was following in her father's wake and being transported to Kilmainham Gaol, screaming at the top of her lungs as the city's streets flew past but out of excitement rather than fear. Much to her surprise she had agreed to go willingly on the back of John's Vespa. It was her first time on the scooter. It was also, ridiculously, considering it was the mid '60s and women's fashions had never been freer or easier to wear, the first time she had ever worn a pair of slacks, which she had had to borrow from Annie for the occasion. It was only common-sense not to ride on the back of a scooter in a skirt. Common-sense or not, Patsy felt delighted out of all proportion at what she regarded as a statement of independence. Never mind the slacks, she had initially been even more self-conscious at the idea of putting a crash helmet on her head but John had insisted and really it was all part of the fun. The neighbours in Warren Street enjoyed the spectacle: Mrs Murphy had certainly lost any of the uppitiness they had enjoyed tutting about in the past: she had become an intriguing character in the street, with new people in and out of her house all the time, taxis calling for her and dropping her off, while her outside toilet was the talk of the terraces after a few of the local kids had positioned themselves atop the wall of the back-yard to have a good gawp at what was going on. And now the grieving widow was climbing on to the back of one of those modern scooter things without so much as a blush. Patsy would have been amused to learn that more than a few of her female neighbours felt positively envious of her.

"That's right, just put your arms around my waist and hold on and we'll be off," said John.

The exhilaration had kicked in before they'd even left the street. Her head tucked in tightly against her brother's shoulder, Patsy thrilled at the feel of the air slamming coldly into her face, at the way John confidently manoeuvred his way through the traffic, neatly swerving this way and that as he dodged his way past cars and buses, hips tilting and rotating from side to side as he steered, and all the time her gasping and laughing as the adrenalin raced round her veins. Patsy felt like a teenager, felt as if she was on a fairground ride, felt more alive than she had felt in years and totally invigorated by such a simple sense of freedom. It didn't take long to get to Kilmainham, much to Patsy's disappointment. She was already looking forward to the return journey.

John had suggested the outing, realising that Patsy would be the one person he knew who would be as interested in visiting the gaol as he himself was. He hadn't been alive when his father had been interned there but he was proud of the family's history and connection with such an imposing fortress and its dark place in the Irish psyche. He had come across a photograph in the old album of Patrick standing in the bleak stone-breakers' yard of the prison at the sacred spot where the Easter Rising leaders had been executed by firing squad. They had been lined up on the rough ground against a high grey stone wall at the end of the yard, all except for James Connolly, who had been so badly injured in the fighting that he had had to be brought to Kilmainham on a stretcher from the hospital and then tied upright in a chair and shot like that. No wonder it had become a place of pilgrimage. On the back of the photograph Patrick had written a small tribute: "This is where you gave your lives for us, and we still owe you so much." In the picture it was easy to see the effect the spot had had on Patrick: there were tears in his eyes and an acute sadness distorted his features.

Their father wasn't a particularly young man in the picture: he was bundled up in a long heavy winter coat, scarf wrapped several times around his neck and a warm trilby pulled down on his head against the weather, but the real chill of the scene wasn't down to the weather. It was the grim emptiness of the yard and the silent volume of the firing squad still lining up against the condemned men and haunting the place. John had been so moved by the photo, by his father's demeanour and message — and by the feeling that John himself had been brought face to face with his own ignorance — that he had determined to visit Kilmainham. His big regret was that he hadn't ever thought to talk to his father directly about those terrible years and about Patrick's experiences and now it was too late. At the funeral it didn't occur to John to pull their Uncle Arthur to one side or to talk to the men who had turned up in their old uniforms, but Patsy had been alive at the time and surely would remember some stories or other. She might be less upset by the memories and his questions than his mammy.

They parked the scooter and walked up to the gate. John realised he hadn't even checked in advance on whether or not the gaol was open and he was relieved to see the chain on the gate not fastened and two men standing outside the main door smoking. He walked through the gate with Patsy and asked if it would be at all possible to go inside and have a look.

"And why would you want to do that?" replied the elder of the two men.

"Our father was held here for a few months in 1920 before he was shipped off to a prison camp in the North," said John. "He died recently and we wanted to pay some sort of respects to what he'd been through but never talked about. Do we need to get special permission?"

The two men shrugged and glanced from John to Patsy as they weighed up the situation. Then they stubbed out their cigarettes and went back in through the huge wooden door. "The two of you come on in then, I don't see the harm," the man said, "but it's at your own risk, we've no insurance for visitors. This way now."

They entered a bright high room rounded at one end and tiered with three rows of cells, the upper two reached by a metal stairway rising up the centre of the hall and dividing off either side.

"Which way do we go?" asked Patsy.

"Please yourself," said the younger man, "but I'm afraid I can't let you go up these main stairs here, otherwise you can wander at will. If you head off to the left, there are stairs will take you up to the padded cells and the rest of the hotel accommodation."

"Padded cells?" said Patsy. She had no idea there were padded cells in Kilmainham.

"Of course," he said. "That's where some poor buggers who had been tortured were kept in solitary and left to go mad."

"And why are these cells in the hall closed off?" asked John tilting his head towards the tiered rows. "I was expecting gloom and dirt and darkness, I can't believe how clean it all looks, as if it's not long been painted."

"That's for the benefit of the Chinese criminal mastermind Doctor Fu Manchu," said the young security man, enjoying the effect his apparently outlandish statement had on the visitors and the look of total bewilderment on their faces. "No really," he said. "There's a film company coming soon to make a film about Fu Manchu so were having to clean up some of the areas. They'll be bringing lots of equipment with them which will all need protecting and kept clean."

"Doctor Fu Manchu? A Chinese film? My God in Heaven, I can't believe they could be so disrespectful," said Patsy. "Isn't that completely out of keeping with what people see as a national shrine to the Republican martyrs and all the other men who fought and were locked up in here?"

"Men like our father," said John, not even trying to disguise the note of pride and ownership in his voice.

"You're no doubt right in what you say but, shrine or no shrine, it costs money to maintain the place even in its basic state and make sure it doesn't just fall into rack and ruin and that money has to come from somewhere," said the watchman. "It's a British film to star Christopher Lee so it's a proper picture, like, it'll bring in a few bob."

"A British film?" gawped Patsy. "As if that doesn't just add insult to injury!"

"Surely they won't be allowed to change anything?" said John.

"They're to build a few Chinese-looking bits of architecture in the exercise yard, I believe, temporary structures, but they won't be touching the stone-breakers' yard where the executions were carried out, that really is too important. And it's not as if it's the first time Kilmainham has starred in a film. Did you not see Brendan's *The Quare Fellow* in the cinema? That was filmed here a couple of years back, although that did include Irishmen locked up waiting for a morning execution so there was an echo of history in that, I suppose you could say. I don't think there were any Chinese involved and I don't think the place was tarted up, though they did have to dig a grave in the yard for one scene. Anyway, you'd best take your look around. You're only here unofficially, so to speak. I doubt we could pass you off as part of the film crew arrived early."

Patsy and John left the brightness of the main hall and set off unescorted down a low damp corridor, the oppressive atmosphere pressing heavier and heavier on their shoulders the further in they went and the walls pressing in closer and closer and seeming to menace their very ability to breathe. Cell doors were left hanging open, their dark interiors just a gaping blackness under the dim spill of the low-watt bulbs along the stone-cold length of the corridors. There were harsh metal staircases and hellish walkways fixed at rigid right angles and the sound of their haltering footsteps made Patsy and John shiver. It was all too easy to hear the threatening beat of booted guards as they patrolled the galleries, rattling their batons along the iron railings and on the doors and shouting smug abuse at the incarcerated prisoners.

"I hate the thought of my daddy being locked up in this place," whispered Patsy, it would have seemed like a flippant intrusion to speak in a normal voice. None of this should ever have been normal, though it had been for the prisoners, both criminal and political alike. "It's far more terrifying than I had imagined," she said. "No wonder Da never spoke of it to us."

They found the padded cells, awful holes, stinking, stained with long-dead piss and blood, the stuffing languishing matted and ragged off the walls in their screaming witness to the past horrors. Images of men tearing at the walls in their loneliness and frustration and helpless desperation, separated from loved ones by the unrelenting thick walls of stone and power, all seemed to inhabit the stagnancy of the gaol. Patsy and John continued down the maze of cells and gangways, one row after another, endless in the hopelessness they contained.

"I can't stay here a moment longer, John. I have to get out."

"I'll come with you, this place is giving me nightmares and I'm wide awake."

They turned and traced their way back to the main hall. This time the brightness was a welcome return to the present rather than a betrayal of the past.

"What did you say your father's name was?" asked the older of the two security men.

"Patrick O'Kelly."

"And he was here in 1920, I think you said. Well, let's just have a look now." He flicked through a heavy ledger he had retrieved from the office and set it down on a table by the stairs: neat handwritten columns filled both sides of every page, not always entered by the same hand and the ink slightly varying in colour every few pages or so. Odd tea splashes specked over some of the entries and some of the pages were freckling with age as if they had developed liver-spots. Finally, the man halted at a page and ran his fingers up and down the lists before stopping to study an entry. "Your father was in a cell up on the top tier," he said, pointing up the central stairway and counting silently. "If you look up to the top row and follow your eyes along to left, there was a Patrick O'Kelly listed as being held in the fourth cell to the left of the stairs towards the middle of 1920. That must have been him. He was here for six months, give or take, according to this, which would fit in with what you said about him being shipped up to the North."

Patsy and John stood staring up at the unyielding cell door, thinking about their da locked up behind it and picturing his daily miserable trudges up and down the stairs, lined up single file with his fellow prisoners, maybe heading out to the exercise yard or to collect a tray of food or to empty their toilet pots, all the time being insulted and assaulted by cruel warders with their sick sticks of authority. They tried to conjure the photos of their father as a young man, the way he would have been when he was a prisoner there and able to cope, but they could only see Patrick as an older man: in Patsy's mind he was the father lying sick in the hospital bed, for John it was the unknown father in the overcoat and scarf and trilby: the images seemed to intensify the horrors of Kilmainham.

"What was the name of the camp he was in?" asked the older man. "Ballykinlar was it?"

"It was," said Patsy.

"And do you still have a small, crocheted string-bag he made for you there?"

"I have, he made one each for me and my two sisters."

"I made one each for my three girls too," said the veteran. "I don't remember a man with your father's name, I'm sad to say, but there were quite a few of us so that's not surprising. I'm sorry to hear he passed away but at least you can now fill in a blank in your family's history.

496

Unfortunately we will have to ask you to leave now but I do apologise for that, you've more of a claim to be here than a film crew and I'm sure you must have questions you'd like to ask. Anyway, I'm usually here so you know where to find me if you want to talk more."

"I'd love that," said John.

"I never want to come near this place again," said Patsy.

They were shown out through the main gate but neither of them was in the mood for chit chat as John unlocked the chain on his scooter and, as they rode back through the city, Patsy experienced no sense of exhilaration at being on the back. The wind on her face now only made her feel cold and she wanted to get home.

"I didn't know you had a bag Da had made in the camp," said John helping her off the back of the scooter outside the house in Warren Street. "I'd love to see it."

"I'll root it out and show you next time," said Patsy. "Were you wanting to come in?"

"Not right now. At some stage I'd like to talk about everything, find out what you remember from when you were little, I just don't think now is the time. It was quite upsetting going to the gaol today, for both of us, I think. It was more like an awful pilgrimage than just a visit to satisfy my curiosity. I'll call in next weekend if I get the chance."

"Thank you, John, for taking me today. I'll see you next week. Remember me to the family."

For a change Patsy welcomed the quiet of the house. She lit up a cigarette and just sat staring into space. She tried to focus her eyes on anything in the room, anything at all, but still she saw only the grimness of Kilmainham, the ripped padding in those awful cells. She offered up a prayer of contrition, ashamed that she had never paid any heed to the prisoners before today: it wasn't only her father who had suffered and even then, she confessed, she had regarded his role in the Irish fight for independence in a ridiculously romantic way. That wasn't the case at all: there was nothing romantic about Kilmainham Gaol.

"I've been to prison today, in case you're wondering why the long face," she said to Jem's chair as she poured herself a Paddy's and lit another cigarette. "It was the one my father was locked up in when he was caught by the Tans. Of course, I was only a child at the time but I knew what was going on, I just didn't know until today what my poor daddy had actually been through. Just think, if it hadn't been for me helping to conceal Jem's secret with a cloak of respectability, your son might very well have ended up in gaol himself. Did you ever think of that? I doubt if a man that-way-inclined would have survived it all, but my daddy did."

Patsy sat staring into the empty grate. She hadn't bothered to set a fire because she was going out with her brother and the plan had been that she would perhaps call in at The Coombe to see Betty in the evening, tell her about the scooter ride. But the gaol had so affected her and John that they had both wanted to just go on home. Now Patsy regretted having no warm fire to look at but she couldn't face setting it for the couple of hours she'd be up before going to bed. The clock ticked on the mantelpiece. Occasional sounds of talking or arguing or laughing filtered in from the well of adjacent back yards. Patsy could hear the sound of her own breathing as she wheezed in drag after drag and, when she struck a match for another cigarette, the scratch of the tip on the rough emery rasped loudly before the sudden phop of the flame bursting into life. It was amazing how noisy the quiet of the house could be.

Everywhere you went in the city you'd hear someone singing the blasted song, literally the blasted song.

Up went Nelson in old Dublin, Up went Nelson in Old Dublin,
All along O'Connell Street, the stones and rubble flew,
As up went Nelson and the pillar too.

For eight consecutive weeks the record was at number one in the Irish charts. Sung to the tune of *John Brown's Body*, the words were as easy to remember as the melody was familiar, celebrating the blowing up of Nelson's Pillar by IRA men to mark the fiftieth anniversary of the Easter Rising. The irony was that the hit song was written and performed by a group of Belfast schoolteachers, so all the proceeds went North: the group went by the name of The Go Lucky Four and the general consensus was that they had indeed struck lucky with the record. The other irony was that many Dubliners were sorry to see the old admiral go. A representative of the former occupying power he might have been but Nelson atop his pillar had over time become an iconic symbol of Dublin.

Nelson had overseen many the start of a burgeoning romance, his plinth offering a safe harbour for those young travellers setting out on their first romantic voyages on the stormy seas of love.

"What do you make of it, Patsy?" asked Margaret. "I have to admit I bought a copy of the record but I also signed a petition in the street to have the column rebuilt, though without Nelson on the top this time."

"I loved Nelson's Pillar," said Patsy. "It was always a must when any nephews or nieces came over from England, a climb to the top of the pillar: round and round and round the spiral steps in the dark, pressing your hand against the wall to keep your balance and stop you getting dizzy, the children religiously counting each of the one-hundred-and-sixty-eight steps on the way, then the reward of being able to stand on the platform and see the city spread out all around you below... until there was such a crowd up there that you had to force your way to the exit and then curl your way down again against the flow of the latest arrivals coming up. And now we're left with just an ugly jagged stump. I think it was a stupid thing to do, blowing it up. I bet if they'd bothered to ask in advance most people would have voted to leave Nelson where he was."

"I'm not so sure," said Margaret. "I would have voted to leave it where it was but a lot of people had been trying for years to get rid of the thing because of what it represented, it was regarded as a terrible insult to have such a huge monument to a British admiral right in the middle of Dublin. And him keeping everything so close to his chest. Why do you think he kept his hand inside his jacket like that all the time?"

"Perhaps he had a cold British titty," said Patsy. They laughed at that.

"Fortunately, or unfortunately, they couldn't do anything about removing it because of some sort of a legal agreement in place for its protection," said Margaret. "I never understood all that, it was too complicated for my brain. Then there was talk of an attempt made during the Easter Rising to blow it up but I don't know which story to believe about that."

"What stories were they?"

"It was said that the men in the GPO tried to blow up the pillar but the explosives were damp and didn't ignite. Of course, that report was used by some in the London parliament and newspapers as proof of the typical incompetence of the eejit Irish. The other story is that none of that happened, that what in fact was the case was that it suited the men fighting in O'Connell Street to have the pillar as a shield, something to provide cover from the British bullets."

"That sounds more credible," said Patsy. "You can still see all the pock-marks."

"One bullet is supposed to have shot Nelson's nose clean off during the fighting," sneered Margaret, "but whether that was a green-white-and-orange bullet or a red-white-and-blue one nobody knows. That'd be some joke wouldn't it, if the British had shot their own hero in the gob. Anyway, he's had more than his snotty nose blown for him now, he's been completely blown away with it."

"I've a friend in work who lives round the back of O'Connell Street in a flat and she was at home when the bomb went off and she said the whole of the building shook and all her dishes fell off the shelves. Imagine that happening in every building in the vicinity of O'Connell Street, the sudden bang late at night and then the shaking. My God what a fright people must have got."

"At least the street was empty and no one was hurt, thanks be to God," said Margaret.

The two friends were sitting in Patsy's back room enjoying a cuppa and a bagel, which Patsy wanted to introduce her friend to. (She herself had become a regular customer at the Bretzel Bakery and had tried all sorts of their bread, including pretzels, which she liked but not as much as the bagels.) Their evenings out had become a thing of the past, everyone's life changes, but with Jem no longer sick in the house Patsy was able to invite Margaret to call again and return her friend's unquestioning hospitality during the isolation years.

"I gather de Valera himself wrote the headline for the newspaper story," said Margaret. "Would you believe that?"

"What was it?"

"Well, I think officially he had to condemn the bombing as an atrocity, as modern parlance would have it, but when he was asked to give a statement to the Irish Press he suggested they call the article 'British Admiral leaves Dublin by air' and that's what they did. That's quite clever, don't you think."

"It is witty, sure enough. My Uncle Arthur worked for a few newspapers and he always said it was as much of an art being able to write a good headline as to write a whole article. What's to happen now with the pillar? Surely they can't leave it as it is, it's an eyesore standing there in the middle of the road."

"The job's to be finished off by the army," said Margaret, "their explosives experts have been called in to demolish the stump but evidently Nelson's head has already disappeared. That was some souvenir somebody was quick to claim."

"A bit heavy, though," said Patsy. "I bet it was students found it and took it. You might say that Nelson's head was kidnapped."

Patsy got the bottle of Paddy's and poured them both a glass in honour of times past and nights out on which the sun had sadly long since set. "What did you think of the bagel?"

"It was just as tasty as you'd promised but perhaps I won't have one with my whiskey," said Margaret. "Here's to Nelson, the old bugger," she said, lifting her glass. "At least you didn't try to introduce me to horse-meat. Did you see there's a butcher shop in the city centre started selling horsemeat? I had a look and it looked tasty and lean enough but I still wouldn't fancy it, would you?"

"Isn't that what they like in France? I wouldn't want to eat it myself, not a horse. With my luck I'd end up eating a bit of old nag that Jem had lost a fortune on at Leopardstown and then it might have given me the runs for my money too."

"He liked his racing all right," said Margaret. "He did leave you with something though, didn't he? You're not struggling for money are you, Patsy? I know you're working but that won't go on forever."

"Is that a subtle way of saying I'm getting on, that you see me ending up as just another poor widow?"

"Not at all. In fact there's no reason why you shouldn't marry again, you're young enough to have a second go. Are there not any favourite stallions in the stables, just waiting to be led out into the yard of matrimony, with you as the jockey? You always looked good in silks, Patsy."

"I did enough mucking out when Jem was ill," said Patsy. "I'm quite content on my own now, thank you."

"But you must miss having a bit of horse-play in bed?"

"Jem was never very active in that department, he was far more concerned with us getting on well outside of the sheets."

"Him and the Bishop of Galway!" said Margaret.

"The Bishop of Galway? Jem didn't know him, as far as I'm aware," said Patsy quickly, slightly shocked at what sounded like a hint of an implication.

"No, the Bishop of Galway, when he was the laughing-stock in all the papers, do you not remember, after the Gay Byrne show?"

"I don't always watch that."

"Well, you're one of the few people in Ireland who don't watch it religiously. Unfortunately, the old Bishop watched it very religiously. What happened was that Gaybo picked out a married couple from the audience, it was only recently, and they agreed to take part in a comical quiz about their honeymoon. I don't remember all the details but, to give you an idea, there was one question to the husband in which he had to say in which part of her body did his wife first feel the cold. He could choose between her nose, her feet or, as Gaybo put it, 'any other part of her body'. You can imagine how the audience laughed at that one. Then the husband was asked what colour his wife's nightie was on their wedding night and he said it was transparent. People thought that was risqué enough and they clapped and laughed some more. But, when it was her turn, the wife said she hadn't worn any nightie, in fact she hadn't worn anything at all because it was her wedding night after all. Well, the audience erupted. I know I had tears rolling down my cheeks just watching it on telly, it was so funny. The look of pretend shock on Gaybo's face was funny enough itself, never mind the hoots and cheers from the audience, but to my mind the husband was the funniest: he had a sort of naughty but delighted look on his face, 'amn't I the lucky one', and all the time his eyes scanning the audience proudly, like a cock in a henhouse. The next day the Bishop of Clonfert in Galway stood up in the pulpit at Mass in all his bishop's embroidered finery — he probably waved his crook as well — and he denounced Gay Byrne and the programme. Seriously, would you believe it? He said he had been disgusted by the disgraceful performance in such a devout Catholic country as Ireland. My God, you wonder sometimes who some of these clergy think people are."

"You do," said Patsy. "Have you met Father Dec at St Kevin's? He called in on a visit and I have to say he's a very modern sort of a priest. He believes the Church places far more responsibility on women in that department than it does on men"

"We're certainly brought up to think women and their bodies are the root of all sin," said Margaret. "It's no wonder we find it so hard to shake off all that guilt instilled in us from an early age. The way the clergy have it, we entice men to commit sins of thought just by walking past them in the street. That reminds me, they're showing that western with Maureen O'Hara and John Wayne again at the cinema, the one with the scene where he has to put her over his knee for a good spanking."

"So that must have the clergy's approval," said Patsy.

"And not a few men's, too. *McLintock*, it's called. Have you seen it already? It's a comedy really."

"No but I'd like to go. I read about it but I missed it when it came out."

"I'm surprised those two never got married," said Margaret. "They always look good together on screen. *The Quiet Man* is still one of my all-time favourites."

"According to the film magazines, off-camera they really are just very good friends. They certainly have a spark between them, you can tell they get on well."

"I wonder what he had to say when his 'very good friend' was caught up in that sex scandal ten years or so ago. That was some story: the red-headed Irish siren caught on the job and not a camera in sight as an excuse. No doubt the Bishop in Galway had something to say about that."

"I never believed a word of it," said Patsy. "I never for a moment thought it likely that a star of Maureen O'Hara's stature would be stupid enough to be having sex in public. Haven't they all got huge houses in Hollywood anyway to get on with whatever they want to get on with in private."

"But you must admit it had all the ingredients," said Margaret. "A red-headed Irish movie actress spotted in a Chinese cinema lying across several seats with a handsome Latino politician on top of her. Sure you couldn't make that up."

"But I think they did, for publicity and because it sells magazines. We should know, Margaret, you and I are still buying them after all these years, and we all enjoy reading a bit of scandal."

"I think the funniest part about that whole thing was when Maureen O'Hara sued for libel and got her sister to appear in court as a character witness. Her sister is a nun."

"And nuns never lie, they just make slaves of young unmarried mothers," said Patsy. "God forgive me, I shouldn't have said that. I was just thinking back to the conversation I had with Father Dec."

"I can't imagine what you must have been talking about to get round to that," said Margaret draining her glass. "Anyway, I'd best make a move before you say something that'll have you rushing round to the confessional, you might not get the understanding Father Dec in the box. I'll leave you to your thoughts on unmarried mothers but, remember, no sinning in those thoughts. Thanks for the tea and the bagel. And for the Paddy's, of course. Pop in and let me know what night you fancy going to the cinema but it has to be soon, it's only on this coming week."

"We should try to make it Tuesday for old time's sake," said Patsy.

"That should be good for me. Let's agree Tuesday then, unless anything unexpected comes up."

Patsy had rooted out the small, crocheted bag Patrick had made in the Ballykinlar camp from the box she kept it in with her letters from Sean Fitzsimmons. While they were secured together with ribbon, the bag was carefully protected in layers of tissue paper with a small card on which her father had written: "To my dear Patsy, my number one daughter, who fills my heart with joy." The original colour of the bag had faded from a strong purple-ink colour to more of a dusty mauve over the years but, as Patsy handled it, every knotted link felt like a direct link to her da: her fingers caressed the work, as if absorbing directly the touch of her father's skin, his dexterity and concentration. She imagined him sitting on a rough wooden chair in a room crowded with other prisoners, intent on crocheting small bags for their wives and daughters, the men's hard-worn hands suddenly called on to do unaccustomed delicate work. Even locked up, surely, they would be making jokes about what they were doing, how instead of threading bullets into a cartridge-belt they were

504

threading strings into farty little hooks.

She carried the bag downstairs so it would be ready to show John if he called. It was a miserable evening, cold and wet and windy outside, so she doubted he'd turn up on a night like that. She'd already had her tea, a few rashers of bacon and a couple of eggs, with bread and butter — on the side, as Jem used to say — and now she wasn't sure what to do with herself. She fetched her father's book of lyrics and hummed through some of the pages and then suddenly remembered that she had a small painting her da had also done in Ballykinlar on a piece of card. She had completely forgotten about it: she hadn't even thought to mention it after the funeral when Annie was talking about discovering their father's artistic side. They had been too busy talking about the painting that had ended up in Molly's coal-shed. This one would be just the thing to interest John. In fact, Patsy decided, she would give it to him: she'd keep the string bag, that was very personal, but she could part with the painting.

The only problem was that she didn't know where the thing was, though she could picture it in her mind. It was a scene of prisoners going to confession in one of the camp's wooden huts. Bare floorboards ran the width of the painting and a barred window on the facing wall let daylight in. At one end was a queue of men waiting their turn and at the other end sat the priest, his long black cassock trailing on the floor, his stole draped around his neck as he administered the sacrament. Kneeling in front of him was a prisoner, head bowed, hands joined, making his confession.

"Now where would I have put that?" she said. "I did show it to Jem once, so I know it's in the house somewhere."

She rummaged in the cupboard, she rifled through the drawers, she hunted upstairs in all the likely places and went back downstairs empty-handed. She sat and lit a cigarette.

"What was that?" she said to the small vibration in the air. "You know, you may be right."

She balanced her cigarette in the ashtray and went into the parlour. Sure enough, the painting was buried in the piano-stool under the sheet music.

"Fancy you knowing that," Patsy said as she carried the picture into the back room. "I suppose you were watching at the time. I suppose you were watching us all the time, which is a bit of an unpleasant idea, not that you'd ever have had anything rude to see, nothing too intimate, unless you were glued to your son's shitting." She paused. "God forgive me for saying such a thing, though I don't know which was worse, the word I used or the unkindness it suggested." She sat down to study the painting.

The unnerving thing about the scene that she hadn't remembered was the contrast between the pared-down figures of the prisoners and the detailed figures of the two British Tommies standing on guard. There was one in each of the two visible corners and they wore full battle dress: tin helmets, bulky great-coats over-strapped with cartridge belts, puttees wound up their legs from their heavy-duty boots and they had rifles held at the ready. Patsy wondered if they had been stationed there to overhear any incriminating confessions.

She wondered what sins the men would actually have had to confess locked up in a prison camp where sources of temptation must have been non-existent. Perhaps they were having unclean thoughts about their wives. Perhaps they were coveting another man's crust of bread. Perhaps they were prey to the deadly sin of pride, seeing themselves as heroes for the cause. Perhaps they were thinking they could be executed at any moment and wanted to be ready to meet their maker. Perhaps lining up for confession was just something to do, a break in the camp routine.

"When I was at school the nuns used to instruct us in what sins we might commit as children," she said. "I'm sure it was the same for you, Mrs Murphy Senior, though no doubt you were one of the goody-goodies. We had to confess every week to any talking in church we were guilty of and try to remember how many times we'd done it since our last confession. That was regarded as a very sinful thing to do, talking irreverently in the house of God, and it demanded a sincere act of contrition. Of course, we also had to tell the priest if we'd been cheeky to our parents or teachers or other adults and how many times; or if we'd used bad words, how many times; been selfish or greedy at the table, how many times. I took it all very seriously but later I got to thinking how bored the poor priest must have gotten, sat there in his dark claustrophobic box for an hour or so listening to all these children filing in to sit on the other side of the grille reciting their lists of how many this-that-and-the-other venial offences they'd committed. And, God forgive me, I got to thinking that the priest must have welcomed the arrival of an adulterer or a thief, someone with something more interesting to relate."

Patsy looked back at the painting. How intensely sad, it was. Perhaps, after all, the men were confessing to the sin of despair.

That was another sin she had thought long and hard about, of how totally lost and depressed a person would have to be to get to that point of despair which the Church considered to be a major sin. How could you possibly go to confession to seek forgiveness for despair when forgiveness was based on a resolution to at least try not to commit the same sin again? You could really try hard not to talk in church but could you be suffering such terrible despair one minute then walk out of the confessional box and everything was fine, no more despair, promise. Patsy could only put it down to one of God's mysteries. She'd be curious to hear John's opinion even though her brother was not a religious type. She rewrapped the painting in the tissue and then put it in a plastic bag. She put on her coat and grabbed her umbrella: she would walk round to John's herself with the picture.

It was dark outside even though it wasn't particularly late. There were bowls of light misting in the rain around the streetlamps and flickering creases of blue television-glow escaping at the edges of curtains: the pavements were shiny and animated, with millions of tiny reflections dancing in the drops and rippling across the puddles of water: Patsy heard her shoes squeak rhythmically on the wet ground and the rain splatter randomly on her brolly. It wasn't nice weather but she was enjoying being out. She could identify the smells of dinners cooked and the smoke from fires burning at the hearth, and she could picture the full bellies settled in for the evening in front of the telly. It was something she always liked about autumn and winter evenings: the homely glow of houses closed in against the elements.

Patsy took the route along the canal. After looking at the crocheted bag and the Ballykinlar painting, her mind easily drifted to the story her da had told them about the night he was captured with Mick O'Shea by the Black and Tans. That was how he had ended up in Kilmainham and then the prison camp and it had been along this very same canal that they

507

were caught, maybe along this very same stretch. Patsy couldn't remember exactly where it was supposed to have happened but she knew it had been dark, just like it was now, and her imagination soon started recreating the scene.

She saw her father with Mick having a cigarette and then them seeing the soldiers and having to run. She saw them being wrestled to the ground, perhaps near this very spot, and them cowering in the grass against the cruelty meted out, when suddenly history repeated itself and she herself was violently pushed to the ground from behind. Her assailants were two young men, they couldn't have been much older than schoolboys, and they stood there laughing and jeering down at her as she floundered in the mud.

"Any money, you stupid old witch?" one of them sneered. "Come on, hand over your bag or you'll be sorry." He put on a foreign accent: "Vee haf vays of taking your bag," he said, cackling and bending to within inches of Patsy's ear so she could feel the stale smell of his breath suffocating her face, and all the time him nudging her with his foot.

Patsy tried hard to resist and not move. She had landed on the painting, which she had been clutching to her chest against the weather, so her attackers couldn't see it hidden under her sprawled body, thank God. It was all she was carrying apart from her umbrella.

"The old witch hasn't even got a bag with her," said the second voice. "Come on, let's go. There's someone along on the other side of the canal."

The first one grabbed the umbrella and kicked Patsy dismissively in the side before the two friends casually walked off sharing the brolly, still muttering about "the stupid old witch".

Patsy lay still on the ground, stunned, hardly daring to look up in case the two attackers had only pretended to leave and were actually just waiting for her to move and invite more punishment for not having a bag. She lifted her head as little as she could and made them out, already several yards away, and she closed her eyes. A rush of relief pounded through her body. She pushed herself up awkwardly on to her knees. The rain was streaming down her face, mixed with tears and with strands of globby mucus hanging from her nose, but she was all right, she wasn't physically hurt. She managed to stand upright and possessively smoothed out the plastic bag: it felt as if the painting hadn't been bent and the bag hadn't ripped so the picture was still dry and for that she offered a prayer of thanks. But her coat was torn and it was soaking and smeared with dirt; a muddy mark was imprinted where the oaf's boot had landed but she was all right, she wasn't physically hurt. But she was shaken and completely unnerved. She felt very vulnerable and violated, her sense of ordinary everyday freedom stolen in one short burst of someone else's power over her, and she had to just stand where she was, shivering and trembling, until she felt able to even move one leg in front of the other.

"Are you all right there, Mrs?" a voice called from the other side of the canal. "Do you need any help?" Patsy would have liked nothing better than to seek the comfort of family around her right now, to be looked after and made to feel safe, but she was cold and wet and too frightened to go any further alone and the kindness of a stranger would do.

"Two men just tried to rob me," she cried weakly.

"Just wait there now, Mrs, I'll be right over."

Patsy saw the man hurry along the canal bank and cross the bridge to reach her and then she recognised him, he was from St Kevin's parish and she saw him regularly at Mass on a Sunday with his family.

"It's Mrs Murphy, isn't it?" he said. "I've seen you at Mass. Do you need the hospital?"

"No, I don't think I'm hurt, only badly shaken," she said.

"Is there anywhere I can take you? Make sure you get there safely?"

"I was on my way to my brother's but now I just want to go straight home, it's only round the corner, Warren Street, but if you've the time I'd appreciate your company."

"I think I saw those two scallies," said the man offering Patsy his arm. "Were they carrying an umbrella?"

"They were when they left," said Patsy, "it was mine."

"You know I once left a packet of biscuits on the back seat of the car and someone broke in and stole them, nothing else was taken," he said as they walked along. "Then I kept looking at every face that passed looking for any tell-tale crumbs around the mouth."

The silliness of the story eased the tension.

"I'm Seamus Hoolihan, by the way, now we're not strangers and you

509

know who you're talking to, though you've probably seen me at Mass," said the good Samaritan. "What's that you're carrying? They didn't manage to snatch that, then."

"I fell on top of it, so they didn't see it, thank God," said Patsy. "It's just a small picture my da painted when he was a prisoner of war," said Patsy.

"Really?" said Mr Hoolihan. "In Germany, was it?"

"No, he was caught by the Black and Tans and sent up to the North with a lot of other Volunteers."

"They were all brave men. You've got some courage flowing round in those veins then," said Mr Hoolihan. "Don't you forget that when you think of the two ignorant eejits who attacked you."

They'd reached Patsy's house and her escort waited while she put the key in the lock.

"You shut the door now, Mrs Murphy, and I'll know you're safe inside," he said.

"I can't thank you enough for your help," said Patsy.

"We've all got a lot to thank men like your father for," said Mr Hoolihan. "Go on in now and get yourself warmed up."

"Thank you again, I couldn't have coped otherwise," said Patsy. "They literally brought me to my knees."

Mr Hoolihan stood there and smiled comfortingly as she closed the door. He waited until she slid the bolt into place before he went on his way.

Once inside, Patsy switched on all the lights simply because it made her feel better to have the house look busy from the street. She put on the kettle for some hot water — she felt an urgent need to clean herself — and then took off her wet clothes. She was mortified to discover that she had unknowingly wet her knickers and the realisation made her cry again at her utter helplessness in the whole incident. She wondered with shame if Mr Hoolihan had been able to smell it. However independent they might feel, women were easy victims to brutal men. Patsy washed and put on her night clothes; she lit a night-light in front of the small Our Lady plaque on the wall and said a short prayer from her Children of Mary handbook: "O Mary, conceived without sin, I wish this day to put myself under your protection." She pulled a blanket around her shoulders and sat down in a chair by the table, poured herself a whiskey and lit a cigarette.

"Don't talk to me now," she said aloud. She decided not to tell anyone what had happened, not even a ghost.

In work the next day, Patsy's colleagues wouldn't leave her alone, asking over and over why she was being so quiet? Why such a long face? Had something awful happened? In the end she blurted it out. "I was attacked near the canal last night," she said, and the admission brought tears to her eyes. Sympathy filled the workroom: she was hugged, given a cup of tea, everyone lit up a cigarette and left their machines as she was called on to give them all the sordid details of what had happened. Better to get it out of your system, she was advised, best not to let it fester and take a hold of you, don't let them win.

"My God, Patsy, the same thing happened to me a couple of weeks ago and it was a couple of young guys too," said Siobhan when Patsy had finished the story. "I hope you reported it to the Gardaí. It's important that you do. Can you give them much of a description? It could well be the same two, preying on women out alone at night."

"I'd feel a bit stupid reporting the theft of an umbrella," said Patsy.

"But you were attacked," said Siobhan. "Going to the police is your way of fighting back and saying 'you can't do this to me and get away with it'. Come on, I'll tell the boss and I'll go with you to the station."

"Why haven't you mentioned before what happened to you, Siobhan?" asked Bernadette as the two women got ready to leave. "I'd never be able to keep something like that to myself."

"Maybe you wouldn't but let's hope you never have to find out," said Siobhan. "We all react in different ways to these things. No matter how strong you think you are, you can end up feeling ashamed and stupid, even though none of it is your fault. In my case, I decided that I wouldn't even give the two men the victory of having me turn their attack into an anecdote. That's why I didn't mention it. I refused to let it take up any more of my time than necessary. Obviously Patsy wasn't going to mention her attack either only we kept pushing. But let's go now, Patsy, you'll feel better after you report it, I promise you. Anyway, you should report it and believe me it will lessen the hurt and make you feel stronger."

The two women didn't have to wait long at the police station before Patsy was asked to make a statement about exactly what had happened the previous night. The officer taking notes was particularly interested in the colour and style of the umbrella that had been stolen.

"It was a red one with a Liverpool badge on it. I know that because my husband bought it at Aintree racecourse when we went to the Grand National a few years back," said Patsy. "It was a miserable day and he bought the umbrella just in case."

"Then you'll be relieved to know we have the two thieves in custody already," said the Garda. "They were picked up late last night trying to break into a car in a backstreet not far from the canal and they had an umbrella exactly like the one you describe. In fact, one of them was holding it up to keep the two of them dry as they tried to force the lock. Perhaps it was the unusualness of the umbrella that made the patrol stop to check. When the suspects were searched, we found a couple of stolen wallets on them. They admitted several robberies so you shouldn't need to appear as a witness, Mrs Murphy, just sign this statement and you can collect your umbrella after the court hearing. You did the right thing in coming in. See how even a detail such as the description of your umbrella is important. Don't you worry now, you can go about your business as normal, Mrs Murphy, the two who attacked you are already in the cells."

"I think we should go for a drink before we get back to work, we both need it after having to relive it all in such a matter-of-fact way," said Siobhan. "You can tell me how it made you feel when you were attacked, never mind what actually happened. It's something we have in common, not that it's something we'd choose to have in common."

"When it was all actually happening, I felt as if I kept my wits about me, it happened so fast that I seemed to just make myself cope without thinking about it," said Patsy. "It was only when they ran off that I could give in to being scared and I could only stand there and be scared, frightened. After that I was just angry, really angry."

"I went through exactly the same process," said Siobhan. "And I'm still angry."

That evening, Father Dec called in briefly to see how Patsy was; Mr Hoolihan had gone to the vestry to suggest that Mrs Murphy might appreciate a visit and the priest had already called a couple of times before he caught Patsy at home.

"I thought you might have taken the day off work," he said, "but I think you did the right thing in getting on with everything as normal."

"What frightens me is that my normal won't be the same any more," said Patsy. "I'm going to be nervous every time I see a couple of young men in the street."

"Quite understandable that you should feel that way," said Father Dec, "but remember that most people are basically good people. It might help if you pray for the two who did it, after all they are the sad ones, they're the ones lacking in any sense of simple decency in their lives and now they're locked up."

Perhaps they were but it would be several weeks before Patsy was able to stem the instinctive panic she felt as soon as she heard the sound of footsteps approaching behind her: she doubted she would ever be able to go out in the dark any more, not alone anyway, her feeling of being carefree was gone. She had a Mass offered up for Mr Hoolihan and his family and she tried hard to pray for her two attackers, which was difficult, but it gradually gave her a certain spiritual strength. Unlike Siobhan, Patsy deliberately turned the incident into an anecdote and that took the edge off it even more. She could talk about it without crying, whatever residue of turmoil still swirled inside, and that was real progress.

4

Patsy got on with things. She had her Singer open in the parlour, out of Sean's sight so he couldn't tittle-tattle to his sisters. She had managed to find a beautiful length of white cotton broderie anglaise at work, perfect for a simple but very special first Communion dress for little Veronica and hopefully with a bit left over to run-up a pretty headdress. Patsy's colleague Bernadette had rummaged out enough oddments of turquois organza with an all-over embossed floral pattern to make a party dress for Maureen. Patsy was particularly looking forward to seeing the delighted surprise on Maureen's face: the girl's brother was the centre of attention with his painting and her sister was the centre of attention over her first Holy Communion and it was obvious to anyone with an eye to see that poor Maureen was feeling not a little left out. The two girls had called round as arranged for Veronica to be measured but Patsy had turned the whole thing into a game in which they all took each other's measurements and noted them down with pencil and paper as if they were working in a fashion house, that way Maureen had no idea that Patsy was going to make her a new frock too. She was working on the dresses of an evening as Saturdays were still taken up with the lavatory scheme but that was in its closing stages and only finishing touches were needed to satisfy Sean's quality demands before the floor and toilet-seat covers could be added and the curtain hung.

"We should have a launch ceremony," said Patsy.

"For a toilet?" said Sean. "All cisterns go!" he laughed.

"Well, it is a toilet, I can't deny that, but it's also a work of art and we should have a special opening like they do in art galleries," said Patsy. "Your mammy and sisters can come and maybe I can invite a few people. I could prepare a small tea and have a celebratory party. Have you any ideas, short of smashing a bottle of champagne against the door which would be a terrible waste, I'd prefer to drink it."

"Well, if it's to be a proper launch you'd have to start with a speech," said Sean after considering the matter for a few minutes. "Everyone could gather in the yard and you could explain why you wanted a lavatory like a jungle — people are always asking me that — and you could perhaps say how we met and had our first business meeting at Bewley's — no one believes me when I tell them that."

"That's a grand idea. I tell you what would be funny," said Patsy. "I could ask Father Dec to come and bless the toilet and all who use it."

"They could flush away all their sins with their poo."

"Like a real cleansing of body and soul," said Patsy. "Then we could declare the toilet open."

"Open for business," said Sean.

"When everyone gets to see the actual opening, when everyone gets to see inside."

"I tell you what we can do. We can make sure the inside curtain is left down and you could fix on a fancy ribbon, then we open the door, people see just the curtain, then we pull on the ribbon and open the curtain back like in a theatre."

"And all is revealed," said Patsy. "The jungle of Warren Street! I think we should be ready by next weekend, do you?"

"My plan is to finish today and that will leave plenty of time for the paint to dry properly. Then I can come round in advance of the launch to do any last-minute touching-up. Shall we make it Saturday or Sunday?"

"I think Saturday afternoon," said Patsy, "that's been our painting day and people are sometimes busy with Mass and family on a Sunday, especially Father Dec."

It was agreed. Sean finished the murals to his satisfaction; Patsy finished all her sewing and the week flew by. Sean arrived early on launch day, very smart in his Sunday best, and helped to hang the curtain and drape it according to plan, then he was responsible for decorating the yard with streamers and balloons while Patsy prepared a table of suitable treats. Finally, all they had to do was sit and relax and wait for their guests. Patsy lit up a ciggie; she had long since given up on not smoking in front of Sean, Saturdays would have been far less relaxed without her allowing herself the odd drag.

"I wasn't able to concentrate at school at all this week," said Sean. "I kept asking myself if the design was right, if I'd painted it well enough, if I had let you down."

"I'd have to answer 'yes, yes and no' to those questions," said Patsy. "I think the design is truly fantastic, as it should be for a tropical toilet plonked down in Portobello, and you've done a grand job with the painting and I love it, it's better than anything I could have imagined. Have you thought yet of what you'd like to do when you leave school? Would you like to be an artist?"

"I think I'd prefer working on designs rather than just on paintings," he said. "I don't know if there's much money in painting pictures unless you're famous and I'd like to be able to help my mammy out with some money."

The first person to arrive was Father Dec, brandishing a small bottle of holy water and his white stole carefully folded in a small drawstring bag. "This is the first time I've been asked to bless a toilet," he said, taking out the stole and draping it over the back of a chair. "It must be something special."

"It's a work of art," said Patsy, "and young Sean here is the artist. He did all the walls and the ceiling."

"Your very own Michelangelo," said the priest. "No doubt there are toilets handy for the Sistine Chapel so you're in good company, Sean. Can I take a peek?"

"Not even a pee," said Sean without thinking that he was addressing a priest. "Begging your pardon, Father, but I'm afraid you'll have to wait, unless you've been caught short and have to go but that would spoil the launch."

"I can hold on," said Father Dec, "though judging by the knocks on the door I might not have to wait too long for the unveiling. It sounds as if the rest of the guests have arrived."

There was indeed a small gathering at the door. By the time Patsy opened it, Betty and Annie were already deep in conversation with Mrs Mulhoney and the girls, as if the families had known each other for years though they'd never met before, and Margaret got there just as Patsy was about to close the door. She was laden down with her Dansette record-player.

"It looks as if you and I are to be outnumbered by the women, Sean," said Father Dec when the new arrivals walked in. "We men will have to stick together."

"Begging your pardon, Father," said Sean, "but I've never really thought of priests as men. They're priests."

"I suppose it's the frocks they have to wear," said Margaret. "Good day to you, Father. Are you here on duty?"

"I'm here to do the blessing," he said.

"That's a relief. I thought for a moment someone might actually be getting baptised in the lavatory. You're looking well, Mrs O'Kelly, and you too, Annie," said Margaret. "I don't know you personally, Mrs Mulhoney, but I've seen you at Mass with the children. This is some strange occasion we're all here for, isn't it? Only Patsy could come up with such a mad idea. Let me just put this down." Margaret put the record-player on the table, being careful not to disturb the simple but tempting spread of titbits and sandwiches and cakes. "I thought such a solemn occasion deserved some suitable accompaniment so I've brought Handel's Water Music." A ripple of amused appreciation animated the group. Margaret sorted out the player ready to go whenever Patsy gave the word.

"Shall we get started?" said Patsy. "I thought we'd do the launch and then have a bite to eat." She led the party out to the yard amid a buzz of genial excitement and yet more delighted appreciation was expressed at how festive it all looked. Fortunately the weather had been kind and the profusion of colourful balloons and streamers bobbed enthusiastically on their strings against the clear blue sky. No one had known what to expect and some of them had thought they actually had better things to do on a Saturday afternoon than come to see Patsy's newly decorated lavatory, even though they'd heard it was a gas, but so far it was obvious there was to be some good craic in store. "Now I'll hand over to my master of ceremonies, the artist responsible for the work you're about to see, Master Sean Mulhoney."

There was a round of gentle applause and the sound of childish giggling added to the general merriment when a row of young heads emerged peering over the yard wall.

Sean felt like the king of the castle. "First of all, I'd like to introduce my patron — I was told that that's what you call people who pay for paintings to be done — Mrs Patsy Murphy here, who had what some people might regard as a crazy idea but to me it was the best idea ever. She wanted her toilet to look like a jungle so she'd have something interesting to look at while she was in there if she was to be there for a while with nothing to read. So she bought a magazine which had lots of photographs of the Indian jungle in it and we looked at them together and decided what to do. She is to say a few words then Father Dec will do the blessing and then you can all see what it is we've been up to."

Patsy thanked Sean as people clapped and his mother beamed with pride. "It was my idea in the first place," said Patsy, "but it's down to Sean's talent that it has turned out so well." She turned and nodded to him and there was more gentle applause: everyone was entering into the spirit of the event. "You all know what a terrible time it was when Jem was ill. I seemed to spend more time out in the lavatory than is good for a person when I had to empty the poor man's chamber-pot non-stop and then clean it in the bowl. The poor neighbours must have been sick of the noise, all the flushing and the waiting for the cistern to refill and then more flushing and more refilling."

"It was like living next door to a waterfall," shouted one of the kids across the wall.

"It wasn't as pleasant as that, believe me, no more was the smell," said Patsy. The audience welcomed the humour but several of them knew it had been no joke at the time. Betty and Annie had offered to help out when Jem was sick but Patsy had seemed determined to keep them away from the house. Only the midwife, Mrs Flaherty, God rest her soul, had been allowed anywhere near the place. Betty in particular had felt offended that she hadn't been called on to help her daughter and was convinced it was to do with the shocking visit that time to the doctor's surgery. "Anyway, after all that I decided I deserved a new toilet," Patsy continued, "one which had no reminders of illness and Jem's dying. I met Sean by accident in the street and, to cut a long story short, he agreed to help me. And he says I have to stress that our first proper discussion was over tea and cakes at Bewley's, and I can report to his mother that he displayed excellent table manners. That's enough from me now. The past can't be allowed to dominate today's ceremony. Back to you, Sean."

"Can I now call on Father Dec to perform the next part of the programme, the blessing," he said.

There was a hushed silence as the priest took hold of his stole, kissed it lightly and put it around his neck. He opened the bottle of holy water and sprinkled some on the toilet door, on which fortunately the last-minute coat of paint had well dried.

"I bless this essential convenience and all who seek relief in its comforts," he said, making the sign of the cross in the air slowly with his hand. "May we recognise that nothing in the workings of the human condition is too humble for the blessing of Our Lord Jesus Christ, and we pray that Patsy Murphy finds both solace and inspiration in her new artistic — what shall we say? — bolt-hole, as she remembers only the good times she enjoyed when her husband was alive. In the name of the Father and of the Son and of the Holy Ghost."

"Amen," came the chorus from the onlookers.

"Thank you, Father," said Sean. "And now if everyone will step back, I'll call on Mrs Murphy to declare the toilet ready and open the door."

"Wait a minute now," said Patsy. "It must be time for the music."

Margaret rushed inside and soon the strains of Handel were powering through the open window to add grandeur to the next point in the proceedings.

Patsy stepped forward and unlatched the toilet door, everyone moving their heads to get a good look and, after all the build-up, seeing only the back of a heavy brown curtain. Then Sean switched on the light, tugged on the ribbon and the drapes were pulled back to reveal the vivid scene within: the tiger, with teeth bared, growling at the monkeys, who were keeping a startled-eyed watch on the big cat's movement from the safety of their tree-top canopy; the tropical flowers, bursting forth in an organised tangle of colour, climbing up through one corner from the floor, swathing the walls and branching across the ceiling to create an arbour of blossom; large-leafed foliage, tall and spiky or flat and saucer-shaped, dripping with hints of rain or dew; the collage undergrowth that carpeted the floor with flowers and grasses and, like a throne fixed centre-stage, the swanky-new low-flush toilet with its foliated cover. The audience clustered close having a good gape, oohing and aahing in genuine astonishment at the surreal scene that greeted them: it was so much more than any of them had expected, so much more... like a jungle... than they had imagined. Sean pointed out that there was a snake in the corner slithering up the wall and behind the door and people took it in turns of ones and twos to squash into the closet to have a look.

"My God would you look at that!"

"Isn't that just marvellous!"

"It's really grand, so it is!"

As the artist's mother, the honour was given to Mrs Mulhoney to perform the inaugural flush and the yard filled with cheers and yet more clapping as the lavatory was brought into full operation. The kids atop the neighbouring wall complained that they couldn't see anything so Patsy invited them to come and join in the party.

When the guests had had their visual appetites satisfied, Sean led them back into the house for the presentation spread. Drinks were poured — wine for the adults, lemonade for the youngsters — and everyone tucked into the treats. Mouths were full of goodies and of congratulations for the hosts and everyone settled down to enjoy the rest of this unusual but warmly sociable afternoon. The children stayed in the yard, creating quite a cacophony of animal noises and Tarzan howls, which in turn set the local dogs barking and yelping.

Father Dec was the first to make a move towards the door, he had Saturday evening Mass to officiate. "I've had a splendid time," he said, "not the usual Saturday at all, in fact not the usual anything actually, I think we'd all agree, and what would life be without the odd injection of the enjoyable but truly bizarre. Again, I want to thank all involved for inviting me and for letting me play a small if significant part in today's inauguration. As for you, Sean, there's a project coming up at St Kevin's which would benefit greatly from your artistic abilities. We're thinking of painting a mural in the parish hall and perhaps your mammy would agree to letting us borrow you and your eye. We can talk about it after Mass tomorrow. I trust I'll be seeing most of you there. I'll see myself out, Mrs Murphy, you carry on with the festivities."

"He's a very nice priest," said Betty. "I didn't realise he was Mrs Doran's son. She must be very proud that all her prayers were answered. And look at how many sons I've had and not a religious one among them."

"The important thing is that you raised your sons to be good men," said Patsy.

"Thanks be to God they are that," said Betty. "Unfortunately, I don't get to see them much, they've got their work and growing families to keep them busy at home. And I think my visits to England are a thing of the past now, I'm not keen on the boat and the idea of being up in the sky in an aeroplane frightens the life out of me. You must hold on to Sean if you can, Mrs Mulhoney. Hopefully he'll find something to keep him in Dublin."

"You have your daughters too, Mammy," said Annie. "Patsy and I are still here and there's John and at least some of your grandchildren. I don't think any of us are going anywhere far."

"Everyone is going somewhere fast if not far," said Betty, "and at the same time it's as if everything has slowed down. Life used to be full of noise and people in and out, there was a pleasant urgency about even the smallest things: the clatter of putting the dishes out on the table for us all to eat our dinner, clearing them away and scraping the plates and washing them up in the sink when dinner was over, then clattering them back again into the cupboard until next time and next time always seemed to come quickly, you never had time to dwell on anything but getting the next thing done. Now there's a terrible quietness settling. I miss Patrick. I miss having the family all still living together. What point is there in being a wife when your husband's gone? Or being a mother when your children have gone?" The wine was beginning to take effect and Annie signalled to Patsy that it was probably time to get Betty home before she became even more morose.

"Well, we still have family waiting on their dinner at The Coombe right now," said Annie, "and it's not far but the faster we get there the better or the noise you're looking for will be all moans and groans. There's little good humour about if there's no dinner on the table."

Patsy helped Betty on with her coat and Annie swept into the yard and quickly cleared it of the neighbours' brood, giving each of them a balloon to ease their sudden dismissal.

"I love it when there are little ones about," said Betty as the youngsters rushed through the house, balls of colour tracing their way out the front door. "I should have had some more, make up for Patsy not having any at all." Betty meant nothing deliberately cruel by her wistful conjecture, nevertheless the room was heavied by a sudden unwelcome silence which Margaret attempted to diffuse by gathering up her Dansette and asking Patsy to put Handel back in his sleeve for his trip home. She left at the same time as Betty and Annie so she could walk part of the way with them. She reasoned that Patsy would be less likely to sink into a mood with Sean and his family than with her own.

"We'd better be off too," said Mrs Mulhoney, who had sensed the change in atmosphere without fully understanding what had happened or what had been said that was out of order: Mrs O'Kelly had seemed a very kindly woman, which made the change in tone all the more puzzling following her last comment. "You'll no doubt want to relax after all the excitement, Mrs Murphy, or would you like some help in clearing up?"

"I can manage, it's not as if I have anyone else but myself to look after," said Patsy carelessly abrupt.

"Well then, we'll be on our way," said Mrs Mulhoney, hurrying her children along and down the hall.

"Wait, wait a minute now," called Patsy recovering herself. The launch had been a great success but there was still one more presentation to make. "The event's not over yet. Let's go on into the parlour, I've something for you by way of thanks."

The Mulhoneys stood there awkwardly at yet another change in temperature as Patsy opened the parlour door. There, laid out under delicate tissue paper, were the two dresses for the girls and next to them a gaily wrapped parcel.

"Veronica, this is your Holy Communion dress," said Patsy, lifting back the tissue to reveal the white confection and the matching headdress arranged in place above it. There had also been enough material to make a small opera-bag to hang from Veronica's wrist by a pretty ribbon. The young communicant's jaw dropped with sheer pleasure as she fondled her special dress and she let out a squeal of joy: she was already seeing herself wearing it for her practised walk down the aisle to the altar. "And there's something for you too, Maureen, you've not been left out," said Patsy, uncovering the turquoise organza party frock. A wide satin sash rested neatly across the middle. Maureen's face broke into the biggest smile that ever could illuminate a face, the happy shock of it all taking away any powers of speech as she too ran her fingers solicitously over the totally unexpected gift before her on the table. "It's a bit late now to try them on here but you can take them home and your mammy can let me know how they fit," said Patsy.

She was besieged by hugs and kisses and uncontrolled gabbles of thanks. There was no way in which the delight on the girls' faces and their cries of excitement could fail to lift Patsy's mood, nor could she be immune to the honest gratitude from their mother.

"And for Sean, here's something you might enjoy," said Patsy handing over the parcel. When Sean ripped open the parcel and discovered the tubes of watercolours, the fine brushes, pencils and proper drawing paper inside, his appreciation shone out of him, as if his head had been filled with sunshine and loaded with imaginary compositions just waiting to be plucked out of his head and captured on paper. It's said that the real joy of gifts is in the giving and not the receiving but, in Patsy's parlour, at that moment, it would have been difficult to tell. Shadows had tried to settle over the Warren Street house but they had been dispersed by the simple application of kindness and the hands of friendship.

5

"I'm going to burn my bra," said Siobhan. She was busy sewing the darts in the bodice of a beautiful brocade evening gown at Jeanette Modes, so her mind was concentrated on bosoms. "If they can do it in America, we can do it in Dublin. Strike a blow for freedom for women's bodies and against the male definition of what we should look like to suit them."

Her declaration wasn't totally out of the blue. The papers were having a field day with the news that hundreds of women had gathered in Atlantic City to protest against the annual Miss America pageant and its cattle-parade treatment of women. The protesters had even crowned a live sheep outside the venue to drive home the point but it was the bra business that had run wild in Siobhan's mind.

"I'm not convinced," said Bernadette, working away at her machine. "Wouldn't the men just love to be able to feast their eyes on a constant menu of bouncing boobs walking past, all their dreams and fantasies there to ogle right in front of them in the street. It might keep them out of the pubs, of course. Why stand propping up the bar with your drunken cronies when you could be outside looking at a free show of women with no bras on."

"Why would any woman want the discomfort of no support?" said Patsy. "Some women have heavy breasts and I can't see how it would be comfortable or good for their posture not to wear something to hold them up."

"And some women have pert little titties pointing forward and I'm sure the men would salivate to see those pert little titties flaunted for their benefit," said Bernadette. "I can remember clearly the very first time I wore a bra. I was wearing a summer dress and no cardigan, it was a lovely warm day, and I was feeling very self-conscious. I was one of those little girls who didn't really want to grow up. Anyway, I was walking home after running a message for my mammy when this boy shouted at me in the street that I looked good in a bra. I nearly died to think it was so obvious, of course I wasn't used to wearing a bra, and I just ran home, I was so embarrassed. But when I got back to the house, I posed in front of the mirror and I was secretly pleased."

"You're both missing the point," said Siobhan. "You, Bernie, are proving exactly that women's breasts are regarded as there to flaunt for the benefit of men. You, Patsy, are failing to appreciate that the bra-burning was just a symbol. They're not saying that we should all ditch our bras, just that we should be able to live in our own bodies without forcing them into shapes that aren't natural. Thank God we don't have to squeeze into laced-up corsets any more or sweat inside a rubber roll-on, having to hold our breath in just to attain an impossibly tiny waist and force a squashed-up cleavage. How ridiculous was that! Here's to Mary Quant and her shift dresses, that's what I say."

"But surely a bra was a silly symbol to choose," said Patsy. "Bras are for our own benefit."

"It wasn't only bras, that was just one element of the protest," said Siobhan. "My understanding is that the women were protesting about the whole double-standards on display. On the one hand are these women, the contestants, parading and posing up and down the catwalk in their skimpy bathing suits, revealing their bodily wares to full advantage, showing how well they match up to men's images of the perfect woman — an hour-glass figure, a beautiful face, long curly hair, preferably blonde…"

"Is that why you got a Twiggy cut?" asked Bernadette but her question was ignored.

"…and a brain the size of a pea. That's the job of women, to try to match up to this stupid male fantasy."

"I bet in America they all have beautiful teeth too," said Bernadette.

"On the other hand, if you'll let me continue," said Siobhan, "those same men have totally different expectations of what a woman should do once she's a wife. Then she should be at home cooking and cleaning, looking pretty in pink and smiling while she slaves in the kitchen making her husband's dinner."

"Anything in pink would get dirty very quickly," said Bernadette, "it wouldn't be practical at all. I always wear a wraparound when I'm in the house but it is a pretty floral one."

"At last you're getting some way there but you're still coming at it from the wrong direction, Bernie," said Siobhan. "That's where the other symbols come into it. The protesters in Atlantic City had what they called a 'Freedom Trash-Can' and into it they threw all sorts of symbols of a woman's place in a man's world: so, as well as the bras and girdles, the high heels and false eyelashes and lipsticks, they also threw into the trash can mops and buckets, pots and pans, and, on top of it all, a load of girlie magazines. And inside the contest venue, two of the protesters unfurled a huge banner that read 'Women's Liberation'. So, there you have it, the message."

"I don't think I could do without my mop and bucket," said Bernadette, "how could I keep the floors clean without them, especially when himself comes home from work and his muddy boots walked all through the house from front to back."

"Exactly," pounced Siobhan, "you have to clean up after he walks his muddy boots through the house, his mud, not yours, but you're the one expected to do the cleaning."

"Of course I am, I don't mind, that's part of my job," said Bernadette.

"And what's the other part? Cooking and washing and ironing and waiting on himself hand and foot? Then putting in a full day's work at this place? My God there's no hope for her, is there Patsy?" Siobhan was rolling her eyes in frustration.

"She's not alone in that," said Patsy from the cutting-table. "Years of tradition have made cooks and washerwomen of us all. Then again, I don't know, to be honest, whether it is tradition or whether it's just the way it is, that men feel more like men if they can keep women in their place, not rocking anyone's boat, only the baby's cradle in the corner."

"And then the next baby and the next baby," said Siobhan. "And if the Pope has his way that's how things will continue."

"What's the Pope got to do with it?" asked Bernadette. "Sure he's not even allowed to get married."

"But he still feels he has the God-given right to tell other men's wives what to do," said Siobhan. "Don't tell me you weren't treated to a hell-and-damnation sermon at Mass this summer about the Pope's latest declaration that all artificial birth control is banned by the Church? It seems you can go to hell for all eternity just for putting a bit of rubber on a man's dick but you can suffer hell on earth if you don't."

"My God did the Pope use the word 'dick'?" asked Bernadette, stopping mid-seam.

"I don't know, "said Siobhan. "I don't know the Latin for 'dick' but I'm sure there must be one with all those Italian Romeos on the prowl."

"I don't think we should question the Pope, he is God's representative on earth and as such he's infallible," said Patsy. "To me the basic issue here is that we women are used to being dominated. We're brought up to know our place, whether at home or at work but preferably at home, and part of knowing our place is knowing that it's the man of the house who makes the decisions and the woman who does what she's told. When I was growing up it was my father, God rest his soul, who made the big decisions about my life."

"What sort of decisions were they?" asked Siobhan.

"That's not important now, none of that can be changed," said Patsy. "The point is that I went along with it, we've all gone along with it, not just Bernie, and now we just have to get on with it. A lot of us have jobs to go to as well but we still accept the housework as our responsibility once we get home."

"Well, my husband refuses to use rubbers and as far as I know he doesn't buy girlie magazines, so that's something to be thankful for," said Bernadette, still not quite following the thread of the conversation or why she felt under attack in what was, she'd thought, a conversation about the treatment of women. She believed herself to be a good wife and a hard worker and she was generally content in her life at home, though sometimes when she got in from work she'd love to be able to put her feet up and let someone else cook the dinner for a change.

"You know it's still the law in this country that a woman has to give up her job in the civil service as soon as she gets married," said Siobhan, "and why is that? So she doesn't get ideas above her station which might make her question her boring mindless duties at home."

"You could say she gets liberated from her job," said Patsy, "though I doubt that's what women's liberation is supposed to mean."

"I like looking at women's magazines," said Bernadette. "Is that all right? I like to look at the fashion pictures and what the film stars wear on the red carpet. It seems harmless enough."

"It's harmless enough if you don't go getting depressed because you don't look as glamorous as they do, that's when the harm starts," said Siobhan.

"Not really because I know I could never look like them," said Bernadette. "But I do like to look nice in my own way if I get the chance to go out, a bit sexy like. I like to dress up and wear something special, it makes me feel good, and I enjoy putting on a bit of lipstick and maybe a bit of powder, otherwise my face can look awfully pale."

"And does himself comment?" asked Siobhan.

"He usually says something like…" — Bernadette put on a funny deep male voice — "'You'll do'." They all laughed and she felt reinstated into the group.

"All the same I wonder what sort of a place America is," said Siobhan. "It's always referred to as the New World but it can't be that new if women are taking to the streets there to complain about men and beauty contests. And what's new about all the killings that go on there? President Kennedy shot in the street and now his brother Robert is after being gunned down in a hotel? It sounds very much to me like the old America of cowboys and Indians. Have gun will travel. Isn't that the motto? Then there's all the marching going on over there regardless of the women — drop out not in, make love not war, civil rights for negro Americans. I think we're better off here in our old world."

"Better the devil you know," said Bernadette.

"Better off here but not in Derry right now," said Patsy. "A lot of Catholics are taking to the streets there too to complain about them not being able to get into a council house while Protestants go straight to the top of the waiting list. Did you not read that story about the teenager, a Protestant unmarried mother, who was given a whole house just weeks after a Catholic family of five was evicted to make way?"

"I read that article," said Siobhan. "The girl just happened to be the secretary of the local Unionist politician."

"At least for a Protestant she obviously wasn't using artificial birth control," said Bernadette. "I bet she never thought she was obeying the Pope."

"Would you not at least try to see the bigger picture here?" said

Siobhan.

"I thought that was quite a funny idea, a Protestant obeying the Pope," said Bernadette, confused all over again.

"That friend of mine I used to go to the concerts with, the one who moved to Cork? He reckoned there was going to be a lot of trouble in the North and that it would likely spread down to Dublin," said Patsy. "He said the Catholics had had enough of all the inequalities there and it could perhaps get very violent. Please God he's proved wrong but that was one of the reasons he wanted to move his family south."

"Maybe I should get away from the whole lot of it and move to California," said Siobhan, "the hippies there seem to have the right idea and it looks as if they have a grand time dancing at their festivals and smoking marijuana. I could see myself in tie-dyed flowing dresses and Indian shawls and lots of beads around my neck. I like the look. And some of the girls don't worry about wearing any bras, Bernie, they just get those pert little titties out that you were talking about and bare them for all to see. Do you fancy coming with me? We could hang out together?"

"I do not," said Bernadette. "It's all right for you, you don't have a family to look after."

Patsy had seen the hippies on the television news and how they handed out flowers to everyone. 'Free Love' was supposed to be their slogan but, according to the Irish newspapers, it was simply a total lack of morality: the so-called 'flower children' were constantly high on drugs, which took away all their self-control, so it was more an excuse for free sex never mind free love. Patsy couldn't fault the message of love and peace, which was after all what Christ himself had taught, and she decided that everyone she knew was taking drugs of one sort or another: she was addicted to tobacco and most men couldn't do without their beer, which was more likely to lead to drunken fights rather than a bit of peace. But the physical immorality was just wrong.

"I can't go along with the free sex," she announced suddenly, her thoughts escaping into words said out loud.

"I beg your pardon?" said Bernadette. "I can't imagine what's going on in your head, Patsy Murphy. Is it widowhood that's turned your mind, talking about free sex?"

"I assume it's not that you'd prefer to pay for it," said Siobhan.

Patsy tried to recover. "I was just thinking that there's no such thing as free sex, just as there's no such thing as a free meal."

"Now you're really making me curious," said Siobhan. "Aren't you the very woman who was always going out for fancy meals with Mr Murphy when he was alive? What was all that about then? On the other hand, I don't think I want to know what price you had to pay for all that fine dining."

There was a letter waiting for Patsy when she called round to The Coombe to keep Betty company while Annie and family went to the pictures. It was addressed to 'Patsy O'Kelly' and the handwriting was unmistakeable and Patsy shook as she looked at the envelope in her hands. It was from Sean Fitzsimmons and just holding it sent a thrill through her body. She was flustered and excited and confused as to why he would write to her after all this time and a horrible welcome explanation irresistibly flashed through her mind that perhaps his wife had died and he wanted to see Patsy again. Then she asked God for forgiveness for having such a terrible, terrible, thought.

"Who would be writing to you here after all this time?" said Betty bustling to get the tea on the go. She had been looking forward to spending an evening with Patsy and having some relaxed conversation as a change from the usual noisy mayhem in the house. "It's obviously from someone who doesn't know you got married and changed your name but it doesn't look formal: it's handwritten."

"It's probably from an old school friend," said Patsy.

"An old school friend?" called Betty from the kitchen. "Sure wouldn't they know you didn't live here any more. They can't have been that good a friend or you wouldn't have lost touch all these years."

"Maybe it was someone who moved away and they're back in Dublin for a visit," said Patsy. Sean's letter was too precious to share with anyone, she didn't know what was in it but whatever it was she wanted to keep it to herself. "I'll open it later when I get home. I'm here to see you, after all. I brought a bottle of Paddy's round for the occasion."

"Did you now? Well, it certainly is an occasion, Patsy, you don't call in much these days. Get a couple of glasses out and we'll forget the tea.

You can forget your whiskey too, take that home, we've a few bottles in the cupboard. Matt somehow seems to keep us well supplied."

The two women sat either side of the fire nursing their drinks. Patrick's old chair was long gone, Annie didn't want to live surrounded by collapsing relics, she'd said, and she'd made the room colourful and modern but still homely. The religious pictures and fonts had gone off the walls too, the hanging lengths of brown fly-paper long since been ejected. All the same Patsy instantly felt at home.

"So why is it you don't call in much these days?" asked Betty. "You know the door's always open to you, Patsy, and you must get lonely in that empty house now Jem's passed."

"I'm usually tired by the time I get home from work and I just want to flop into the chair," said Patsy.

"I don't think that can be the only reason," said Betty. "You often used to call in on your way home, maybe with some Hafners."

"So that's it," said Patsy, "it's the free sausages you miss."

"Actually, I do miss them," Betty laughed. "Annie and Matt have different ideas now on what we should eat. Annie likes to cook fancy things and sometimes I think if I ever see another grain of rice I'll scream. And she throws in leaves that look for all the world as if she'd just pulled them off someone's garden hedge. Jem liked his food too, I remember."

"He got into Chinese food once but the phase didn't last. Jem was more inclined to a good cut of meat or a nice piece of steak on his plate, with vegetables you could recognise. I thought, to be honest, it was because the foreign food didn't go down so well with his whiskey."

"I'd say this here is going down well," said Betty, raising her glass. "Your father would turn in his grave if he saw me just sitting and drinking, God rest his soul."

"You've earned your sitting and drinking, Mammy, you've worked hard for the family all your life."

"I have," said Betty.

"Would you say you've had a hard life, Mammy?"

"Not really, I've had an ordinary life, I'd say. Of course there were hard times to go through, the same as with everyone else, everyone goes through those, but on the whole I've no complaints. Your father was a good man."

"Aye, deep down," said Patsy involuntarily. She suddenly felt Sean's unopened letter burning a hole in her pocket.

"But you two were very close. Is that why you don't come round so much, because he's not with us now?" said Betty. "There must be some reason. And you always get on so well with young Marie, she often asks when you're coming next and I never know what to tell the girl. You know she sees things, the way you do. I hear her whispering sometimes in her room. She says she has a couple of invisible friends but I know it's more than that, I think she's like you in lots of ways. Should I worry, do you think?"

"Not as long as she doesn't end up too like me." Patsy took a slow sip of her Paddy's. "It's hard for me coming here, Mammy," she said, "not because it's without Da but because of who it is with. All the others have families of their own but they're in England," said Patsy, "I don't have to watch them all growing up and getting on with their lives. Here there's Annie and her children and it's all too much of a reminder that I'm on my own. I love talking to Marie but it's too easy for me to sit wishing she was actually my daughter. It's as simple and awful as that, Mammy."

They sat there in silence, Patsy with nothing more to say, Betty not knowing what she could say; she didn't feel in the circumstances that she could chat about the various family members so gradually she steered the conversation to bits of local gossip and what various neighbours were up to, but she realised that Patsy had got fidgety and wasn't surprised when her visitor made a move to leave. The evening hadn't gone quite as Betty had hoped and she didn't argue when Patsy wanted to leave before it got dark for the walk home alone. The mugging was still fresh in everyone's minds.

Back at Warren Street, Patsy placed the letter on the small table in the parlour. She didn't take her eyes off it as she threw her coat on the back of the armchair and sat down. She put it up to her nose to try to inhale some of Sean's scent; she touched her lips to the writing and to the flap where the envelope was sealed, where his own precious lips had hovered as he licked the glue to stick it down; she stared at the address he had written and marvelled that his hand had moved left to right over that same envelope just days earlier; she felt a powerful sense of his presence. She opened the envelope, very carefully, not wanting to cause even the tiniest rip in the paper. The letter wasn't on the same lined paper he used to write on in the past but it had the same appearance, the same organisation, the same careful script, the same neat fold across the middle.

'*My Dear Patsy,*" he wrote, "*I had to stop myself writing Streaks as that wouldn't have seemed right and forgive me for not knowing your married name or your address. I hope this letter reaches you. I just took a chance that some of your family would still be living at the house on The Coombe.*'

Patsy lit a cigarette.

'*I heard via Mrs Doran that you had been attacked and robbed in the street and I wanted to send you my heartfelt sympathy and best wishes. As you'll know, Mrs Doran's son is a priest in your parish and she herself was a great friend of my mother and she still comes to visit me and the family even though my mammy sadly passed. I always pick her up in the car and then drive her home as the poor woman suffers so with her knees. I was quite upset when she told us what had happened, to think of poor you and what you went through. Believe it or not, you're still in my mind often, probably far too often, and I hated that you were out alone and unprotected. None of us are getting any younger but I still feel that strong bond we had between us and that somehow I should have been there for you.*'

Patsy couldn't help it, she kissed the letter.

'*You haven't had a good couple of years, from what Mrs Doran tells me, what with your husband dying — forgive me for not knowing his name, I'm sure he was a good man as you married him — and then losing your father too. Of course, Mr O'Kelly and I didn't get on, but I was sorry to hear of your loss.*

Hopefully you're in better spirits after your ordeal and, if knowing I'm thinking about you helps at all, then know that you are wrapped up safely in my thoughts and in my heart.

Yours as ever, Sean F.'

There were no kisses. Patsy read the letter over and over and then just sat nursing it to her bosom; her eyes were closed, her pulse was racing, her emotions were fit to explode. And she couldn't fight the thought from invading her head that Sean's wife was obviously still alive.

It had gone very quiet at Patsy's house. The fuss surrounding the toilet had subsided and the neighbours had long since stopped calling asking to have a look at the jungle novelty; they'd all seen it by now and Patsy had enjoyed her moment of what she regarded as her temporary notoriety. She realised that they probably all thought she was a bit eccentric but that was a sort of fame in itself. There didn't appear to be too many eccentrics living in Warren Street. Alas the Saturdays spent painting with Sean were a thing of the past too because he was busy helping with the mural in the parish hall. It was a major undertaking after school and at weekends and he had no time to spare for the proposed piano lessons with Patsy. She tried not to mind, art was Sean's main interest, but she had to admit to being disappointed. He still called to see her and show her any small sketches and watercolours he'd done with the materials she'd given him. He had even done a picture of the outside of Bewley's, which he had mounted in a cardboard frame and given to her a few days before Christmas as a reminder of their first business meeting. Mrs Mulhoney had also kindly sent round a photograph of Maureen and Veronica in their dresses. That too was mounted on card, this time with a 'Happy Christmas' message written underneath. The Bewley's painting had since stood in pride of place on the mantelpiece where Patsy could see it every day, but it wasn't the same as enjoying Sean's company regularly. When she examined her feelings, Patsy had to admit that she had been in danger of trying to turn Sean into the son she never had and that wouldn't have been right.

She had spent Christmas Day at The Coombe but had left late afternoon straight after dinner, before it got dark and the streets were deserted. Matt had offered to see her home if she'd wanted to stay but she had no wish to sit on the side lines of other people's children absorbed in their presents while the adults dozed in front of the television: she might as well be at home dozing in front of her own television.

Then, of course, Midnight Mass on New Year's Eve had been out of the question: she wouldn't take the risk of walking home alone and no one else about. The evening had instead passed in a fog of cigarette smoke and lonely glasses of Paddy's as Patsy listened to the time ticking away. Memories of Jem and his enthusiastic insistence on a big celebration to welcome in the New Year did bring smiles to her face but, when the memories and smiles had run their course, Patsy's solitary glass of Paddy's seemed even lonelier. She made a half-hearted resolution to go out more and stop being such a scaredy-cat but, as January trawled into February, the long nights seemed endless and she never had the will to put her resolution into practice, telling herself that there was a whole year in which to implement the promise to herself. Going to work kept her going. The companionship she enjoyed in the workroom was becoming more important to her than her pay packet.

Patsy spent a lot of time gazing out of the back window on to her yard while she sat at the table smoking.

"You know the only bright spot out there is the lavatory door," she said to her floaty lodger. "Otherwise it's just rows and rows of bricks. I've been studying them. Some are still fairly red but others are blackened or whitened, now isn't that strange? Why have some turned black and some turned white?" She took a drag on her cigarette. "I suppose it could be a combination of smoke on some and damp on the others, that would do it."

At the bottom end of the yard there was a shallow slanting roof and protected underneath it was the press, a small, aerated cupboard in which Patsy kept her butter and milk and perhaps a few slices of ham cool during the warmer weather. There was one exactly the same at The Coombe. Patsy suddenly missed the coo-rooing of the pigeons and that constant feeling of life and movement they had added to the back of the house. It was like a bit of nature itself thriving right there behind the house.

"I should do something to the yard," she said, "brighten it up a little." There was a stirring in the air. "What was that? What did you say Mrs Murphy Senior? Plants? You always wanted some plants out there?" Patsy surveyed the yard again with a critical eye. "You know, I think you're right. Thank you, Mrs M. You see, you are appreciated. Sometimes anyway."

Another scheme began to form in Patsy's mind. It would have to wait until the evenings started to draw out and the spring sunshine dawned but meanwhile the idea would keep her busy. She would paint foliage directly on to the yard walls, as if the lavatory jungle had outgrown its small enclosure and encroached into the outside space. An arrangement of real potted plants would then be dotted about to create a natural feel and she would ask Matt to fix up a trellis around the back door to support a climbing plant, perhaps with a couple of fixed planters at the bottom on each side. And he could put up a few hooks along the edge of the sloping roof to hold hanging baskets, so a curtain of leaves and flowers would eventually trail down turning the yard into a woodland grotto.

Now as Patsy gazed out of the back window, that was the scene she saw in her mind's eye.

She wondered if she could look forward to all the neighbours calling in again. They really would think she'd gone mad, and she wouldn't mind that at all. She already felt she added interest to the street.

The very next weekend, Patsy called in at the newsagents where she was greeted like an old friend.

"You're back from your safari, I see. I trust you didn't get mauled by any lions," said the newsagent.

"No, but I've got a tiger in my backyard," said Patsy.

"Now isn't that a grand thing to have," he said. "I've only got a tiger in my tank but I do have my very own lioness in the kitchen. What is it that's grabbed your attention this time?"

"I'm looking for some guidance on outdoor plants," said Patsy, "the sort you can grow in containers."

"Is that right? My wife loves plants, we have them all over the house, every room has something growing in it even if it's just a small prickly cactus, and aren't they the very devil if you happen to catch them with your finger, but of course I'm the one who has to do any heavy lifting required when she takes it into her mind to move everything around for a change of scenery. Some of those pots can get very heavy. I've seen little wheeled contraptions advertised for moving them around but I can't see those working on the carpets. You may find what you're looking for along to the left, bottom shelf."

Patsy picked and flicked through the limited selection of gardening magazines, a few already a couple of months out of date but that didn't matter, surely the basic information never changed. There were photographs of glorious displays of growth in the gardens of great country houses, where separate areas were devoted to maybe a collection of tropical ferns — Patsy loved the ones that grew like trees, wouldn't one of those be great towering in the yard, though it would eat up the space and then going to the toilet really would be like going on a safari. Other photos showed swathes of drifting flowers of different reds and purples, added interest created by varying heights and density. 'Remember the geometry of your scheme,' was the advice but there wasn't much scope for geometry behind a Warren Street terrace house. There was even guidance on growing edible plants in what was designed to look like a natural setting, with savoury and medicinal herbs interspersed between the larger plants. None of this was of any real use to Patsy for her backyard but she enjoyed looking at the pictures and they made her think back to her day out with Sean Fitzsimmons when they had strolled round the gardens of Howth Castle like the young lovers that they were. Back in the day! Fortunately, one of the magazines did include an article aimed at people living in fancy high-rise apartments with broad balconies to green up. That was the target audience but the spread was simply about growing plants in containers and that's what Patsy was looking for.

"I'll take this one," she said, taking the magazine over to the counter to pay.

"I'm just looking at your fingers there and I'd swear they're already turning green," said the newsagent.

"Green with envy is what I am," said Patsy. "Imagine having a garden like some of them in the photographs."

"It's the green-backs that cultivate those," said the shop-owner, "and that pay for the teams of gardeners needed to look after them. I'm thinking you'll be doing all your work yourself."

"I have such a small backyard you wouldn't even be able to fit a team of leprechauns in it. It's a team of little green men from Mars I'd need."

"Then you might be in luck," he said. "I see the Americans are trying to get to the Moon. It could be Mars next stop and then your problem could be solved."

"I don't think I could wait that long," said Patsy. "I want blooms this summer to enjoy."

"A blooming good idea," said the newsagent. "I look forward to your next venture. I have to say you're not in the least predictable."

"Is anything in life predictable?"

"I am, according to my wife. But then I'd have to say that nothing she does surprises me either," he said. "I always know it will mean more work for me so no surprise there."

"I'll take a pad of paper too, please, so I can jot down my ideas," said Patsy. "Actually, a child's small notebook will do, perhaps the lines will help me keep everything organised."

The newsagent put the purchases in a bag. "Enjoy yourself now, but be careful," he said handing Patsy her change, "you don't want to hurt your back. I got an awful twinge the other day when my wife asked me to move a chest of drawers. It was one that didn't have a heavy plant on it but it does now right enough."

The very first entry Patsy put in her notebook, written in big bold letters, was 'nasturtiums'.

6

Patsy held her breath along with the rest of the world. The silence in the bar spoke volumes, eyes popped in their sockets and mouths hung jaw-dropped open while beer glasses were held unsupped mid-air, and anyone who dared speak got a sharp dig in the ribs. Mission Control was in charge in every pub that had a television set. While Houston was guiding Neil Armstrong in how to descend the last rungs of the ladder on to the surface of the Moon, customers in the Dublin city bar — Patsy didn't really know which one she was in — were also hanging on every word that came out of NASA.

"I'm at the foot of the ladder," said the astronaut. "The surface appears to be very, very fine sand, almost like a powder, it's very fine. I'm going to step on to land now."

"This is Houston, we're copying."

"Oh, dear God," someone whispered as everyone focused on the slightly blurred image of a man in a huge white suit gingerly putting a huge-booted foot on to the ground that was actually the Moon.

"That's one small step for man, one giant leap for mankind," announced Armstrong quite humbly, putting his feet down on that very, very, fine sand where no human being had ever set a foot down before. The reportedly 600-million people watching on televisions around the world, be it in community huts or cosy individual homes or jam-packed school assembly halls, be it in the middle of the night, early morning or late afternoon, everywhere people were able to exhale at last and share in a global grinning frenzy. Patsy was just one of the millions to sigh and smile with relief. She joined in as the bar around her erupted with cheers and applause and prayers of thanks. Glasses were clinked and mid-air drinks finally got to be drunk.

"Quiet now," shouted someone. "This is history happening right now, right in front of us." All eyes turned back to the screen and an engrossed silence returned.

Armstrong was still at the bottom of the ladder of the lunar module but he had started to move his foot. "I can move the powder with my toe," he said, and in the bar customers acted reflexively and unconsciously started circling their feet gently on the wood floorboards. "This is Houston, we're copying." Everyone was copying.

Finally, it was Buzz Aldrin's turn to join his fellow spaceman and leave the lunar module through the hatch. "I'd better be sure not to lock it on my way out," he said.

The black humour behind his remark had everyone laughing and served to release the tension. "Jesus wouldn't that be a terrible thing to do," said someone in the bar. It was difficult on such a suspense-filled occasion not to identify with the two human beings who were both now landed on the Moon, on the very Moon that until now had been just a glowing ball you could see high above in the night sky. Poets wrote about it, singers sang about it, lovers gazed at it through dreamy eyes and now two men were actually up there.

"What sort of a name is Buzz?" asked Siobhan quietly, seizing the opportunity to speak as Buzz himself was now being guided down the ladder and for some inexplicable reason being instructed to jump from the ground up to the lower rung and back again several times. "It can't be short for anything, surely."

"It sounds very American," said Patsy, "like Chuck or Kirk or Randy."

"Well I know what randy means, right enough," said Siobhan taking a gulp of her Guinness. "But Buzz, now! A buzz of excitement, maybe, or the buzz of the bell on the bus. Wouldn't you think you'd use your proper name if you knew you were going to be written up in the history books," she said, "surely Buzz isn't a proper name."

Patsy had intended to watch the Moon landing at home but Siobhan had suggested it was an event to share with other people and she had known just the pub in the city to go to, though it was a new one to Patsy. It was compact but lively in there and as good humoured as you'd expect when everyone was enjoying the same spectacle.

A man stood next to them with his mates had overheard Siobhan's comment and he was intent on drawing the two women into his circle, especially the young one; it would be a bit of a notch on his belt in front of his friends if he did.

"Do you not know the name of the man left in the command ship?" he said, as if Ireland hadn't been awash with the information for weeks and he was telling Siobhan and Patsy something they didn't already know but camaraderie was abroad so they didn't mind. "It's Michael Collins. Would you believe that? Michael Collins?"

"Sure everybody knows that!" said Siobhan. "A Cork family, I believe, his grandfather was a farmer there before he emigrated."

"Is that right?" said the man, pleased with his success and with the growing attention of his mates who were now all turned towards the two women. "And did you know that our very own hero Michael Collins was also a County Cork man?" he said.

"I knew that," said Patsy but she was ignored.

"And what about the others, the men actually on the Moon?" asked the stranger directing his half-closed eyes at Siobhan. "What can a knowledgeable girl such as yourself tell me about them?"

"A girl such as myself who bothers to read an ordinary newspaper can tell you that Neil Armstrong is supposedly descended from Ulster cattle-rustlers but I don't know whether they were Orange or not and until I do I'll not enthuse too much about his ancestry," said Siobhan. "But you haven't answered the question, is Buzz short for a proper name?"

"I think it's just a nickname," said the man. "Perhaps his arrival did cause a buzz of excitement, like when you walked into the bar earlier. I definitely felt some sort of a buzz, a sort of a buzz of expectation, if you get my meaning."

Siobhan rolled her eyes up. "Is it not possible for a woman to watch a great scientific achievement like man landing on the Moon without some eejit having to seize the opportunity to try it on?" she said. "You were doing all right up to your pathetic chat-up line, I thought perhaps we were two people just having a conversation."

"Talk is cheap," said the man. "Let me buy you a drink while we stand gazing up at the Moon together."

"My drink is cheap enough that I can pay for it myself," said Siobhan and the stranger's mates burst out laughing at him.

"You feckin' little tart," sniped the man as he turned his back.

Siobhan sucked in her cheeks and looked back at the screen. One of the astronauts was now sweeping a camera around to get a panoramic shot of the Moon but it just looked like a white blur on the television transmission. Then it was a case of Houston instructing left-a-bit right-a-bit as the spaceman attempted to position a fixed camera to capture what tasks the two men had still to perform. Some equipment or other had to be assembled and/or fixed near the lunar module but the picture was quite grainy and it was hard to tell what was going on. Back on earth it was easy to tell what was going on: yer man kept making sniggering remarks to his friends and sneering at Siobhan.

"I hate to say this, Patsy, but it's getting a bit samey now," said Siobhan. "Shall we move? I wouldn't mind a change of scenery."

"I think I've had enough too," said Patsy. "I'm sure it will all be shown again tomorrow so we won't miss anything. Where do you want to go next?" she said, picking up her cigarettes and matches and stowing them away in her bag.

"Let's just get out of here," said Siobhan.

It was good to be out of the smoky bar. The street outside was fairly deserted and the two women walked towards the Liffey, looking up at the moon every few yards.

"Can you believe that loser in the bar?" said Siobhan. "Men have a great knack of spoiling things. It's impossible to have a normal conversation without them sniffing at your pants and then insulting you if you're not interested."

"I don't think he was interested in sniffing my pants," said Patsy. Siobhan linked her arm and laughed. They reached O'Connell Bridge and stood leaning on the balustrade looking up to the heavens.

"It's hard to imagine the two of them up there, being so far away they can look at the earth the way we look at the Moon," said Siobhan. "Let's hope they get back safe."

"Can I ask why you asked me to meet you this evening?" said Patsy. "I was glad you did, it wouldn't have been the same watching at home on my own, but I was surprised when you suggested it."

"If I'm to be honest I'd have to tell you I was using you in a way," said Siobhan. "I finished with my boyfriend last week but I haven't told my ma and da yet and it had been arranged that I'd watch the Moon landing with him. I thought you wouldn't mind, you being on your own now. Was it an awful thing to do?"

"Not in the least and if you'd explained I still would have been happy to come," said Patsy. "What happened with your boyfriend? Had you been seeing him for long?"

"Long enough, over a year, but I liked him, at least I did until I caught him necking some other girl in the pub," said Siobhan. "And it was so — what should I say — common. She'd gone to the toilet and he'd followed her out and there they were, stood in the smelly hallway outside the lavatories, kissing and slobbering over each other in a frenzy and me looking at them through the open door. No shame, no embarrassment. Where was their self-respect? Then he had the cheek to come back to the table and ask me if I wanted another drink. Would you believe that? I stood up and left but I poured my last drop of Guinness over him before I did, just like in the movies. It felt great."

"And the revenge would have lasted, it would have left him with a sticky head of hair to wash," said Patsy.

"You're right, especially as he's one of these types with long hair who think they look like Christ," said Siobhan. "I should have let him buy me another drink and poured the whole lot on him. Shall we get a bag of chips or are you in a hurry? I don't want to get home too early, there'd be an inquisition."

"Let's cross the river. You don't live that far from me and we can get some to eat on the way home," said Patsy. "They always taste better out of the paper. Did you not want another drink?"

"I've had enough with pubs for a while," said Siobhan. "There's always men in them."

They bought their chips and strolled along.

"What was it you meant that day at work when you said all the important decisions in your life had been made by your father?" asked Siobhan. "You said at the time that it wasn't important, it was all in the past, but I think those things stay with you, they're always important, they don't go away, they can't, because as a result of them your life is changed forever from what it might have been."

"For a start he stopped me taking up a music scholarship I was offered to study the piano," said Patsy. "That was when I was just leaving school. My music teacher said I had the talent to become a professional pianist but I never got the chance to find out."

"So your father's interference was incredibly important. It meant you ended up working in a sewing factory, which isn't quite the same," said Siobhan. "You might have ended up playing at concerts in big swanky halls or for some hot jazz band in a New York speakeasy. That would have been the life. Your father had no right to do that."

"He did, he was my father, he made the decision and that's how things were done," said Patsy. "And maybe I wouldn't have been good enough anyway so perhaps in the end he protected me from a great disappointment. I've a piano at home which I hardly ever play so maybe he was right, maybe it was just a schoolgirl's fancy."

"But the point is that you'll never know," said Siobhan, "that was robbery, he robbed you of a great opportunity. I believe it's everyone's duty to take whatever opportunities come their way, to make the most of the life God's given them, especially if you're lucky enough that God has given you a talent. Isn't that what life is all about, otherwise we'd all end up doing the same things from cradle to grave. Jesus, that'd be too dreadful. I just can't imagine ever not being able to make my own decisions. I do listen to my da and I love him, don't get me wrong, but he has no right to tell me how to live my life just because I'm his daughter. It's my life. My God, Patsy, it's 1969, I'm not going to let any man dictate to me what to do."

"I think what was worse was when my father made it clear he didn't want me to marry the young man I'd been seeing for quite a while. That was very hard, we were very close."

"Jesus, Patsy, that was a terrible thing for him to have done. Unless, of course, you'd lost your heart to a mass murderer or some ruthless gangster. Is that what it was? Come on now, tell me: did you fall for a Mafia man?"

"I did not, unless the Mafia were recruiting innocent young bakers in Dublin at the time," said Patsy. "I never noticed him splash the cash, only his dough," she said laughing.

"Did you love him very much, your innocent young baker?"

"Yes actually, I did," said Patsy, "very much."

"And had your innocent young man proposed?" Siobhan said, lowering her voice as she realised that Patsy was actually putting on a show, trying too hard to be casual.

"He did propose but I turned him down and stopped seeing him altogether. I couldn't go against my da. I hated it but I could understand his strong feelings against the marriage when he explained it to me, at least I thought I did at the time, and like a good daughter I went along with it. Then again maybe it was me just using my da as an excuse to get out of something I wasn't sure about."

"It sounds as if you're sure enough about it now to have regrets," said Siobhan. "I'm so sorry that happened to you, Patsy, that you weren't allowed to marry the man you loved. Not many fathers these days would even attempt to have a say in such matters. I'm glad I wasn't young when you were. At least if I go out with a dickhead it's my own choice to pour Guinness over him as I take my leave."

"I'm sure your father would have been cheering you on," said Patsy. "You girls all have a lot more freedom nowadays but that can be hard too. Expectations can be high and you only have yourself to blame if things go wrong."

"I'm happy to take responsibility for my own mistakes," said Siobhan. "I'm young but not entirely stupid, at least I don't think I am. What about the man you did marry?" asked Siobhan. "Did you not love your husband?"

"He was a good man, very caring, very considerate, he was great company, and we'd talk about all sorts of things, life was never dull, but I didn't love him, not in the same way," said Patsy. "The young man was the love of my life, isn't that what they say?" She laughed. "Anyway, he married someone else and had a few children. I saw them all once passing in the street. Of course I never had any children of my own. I looked at them in the street and thought that in a different life those children would have been mine, that would have been my family. So yes, I do have regrets."

"Well, it might be a bit late for you to do anything about the mother bit but you're still young enough to meet someone else," said Siobhan. "Nothing is impossible."

"Well, I'll be old enough to retire in a few years but if they can put man on the Moon then nothing is impossible."

"I might go to America after all and find myself an astronaut," said

Siobhan, "even one descended from some Ulster castle-rustlers. The sky's the limit, Patsy, we can both aim for the stars."

"First let's finish our chips."

The impossible sometimes seems just that, impossible. The coming together of the whole world in one glorious moment of peaceful unity for man's first steps on the Moon didn't last long. In Ireland alone, just two weeks later, the violence that had been increasing in intensity and hatred in the North burst its way into Dublin when a bomb planted by the Ulster Volunteer Force exploded in the RTE television centre at Donnybrook. The day, August 5, 1969, signalled the eruption of the Troubles into the Republic itself and no one could believe it. It was in August only twenty years earlier that the Irish Republic had finally been declared totally free of Britain and its monarchy. People who had lived through the dark days of the struggle for independence thought all that violence was a thing of the past and now suddenly King Billy was back on his warhorse. Ireland south of the border was not a sectarian place, nobody really cared what religion their neighbour might follow. Patsy counted more than just Catholics in Warren Street and none of them were at each other's throats. That an Orange bomb had exploded in Dublin was unimaginable. It had gone off during the night when there weren't many people at the television studio, just a few cleaners and night workers, but it was thanks to God that no one had been killed.

A week later, refugee camps and field hospitals had sprung up in Ireland along the border with the North. So much for 'Make Love Not War'. Thousands of Catholics had been forced to flee their homes and businesses or stay and risk being burned alive after riots in Derry and a battle raging in the Bogside area pitted Catholics against Protestant unionists and the local police. Nowhere in the North offered sanctuary or safety. The only alternative was to flood into the South. Patrick's fears during his last days had been justified. James and his reasons for moving to County Cork had been proved right.

Patsy felt guilty as she spent her weekends painting a forest of foliage in the backyard or went shopping for plants: Matt had fixed up the trellis for her and she was trying to enjoy her magazine and the various suggestions for climbers in containers — she fancied clematis but it sounded tricky to get established — but her mind constantly dwelt on what the poor people in the North were having to endure, and not just the Catholics. She remembered too well the horror of civil war. Here she was, calmly painting her yard, trying to make a silk purse out of a sow's ear, a woodland grotto out of brick walls, yet all the while the news coming out of the North was that of a war zone. There the brick walls were tumbling down and then used as missiles. Even the British Army had been deployed to patrol the streets. Everyone was suffering up there, there were terrible atrocities being committed daily on both sides of the divide, unforgiveable and merciless atrocities. So many men seemed to relish the excuse to have guns cocked and ready to fire while women shouted and screamed venomous obscenities at other wives and mothers across barricades; young people were being schooled in the art of throwing stones and coins and petrol bombs. Casual and vicious violence had become the norm. Why was that? Patsy couldn't understand the depth of the hatred and bigotry and she wished her da was still around to give his opinion on what was going on. What parallels would he see, if any? She recognised that his attitudes had mellowed over the years and now she longed to know why, whether it was just age or his conscience over the people he had killed or a deeper loss of faith in the justification of any cause to commit murder.

Yet here she was, stuck with Mrs Murphy Senior's spirit and not that of her da. She tried talking to her ghostly visitor but there wasn't much feedback.

Patsy and lots of other parishioners daily filed into St Kevin's for series of novenas and rosaries offered up for peace but Patsy herself was confused. Mixed messages were being bellowed out through microphones and loud hailers at mass gatherings in the North and often the voices were those of religious leaders and often those voices were goading people on to more violent confrontation. Yet they were all supposed to be Christians. Patsy hung around one evening after rosary and sought out Father Dec.

"Have you a few minutes, Father? I know you've just finished the service and I don't want to delay your time for relaxing."

"Come in, of course I've a few minutes, Mrs Murphy," he said. "Let's go through into the priests' house, it's a bit warmer than here at

547

the back of the church."

His office was dark but quite cosy: there was a fire lit in the grate and a couple of worn leather armchairs at either side; the walls were lined with bookshelves and there were papers strewn on the table and piled up on the chairs, the tidy mess Patsy associated with people whose intellectual attention was constantly being pulled this way and that.

"I'll make us some tea?" he asked. "I'd offer you something stronger but I've to go out on a house visit later and it wouldn't do for me to be administering Holy Communion and breathing whiskey fumes over the sick at the same time. Though come to think of it, it could help speed their recovery."

"Tea is fine," said Patsy.

"There's an ashtray on the mantelpiece," said Father Dec. "Of course I'm glad of your company, but I assume there's something specific you want to talk about and I know you like your cigarettes."

"It's all the trouble in the North that's bothering me," said Patsy. "I don't know which side I should be on, if any. I can't understand why some priests and Protestant ministers are encouraging people in their hatred when they're all supposed to be Christian. I was brought up in a family that fought the British for independence — God knows, the O'Kellys have a bloody history in that respect — so instinctively my sympathies lie with the Catholics and the nationalists in the North but this all seems different to me. It seems to be based more on religious bigotry than on anything else. I follow the news and read about the terrible bias against Catholics in everyday life and I can understand their frustration at the unfairness of it all. And the way they're treated can only be rooted in hatred and suspicion. I just don't understand that, it's not what Christ taught, so how can any of them condone what's going on, the ambushes and the killings, people beaten to death in the street or shot in their homes in front of their families. Each side is as guilty as the other."

"Well now, if I had the answer to that one..." said Father Dec. "Contradictions and conundrums beset us on all sides. What's a just act to one person is to another person just an act of terror." He brought the tea over to the fireside table. "Weren't there hundreds of genuine pacifists during the Second World War who believed that any taking of another's life was wrong but then there were thousands of genuine people who thought it was a just and necessary war and that the killing was an inevitable evil."

"But they're not really at war in the North. They're fighting over how the country is governed to the benefit of just the minority," said Patsy. "It seems to me that they're fighting because some are Catholic and some are Protestant and that's what they really hate about each other. And when I hear someone like Ian Paisley talk about 'the Papists' it's like listening to a wild dog spitting and snarling and baring its teeth ready to attack. Yet he's the Reverend Ian Paisley, a churchman."

"Religious faith has been at the root of wars throughout history, or at least it's always been cited as a valid reason to go to war," said Father Dec. "The leading religions throughout the world teach peace and teach us to honour God, whatever name we might use for God. They also teach us to honour and respect our neighbour. Didn't Jesus himself tell us the parable of the Good Samaritan? Yet how many of us actually manage to do that? How many of us are totally free of judging people based on simple things like their social status or their level of education or their regional accent, where they live and where they come from? It can make us feel better about ourselves, a little superior, if you like. And these differences can make us feel nervous, out of our depth, frighten us, even shake up our sense of security. How does a person from a comfortable background relate to a person living in poverty in a tenement building? The answer is 'with great difficulty'. So what chance is there when you move up to the great fundamental differences of colour or culture or religion? Difference makes us wary."

"But surely the clergy should know better, they should be teaching the basics of 'love they neighbour', trying to get Catholics and Protestants together to sort out their differences, peacefully, for the love of God, without bloodshed."

"I think a difficulty a lot of us have is in recognising that basically we're all just human beings, even us clergymen, and as such we aren't always rational and we're certainly not perfect. We study the word of God and what's right and wrong, but we have our weaknesses, our failings, our own cherished opinions and a common failing — perhaps one we can all suffer from — is the belief that we ourselves hold the right opinion and that other people are therefore wrong and pose a threat to what we hold dear. Once that's taken to the extreme, like in Northern Ireland at the moment, then it's a short step to trying to impose that 'right' opinion by any means necessary. And if you can do it in God's name, all the better. Paisley rails against Papists but you might wonder what it is about us that makes him so frightened. Is it because he's uncertain of the strength of his own religion? Help yourself to milk and sugar."

"But surely the clergy in the North should preach peace and justice," said Patsy.

"No doubt some brave souls said the same about the clergy during the Spanish Inquisition, when people were put to the stake for any transgressions against the Church's teachings or for refusing to convert to Catholicism, and didn't that have the backing of the Holy Roman Church?" said Father Dec. "You know, Patsy, when they exported the Inquisition to South America, natives were tortured and killed for not being able to recite the Lord's Prayer when actually they had never been exposed to learning it so how could they possible recite it. There's justice for you carried out in the name of religion. And what about when you learned your catechism: doesn't it say in there that Catholicism is the only one true religion? Do you really believe that, Patsy, that all the devoted Muslims and Buddhists and Hindus or whatever are destined for hell just because they're not Roman Catholics? Or that an innocent baby is condemned to an eternity in purgatory just because that poor baby died before receiving the sacrament of baptism? Surely you don't believe any of that?"

"No I don't but I used to, I took it all at face value, I think I was even smug to know that I belonged to the one true religion," said Patsy. "Then when I started to think about it, none of it seemed to fit with my belief in a loving God. But I find what you're saying doesn't leave much room for hope, Father, not in the face of so much ingrained arrogance taught and accepted without question."

"There is always hope," said Father Dec. "Most people want a peaceful life but conflict does seem to be a part of the human condition. Tribe has always fought tribe. There's a lot of history being repeated in the North, the sins of the fathers, perhaps, the unionists versus the nationalists. Wasn't it predicted when the Treaty was signed and the six counties split away? Wasn't that what the Civil War in the South was all about? Perhaps after all, Patsy, it's the same fight going on in the North now as it was in your father's day but with a heavy dose of religion thrown into the mix."

"That's partly why I came to see you, Father Dec. I'd love to be able to talk to my da about it all but he's gone and I'm stuck with my mother-in-law and she hasn't anything to say on the matter."

"I thought your mother-in-law died a long time ago. I thought you lived on your own, Patsy."

"I do but the late Mrs Murphy Senior is still hanging around, she's literally there in spirit."

"Is that right?" said Father Dec. "And how does her presence manifest itself?"

"Oh, she just sits there in the chair watching and making the odd comment."

"And do you see her?"

"Sometimes but not always, sometimes she's little more than a sort of fuzzy movement in the air."

"Really? Would you like me to try to put her soul to rest?"

"Not at all," said Patsy. "She seems happy enough. She doesn't do me any harm, she's just a link to the other side."

"I have to go out on my home visit now, unfortunately Patsy, but I'd be fascinated to carry on this conversation. Is she your only direct experience of the spirit world?"

"There have been spirits of all ages visiting me since I was a child," said Patsy. "I'm well used to them."

"Well now isn't that something? We'll have to talk more about it," said Father Dec. "Meanwhile don't despair too much about what's happening in the North. I'm a great believer in the power of prayer even if we don't always appreciate exactly how that power translates down here on the ground. We always want instant answers when sometimes the answer can only come through long-term changes in attitudes. The Catholic Church isn't burning heretics any more but it didn't stop overnight. I'll just get my coat and see you home, it's on my way."

Patsy didn't know how much better or not she felt after her conversation with Father Dec but just having the conversation had helped rein in her mind. Human beings weren't perfect, as the priest had said: all the more reason to pray for them.

The immediate outrage at the whole awful situation was dampened as the horrific reports coming out of the North took on a routine, numbing familiarity and gradually even the church service rota returned to normal. Inevitably over the months the shock of the RTE bomb subsided and a complacent sense of ease settled once again over Dublin. Despite her feelings of guilt, Patsy determined to keep the light of hope burning in her heart by adding her own little touch of beauty to the world and the transformation of the backyard got finished. Young Sean had been able to help occasionally, making suggestions or helping with the brushwork, but he was busy with school, studying hard to win a place at the National College of Art in Dublin: he had taken various photographs of the toilet project and the mural to support his application.

"I don't know what's got into people," said Margaret. Patsy had invited her friend round to enjoy a glass of wine in the new tropical setting: she hadn't felt like going overboard with another party but Margaret's company was always welcome. The sun shone down on her planting efforts but it was a late autumn sun and the women had to sit wrapped up. "Why would the UVF want to blow up a power station in Donegal?" asked Margaret. "That lot are nothing but trouble."

7

Molly was in Ireland with her youngest daughter, Margaret, who had insisted that she wanted to see more of the country than just Dublin. She had taken her mother on a hitchhiking jaunt from one side of the country to the other. They'd headed west from Dublin up to and beyond Galway to the bleak wilds of Connemara, where Margaret had registered with an estate agent for any small cottage that might come on the market. From the coastal village of Roundstone, a refreshing lift in the cab of a Harp Lager wagon had dropped them at Lisdoonvarna, where they were too late for the annual matchmaking festival but had plenty of music and dancing to enjoy in the town's bars. A bespoke-suited businessman had driven them in his Rolls to the lakes of Killarney, where he treated them to a slap-up dinner in a fine establishment looking out over the water. Whatever the age difference, mother and daughter were both quite taken with the older man's charm and gentle manners. Less luxurious was their lift with a priest in a rather battered old Ford truck but he and his truck got them along a stretch of the south coast in the general direction of Cork. The return leg back to Dublin took them via the Curragh. There they had gone in search of a horse trainer who had given them a lift earlier in the week in his fancy car, stopping at every pub along the way while he tried to guess Molly's age by the state of her teeth.

"As you know, Patsy, I was never blessed with good teeth and it was a bit disturbing to be studied as if I was a horse," said Molly. "I kept thinking I should make it easier for him by pulling my lips back over my gums and opening my mouth wide to bear my choppers in a neigh. But for all the unwanted dental attention, this was the freest, best holiday I've ever had."

"Were you not nervous getting into cars with complete strangers?" asked Patsy. "I thought hitch-hiking was terribly dangerous."

"We didn't have any trouble. I think the drivers were taken by the novelty of seeing a mother and daughter thumbing a ride at the side of the road," said Molly.

"We were picked up by what my mum called 'one of the boys' when we were up near the border," said Margaret. "That was a bit weird. We drove along a really lonely stretch of road with dense forest on either side, the sort of scenery when you see it in movies you know something awful's going to happen, and the driver kept asking questions about who we were, where we were from and where we were going and why. He wasn't being chatty. We were definitely being questioned. Then he suddenly stopped the car in the middle of nowhere and told us to get out. Then he drove off and just left us there."

"Jesus, Mary and Joseph," said Patsy, "were you not scared?"

"I would have been but he also looked like a character from a movie," said Margaret. "He was wearing a shiny black fake leather trench coat, belted and with the collar turned up, and he had driving gloves on and a trilby hat pulled down at the front. He was straight out of the wardrobe department. It was like a big joke."

"It's no laughing matter," said Patsy. "There are gun battles going on in the streets not that many miles from where you were, you might have been kidnapped and held for ransom."

"Our family's got no money," said Margaret.

"Maybe not but your lives would be worth something politically."

"The scariest time we had was actually nowhere near the border, it was in the Wicklow Hills on the way back to Dublin," said Molly. "We got a lift with a very artistic-looking type. He had long dark hair and a full beard and he wore heavy-rimmed glasses. He was quite handsome, in an interesting sort of a way rather than in a good-looking one. He had leather gloves on too but they were those expensive driving gloves, with press studs round the wrists and fancy cut-out holes on the back. Margaret was sitting next to him in the front and the two of them were getting on like a house on fire but of course she couldn't see what I could see. There was a rifle just lying there on the floor of the car right in front of me, in broad daylight. I couldn't take my eyes off it. It was right by my feet. I was frightened to move in case I dislodged the trigger."

"My God, a rifle?" said Patsy.

"A proper real rifle, and it wasn't in a bag or anything, it was just there for anyone to see," said Molly. "I kept trying to nudge Margaret in the back through the seat or I'd pretend I was trying to get more comfortable, all the time trying to catch her eye in the mirror, you know? But she just wouldn't look at me. The two of them were too busy talking. The next minute your man stops on the top of a hill and insists that we all get out to look at the view. I thought 'this is it, we're going to be shot'. I nudged and nodded and winked at Margaret to look in the back of the car and finally she saw the gun and didn't her face drain then. We tried to linger by the car doors, we didn't want to give him the chance to fetch the rifle out of the back, and all the time he was telling us to get closer to the edge of the hill, closer and closer, for a better view, he said. I know I was petrified. I really thought we were going to be killed and our bodies thrown over the edge. Margaret and I looked at each other as if it was the last time, as if we were saying our final farewells, and we inched closer to the side of the hill arm in arm. He was busy talking about the rolling hills and how beautiful it all was and we were just agreeing and trying to be enthusiastic. If we were pleasant, he might let us live."

"And what happened?" asked Patsy.

"He was right, it was a great view, and absolutely nothing happened, we lived to tell the tale," said Margaret. "In fact I need to be off. The guy lives in Dublin, he's got a small house that backs on to the Bay and it sounds great. I said I'd call in for a coffee and have a good nose."

"But what was he doing with a rifle in the back of his car?" said Patsy.

"I'll let you know if I find out," said Margaret. "I'll see you back at Nora's, Mum, I won't be late. Evenings at Nora's are too good to miss. I can see why she has regular guests staying there so often, they probably have more fun than they do at home. Maybe I'll run a B&B in Connemara. See you tomorrow, Auntie Patsy. I assume you don't work Saturdays."

Patsy poured herself and Molly a glass of Paddy's and they settled down in the parlour.

"I thought you might have given up work by now," said Molly, "but then you're the same as me, we've always liked working whereas Theresa only went back to it out of necessity. She must have found that hard. I'm a Civil Servant now, of course. Kevin filled in the application form and lied about my age to get me in, he knocked a few years off. I think he inherited his ease with dirty tricks from his mother. The problem is I can never remember how old I'm supposed to be but fortunately it doesn't come up much in conversation. People don't really like to discuss their age once they start counting the years passing, I know I don't."

"I'll carry on working until I have to stop," said Patsy. "Sadly, that day is getting nearer. I don't want to retire but at the same time I think we should make way and let the young ones have the jobs. I hate the idea of being stuck at home."

"At least it's a comfortable home and you've certainly brightened it up a lot," said Molly looking around. "I don't think I've been here since Father's funeral. I can't believe how long ago that was, six or seven years it must be. And here you still are, and there I still am. Some things have changed, of course, Theresa and Billy had to sell their house as she'd expected. It must be an awful thing, heavy gambling."

"I suppose the signs were there for all to see," said Patsy. "Jem used to wonder at Billy's casual way of losing money on the horses, always confident that the next bet would be a winner. Where are they living now?"

"They moved into a small ground floor flat, still in Cheltenham, but it's rented, it's not their own, and they have no garden any more. It only has a kitchen and one big sitting-room-diner, as they call it, but nice big windows look out on to a tree-lined street so it's nice and bright, it has the feel of space. Theresa has tried to make it look special. She has white shaggy fur rugs thrown on the floor and coloured scatter cushions everywhere, I think she likes the magazine look but I was conscious of not wanting to dirty anything with my feet or disturb the cushion arrangement when I sat down and I wouldn't want to live like that. And I didn't want to invite that pursed-lips expression Theresa's always been good at."

"Did you see any of the others when you were there? How are they all getting on?" asked Patsy, who hadn't been to Cheltenham or Liverpool since Jem had passed.

"Ciaran's doing well and he has a lovely home, a close family, but Mikey, he's a different story. He drinks a lot," said Molly. "He hits Cissie when the drink's on him and Theresa was telling me that sometimes Billy has to go round to calm him down. Cissie has called the police out a few times when Mikey's been really violent but of course they won't do anything, they're not supposed to interfere in domestic problems between husband and wife. Poor Cissie can be standing in the street with a black eye and her nose bleeding waiting for the police while Mikey's lurching in the doorway screaming blue murder at her and then the police turn up and basically just tell him to behave himself. I can't see her putting up with it much longer."

"He always had a slow way about him, Mikey," said Patsy. "Did you know I caught him once being very cruel to one of the pigeons? He'd taken it out of the loft and seemed to be twisting the head around on the neck to see how far it would go and the poor bird's eyes near popped out. I went mad at him, and he was broken-hearted with remorse in that simple way he always had so I didn't tell Daddy or Eddie about it. I thought it must be a one-off, children can be very cruel with animals, but you never know with these things."

"He was too much in awe of Ciaran, I always thought," said Molly. "Whatever Ciaran did or said, Mikey tried to copy."

"From what you say, it's a pity he's still not trying to copy Ciaran."

"Mother seems well enough," said Molly. "I never know how she's going to be when I come over and it was a relief to see her looking so well."

"It's thanks be to God that Annie lives with her, she really takes care of her mammy, and Matt's a godsend however he makes his money. He's been good to me, too, he always seems to know someone who can do whatever job needs doing. It was Matt who sorted out the new toilet fittings for me."

"That looks grand. And what about you, Patsy? That must have been awful getting knocked down in the street."

"It shook the life out of me at the time, Molly, and I was frightened to go out in the dark until the evenings drew out. I must admit I'm still nervous, you know, and I still go cold when I hear footsteps coming up behind me, but I can't be a prisoner in my own house. Imagine how frightening it must be going out in the street in Belfast or Derry. I wouldn't even want to go to the shops."

"Kathleen had a friend she wrote to in Belfast for a while. We met the family when we were all on holiday at Butlin's in Mosney, you know, just north of Dublin. Did you ever go?"

"I didn't, I thought it was probably a place for young families."

"I suppose it was mainly," said Molly. "Anyway, we made great friends there with this other family, a Protestant family but that didn't matter, and we spent most of the holiday together. They were great company, even Kevin would come out to the bar every evening and you know he never goes in pubs, he's not a drinking man. After that we used to send each other Christmas cards but Kathleen kept in touch with the son for quite a while, like penfriends, I suppose you'd call them. Then suddenly last year Kevin got a letter from the boy's family and you wouldn't believe the bad language and the physical threats they made to us if our Papist daughter ever wrote to their son again. They had people in Liverpool who wouldn't have to be asked twice to kill a Catholic, they said. I couldn't believe it. It was ugly but at the same time ridiculous, you couldn't imagine anyone would seriously sit down and write a letter like that and then stick a stamp on it and post it. We showed it to our parish priest and he actually read it out at Mass the following Sunday during his sermon."

"My God that's something when people can't even write letters to each other without bigotry coming into it," said Patsy. "And was Kathleen all right after that?"

"She was, I don't think she had any romantic interest in the boy, it was just a friendship, but she decided to stop writing. She sent him one last letter saying what a pity it all was."

"It was a pity all right. You think it's only the real hot-heads you have to worry about, the ones throwing the bombs and doing all the killing, but it seems as if the whole anti-Catholic attitude is becoming more common."

"It's always been a bit like that in Liverpool, in my time anyway," said Molly. "When the schools let out at four in the afternoon it was routine for the children to call each other names in the street on the way home, like 'Proddy Dogs' or 'Red Necks', that was every day and that was just the kids. Then last year our Margaret had a summer job at Jacob's biscuit factory and she enjoyed it, she got on well with the other girls and they had a laugh together. She went to clubs with them a few times at weekends and they seemed to become friends. As it turned out, some of the girls were in the Lodge and when the glorious twelfth came round they stopped talking to Margaret altogether other than to make remarks about 'dirty Papists' every time they passed her desk. These were the very same girls she'd been out dancing with. They all took a day's holiday for the big Orange parade through Liverpool and the television showed pictures of the marchers all waving their little flags and carrying banners saying 'Down with the Pope'. A couple of days later everything went back to normal at the factory and they started talking to Margaret again as if nothing had happened but she left not long after, it was all a bit two-faced."

"I didn't know they had marches in Liverpool."

"Nor did I," said Molly. "I think last year maybe it was more in the news because they decided to put on a bit of an extra show with what's going on in Northern Ireland."

"I think the curtain's certainly being raised on our show," said Patsy. "When he was in hospital, Daddy warned me that he thought the problems north of the border would move south and a few bombs have gone off already here, planted by the UVF, that's what they claimed anyway. Just after Christmas, a car-bomb exploded outside the Gardaí headquarters in Dublin and the previous day or the day after Daniel O'Connell's statue in the city was damaged by a bomb hidden behind one of the four cast iron angels."

"I didn't hear about that. I always liked that statue. Was anyone hurt?"

"No, thank God. They must have been guardian angels right enough because there wasn't anyone hurt and not much damage to the statue, though a lot of nearby windows were broken. Ulstermen obviously don't like our Irish heroes. They'd already tried to blow up Wolf Tone's grave in County Kildare late last year. Anyway, God willing that's it and they've made their point," said Patsy. "But God help us if things get as bad here as in the North. At least they're not likely to bomb anywhere in England. Do you remember much about the fighting when we were children?"

"Not really, I just have odd vivid images," said Molly, "like the night the Tans raided us on the Quays. I can still picture Mammy running in to hide a gun and signalling to us to be very quiet and not breathe a word.

Otherwise, I don't recall that much: all the rubble and the buildings bombed out and tanks in the streets, of course, that seemed normal at the time, then I have odd memories of Father going out late at night. I do remember learning that he had been arrested."

"Did you know that John and I went to visit Kilmainham?"

"Annie mentioned it and Margaret said she'd love to go," said Molly. "She reads a lot of Irish history."

"She must feel a strong connection with Ireland," said Patsy. "She's got her granddad's blood in her veins. I didn't know she wanted to live in Galway."

"I think that was a spare of the moment decision but she's more likely to come over here to live than I am, and God knows I miss it," said Molly.

"And how are things in Bootle?"

"Nothing ever changes there."

"Would you not be tempted to come back? You always seemed to enjoy life here so much more and I'd like to have you nearer," said Patsy. "I didn't expect you to stay in England all this time, you and everyone else. What about Kevin? Would he not like to move over to Dublin?"

"He says he would and when he gets on the piano he always plays and sings 'I'll take you home again, Molly'. But then that's it, the lid goes down on the piano and he rushes round to see if his mother needs anything doing."

"Mothers and their sons!" said Patsy. "I know a bit about that."

8

Jeanette Modes had been involved in making some of the costumes for the Eurovision Song Contest which was being hosted at the Gaiety in Dublin after Dana had won the contest the previous year. There were no complimentary tickets handed out to the sewers — tickets were like gold dust, anyway, impossible to get unless you knew someone who knew someone — but Patsy had arranged to meet up with Siobhan and Bernadette outside the theatre to watch the comings and goings. The Eurovision wasn't normally a big thing for most people but the staging of it promised to be a novel occasion.

There had already been a fair amount of controversy over the UK entry. With all the troubles in the North, it was no surprise that politics got involved. In what was generally regarded as a rather pathetic attempt at diffusing tensions across the divide, it was a Catholic singer from Northern Ireland, Clodagh Rodgers, who had been chosen to carry the British flag. There was even more controversy when some in the Church complained about the sparkly tight-fitting hotpants she was to wear — and her supposed to be a Catholic symbol! — brought into sharper focus by the item in the news that claimed her legs were insured for one million pounds.

"I thought it was only Hollywood stars like Cyd Charisse who had their legs insured," said Patsy.

"And who in God's name is Cyd Charisse?" asked Siobhan.

"She was a great dancer in films," said Patsy. "Have you never seen *Singin' in the Rain*?"

"It's going back a bit then," said Siobhan, "she's a bit before my time."

"Sure, I know that film, I loved it," said Bernadette, "but I thought it was Debbie Reynolds in the yellow mac."

"She played the main female character, she was a great tap-dancer, but it was Cyd Charisse who did that strange ballet scene when they have the wind blowing her long trailing scarf up in the air behind her, really classy," said Patsy. "I read in a movie magazine that her legs were insured for five million dollars."

"Imagine that," said Bernadette. "I'd be happy to have the money for a decent pair of shoes." Bernadette's husband had thought his wife crazy wanting to go and stand in the street to see a load of nobodies walk into a theatre but he was happy to stay in with the kids and then have the television to himself. "Isn't this grand?" she said, thrilled to be out with her friends from work. She loved going out with himself, of course she did, but she had a better laugh with the girls. "My God what's going on over there?" she cried suddenly, waving her arms excitedly "Would you look at them."

A crowd of shouting women had marched along the road and taken up position outside the Gaiety, carrying banners and shoving leaflets into people's hands. It was a protest by the Irish Women's Liberation movement complaining about contraception being illegal in the country.

"Irish women have nothing to sing about, Irish women have nothing to sing about," they chanted over and over.

"They must be the opening act," said Siobhan. "Shall we join in?"

"We will not," said Patsy.

"Let's get a leaflet at least," said Siobhan.

"I've read their leaflets before and they're all about sex," said Patsy.

"Then I definitely want one." Siobhan laughed and pushed her way through to one of the demonstrators and was soon involved in a conversation with the woman. Patsy and Bernadette could see their friend's face contorting with interest in whatever the protestor had to say and she was obviously asking lots of questions. Bernadette couldn't wait to find out what they were talking about. Siobhan was beaming when she returned waving the leaflet.

"This is probably of more use to you right now than me, you being a mother," she said handing it to Bernadette, "unless you want to keep having babies in the Irish tradition. It's about having sex without the consequences and, if you're interested, Bernie, there's what they call the Contraception Express, a regular train from Belfast to Dublin smuggling contraceptives across the border into Ireland. I'm sure you'll find the relevant information in there, a phone number at least."

562

Before Patsy had time to object to Bernadette being tempted into sin, another kerfuffle broke out around them: another demonstration had formed up on the pavement and in the road, with more placards and more chanting.

"My God I bet it's more fun outside than in the theatre," said Siobhan. "They could have sold tickets for this."

The second protest was a contingent of trade unionists representing the workers at the television studio. They were lobbying against the high cost of the whole shenanigans — RTE was evidently engaged in only its second ever outside broadcast in colour — while their members had to fight for better pay and conditions.

It was all very good natured but it wasn't long before more police had to be summoned to keep some semblance of order as people got too involved in the spirit of the events and the inevitable jostling started and more people joined in with the various chants, not necessarily out of solidarity. It was like enjoying great communal craic right there in the street. Apart from the chanting, the predominant sound was of laughter and chatter. Still, the Gardaí policy was that it wouldn't do for any of the theatre guests to be harried by a bunch of barracking commoners gathered in the street, especially with the world watching.

The crowd ogled as the glitterati filed into the Gaiety in their fancy evening wear. Bernadette said she felt as if she was in the opening scene of *Singin' in the Rain* when all the fans turn out to see the stars arrive at a movie premier: "Dignity, always dignity," she quoted but it was lost on Siobhan.

Eventually there was nothing more to see: everyone who was anyone had already entered the theatre and the protesters dispersed, taking their side-shows with them. The atmosphere of anticipation slowly evaporated in the absence of anything more to anticipate and the street crowd began to move off. The three friends headed to a bar to have a drink before going to their various homes to watch the song contest results on the television. It was full of people who seemed to have the same idea.

"You're full of surprises, Patsy Murphy. Fancy finding out that in your innocent and distant past you'd read literature put out by the women's libbers," said Siobhan. "And all about sex, was it?"

Patsy couldn't help her instinct to look around in case anyone had heard Siobhan's comments and use of the 'sex' word but the pub was too noisy for anyone to be paying attention to anything but their own conversations. She relaxed a little and leaned into the table.

"It was a long time ago," she said, "not that long after I started working at Jeanette Modes."

"Oh good, are we going to hear a story?" said Bernadette. "I love it when people tell stories about when they were young, it's like listening to history."

"History! How old do you think I am?" said Patsy with pretend annoyance. "Mind you, it's true I've lived through some important events in Irish history."

"Let's concentrate on the women you got involved with," said Siobhan.

Patsy related the tale of her decision to go to a women's meeting she had seen advertised, thinking it was to discuss women in the workplace and their entitlements to better wages but finding out too late that it was about something altogether different.

"It was all about contraception and women's rights to use their own bodies as they saw fit and not as society demanded," she said in as quiet a voice as she could manage and still be heard. "Then they handed out leaflets about different forms of birth control and told us all we had the right to enjoy sex just as much as men: the only difference was that men didn't have to worry about having babies, so why shouldn't we be free from that worry too."

"But that's ridiculous," said Bernadette. "Men don't have to worry about having babies because they can't have babies, they're men, they're not built for it."

"Exactly," said Siobhan, "so they have no understanding of what it's like for women. The men can just thrust away until they come and they're done, they don't lie there worrying if this is going to be the night the sperm hits the egg jackpot. How can women enjoy sex to the full when they can't relax? When they know they're treated like just a baby-making machine, in this country anyway?"

"I'm pregnant again," said Bernadette. "I'm three months gone."

She made the announcement in such a matter-of-fact way that it took a moment for Patsy and Siobhan to respond. They were trying privately to gauge exactly how Bernadette had delivered her news, trying to assess whether she was pleased or slightly broken by the situation. It was a predicament: neither of them wanted to congratulate too much if it was commiserations that were needed. In the end it was Siobhan who managed just the right reaction.

"Well, here's to you," she said and raised her glass in a toast. The tension dropped.

"So, I won't be needing the contraceptive express," said Bernadette, not quite light-heartedly but smiling now, relieved that she had been accepted again when she had expected perhaps to have ended up feeling she'd fallen short as a modern woman. "I'll stay at work as long as I can, though, I'd miss the company of you two specially. Don't we have great gas together?"

"We do that," said Patsy, toasting Bernadette again so she could lift the glass to her mouth and hide her twinge of jealousy.

"I tell you what was more great gas about the Eurovision contest," said Siobhan. "There were two other protests apart from the ones we ourselves witnessed. Apparently, the Celtic League, a worthy institution no doubt, criticised the Irish organisers for not entering a song in Gaelic. As if the vast majority in Ireland would understand a word if they had! Meanwhile the Irish Council Against Blood Sports, another worthy institution I'm sure, also got in on the act, criticising the Irish tourist board for showing a promotional video at the contest that included film of a fox hunt in Galway."

"I can only remember a bit of Gaelic from school, we had to learn it," said Patsy. "I'd be interested to know if the Celtic League made their protests in Gaelic. Maybe that then was the problem, no one could understand what they were protesting about."

"I don't know any Gaelic other than what you see on signs, like the one for the public toilets," said Bernadette. "I know they have the destinations on the buses in Gaelic but I only look at the ones in English."

"But don't you think it's all a bit mad?" said Siobhan. "Here we are in Dublin, hosting a major international competition, with television cameras and visitors from all over Europe, and outside the venue we have a women's group shouting for contraception to be made legal, we have a bunch of trade unionists questioning the cost of the whole shebang, and behind the scenes we have the Gaelic lobby pushing its language mission and the anti-fox hunting brigade taking aim at the tourist board and all on the back of a song competition. I just love this country. I'll certainly miss it."

"What do you mean you'll miss it?" asked Bernadette.

An ear-to-ear grin spread across Siobhan's face. "I'm emigrating," she said, pausing to pick up her glass for maximum dramatic effect. She looked from one astonished face to the other, waiting as her words sank in. "I'm moving to America."

Patsy's face turned pale. "America?"

"I didn't know how to tell you both," said Siobhan, "I've rehearsed it time and time again in my head and now I've just blurted it out. No one else in work knows yet, I'll be giving my notice in next week, but I wanted you two to be the first to know. I've always felt we were our own little trio in the workroom."

"America? Sure, what's in America?" said Bernadette. "Aren't your family and your friends all here?"

"I've family over there already," said Siobhan. "One of my mammy's sisters moved there in the fifties, to New York, when a lot of Irish people went. My mammy said there wasn't much work to do on their farm and her sister was always the headstrong type, always impatient for something new. She had no intention of being stuck in the Irish countryside watching the potatoes grow and herself grow old. We can all understand that. I can anyway, she sounds a lot like me. And a lot of her friends had already left."

"So how in those days would she get from a farm in the middle of Ireland to America?" asked Bernadette. "I live in Dublin and even now I wouldn't have a clue where to start."

"Well, what do simple Irish people do when they have any sort of problem?" said Siobhan. "They ask the parish priest, of course. Her parents, my granny and granddad, did the same, they asked their local priest for advice and, good enough, he ended up helping to organise everything. Evidently there was already a great network in place in New York then for people arriving from Ireland, I suppose because they were mostly young women, as it happens, and the Church was determined to stop any of them going astray. They even had boarding houses especially for young Irish girls. That was one sure way of keeping an eye on them."

"Still, it must have been a great help," said Bernadette. "It can't be easy leaving home to move to a completely different country, even if they do speak the same language."

"You're probably right, Bernie, and my auntie was only a country lass straight from the bog no matter how independent she thought she was. But the network also found her a job in a supermarket and she loved her new life so much that she stayed. She preferred selling potatoes to picking them. She eventually married a Yank and had a family, so I've got cousins there, still in New York," said Siobhan. "They said I'll have no trouble getting a job and I'll be able to stay with them while I find my feet."

"My God, Siobhan, imagine you living in New York. I'd love to see those sky-scrapers for real, to stand at the bottom and look up and up," said Bernadette. "When are you planning on going?"

"I bought my ticket last weekend and I leave in a month's time," said Siobhan. "I can't wait. Just a couple more weeks sitting at that blasted sewing machine in work and I'll be off. I'll be making love not war and I might even find that astronaut we were talking about. What do you say, Patsy?"

"That I've been sitting at that blasted sewing machine for forty years."

That quite bitter reply kept running through her head as Patsy made her way home. "And I've been putting this same key in this same lock for twenty-five of those years," she thought, pausing at the door and looking up and down the street with all its same doors, same windows, same houses. "Jesus, Mary and Joseph."

She went in and turned all the lights on, as if the light would make life look brighter, then she took off her coat and put the kettle on. The night out had been great fun and here she was in danger of ruining it all with another attack of melancholia, frustration, resentment. She said a prayer thanking God for all he had given her, conscious all the time that God would know too well what was going on deep inside her and that her thanks weren't completely heartfelt at that moment.

"I'm fine," she said to the chair. "I've had a good time with my friends, a really good time, but unfortunately they won't be around for much longer. One's having another baby and one's leaving the country so I'm feeling a little sad, that's all."

That wasn't all and she knew it. As soon as Siobhan had announced she was emigrating to America, Patsy had felt the blood drain from her face but it wasn't so much the news itself, which did come as a total surprise, so much as the easy way, it seemed to Patsy, in which Siobhan had arrived at a huge conclusion and reached a huge decision to act upon it herself: she was going to give her idea a shot. All the previous joking references about moving to America had obviously sown a seed. Patsy would never in a month of Sundays have had so much courage. What she was feeling wasn't sadness, it was inadequacy.

"Is that why you're still here, Mrs Senior?" she said. "Was there something you wanted to do in your life but you didn't and now you're hanging around to — what — I don't know — see if you can still capture whatever it was you let escape? Sorry to inform you, madam, but it's too late now." Patsy poured the tea. "Twenty-five years drinking tea in the same house, while there's a whole world of different people and different places outside, beyond my reach," she said. "We've much in common, you and me, Mrs Senior. Perhaps after all you're actually just here to keep the chair warm for me."

Part 7

While the world is full of troubles
And is anxious in its sleep,
Come away, O human child,
To the waters and the wild.

—   W B Yeats

1

Patsy was walking home from Jeanette Modes for the last time. She was laden down with flowers and chocolates and a huge card signed by everyone to wish her a happy retirement. Organised casually around her neck was a beautiful silk scarf, held in place by an ornate gold pin, both presented to her by her boss, and in her bag was a sexy French negligée, which the girls had given her as a reminder of the tale she'd once told of Jem advising her on the tactile qualities of French lace next to the sleeping body. And indeed, it was trimmed with French lace, though the trim had been bought separately and stitched on to an otherwise pretty but ordinary cotton lawn nightie: a whole French creation would have been out of the question for these working women even with the generous whip-round collected for Patsy's leaving present. The girls had joked that the negligée wouldn't warm her up much on a cold night, so they had given her a couple of character hot water bottles too and, they said, if they didn't work, then she'd have to take matters into her own hands to get some heat going round her body. The girls had cheered and applauded when the joke elicited the usual Patsy blush of humorous disapproval. She blushed again as she stopped in front of her usual window on the way home — it was a habit she had never managed to shake — and admired the scarf and the air of specialness that the bouquet added to the image. The bouquet was her window-hyphen, she reflected, a link between her beginnings at the fashion house and her last day there. A shiver of fear went through her, her last day, she would no longer be a member of the city's daily workforce, this journey marked the end of all that.

She strolled home casually, without the least hint of urgency, the evening ahead had already taken on a lack of significance; it would be finite, not just a period of relaxation before the routine of her next day at work, and she wasn't anxious to embrace it too soon. Also, she was enjoying the certain air of sentimental importance she knew she was giving off in the street. Total strangers hurrying past managed warm smiles in her direction, as if sharing in something very pleasant.

She lingered outside Bewley's, trying to decide whether or not to go in — she wouldn't want any of the beautiful flowers to get damaged by a careless customer shoving past the table — when she heard a familiar voice reaching her from the door.

"You're not going in now are you, Patsy? What a pity, I'm just leaving, I have to get the guests' dinner ready or they'll desert me in droves and then where would I be." It was Nora. Over the last few years Patsy had avoided Bewley's at certain times if she thought there was a chance she might coincide with Molly's friend: she hadn't forgotten Nora's speculation about Jem's reasons for drinking a whole bottle of whiskey against the doctor's strict advice and she wasn't open to having that conversation revisited. It hadn't obviously crossed Nora's mind. "My God what are you carrying?" said Nora. "You're weighed down with, what is it, flowers and chocolates? Is it somebody's birthday?"

"I retired today," said Patsy. "These are my leaving presents."

"Retired, is it? I never thought you'd ever retire, Patsy, you've always been really modern when it comes to having a career and sticking at it."

"I'm not sure sitting at a sewing machine all your life amounts to a career. Anyway, you get to the point when you need to make way for other people to have the work and I reached that point," said Patsy.

"They'll find it hard to find anyone as good as you," said Nora. "Molly always said you were the most talented tailoress she knew."

"Did Molly say that?"

"She did and she meant it. She said you were one of the best pattern-designers and cutters and that you were as deft with a needle as a surgeon. As good as any man tailor, she said, and don't they get all the credit the way men do."

"Well, I never knew that was her opinion," said Patsy, quite touched by her sister's hitherto unknown compliment. "Still, it's all behind me now, I won't have to get up early every morning if I don't want to, I can lie on in bed."

"Now you don't want to get into that bad habit," said Nora. "It's just a short step from that to staying in your nightie all day and you've always taken such a pride in your appearance. Look at the beautiful scarf you've got on today."

"Isn't it beautiful?" said Patsy. "It was a present from the boss, and this gold pin with it."

"Like I said, you must have been a highly valued member of staff. Anyhow I must rush now to catch the bus and get busy in the kitchen. Not all of us are retired into a life of leisure. We'll no doubt meet up in Bewley's one of these days, Patsy, you'll be able to call in on a weekday afternoon now and I'm often here," said Nora, "it's my treat to myself. We'll catch up on all your news next time, make it soon."

Nora swept off across the road and Patsy felt as if she had been dropped suddenly in the wake of a gust of wind. Nora always had that effect. It seemed to go with the cupid-bow lips, as if Nora herself had been shot like an arrow and had a target in sight. All the same Patsy was left feeling guilty for having deliberately avoided the woman for so long over something that might after all have just been in her own head. She might have read something into Nora's words when all the time it was her own words she was actually hearing.

She decided to give Bewley's a miss and carry on home, enjoying the last bit of the walk along the canal, though she kept to the road and didn't stray on to the grass. Warren Street looked its usual self but Patsy imagined colourful bunting tied across the street to celebrate her retirement with a neighbourly flutter. None of her neighbours actually knew she had just stopped work but no doubt word would get round soon enough. She put the key in the lock, opened the door and shut it behind her.

"I'm back," she called, "for good, whether you like it or not." She walked down the hall and into the back room. "I don't know yet whether I like it or not," she said, "we'll have to wait and see, but whether or not I'm looking forward to the wait-and-see is another matter."

Patsy draped her new silk scarf round the back of a chair and pinned it in place with the gold clasp, as if the chair was the torso of a tailor's dummy, then she arranged the flowers in a tall vase and placed them in the middle of the table. She put a match to the fire and poured herself a small Paddy's to mark the occasion of her last day at work and sipped at the whiskey while studying the selection in the box of chocolates. She chose a couple and closed the lid back on the box.

"It's not a nice feeling," she said. "It's an awful mixture of feeling redundant and old. I suppose they go together. Sure you don't retire unless you're getting old. Or unless you have lots of money and can give up work while you're still young enough to enjoy a life ahead." She ate a chocolate, a coffee cream, which with the whiskey reminded her of Tuesday nights out at Bewley's with Margaret, chatting about this and that, scrutinising the other customers, discussing movie stars. She sipped at her drink, it heightened the reminder of years past, or was it passed? She couldn't decide.

"As far as I know you didn't work much outside the home, Mrs Senior, so it's not something you'll have gone through." Patsy ate the second chocolate. "These are very nice," she said. "I'd offer you one but it would only end up sitting on the chair and turning gooey." She laughed. "Imagine that. I would put a chocolate in what looks like your mouth but there is no mouth, because you're not really there, so it would go right through you and just fall on the chair." She laughed again. "Then I might forget all about it and sit on it and I'd have a shitty-looking spot on the back of my skirt. Nora would be astonished. Haven't I always taken such pride in my appearance! I can hear her now. 'Did you know, Patsy, you've got chocolate smeared all over your arse?'"

Patsy stood up and gazed out of the window. She could still make out the shapes and colours of her little oasis in the early evening light though a diagonal of shadow had already forced closed the petals on some of the flowers. They'd have their own night of relaxation before opening for business the next day. "For bees-ness," thought Patsy. She was in a bit of a silly mood, not to say even a bit rude, perhaps she should have gone for a farewell drink after work, she might have enjoyed it after all. A group of her colleagues had tried to persuade her, but she had declined with a lame excuse of having to feed the cat she didn't have. They knew she didn't have a cat and she knew that they knew. In actual fact she would have gone if Bernie and Siobhan had still been around but Bernie hadn't returned to work after her new daughter was born and Siobhan was long gone in search of her American dream. Also Patsy hadn't trusted herself not to get embarrassingly emotional. It hadn't been her choice to retire. It hadn't been her genuine choice. All the same, she thought, the women might have worked a bit harder in trying to persuade her to go out: they were going anyway, having already organised to be home from work later than usual as there was to be a retirement party.

She took out the farewell card from her bag and studied the photo on the front; it looked like a scene from Killarney or thereabouts — she had never actually been to that part of the country — with a small rowing boat pulled on to the dry bank of a calm lake and, rising out of the water, breezy grassy banks which sloped upwards and gave way to tree-covered hills and distant mountains. It was a pretty scene and she offered up a quick prayer of thanks that God had created such lovely places on the earth. She started reading the messages. Most of them were five or six words long, including the names, and included best wishes for the future, for good health, for happiness, for good luck. They were sincere enough but Patsy was disappointed that after all her years at Jeanette Modes no one had thought of anything more personal to write, just the usual routine comments you scribbled when a card was shoved in front of you to sign when you were busy concentrating on something else. One of them seemed to shout at Patsy, not for any particular difference in sentiment but for the way it was expressed. "The best of luck in the future," it said. Now what does that mean? Patsy wondered. She speculated on the unspoken part of the message: "The best of luck in the future, you'll need it," maybe. "The best of luck in the future, what future you have left," maybe. No. She took another sip of whiskey and read the printed verse.

When you retire, it's natural to do some looking back
Along the way you've travelled, yes, the same familiar track.
But now the way is opening up and promising for you
Great opportunities to try, just all you've wanted to.

It tried to strike an encouraging note but to Patsy it sounded a discordant mix of misplaced nostalgia and totally unrealistic optimism, of the losses suffered and eaten up by the past now inexorably merging into the inevitable *familiar* losses awaiting in a future of growing older and more alone. Sure, at this time in her life she'd naturally look back but wasn't she always looking back? That was one of her things, to look back. She doubted she'd now look back through any rosier eyes on that *same familiar track*, a track through life that had been altogether too much the same and far too familiar to allow for any exciting change of direction. Another unspoken message entered her head: 'Familiarity breeds contempt.' Her past had been one of unfulfilled dreams and opportunities and now the card was telling her that the way was finally opening up to *Great opportunities to try*. She wondered what they would be that would make them so great and, besides, it was already too late for her to try all she had ever wanted to try. And how was a widow supposed to pay for these *Great opportunities*. Jem had left her with enough money to live and eat and pay the bills but not enough to seize any new *Great opportunities*. Patsy stood the card on the mantelpiece feeling guilty that she had almost come to resent it and its jaunty but phoney pleasantries when the colleagues who gave it to her had been kind and thoughtful enough to present her with such lovely gifts.

She took the nightie out of its fancy wrapping and again warmed to the women she had worked with and chatted with across the rows of sewing machines and cutting tables all these years. She believed that the workroom would miss her presence; everyone, including herself, had enjoyed those moments of laughter when she had displayed the expected disapproval at some funny but rude remark, a disapproval sometimes genuine, sometimes feigned for the welcome affect it had on the others, an affect that made her feel appreciated in her role as the contrary part of the intimate sewing room community.

"Well, all that's gone now, disappeared down that *same familiar track* along with everything else, including the stinking commode," she said nodding to the chair.

Then she stopped and stood looking at the corner of the room where the chamber-pot contraption had been sited during those long smelly times. She sat down again, her gaze still fixed on the same spot; she chose another chocolate and helped it down with another sip of Paddy's. "Here's cheers to the future and to my first great opportunity," she said raising her glass. "Before that I need to use the lavatory, I don't want to be caught short just as I'm about to begin an adventure."

She went out to the toilet and the sound of the flush seemed to echo sharply off the brick walls in the still of the evening. She paused to look up at the night sky, shivered with the cold, and hurried back into the house to sit in front of the warm fire. She picked up the two hot water bottles that had sat propped up on a dining chair since she had got home, the same chair that served as the tailor's dummy for her scarf, and she looked at them properly for the first time. The head of one was shaped like a duck, with a large Donald Duck beak: the other had a head moulded like a monkey, complete with a set of large rubbery lips. Both of them had large open eyes which smiled child-like at Patsy. She smiled back. She hugged them in close, these comical symbols of her working life being over, and held them tightly in her arms, rocking backwards and forwards seeking some element of comfort as her tears flooded out, christening the bottles.

2

Bloody Sunday in Derry: twenty-six unarmed civilians shot dead by British soldiers during a civil rights march protesting against the policy of internment without trial. Bloody Friday in Belfast: more than twenty bombs detonated by the Provisional IRA in Belfast, injuring more than one hundred and thirty people but killing nine, their bodies so badly mutilated by the blasts that one explosion left a head stuck to a wall while elsewhere a ribcage and vertebrae were found scattered across a roof top. Reprisals carried out on each side claimed more lives, more maimings. In between, the British Embassy in Dublin had been burned down and there had been blood spilt at an army barracks in Aldershot and at the law courts in London. More dead. More injured. Life had turned bloody. Along with most people in Ireland, Patsy was both sickened and ashamed of what was being perpetrated in the name of the IRA: its noble credentials had been stolen. In a letter from Bootle, Molly had written that she had started to try to hide her accent because of some of the looks she got when she spoke in the shops: some people had even sworn at her and told her to go home if she was so anti-British.

"I don't see the sense in any of it," said Margaret. "Live and let live is my motto. Poor Molly, and she married to a man who fought the Germans and her pregnant at the time."

"A lot of Irishmen fought in the war alongside the English," said Patsy. "My Uncle Arthur, my daddy's brother, worked with the French Resistance until they were liberated. People have short memories, allies one day, enemies the next. But the fact is, Margaret, that some things are right and some things are wrong and, in my opinion, if the Catholics in the North have right on their side, you know, with all the problems over their lack of rights, then their actions should be above reproach, not wrong. They shouldn't try to win those rights by being as bad as the Protestants. There's no point in asking for justice, on the one hand, and, on the other, murdering and planting bombs."

"But, as far as I understand it, they were just marching in Derry when those people got shot."

"And after that was the very time the Catholics should have responded in a peaceful way," said Patsy, "not with planting all those bombs to go off one after the other in Belfast. Their retaliation should be to turn the other cheek. They should be demonstrating that they are above all that, that they are the good Christians and it's the Protestants who deserve to be condemned. As it is, they're all as bad as each other. I think they're enjoying it all, like little boys playing at soldiers only with real guns and real bullets."

"And isn't that a strange idea, to have bullets made of rubber?" said Margaret.

The two women were sitting in the back room at Warren Street. The air was foggy with cigarette smoke — Patsy was smoking more than ever since she stopped work — and fumes from the fire.

"What are those things doing there?" asked Margaret. She'd spotted the two hot water bottles lying on the floor in front of the fire. "They're going to get hot even before you fill them, Patsy. Let's hope they don't perish before bedtime." She picked them up and studied them as she put them on the chair. "Would you look at them," she said, "a duck and a monkey."

"Have I not shown you them before?" said Patsy. "Actually I like having them down here during the day as a bit of company, I like their cute little faces. They were part of my retirement present from the women at work, them and a beautiful French nightie."

"Imagine that, a beautiful French negligee and you a widow and no one to coax into bed with it," said Margaret. "You'll have to cuddle up to the monkey and the duck instead of Jem, though they're no substitute whatsoever for Jem, God rest his soul. By the way, did you ever hear from that friend of Jem's, the one who went to live in County Cork a few years back?"

"James? No, I've not heard a word since he left. He promised to keep in touch but he never did and I don't have an address for him, he was supposed to send it to me."

"It was probably his wife who told him not to write."

"His wife? Now why would she do that?" said Patsy.

"Jealousy, of course," said Margaret. "You used to go out with her husband regularly, just the two of you out in Dublin on a Friday night, and no doubt the two of you got dressed up for your concerts or whatever they were and she at home with the children. Of course she'd be jealous, what wife wouldn't be? And if not exactly jealous, she might have wondered what you were up to, going out with her husband. Did you never think of that?"

"It never crossed my mind," said Patsy. "His wife didn't like going to concerts and he did, and I did, so it suited everybody."

"How do you know she didn't or that it suited her? Was it himself who told you that? Did you ever get to meet her and ask her yourself?"

"No, I never met her, James told me she didn't want to go."

"There you have it then," said Margaret. "It obviously didn't suit her at all and, when they moved, she took the opportunity to nip the relationship in the bud and forbade him to write."

"But there was no relationship," said Patsy. "We were just good friends."

Margaret laughed. "And how often have you read that very same thing said by film stars or politicians caught up in a scandal they're trying to deny. 'We're just good friends,' they always say that. Then before you know it there's a divorce on the cards."

"But I never once thought of James as anything other than a good friend."

"Perhaps you didn't," said Margaret, "but can you speak for him? You are so innocent, Patsy. Not everyone manages to be as morally upright as you. In fact it's only because I know you so well that I never once thought anything untoward about your Friday concerts. I bet you wore a bit of lipstick, did you? And did you sometimes link his arm?"

"Only if the pavement was wet and he didn't want me to slip over. There was no more to it than that," said Patsy.

"Maybe he welcomed the excuse to have your arm in his. It's possible that one of his wife's friends saw you at that precise moment when he was being, as you thought, a gentleman and she put two and two together and made five. The next minute the wife's been informed and the 'just good friends' comes into play."

Patsy was mortified. It hadn't occurred to her that she was doing anything inappropriate, especially with another woman's husband.

"Do you think I might be right about his feelings?" asked Margaret. "You always said how well the two of you got on and how much you had in common. Perhaps you dazzled him."

A vivid memory crept into Patsy's mind of the last time she had seen James. They had been to the Feis Ceoil music competition and gone on to The Brazen Head. He had complimented her several times and, although she brushed it off at the time, she had been aware of an extra something, an extra closeness or lingering in the way he had hugged her before she got into the taxi to leave. She could still picture his face as the taxi drove off and she watched him out of the window, waving until he was out of sight. Now as she remembered his face, she saw in it an expression of loss, of longing. She blushed at the realisation.

"I can see from your face that I'm right, Patsy Murphy," said Margaret. "You dazzled him so he had to leave. End of story."

"I'm an idiot," said Patsy. "I've always been an idiot."

"You're one of the brightest women I know so we'll have none of that nonsense. You've just gone through your life not realising how attractive you were."

"I notice you used the past tense," said Patsy. "Perhaps you're telling me all this too late. I am retired now."

"Come on now, I've told you often enough, but you've never let yourself relax where men are concerned and we all know it's never too late," said Margaret. "But let's change the subject before you turn pious on me. How are you getting on with being retired? Are you any more used to it?"

"I've no option but to accept it and get used to it," said Patsy. "I still feel guilty if I'm not doing something positive, something real. Work was always real. I don't know what to do with myself now, I just know I want it to be something proper, with a purpose to it other than waiting for the hands on the clock to go round."

"You need to start pampering yourself, Patsy. You did a grand job with the toilet and the yard, find something else to occupy your time."

"If anyone else says that to me I'll scream. The idea of suddenly having to 'occupy my time' is a terrible thought, as if I'm just filling in what's left before my time is up. I might have another thirty years and that's a long time to just keep myself occupied. You have your children and your grandchildren, I'm on my own."

"You have your family still. There's a few of them still in Dublin and don't you have family in Tullamore?"

"I've not seen any of them since my da died. I don't even know who's there and who isn't or how many of them there are now."

"Well then find out, woman. Meanwhile you have me, Patsy, and I'll not be dismissed. I'm as good as family, we grew up together: you, me and Maureen O'Hara. So stop your nonsense and stop feeling sorry for yourself. Whoever heard of using silly hot water bottles for company. I'm your friend so I can say that Patsy, you're in danger of wallowing and self-pity is boring for everybody else. You need to establish a routine to stop you moping." Margaret paused, wondering if she had gone too far. "You know what you could do? Why not explore Dublin? I'd love to have the time to do that. You've lived here all your life and I bet there's still lots you don't know. You used to love your days out with Sean Fitzsimmons and all the information he had at his fingertips, well now's your chance to do the same. I remember you said you enjoyed your visit to Kilmainham with John to see where your daddy was locked up: well, you could follow in history's footsteps and explore different trails round the city and find out what happened where, gather up your own information to have at your fingertips."

"That's actually a good suggestion," said Patsy. Her silent voice inside, however, told her that it wouldn't be much fun doing any of that alone.

Routine was hard to establish because there was no set timetable, nowhere she had to be, and Patsy struggled to occupy her time in what she felt was any meaningful way. She read fiction books but fidgeted all the while: it was too idle a pleasure to enjoy without the guilt setting in, so she decided to give Margaret's suggestion a go. She didn't want to be a wallower.

Phoenix Park promised as good a place as any to start her preliminary research. She borrowed a guidebook from the library which said that the original scheme had been laid out in the 1840s as a deer park, with a lake and water features, a walled garden added later, and flower beds designed after the Victorian fashion. The park was opened to the public and was free to get in, the idea being that the lake would engender a desire for cleanliness in the city's poor.

"Would you believe that?" said Patsy. "The problem for the poor was not a lack of desire for cleanliness but the lack of anywhere to get washed in other than the kitchen sink and no hot water without putting a pan on the stove. Then there was the gas to pay for."

She carried on reading.

"Would you believe that?" she said. "The paths were gravelled and made nice and wide to accommodate the ladies' dresses. How many of the poor women in Dublin had gowns with such long full skirts that needed to be accommodated?" The air agitated around her. "All right, I'm complaining," said Patsy, "and you're right, I have to admit it is a beautiful park. Your son took me round it once in a horse-drawn carriage and it was magical. It was early evening, it was summer time but a bit cool and the driver lent us a big woolly blanket to put across our knees. Jem even sang as we trotted around the paths. It was almost romantic but, of course, I was with Jem and any romantic ideas he had weren't aimed in my direction. Still, it was a precious experience."

She turned back to the guide and looked at the chapter on the Grand Canal, the very one which ran past the bottom of Warren Street. That had been constructed in the 1880s, she read, as a cargo and passenger corridor stretching all the way from Dublin to the River Shannon.

"Yes, I know all that, but the book doesn't say the canal went on to serve as a place for people to be ambushed," she said.

She flicked through the book. "Here we are now, Glendalough, founded by St Kevin and aren't we in St Kevin's parish so that's appropriate." The name 'Glendalough', it seemed, signified 'the valley of the two lakes'. Patsy looked at the pictures and it did look very picturesque, with lush green hillsides climbing up from clear still waters. "No wonder St Kevin was taken by it all those years ago," she said. "Concentrate now, Mrs Senior. According to this, he founded a monastery there in 618AD and spent his life there from then on in solitary prayer and meditation. He'd be at home in this house, then. When he died, it says, pilgrims from all over went to visit his tomb. And, wait now, here we go... the place was destroyed by English forces in 1398.

Wouldn't you know it?"

Patsy lit a cigarette. "All the same there are some ruined buildings left to explore. It would be a lovely day out if you got the weather, I think. I might suggest to Father Dec that we organise a parish outing. St Kevin's feast day is coming up in June so that would be a good way to mark it and it would be something very positive for me to do. Margaret would be impressed."

Conscious that she had joined the congregation of solitary women who frequented the pews for morning Mass every day — she was one of them now even if she didn't don any widow's weeds — Patsy waited after the service the following day to put her idea to Father Dec. She took the guidebook with her and together they read about St Kevin's bed, St Kevin's cell, St Kevin's kitchen and St Kevin's tower, with its entrance some seven or eight feet above ground level. They learned that oak from trees in the valley had been used to construct the second-longest Viking ship ever recorded and also that there had been a lead mining site just up the lake from the monastery.

"I've heard of Glendalough, one of the holiest sites in Ireland, of course, but I'm embarrassed to say I've never been there even though it's not that far from Dublin," said the priest. "But I love the idea of a coach trip from the parish to mark St Kevin's feast day, there's obviously a lot to see there. I'll have to run it past the parish priest but I can't see him objecting. We could hire a coach and everyone could bring something for a picnic. Maybe we could hold a Benediction there too. Good on you, Patsy, it's a great suggestion. I'll start on it right away."

A notice soon appeared in the back of the church with details of the planned outing and gradually the columns filled up with the names of parishioners signing on for the day trip. Surely there were plenty enough to fill a coach. The place was abuzz with excitement as people gathered after Sunday Mass: families got together to plan combined picnics, who'd bring what and maybe all take their own cutlery and don't forget a couple of blankets to sit on, they could be stored out of the way in the back of the coach; some of the men wondered if it would be totally inappropriate to take a few beers along but a drink would certainly help what was essentially a mini-pilgrimage and help take the 'grim' out of it; young boys wanted to know if there would be space for a game of football after the tour and could they fit a couple of the school goalposts

585

in the coach or would they have to use their cardigans; the young girls thought the boys were being stupid and said they could all join in one big game of chase or hide-and-seek. And did anyone know if it was safe to swim in the lake? Was it allowed at such a holy place? Did that mean that they would be swimming in Holy Water? Wouldn't that be a gas! No piddling in there, now.

Father Dec had mentioned Mrs Patsy Murphy at the end of his sermon, saying everyone owed her a debt of gratitude for suggesting the trip, and Patsy felt quite proud of herself as people did indeed pass on their thanks at the door of the church. Her old rescuer, Mr Hoolihan, particularly inquired after her well-being and said he planned on taking the whole family on the outing: their names were first on the list, he said. Some of the parishioners from Warren Street commented that they'd wondered what their eccentric neighbour would dream up next: she'd been keeping a low profile since she'd intrigued everyone with her jungle installation.

The trip was set for Saturday. The day before, Patsy went out to buy a few treats for the picnic. She had decided to make a pile of salad sandwiches with chicken and stuffing and perhaps get a few special cakes at the Bretzel Bakery the following morning on the way to catch the coach, she could make a flask of tea last thing and box-up a few chocolate biscuits. Both hands were taken up with carrying heavy bags but on impulse Patsy made a short detour to call by the church on her way back from the shops to have a last look at the list of trippers. She had been designated the job of ticking everyone off as they arrived and boarded the bus and she felt obliged to make sure she knew whom to expect. She remembered a phrase she'd heard somewhere, 'meet and greet', and that was to be her job. It made her feel very responsible.

Father Dec was adding a couple of last names to the list when Patsy walked through the church door. "There now, Patsy, we're full up," said the priest, "that's the last two seats taken. My mother is coming with a friend as she has to use a wheelchair to get about now and she needs someone to push it. I offered but she didn't want to distract me from mingling with my parishioners. She said I'll be on duty as a Father and not as a son."

"Thank God there were two seats left then," said Patsy. "It'll be a lovely day out for her. They get so many visitors at Glendalough, I'm sure the pathways will be suitable for wheelchairs. I didn't realise your mammy's legs had gotten so bad," she chattered on as she consulted the list. There, in Father Dec's hurried scribble, she read the two last-minute names: Martha Doran and Eileen Fitzsimmons. It was as if a blow had been struck across Patsy's face: she flushed red, then drained white fit to faint, then stood with her mouth hanging open.

"Are you all right, Patsy? You've gone a bit odd looking," said Father Dec with concern. "Can I get you some water to drink?"

"No, thank you but I'm fine, Father," said Patsy. "It's the weight of the shopping bags, they suddenly seemed to get heavier. I'd best get on home with them, give my arms a rest."

"I can carry them back for you, it wouldn't take me long. I'd be well back in time for Friday prayers."

"Not at all," said Patsy. "I can manage, honestly, but thank you." She turned quickly and headed out of the door.

"I'll see you in the morning, then," called Father Dec to her back.

"Yes, bright and early," she called.

Patsy hurried along lest the priest decided to follow her and she was relieved to be able to close the door of the house behind her. She had been a little abrupt with some of the neighbours, who had only wanted to chit-chat happily in anticipation of the morrow's expedition, but she wasn't in any mood for small talk. She dropped the bags on the floor and sat down and lit a cigarette, drawing in deeply with each puff.

"I can't go," she said. "I couldn't face it." She kicked the shopping with her foot: the lettuce and a few tomatoes spilled out on to the floor, the cucumber rolled under the table. "I'll be picnicking at home in the jungle while everyone else enjoys my day out, the day I had planned, it was my idea." She took aim at a tomato with her foot and it wobbled its way across the room.

"You keep your comments to yourself, I don't need an old woman who's not even there telling me what to do," said Patsy to the chair. "Of course I can't go and I won't make myself go. I can't meet Sean's wife face to face, especially after that last letter he wrote. I'd feel like 'the other woman'. Mrs Doran is bound to introduce us, then she'll explain that I knew Mrs Flaherty too and how we all met and then she'll tell Eileen Fitzsimmons that my father worked in the same bakery as her husband. For all I know, the woman would recognise the name and I couldn't stand for her to know who I was, who my father was and how he'd treated Sean. I'd be thinking of it all day. How could I enjoy the trip? Then she'd go back and report to him, 'guess who I met on the trip'. I feel sick just thinking about it. I'm not going and that's the end of it."

In the morning, Patsy wrote a short note to Father Dec saying that she must indeed have taken a funny turn in the church because she'd woken up not feeling well at all and couldn't possibly go on the coach trip. The priest was not to worry, she wrote, and covered herself with a jokey reference to 'women's problems'. That would stop him rushing round out of undue concern. She expressed great regret but wished them all a great day out. She looked forward to hearing all about the grand time they were sure to have.

Patsy reread the note and was satisfied it sounded ill but healthy enough. Then she splashed hot water on her face to make it look as if she was a bit feverish and held a cut onion next to her eyes to make them look runny, then she called at a neighbour's house and asked for the letter to be delivered to the priest.

All day she felt as if she was in hibernation. Either that or as if she was in hiding. She certainly wasn't following in St Kevin's footsteps, practising solitary prayer and meditation, instead she was following the footsteps of St Kevin's parishioners. She imagined their laughter and their comical banter on the coach as it made its way out of Dublin and into the countryside, all the passengers in an excited, exuberant mood. The kids would all be kneeling up on the seats and ignoring parental instructions to get their feet off the plush. People sitting by the windows would be busy pointing out this and that as they drove past and those sitting in the aisle seats would be straining to catch a glimpse of whatever it was before it flashed out of sight. Patsy, alone, looked at the guidebook again, imagining who might be looking at St Kevin's cell in reality at the precise moment she was looking at it in the photograph. She made up the chicken and salad sandwiches and ate them in the yard, pretending she was enjoying a picnic on the banks of the lake at Glendalough. And she wondered who'd start the inevitable sing-song on the bus on the way back. She would have loved that; she didn't have a bad voice and knew all the words to most popular songs.

Patsy tried not to resent Mrs Doran's decision to go on the trip but in her heart of hearts she did. She prayed to God for forgiveness but her attempt at true remorse was sorely tested when she heard the neighbours at last streaming back home, noisy and fussing at their doors as they said goodnight to each other after their day out.

Unexpectedly Patsy realised someone was knocking on her own door. It was Mr Hoolihan, calling to check how she was and to thank her again for having had such a wonderful idea.

"We look forward to the next outing," he said.

"Me too," said Patsy. "I'll get my thinking cap on now that I'm feeling better. I'll have to study the guidebook for some more inspiration."

"It was great to see Father Dec's mother having such a nice day out too," said Mr Hoolihan. "It must be quite frustrating having to spend your final years in a wheelchair after being active all your life but the young woman wheeling her round seemed very friendly, very caring of her charge."

"The young woman wheeling her around?"

"Yes, her goddaughter, the granddaughter of an old friend, I believe, a nice girl. Anyway, Mrs Murphy, I hope you're well enough that we might see you at Mass tomorrow. Goodnight to you now."

Patsy went back inside and lit a cigarette. "'A young woman, the granddaughter of an old friend!' I could have gone after all," she said. "God forgive me but it serves me right for my uncharitable thoughts about poor Mrs Doran having a day out." She noticed the stray tomato was still on the floor. She picked it up and held it in her hand, appreciating the round plumpness of it, the shiny red colour of it, then she dug her nails into it and squashed it between her fingers. She wouldn't study the guidebook any more: she would return it to the library.

3

Patsy was slipping into an insidious but dangerous habit: she had started watching television, really started watching it, day and night. It had become all too easy to switch on to bring a bit of life and the sound of human voices into the house, at least the illusion of life, at least the sound of recorded human voices, and gradually she started to switch on without even thinking. She had particularly been sucked into the rural goings-on of *The Riordans*, a soap-opera set in a farming community. It was supposedly set in Kilkenny but actually it was all filmed on location in County Meath, not that far from Dublin, so perhaps not totally unlike the area around Tullamore. Patsy used that fact as a justification for her devoted viewing. She told herself it was like keeping in touch with her country cousins: the show dealt with important issues about life in rural Ireland, exactly the sort of issues they would be facing. It put the problems into a story setting but was very informative, like who could inherit what — she thought about Michael and how his health might be, she was completely out of touch — and the price of silage, whatever that was, she hadn't seen anything called 'silage' in the shops. She got to know the *Riordans* characters as if she lived among them, as if they were indeed Michael's and Robert's neighbours. She enjoyed all the machinations and ups-and-downs of the fictional community, the feuds and rivalries, the messy relationships and the different attitudes of the well-to-do contrasted to the labourers' approach to the various issues covered, and she found herself joining in their conversations or making comments as she watched the storylines play out. The cast became like family. Then there was the priest in the series, a Father Sheehy, he sounded as if he was from the same mould as Father Dec while Patsy herself might well be one of his more traditional flock. She certainly didn't approve of the daughter-in-law using contraception. Siobhan would have been on the girl's side.

To back up her viewing habit, she read any articles which appeared in the newspapers about the soap. Readers and writers of the various gossip columns obviously took great delight in their own gossiping about the *Riordans'* own village gossip. In the programme she was an elderly resident, in real life the actress who played the role was married to the actor who played the leading man in the series, 'Tom Riordan' himself, and even in real life she was much older than him, twenty years his senior, would you believe. Patsy found that very unusual and the letters to the editor's column showed she wasn't alone.

She mentioned it to Margaret. "You've already told me that, Patsy," her friend said. "Have you forgotten or are you really trying to tell me something else? Have you met a younger man? If you have then just spit it out and stop with the hints."

Not only had Patsy become addicted to *The Riordans*, to the nightly news, to Gay Byrne's late shows and anything else on, really, any films, documentaries or dramas — she wasn't particularly selective — but she had also started to watch children's programmes. She particularly loved *Wanderly Wagon*, in which a cast of humans and puppets travelled around Ireland in a brightly painted wagon.

"You two will enjoy this," she said, sitting down with the hot water bottles on her knee in front of the television. "We can watch it together; won't that be nice? And just wait until you see the wagon fly." Her favourites in the programme were not the humans but the puppets, she was very fond of Judge the Dog, with his woolly scarf always thrown round his neck, and of Mr Crow, who sported a sort of bib with 'Mr Crow' spelled in large letters across it. She wasn't mad about Sneaky Snake, with his wide green hissy head, but really, he was as harmless as the snake in the outside toilet and, after all, he'd escaped the rod of Saint Patrick.

"I could make you both some little clothes of your own," Patsy said to the rubber monkey and the rubber duck: the hot water bottles were snuggled on to her lap and she unconsciously stroked their faces with her fingers while she kept up a commentary on the adventure playing out before them in the magic wagon that could fly. "We'll have to give you names first. What about Monty Monkey and Daisy Duck? A boy and a girl. Yes, I like that."

After the programme, Patsy went upstairs to have a root around in the cupboard for any fabric remnants she might have stowed away. She wouldn't need much to make a couple of baby outfits. She remembered an old floral blouse she had, which would be perfect for Daisy Duck, and she found it stuffed into one of the dressing table drawers. She was holding it up in front of her when she saw herself in the mirror, arms outstretched as she held up the blouse for suitability, and a rush of eye-to-eye sanity stopped her in her tracks.

"You want to make baby clothes for two hot water bottles?" she asked herself. "Seriously?" And she threw the blouse on to the bed.

Back downstairs Patsy poured herself a Paddy's, lit a cigarette and stared out of the window. The yard needed weeding. The plants needed watering. The ground needed sweeping. All that would have to wait even longer: she needed to get out of the house; she was going stir-crazy. She gulped down her whiskey and set off into the city to go to the pictures, it didn't matter what was on: it would still involve looking passively at a screen but somehow it seemed more worthwhile than watching the television because it didn't involve just sitting at home.

As she queued at the box office, Patsy felt quite self-conscious among the couples and groups of friends waiting in line but she liked that this would be a first for her, she had never been to the cinema on her own before, ever. All the same she had to fight down her preconceived notion that it would signify she was looking to be picked up. At the back of her mind was that common belief years ago that prostitutes would go to the pictures alone touting for customers. (That's what people said.) Right now, however, a different idea appealed to Patsy, that she would sound very independent should anyone ask, and she could tell them casually that she'd been to the cinema on her own. It suggested she could do things on the spare of the moment, be out and about, devil-may-care even. All the same, she would sit on an end seat, just in case she had to escape some nuisance man who was himself on the pick-up. The thought amused her, "Who'd be interested in me at my age?" Then she remembered the *Riordans* actress who was twenty years older than her husband. "Well, you never know," Patsy grinned to herself.

She bought a bag of sweets and had them open ready when the film started, a brand-new spy thriller starring Paul Newman called *The Mackintosh Man*. Paul Newman was a favourite with most women, including Patsy; those blue eyes of his were irresistible. She had loved him in *Cool, Hand Luke*, he was so cool and manly in it and a lot of the fan magazines had likened his role to Christ and referred to the Christian symbolism used throughout the film. The main thing Patsy remembered was that she hadn't been able to eat a boiled egg for months after seeing it. But that was then and this was now and this time the American star's attempt at an Australian accent took some getting used to. One had to be prepared to forgive, thought Patsy, suspend belief: that's what the movies were all about.

As it happened none of that mattered. Some early scenes of *The Mackintosh Man* had been shot on location in Kilmainham Gaol so it was all too redolent to Patsy. She knew that beyond the brightness of the main hall where Newman and the other prisoners congregated was dirt and decay and matted walls and a dark horror full of ghosts and her experience of the place distracted her from the film. Not even Paul Newman could hold her attention.

Then when the action moved to a remote countryside setting it was in fact Connemara and the small fishing village of Roundstone, some of the very places Molly and Margaret had talked about after their hitch-hiking holiday. Hadn't they stayed in a B&B in Roundstone, in a small terrace house facing the harbour wall, the family had had to debunk to make way for them and earn a night's tariff. Patsy's mood lifted as she looked at the scenery through their eyes. She could understand why Margaret had fallen for the place with its romantically green and rocky bleakness; something about the wild and windswept landscape blew right into the soul. It was different to the lushness of *The Quiet Man* and Patsy decided that young Margaret must have a sense of the Irish melancholy in her longings.

It was dark when Patsy filed out of the cinema and took the bus home. There had been no unpleasant or unwelcome encounters by sitting watching the movie on her own and it was something she could comfortably repeat. Even travelling through the city on the bus with everyone else making their way home felt good. She missed being out in Dublin, with its lights and people; she felt invigorated.

Until she walked back into the house. The hot water bottles were there on the chair in front of the television where she had left them and

593

she felt a twinge of guilt at having abandoned her two little companions for the evening. It was ridiculous, she knew, but that was how she felt. She took Monty and Daisy upstairs and put them to bed. She kissed them goodnight and laughed at herself.

4

"We'll have a full day of culture together to make up for me not having seen you for a while." That's what Sean Mulhoney had written on an invitation card he'd posted to Patsy, asking her to join him to explore two recent developments in the city, and she had immediately replied that she would love to join him and couldn't wait to learn what he had in store. Her condition was that he would allow her to treat him to lunch.

Patsy got up earlier than usual, impatient for her day of culture to start and anxious to see Sean again. It had indeed been some time since she'd seen him: she was touched that she was still in his thoughts. He must be well into his studies at the art college and Patsy felt she could justifiably take some of the credit for his having found his true vocation. She recalled their tea-and-cakes session in Bewley's and how the ideas for the jungle toilet had just poured out of his imagination non-stop. It was obvious even then that he was a natural when it came to art.

They met up in The Brazen Head. Sean had suggested it as he knew it was one of Patsy's favourites and they could have their lunch there, get plenty of fuel inside them for the busy hours head.

"I've a full programme planned," he said when they settled at their table.

"I can't believe how long your hair is now," said Patsy. "You look like my idea of what an artist should look like. How are you getting on at the college?"

"I love it," said Sean. "It took time for me to settle and find my feet, of course. The other students certainly gave the impression that they knew a lot more than me about art and painting and at first I was nervous of doing any work in front of them. Just picking up a pencil made me shake with a feeling of inadequacy, as if I couldn't draw even the simplest thing. I thought they must all be more talented than me."

"Don't be so modest, Sean. You know your ability as well as I do," said Patsy.

"It's not false modesty," he said. "It was hard. I'd never been up against what you might call 'competition' before. The worst day was near the very start of the course, when we had to do life drawing. I was so embarrassed when the model walked in with no clothes on, it was the first time I'd ever seen a naked woman and for the life of me I didn't know where to direct my eyes. And all the while the teacher was telling the model how he wanted her to stand. She had to lean with her back against the wall and stretch her arms out either side along a pipe on the wall, for all the world like a ballet-dancer's bar, I suppose. I thought I couldn't imagine why anyone would ever stand like that, it didn't seem a natural way of standing, especially with no clothes on and everyone staring at your body. But I think I was the only one squirming with embarrassment. Fortunately, I soon got used to the life-class — that's what it's called — and realised it's one of the best ways to learn how to draw. But then we don't really see the model as naked, we see her as nude."

"I suppose there must be some subtle difference," said Patsy, unconvinced that she'd be able to define it. "And what about now, you must be very good by now?"

"I'm not the best but I'm certainly not the worst," he said. "We all have our own strengths, I suppose. I love to design something, have ideas and schemes, but I have little patience for having to concentrate on finishing the details for assessment. You'll have to come to our end-of-year exhibition and see for yourself."

"And how is your mammy and your sisters? They must be quite grown up too now."

"My mammy's fine. In fact at long last she's seeing a nice man, she'd been on her own for too long. We all get along grand and he's very kind to her. He's a fireman in the city. He was involved after the bomb that went off at the British Embassy that time. Very frightening that was. Maureen is a nurse, she's in a hospital in Limerick so she's not living at home any more. I've been to visit her a couple of times though I wouldn't say it would be my favourite city. Veronica has grown into a typical teenager. She's always flouncing round the house putting on a performance and says she wants to be a singer and represent Ireland at the Eurovision."

"I went to see that with a couple of friends when it was in Dublin," said Patsy. "We weren't actually in the theatre, we stood outside to watch all the fancy people arriving, and the next minute there were demonstrations going on all around us and the street entertainment was a gas."

"I vaguely remember all that," said Sean. "I gather some of the female students went along to join one of the protest marches. Anyway, let's get down to the day's schedule."

"I'm intrigued."

"Well, we're going to start on Wood Quay along the Liffey, behind Christ Church Cathedral. It's not far to walk but I hope you have comfortable shoes on because we'll be going on somewhere else after that and there's a bus strike on. So, first on the agenda is an archaeological dig."

"My God that sounds interesting but I can't picture anywhere along the quays where there could be ancient buried treasure. It's either mud or docks or roads all the way along."

"It's not the usual sort of treasure, though I'm sure there will be some precious finds." said Sean. "As someone born and brought up in Dublin, what they've discovered is to me far more interesting than old bronze trinkets. They've unearthed a huge settlement dating back to the Vikings, Dublin's founding fathers. They're excavating a four-acre site and they have already amassed a collection of artefacts that have lain buried there since the ninth and tenth centuries and, what I think is the most exciting of all, a huge area of wooden docks. Some are Viking and some later ones go back to mediaeval times. Unfortunately the city's current fathers might in their wisdom cover the whole lot under concrete soon."

"It rings a bell now," said Patsy. "Isn't Wood Quay where Dublin Corporation wants to build new offices? I saw the plans in the paper, and it said that the museum people had insisted on exploring the site before any new building went ahead."

"The bell is ringing true," said Sean "That's the very place. Don't tell me you've been to see it already?"

"No, I've not. To be honest it hadn't occurred to me."

"I walked past it quickly the other day and it was full of activity. Shall we set off?"

"But you haven't told me about our second destination yet?"

"All will be revealed," said Sean. "I thought after the dig we could have a coffee or some tea and that's when I'll tell you about the next item on the agenda."

The excavation site was surrounded by a boarded fence but it was easy to see what was going on. A vast expanse of what looked like sludge was populated by people squatting or on their knees, bending over in the mud, each intent on their own tiny patches of ground, scraping with little trowels and brushing away carefully to reveal something that might turn out to be something important. Strings were laid out in a grid and identity tags fluttered like paper chains marking what was found where and how deep down, buckets and shovels littered the site, trays and tables held blackened objects, retrieved in the dig and then labelled. Low walls of stones traced what were obviously once the walls of houses, but Patsy and Sean couldn't see over as far as the river, where the Viking dockside had been unearthed. One man, who was obviously in charge, was constantly being summoned by the diggers for some on the spot consultation.

"He's coming towards us," said Patsy. "Do you know him, Sean?"

"Not at all. The only time I go to the museum is to draw something on display, a beetle or a butterfly or something I might add to your jungle one of these days."

"I'm afraid the jungle isn't looking quite so fresh now."

Just then the supervisor stopped right next to them, where a reporter and a photographer were waiting to interview him.

"What we have here are the very origins of today's Dublin," he explained to the journalist. "We're finding the detritus of everyday life in Viking times, utensils and tools, what was used for clothing materials, remains of food. After all people lived their lives here, they worked here, they traded here, and you can see from the layout of the walls we've uncovered that they thought about their living space, their huge settlement was carefully laid out. We're uncovering the foundations of one-hundred-and-forty houses. It's an example, if you will, of early town-planning. It's probably the best urban archaeological remains of any town in Europe. Unfortunately, we don't have a lot of time on site before the corporation bulldozers move in and we have twelve different layers to sift through so we're having to work around the clock to rescue and save as much as we can."

Patsy couldn't believe that the corporation would want to bulldoze any single part of such a valuable and historic site, especially just to put up a new office block.

"That's how it is," said Sean. "When you think about it, every town or city is built on top of the remains of earlier ones. We're all living on top of history's kitchen scraps. There's no such thing as virgin ground."

They left Wood Quay and headed in the direction of Trinity College. "Did you ever the see the film, *The Vikings*?" Patsy asked Sean. "They were certainly made to seem a bloodthirsty lot, raiding and killing. Imagine them sailing up the Liffey and pulling their long ships ashore and then rampaging through the countryside. You know, they used oak grown in the valley round Glendalough to build boats, that's what it said in a guidebook I read, so they must have at least got that far in from the river."

"I think I saw that film on the television, not in the cinema," said Sean. "I vaguely remember two things: Kirk Douglas wearing an eye-patch and Tony Curtis having his hand cut off and that's about it. Let's get a drink somewhere, shall we? I'll pay as you got the lunch."

As they sat with their coffees, Sean produced a small thin book. It was to provide background information for their next destination. "We're going to Nassau Street near Trinity," he said, "and this book is the clue."

Patsy saw that it was a child's book, relating the story of Irish folklore about the hero, Cúchulainn, who single-handedly beat off an invasion of Ulster by Queen Maeve of Connacht, who was bent on stealing the sacred Brown Bull of Cooley.

"A sacred brown bull?" said Patsy, furrowing her eyebrows.

"You don't have to read it all now, Patsy," said Sean, "you can keep the book and absorb all the details later. Suffice to say it's a mystical tale of pagans and Druids, of wild dogs and magic curses, sun-gods and supernatural beings and warring warriors, beaten to a man in hand-to-hand combat with our hero. And all to save the sacred Brown Bull of Cooley. How does it grab you so far?"

"I'm ashamed to say I've never heard of this particular Irish hero," said Patsy. "Perhaps because it's all rooted in paganism and not

Christianity the nuns never taught us about it at school. So what are we to go and see? Is it the sacred bull?"

"We're going to see a huge mosaic being constructed along a wall in Nassau Street, piece by piece, the work of an artist called Desmond Kinney. He's actually from Belfast, though as far as I know the Ulster of the story is not the Ulster of the North, but he was obviously very inspired by the myth and he's on site himself fixing on the bits of mosaic. Would that be of interest to you?"

"It'll be grand to look at it with the benefit of my personal artist alongside to point out the various elements," said Patsy. "How did you find out about it?"

"Somebody was talking about it in college. We'll go and have a look and then, when you read the book, you'll have some fabulous images to call to mind. You might even get more inspiration for another installation in your yard."

The traffic was dense as they set off walking to locate the mural. It was rush hour by now and, with no buses running because of the strike, the city centre roads were clogged with more cars than usual. South Leinster Road was no different and Patsy and Sean had to negotiate their way to nearby Nassau Street along pavements jammed with people going home from work, happily looking forward to their weekend ahead.

"I hope they don't all stop to look at the mural," said Patsy. "If it's as big as you say, we'll need to stand well back to take it all in."

"It must be a good twenty-feet long at least and maybe half that in height," said Sean. "Imagine how many little squares of ceramic that would…" But his words were drowned out by the sound of a terrible deep bang and everyone stopped stock-still mid-stride, looking round trying to identify the cause or the direction of the sound. Almost immediately another loud boom shot through the airwaves, closer this time, and people started to get panicky. Voices rose in agitation and confusion above the cacophony of car horns and idling engines.

"My God that sounded like a couple of explosions the other side of the river," said Sean.

Then suddenly they were almost blown off their feet when a car-bomb exploded right by the railings of Trinity College, less than a block from where they were standing. Everything happened in an instant but seemed to decelerate into slow motion as a ball of flame burst out with a terrible expanding heat-blast from where the bomb had gone off. A dense storm of broken glass and building debris erupted like some mad confetti flung violently into the air. Metal shards were fired, lethal missiles darting out from all the cars and bits of railings that had been ripped apart by the blast, cutting and impaling people where they stood, transfixed now by the shock and by the darts finding their random targets.

People started screaming and running in terror. Sean threw Patsy to the ground to shield her and their clothes and hair were immediately covered in a thick layer of dirt dust sparkling with myriad splinters of glass. Patsy peered out from under Sean's arm: in the narrow slit of her vision she saw a man crouched hugging himself on the ground, he was on fire; she saw two young women almost welded together, with horrific slashes and cuts to their faces, their clothes burned off their bodies; she saw one girl with the back of her leg missing; Patsy closed her eyes, she didn't want to see any more. Someone started shrieking that there was to be another bomb and people rushed to find shelter or ran in whichever indeterminate direction the urge drove them but where could they shelter, where would they be safe? Palls of black smoke retched into the sky. Victims retched on to the ground.

Minutes ticked away without further explosions as the dust settled over the scene and a ghostly heavy silence took over, everything muffled into a lonely, isolating deafness. Even the crying and moaning from the injured who lay where they'd fallen and the words of optimistic comfort and encouragement offered them by friends and perfect strangers alike didn't register: neither the victims nor the comforters could hear each other. The faces of horrific injuries and the anxious attempts at soothing were merely discernible in moving blurs of black, white and grey, like in an old silent movie. The terrified hysteria had died to a dazed, uncomprehending numbness.

The awful stillness was interrupted by the sudden arrival of a group of dental students who'd hurried out from Trinity College, bringing an element of hope as they took initial charge, tending to the wounded and administering as much comfort and reassurance as they could. Gradually the sound of police and ambulance sirens slowly filtered through as if from a great distance. Of course they were at a great distance, stuck in all the traffic which had braked to a halt. Three bombs had gone off almost simultaneously in the city and both life and death had been put on hold.

Sean helped Patsy to her feet. All around them the scene was of total carnage and the bodies of two lifeless women lay on the pavement, a coat thrown over their destroyed and bloody faces to provide some makeshift element of respect. It was awful, inhuman. Patsy and Sean were both apparently without serious physical injury, just scratches and grazes, but, like everyone else who'd been close to the explosion, they were traumatised and could only stand and stare, helpless and disbelieving, holding on to each other for support. One of the medical students asked if they needed any urgent help; he had to shout and mime to get through to them until they understood enough to wave him away to tend to the seriously injured.

At last ambulances and police arrived and some semblance of organised activity took charge. Somehow their sudden arrival added a horrific clarity to the scene, to the reality of what had just happened, to the dreadful aftermath of a bomb that had killed and injured ordinary people going home from work on a Friday afternoon. As doctors and paramedics got to work and a constant tide of stretchers were carried to and fro, their matter-of-fact response helped defuse the madness into a bizarre sanity.

Blankets were issued to warm people suffering from acute shock but with no apparent physical injuries and, from a mobile van, cups of sweet tea were produced and handed out to the survivors. Patsy and Sean were still supporting each other as a Garda wrote their names and addresses down and took brief statements from them before moving off to talk to other lost witnesses.

"Have your ears cleared yet?" Sean mouthed to Patsy.

"More or less," she said.

"Can you walk?"

"I think so, yes," said Patsy.

"Then come on, lean on me and I'll get you home."

Patsy's nights were tortured with nightmares, constant replays of what had happened switching on the moment she put her head on the pillow and closed her eyes. She tried sitting up in bed, leaning with her back against the headboard and clutching her knees to her chest but it didn't help. It was like closing in on herself with no one on hand to share her pain, to hold her, to protect her, smother her in care. She shivered helplessly and had no one to still her nerves. More than thirty people had died in the bombings and more than three hundred had been seriously injured, the victims mostly young women. Patsy and Sean had had a narrow escape. Had they not lingered over their coffee while she looked at the children's storybook they would have been closer to the explosion and suffered the full force of its horrific impact. Patsy felt guilty that she had survived, so many with their lives still ahead of them had died, including a woman who was nine months pregnant. Nothing helped calm her state of mind.

Annie called in every day to see her, ask how she was, was there anything she needed doing, would she not like to go out on a bit of a walk? Patsy preferred to stay at home and eventually Annie decided it was best to leave her sister to recover in her own time.

Father Dec called to see her, ask how she was, was there anything she needed doing, would she not at least like to walk over to St Kevin's with him. The priest didn't give up, he had his work cut out and not only with Patsy. She was just one of several in the parish who had been caught up in the blasts; family members had been killed or injured and a series of requiem masses and novenas for those in hospital had been organised at the church. Father Dec established a rota of parishioners, volunteers to accompany the vulnerable to Mass to give them support as they ventured into the street after the trauma. Patsy didn't put her name down but her Good Samaritan, Mr Hoolihan, was dispatched to Warren Street regardless. He knocked on her door and insisted on walking her to the church. "I think of myself as your official escort now," he said. "You know, Mrs Murphy, we are on this earth to help each other and I think God has assigned me to you."

John arrived too and suggested another outing on the scooter. She had enjoyed her first foray, he said, and another excursion would be the very thing to distract her. They wouldn't need to ride about in the city but could go into the country where she might feel more relaxed. Patsy preferred to leave it for another day.

When young Sean visited, it was his company that allowed the personal release Patsy craved: she was more comforted by his presence than that of her own family members. She was able to talk more freely about her soaring emotions and the terrible dreams that recurred and recurred because he understood where they came from, he was dreaming them too, he had lived through the same horrors with her, at her side. It was a tragedy they shared and it had created a precious bond between them. He checked on her regularly after the explosions but he was trying to come to terms with what had happened in his own way: his end-of-year exhibition was looming and he decided to immerse himself in his college work.

Of course, Patsy had to go out. Whatever her fears of further attacks, on a mundane level she was a habitual smoker and needed a constant supply of cigarettes, never mind food, but she confined herself to the shops nearest the house and was forever on the alert for any unfamiliar sounds. She gave a wide berth to any vehicles that were double-parked where they shouldn't be. When there were cars pulled up idling bumper to bumper, she would turn back and go down the next street instead. Tears would come to her eyes unexpectedly. She jumped at any sudden loud noises. If a car backfired, she was sometimes forced to rush back to the house to change into clean underwear.

It took time but slowly Patsy was able to be outside again with some sense of controlled ease, but she would breathe a sigh of relief immediately on getting home and closing the door behind her on her own safe world. Monty the monkey and Daisy the duck would be waiting for her and she would reward them with hugs. While the nights were filled with gruesome figures, some screaming without faces, some running without limbs, haunting her sleep relentlessly, the days were soothed with the cute eyes of the two little rubber creatures who looked back at her without any hint of threat.

"Aren't they adorable," she said to the chair. "Do you like their little outfits?"

Patsy had been busy in her isolation and now Monty was dressed in a smart pair of brown dungarees, with a large red M appliqued to the front and a pair of stuffed legs dangling from below the body of the hot-water bottle. Daisy was floral to the extreme, the old blouse had been fashioned into a dress, with feathered-cotton arms padded on to the sides and cut-out daisies sewn on to the bodice, yellow webbed feet hung down.

"They're like two little babies," she said, "tiny toddlers, really, perhaps they look too old to be babies. Ugly little toddlers, you're probably thinking, but I'd say they are beautiful in their own way."

Monty and Daisy went everywhere in the house with Patsy. She was never without them. If she went upstairs, she carried them up too in her arms. If she was sitting at the table, they sat propped on a chair opposite, always in sight. When she watched television, they were companions in her viewing. She told herself it was because they had become her lucky mascots but really, they were something to cling on to, like a child's security blanket.

The psychological prop worked. After five or six weeks, Patsy took herself off to morning Mass, striking out for independence without Mr Hoolihan's help and planning to call in at the Bretzel on the way home to buy half a dozen bagels. She would invite Father Dec to visit and he did like his bagels. Unfortunately the priest was too busy and wouldn't be able to join Patsy until later in the week but she lingered on the steps of the church chatting to different people. The light sociability proved a tonic. The handful of parishioners had approached her after the service, charitably perhaps but expressing eagerness to know when the next coach trip would be because, as everyone agreed, they couldn't allow a few bombs going off to stop them living their lives. Patsy was conscious of sporting a wide grin during the friendly chatter, pleased with the attention she was receiving, and she thought maybe she would borrow the guidebook from the library again after all. Finally, the small group dispersed and Patsy went on to the bakery to buy the bagels as planned.

"I can't imagine what's keeping him," she said later, waiting to pour the boiling water fresh on to the leaves, two of her best china cups and saucers waiting on the table. Father Dec was usually a mug man where tea was concerned but she wanted to make everything a bit special for a change: she felt she was emerging out of the blackness at last. "I know he's busy but he said he'd be here." She lit a cigarette. "Did he say today, is that what you're asking me?" she said to the chair. "Do you think I'm that daft, Mrs Senior? He definitely said he'd be here Thursday."

There was quite a stirring in the air.

"What's that? Are you sure? And how would you know, you're not even real?"

But Mrs Murphy Senior was right and Patsy remembered that it was actually still only Tuesday. She must have got confused by all the conversation after Mass. She put her elbows down heavily on the table in exasperation with herself and the cups and saucers clattered as they parted company. She picked them up and put them back in the cupboard before switching on the television.

5

There was a general feeling in the city that the authorities and the police were being somewhat lax in their inquiries into the May bombings, three in Dublin and one in Monaghan. The attacks accounted for more deaths in a single day than any of the atrocities committed so far during the Troubles, either north or south of the border, yet little by way of constructive investigation was reported in the papers, other than that the three cars used in the Dublin explosions were identified as having been stolen in Belfast earlier that same day. No one understood why Dublin was dragging its heels. Meanwhile rumours were rife that British security forces must have been involved because the bombs were fairly sophisticated, while a few vociferous Ulstermen denied the connection, bragging that they needed no technical help when it came to blowing up a few Paddys. "It was a happy day for us," they were quoted as saying when asked by the press for a reaction to the bombings in the South.

The attacks were regarded as having been the work of Unionists violently opposed to the Sunningdale Agreement between the UK Government and the Northern Ireland Executive. Unionists had no intention of accepting it, they had declared: they had no intention of accepting any agreement which gave the South a say in cross-border issues, even on such seemingly non-contentious matters like tourism and animal welfare, and they would stop at nothing to prevent the agreement coming into force.

The Unionists stopped at nothing and had won the day. The Dublin and Monaghan massacres sabotaged the accord. When it was repealed, some individuals in Dublin breathed a sigh of relief — perhaps now the paramilitary loyalists would leave their city alone — and the streets had returned to their noisy, crowded familiarity.

"I might go in to do a bit of window-shopping in town, do you want to come?" Margaret asked. "It's safe enough now, Patsy, and we can come home if you don't feel up to it. I thought with me you might feel more able to face it, I know you've not been into the city since, you know, the explosions."

Patsy knew Margaret was right, she needed to get beyond Portobello and The Liberties for sanity's sake. "I wouldn't mind having a look round Clery's basement too, see what new bargains they have in, and perhaps we could treat ourselves to a bite in their restaurant."

"I'm all for that," said Margaret. "You must fancy making up for lost time. I've a whole day free tomorrow, we could go then."

Early the following day they took the bus to O'Connell Street and Patsy again felt her lungs fill with the bustling atmosphere of the city. Margaret made sure they avoided Parnell Street and Talbot Street, where the first two of the May bombs had gone off: she wasn't sure if there was any debris still waiting to be cleared or windows still boarded up even after two months and she didn't want Patsy's day spoiled by any direct reminders of her near-miss. They both had a good rummage in the special-offer bins in Clery's and bought a few bits and pieces between them, nothing either of them particularly needed but a bargain was a bargain and would always come in handy.

As they were enjoying their refreshments in the cafeteria, they heard a couple of young women at the next table talking loudly and excitedly about a demonstration they were off to that was set to cause quite a commotion down by the Bay. The television cameras would be there and the two girls thought they might see themselves on the telly later if they found a good place to stand. They might even get spotted and offered parts in a show.

"Excuse me but I couldn't help overhearing you talking about a commotion about to go off," Margaret asked them. "Would you mind telling us what's happening?"

"Not at all," said one of the girls. "There's a group calling themselves... what is it now?"

"The Dublin City Women's Invasion Force," answered her friend.

"That's it, The Dublin City Women's Invasion Force. It's quite a mouthful of a title they chose. Anyway, they're going to invade the Forty Foot, you know that rocky bit at the end of Dublin Bay where men go to swim in the nude? Women aren't allowed to swim there, the men have had the cove all to themselves evidently for one-hundred-and-fifty years and this Dublin City Women's Invasion Force says it's time to put a stop to all that nonsense. We thought we'd go down for a laugh. You should come with us, show solidarity with the sisterhood and all that, and, you never know, we might get lucky and see a few naked men. Us women can ogle them for a change."

"I'm up for that," said Margaret. "What do you say, Patsy, shall we join the sisterhood?"

Patsy had no desire to put herself in the position of being faced with naked men but obviously Margaret was keen to go and it was thanks to Margaret that she was out at all. Patsy also remembered the fun it had been hearing all the chanting from the protests at the Eurovision contest and now the idea of women making their voices heard over something as stupid as men telling them where they could and couldn't swim seemed quite attractive. She could be a part of it and why not. It was decided that they would go.

"If you don't mind us tagging along, we'd love to join you," said Margaret. "My name's Margaret and this is Patsy."

"And I'm Deirdre and this is my friend, Shelagh. We'll just finish up here and we'll be off, shall we."

It was agreed that they'd share a taxi as there were four of them and they wanted to get there in time for the action. It was as well they did, the place was filling up fast. They found a free spot to stand very close to the ramp that led down into the water and looked on as a shoal of men messed about in the tide, doing this stroke and that stroke, jumping up out of the water and then sinking down again for all the world like anchors, some of them determinedly putting on a show as if they were Olympic swimmers in front of sporting aficionados. And some of them were indeed naked and obviously proud of their accoutrements. By the time the invasion got underway there were hundreds in the audience watching the men's display.

"I've never seen so many balls floating in the sea all at once," said Shelagh.

"I think they're ping-pong balls," said Deirdre, "punctured ping-pong balls."

"They do look a bit cold and shrivelled," said Margaret. "Should we try to net a few?"

"I wouldn't bother," said Deirdre. "I doubt there's much bounce left in any of them."

"Maybe they're not ping-pong balls at all," said Shelagh. "On closer inspection — and I am inspecting them closely — they look more like floating walnuts."

"They're certainly not hiding in their shells," said Margaret.

There was a lot of similar rude banter in the air from the onlookers but, when the group of women protestors arrived, the men swimmers turned very shirty. Their apparent spokesman stood shouting at a reporter to "hop it, clear off". He eventually agreed to make an official statement: "We wouldn't go into your canteen and demand we have cups of tea, we'd have no right," he said, "and these women have no right to swim here." He indicated the sign on a wooden board by the ramp which declared: *Gentlemen's Bathing Place*. He was puce and his jowls wobbled in his outrage.

When the determined invaders stripped down to their cozzies and bikinis, however, and ceremoniously entered the water, the men's self-righteous shirtiness soon changed. They chorused a stream of far-from-gentlemanly obscenities and the members of the Dublin City Women's Invasion Force were crudely advised that it wasn't a swim they all needed but a good fuck.

"There's really no need for that sort of language," said Patsy.

"That's gentlemen for you," said Shelagh.

"Would you look at that?" said Deirdre, almost guffawing with the sheer comedy of the proceedings. All heads turned in unison and everyone burst out laughing. Some of the naked men were stood in the waves waving their genitals at the invasion force.

"Are they dick-heads or just dicks?" said Deirdre.

"More like wee willy wankers," said Shelagh.

The next minute the erstwhile spokesman was complaining to the reporter at the disgraceful behaviour of the women, and in Ireland, of all places, a puritanical country if ever there was one. "These women are intimidating the men," he protested.

"But it's the men who've got their cocks out," shouted some perceptive joker in the crowd.

The event could only go down as a great result for the Dublin City

Women's Invasion Force. They had made their point, had a good dip in the sea and then sat calmly on the rocks, sunbathing and laughing as they towelled themselves dry, relishing both the publicity for their cause and the pathetic response of their opponents, whose only recourse was the lowest common denominator of the crudest type of sexual harassment. The men had made asses of themselves.

"Aren't you glad you came?" Deirdre asked Patsy and Margaret. "Wasn't that better than any of us could have imagined?"

"I'm glad I butted in on your conversation," said Margaret.

"We only came out to do a bit of window shopping," said Patsy.

"Well, you got an eyeful you didn't expect," said Shelagh, "not that I can imagine you wanting to take home any of the goods on display."

"They look very second-hand," said Margaret.

"But exactly whose hands?" said Shelagh. "There's a lot of intimate macho camaraderie on show."

"There's far too much intimacy on show for me," said Patsy.

"We'll be off now," said Margaret, picking up on her friend's growing discomfort. "Thanks again for the invitation, girls, I wouldn't have missed it for the world."

"We're going to hang round," said Deirdre. "With a bit of luck one of us might get interviewed for the television."

"We'll look out for you on tonight's news," said Margaret.

"See you ladies around," said Shelagh. "We're all part of the sisterhood now."

"It's certainly a different sort of sisterhood to the nuns," said Patsy.

"Aye, too many bad habits," said Shelagh. "Take care now. Up the revolution!"

Patsy and Margaret walked off waving to Deirdre and Shelagh, who stood there smiling with upstretched arms and fists clenched.

"They were great fun, the two of them," said Margaret. "Don't I envy young women now and the freedom they have, nothing like in our day."

"Perhaps we enjoyed a different sort of freedom," said Patsy. "I for one wouldn't want to go swimming even in a one-piece with crude men like that around."

"Yes but the point is surely that it's the men who have the problem.

What a fuss over a stretch of sea. As Shelagh said, they can be real wee willy wankers."

"Margaret!"

That evening Patsy couldn't wait to watch the news and see if Deirdre and Shelagh had made it on to the television report. They had indeed and, of course, standing right next to them cheering and laughing against the background of naked men flapping about in the sea were Margaret and Patsy herself.

"I see you're managing to get out and about again," said one of the neighbours the following morning. "I didn't have you marked down as a women's libber but you flew the flag well."

The amused novelty value of Patsy's unexpected TV appearance eventually died down and she was able to appear in the local shops or at Mass without comments being aimed in her direction, friendly enough comments, some of them very funny, but she was relieved when the novelty had worn off. She had started to repeat her funny retorts, probably to the same people. The whole incident slipped into the past and the normal way of things was re-established, the difference being that now Patsy dared go into the city centre again, alone, though only after certain rituals had been observed.

First of all, she would pack a small bag containing her prayer book and rosary beads; a couple of hankies, in case she found herself inexplicably crying; a clean pair of knickers, in case she was startled into incontinence by any sudden loud bang and had to find a ladies' toilet rather than make her way home risking embarrassment, and a neatly written list detailing her address and who to contact in the event of any mishap. Of course this was her family on The Coombe. Also into the bag went a small box of sticking plasters, a few bandages and a pair of scissors. She also checked that her Child of Mary scapula was still in place around her neck and hadn't come off without her noticing. Everything went into the bag in the same order each time then she would sit and have a cigarette and tell herself to be brave. Occasionally her courage still failed her and she would empty the bag, put the stuff away and stay at home. Often enough, fortunately, the system worked.

She even allowed herself to take another look at the Wood Quay excavation.

"You wouldn't believe the activity going on there," she said towards Jem's old chair. "It's far busier than when I went with Sean and the tables are covered in stuff they've collected, not that you can tell what they are from looking over the fence. I'm sure there are far more tables now than before. It must be very interesting to be digging up the past instead of living in it, like some of us, Mrs Senior. What's that? Some pasts shouldn't be relived? I know that but some pasts just won't go away and you can't help but relive them," said Patsy. "If you find my bag of preparations so annoying, then don't look when I'm packing it. Thank you for your unwelcome reminder. I know only too well what happened after my first visit to the Viking site but this time I was ready."

The nightmares had actually eased in as much as they were no longer recurring every night. Patsy wasn't waking up in cold sweats as frequently, she wasn't as afraid to close her eyes again after a bad dream as now she didn't always immediately find herself submerged back into the same horrific replay.

It was the same for Sean. Patsy had gone to see his end-of-year exhibition, a wonderfully enthusiastic occasion attended by the exhibiting students' families and friends, each group convinced that their 'very own' artist stood out from the rest.

Each student had several personal display boards arranged to create private viewing corners, their year's progress easily followed from the first board on. Sean's work started with those wonderful combinations of colour he had explored doing the jungle scene: he had designed a game of inter-matching interchangeable animals and birds, almost the inevitable extension of that first jungle foray. There were silk-screened posters of exotic foliage and flowers; lithograph prints of various subjects and products that might be advertised; colour photographs of surreal still-lifes, showing the profusion of the imagination coursing through his creative mind. Then the last couple of boards showed a series of soul-searching self-portraits, pencil and charcoal drawings which had been developed into more prints, this time limited to a palette of just black and white. It was a total change. Patsy and Sean had managed to fit in a quiet word, just the two of them, on how they were recovering. While Patsy's dreams were still of mangled bodies and faces, Sean's were dominated by a deathly silence in which he kept struggling to escape heavy layers and layers of clinging black dust sparkling with glass but he couldn't get out from under the shifting weight: the more he struggled to push through and breathe, the more the dust and shards settled in over him again.

"But we're getting through it all, Patsy," he said. "This time next year our minds will be freed into the sunshine again."

Mrs Mulhoney had greeted Patsy with a warm hug and words of reassurance while Patsy was able to tell her that her son had proved himself quite a hero. All the same it was noticeable that the last few months of his artwork had taken on a much darker tone than his earlier, pre-bombing projects. To Patsy, her nightmares were more understandable, definitely rooted in the experience of what she had witnessed in the explosions: she thought that Sean's had become more disturbingly psychological. She prayed hard for her friend.

"He's a young man, he should get over it," Father Dec had advised when she mentioned her concerns. "He has a great outlet for expressing his fears, his pre-occupations, he can illustrate them in his art in a way not open to most of us. In theory you should take longer to recover, Patsy, but you seem to be managing well."

"The memory isn't fading but the immediacy of it obviously has eased," said Patsy. "I wonder how my father managed during the struggles, especially as he was actively involved with those responsible for planting bombs and blowing places up, killing people. We don't seem to have come very far from those days, Father. I hate to be one of those doubters but it's hard not to ask the question: why does God allow such things to happen?"

"It's not that God allows these things to happen," said the priest, "it's that he allows people to happen. He gave us all free will and he allows us to use that free will and it is human beings who commit these atrocities, not God. So the question is really not why does God allow these things to happen but why do people allow them? Why do people do such awful things to each other?"

"Sometimes when I'm praying, I don't know what to pray for," said Patsy. "There is so much trouble in the world, not just in Ireland, and, when I want to pray for peace, I don't know where to begin or how to start. I pray for the victims and I pray for the perpetrators but I get overwhelmed with the enormity of it all. It's like praying for mankind to fundamentally change what seems to be an inbuilt part of human nature and, if it's inbuilt, how can it change? Will it ever change? There has always been violence between people and if that's how it is then I wonder if I'm wasting my time praying for peace."

"I don't believe that prayer is ever wasted," said Father Dec. "At the very least it is adding to an atmosphere, a preponderance, if you like, of good, peaceful thoughts to hopefully counter the bad and the aggressive. You know when people say they can sense something terrible in the air? Well, I believe they can also sense something wonderful and kind in the air and your prayers add to that accumulation of kindness, to that gathering of love you can feel around you. And that in its turn influences people and, fortunately for all of us, helps to outweigh the hate, certainly on a day-to-day level. Isn't something as simple as laughter wonderfully contagious? That's a sharing of a goodness in the air. We all know how precious it is to get a warm smile from a perfect stranger. And weren't there lots of strangers helping each other after the bombings? I've said to you before, Patsy: if you really think about it, there are far more good people than there are bad."

"It still doesn't seem fair that ordinary men and women and families get ripped apart for no good reason," said Patsy.

"And most people would agree with you. I had a friend once who saw things from the opposite direction," said the priest. "He used to say that he expected the worst and so delighted even more when he met the best. I don't personally agree with his starting point but I can accept that it's a way of looking at things that can give a comforting jolt to the pessimists among us. But I still think it's better to try to remain optimistic, Patsy. Otherwise, what hope have any of us."

"That's not what I'd expect a priest to say."

"We're all just struggling along, don't forget that, struggling and juggling with the obstacles life throws at us," said Father Dec. "We owe it to ourselves to at least try to keep all the balls in play but, if we do drop one or if one is knocked out of our hands, we just have to make sure we bend down to pick it up and start again. The secret is not to give up. Isn't that what life's all about? Then the sudden delight in meeting the best can be reward in itself."

There was no delight, no best to be welcomed when some thirty people were killed and hundreds injured by purported Provisional IRA bombs detonated in pubs in England a few months later, when people were already turning their minds towards Christmas. Murder was hardly a suitable gift from supposed Christians to present at the feet of the Christ Child as he lay in his crib. Shops and pillar-boxes were also targeted or fitted with explosive devices.

"My God not even Christmas cards are safe," thought Patsy. "You can't even wish someone the peace of Christmas time with a nice card. There is no peace." She thought of what Sean had said, that this time next year their minds would be freed into the sunshine again. It seemed a long way away.

Yet the seasons moved through their cycles, the bare trees burst forth and shivered with new leaves after their winter rest, their canopies filled with birds' nests and the sound of insistent young chicks; spring-bulbs and apple-blossoms flowered and browned and drooped and the sun at last shone down with the golden warmth of summer. Patsy's backyard was aglow with the hot colours of the persistent nasturtiums and the yellows of the happy honeysuckle climbing up the trellis round the kitchen door. Then the members of the Miami Showband from Dublin were massacred at a phony checkpoint in the North and it seemed not even music was to be allowed to cross the dark divide. There was no sunshine to be had.

Patsy began to shrink in on herself again. News stories detailed more attacks, more slaughter, as the days passed. Locked away on her own for most of the time, Patsy felt as if the world outside the safety of her little house was beset by violence and danger. The fictional life of *The Riordans*, for all the contrived problems and story-line squabbles, offered the simple comfort of a countryside idyll while *Wanderly Wagon* offered simple if ridiculous escapism from harsh reality. Monty and Daisy took Patsy even further out of herself. Their company in front of the television represented an innocent ignorance which helped dilute the tension she felt mounting relentlessly inside, partly because she played the role of the protective mother. She could raise little enthusiasm for doing anything outside the house on her own. Her visits to The Coombe were few and far between and Annie took to calling in unexpectedly to check on her sister. She was surprised to see that the hot water bottles now had bibs over them to protect their clothes.

"Where on earth did they come from?" she asked.

"I made them," said Patsy. "I cut up an old towel. I thought the bibs would keep the young ones clean."

"But they're not young ones, Patsy, they're hot water bottles," said Annie.

"Don't be silly, I know that," said Patsy. "It gave me something to do, and the towels were too old to be of much use. When we watch our programmes, I like to nibble on a bit of cheese or chocolate, ice-cream too if I have any, and I don't want to dirty their clothes if I drop any."

Annie looked at her sister with a mix of alarm and pity. "I'm worried about you, Patsy, we all are. You spend far too much time on your own."

"Well, I'm a childless widow, I am on my own," said Patsy directly. "That's the truth of the matter. I can't keep going out for the sake of it. Walk round this block, walk round that block, go up this side of the road, cross over and go back down the other side. And then you never know what's going to happen if you're out and in the wrong place at the wrong time. By the way you must thank Matt again for the television set. I don't think I ever paid him for it but I'm a big fan, I'd be lost without it. Do you ever watch *The Riordans*?"

"Mammy does," said Annie, glad of the change of topic. "She's convinced she recognises some of the locations. I don't think her mind is as sharp as it was. She's taken to reminiscing about some young man she was set to marry out in Tullamore. Then she gets him mixed up with our da and they seem to merge into one person."

"I vaguely remember that she had an understanding with a young farmer before she came to look after us when my real mammy died. I think his mother was supposed to be a bit of a dragon, either that or he was just a mammy's boy," said Patsy. "Whatever, he did what he was told. I'm sure Uncle Michael felt Betty had had a narrow escape even though, as I recall, the young man was regarded locally as being a good catch with a farm to inherit."

"Well, I wouldn't be here but for all that coming to an end," said Annie. "What do you think, Patsy, is there such a thing as a narrow escape or is it actually fate taking control to set everything on its destined path?"

"It was certainly a narrow escape Sean and I had that day, it was a mercy we weren't injured or killed."

Annie didn't want the conversation to get maudlin again. "But was Mammy fated to marry our da so that we'd be born and the other young man was never on the cards, never written in the stars?" she said.

"Things happen as they happen, through a meeting of chance circumstances which we may or may not have had a hand in bringing about," said Patsy. "Things happen and we choose to go with them this way or that way and we live to regret it, or we live pleased with how things turned out. The only stars I believe in are the Hollywood variety."

"As you said, you are a childless widow, so was it a meeting of chance circumstances that meant you had no children? Was it because you married Jem and he made a decision and you went along with it? I know you miss not having any children of your own and I can't believe you would be the only sister of the fertile O'Kelly bunch who couldn't conceive. Or was it a physical problem with Jem?"

"In a way it was," said Patsy. She paused to light up a cigarette. She looked at Annie and puckered her lips as if trying to decide what to say. "I might as well tell you, perhaps it's time," she said. "The physical problem with Jem was that Jem never wanted to have sex, he told me that right from the beginning, when he proposed, and I went along with it."

"Never?"

"Never."

"You mean...?"

"I mean I'm still a pure virgin even though I was married for all those years. Through a meeting of chance circumstances, I remain, as they say, intact." Patsy raised her eyebrows and drew on the cigarette. "So there you have it."

"My God, Patsy, I had no idea," said Annie. "He was such a lovely man and you seemed to have such a happy marriage."

"We did, we got along well and enjoyed ourselves together, so why would you have had any idea?" said Patsy. "It wasn't what you'd call normal so why would it even enter your head? Why would it enter anyone's head? To all appearances we were ideally suited and in a way we were. Jem was a great partner. My marriage was full of fun."

"Fun but no passion," said Annie. "Did you ever tell anyone?"

"Betty knows, only Betty and now you and I'd like to keep it that way. Mammy marched me off to the doctor's once to find out why there were no babies on the way. I knew why, of course, but she wouldn't take no for an answer, she insisted I had a medical examination. So eventually I had to go with her to the surgery and I had to suffer this awful internal, as they say, I remember it was very painful and humiliating, and then the doctor told her, in front of me, exactly why I hadn't yet conceived. I asked her to keep it a secret, it wasn't something I wanted the family to be tittle-tattling about."

"We wouldn't have tittle-tattled, we would have been understanding I hope," said Annie.

"I'm sure you would have been but there would still have been plenty of talk behind my back, not cruel talk, necessarily, maybe gossipy talk, speculation, pity for me, probably, and I didn't want that. I was too embarrassed, even a little ashamed."

"And what about now? Why have you told me now?"

"Because you're sitting here and we're talking," said Patsy. "And I'm too old to be embarrassed. Well, perhaps I am still a bit embarrassed but I'm not ashamed any more. I took a personal vow of chastity when I was young and I kept to it and for that I feel proud, hopefully not in a sinful way, God forgive me. Perhaps it was God or fate or whatever that organised the chance circumstances in which I would find a loving husband who offered no threat to my vow. Jem was a loving husband, despite all. I had the best of both worlds in that sense."

"And do you regret any of it now?" asked Annie. "I can't imagine being with Matt and not being with him. Even after all these years I sometimes look at the man and just want to leap on him."

"I must admit I've been curious about that side of things, about what I've missed out on, but I'm a bit of a prude. No doubt the comfort of lying in someone's arms would have been nice but any more than that I would have found difficult. I am basically a disapproving prude and always have been, Annie, the sex aspect of it has always struck me as being a bit base, a bit coarse. My private parts are my private parts. It was drummed into me from an early age that my body was a tabernacle for God and that I was to pay it no regard for its own sake, to do otherwise

619

would be sinful. That became an unshakeable attitude, even after I grew up and should have had more sense, perhaps. But I was the naïve young country girl besotted with the stories of martyrdom and sainthood, of the holiness and purity of young girls throughout history who had given up their lives rather than surrender their chastity and were then revered for their sacrifice and declared saints. And wasn't Our Lady the ultimate example? God chose a virgin to be the mother of his Son because only a virgin could be pure enough. And weren't we taught to emulate Our Lady? I was like blotting paper soaking it all up, believing every word. I wanted to be pure and saintly too."

"So does that mean you do have regrets?" asked Annie.

"If I do it's that it's because of who I am that I've lived my life the way I've lived it, I made the choice. It's no one else's fault, not Jem's, not the Church's but all mine. I, me, could never allow myself to get physically passionate, the guilt would have been too much to bear, that's how much the nuns' teaching and the Church's message hit home but I don't blame them. Most women learn how to shrug off all that nonsense and I never did. But I can only be me, Annie, I can't regret who I am. If I did, I'd collapse with the sad tragic waste of it all."

The two sisters sat without speaking. There was nothing more to be said, nothing that wouldn't have sounded too light-hearted or heavy-handed in the circumstances. The one looked at the other wondering what it would be like to not make love to the man who churned your stomach inside out with an honest human desire. The other returned the gaze, wondering what it must be like to want to leap on your man because of what she now realised, too late, was an honest human desire.

6

Patsy went to Christmas Midnight Mass. She wasn't nervous, the streets were full of people heading in the same direction, some straight from home, others finding their way straight from the pub. Patsy had to admit that one of the things she loved about Midnight Mass was the distinct waft of boozy fumes in the air. It wasn't so much the smell she enjoyed, though the smell of alcohol was part and parcel of the season's familiar aromas, it was the thought that people had rounded off their night in the bar to celebrate Christmas in the church. It seemed like an affirmation of priorities.

The altar at St Kevin's was festooned with flowers and the windowsills down each side of the church were decked with holly, a candle burning in each display atop a tall sconce wrapped in silver tinsel. A decorated tree stood at one side of the altar; as well as shiny baubles and draping glitter, cut-out stars of various colours dangled from the branches bearing the names of the recently dead and the sick of the parish, adding an important sense of local continuity, a personal investment in the truth of the festive message. The crib was set to the other side, the central figure of the Baby Jesus waiting to be delivered during this first Mass of Christmas Day. The scene was a beautiful sight to behold, a real mood-setter to gaze upon and enjoy before the service began. Whispers of admiration could be heard in appreciation of the team of women who had done all the work. Hadn't they done a wonderful job! Didn't the whole church look grand! God, it must have taken them hours to do it all!

A fresh crop of children now considered old enough to be allowed to go to Midnight Mass sat there in their new clothes, fidgeting as children do while at the same time oozing the simple confidence of feeling very grown up. They squirmed and turned on the benches, greeting all eyes with a radiant smile. They nudged their parents to take a quick peek at the latest arrival of the beery worse-for-wear contingent,

621

perhaps a normally grumpy neighbour; perhaps, even more worth a titter, one of their teachers. The parents nudged them back with warnings of not to stare, though they couldn't themselves resist the quick peek.

At last, the doors at the back were opened and the congregation stood and turned as one. Service booklets fluttered like paper doves in people's hands and the glorious anticipation of the first Christmas Mass was tangible. It was somewhat marred by a few discernible groans, which could be heard from the pews as the priests and servers processed up the aisle in a cloud of incense to begin the service: it was the parish priest, Father Dannagher, who was to be the main celebrant, not Father Dec, as everyone had hoped. Glances exchanged suggested everyone knew they were in for a long service. Father Dannagher was well-known for never being able to finish a sentence, so his sermons tended to ramble on and on as he inevitably lost his plot. Even at the end, just before the final blessing, he would wish everyone a happy and a holy Christmas, but it would take him a good ten minutes to do it. In a way it had become part of St Kevin's festive tradition and even the complainers had to accept it as such.

All the same when the organ started up with the introductory strains of *Adeste Fideles* and voices of all ye faithful rang out loud and clear, the joy of Christmas was irresistible whatever the aging bumbler had in store.

The church was full to bursting, full enough that all singing abilities were represented and there were none of those awkward moments when the notes were too high for most of the congregation to reach and only the smoker's croak of the parish priest was left to carry the tune. No carol was left hanging in the air. A choir of angels couldn't have performed with more spirit.

But, with so many at the Mass, an organised system for taking Holy Communion would have been useful, especially as the ends of the pews were so popular. Parishioners had their favourite fixed spots right next to the aisle for nipping in and out and they were determined not to give them up to any once-a-year worshipper, which resulted in a lot of bobbing up and down constantly as people seated further along the benches decided at will when to go up to the altar to receive the host. Parishioners also had their pet approaches to going to Communion: some stood up immediately after the priest's own and filed up somewhat early to be first in line; others liked to wait until the last stragglers joined the queue but this could be a fine balancing act as no one actually wanted to be the very last, with the whole church looking at their backside as they walked up the aisle, or wobbled, or teetered, the women with their hands joined and their stomachs held in, the men drawn up to full height and their arms swinging, all the time trying to look humble and reverential.

Patsy liked to sit about three rows from the front, not too close to appear ostentatiously devout but near enough to hear all the prayers and responses. She was one of the end-of-pew regulars. This too had its disadvantages when the church was full: she preferred to sit for a few moments to say her private prayers before getting up to leave at the end of the service but her routine delay was impossible with so many crowded in beside her, everyone anxious to be up and moving and exchanging their greetings to anyone with a hand to shake.

This year Father Dec had invited everyone who could spare an extra half hour or so to join the clergy and the servers for tea and mince pies in the church hall after the service. Patsy wasn't keen on being out even later than it was — thanks to Father Dannagher the Mass had taken almost an hour and a half — and she exited the bench quickly behind the closing processional to *Hark the Herald Angels Sing* to make her escape. Her particular balancing act had backfired. Standing at the door right in her path was Mr Hoolihan waiting for his family to emerge. He had had to remain at the back to help with the collection, always full plates at Christmas.

"Mrs Murphy," he called, lightly taking Patsy by the elbow. "And a merry Christmas to you this fine evening, though by rights, of course, it's morning already. Wasn't that a beautiful service? I'm glad you decided to venture out. Will you be going to the hall for some jollity? I believe there might be something a bit stronger on offer than tea to wash down the festive fare. One of the local pubs has kindly donated the odd bottle or two and maybe — though I shouldn't say this — we all need a wee drop after Father Dannagher's customary ramblings."

"I should get on home," said Patsy. "It's a busy day tomorrow."

"For us all, Mrs Murphy, for us all," said Mr Hoolihan. "But it truly is Christmas night and if we can't put up with a bit of sleepiness tonight of all nights then it's a sad business indeed. You could argue that this is the very time when we should be celebrating. Jesus has just been born, it's his birthday. Come on now."

At that moment Mrs Hoolihan and the children appeared at the church door and Patsy found herself being swept along on their enthusiasm and into the parish hall. Fifty or so parishioners had taken up Father Dec's invitation and the hall was abuzz with Christmas cheer. There was indeed the odd bottle or two, not only from the pub but some enterprising men, who'd been tipped the wink, had also contributed to the makeshift bar while their wives had obviously prepared more than just a few mince pies for the after-Mass social. Busy day tomorrow or not, the members of the erstwhile congregation were definitely in a party mood. Even Father Dannagher put in a brief appearance.

Women discussed the difficulties they'd had buying food and presents, money being tight during the current recession, and the best way to cook the turkey was debated. Men talked about the season's sporting calendar and how they looked forward to being able to fall asleep in front of the telly after the big dinner. The younger ones talked about their annual visit to see the Moving Crib in Parnell Square, where all the figures and animals were animated mechanically: they affected a blasé approach to the tradition but the Moving Crib had been a part of their Christmas since they were old enough to walk and the visit was as precious as their dismissal was feigned. The mood in the hall was happy and bubbly and pies and pints went down equally well.

It wasn't long before the singing began. Patsy was commandeered by Father Dec into sitting at the piano and all the old festive favourites were on the programme. People might have got fed up listening to them in the shops but it was different having a communal sing-song on Christmas night itself.

"Can you play Bohemian Rhapsody?" a teenaged boy asked Patsy. "You must know it, by Queen, it's top of the charts. We've had enough of all these old tunes." The lad stood by the piano and started to sing the opening lines about life being a fantasy and soon other young people in the room were joining in. Patsy followed as best she could on the piano. "*Open your eyes, look up to the skies and see,*" they sang and all together they bent their heads back to look up. Even some of the adults joined in with the *oooo-oo-oo-oo-oooh* easy bits, the *easy come, easy go*s, and at the end there was a round of applause.

"Not bad for an old-timer," the teenager said to Patsy by way of appreciation.

"I think she's earned a break," said Father Dec. "Come along, Patsy, get yourself another drink and a mince pie and we'll finish with a couple of dances. We could all do with moving a bit after sitting through a long Mass on wooden benches and it will help the drink go down." He uncovered the record-player and produced a few 45s of fifties and sixties music and put on *Rockin' Around the Christmas Tree*. People formed into a circle and danced in individual choreography around an invisible tree. People had a grand time.

It proved to be a great impromptu party but gradually the revellers started leaving for home full of the Christmas spirit in more ways than one. Patsy walked back with a couple of her neighbours, pretending all the while to look out for Santa's sleigh in the night sky.

"Will there be anything in your stocking tomorrow morning?" they asked Patsy.

"Only my foot," she said, "but I'll have to wash it first after my turns around the dance-floor."

More greetings for the festive days ahead were swapped, doors were opened, doors were closed. Patsy wasn't even tempted to linger in the kitchen but went straight upstairs, ready for her bed and hopeful of a good sleep for the few hours left before morning. She knelt down to say her prayers.

"Dear God, thank you for inspiring Mr Hoolihan into giving me the shove I needed to celebrate Christ's birthday in such a joyful way with the members of your church. I know I wanted to disappear unnoticed, but you always notice and for that I am eternally grateful. I am also thankful for the bit of talent on the piano you gave me, which allowed me to contribute a small measure to everyone's enjoyment. At least I hope I did, I wouldn't want to commit the sin of pride during my prayers. I haven't much to offer as a birthday gift this Christmas, only myself and the promise that I will try not to be such a miserable stay-at-home but will instead endeavour to make the most of this wonderful life you have given me. I offer up any misdirected disappointments I might have had and think only of the good things you have bestowed on me in my life. I have nothing to regret when I know there are people in the world starving, living in terrible poverty and war. Please God, let the ceasefire over the troubles in the North lead to a lasting peace up there. May the Christmas message be for everyone, Catholic and Protestant alike. Through Jesus Christ, Our Lord, Amen."

Patsy climbed into bed and snuggled down, feeling better than she had in a long time. She slept the sound sleep of the pleasantly intoxicated.

Moore Street market was bustling. Patsy had never been a regular, preferring the convenience of the local market at Meath Street in The Liberties, but she had read in the paper that Moore Street was the oldest food market in Dublin as well as being a site of major historical significance and her curiosity had been piqued. She had pulled together a short itinerary that also appealed to Margaret: Patsy had described it as being in line with her friend's suggestion of getting to know the city better and they could do it together. They agreed that a short informed ramble combined with their weekend shopping would be a good way to pass a couple of hours one Friday. They could round it off with some refreshments in Bewley's.

The area round Moore Street was referred to as the battlefield site of the Easter Rising so Patsy and Margaret started their walk at the General Post Office, which had been the main command post of the Rebellion. They were both very familiar with the events of 1916 but not so much with the drama and geography that spelled the end of the GPO siege. They consulted Patsy's guidebook and learned about the trail taken by Patrick Pearse and the other Rising leaders and Volunteers when they had had to flee their control base, flames turning the inside of the post office into an inferno. Patsy and Margaret retraced the men's steps.

They had scattered with an urgency through the patchwork of smoke-clogged back alleys behind the post office building and on to Moore Lane and Henry Street, all the while bullets flying as British soldiers tried to pick them off. Those who didn't catch a bullet in the chase ran on into Moore Street, where they took cover in a row of terrace houses. This was to be the scene of the last stand of the 1916 Easter Rising combatants before the decision was taken that they couldn't win the battle. The survivors had emerged from the houses and laid down their weapons and surrendered to the British troops. Moore Street had had to be restored after the onslaught, like so much of Dublin city centre.

"It's hard to believe this was where it all came to an end," said Margaret. "You look at all the shops and the stalls and you hear the traders shouting their wares and everybody busy with their shopping and then you think of those brave men fighting with their backs against the wall until they could fight no more. And in this very street! You can just picture them lining up there and standing with their arms in the air in surrender and all the rifles trained on them before they were marched off like scum. It must have been a heart-breaking sight."

"My da always said it was the end of the beginning," said Patsy. "It proved what was possible and many more volunteers came forward as a result, especially after the executions at Kilmainham. It's strange that there's no real evidence or indication left of what an important event in Ireland's history took place here. If it was in England there'd be some sort of re-enactment, like they do those mediaeval battles, something anyway, and coachloads of visitors would come to watch."

"Maybe it's still too soon after," said Margaret.

"I wouldn't have thought sixty years too soon but look around you, it's just business as usual."

Indeed today it was the usual riot of colour and noise, wooden stalls laden with pyramid displays of fruits and vegetables, buckets and bouquets of flowers lining both sides of the street, hawkers boasting the merits of old clothes and boots that still had some walking potential. Chickens and rabbits and strings of sausages and white pudding were disappearing fast off their hooks, slapped and wrapped in paper before being stowed into bulging shopping bags. Liver was popular — it was cheap and tasty — and bundles of herbs and scallions were being sold by old women out of old prams. Some of the daily produce was still delivered to the market by horse and cart and small cannons of straw-marbled manure dotted and composted into the tarmac.

The origins of Moore Street and its open-air market stretched back to the eighteenth century and little had really changed in that time, with stalls being handed down through generations of trader families.

"Imagine inheriting a family business that meant you'd be out working in all weathers," said Margaret. "I think I'd have to decline politely or at least argue for moving indoors into a shop."

"No different to working on a farm, I suppose," said Patsy. "People work hard to put the food on our tables. It must be in their blood, I don't think there can be much money in it. My relatives out at Tullamore have been working their land and animals for God knows how long and babies keep coming along to grow up and keep it all going. More babies means more mouths to feed, they're lucky to make ends meet. I remember the debt they got into just trying to get electricity installed."

"My God, imagine if we still had to rely on candles," said Margaret. "Then again I wouldn't be able to see all my wrinkles quite so clearly." She looked at all the packing materials, the trestles and table-tops, the tarpaulins, scales, bags and goods. "At least on a farm everything's more or less to hand, it's all already there," she said. "I wouldn't like to have to pack boxes and crates into the back of a van every morning before even starting out for work, then have to take them all out again to set up the stall before the first customer arrives, then to have to pack the whole paraphernalia away again at the end before going home. Imagine having to do that every morning and afternoon. Give me a job in a sewing factory any day."

Patsy, as the mini tour guide, related that way, way back, before food became the main produce, the Vikings reportedly sold slaves in the Moore Street vicinity.

"Imagine that!" said Margaret. "That's almost a reflection of the end of the Rising: men captured by an occupying force and standing in line at sword-point or gun-point, then being marched off to an unknown fate." She pondered the parallels. "Still, I suppose we should be thankful to the Vikings for founding Dublin in the first place, even if they were marauding invaders. I wonder if many of them looked like Kirk Douglas or Tony Curtis."

"I'll have to take you down to Wood Quay to see the archaeological dig," said Patsy. "They're uncovering all sorts of Viking bits and pieces there and it's easy to watch over the fence. We could go home that way today, if you like."

"I think by the time I've bought the weekend's food I'll have enough to carry without making any detours. Another day, perhaps. Wasn't that where you'd been when the bombs went off?"

"It was, I was with young Sean," said Patsy.

"Fortunately lightning never strikes twice, they say," said Margaret. "I'm going to get some of that liver for our dinner tonight and maybe one of those chickens, they look plump enough to cover a few meals. You could come round to eat with us tomorrow if you fancy it, Patsy, assuming you like chicken."

"I do if it comes ready for the oven and you don't have to kill it yourself. My mammy used to have to do that in the yard if Uncle Michael had brought a live one up from the farm and it was always funny but brutal at the same time, seeing the poor thing flapping about not realising it was already dead. Shall I bring the vegetables?"

"Not at all, I'll have the whole dinner on when you arrive."

"Don't those oranges look sweet and juicy? I'm going to get some," said Patsy. "Oranges remind me of childhood. Do you remember when they used to be individually wrapped in tissue-paper, with the producer's name and design printed on? I used to love those wrappers. They were so delicate. Oranges were a real treat — we always had to share just the one between the five of us — and I'd smooth out the tissue and keep the wrappers pressed in a scrapbook to look at, trying to imagine all those hot places my mammy described where the oranges grew and how it would be to visit them. I've never been to one, Margaret, so your house will have to do. I'll bring some round tomorrow."

"This little outing has made you nostalgic, Patsy, talking about when you were growing up."

"I'm just adding a bit of personal perspective to our history tour. Time flies, doesn't it? My God, think of it: Vikings used to walk on this very ground but that was centuries ago and now it's us walking here," said Patsy. "When you're a child you learn about history and the past but, even though you know all that, it still seems as if life as you yourself know it will go on forever."

"Well it doesn't and maybe we should be grateful for that," said Margaret. "Not that I'm ready to go yet, mind, but I wouldn't want to live to be a hundred and having to rely on others to take care of me."

"Well Jem was a lot younger than that when I had to take care of him."

"Let's stop now and not get melancholy, Patsy. Let's buy what we need and go for that drink."

The banter from the stallholders was great entertainment. Of course they were after as many customers as they could attract from their competitors but their joking and their sales pitches took the chore out of shopping. Patsy's purchase of half a dozen oranges passed without comment but Margaret was invited to caress the plump bellies of the chickens on offer.

"Imagine it's a line-up of naked men and you're after the biggest for a wealth of stuffing," said the butcher.

"They're not as hairy as I'm used to," she replied.

"Then it's time you tried your hand at a bit of smooth flesh, all well plucked," he said.

The minute the chicken was wrapped and bagged, the butcher had moved on to the next customer with advice on meatiness, on the best way to get the juices flowing, on the various ways to handle sausages. It was hard even for Patsy not to laugh. Good nature came free in the thriving market.

It was difficult to make the sounds out at first over the animated hubbub of the street. There was one deep boom and then a series of loud pops, followed by drifts of smoke rising up from somewhere towards the bottom of Moore Street. Nobody moved as their ears strained to detect either direction or explanation for the sounds. Eyes focused on the billowing and thickening black smoke gradually smothering the air.

"Bombs!" someone yelled. It took but split seconds for pandemonium to break out and stalls were overturned and toppled as the crowded street became a tangled rushing knot of people trying to flee in all opposing directions. Children were snatched up into mothers' arms. Elderly shoppers not able enough to join the fray were left clinging helplessly to street posts and door jambs or risk being knocked down in the crush. Men put protective arms around women, any women, and tried to usher them to safety. Items of fruit and vegetables became potentially lethal obstacles as they rolled around on the ground under hurrying feet. And as it gradually became clear that the smoke funnels were rising from distinct points in the direction of nearby Henry Street, the crowd learned which way to run and a human stampede charged back up Moore Street.

Patsy wasn't part of it. She was transfixed, rooted to the spot.

Margaret had initially run to find some sort of shelter, thinking Patsy was right behind her, but, when she realised they had been separated, Margaret had fought her way back through the throng, pushing and shoving frightened people out of the way in her desperation to find her friend. The open-air market hadn't taken long to empty but it felt like an eternity in all the panic and customers were still pouring out of the shops fleeing for their lives and all the time the sky darkening with smoke. Finally, Margaret could make out Patsy in the midst of the bedlam and she rushed to her friend shouting all the time, "you're not alone, Patsy, I'm here now". She tried to drag Patsy away from the danger but Patsy was a dead weight, like a stone statue cemented to its plinth, eyes wide open but unseeing.

"You both need to move, Missus," a young man urged them.

"My friend can't move and I can't leave her," said Margaret. "She's already been through this once and she's petrified with fright."

"Wait now and I'll give you a hand," he said. "You take her bags and my stuff for me and I'll get her going. I'll drag her along if I have to."

Margaret, relieved, did as she was told and let the young man get on with it. He stood behind Patsy and threaded his arms through hers and, holding her firmly at the elbows, he frog-marched her forward along Moore Street. It was awkward and it was a stumbling, ugly sight — Patsy was too dazed to help her rescuer as he struggled to get some distance between them and Henry Street — but it worked. Patsy slowly became aware that her feet were actually walking on someone else's and she snapped out of her stupor.

"Can you manage to walk a bit now, Missus?" he asked her. "I'll keep hold of you but I doubt my feet can take your weight for much longer. They're ready to drop off, so they are, and I wouldn't mind holding on to them, if it's all the same to you."

Patsy slumped into him but managed to stumble along on her own two feet. They got down to near the bottom of Moore Street and Margaret led them off into the back alleys she and Patsy had explored earlier. When they stopped finally, the man helped ease Patsy down until she was sitting resting on the ground, her head back leaning on the wall, her face white, her body limp, her mouth hanging open.

"I can't believe this has happened again, not again," murmured

Patsy, staring vacantly, lost inside herself. "I'm out, just enjoying the life God gave me as I promised him I would, then there's another bomb, then I'm so pathetic I have to be helped by a young man again instead of me helping others. That's what a good person would do. I can't be a good person. I'm being punished for the artificial life I've led, that I've thrown back into God's face."

"Whisht now Patsy," said Margaret, leaning in closely and gently stroking her friend's face. "We should be safe here until the police come."

"The police?" said Patsy, still somewhat out of it. She gazed at her companions, from one to the other, and was back in the moment as her head cleared. "Of course," she said. "Last time we all had to give them statements."

"If it's all the same to you I'll be off now," said the man. "Me and the police aren't what you'd call the best of friends. Take care now, the two of you."

"Thank you for your help," said Patsy, looking at him properly for the first time. "I hope your feet recover and there's no lasting damage."

"You're welcome and I'm sure the feet will be fine," said the youth. "You're not that heavy, I exaggerated a little for humour's sake. Cheerio, now. I hope you manage to get home safe."

He gathered his stuff from Margaret and hurried off down the alley steering away from Moore Street, obviously being careful to stay out of sight as much as possible but turning to give a last nod to the two women.

"Thank God he came along," said Margaret. "I couldn't budge you from where you were standing. It was like trying to shift a ton weight."

"Do you know who he is?"

"Now how would I know who he is. Why? Do you want to send him a thank-you letter or a Mass card, is it?"

"He's one of the two men who mugged me that night down by the canal."

"No! Are you sure? But he was so kind," said Margaret.

"How could I forget his face?" said Patsy.

"So why are you grinning?" asked Margaret, not knowing whether or not her friend had totally lost it in the convergence of violent incidents.

"I've been praying for him every day since then and I think my prayers must have been answered. He's changed from being my attacker to being my knight in shining armour."

"Perhaps so," said Margaret, "but I got the distinct impression that the police might not agree. Can you get up now?"

The madness in the streets had subsided and now people were standing about huddled in groups for safety and comfort, seemingly reluctant to leave the scene they had minutes earlier been frantic to escape. Patsy and Margaret lingered in case the Gardaí wanted to talk to them but the police obviously had their hands full elsewhere for only one patrol car took up position across the end of Moore Street. No one seemed to have been hurt in the market, which, it was clear now, had not been the target of the attack. The traders got together to discuss whether or not to set up their stalls again to try to save the day's business and help restore some sort of defiant order in the process, but the mood had changed too much, and they packed up for home. Spilt fruit and vegetables would be left for people needy enough to be scavengers.

Eventually Patsy and Margaret decided to make their way through to O'Connell Street to catch the bus home though it was like joining a stream of refugees like they'd seen in Pathé news reports about war zones. The pavements were crowded with people, slowly but determinedly moving forward, but traffic on the roads was at a standstill and the siren sounds of fire-engines and police cars and ambulances rose and fell in the ears. The planned call at Bewley's was definitely off the day's agenda but the nearest open pub would do. Both Patsy and Margaret were in need of a stiff drink.

The bar had customers in but not too many and they found a couple of free seats at a table. Patsy kept their place and lit up a cigarette while Margaret went to the bar and ordered two doubles of Paddy's. The combination of the warming whiskey and the bizarre normality of the pub — bizarre only in the circumstances of the city being under attack — certainly helped soothe the nerves. Margaret noticed that her friend had started shaking uncontrollably, which was perfectly understandable.

"We both needed that," said Margaret after taking a long gulp of the alcohol. "I hope it doesn't take too long for the traffic to clear. If I don't get home soon and Duggie hears what's happened, he'll be worried sick. And poor you, Patsy, having to live through all that again."

"At least I did just that," said Patsy, "I lived through it, again."

"Wait now," the barman suddenly called out at the top of his voice. He was listening to a radio behind the counter and the bar fell silent waiting for his news. "The Gardaí said that a bomb had gone off in the Shelbourne Hotel and that they think at least eight incendiary devices had been planted in shops and stores in Henry Street and Grafton Street." Customers looked at each other with growing alarm. The barman listened in to the radio again. "The devices set off a series of fires but…" he paused, listening. "Thank God for that." He looked up and smiled, an expression of encouragement on his face, "it seems there were no casualties or serious injuries."

A general cheer went round the pub and glasses were raised in relief.

"A round for everyone on me," shouted a man at the bar, a business type in a well-tailored suit, noted Patsy.

Another general cheer erupted. The barman scanned the room, remembering the various orders, and set to delivering the drinks.

"Thank God no one was hurt," said Margaret. "I wouldn't be surprised if all the rushing and pushing in the market caused more mishaps."

"Did your chicken survive?" asked Patsy.

Margaret rummaged in her bag to examine the bird. "Just as tempting and well plucked as when I bought it," she laughed, "it's just waiting for me to get busy massaging it with butter, but I might ditch the liver, I've gone off the idea of all that bloodiness. It'll be fish and chips after all this evening."

"That'll be me too."

"How are you feeling, Patsy? I can't believe the coincidence. Was it like before?"

"That's what had me rooted to the spot, I thought it was going to be the same thing over again and I couldn't move for fear, but the worst never happened. We were lucky."

"Everyone's been lucky today," said Margaret, "if you can call going to do your shopping and not actually getting killed 'lucky'. I wish to God they'd settle it all. Wasn't it grand over Christmas when there was a ceasefire? Why can't they just continue that? I'm feeling guilty now for bullying you into going out after your first experience. I had no real grasp of what you'd been through."

The friends finished their doubles and started on their free drinks. They called out a thanks and a cheers to the man who'd paid for them and clinked their glasses in his direction. His generosity had given them back some faith in human nature, in the relaxed companionship of strangers.

7

However brave a face she put on to reassure her friend, in the solitude of the house Patsy was far from all right. She moped about the house, moving things around from place to place for the sake of it, smoking heavily, drinking more than she realised. Her appetite had deserted her and her diet became as basic as mashed potatoes and carrots: too often the butcher's shop seemed just that little too far to venture. She refused all pleas from Margaret to take a short walk with her, maybe to the park, maybe to see the Viking dig as she'd promised: Patsy didn't want to go anywhere, nowhere was safe. She felt more secure in the house with Monty and Daisy.

Except when the nightmares returned, when the nightmares returned and were so vivid that they never completely went away even when she was awake but lingered as if monstrous threats hid in every room, waiting for her to just open the door. Only then would she leave the house to escape.

Death was the recurring presence in her dreams, her own imminent death always providing the shocking jolt that forced her awake. The scenarios were always the same though not identical, more like variations of the same hideous theme, as if she was doomed to live through the same hideous story over and over until the last time, when the jolt back into life wouldn't work.

She would be out with friends in the city. They would be laughing and conversing and enjoying each other's company and all was full of a sense of belonging and camaraderie, until someone would suggest moving on somewhere else. That was when the nightmare took over. Whatever she did, Patsy always ended up lagging so far behind her friends that she would lose sight of them in the distance and get lost. She'd see buildings that she knew but they were out of place, out of context, looming and dark, shapes lurking in the shadows, and she would be caught in a maze of the familiar and the unknown, getting more and more confused and desperate, not knowing where she was, where to go, what to do. Footsteps would follow staccato sharp behind her, forcing her to try to get away from she never knew what: maybe British soldiers, maybe muggers. She'd run, stumbling, falling, booming sounds going off all around her. Sean would appear, arm outstretched to secure her but always it had gone by the time she reached out and she would fall. Once she ended up on a wooden bridge, water beckoning her from below, liquid and inviting and pressing its welcome in the moonlight with a gentle rush of wind fingering through the reeds and up through her hair. But there were moving figures in the greenery and she fled. One time she ended up in the train station but it had changed: she wanted to buy a coffee to steady her nerves but the café had moved, gone, replaced by people with grotesque faces covered in dust and blood, all sitting at tables and calling to her with their hollow eyes. Sean would appear at the door calling to her but he'd vanish before she could get to him and his protecting arms.

The culmination of the nightmares was a dream so frightening that she would never fully recover even on waking. This time her flight took her into an arched stone tunnel, its ground cobbled and cold, echoing and reverberating with the noises of bangs and blasts coming from way beyond the tunnel entrance behind her but exploding right inside her ears. She had nowhere to flee; there was no respite, either end of the tunnel spelled danger and chaos: at one side, a tiger growled and snakes slithered through lush foliage, at the other the sky was repeatedly illuminated with sudden flashes and bursts of flames. She crouched at the bottom of the wall, wrapping in on herself, looking this way and that and praying to God Almighty to intervene when a horse-drawn carriage clip-clopped like a raging vortex into the tunnel and reared to a halt beside her. Pulling the coach was a tall black horse, its mane, gathered and plaited into ribboned sections like exotic plumage, its coat shining like polished ebony. The horse neighed and pawed a front hoof on the cobbles and turned its head to snort in Patsy's direction, the air from its nostrils puffing dense white in the darkness. A bony hand appeared, gripping the edge of the window, and the carriage door was thrown open to invite Patsy inside. She moved to accept the welcome shelter of the coach when to her horror she saw that it was no rescue from the tunnel but an ascent into the absolute unknown. She couldn't breathe, her lungs were being sucked and emptied of air as she realised that the beckoning passenger was Jem's mother, now turned into the banshee.

Patsy woke gasping for breath. She leapt out of bed and made herself walk round the room. She needed a cigarette but was too frightened to go down the stairs. She felt as if death was getting relentless in its pursuit and could be lurking anywhere in the house. She knelt down to pray, clutching her scapula.

"My Queen and my Mother," she prayed, reciting her Child of Mary morning devotion, "I offer myself entirely to Thee. And to show my devotion to Thee, I offer Thee this day, my eyes, my ears, my mouth, my heart, my whole being, without reserve. Wherefore, good Mother, keep me and guard me as thy property and possession. Amen."

She repeated the prayer over and over, fervently, not daring to stop, oblivious to the moment when at last she drifted into an empty sleep. When she awoke, half-kneeling, half-slumped over the side of the bed, it was morning. She looked around, not sure if she was alive or dead, but she saw weak daylight filtering through the curtains and stumbled to her feet. Cramps shot through her legs after her twisted posture but she didn't care. She knew she had survived the night.

Patsy came to realise, with a mixture of relief and a sense of having been abandoned, that she was suddenly, for the first time, completely alone in the house. Her spectral companion had gone. There were to be no more comments from the other side, no further reproofs or encouragements, no unwanted reminders of what was or what might have been, no psychological sparring across the ether. Mrs Murphy Senior had vanished with the death-coach. Patsy feared it was a dreadful portent.

But the habit of talking aloud when she was alone in the house was hard to shake. For years Patsy had found a begrudged comfort in her unseen visitor and now was at a loss as to where to direct her conversation. Monty and Daisy took over the role. Confining herself as much to staying indoors as possible, Patsy created her own interior world in which the hot water bottles took on a life of their own. In the absence of anyone else, she talked to them, her language becoming simpler and simpler as the days wore on until it was the way she would talk to a small child. Monty and Daisy became the recipients of all Patsy's frustrated motherhood and she started making porridge to feed both them and her escapism.

Margaret called in regularly but had stopped making suggestions for short excursions. Instead, she would knock on Patsy's door and say that she needed a few things, did Patsy fancy going to the shops with her? Then they would sit over a cup of tea and Margaret would try to make ordinary conversation.

"Did you see those photographs in the Sunday newspaper?" she asked. "Some people have no shame. It seems to run in that family."

"What photographs? Which family?"

"The royal family, in London," said Margaret. "The newspaper was full of pictures of their Princess Margaret splashing about in the sea with a young gardener she's taken up with. At least he's supposed to be a gardener but which flower he's looking after God only knows. Though of course everyone knows now."

"I didn't think there was any sea at London," said Patsy.

"Not in London, eejit, she's on that island, Mystique or Mustique or whatever they call it, musty anyway, judging by what goes on. She has a huge house there, it's all very exclusive and she's there with a young man young enough to be her son. Evidently she took him there years ago to do the garden and he's been back and forth with her ever since. Or up and down, or in and out, as the paper would have us believe."

"I thought she was married to a famous photographer."

"And so she is, that's what I mean, no shame," said Margaret. "Didn't her uncle have to give up the throne after cavorting all over Europe with his American fancy-woman? She was divorced too, as I remember."

"I remember that business well enough," said Patsy. "The woman had a great sense of style, her clothes became all the rage."

"Well, the princess obviously has her own sense of style too, the style of living that goes with privilege and being one of the royals. The article said that if any English holidaymakers happen to coincide with her on the beach, the women all have to curtsy even if they're only wearing skimpy bikinis. Can you believe that? And she's always partying and drinking and evidently does a good attempt at singing dirty songs if anyone's willing to sit at the piano for her. Like I said, no shame."

"I think the real shame of it is that she's carrying on like that while there are bombs going off and killing people and some of them in the very country she's supposed to represent," said Patsy.

Margaret didn't really care one way or the other about the British princess and her love life, she had mentioned it by way of some gossipy conversation and despaired when even a juicy newspaper article led Patsy back to the bombings. She decided to try a different tack.

"There's a new John Wayne movie coming out. We could go to see it when it opens."

"And what's that?"

"It's another western and it should be fun," said Margaret. "The story is about an old gunslinger who's dying of cancer, but the film starts with lots of clips from John Wayne's old movies and it would be fun to spot how many we've seen together."

"More guns," said Patsy, "more dying, more killings. I'm not in the mood for that."

"Patsy, you can't keep dwelling on what happened, it's not good for you."

"Well going out doesn't seem too good for me any more. What would you have me do, Margaret? Go out and maybe it would be third time unlucky?"

Margaret didn't know what else to try and finally sought the help of Father Dec. Patsy was so devoted to her religion that perhaps, thought Margaret, a firm word from the priest might work. He could talk about God's will and God's plan and whatever else he could find in the scriptures to bully Patsy out of her despair.

Father Dec did his best. He arranged times when he would visit Patsy, suggesting she bought in some bagels for his visit, mainly as a way of getting her out of the house and talking to people she knew and trusted. He had to stop that when the bakers felt obliged to tell him that Patsy had started going into the shop a couple of times in the same day to buy bagels for the priest's visit, having forgotten she had already been in earlier and being quite adamant that she hadn't.

So he took to turning up unexpectedly, knowing that Patsy hardly ever went out. He would talk to her about what was going on in the parish, suggest she might go over to the hall and play the piano at a social that was planned; he was anxious to get her back into the habit of leaving the house casually and without constantly fearing the worst.

For something to say he asked her about her resident ghost. He'd been reading up on the Church's attitude to the supernatural world, he said, and he could reassure Patsy that there was no particular doctrine on the matter, so she wasn't to think she was doing anything sinful or against the Church's teaching through her conversations with her dead mother-in-law.

"In fact you're in good company, Patsy," he said. "St Thomas Aquinas evidently saw spirits and angels on many occasions as he slept and he is regarded as one of the great scholars and philosophers of the Catholic Church. We still use his writings as the basis for our studies in the seminary. And didn't we used to refer to the Holy Spirit as the Holy Ghost? And don't we pray for the souls of the dearly departed, the souls who have passed on beyond the physical world?"

"I don't have a resident ghost any longer," said Patsy. "It turned out that Mrs Murphy Senior was none other than the banshee in disguise. She only comes now during the night, in her death-coach, and she invites me to climb aboard." Patsy laughed. "I keep refusing the invitation, the old witch."

"But that's just Irish myth," said the priest. "That was a nightmare, perfectly explainable after all you've been through."

"Isn't a myth just an earlier way of describing something we now recognise as something else?" said Patsy. "Surely the banshee was just another name for the Angel of Death, and haven't you just told me that it was in his sleep that St Thomas Aquinas was visited by angels? I don't see any difference between him being visited by angels in his dreams and the banshee visiting me in mine. We were both asleep at the time."

"Patsy you're getting too morbid, it's not healthy," said Father Dec. "God doesn't want you holed up in the house away from your friends and neighbours. He didn't put us on this earth to live alone, we're social animals, we need each other. Can I not persuade you to come to the church event this weekend? You had such a good time at Christmas after Midnight Mass. It was a bit impromptu but everyone appreciated your participation on the piano, it added to the surprise flavour to the occasion."

"Thank you, Father, but there's a programme on the television I don't want to miss."

"I didn't even say which night we're holding the party so how do you know there's a special programme on that you don't want to miss?"

"Because it's the weekend and there are special programmes on every night," said Patsy. "Besides, it's not fair to leave Monty and Daisy on their own all evening. They enjoy the television too and how can they watch it without me?"

"But they're not real company," said Father Dec.

"They're real enough for me," said Patsy. "And they pose no threat."

"They pose a different sort of a threat, Patsy, don't you see that?" said the priest. "They're just physical objects and it's dangerous to invest more in them than what they are."

"Sure Monty and Daisy are harmless, good little souls, Father," she said. "And don't you worry, I've already baptized them in a bowl in the kitchen so they're like two little saints."

The normal basic reference points that in the past had kept Patsy grounded for most of her life — getting up and going to work, coming home after work and preparing the dinner — had long since disappeared from any daily schedule. The fingers forever circling on the clock no longer signified any pressing need to do this or that, go here or go there. She was a free agent. Her time was her own though she neither occupied it nor was occupied by it. Dull sameness was the same dullness regardless of the hour. The only day different to any other was a Sunday. That's when Patsy would go to the eleven o'clock sung Mass at St Kevin's, which was longer and richer in litany than the regular early morning Mass. She felt instantly holy when the incense entered her nostrils and filled her lungs, when the soaring singing of the hymns was absorbed through her ears and, she felt, entered into her very soul. She was detached from everything else. Prayer was all, safety was paramount, faces on the television became surrogate friends. Patsy didn't even realise how acute was her loneliness. The eccentric whom the neighbours had loved to marvel at became the slightly mad recluse whom the neighbours avoided meeting in the street.

As Margaret had sought his help, Father Dec in turn sought the help of Sean Mulhoney, thinking that the young man might have more success in getting through to Patsy as he had been in Leinster Street with her during the bombing. Sean had taken the experience badly too but he was working it out of his system and refused to let it define his life. The priest hoped that her friend's determination to remain positive would shake Patsy out of her despondency.

Her face lit up at the door when she saw Father Dec on the step with Sean. "My two favourite men," she beamed, ushering them down the hall. "Isn't it grand now that you happened to knock on the door at the same time. I detect the guiding hand of God in the coincidence."

She led them into the back room where the visitors struggled to hide their astonishment at the state of the place. Father Dec in particular couldn't believe how bad things had gotten in just the short week or so since his last visit. The floor obviously hadn't seen a sweeping-brush for far too long, with crumbs and clumps of fluff lying undisturbed under the table, and a layer of dust and soot had settled gently on the mantelpiece and on the pictures and memorabilia displayed there. The chairs were hidden under old newspapers and film magazines and discarded clothes which might or might not have been waiting to go in the wash. The tablecloth was marbled with stains and dried spillages, dropped food ground into the fibres.

"Excuse the state of the place," said Patsy, "I wasn't expecting anyone to call. Sit down and I'll pour us all a drink."

"Isn't it a bit early?" said the priest. It was still morning. "I'd love a cup of tea, though, Patsy."

"Tea's fine for me too," said Sean. "It looks as if you're having a clear-out," he said looking through the magazines on the chair. "I didn't know you were such a movie fan, Patsy."

"I've always loved the cinema and the fan magazines," she called from the kitchen. "You used to like them too, I seem to remember, Sean. I don't know why we stopped going."

"Here's that old National Geographic we studied for ideas for the outside toilet. You kept it all this time," he called out. "See that, Father, that's partly why I went to art college, after looking at the photographs to get inspiration with Patsy and realising that it was something I could do and enjoy. She had invited me to have tea in Bewley's. It was my first time there and I couldn't believe cakes could be so delicious."

"Then you're one up on me," said Father Dec. "I've never been there even though I know it's a bit of a Dublin institution."

"I don't think we were ever there, were we Sean?" called Patsy. "In Bewley's? I know I used to go with Margaret all the time."

"Of course we went, you took me and said I could have as many cakes as I wanted," said Sean. "You called it our first business meeting and later I did that small painting of Bewley's for you that's still on your mantelpiece. It was a Christmas present. It was all a while ago but I've not forgotten how much of a treat it was to go to such a posh café. I was only young, of course, maybe I was easily impressed. I was just telling Father Dec how that helped me decide to go to art school, after we sat there looking at the pictures of India and the jungle when we were talking about your toilet plan."

"That was a great plan, wasn't it, and you did a grand job in making it happen. Sometimes when I go to use the toilet, I'd swear the animals have come to life" said Patsy bringing in the tea-pot. "I'm afraid there are no biscuits so help yourself to extra sugar if you need sweetening up."

Father Dec and Sean felt awkward standing but every seat, every chair was a receptacle for something other than human bottoms and they didn't want to shove stuff to one side in case Patsy got flustered so they just stood.

"So how are you, Patsy?" asked Sean. "Father Dec was telling me you don't go out much these days. That doesn't sound like the Patsy I know. We'll have to arrange another outing. I'll have a look and see what's on and we can go along together. I don't think either of us would be keen on going back to find the mosaic, it must be finished by now, but I personally never go near South Leinster Street if I can avoid it. Are you over it all now? I gather you've been having bad nightmares."

"You said the sunshine would come out again, didn't you Sean, and here you are, bringing it with you. But then you always brought sunshine into my life," said Patsy. "All those times we used to go out and I never dreamt you were so good at painting and drawing. You should have had a sketchbook when we went out to Howth. What a beautiful day that was. Do you remember seeing the horses galloping along the sands? You could have painted them. You might have even caught the one that won the Grand National a few years later. Sean's a very good guide, you know, Father. He always researches what we're going to see and then he passes all the information on to me and makes it all come alive. He knew all about the mosaic and the Irish myths it was based on, though I don't think you put much store by myths, do you Father?"

"Wait now, Patsy," said Sean, "I think you must be getting me mixed up with someone else."

"Sure there's only one Sean," said Patsy, reaching out to take his hand.

Father Dec saw that the young man was getting confused and he asked Patsy to pour him another cup of tea so that she would have to let go her hand.

"So, what is all this, Patsy?" said the priest. "Is it a big clear-out you're having? If you have stuff to get rid of, I can organise some help to come and collect it for you, get it out of your way."

"It's not in the way, it's just stuff lying around. I think it makes the place look more homely, more lived in, don't you?" said Patsy. "Mind you just a minute," she said, her face breaking into a cheeky smile. "There's something I've just remembered upstairs." Patsy flashed a flirtatious grin at Sean and hurried out of the room.

The two men looked at each other.

"Have you any idea what's going on here?" Sean asked the priest. "She seems to know who I am and then suddenly goes off talking about things that don't mean anything to me. I've never been to Howth with Patsy, ever; or to the cinema, and I've never seen horses galloping along the beach. Do you know any other Seans she knows?"

"I don't. I know that her husband's name was Jem but I'm afraid she's been locked away alone in the house for far too long she's obviously losing it a bit," said Father Dec. "She went through a bad time after that first bombing when the two of you were out but she seemed to rally and was doing well enough, going out into the city again, shopping with her friend. I know she also went to your exhibition at the college because she told me all about that, she was very proud of you. So I'd say she was definitely over the worst but then she was in Moore Street market when that second lot of bombs went off in the shops back in February and she hasn't been right since. I told you about her nightmares and her growing fixation with her own death. What's very sad that I didn't tell you about are the two hot water bottles she's got that she thinks of as her babies. She told me that she'd even baptized them in the sink."

"My God, poor Patsy," said Sean. "I feel guilty now for not calling to see her more often and it's only because I was being selfish; she was too much of a reminder of that awful day. I struggled to keep visions of what we saw from coming into my head and I didn't want to see Patsy and have them all come flooding back. I was too busy trying to get over it in my own way to really think about her as much as I should have."

"I don't think there's any need for you to feel guilty," said Father Dec. "I know she's been a sort of a friend for a long time and was very helpful to you and your family but perhaps she grew to rely on you too much when you were young, she seemed to treat you like a son. Perhaps without realising it she was using you all as a substitute for the family she never had. But you're a young man, Sean, you must look to your own future. It's not your fault that circumstances have served to throw Patsy back into her past."

"All the same I feel bad about it," said Sean. "She was always so generous, so open to crazy notions, and fun, she was fun. Now it's as if that person has disappeared."

"Disappearing and getting further away as the days pass," said the priest. "I feel guilty in my own way too because I don't know how or what I can do. I thought you coming here would be a help but I'm not so sure now. She doesn't seem able to distinguish you from this other Sean, whoever he was."

"I'll do anything I can to help, I owe Patsy so much," said Sean, "but I wouldn't like to think that my presence was causing her too much confusion. I honestly don't know if I could pretend to be someone else just to humour her, that would be too much of a lie, too unfair."

Before Father Dec could say anything more, Patsy burst back into the room. She had changed her clothes.

"So, Sean," she said, twirling and holding out the skirt of her dress. "Remember this? It was always your favourite and so it always reminds me of you."

Patsy had put on the black and white patterned dress that she used to wear on outings with Sean Fitzsimmons. She made a comic but tragic sight. After fifty-odd years, the dress didn't fit her any more; it was stretched across her stomach and around the waist and some buttons would no longer fasten so she had put a belt around the middle to hold it together.

"Well Sean, do you approve?" she asked.

"You look as beautiful as ever," he replied at a loss. "I can see why it would have been a favourite. What do you say, Father Dec?"

"I would have to agree," said the priest. "Patsy Murphy, you never fail to astound. However, I know that Sean has lots of work he needs to do at his college so perhaps we might take our leave of him and let him get off." Father Dec stood and held his hand out to Sean. "We'll no doubt be seeing you soon," he said. "I'll see Sean to the door, Patsy, while you pour me that drink you offered earlier."

"Of course, Father," she said. "And don't you get nasty with Sean while he's leaving, you're not at the bakery now."

Patsy busied herself with fetching a couple of glasses and the Paddy's and the two men went down the hall to the front door.

"Thank you for that, Father," said Sean. "I do actually have work to get on with but I didn't know how to leave without seeming to be running away. I have a major project to finish for my final year assessment and that future of mine you were talking about could depend on it. Should I come back later, do you think?"

"I shouldn't come for a while if I were you, Sean, but don't feel bad about it, Patsy may need time to come back from wherever she is. We wouldn't want her leaping on the wrong Sean, would we, that would be a very tricky situation to handle. I'll stay a bit longer now and have a drink with her — God, it's still early in the day for whiskey but what can you do? Then I'll see about getting one or two of the parishioners to start calling in to see her regularly. I'll call in to alert her sister at The Coombe too."

"Thank you, Father," said Sean. He stood at the door shifting his feet and looking pained as he studied the outside of the house with an inner nostalgia. "Obviously let me know when you think I can be of some help. Bye now."

Father Dec watched as the troubled young man walked off down the

647

street, hands in his pockets and shoulders hunched over. Then he shut the door and said a quick prayer before going to rejoin Patsy.

She was waiting with the drinks when the priest edged back into the room.

"He's a good young man," said Father Dec.

"He is and I'm very lucky that he wants to marry me," said Patsy. "I just don't know why my father is so against him. Perhaps you could have a word, change his attitude, he might listen to a priest."

"I could certainly try," said Father Dec. He downed his whiskey and, in the circumstances, enjoyed it far more than the time of day and his conscience should have permitted.

Annie went to see Patsy's situation for herself and found the place just as the priest from St Kevin's had described. He'd called to The Coombe a few days earlier and Annie had taken the first opportunity she had to go to Warren Street. She was up to her eyes in work at the moment and at home she also had her mammy to look after; Betty was quite elderly and becoming somewhat hunched after her years of constant childbearing and then looking after all the grandchildren who'd come along in rapid succession; both Annie's kids and John's had benefited from their granny being a convenient childminder

On Annie's previous visit, Patsy had been wandering somewhat in her conversation but the house itself was clean and tidy and Patsy had seemed to be taking care of herself. This time the deterioration was obvious from the moment Annie walked through the door. It was a complete mess and distinctly smelly. Patsy, who had always been so fastidious in her appearance, was wearing a grubby old frock held in place by a belt and she was flouncing around with a bizarrely glamorous air. She even had a smear of lipstick on.

While Patsy was making tea in the kitchen, Annie went to sneak a quick look into the parlour to see if that was any better. It was a bit untidy but only in the way it is when someone has been watching television and then gone to bed without straightening the seat covers or the cushions. The curtains were still drawn, making the room look dark and depressing, and Annie pulled them back to let in some daylight. She was surprised to see that the window was wide open; the bottom sash was pushed right up so she hadn't noticed it from the street. She was also surprised to see a couple of blankets thrown on the floor and that the television set had gone.

"Patsy, where's your telly?" she shouted. "Did you move it upstairs? Matt could have helped you with it, you shouldn't have lifted it on your own, it's far too heavy and awkward to carry anywhere, let alone up the stairs."

"I haven't moved it upstairs," said Patsy coming through from the kitchen. "Isn't that strange, now? I was only watching it in here last night."

"Did you not realise it had gone?"

"I haven't been in here this morning since I got dressed," said Patsy.

"You must have left the window open when you went to bed last night," said Annie. "Somebody must have got in and pinched the television while you were asleep."

"I don't think I went up to bed last night," said Patsy. "The newly-weds who've moved in next door are very noisy at night and I can hear everything coming in from the other side of the bedroom wall so I decided to sleep in here last night. I don't want to be listening to all that carry-on. I remember it was a very warm evening so I opened the window a little. I didn't wake up until I heard the milkman put the bottles on the step and then I just got up and went upstairs to get dressed."

"Well, the window is wide open now," said Annie. "Whoever it was must have climbed in and managed to pick up the television and manoeuvred it through the window while you were asleep in the chair. My God, Patsy, anything could have happened. You could have been attacked where you slept or, my God, imagine if you'd woken up and caught them in the act. You could have been raped or murdered. Did you not hear anything?"

"Nothing at all."

"Thank God for that," said Annie. "I dread to think of you disturbing them and what they might have done. They might have even thrown the damned thing at you so they could get away and you might have been pinned down under it for hours."

"I'd better report it to the police," said Patsy. "Can you remember what model it was? It was the same make as the one Matt gave to

Mammy."

Annie bit her lip, thinking quickly that she didn't actually know how Matt had gotten hold of the two television sets and that it was perhaps best not to bring the matter to the attention of the Gardaí even after all these years.

"I wouldn't bother doing that," she said. "I'm sure the police have more to investigate than wasting time over a telly because someone was daft enough to leave the parlour window open. That's an open invitation to a thief and you'd probably let yourself in for a lecture and no chance of catching the thief. It was an old telly anyway, Patsy, and it's probably time you had a new one. I'll have a word with Matt. Just make sure all the windows are closed in future. You're alone in the house, you can't afford to be so careless."

Annie left Patsy's house more worried than she had been after listening to the priest. He hadn't exaggerated at all about the state Patsy was in and Annie hurried to see John to get his thoughts on what was best to do about their sister. Father Dec had told her, as something to consider if things got really bad, that there was a Catholic residential-care home in the north of the city; it was run by the Sisters of Nazareth, and was a modern building set in beautiful parkland. He could make enquiries, if Annie thought it a good idea.

"We might have reached that point, I think things are really bad with Patsy already," Annie told John. "She's not looking after herself and she's leaving herself very vulnerable. Anyone could get into the house. I hate to say it but I think she's creating dangers for herself, not to mention her state of mind and the way she thinks those hot water bottles are babies. That's not healthy and it's getting worse."

"It was all those bloody bombs," said John. "She never got over any of it. I should have been more supportive, visited her more."

"I'm sure we could all look to our consciences where that's concerned," said Annie. "You read about these explosions and people dying in the street and you see it on the television, but you have no real sense of what it must have been like for the people at the scene and you just go and put the kettle on or get the dinner ready, in a way I think you dismiss it from your mind. We none of us appreciated properly what Patsy had lived through, what she'd nearly died through."

"It's the human way of things," said John. "You get on with everyday life and take everything for granted, especially you take your family for granted. It's as if you think to yourself that they're there and that in itself becomes sufficient, knowing that they're there. You're getting on with everything and you just assume they are too because you know they're there, that's what's important, that you know they're there. So you end up not giving them a second thought," he said. "My God, that's a terrible thing to have even thought let alone to have said, to admit that I never gave my sister a second thought and there she was all the while falling apart."

"I suppose with Patsy being the eldest out of all of us, she was never a part of our lives in terms of growing up. We were much younger, the last arrivals in Da's second family, with years and years difference between our ages. When we were just small children Patsy was already going out to work, so to us she was mature and capable. She was always an adult. It never occurred to us that she might need us and that's an attitude that's hard to change."

"I'm not sure that makes me feel any better," said John. "She had a great day out with me on the scooter and we both enjoyed each other's company, it wasn't all one way. Why couldn't I have found time to do that again, take her somewhere else? God forgive me, I've no real excuse."

"Well, we can both do something now. What do you think, shall we go and take a look at this Nazareth House from the outside? Try to gauge some sort of an impression?"

"The three of us could go in the car — you, me and Patsy — and we could just see what she says about the place without saying why we're driving past," said John. "We could maybe make a trip out of it, take a drive into the country, perhaps to Larch Hill, isn't that where they used to live?"

"That's a grand idea," said Annie. "And, depending how it goes, I could ask Father Dec to look into getting Patsy a place in the home."

John arranged to take a day off work from the bakery citing 'family reasons' though he needn't have made any excuse; he was no shirker and didn't have days off sick and, even after all these years, his father's name still carried some weight. Annie had arranged to meet him at Patsy's as she wanted to make sure that her sister was clean and presentable, just in case they actually went into Nazareth House. The brother and sister had also agreed that a pub lunch out in Rathfarnham would add to the treat. All the more reason for Patsy to look her best.

In fact Patsy didn't object to Annie's rummaging about in the wardrobe choosing something suitable for the trip, the ghost of the old smart Patsy re-asserting itself in the excitement of a day out.

There was noisy conversation as they climbed into the car and set off from Warren Street. Annie suggested that Patsy might like to sit in the front seat to have a clearer view out of the window but Patsy opted for the back, where she could stretch out and choose whether to look right or left as they drove along and where there would be more room for Monty and Daisy, who couldn't be at home on their own for a whole day.

The journey took them right through the centre of Dublin and out the other side. Nazareth House was situated on Malahide Road in the Artane direction but wasn't too far out of the city. The home looked to be mainly a complex of very modern three-storey buildings, very bright, with picture-windows on each floor adding a sense of weightlessness. It certainly wouldn't be dark and pokey inside. Up one facade rose a series of seven multi-coloured stained-glass windows, abstract rather than figurative in design, and the site was indeed set in a lush environment of woodland and lawned gardens.

John parked the car at the front, ostensibly so they could get out and stretch their legs and have a closer look. Patsy wondered why on earth they were there at all, it wasn't her idea of a trip to the country.

"Isn't this beautiful?" said Annie letting her eyes wander over the house and grounds. "I wouldn't mind living in a place like this. I bet there's all mod-cons in there and proper heating. And the trees! Sure, you'd never get tired of seeing them out of your window every day, much nicer to look at than boxy backyards and rows of houses leaning on each other. Can you imagine waking up to that view every morning, Patsy, and watching the seasons change through those huge windows? I bet there are lovely walks through the woods too, pathways and probably benches to sit on and rest your legs and just enjoy the setting. Isn't it grand, John?"

"It certainly is," he said. "We could pop inside if you fancy, Patsy. I wouldn't mind seeing what's on the other side of those beautiful stained-glass windows. It looks as if it might be a chapel."

"Come on, let's go in," said Annie. "I'm sure it must be allowed. Surely we can just go through the doors without getting into trouble."

John led the way and held the main door open for Patsy and Annie. It gave on to an entrance lobby with one or two easy chairs and a counter. A collection of brochures was on display and a receptionist asked if they needed any assistance. John took her to one side and explained why they were there but cautioning that Patsy wasn't yet aware of the full situation. Patsy could see the two of them nodding their heads at whatever was being said. Then John rejoined his sisters.

"We can take a look around the ground floor, no problem," he told them. "Those coloured windows are in a chapel. Shall we go and see, Patsy?"

She didn't reply one way or the other, she just waved a brochure in his face. The brochure bore the simple heading: Nazareth House Care Home.

"Well, I want to have a nose now that we're here," said Annie quickly and she linked her arm through Patsy's and they all headed off to the chapel. They were also allowed to see an example of the living quarters and the various care facilities available on site and the specific areas arranged for communal use. Annie and John waxed lyrical in their praise of everything they saw but Patsy remained silent.

Finally she said: "Can we go to the country now? I thought we were going out to Larch Hill."

"Of course, we can go now," said Annie. "I just wanted to see this place. Father Dec had mentioned it and I suppose I was curious."

"When did you see Father Dec?" asked Patsy.

"I bumped into him in the street, a few weeks ago now, it must be."

"And how did he happen to mention this place?"

"I can't remember how it cropped up in conversation but it's not important," said Annie, indicating silently to John that perhaps it would be best to leave the matter there for the moment. "Let's be on our way. We'll have a walk round your old neighbourhood, Patsy, you can show us where you used to live and by then I'll be ready for that pub lunch."

The drive out to Rathfarnham was more subdued than when the party had first set out. Patsy sat clutching Monty and Daisy in the back while in the front Annie and John attempted diversionary small talk before giving up and the rest of the journey passed in silence. It was only when they had left Dublin behind and were travelling along the roads on the outskirts of Rathfarnham that Patsy's enthusiasm returned and she sat bolt upright in the back of the car to feed on the memories.

"I used to go to piano lessons in that house," she said, pointing to Miss Bourke's old residence and twisting round so her eyes could linger on it as they drove past. "She always said I was very talented but then Daddy put a stop to all that."

"I heard that he'd refused to allow you to take up a music scholarship," said Annie. "He could be a hard man."

"I'm sure that's where Molly saw the leprechaun," Patsy suddenly interrupted as they drove along the lane up to Larch Hill. "We were in the pony-and-trap and Seamus — that was the name of the horse — suddenly reared up at the front before galloping all the way home. We nearly fell out of the trap. I was very jealous of Molly because I didn't see the little man but I think Mammy and Daddy did because they suddenly threw a blanket over us in the back. Molly was very annoying afterwards, boasting to me deliberately about what she'd seen and knowing how jealous I was even though I pretended not to care."

"So do leprechauns really exist?" asked John. "I thought the stories of the little people were just part of Irish folk lore."

"Of course they exist and why not? You're as bad as Father Dec," said Patsy. "He tried to tell me there was no such thing as the banshee but didn't the banshee visit me one night in bed so what does he know."

"That must have been very frightening," said Annie.

"It was at the time," said Patsy. "I woke up and I was desperate with fear, I didn't dare get back into bed and in the morning when I woke up I was on the floor, but then I got used to the idea. Doesn't the banshee come for all of us in the end?"

"Has it changed much here since you were a girl?" said John steering the subject in a healthier direction. "It's certainly beautiful countryside. It must have been quite hard to leave it when you moved into Dublin."

"Well Mammy died and it was never the same," said Patsy. "She died in my arms, you know, while I was reading her a story. Daddy and

654

Molly and Theresa had gone into the village in the trap to shop and I stayed home to look after Mammy. She was dead before they got back. Look now, see that field?" said Patsy. "That's changed. That used to be full of haystacks that we could play in. We'd scramble up and then jump down from the very top and land in all the long grass."

"I bet you got a few bruises doing that," said Annie.

"Never," said Patsy. "It was always a lovely soft landing. And then we'd hear Mammy calling us in for our dinner and we might sometimes splash our way back along the river and Daddy would make us clean ourselves up before we were allowed to sit at the table. Here's the gatehouse now, this is where we used to live," said Patsy.

John parked the car and Patsy immediately leapt out, not paying any mind to Monty and Daisy.

"It's definitely seen better days," said Annie but Patsy only saw her old home through the eyes of childhood. The flowers were still growing round the door, the vegetable patch was still thriving, the pretty curtains her mammy had sewn were still hanging gaily in the windows. She ran her fingers over the door, not noticing all the splinters through the peeling paint, and pretended she was putting the key in the lock. She knelt to put her nose to the ground, inhaling deeply the smell of the familiar earth. She stood and twirled as if she was a little girl.

Before Annie or John could react, Patsy had disappeared round to the back of the cottage and skuttled across the field, arms outstretched, and head thrown to the skies. She felt more alive than she had in a long time.

"Shall we go after her?" asked John. "She might fall and hurt herself. The ground might not be as soft as she remembers."

"Let's give her some time, she's obviously enjoying all her memories but I'm sorry, John, to be honest none of it means anything to me. I haven't heard any of these stories or about their life before Dublin. I know our mammy lived here for a while looking after Patsy and Molly and Theresa when their real mammy was ill but that's about all I know. I'm sure she'll be fine. She probably wants to be on her own for a while. We can sit and wait for her in the car, keep Monty and Daisy company. I'll be ready for something to eat soon, will you?"

"I will that," said John. "But I don't mind waiting a bit longer,

Patsy's loving every minute of it and that was the whole reason for coming out here. It's been a real tonic for her. I think today was a grand idea all round. And I liked what I saw of Nazareth House, didn't you?"

"I did but it might take some coaxing to get Patsy to come round," said Annie. "She seemed quite reluctant when we were there."

"I put a couple of brochures in my jacket," said John, "we can look at them while we wait."

"As long as we hide them out of sight before she gets back."

Nazareth House was the last thing on Patsy's mind as she happily brushed her feet through the tall grass and bent to pick some wildflowers to make into a small posy, like the ones she used to present to her mammy. She sniffed the fresh air and filled her lungs with the rich smells of the countryside. She listened to the birdsong and marvelled at how green everything was, greener even that she had remembered. She strolled idly through the field, loitering to savour every experience that enlivened her senses, and made her way down to the river.

She was delighted to see her floaty woman was there, still working, still fishing around in the water, still wearing the same old clothes. The woman looked up and waved when she saw Patsy and Patsy felt an overwhelming sensation of comfort and belonging.

"Hello," she said to the old woman, "it's grand to see you. You haven't changed one bit."

"I've been expecting you, Patsy," said the woman, her face beaming a welcoming smile. "I knew you'd come back, this is where you've always belonged."

"It's a magical place, all right," said Patsy, "I always felt a part of it and that it was part of me."

"You were right, and it's been here waiting for you to come back," said the old woman. "Come here to me now and we'll explore it together, I'll take you somewhere you'll never ever want to leave."

She stretched out her arm to Patsy and offered her hand, her bony fingers so translucent that they melted into the green of the field, the rush of the water, the leaves of the trees. "Come, Patsy, look now, have you ever been anywhere so beautiful, so peaceful? It's been waiting for you all this time and at last you're here, home."

Patsy's eyes opened wide. Guided by the old woman's hand, she was transported into a place that was somehow familiar but more real than anything she had ever known: she was standing by a rippling lake; there was a small rowing boat pulled up on to the bank and a breeze was wafting carelessly through the reeds and tickling the leaves on the trees into a happy dance; across the water, gentle slopes tilted upwards and above their treeline mountains were visible, standing proud against the clearest blue heaven Patsy had ever seen. She recalled some distant words about the way opening up for her beyond the familiar track, a way that promised all she had wanted.

"Yes," said Patsy to the old woman. "You're right, this is all I had wanted. I'm here at last, now I'm home."